# Down Here

## Strega
## Blue Belle
## Hard Candy

A BURKE OMNIBUS

ANDREW
VACHSS

Quality Paperback Book Club
New York

# Down Here

A BURKE OMNIBUS



Printed in the United States of America

# CONTENTS

# INTRODUCTION

I DIDN'T START OUT TO BE a novelist. Before I ever wrote a book, I was a federal investigator in sexually transmitted diseases, a field caseworker for the infamous New York City "Welfare" Department, and a community organizer. I was on the ground during that tribalistic, genocidal insanity in Biafra (now called Nigeria, because winners get to write the history books). Having survived that, I ran an advocacy agency in Chicago's notorious Uptown district, then a reentry center for ex-cons, and finally a maximum-security prison for violent juveniles in Massachusetts. There the connection between child abuse and neglect and America's worst social problems finally hit home. Hard.

Realizing I could never contribute to systemic change working for institutions or agencies (and wanting to be in control of my own mission), I then went to law school. Once I finished, I split my caseload between shooters, stabbers, and stompers (who paid the bills), and abused and neglected children (who couldn't).

I thought I had learned quite a bit along the way (especially if it's true you learn from your mistakes). I wanted to share that knowledge. So I wrote a textbook. It got great reviews, but it had no impact outside the "profession."

I knew if I couldn't reach people, I couldn't make change. I wanted a bigger jury than I'd ever find in a courthouse. So I turned to "crime fiction." I've continued both careers (representing children and writing books) ever since. The success of the books freed me to represent children exclusively. Literally, a dream come true.

Why I wrote was never a secret, although I didn't know there was a term for the kind of writing I do. I am indebted to a German reviewer for the French term he used to describe my work: "*littérature engagée*." If I understand it correctly, it's right on the money.

In English, the books have come to be called "investigative novels."

But not at first. In *Strega*, I wrote about predatory pedophiles trafficking in kiddie porn using linked computers. Today, such crimes are daily newspaper fare. But *Strega* came out more than thirteen years ago. Because I was reporting what I saw from my ground zero perspective long before it became common knowledge, much of my material was dismissed as total fantasy. One reviewer called it "the product of a sick, fevered imagination."

I wanted to show people what Hell really looked like . . . and I didn't think an angel would make the best guide. Burke, my protagonist, is a member of that vast tribe I call "The Children of the Secret" (formerly abused children, now grown). Burke is also an ex-convict, a hijacker, a thief, a gunrunner, a scam artist. And, some would say, a killer. In short, he's a career criminal, with no plans to join a society that has rejected him from birth.

These three books are an ideal introduction to Burke and his world, because they so clearly illustrate the connectivity of all the books. Unlike some "PI series" where the protagonists never seem to age, and simply handle one "adventure" after another without it affecting them in any meaningful way, the Burke series moves in two directions, simultaneously. Burke changes with each book, as do all those around him. And, with each book, you learn more of his origins and that of his "family of choice." The title character in *Strega*, for example, reappears in *Hard Candy*, which is the "sequel" to *Blue Belle*.

If your idea of "realism" is based on Hollywood's output, these books will read like science fiction. But if you live or lurk anywhere in the predator-prey-hunter food chain, you'll know the truth when you read it. And if your mind is open, if you're coming to Burke's world the way you come to a blues club—to hear whether the musicians can really bring the truth—you've come to the right place.

Andrew Vachss
March 2000

# Strega

## ACKNOWLEDGMENT

To Ira J. Hechler, the master-builder content to allow others to engrave their names on the cornerstones of his achievements, I acknowledge my gratitude and proclaim my respect.

✦

For Doc, who heard it all while he was down here.
For Mary Lou, who can hear it all now.
For Sam, who finally gave up his part-time job.
And for Bobby, who died trying.

Different paths to the same door.

# 1

IT STARTED WITH a kid.

The redhead walked slowly up the bridle path, one foot deliberately in front of the other, looking straight ahead. She was dressed in a heavy sweatsuit and carrying some kind of gym bag in her hand. Her flaming hair was tied behind her with a wide yellow ribbon, just as it was supposed to be.

Forest Park runs all through Queens County, just a dozen miles outside the city. It's a long narrow piece of greenery, stretching from Forest Hills, where Geraldine Ferraro sells Pepsi, all the way to Richmond Hill, where some people sell coke. At six in the morning, the park was nearly deserted, but it would fill up soon enough. Yuppies working up an appetite for breakfast yogurt, jogging through the forest, dreaming of things you can buy from catalogues.

I was deep into the thick brush along the path, safely hidden behind a window screen. It had taken a couple of hours to weave the small branches through the mesh, but it was worth it—I was invisible. It was like being back in Biafra during the war, except that only branches were over my head—no planes.

The redhead stopped on the path, just across from me, about twenty feet away. Moving as if all her joints were stiff in the early-spring cold, she pulled the sweatshirt over her head, untied the pants, and let them fall to the ground. Now she was dressed in just a tight tank top and a skimpy pair of silky white shorts. "No panties, no bra," the freak had told her on the phone. "I want to see everything you got bounce around, you got it?" She was supposed to do three laps around the bridle path, and then it would be over.

I had never spoken to the woman. I got the story from an old man I did time with years ago. Julio called me at Mama Wong's restaurant and left a message to meet at a gas station he owns over in Brooklyn. "Tell him to bring the dog," he told Mama.

Julio loves my dog. Her name is Pansy and she's a Neapolitan mastiff—about 140 pounds of vicious muscle and dumb as a brick. If her entire brain was high-quality cocaine, it wouldn't retail for enough cash to buy a decent meal. But she knows how to do her work, which is more than you can say for a lot of fools who went to Harvard.

Back when I did my last long stretch, the prison yard was divided into little courts—every clique had one, the Italians, the blacks, the Latins. But it didn't just break down to race—bank robbers hung out together, con men had their own spot, the iron-freaks didn't mix with the basketball junkies . . . like that. If you stepped on a stranger's court, you did it the same way you'd come into his cell without an invite—with a shank in your hand. People who don't have much get ugly about giving up the little they have left.

Julio's court was the biggest one on the yard. He had tomato plants growing there, and even some decent chairs and a table someone made for him in the wood shop. He used to make book at the same stand every day—cons are all gamblers, otherwise they'd work for a living. Every morning he'd be out there on his court, sitting on a box near his tomato plants, surrounded by muscle. He was an old man even then, and he carried a lot of respect. One day I was talking to him about dogs, and he started in about Neapolitans.

"When I was a young boy, in my country, they had a fucking statue of that dog right in the middle of the village," he told me.

"Neapolitan mastiffs, Burke—the same dogs what came over the Alps with Hannibal. I get out of this place, the first thing I do is get one of those dogs."

He was a better salesman than he was a buyer—Julio never got a Neapolitan, but I did. I bought Pansy when she was a puppy and now she's a full-grown monster. Every time Julio sees her, tears come into his eyes. I guess the idea of a cold-blooded killer who can never inform on the contractor makes him sentimental.

I drove my Plymouth into the gas station, got the eye from the attendant, and pulled into the garage. The old man came out of the darkness and Pansy growled—it sounded like a diesel truck downshifting. As soon as she recognized Julio's voice her ears went back just a fraction of an inch, but she was still ready to bite.

"Pansy! Mother of God, Burke—she's the size of a fucking house! What a beauty!"

Pansy purred under the praise, knowing there were better things coming. Sure enough, the old man reached in a coat pocket and came out with a slab of milk-white cheese and held it out to her.

"So, baby—you like what Uncle Julio has for you, huh?"

Before Julio could get close enough, I snapped "Speak!" at Pansy. She let the old man pat her massive head as the cheese quickly disappeared. Julio thought "Speak!" meant she should make noises—actually, it was the word I taught her that meant it was okay to take food. To Julio, it looked like a dog doing a trick. The key to survival in this world is to have people think you're doing tricks for them. Nobody was going to poison my dog.

Pansy growled again, this time in anticipation. "Pansy, jump!" I barked at her, and she lay down in the back seat without another sound.

I got out of the car and lit a cigarette—Julio wouldn't call me out to Brooklyn just to give Pansy some cheese.

"Burke, an old friend of mine comes to me last week. He says this freak is doing something to his daughter, making her crazy—scared all the time. And he don't know what to do. He tries to talk to her and she won't tell him what's wrong. And the daughter—she's married to a citizen, you know? Nice guy, treats her good and everything. He earns good, but he's not one of us. We can't bring him in on this."

I just watched the old man. He was so shook he was trembling. Julio had killed two shooters in a gunfight just before he went to prison and he was standup all the way. This had to be bad. I let him talk, saying nothing.

"So I talk to her—Gina. She won't tell me neither, but I just sit and we talk about things like when she was a little girl and I used to let her drink some of my espresso when she came into the club with her father—stuff like that. And then I notice that she won't let this kid of hers out of her sight. The little girl, she wants to go out in the yard and play and Gina says no. And it's a beautiful day out, you understand? They got a fence around the house, she can watch the kid from the kitchen—but she's not letting her out of her sight. So then I ask her, Is it something about the kid?

"And then she starts to cry, right in front of me and the kid too. She shows me this brown envelope that came in the mail for her. It's got all newspaper stories of kids that got killed by drunk drivers, kids that got snatched, missing kids . . . all that kind of shit.

"So what? I ask her. What's this got to do with *your* kid? And she tells me that this stuff comes in the mail for weeks, okay? And then this *animale* calls her on the phone. He tells her that *he* did a couple of these kids himself, you understand what I'm saying?—he snatches the kids himself and all. And her kid is going to be next if she don't do what he wants.

"So she figures he wants money, right? She knows that could be taken care of. But he don't want money, Burke. He wants her to take off her clothes for him while she's on the phone, the freak! He tells her to take the clothes off and say what she's doing into the phone."

The old man's eyes were someplace else. His voice was a harsh prison whisper, but reedy and weak. There was nothing for me to say—I don't do social work.

"She tells me she goes along with it, but she don't really take nothing off, okay?—and the freak screams at her that he knows she's not really doing it and hangs up on her. And that's when she hit the fucking panic button—she believes this guy's really watching her. All the time watching her, and getting ready to move on her kid."

"Why come to me?" I asked him.

"You know these people, Burke. Even when we were in the joint, you were always watching the fucking skinners and the baby-rapers and all. Remember? Remember when I asked you why you talk to them—remember what you said?"

I remembered. I told the old man that I was going to get out of that joint someday and I'd be going back to the streets—if you walk around in the jungle, you have to know the animals.

"Yeah," I told the old man, "I remember."

"So what am I gonna fucking do, ask one of them psychiatrists? *You* know about freaks—you tell me what to do."

"I don't tell people what to do."

"Then tell me what's going on—tell me what's in his head."

"He isn't watching her, Julio," I told him. "He just figured she wasn't going along, that's all. He's a freak, like you said—you don't ever know why they do something."

"But you know *what* they're going to do."

"Yeah," I told him, "I know what they're going to do." And it was the truth.

We smoked together in silence for a bit. I knew Julio, and I knew there was more coming. Finally, he snubbed out his skinny, twisted black cigar on the Plymouth's faded flank and stuck it in his pocket. His old, cold eyes grabbed mine:

"He called her again. . . ."

"And . . . ?" I asked him.

"He told her to come to the park, you know, that Forest Park, near her house in Kew Gardens? And he says she has to go jogging in the park Friday morning, okay? And not to wear no underwear, so's he can watch her bounce around. He says if she does that, they'll be even and he'll let her kid off the hook."

"No," I said.

"No fucking *what*?" shouted the old man. "No, she don't go to the park—no, he don't let the kid off the hook . . . what?"

"The kid's not on the hook, Julio; this freak is. He's a degenerate, okay? And they never stop what they do. Some of them step it up, you understand? They get into more freakish shit. But they don't stop. If she goes into that park, he'll call again. And the next time he'll want more."

"He's gonna rape her?"

"No, this kind doesn't do that. He's a watcher—but he wants to hurt women just the same. He wants to make them dance to his tune. And the ones that dance, he speeds up the music."

The old man slumped against the fender. All of a sudden he looked ancient. But an old alligator can still bite.

"She's good people, Burke. I never had a daughter, but if I did I wish it would be her. She's got a heart like steel. But this kid of hers, Mia, she turns her to water. She ain't scared for herself . . ."

"I know," I told him.

"And she can't tell her husband. He'd wanna file a fucking *lawsuit* on the guy or something."

"Yeah," I agreed, sharing the old man's profound respect for citizens.

"So what do we do?" the old man asked me.

"Where did this 'we' come from, Julio?"

"You do bodywork, right? I heard around for years—you do this kind of work, like private-eye shit and all."

"So? This is different."

"What's so different? Just nose around and find out this guy's name for me—where he lives and all."

"Not a chance," I told him.

The old man looked into my eyes, slipping into a new game quicker than a striking snake.

"Burke, this is family."

"Yeah," I said, "*your* family."

"In the joint, we was like family," he told me, his voice quiet.

"You been reading too many books, old man. I was never in your fucking family."

"Hey, come on, Burke. Just 'cause you ain't Italian don't mean nothing to me," he said, with all the sincerity of a real-estate broker.

"I went to prison because I wasn't going to spend my life kissing ass," I said, "and kissing some old man's pinky ring don't race my motor either. A boss is a boss—I don't have much but at least I don't have a fucking boss, you hear me?"

The old man kept his face flat against this sacrilege, but his lizard eyes blinked. He said nothing, waiting for me to finish.

"I showed you respect then—and I show you respect now," I said, letting him save face. "But don't disrespect *me* with this bullshit about 'family,' okay?"

The old man thought he got it. "You want money?" he asked.

"For what—for doing what?"

"I want to make this freak stop hurting Gina."

"Will she do what you tell her?" I asked him.

The old man made a clenched fist, pounded his chest where his heart would be if he had one. It was all the answer I needed.

"I'll take a shot," I told him. "Tell her to go to the park on Friday, just like the freak told her to. I'll be around, okay?"

"Burke—you'll do it right?"

"There is no 'right' about this, Julio. I'll get it done or no charge, how's that?"

"How much?"

"Ten large," I told him.

The lizard eyes didn't blink. "You got it."

I climbed back into the Plymouth. It was only two days to Friday and I'd need some help for this one. The old man's small hand reached for my arm—I stared down at the hand the way you do in prison when someone touches you who shouldn't—it was boneless—nothing but parchment skin and blue veins.

The old man looked at me. "Burke," he pleaded, "take him off the count."

"I don't do that kind of work, Julio."

The old man's eyes shifted again. "You said thirty large, right?"

"I said *ten*, old man. I don't do that kind of work. Period."

Julio tried to look injured. "You think I'm wearing a wire?"

"No, old man, I don't think you're wired. But you know better than to ask me to drop someone. I'll do what I said I'll do. That's it. Say yes or say no."

"Yes," said the old man, and I backed out of the garage, heading back to the city.

# 2

IT TOOK US MOST OF THE night to get everything in place. I couldn't bring Pansy on a job like this—if I kept her in the blind with me and some fool let his dog lift a leg against a nearby tree, the emergency ward would have some new customers. She's perfect on a job when you're working people, but other dogs annoy the hell out of her—especially male dogs.

Max the Silent was somewhere in the nearby brush. He's a Mongolian free-lance warrior who works for only those he wants to, and walks where he will. Calling him a karate expert is like calling a politician crooked—it doesn't tell you anything special. A strange little guy we call the Prophet was trying to explain Max to some of the young guys on the yard once. He did it much better than I could—when the Prophet talks, it's like being in church, only he tells the truth:

"Max the Silent? Max the life-taking, widow-making, silent wind of death? Brothers, better to drink radioactive waste, easier to reason with a rattlesnake, safer to wear a gasoline overcoat into the fires of hell than to mess with that man. You go to fuck with Max, people, you best bring your own body bag."

But he's not called Max the Silent because he moves so quietly. Max doesn't speak and he doesn't hear. He may be able to read lips—nobody knows—but he communicates perfectly. I showed him some of the clippings the freak had mailed to the redhead; then I made the universal sign of the maggot—two palms pressed together, one opened to show a rock being overturned, and a disgusted face at what I was looking at underneath the rock. Then I made the sign of using the telephone, and started to unbutton my shirt with a horrified look on my face. He got it all, and he dealt himself in. We'd split the money.

It was quiet and peaceful in my concealed blind. It made me think of Biafra again—comfortable isn't the same as safe.

I watched the redhead jog off along the path, her face set and hard but her body doing what the freak wanted it to do. She'd make the three circuits, standing up all the way—just like Julio promised.

He had to be out there somewhere. I didn't know his name, but I knew him—he'd have to see the redhead dance for himself. But I'd been there for hours; if he was anywhere nearby, I'd know it by now. The bridle path was about a half-mile around. The freak could be anywhere out there—but so could Max the Silent.

Minutes passed, but I never moved. I'm good at waiting. Then I heard the car: someone was driving along the road parallel to the bridle path, moving too slowly to be an early commuter. I froze as I heard the tires crunch gravel—he was off the road now, heading over to right across from where I was hidden. Perfect.

The tan Pontiac rolled to a gentle stop deep into the branches on the other side of the path, about fifty feet from where I was hidden. The engine died and the forest went silent, wondering at this new intruder. The side window of the Pontiac was heavily tinted—I couldn't even see movement inside. Then the door opened and the freak cautiously stepped out. He was tall, well over six feet, and rail-thin. He was wearing one of those jungle camouflage outfits they sell in boutiques, complete with polished black combat boots. He had a military field cap on his head, and his eyes were covered with mirror-lensed sunglasses. A long survival knife was slung low on his left thigh.

The freak started chopping at tree branches with the knife, covering the nose of the car so it would be invisible. His movements were quick, frantic. Maybe in his mind he was a soldier building a sniper's roost—to me he looked like a freak in a raincoat bouncing up and down in his seat, waiting for a porno movie to start.

The little telescope brought his face right into the blind with me. I couldn't see his eyes, but his lips were working overtime. Then we both heard the measured slap of sneakers on the path and we knew the redhead was making another circuit. He dove back into the Pontiac. I watched until I saw the driver's window sneak down and there he was, his face swiveled on a scrawny neck, eyes glued to the bridle path.

The redhead came along at a dead-even pace, running in the middle of the path, looking straight ahead. The freak's head turned with mine as we watched her approach and watched her disappear around a bend. I could see his face, but not his hands—I knew what he was doing with them.

The freak never moved. His window stayed down. Now I had to wait—was one circuit enough for him to get where he wanted to go? Would he take off now? I couldn't read the license number on his car. If he took off I'd have to make my move without Max.

But he stayed where he was—going back for seconds. I slowly twisted my neck back and forth, working out the kinks from staying too long in one spot, getting ready to move out. I felt a sharp sting against my face—I slapped the spot, looking all around me for the offending hornet. Nothing. Then a snake's hiss, amplified a dozen times, penetrated my foggy brain and I knew Max was close by. It took me another half-minute to spot him, crouched motionless not ten feet from my blind. I pointed over to where the freak was parked and Max nodded—he knew.

I held up one finger to Max, telling him to wait a minute before he moved. Then I used the same finger to draw a half-circle in the air, made a motion as if I was getting to my feet, and grabbed my left forearm with my right hand. Circle around behind the freak, I was telling Max, wait for me to show myself, and then make sure the target doesn't move. I had grabbed my forearm instead of my throat for good reason—I wanted the freak to stay where he was until I could talk to him, not get planted there forever.

Max vanished. The park was still quiet—we had some time, but not much. How long does it take a woman protecting her cub to run a half-mile?

We both heard her before we saw her again, just like the last time. I knew where the redhead had left her gym bag, up ahead of where she rounded the corner. This would be the last time we saw her, but maybe the freak didn't know that. He had missed the first circuit—maybe he thought there was another lap still to come.

The redhead jogged past us exactly like before—a reluctant machine unable to overcome its programmer. I could feel the freak's eyes burning.

I waited a couple of seconds after she rounded the bend, watching carefully, but the freak didn't start his engine. I knew Max was in place. No point in trying to be quiet about this—it would take me ten minutes to slither out of the blind without giving myself away.

I grabbed both knees, rocked back until I was flat on my back, and kicked out with both feet. The blind went flying, the birds started screaming, and I heard the freak trying to start his car. His engine fired into life just as I was charging across the road to where he was hidden, but he never had a chance. His rear tires spun in a frantic dance, but his car never moved. It wouldn't go anywhere, not with the concrete wedges Max had stuffed in front of each front wheel.

The freak saw me moving toward him; his head was whipping wildly on its thin stalk of a neck looking for a way out, and then Max materialized at the side of the car. Another split-second and he reached into the car and pulled out the freak, the way you'd pull a dead fish out of a tank. The freak started to say something and Max twisted his neck—the something turned out to be a scream. Max flashed his spare hand into the freak's belly, palm out, and the scream turned to silence.

The Pontiac was a coupe, so I went around to the passenger side and climbed into the front seat. Then I pushed the driver's seat forward and Max climbed in too, holding the freak at arm's length until I shoved the seat-back forward to give him room. He deposited the freak next to me on the front seat, keeping his hand on the scrawny neck.

We all sat there for a minute. Nobody spoke. Three strangers at a drive-in movie with nothing on the screen. When the silence got too much for the freak, he opened his mouth—it only took a slight pressure from Max's hand for him to realize that talking would be painful. I reached over and snatched the mirror lenses from his sweaty face—I wanted to see his eyes. They darted around in their sockets like half-drunk flies on a Teflon pan.

"Give me your wallet," I told him, in a calm, quiet voice.

The freak hastily fumbled open his camouflage suit and handed me a billfold. Just what I expected—a miniature police badge was pinned to one side, almost two hundred in bills, an honorary membership card from the PBA, credit cards, and other assorted crap. The driver's license and registration were my targets, and I found them soon enough.

"Mark Monroe," I said, reading from the license. "That's a nice name . . . Mark. You think that's a nice name?" I asked Max, who said nothing.

The freak said nothing too. I took my .38 from one pocket and the silencer tube from another. He watched as I carefully screwed them together, assembling a quiet killing machine.

I made a gesture to Max and his hand vanished from the freak's neck. "You made a big mistake, Mark," I told him.

The freak looked at me. He tried to talk but his Adam's apple kept bobbing into his voice box. "Just calm down," I told him, "take it easy, Mark." It took a while before he could speak.

"Wh . . . what do you want?"

"What do I want, Mark? I want you to leave people alone. I want you to stop threatening their kids. I want you to stop getting your kicks by torturing people like you did this morning."

"Could I explain this to you . . . could I tell you about . . . ?" he wanted to know.

"Mark, if you want to tell me you're a sick man and that you can't help yourself, I got no time to listen, okay?"

"No," he said, "I don't mean that. Just let me . . ."

"Or maybe you want to tell me how the bitch asked for it—or how she really enjoyed the whole thing—is that it, Mark?"

"Well, I just . . ."

"Because if that's it," I told him, leveling the pistol at his eyes, "I'm going to blow your slimy face all over this car, you understand?"

The freak didn't make a sound—I'd just used up his only two options and he couldn't think of another. I pulled the keys from the ignition and got out of the car, leaving him inside with Max. The trunk had two cartons of newspaper clippings about kids, plus an assortment of magazines that made *Penthouse* look like *House & Garden*—*Bondage Beauties, Women in Chains, Leather & Discipline*, all hand-job specials for long-distance rapists. I took the stuff out and piled it on the ground; then I got back in the car. The glove compartment had two canisters of the halfass "mace" they sell over the counter, a billy club, and a roll of Saran Wrap. A Saint Christopher's medal dangled from the rearview mirror. Still no surprises.

"Where do you work, Mark?" I asked him in a friendly tone.

"Con Edison. I'm an engineer. I've been with them for . . ."

"That's enough, Mark!" I said, jabbing him in the ribs with the silencer. "Just answer my questions, okay?"

"Sure," the freak said, "I just . . ."

I jabbed him again, harder than before. "Mark, you and me have got a problem, understand? My problem is how to stop you from doing this stuff again, okay? And your problem is how to get out of here alive. You got any good suggestions?"

The freak's words were tumbling all over themselves, trying to get to the surface. I guess he was better on the phone. "Look, I'll never . . . I mean, you don't have to worry. . . ."

"Yeah, Mark, I have to worry. People *paid* me to worry, you understand what I'm saying?"

"Sure, sure. I didn't mean that. I'll never call her again, I swear."

"Yeah, that's right—you won't," I told him. "Now get out of the car, okay? Nice and slow."

He never tried to run. Max and I walked him back deep into the woods until I found what I was looking for—a flat stump where the Parks Department had chopped down a monster maple tree for some stupid reason.

"Mark, I want you to kneel down and put your hands on the tree—where I can see them."

"I . . ." the freak said, but it was a waste of effort. Max's clenched hand drove him to the earth. I let him kneel there as though I had all the time in the world.

"Mark, I notice you're all dressed in survival gear—it's real nice. When you drive yourself to the hospital, you tell them you were out in the woods fucking around and you fell and hurt yourself, okay?"

"Hurt myself?" he whined.

"Yeah, Mark, hurt yourself. Because that's just what you did today—you hurt yourself. You always hurt yourself when you try and fuck with people, right?"

"Please . . . please, don't. I can't stand pain. My doctor . . ."

I nodded to Max. I saw his foot flash in the morning light and I heard the crack—now the freak only had one thighbone that went from end to end. His face turned dead-white and vomit erupted from his mouth, but he never moved his hands. Even slime can learn.

"Every time you try and walk straight, Mark, I want you to think about how much fun you had in the park this morning, okay?" I asked him.

The freak's face was contorted in pain, his lips bleeding where he had bitten into them. "Yes!" he gasped out.

"And every time you try and dial a phone, Mark, I want you to think about today—will you do that?"

"Yes, yes!" he blubbered again. Max reached over and took one of his hands gently from the tree stump. A quick twist behind the freak's back, another loud snap, and the arm was useless. They call it a spiral fracture—the doctors would never get it set right. The freak had opened his mouth wide, set for a desperate shriek, when he saw the pistol six inches from his face. The scream died—he didn't want to.

"Mark," I told him, "listen to me real good. I know your name, your address, your Social Security number . . . I know everything. If this ever happens again—if you ever so much as use a scissors on a newspaper or make a phone call again—I'm going to pull your eyes out of your head with a pair of pliers and feed them to you. You got that?"

The freak looked at me; his body was working but his brain was on the critical list. All he could say was "Please . . ." It wasn't enough.

"Mark, when you get to that emergency room, you better tell them you hurt *yourself*, right? You bring anyone else into this, and you're a piece of meat. We're going to be leaving in just a minute. You can still drive, and the pain will pass. But if you ever forget the pain, there's lots more coming, okay?"

"Yes," the freak said.

"Oh, just one more thing," I told him, "I got to make sure you don't forget, Mark. And, like I told you, pain goes away. So I'm going to leave you something permanent as a souvenir of your little war-games today."

The freak's eyes turned crazy when I pulled the butcher knife from my coat, watching his one hand resting on the tree stump.

"Don't move," I told him, but he whipped back his hand and tried to run. You can't run on a broken leg. This time we let him scream.

Max hauled him back to the chopping block, holding the freak's forearm down like an anvil on a feather.

"Now, see what you did to yourself, Mark?" I asked him. "You turned a nice clean broken leg into a compound fracture. You jump around too much now and you're liable to lose an arm instead of just a hand, okay?"

The freak's slimy smell mingled with his urine as he lost all control. He was making sounds but they weren't words. Max grabbed the freak's fingertips, stretching the hand out for me. I raised the butcher knife high above my head and brought it flashing down. The freak gasped and passed out.

I pulled the knife short, looked back at Max. He immediately grabbed the freak's hand and stretched it again, but I waved him away. If the freak hadn't learned from what had happened to him already, he was past anything we could do.

Time to go. Max picked up the two cartons of filth in one hand and we worked our way back to the blind. I pulled out the screen and carried it to the hidden Plymouth. Another two minutes and we pulled out of the forest onto the pavement. I left Max in the car and used some branches to sweep away the tire tracks.

Another five minutes and we vanished onto the Inter-Boro, heading for Brooklyn.

# 3

IT SHOULD HAVE BEEN over then, except for picking up the money. You don't get cash in front from a man like Julio—it's disrespectful. Besides, I know where he lives, and all he has for me is a pay-phone number in Mama's restaurant.

I gave him three weeks and then I called the gas station from a pay phone near my office. You have to call early in the mornings from the phone—it belongs to the trust-fund hippies who live in the loft underneath me. They generally stay up all night working on their halfass stabs at self-expression, and they usually fall out well past midnight, dreaming of a marijuana paradise where all men are brothers. Good thing they never ride the subways. I don't pay rent for the top floor and I never expect to, unless the landlord sells the building. His son did something real stupid to some people a few years ago, and I passed the information only as far as the landlord. Like I told him one time, the top floor has lots of room to store information like that, but if I had to move to a smaller place . . . you never know.

I don't abuse the privilege—never stay on the phone for more than a minute, no long-distance calls. I put a slug into the pay phone—another slug answered.

"Yeah?"

"It's Burke. Tell your boss I'll meet him tonight on the third shift."

"I ain't got no boss, pal. You got the wrong number," he said, slamming down the phone. The Strike Force is making all Italians nervous these days.

The "third shift" means eleven at night to seven in the morning, just like it is in prison. When you're doing time, you learn that each shift has its own personality. The first shift, the joint is on its best behavior; that's when the visitors are allowed in and that's the only time the Parole Board comes around. The jerkoff therapists and counselors and religious nuts all make their appearances on the first shift too. The second shift is where you settle all your disputes, if you're serious about them. Prison fights only last a few seconds—someone dies and someone walks away. If the guy you stab lives, he's entitled to a rematch. And the third shift is where you check out of the hotel if you can't stand the room—that's where the young ones hang up in their cells. Prison's just like the free world: bullshit, violence, and death—only in prison it's on a tighter schedule.

Maybe you never really get out of prison. I don't have bars on my back windows—the fire escape rusted right off the building years ago except for the stairs to the roof—and Pansy was ready to discuss the ethics of breaking and entering with anyone who might show up—but it was another day coming on and my only goal was to get through it.

Inside the walls, they don't leave you with much. That's why the body-builders treasure their measurements more than any fashion model.

You can die for stepping on another man's little piece of the yard—or on his name. You either stand up to what they throw at you or you go down—it's that simple. In prison, you go down, you stay down.

The redhead was a standup broad. She didn't like doing that number in the park, but she went the route for her kid. She did the right thing—it made what I did right too. I'd never see her again. I didn't want to—the whole thing made me think of Flood.

Until Flood came along, I had survival down to a science. Like the redhead, she had a job to do, and I got brought in. She took her share of the weight and carried it right to the edge.

Flood was a state-raised kid, like me. "I'm for you, Burke," she told me just before she went back to another world. I was okay before I met her—I knew what I had to do and I did it. You don't miss what you never had. But ever since Flood, the pain floats around inside me like a butterfly. When it lands, I have to do something to forget. A piece of that song Bones used to sing in his cell late at night came to me:

I wish I had a dollar,
I wish I had a dime.
I wish I had a woman,
But all I got is time.

"Maximum Security Blues," he used to call it. Bones wasn't used to big-city jailing. He'd done most of his time down in Mississippi, on the Parchman Farm, a thirty-thousand-acre prison without walls. They didn't need walls—a man can't run faster than a bullet. Bones said he got his name years ago when he was working the dice circuit, but we called him that because that's all there was of him—he was about a hundred years old, as sharp and skinny as an ice pick. Bones did things the old way—he'd be so respectful to the guards with his thick Southern voice that they'd never listen to what he was really saying.

One of the young city blacks didn't listen so good either. Bones was sitting on a box on one of the neutral courts in the Big Yard, playing his battered six-string and singing his songs. The young stud came up with his boys, all dressed in their bullshit back-to-Africa colors, "political prisoners" one and all. I didn't know mugging old ladies for their welfare checks was a revolutionary act, but what the hell do I know? The only Marx who ever made sense to me was Groucho. The leader insisted everyone call him by his tribal name, and the new-breed guards went along with it. He rolls up and tells Bones that he's a fucking stereotype—a low-life Uncle Tom ass-kissing nigger, and all that. And Bones just strums his guitar, looking past the punk to someplace else.

The only sounds on the yard were the grunts of the iron-jockeys and the slap of dominoes on wood—and Bones's sad guitar. Then we heard a loud slap; the guitar went silent but the rest of the joint started to hum. The cold gray death-shark was swimming in the prison yard, but the guards on the catwalks didn't know it yet. Men were getting to their feet all over the yard, drifting over to where the punk was standing over Bones, holding the old man's guitar in his hands.

"This thing is nothing but an instrument to play slave music with, old man," the punk leered at him, holding the neck in one hand and the body in the other. "Maybe I'll just snap it over my knee—how you like that?"

"Don't do that, son," Bones pleaded with him.

The punk looked back at his friends for approval, all alone in his power-world now, never seeing the human wall closing around him. I looked past Bones to where Virgil, my cellmate, was closing in. Virgil wasn't raised to take up for blacks, but he'd back my play like he was supposed to when it went down. I hated Bagoomi—or whatever the fucking fool called himself—anyway. His revolutionary mission didn't stop him from raping fresh young kids when they first came on the cellblock.

But I was too late. The ancient guitar snapped across his knee as easily as a toothpick and he held one piece in each hand, his gold-toothed mouth grinning down at Bones. The old man's hand flashed and the fool's smile died along with the rest of him. By the time the guards smashed through the dense clot of prisoners, all they discovered was one more weasel who'd found the only true path to the Promised Land, a sharpened file sticking deep between his ribs. The guards paid no attention to Bones holding the pieces of his guitar and crying to himself. Their investigation determined that someone had settled a gambling debt with the punk, prison-style, and that the old man's guitar had been a casualty of the collection method.

I didn't know Flood when I was doing time—I didn't know there were women like her on this earth. I should have known that when love came to me, it would only be for a visit.

When the blues come down on you this hard, you don't want to be locked up. In prison, I had no choice. But in prison, I never had the blues like this. It was time to hit the streets.

# 4

I CALLED PANSY DOWN from her roof, locked the place up, and climbed down the stairs to the garage. Sometimes when I get the blues I sit and talk with Pansy, but she was being a real bitch lately. She was in heat again—I didn't want to have her fixed—and every time she went into heat she'd rip up pieces of the office until she got over it. It didn't change the look much, and my clients aren't the particular type anyway.

The docks were quiet—a few sorry hookers hiding empty faces behind cheap makeup, a leather-laced stud hustler not smart enough to know the action didn't start until it got dark, a few citizens late for work. I was looking for Michelle, but I guess she'd taken the day off.

I thought about going up to the Bronx and scaring up the Mole, but I wasn't in the mood for a conversation about Israel today. The Mole loved the *idea* of Israel, but he'd never go.

Then I thought I'd find Max and go on with our gin game. We'd been playing almost a dozen years now, and he still had every single score-sheet. I was about forty bucks ahead. But the warehouse was empty.

The light at Bowery and Delancey held me up—long enough for one of the bums to approach the Plymouth with a dirty rag in one hand and a bottle of something in the other.

"Help me out, man?" the bum asked. "I'm trying to get together enough to get back home."

"Where's home?" I asked him.

"Used to be Oklahoma—I don't know."

"This is home now, brother," I told him, handing him a buck and watching his face light up. Maybe I'll never buy the world a Coke—although I know some Colombians trying to do just that—but at least I can buy a man a drink. Even so, the blues were still winning.

Across Fourth Street near Avenue C, another light, another stop. Paul Butterfield was singing "I've got a mind to give up living" through my car's speaker and the music wafted out into the thick city air. I had lit a smoke, and was thinking my thoughts, when I heard her voice—"You like that sad old music, *hombre*?"—and my eyes were pulled to a Puerto Rican flower: glossy raven hair hanging loose and free, big dark eyes, lips as red as blood before it dries. She was perched on a stoop near the curb, a shiny white blouse tied just under her heavy breasts, creamy skin tapering to a tiny waist and flaring out dramatically in pink toreador pants. One spike heel tapped out a rhythm on the hot sidewalk.

"The blues are the truth, little girl," I told her—and she swivel-hipped her way up to the Plymouth to hear what else the stranger had to say.

She was fifteen years old—or thirty—I couldn't tell. But she'd never again be as beautiful. Every eye on the street followed her. I looked over to the stoop where she'd been sitting and I saw four men sitting. Watching.

The Puerto Rican flower was no whore—she was a fire-starter. She bit into her lower lip, making it swell against the pressure, leaning one perfect hip against the Plymouth.

I only had a minute to make up my mind, but it was no contest—she was for sale all right, but the price was a war with at least one of the watching young bloods. I wasn't buying—young blood gets hot, and hot blood gets spilled.

"What's your name, honey?" she wanted to know. And I knew she never would. I took one of her hands in mine, the red-lacquered nails gleaming in the sun. "Make today last, beautiful girl," I told her. I kissed her hand, and drove off.

It wasn't going to be my day—I knew the feeling. I drove aimlessly, the music playing, getting it under control. It wasn't nice, but I'd do the time—I'd done it before.

I went back across the bridge, past the House of Detention, telling myself that being depressed on the street was better than being depressed in jail, but it only worked for a couple of blocks.

I parked on Nevins Avenue to get some smokes, sat on the hood of the Plymouth, and lit one up. In no hurry to go nowhere. Right across from me were three old black guys—impossible to tell how old—wearing winter coats in the warm weather, sitting on some milk crates, passing around a bottle of wine, talking to each other about something. Minding their own business, sitting in the sun. Not all clubhouses have doors and windows.

Then I saw the pack of punks bopping up the street on the same side as the old men. Four white kids; they all had those weird haircuts, short and spiky in front, long in back, streaks of bright color and sticking up. They were dressed in short-sleeved leather jackets. One sported a long black cane with an eagle's head on top and probably a sword inside. Another one had a collar around his neck that looked like it belonged on a bulldog. They all were wearing black half-gloves, the kind that leave your fingertips out and knuckles bare. The punk with the cane came first, the others fanning out behind him. Then the biggest one moved up on the outside wing of the flying wedge, bouncing up the street throwing left jabs at anyone who came by—the others laughing as people fell over themselves to get out of the way.

As they passed by the old men, the big one fired a vicious jab square into the chest of one of them, knocking the old-timer right off his crate. I stepped off the hood of the Plymouth, reaching into my pocket for the roll of quarters I always keep there to pay tolls—but before I could move, the old man shook his head violently and struggled to his feet. He rubbed his face with both fists, drew a deep snarfling breath through his nose, and shuffled forward, suddenly hooking with both hands. The big kid threw up his own hands in some feeble imitation of boxers he'd seen on television, but he never had a chance. The old man drove the kid back against the side of a van like it was the ropes in the ring he must have fought in years ago, firing punch after punch to the kid's unprotected face and stomach—hard, professional punches, coming unpredictably from both hands. The big kid dropped to the street; the old man turned and went to a neutral corner, running on automatic pilot.

The street was quiet, but you could feel the joy swelling out of the bodegas and the bars. The big kid lay where he dropped—I scanned the street, but his running buddies were nowhere in sight. About what you'd expect. And the old man was back on his milk crate, being with his friends.

When the old man heard the bell, he knew what he had to do. Maybe he was past talking about it, but he could still do it. When I looked around again, the big kid was gone. And so were my blues.

# 5

THE THIRD SHIFT WAS JUST getting started when I wheeled the big Plymouth up Flatbush Avenue to the gas station. I pulled up to the high-test pump, told the jockey to fill it up, and watched the shifty-eyed slob pour an extra twenty-eight cents' worth of gas down the side of my car just so the total would come out even and he wouldn't have to count to make change. When he came around to the window, I just said "Julio?" and he nodded toward the back. Before he could ask for his cash, I flicked the lever into Drive and took off.

As soon as I pulled behind the station and saw the white Coupe de Ville I knew Julio had sent one of his stooges to make the payoff—the old man's idea of a class act. The white Caddy had the driver's window down—the guy inside picked up the Plymouth and was opening his door even before I came to a stop. Just what I expected: a full-race Cheech—about twenty-five years old, blow-dried hair over a blocky face sporting an Atlantic City tan and dark glasses, white silk shirt open to his chest so I could see the gold chains, dark tight pants, shiny black half-boots. His sleeves were rolled up enough to show me muscular forearms, a heavy gold bracelet on one wrist, a thin gold watch on the other. Central Casting.

The Cheech stepped out of his Caddy, flicking the door shut behind him, strolling over to me.

"You Burke?" he wanted to know.

"Sure," I told him. I wasn't there for the conversational opportunity.

"I got something for you—from Mr. C."

I held out my left hand, palm up, keeping my right where he couldn't see it.

"I got ten big ones here," he said, tapping his front pocket.

I didn't say anything—the jerk was unhappy about something, but it wasn't my problem.

He peered into the Plymouth, watching my face. And then he came out with it. "You don't look so tough to me, man. Whatever you did for the old man—I coulda done it."

"Give me the fucking money," I told him pleasantly. "I didn't drive out here to listen to your soap opera."

"Hey, fuck you, you don't want to listen! Money talks, right?"

"I don't know, kid. But the money you're holding for me better *walk*, you understand?"—opening and closing my hand a couple of times so he'd get the message.

The Cheech took off his dark glasses, hooked them over his dangling chains, acting like he was really thinking about not paying me—or acting like he was really thinking, I couldn't tell which. Then he decided. He handed over the envelope without another word, something still on his mind. I tossed it into the back seat, giving him something else to think about. I took my foot off the brake and the Plymouth started to roll forward.

"Hey!" he said. "Wait a minute."

"What?"

"Uh . . . look, man. You ever use anyone else on jobs . . . you know. I could always use some extra coin, right?"

"No," I told him, my face flat as a prison wall.

"Hey, just *listen* for a minute, okay? I got experience, you know what I'm saying?"

"Kid," I told him, "I got warrants out on me older than you," and started to roll forward again.

The Cheech's hand went in his pocket again, but this time he came out with a snub-nosed revolver—he stuck it through the open window, holding it steady, about six inches from my face.

"Don't fucking *move*! You got that? You fucking sit there and you listen when I talk, you understand? I ain't no fucking nigger you can just walk away from—I'm *talking* to you."

I looked at him, saying nothing. There was nothing to say—Julio sent me a messenger boy with some dangerous delusions. It's hard to get good help nowadays.

"You show me some respect, huh?" barked the Cheech. "You ain't no fucking better than me."

"Yeah, I am," I told him, nice and calm and gentle. "I think about what I'm going to do before I do it. Now *you* think about it. Think about me coming here alone. Think about how you're going to get out of this alley if you pull the trigger. Think about what you're going to tell the old man. Think about it . . . then think about what you have to say—and say it."

The Cheech tried to think and hold the gun on me at the same time. It was too much work and his brain overloaded. The snub-nose trembled in his hand for a second and he looked at it as if it had tricked him. When his eyes came back up to me, he was looking at the sawed-off shotgun I was holding in my right hand.

"I'm listening," I told him. But he had nothing to say. "You know how to load that thing?" I asked him. "Or did someone do it for you?"

"I know . . . " he mumbled.

"Then fucking *un*load it, kid. And do it slow—or I'm going to blow your pretty gold chains right through your chest."

He pointed the pistol up, popped the cylinder, held it upside down, and slowly dropped out the bullets. They made a soft plopping sound as they hit the ground. There was so much wet garbage in that alley you could have dropped a safe from a ten-story building without too much noise.

"Listen to me," I said, calm as an undertaker. "You made a mistake. You even *think* about making another one, go make out a will, understand?"

He just nodded. It was an improvement.

I tapped the gas and the Plymouth rolled out of the alley, heading home. By the time I crossed Flatbush Avenue, my hands had stopped shaking.

# 6

THE PLYMOUTH SLOWLY MADE its way down Atlantic Avenue. It wasn't the fastest way back from Brooklyn, but it was the quietest. I eyeballed all the antique shoppes and trendo restaurants which had sprung to life in the last few months—the wino-rehab centers and storefront churches never had a prayer. The new strip runs from Flatbush all the way down past the Brooklyn House of Detention—pioneer-yuppie lofts with stained-glass windows sat over little stores where you could buy fifty different kinds of cheese. Some of the stores still sold wine, though not the kind you drank out of a paper bag. But news of the urban renaissance hadn't filtered down to the neighborhood skells yet—it still wasn't a good idea to linger at a red light after dark.

I turned up Adams Street, heading for the Brooklyn Bridge. The first streaks of filthy daylight were already in the sky. The Family Court was on my right, the Supreme Court on my left. It works good that way—when the social workers are done with the kids, the prisons can take them.

The newsboy was standing on the median strip just before the entrance to the bridge. He had a stack of papers under one arm, hustling for an honest buck. Motorists who knew the system beeped their horns, held their arms out the window, and the kid would rush over, slap a paper into your hand, pocket the change, and keep moving. Every once in a while a patrol car would decide the kid should work some other corner, but mostly the cops leave the kids alone.

I pulled into the Left Turn Only lane, ignoring the sign like everyone else. When I hit the horn, the kid came over. I pushed the switch to lower my window and took a close look: black kid, about fifteen, husky build, Navy watch cap over a bushy Afro. I waved away the *Daily News* he offered.

"Roscoe working today?" I asked.

"Yeah, man. He working. 'Cross the way, you know?"

I already had the Plymouth rolling, timing it so I'd get caught at the light. I watched the black kid fly back across the street to tell Roscoe he had a customer. The twenty-four-hour news station was saying something about another baby beaten to death; this one in the Bronx. So many cases like that now, all they do is give you the daily body count.

The light changed. The Plymouth rolled forward until I spotted Roscoe standing on the divider, a bunch of papers in one hand, a big canvas bag held by a thick strap around his neck. Roscoe's about thirty, too old to be selling papers.

He recognized the car—looked close to be sure he recognized the driver too.

"Paper, mister?"

"Yeah, give me *The Wall Street Journal*," I said, holding a twenty out toward him at the same time.

"Oh, yeah. I got one around here someplace," he mumbled, rummaging in his canvas bag.

While he was looking down at his bag, I did a quick scan of the streets, knowing he was doing the same. Nothing. I reached my left hand out for the paper Roscoe was holding over the open top of his bag, snapped the twenty toward him, and dropped the sawed-off into his bag at the same time. Gravity is one law nobody fucks with.

Roscoe comes honestly by his name, if not his income. I tossed yesterday's *News* on the front seat and drove off, heading for Chinatown. I don't like to carry heat across the border.

# 7

THE CHINATOWN STREETS WERE just getting organized: young men pushing hand trucks loaded with fresh vegetables, older women lumbering toward another day in the sweatshops. I spotted Hobart Chan cruising the Bowery in his sable Bentley, a shark looking for blood in the water. Even gangsters go to work early in Chinatown.

I rolled past Mama's checking the front window. The white dragon tapestry was in place—everything cool inside. I tooled through the narrow alley and left the Plymouth in its usual spot, right underneath some Chinese writing on the wall that warned the local hoods not to park there. It didn't bother me—it was Max's writing.

I went through the kitchen and into the back like I usually do. When I opened the door, one of Mama's alleged cooks smoothly slipped his hand inside his white coat—he pulled it back empty when he recognized me. I walked to the front, pulled the two-star edition of the *News* from underneath the register, and walked to my table in the back, next to the kitchen. No one approached my table pretending to be a waiter, so Mama was around someplace. I read through last night's race results from Yonkers and waited.

I caught a shadow across the newspaper and looked up. It was Mama—looking as though she just stepped out of a 1950s beauty parlor, hair black and glossy in a tight bun at the back of her head, plain high-collared blue silk dress that almost covered her shoes, a jade necklace setting off her dark-painted lips. She's somewhere between fifty and ninety years old.

"So, Burke. You come to eat?"

"To eat and to see Max, Mama. He around?"

"Burke, you know Max not come around so much anymore. Not since he take up with that bar girl. You know that bar girl—the one from Vietnam?"

"Yeah, I met her."

"That girl no good for Max, Burke. He not keeping his mind on business—not reliable like before, right?"

"He's okay, Mama. There's no problem."

"You wrong, Burke. *Plenty* problems. Problems for me, problems for Max, maybe problems for you, okay?"

"I'll talk to him," I told her, more to stop this broken record than anything else.

"Yes, you talk to him. I talk to him, he not listen, okay?"

"Okay. You got any hot-and-sour soup?"

But even the mention of her favorite potion didn't calm her down. Mama was a businesswoman in her heart. She wanted me to get on

Max's case about the girl, but she hadn't been there when they first met. I had.

WE WERE WORKING THE box system that night on the subway: me lying across three empty seats on the uptown express, dressed in my Salvation Army suit and a smashed old fedora, Max right across from me wearing an old raincoat, staring straight ahead like he was on his way to some early-morning cook's job, the Mole at the other end of the car, Coke-bottle lenses fixed on pages and pages of his "calculations" on some greasy paper. I had the papers we had contracted to deliver sewn into the lining of my suit jacket. I don't carry heat on this kind of job. The Mole was packing enough high explosive to turn the F Train into a branch of the space shuttle. Max had only his hands and feet—he was more dangerous than the Mole.

I didn't need a disguise—it's no great feat for me to look like a used-up wino. And the Mole always looks like the lunatic he is—not the kind of human you'd want to make eye contact with on the subway. Max can adjust his posture and muscles in his face so he looks like an old man, and that's what he was doing.

The deal is this: If anybody hassles me, I take any amount of abuse that won't cripple me or make me lose the papers. If anyone moves on the Mole, Max steps in, leaving me carrying and clear. And if anyone moves on Max, me and the Mole just sit there and watch. It never takes long.

But that night we weren't alone in the subway car. First this Oriental woman gets on at 14th Street. She was wearing a black cape with a red silk lining over a white silk dress. It buttoned to the throat, but the straight skirt was slit to past mid-thigh. Heavy stage-type makeup, overdone eye shadow, spike heels. Maybe some Off Broadway lames were reviving *Suzie Wong*. She looked at me without expression, didn't even glance at Max or the Mole. She sat there primly, knees together, hands in her lap. Her eyes were unreadable.

And we rode together like that until we got deep into Brooklyn, where the wolfpack boarded the train. Two white kids and a Puerto

Rican, dressed alike in the standard hunting outfit: leather sneakers, dungaree jackets with the sleeves cut off, gloves that left their fingertips exposed, studded wristbands, heavy belts with chains dangling. One carried a giant radio, the others were empty-handed. They checked the car quickly, eyeballing the girl.

But they were looking for money, not fun. A fast score from some working stiff. And Max was the target.

Ignoring me, they surrounded him. One sat down on each side; one of the white kids remained standing, facing Max. The spokesman.

"Hey, Pop—how about twenty bucks for a cup of coffee?"

Nobody laughed—it wasn't a joke.

Max didn't respond. For one thing, he doesn't speak. For another, he doesn't pay a lot of attention to bugs.

I glanced over at the Mole under the brim of my hat. The yellow-orange subway lighting bounced off his thick glasses as he buried his head deep into some papers. He never looked up. The skells weren't paying any attention to me, just concentrating on Max. One of the white kids snatched Max's old raincoat, jerking the lapels toward him to pull Max to his feet. But nothing happened—I could see the muscles ripple in the kid's arm as he strained, but it was like he was trying to pull up an anchor. The other maggots crowded in, and the Puerto Rican kid snarled, "Give it up, old man!" The other white kid started to giggle. He pulled out a set of cheap brass knuckles, the kind they sell to kids in Times Square. He slowly fitted them over one hand, made a fist, smacked it into an open palm. The slapping sound brought the Mole's head up for a second. Max never moved.

The kid with the brass knuckles went on giggling to himself while the other white kid struggled to pull Max to his feet and the Puerto Rican kept up a steady stream of threats. None of them was in a hurry.

Then the girl got to her feet. I could hear the tapping of her spike heels as she closed the gap between herself and the maggots. They never looked her way until she hissed at them: "Hey! Leave the old man alone!"

Then they spun to her, delighted with new prey, abandoning Max.

The Puerto Rican kid was the first to speak.

"Fuck off, bitch! This ain't your business!"

But the woman kept closing on them, hands on hips. Now the whole wolfpack had its back to Max, moving toward her. The white kid was still giggling, still slamming his brass knuckles into an open palm. The woman walked right into the center of the triangle they formed. As the white kid reached a hand toward the front of her dress, I lurched to my feet in a drunken stupor and stumbled into him. He whirled to face me, brass knuckles flashing. I threw up a weak arm to try and fend him off as the Oriental woman unsheathed her claws and the Mole reached into his satchel. But then Max the Silent shed his dirty raincoat like an old scaly skin and moved in. It was too fast for me to follow—a hollow crack and I knew the Puerto Rican kid would never reach for anything again without major medical assistance—the flash of a foot and the biggest white kid screamed like ground glass was being pulled through his lungs—a steel-hard fist against the skull of the punk with the brass knuckles and I saw the front of his face open like an overripe melon too long in the sun.

The subway car was dead quiet inside, rumbling on unperturbed toward the next express stop. The Mole took his hands out of his satchel and went back to whatever he was reading. The three maggots were on the ground, only one of them conscious enough to moan—it was the Puerto Rican kid, blood and foam bubbling out of his mouth.

The woman stood shock-still, her face drained of color, her hands frozen at her sides. Max the Silent looked into her face, and bowed deeply to her. She caught her breath, and bowed back. They stood looking at each other, seeing nothing else.

Max gestured for me to stand, pointed at his mouth and then at me. The Oriental woman's eyes flashed, but she seemed beyond surprise now. She stood swaying slightly with the train's rhythm, balancing easily on the spike heels, dark-lacquered talons on silky hips. She watched the wino remove his hat and smooth out his tangled hair. If she was expecting another transformation, she was deeply disappointed. The distance between the real Max the Silent and a helpless old man was cosmic—the distance between the real me and a bum was considerably less. But I bowed to the woman too.

"My brother does not speak or hear. He can read lips, and those who know him can understand him perfectly. He wishes to speak with you, through me. With your permission . . . ?"

The woman's eyebrows arched, and she nodded, saying nothing . . . waiting patiently. I liked her already.

Max gestured toward her, two fingers held against his thumb. He turned that same hand back toward his heart, tapped his chest lightly, bowed, reached his left hand back to the old, discarded raincoat, held it in one hand, touched his eyes, one at a time, with the other. He touched his heart again.

"My brother says you are a woman of great courage, to protect what you thought was an old man against such dangerous people."

The woman cleared her throat, smiled gently with the side of her mouth. She spoke as gravely as I had, with just the trace of a French accent in her speech.

"Your brother is quite deceptive."

Max absently swung his foot into the rib cage of one of the maggots lying on the floor, never taking his eyes off the woman. I heard a sound like a twig snapping. He touched his eyes again, shook his head "no." He expanded his chest; his eyes flattened and power flowed from his body. He turned to me.

"My brother says a maggot cannot see a true man," I told her.

Still with the same half-smile, she asked, "Can a maggot see a true woman?"

Max took a pair of dark glasses from my coat pocket—he knows where I keep them—and put them on his face. He made a gesture like tapping with a cane, took off the glasses, threw both hands toward the woman, and smiled.

"My brother says even a blind man could see a woman such as you," I translated, and she was smiling too, even before I finished.

That's how Max met Immaculata.

# 8

TO MAMA, IMMACULATA WAS a "bar girl," her catchall phrase for anything from prostitute to hostess. A Vietnamese was bad enough, but one of mixed parentage was suspect beyond redemption. As far as she was concerned, a true warrior didn't need a woman, except on an occasional basis.

Mama never seemed to move from her restaurant, but nothing escaped her sight. She knew Max still lived in the back of the warehouse near Division Street, where his temple lay hidden upstairs. But he didn't live alone anymore. For Mama, anything that wasn't business was bad.

Immaculata had been working as a hostess in a Manhattan bar before she met Max. She had been trained as some kind of psychotherapist in France, but she couldn't practice in this country until she completed enough courses and got a license.

I saw her work one day when I went over to the warehouse looking for Max. I pulled the Plymouth into the garage on the first floor. It was empty—it always was. I got out of the car, closed the garage doors, and waited. If Max was around, he'd be there soon enough. If he didn't show in a couple of minutes, I'd just chalk a message to him on the back wall.

I heard the sound of fingers snapping, looked to my left, and there was Max. He was holding a finger to his lips—no noise. I climbed out of the Plymouth, leaving the door open, and walked over to where Max was standing. He motioned for me to follow him upstairs.

We padded along the narrow catwalk past the entrance to his temple. When we came to the blank wall behind the temple door, Max reached up and pulled back a curtain. We were looking through some one-way glass into what looked like a kid's playroom: kid-size furniture, brightly painted walls, toys all over the place. Immaculata was seated at a small table. Across from her was a little girl—maybe four years old. They were both in profile to us. It looked like they were playing with some dolls together.

I shrugged my shoulders, spread my hands, palms up. "What is this?" I was asking Max. He patted the air in front of him with both hands and pointed to his eyes: "Be patient and watch."

There were four dolls on the table. Two were bigger than an average kid's doll; the other two were a lot smaller. From their clothes and their hair I could see that two were male and two female.

Immaculata put the dolls to one side of the table and asked the kid something, looking calm and patient. The little girl took one of the small dolls and started to undress it, slowly and reluctantly. Then she stopped. She took the big male doll and made it sort of pat the little girl on the head. The little doll pulled away from the pat, but not too far. Finally, the big male doll helped the little girl doll get undressed. The big male doll unbuttoned his pants. It had plain white boxer shorts underneath. The child took off the shorts, revealing a set of testicles and a penis. The little girl doll was pushed over toward the big doll. The child kept lifting the male doll's penis, but it always flopped back. Finally, she put the little girl doll's mouth against the male doll's penis. A couple of dead-weight seconds went by. Then the child pulled the little girl doll away from the big doll. She put the little girl doll face down on the floor—then she had the big male doll pull up his shorts and pants and walk away.

The little girl was crying. Immaculata didn't move—but she was talking to the child. You couldn't hear a thing outside the window. She put out her hand to the child. The little girl took her hand, and Immaculata gently pulled her around to where she was sitting. She put the little girl on her lap, one arm around her back. She kept talking until the child nodded agreement to something.

Then Immaculata reached out for the big male doll and put it right in front of the child. The little girl grabbed the doll and started to shake it, screaming something. Her face was contorted in rage. She ripped at the big doll. Suddenly, the big doll's arm came off in her hand. The child looked at the arm she was holding, then back to Immaculata, who nodded something to her. The child ripped off the other arm.

Then she started talking to the big, armless doll, shaking her finger in some kind of admonishment. Then she started to cry again.

Max motioned for me to follow him again. He pointed back toward his temple, telling me to wait for him.

I walked through the temple, being careful not to step past the black lines painted in a rectangle on the bleached wood floor. Then around to the back stairs, and from there into the small room that opened onto an alley behind the warehouse. I went over to the battered wood desk and pulled out the last score-sheet from our endless gin-rummy game.

I heard a knock at the back door. Then another. And then three raps, short and sharp. Max. I opened the door to let him in. If the three raps had come first, I wouldn't have opened the door without a gun in my hand.

Max and Immaculata came in together. She greeted me the way she always does—a slight bow of her head over her hands clasped in front. Always formal. She sat down across the table from me. Max went around behind me so he could watch her lips when she spoke.

"What was that I was watching?" I asked her.

"That was what we call a 'validation,' Burke."

"Validation?"

"That little girl has gonorrhea—a sexually transmitted disease. It was my job to find out how she contracted it."

"And she showed you?"

"Yes. The large doll is her father. Many children, especially very young ones, have no ability to use a narration. Most of them don't even have the words for what has been done to them."

"I never saw dolls like that," I said.

"They're 'anatomically correct' dolls. Under the clothes, the bodies have genitals proportionate to their size. They have to be specific, especially when the children don't speak."

"You mean when they're too young?"

"Not necessarily. The child you saw is almost six years old. But she had been told that the 'game' Daddy plays with her is their special secret and she isn't to tell anyone."

"Did he threaten her?"

"No. In fact, most incest offenders don't use threats until their victim is a lot older than this one. The child almost instinctively knows something is wrong with the activity, but the combination of guilt and fear is usually enough to ensure silence."

"What was that thing at the end—with the arms on the doll?"

"Just what it looked like to you. Rage. Sexually abused children are often consumed with anger at the person who hurt them. And sometimes at the person who failed to protect them as well. Part of the treatment process is letting them know it's okay to say 'No!'—it's okay to be angry. The arms and legs of the dolls are attached with Velcro; the children can tear them apart—and maybe put them together later, if they come that far."

"Doesn't the kid live with her father?"

"She lives with her mother. The incest happens during the time she visits him."

"No more visits for him?"

"That's really up to the courts. When the child showed signs of having been sexually abused, the mother took her to a doctor. She didn't know what was wrong, but she knew *something* was. The doctor didn't find anything physical—he never thought to check for V.D., it never occurred to him. The actual diagnosis wasn't made until weeks later—when the mother took the child to the emergency ward because of a vaginal discharge. The child was referred to a program where they do therapy and also teach the children physical and emotional self-defense. I work there too—I need the supervision to qualify for my license here. What I was doing in the playroom was preparing the child for supervised visitation with her father. She has to know she can confront her father and tell him to stop, and she has to feel protected if she is to do that."

"Why should this maggot get *any* visits with her?"

"That's a good question," she said. "The answer is that the child must work through her own rage at what happened to her. She has to recapture a sense of control over her life. The supervised visits are not meant to benefit the father—they are therapeutic for the daughter. And, at the same time, the father can start his own treatment."

"How about if he denies the whole thing?"

"They usually do, at first. But eventually, most of them do acknowledge what they have done—covering it, of course, with a thick layer of self-justification."

"What justification?"

"Oh, that the child was the instigator . . . that this was nothing more than showing his affection in a special way . . . minimizing."

"What bullshit. Is he going to be tested for gonorrhea?"

"Yes, he will be tested. But it takes less than twenty-four hours for all traces of the disease to disappear if he gets treatment. However, the courts will consider the presence of a sexually transmitted disease together with my validation. And find against him."

"You're telling me there really is treatment for these people?"

"That's one of the major arguments in the profession today—I don't know the answer."

"I don't know about incest like this. But the maggots who like sex with kids *never* stop."

"Pedophiles may well be incurable. I don't know. I work only with the victims."

Max crossed over to stand behind Immaculata. He shook his fist tightly to show me how proud he was of his woman. She looked up at him and I knew this wasn't a day for gin rummy.

# 9

EVERYTHING PROBABLY WOULD have blown over between Immaculata and Mama except that Max brought his woman to the restaurant one night. In honor of the occasion, we all took one of the big tables near the back. There's no air conditioning in Mama's place, but the atmosphere was like a meat locker anyway. Mama wasn't insane enough to openly insult Immaculata, so they fought their battle with the subtle fire only women of character ever truly master.

One of the thugs brought a huge tureen of hot-and-sour soup.

Mama bowed to Immaculata, indicating she should serve everyone—that's what bar girls do, right? But Immaculata never flinched—she took Max's bowl off his plate and spooned in a generous helping, being extra-careful to serve it properly, a full measure of all the ingredients, not just the thin stuff on top. Mama smiled at her—the way the coroner smiles at a corpse just before the autopsy.

"You serve man first, not woman. Chinese way, yes?"

"Not the Chinese way, Mrs. Wong—my way. To me, Max comes first, you see?"

"I see. You call me 'Mama,' okay? Like everybody else?"

Immaculata said nothing, bowing her head ever so slightly in agreement. But Mama wasn't finished.

"Immaculata your name? I say that right—Immaculata? Is that Vietnamese name?"

"It's the name the nuns gave me—a Catholic name—when the French were in my country."

"Your country Vietnam, yes?"

"Yes," said Immaculata, her eyes hard.

"Your father and mother both from Vietnam?" Mama asked innocently.

"I don't know my father," Immaculata responded flatly, "but I know what you want to know."

The table was dead quiet then. Max watched Mama, making up his mind—Mama had survived two wars but she was never as close to death as she was at that moment.

Max pointed one steel finger at my face, then opened his hands, asking a question.

I knew what he wanted. "No," I told him, "I don't know who my father was either. So what?"

Max wiped his hands together: "All finished," he meant. The discussion was over.

But he wasn't going to pull it off that easy. "You want to know my father's nationality, yes?" asked Immaculata.

"No," Mama said, "why I want to know that?"

"Because you think it would tell you something about me."

"I already know about you," Mama snapped.

"And what is that?" asked Immaculata, the air around us crackling with violence.

But Mama backed away. "I know you love Max—that good enough. I love Max—Max like my son, right? Even Burke—like my son too. Have two sons—very different. So what, yes?"

"Yes, we understand each other," Immaculata told her, as Mama bowed her agreement.

"You call me 'Mama'?" the dragon lady asked.

"Yes. And you call me Mac, okay?"

"Okay," said Mama, declaring a truce, at least when Max was around.

## 10

BUT MAX WASN'T AROUND NOW, so I'd have to leave the money with Mama. No big deal—anytime I make a score, I stash some of it with Max or Mama. It's not that I have such good savings habits—it's just that it's a long time between decent scores for me. I didn't mind working without a license, but I wasn't going to try it without a net.

The last time I went back to prison changed everything. When you're raised by the state, you don't think about the same things citizens do. You find out sooner or later that time is money—if you don't have money, you're going to keep on doing time. Most of the guys I came up with were doing life sentences on the installment plan. A few years in—a few months out.

I thought I had it figured out before I took my last fall. Up to then, I kept making the mistake of involving citizens in my business. There's a different set of rules for them and for us. You stab a man in prison, you might end up in the Hole for a few months—you stick up a liquor store on the street and you're looking at telephone numbers behind the walls, especially if you've been there before. I'd taught myself some things by then, and I knew better than to work with partners who wouldn't stand up. And I knew where the money was—if I wanted to steal without making citizens mad at me, I had to steal from the bad guys. Back then, the heroin business was strictly European—the blacks were only on the retail end and the Hispanics hadn't made their move. The Italians were moving pounds and pounds of junk all through the city, and they weren't too careful about it—they had no competition. Max wanted to hijack the gangsters when the money changed hands, but that wouldn't work—the Italians transported the dope without a care in the world, but they got paranoid as hell when it came to cold cash. Too many bodyguards—I wanted a nice smooth sting, not the O.K. Corral.

Finally, I came up with the perfect idea—we'd hijack the dope, and then sell it back for a reasonable price. It worked fine at first. Max and I watched the social club on King Street for a few weeks until we saw how they did it. Three, four times a month, a blue pastry truck with Jersey plates would pull up to the front door, and the driver would offload the covered trays of pastries and the metal tubs of tortoni and spumoni. Within a couple of hours, a dark blue Caddy would pull up outside and the same two hard guys would get out. They looked enough alike to be twins: short, muscular, with thick manes of dark hair worn a little too long in the back.

Max and I watched them walk up to the dark-glass front of the social club. If a couple of the old men were sitting outside—always wearing a plain white shirt over dark suit pants, polished shoes, talking quietly—the young guys would stop and pay their respects. They were muscle all right, but family muscle, working their way up the ladder.

The young guys would go in, but they wouldn't come out for hours. It didn't add up—boys like that might be allowed in the club to get an assignment, or on a special occasion, but the old guys wouldn't let them just hang around.

Max and I learned to be patient in different places, but we both learned it well. It took another few weeks to work our way around to the back of the club and find a spot where the constantly watching eyes in that neighborhood couldn't see what we were doing. Sure enough—ten minutes after they went in the front door, the muscle boys went out the back. One carried a suitcase, the other held a pistol parallel to his leg, barrel pointed down. The guy with the suitcase tossed it into the open trunk of a black Chevy sedan, slammed it closed, and got behind the wheel while the gunman watched the alley. A minute later, the Chevy took off with both of them in the front seat.

I didn't have the Plymouth then, so Max and I followed them in a cab—me behind the wheel and Max as the passenger. I didn't mind taking some reasonable risks to make some unreasonable money, but I wasn't about to let Max drive.

The muscle boys took their time—they cruised up Houston Street to the East Side Drive. When they crossed the Triboro into the Bronx, I looked a question at Max, but he just shrugged his shoulders—they had to be going to Harlem sooner or later. Sure enough, they circled Yankee Stadium, hooked onto the Major Deegan Expressway, and took the exit to the Willis Avenue Bridge. At the end of the exit road all they had to do was make a quick right and they were back over the bridge and into 125th Street, the heart of Harlem. Another few minutes and they parked in the back of a funeral parlor. We didn't follow them any farther.

The next two runs followed the same route—we just had one more piece to check out and we were ready to operate. We met in Mama's basement—me, Max, Prophet, and the Mole.

"Prof, can you get a look at how they transfer the stuff? It's in the back of the Golden Gate Funeral Parlor on Twenty-first," I said.

"The next time the move goes down, the Prof shall be around," he assured us.

"Mole, we need three things, okay?" I told him, holding up three fingers to let Max follow along. "We need to disable their car real quick, get the trunk open, and get in the wind."

The Mole nodded, his pasty skin gleaming in the dark basement. "Tiger trap?" he wanted to know. He meant one of his bombs under the lid of a manhole cover—one flick of a switch and the street would open up, dropping the car into the pit. That would sure as hell disable the car, open the trunk, and give us all the time in the world to walk away. It wasn't exactly what I had in mind—the

Mole's heart was in the right place, but it would take years of therapy to reduce him to a lunatic.

"Mole, we don't want to *kill* them, okay? I had in mind maybe the Prof gets their attention for a second, Max and me hit them from either side and brace them—you pop open the trunk, grab the suitcase, and slash the rear tires. How's that?"

"How does the trunk lock?" the Mole wanted to know. It was all the same to him.

I looked over to the Prof and he nodded—we'd know soon.

"You can get us an old Con Ed truck, Mole?" I asked him.

The Mole made a face like "Who couldn't?" It was true enough for him—he lived in a junkyard.

# 11

THE NEXT TIME THE MUSCLE boys stopped at the red light before they turned onto the bridge for Harlem, things were a little different. The battered Con Ed truck was nosed against the metal support for the traffic light, blocking most of the intersection. The black Chevy slid to a smooth stop—running red lights wasn't the best idea when you were carrying a trunkful of dream dust.

I climbed out of the driver's seat, wearing a set of Con Ed coveralls and a thick leather tool belt around my waist with another strap over one shoulder. My eyes were covered with blue-tinted sunglasses—I had pasted on a heavy mustache a few minutes ago. The Con Ed cap covered a thick blonde wig and the built-up heels on my work boots made me two inches taller. The Prof was slumped against a building wall, an empty bottle of T-Bird by his side, dead to the world.

I walked toward the Chevy, spreading my hands in the universal civil-service hostile apology: "What can I do?" The driver wasn't going for any delay—he spun the wheel with one hand to pull around the truck: I could get out of the way or get run over. His hard face said it was all the same to him. He was in control.

Then it all went to hell. I tore open the snaps on the coveralls and unleashed the scattergun I had on a rawhide cord around my neck just as the Mole threw the truck into reverse and stomped the gas. The truck flew backward right into the Chevy's radiator, and one chop from Max took out the guy in the passenger seat before he could move. The Prof flew off the wall, an ice pick in his hand. I don't know if the driver heard the hiss from his rear tires—all he could see were the twin barrels of the sawed-off staring him in the face from a distance of three feet.

I flicked the scattergun up a couple of inches and the driver got the picture—his hands never moved off the wheel. He didn't see the Mole slither out of the truck and around to the back of the Chevy—another couple of seconds and the trunk was open and Max had the suitcases.

I patted the air in front of me to tell the driver to get down in the front seat. As soon as his head started to drop, I cut loose with the scattergun right into his door. I blasted the second barrel where his head had been a second ago, taking out most of the windshield, and sprinted for the side of the warehouse where the cab was waiting. Max was at the wheel, with the Mole beside him, the engine already running. I tossed the empty scattergun to the Prof in the back seat, dove in beside him, and we were rolling. Everyone knew what they had to do—we were pretty sure there was no backup car, but it was too early to relax. The Mole had his grubby hands deep in his satchel and the Prof was already reloading the shotgun for me.

# 12

WE LEFT THE SUITCASES with the Mole in his junkyard and split up. We didn't make our move for a few weeks—the mobsters were too busy murdering each other to answer anonymous telephone calls. I don't know if they dusted the driver and his partner or not—probably kept them alive long enough to make sure they were telling the truth, and then started looking. But they weren't looking outside the family. Me and Max and the Prof were sitting in Mama's restaurant when we read the headline in the *Daily News*—"Torched Building Was Gangster Tomb!" It seems someone had wiped out a whole meeting of the heroin syndicate and then set fire to the building—the Fire Department hadn't discovered the bodies for a couple of days, and it took another few days for the cops to make positive identifications. That kind of massive hit didn't sound like it was connected to our little hijacking, but we didn't know who we could ask.

The Prof looked up from the paper. "Sounds like Wesley's work to me," he whispered.

"Don't ever say that name again," I snapped at him. Wesley was a guy we had done time with before—if I thought he was operating in New York, I'd move to the Coast.

Anytime you pull a snatch-and-switch, the last part is the hardest. You can grab the goods easy enough—the mark isn't expecting the move—you just disappear and let them look in their own backyard. But when it gets down to exchanging the goods for cash, you got major troubles. It's easy enough to do if you don't mind losing some of your troops along the way, but our army was too small for that kind of sacrifice.

We agreed to wait another two weeks. It was fine with the Prof. Max looked unhappy. I spread my hands, asking him "What?" He just shook his head. He'd tell me when he was ready.

## 13

WE WERE IN THE SUB-BASEMENT of Mama's restaurant, planning the exchange. It was simple enough—I'd make contact over the phone, explain my problem, and wait for the solution to come from them. Sooner or later they'd agree to use one of the free-lance couriers who work the fringes of our world. These guys worked off a straight piece, no percentage—maybe ten thousand to deliver a package and bring something back. You could move anything around the city that way—gold, diamonds, blueprints, funny money, whatever. None of the couriers were family people, although one was Italian. They were men of honor—men you could trust. Even back then, there were only a few of them. There's even fewer now. Anyway, the scam was for them to suggest some halfass plan that would get me killed, and for me to act scared and start to back out. They'd eventually get around to suggesting one of the couriers, and Max was on that list. We'd agree on Max, and that would be it. Simple and clean—the heroin for the cash. I laid it out for the others, figuring on scoring about fifty grand apiece when this was over.

"No," said the Mole, his pasty face indistinct in the candlelight.

The Prof chipped in, "Burke, you know what the people say—when it comes to junk, the Silent One don't play."

And Max himself just shook his head from side to side.

I knew what the Prof meant. Max would carry anything, anywhere. His delivery collateral was his life. But everybody knew he wouldn't move narcotics. If he suddenly agreed to do this, it'd make the bad guys suspicious. Even if they let him walk away, he'd have to make dope runs from then on. No matter what kind of sting we pulled off, if Max was the courier he was finished.

There wasn't much to say after that. I watched the candle flame throw shadows on the walls, burning up my plans to be free of this nickel-and-dime hustling once and for all. I wasn't going into the dope business, and I wasn't giving this up without another try.

"Prof, your cousin still work for the post office?"

"Melvin's a lifer, brother—he's hooked on that regular paycheck."

"Would he hold out a package for us if we paid him?"

"Have to pay him a good piece, Burke—he *loves* that joint. What's the idea?"

"The idea is, we *mail* the stuff back to them. Mole, how much was in the suitcases?"

"Forty kilos—twenty bags in each case. Plastic bags. Heat-sealed."

"Prof, that's worth what on the street?"

"Depends—how pure is it now, how many times you step on it. . . ."

"Mole . . . ?"

"It's ninety, ninety-five percent pure."

"Prof . . . ?"

"They could hit it at least ten times. Figure twenty grand a key, at the least."

"So they'd pay five?"

"They'd pay the five just to stay alive."

"That's two hundred thousand, okay? How about we mail them four keys, okay? No questions asked. Just to show good faith? And we give them a post-office box number, and tell them to mail us the money for the *next* installment. We keep running like that until we're near the end. All they can beat us for is the first and last piece, right?"

"No good," said the Prof. "They'd trace the box, or have some men waiting. You know."

"Not if Melvin intercepts the shipment. He still works in the back, right? All he has to do is pull their package of money off the line when it shows up."

"Melvin don't work twenty-four hours a day, man. He's bound to miss some of them."

"So what? We don't need *all* of them. Every exchange is twenty grand coming from them. If Melvin can pull ten out of twenty, it's *still* fifty apiece, right?"

"It's shaky, man. I don't like it."

I turned to Max. He hadn't moved from his place against the wall, standing with his corded forearms folded, no expression on his face. He shook his head again. No point asking the Mole. We were back to Square One. The Prof was looking at me like I was a bigger load of dope than the one we'd hijacked.

I lit a cigarette, drawing into myself, trying to think through the mess. Keeping the dope wasn't a problem—the Mole's junkyard was as safe as Mother Teresa's reputation, and heroin doesn't get stale from sitting around—but we took all this risk and now we had nothing to show for it. Waiting didn't bother Max, and the Prof had done too much time behind the walls to care. I watched the candle flame, looking deep into it, breathing slowly, waiting for an answer.

Then the Mole said, "I know a tunnel." He didn't say anything else.

"So what, Mole?" I asked him.

"A subway tunnel," he explained, like he was talking to a child, "a subway tunnel from an abandoned station back out to the street."

"Mole, *everybody* knows about those tunnels—in the winter, half the winos in the city sleep down there."

"Not a way in—a way out," said the Mole, and it slowly dawned on me that we could still pull it off.

"Show me," I asked him. And the Mole pulled out a mess of faded blueprints from his satchel, laid one flat on the basement floor, and shone his pocket flash for us all to see.

"See here, just past Canal Street? You come in any of these entrances. But there's a *little* tunnel—it runs from Canal all the way up to Spring Street . . . see?"—pointing a grubby finger at some faint lines on the paper and looking up as though even an idiot like me would understand by now.

When he saw I still wasn't with him, the Mole's tiny eyes blinked hard behind his thick lenses. He hadn't done this much talking in the last six months and it was wearing him out. "We meet them in the tunnel near Canal. We get there first. They block all the exits. We give them the product and we take the money. We go out heading west . . . see, here? . . . they go out heading east. But we don't go out the exit. We take this little tunnel all the way through here"—tracing the lines—"and we come out on Spring Street."

"And if they follow us?"

The Mole gave me a look of total disgust. He was done talking. He took his satchel, pushed it away from him with his boot, so it was standing between us. "Tick, tick," said the Mole. They wouldn't follow us.

Now I got it. "How long would it take us to get to the Spring Street stop?"

The Mole shrugged. "Ten minutes, fifteen. It's a narrow tunnel. One at a time. No lights."

Yeah, it could work. By the time the wiseguys figured we weren't coming out any of the Canal Street exits, they'd have to go back inside to look for us, and we should be long gone by then. They'd figure we'd be hiding out, waiting for darkness to fall, or that we'd try to slip away in the rush-hour crowd. And even if they did tip to the plan, we'd have too much of a head start.

"It's great, Mole!" I told him.

The Prof extended his hand, palm up, to offer his congratulations. The Mole figured the Prof wanted to see his blueprints, and tossed the whole bundle into the Prof's lap. Some guys are just culturally deficient.

I looked at Max. He was watching the whole thing, but his face never changed. "What's wrong *now*?" I asked him with my hands.

Max walked over to us, squatted down until his face was just a few inches from mine. He rolled up his sleeve, pulled off an imaginary tie, and looped it around his bicep . . . he put one end in his teeth and pulled it tight. Then he drove two fingers into the crook of his arm, where the vein would be bulging, used his thumb to push the plunger home, and rolled his eyes up. A junkie getting high. Max watched my face carefully. He folded his arms in the universal gesture of rocking a baby, then opened his arms to let the baby fall to the floor. And he shook his head again. Max the Silent wasn't selling any dope.

I pointed to my watch, spread my hands again. "Why *now*?" I wanted to know.

Max tapped his heart twice with a balled fist, nodding his head "yes." Then he rubbed his fingers together to make the sign for "money," moving his hands back and forth with blinding speed. He was a warrior, not a merchant.

Fuck! I threw up my hands in total disgust. Max watched my face, his own immobile as stone. I used my hands to shape the one-kilo packages of dope in the air, laid them end to end until Max got the idea. We had a whole pile of heroin between us. Then I rubbed my first two fingers and thumb together the way he had before. Money, right? Then I separated my hands, and crossed them in front of my chest, opening them as I did so. Exchanging one for the other. "How?" I wanted to know.

Max smiled his smile: just a thin line of white between his flat lips. He bowed to the Mole and the Prof, then to me. He made the same signs for the dope as I had, and followed it with a gesture that meant throwing something away. Okay, we disposed of the dope—maybe threw it in the river. And then?

Max pointed to the blueprints, nodding his head "yes." We'd make the meet in the tunnel like the Mole wanted, only we wouldn't have any dope with us. I spread my hands wide for him again—how would we get out of there with the money? Max bowed, stepped back out of the circle of light cast by the candle, and vanished. It was dead silent in Mama's basement. I watched the candle burn down, along with my hopes of making a respectable score for the first time in my life.

"Hey, Burke," called the Prof, "when Max comes back, I want you to say something to him for me, okay?"

"Yeah?" I asked him, too depressed to give a damn.

"Yeah. You know how to make the sign for 'chump'?"

The Prof was good at this. Plenty of times he'd cheer us all up on the yard when nothing was happening. It didn't even bring a smile this time.

It got darker and darker in the basement, so quiet I could hear water dripping off in the distance. All of a sudden, the Prof shot straight into the air as if he'd been hoisted by an invisible crane. "Put me down, fool!" he barked, his short legs dangling helplessly. Max stepped into the tiny circle of light, holding the Prof by his jacket in one hand. He opened the hand and the Prof unceremoniously dropped to the floor. I pulled a fresh candle from my pocket and lit up. The shadows flickered on the walls and the darkness moved back another few feet. Now I understood.

"You get it, Mole?" I asked.

"Yes."

"Prof?"

"Yeah. We meet them in the tunnel, Mole kills the lights, and Max does his thing, right?"

"Right."

Max bowed to each of us, waiting for recognition of his superior problem-solving ability. The Prof was right—he *was* a chump.

"It's no good," I told them. "It'll take too long. If Max jumps them all in the tunnel, we'll be running for our lives, okay? And even if we get away with it, they'll never stop looking for us. It doesn't play, okay? It's not what we planned."

"You mean it's not what *you* planned, man," countered the Prof. "We took the shot to score a lot. Max don't want to give them the dope, and you don't want to rough off the money. That leaves us with what?"

That's when I got my brilliant idea that saved me twenty years in the joint. "Mole, you said the stuff was near pure, right?" He didn't answer —the Mole doesn't say anything twice. "Okay, how do you know?"

"Test," said the Mole.

"Test?"

"Heroin is morphine-based. You add something to it, it turns a certain color, you know it's good."

"Mole," I asked him, trying to keep the hope out of my voice, "can you make it turn the right color even if it *isn't* real dope?"

The Mole went into one of his trances—lost in thought. We all kept quiet, like people do around a volcano that might go off. Finally he said, "There would have to be *some* of the morphine-base—or else they would have to pick the right bag to test."

"How far down could you cut in and still make it pass the test?"

"I don't know . . ." said the Mole, his voice trailing off. He pulled out a pencil as stubby and greasy as he was, and starting scribbling formulas on the side of the blueprints, lost to the world.

Finally, he looked up. "How will they pick a bag to test?"

"Who knows?" I told him, looking over at the Prof, who nodded in agreement.

"Two bags of pure," said the Mole, "six bags cut deep. The rest no morphine-base at all. Okay?"

*"Okay!"* I told him. The Prof's grin split the darkness. And then there was Max. But before he could say anything, I took a deck of cards out of my pocket, held it up for him to see, and motioned for him to come close with the others. I dealt out forty cards, one for each bag of dope. Then I separated the cards into four stacks, shov-

ing one in front of each of the others, and keeping one in front of me. I reached over and took the stack away from Max, held it up before his eyes, made a motion like I was spitting on the cards, and tossed them into the darkness of the cellar. I did the same thing with the Mole's share. And then with the Prof's. From my stack, I slowly counted off two cards, then six more—the amount the Mole said he needed to work the scam. And I threw my other two cards away too. I looked at Max, caught his eyes, then took six cards from my little remaining stack and tore them into small pieces. I threw away the big pieces, leaving only scraps behind—and two untouched cards.

There was a long count. Then Max slowly nodded, and we had a deal.

## 14

I WAS ONLY ON THE PHONE for a few minutes with the wiseguys. Two hundred thousand in cash in exchange for forty kilos of their product. And I told them where and when. The gangster who answered the phone listened patiently—I could feel his desire for my death coming over the wire, but he kept his voice quiet. Sure, sure . . . whatever we wanted, no problems . . . very reasonable.

The meet was for five-fifteen on a Thursday evening. Maximum rush-hour mess, so they'd think we planned to lose them in the crowds after we made the switch. We got there just after eleven the night before, set up camp, and started to do what we all did best—wait.

We waited at the apex of the tunnels. The wiseguys would have to come from the east, and they'd have people planted in the tunnel from the west. Plenty of room to do whatever they planned. All we needed was a few minutes to get lost, and I had something with me that would take care of that. I didn't care if they sent Godzilla down the tubes after us—we had it wired.

It was five-fifteen on the dot when Max snapped his fingers and pointed to the east. I couldn't see anything at first, but then I glimpsed a faint beam of light moving slowly in our direction—from the west, where they weren't supposed to come from. And then I heard footsteps, lots of footsteps, coming from the right direction. The Mole put his satchel on the ground, one hand inside. The Prof thumbed back the hammers on my sawed-off, and I fingered the baseball-shaped piece of metal in my jacket pocket. It was going down.

And then the wheels came off. "This is the police!" came a voice on a bullhorn. "You men are surrounded. Drop your weapons and walk toward the sound of my voice with your hands in the air!"

The miserable fucking maggots! Why take a chance of dealing with renegades when they could get their dope back and hand their cop pals some major felony arrests at the same time?

I had to stall them, get time to think.

"How do I know you're the cops?" I shouted back down into the tunnel.

"This is Captain Johnson, N.Y.P.D., pal. Precinct Number One. You are under arrest, you got it? You got two minutes—I don't see hands in the air, I'm going to see blood on the ground."

It was the cops all right, and not the Transit Police either—only the bluecoats talk like that—and only when they've got an audience.

I turned to face my brothers. There was nothing to discuss—the Mole wouldn't last an hour locked up. If the Prof took another fall, they'd hold him for life. And without someone to watch out for him, Max would kill a guard sooner or later. "Prof," I snapped at him, "hit the little tunnel, okay? Take the bags with the real dope with you, leave me the rest. You go first—make sure it's clear on Spring Street before you step out. The Mole follows you. Max brings up the rear in case anyone gets past me. You know where the car is. Got it?"

"Burke," the little man said, "I'm down for the next round. Fuck these blue-coated thieves!"

"Get in the tunnel, Prof. The Mole can't make it without you. Don't let Max do anything crazy."

"Come with us," the Mole told me, hefting his satchel.

"Not a chance, Mole. It won't give us enough time. It's the Man, brother, not the mob. We can't outrun a fucking radio. Go!"

"What're *you* going to do?" asked the Prof.

"Time," I told him.

The Prof looked back for a second, squeezed my arm hard, and hit the tunnel, the Mole right behind. That left Max. I pointed into the tunnel, patted my back to show he had to protect the others, and Max touched his chest, made a motion like he was tearing out his heart, and put his fist in my open palm. He didn't have to tell me—I knew.

I turned in the direction of the bullhorn. "I'm not going back to jail!" I screamed at them. "I'll hold court right here, you understand!" I'd been waiting to use that line since I got out of reform school the first time.

"Give it up, buddy!" came back the cop's voice. "You got no place to go."

"Any of you guys ever been in 'Nam?" I yelled down the tunnel shaft, buying time with every word.

Silence. I could hear mutters, but no words. They'd move in soon.

Finally a hard voice came back down the tunnel to me. "I have, friend. Eighty-seventh Infantry, Charlie Company. Want me to come back there alone?"

"Yeah!" I shouted back. "I want you to tell your cop friends what *this* is!" I pulled the metal baseball out of my pocket—a fragmentation grenade with the pin still in—and lobbed it down the tunnel in their direction. I listened to it bounce around the walls and then everything went quiet. It must have fallen onto the tracks.

"What was that, friend?" my Vietnam buddy wanted to know.

"Shine your light and see for yourself," I told him. "But don't worry—the pin's still in!"

The place went as quiet as a tomb—because that's what they all thought it had turned into. I saw flashlights bounce off the dripping walls of the tunnel, but none of them came closer to me from either side. Then I heard "Holy shit!" and I knew they'd found it.

"You know what that is?" I called out to them.

"Yeah," came back the infantryman's weary voice, "I seen enough of the fucking things."

"You want to see more, just come on back," I invited him. "I got a whole crate of them just sitting here."

More silence.

"What do you want?" he called down to me.

"I want you guys to clear out of this tunnel, okay? And I want a car full of gas at the curb on Canal Street. And a ride to J.F.K. And I want a plane to Cuba. You got it? Otherwise, the Number Six Train's going to have a major fucking detour for the next ten years."

Another cop yelled back to me. "I want to talk to you, okay? I want to talk about what you want. Let me walk toward you. Slow . . . okay? My hands in the air. I can't talk to you about this and scream down this tunnel. Okay?"

"Let me think about it," I told him, "but no fucking tricks!"

"No tricks. Just take it easy, okay?"

I didn't answer him, wondering where the Prof was by now.

I stretched it out as long as I could. Then I called down to the cop, my voice shaking more than I wanted. "Just one cop, okay? I want the soldier. Tell him to come *alone*, you understand—and *slow!*"

I heard the soldier's footsteps before I saw him. He rounded the bend in the tunnel from the east, shirt unbuttoned, hands over his head. He was short, built solid and close to the ground. I couldn't make out his features in the dim light.

"Stop!" I barked at him.

"Okay, friend. Just be easy, okay? No problems, nothing to worry about. All we're going to do is talk."

"I want to show you something first," I told him. I held another grenade in my right hand, high up, where he could see it. Then I palmed one of the spare pull-pins I had with me in my left. I reached over to the grenade and pulled hard; my left hand came away with the extra pin. I flicked it backhand at the cop, listening to it skim down the tunnel, like a kid skipping stones on a lake. "Pick it up," I told him.

I watched him bend down, grope around until he had it.

"Fuck!" he said—not loud, but clear enough.

"Now you got the picture," I told him. "I'm sitting on a couple dozen of these little bastards and I pulled the pin on the one I'm holding, okay? You get one of your fucking sharpshooters to drop me with a night-scope and the whole tunnel goes into orbit. Now, what about my plane?"

"Those things take time, friend. We can't just make a phone call and set things up."

"All it took was a phone call to set *this* thing up, right?"

"Look, friend, I just do my job. Like I did overseas. Like you did too, right? I understand what you're feeling. . . ."

"No, you don't," I told him. "Where'd you see combat?" I asked him.

"Brother, for all I know, I was in fucking Cambodia. They sent us into the jungle and some of us came back. You know how it is."

"Yeah, I know how it is. But I did my stretch in prison, not 'Nam. Too many times. And I'm not going again. I'm going to Cuba or we're all going to hell."

"Hold up!" he barked at me. "Give us a chance to work this out. I didn't say we *couldn't* do it . . . just that it takes a bit of time, all right? I have to walk back down and talk to the Captain, let him use the radio, call outside, you know . . . ?"

"Take all the time you want," I said to him, the most truthful words I ever spoke to a cop in my life. I watched him back down the tunnel.

A few more minutes passed. I was looking around, checking to make sure there was nothing left in the tunnel to add to my sentence, when I heard his voice again.

"Can I come back down?" he shouted.

"Come ahead!" I yelled back.

When he got back to where he'd been standing before, he was talking in a calm, quiet voice, like you'd use on a crazy person. Good. "It's all in the works, my friend. We've got the process started, but it's going to take some time, you understand?"

"No problem," I told him.

"Man, this might take *hours*," he said. "You don't want to sit and hold that thing without the pin for that long."

"I got no choice," I replied.

"Sure you do," he said reasonably. "Just put the pin back in. You can sit right by the grenades. You hear anyone coming or anything at all, you just pull it again. Okay?"

I said nothing.

"Come on, friend. Use your head. You're going to get what you want—we're doing it for you—we're cooperating. No point in blowing yourself up when you're *winning*, right?"

"How . . . how do I do that?" I said, my voice trembling badly. "You have the pin."

"I'll give it back to you, friend. Okay? I'll walk nice and slow toward you, okay? Nice and easy. We got a piece of wire—I'll wrap it around the pin and tie it to my holster belt, okay? I'll throw the whole thing down to you. Nice and easy."

"You won't try anything?" I asked, distrust all over my voice.

"What's the point, friend? We try something and you blow us all up, right? I'll be standing right here—I'll be the first to go, okay? I didn't walk through that fucking jungle to get killed on the subway."

"Give me a minute," I told him.

He gave me nearly five, playing out the string, doing what he was supposed to do. The cop and I were the same right then: I was holding the point for my brothers so they'd make their break—and he was a hundred yards ahead of the rest of his boys. It was only him and me that'd get blown to hell if this didn't work. The soldier had a lot of guts—too bad he worked with such a lame crew.

"You're really getting the plane?" I asked him.

"It's in the works," he said, "you have my word. One soldier to another."

Maybe he did understand it. I was running in luck—an infantryman would know all about falling on grenades. If he'd been a Tunnel Rat in 'Nam he'd be thinking flamethrowers by now. But he was just doing his job. I let him persuade me.

It took another ten minutes for us to work it out, but he finally came back down the tunnel with the belt and lofted it gently in my direction. I could see it gleaming in the tunnel's soft light. I reached out for it gingerly, feeling the sniper's telescope on my face. Fuck them—I'd have the last laugh in hell.

But they didn't shoot.

"I got it!" I yelled to him.

"Just like I promised," he shouted back.

"I'm putting it back in," I said, my hands shaking for just the right touch of authenticity. I swear I could feel all their breath let out at once when I went back into the blackness.

"I'm going to sit right here," I yelled. "Just like I said. If any of you come even *close* . . ."

"All you need now is patience, my friend," said the cop. "I'll sit right down here and wait with you." And he was right about both parts.

# 15

IT WENT ON FOR HOURS. I knew the game—the soldier kept coming back down the tunnel to talk to me, reassure me everything was okay, ask me if I wanted some cigarettes, some coffee, anything—waiting for me to get sleepy. They had all the time in the world.

It was well past midnight. Either my people had made it or they hadn't. I was seeing spots in front of my eyes, jumping every time the cops made a noise at their end. I don't drink coffee, but I knew what would be in the coffee they kept offering me, so I finally said yes.

The soldier brought two Styrofoam coffee cups down on a tray, halfway to me, turned around, and went back. I told them it wasn't close enough, so he brought it even closer.

Then he played out the string. "Pick one, friend. The other one's for me." It didn't matter which one I picked—they'd have pumped the cop so full of stimulants that I'd pass out before he would anyway. I popped open the lid of the one I picked and drank it all down like a greedy pig. The drugs hit me like a piledriver before I could even take the cup away from my mouth. I remember thinking just before I passed out how I wouldn't even feel the beating I was going to get.

## 16

SO I WENT BACK TO PRISON, but only for possession of explosives. Possession of thirty-two kilos of sugar and quinine isn't against the law. And even Blumberg the lawyer was able to make something out of the fact that I was drugged and unconscious at the time of my arrest, so they didn't hit me with too stiff a jolt.

I wasn't in population more than a week before one of Julio's gorillas asked me where I'd stashed the heroin. I told him I didn't know what he was talking about—as far as I knew, the cops had the stuff. And, anyway, I told him, it hadn't been me who roughed off the stuff in the first place. Some guy had contacted me—offered fifty grand for me to handle the exchange.

Another man came to see me in the prison about the dope, but this guy came through the front gate. When the hack told me my attorney was there to see me, I knew something was wrong—Blumberg wouldn't make the trip to Auburn even if I *had* paid him for representing me at the trial. This guy was all pinstripes and old school tie, with a pretty leather briefcase and a gold wedding band to match his Rolex. The new breed of mob lawyer, although I didn't know it then. He didn't even pretend he was representing me—he came there to be judge and jury, and I was on trial for my life.

Okay—I was ready for him. We went over the thing a dozen times. He had me tell my story out of sequence, did his best to trip me up—it always played the same. But slowly he got a few more details out of me.

"Tell me again about this guy who approached you."

"I already *told* you," I said. "About thirty years old, long hair, almost like a hippie, dirty army jacket. He was carrying a piece in a shoulder holster—didn't care if I saw it or not. Said his name was Smith."

"And he told you . . . ?"

"He told me he had this stuff, right? And it belonged to your people, okay? And I should make arrangements to sell it back to him for two hundred grand. And all I had to give him was one fifty—the rest was for me."

"You thought he stole it?"

"I didn't know *how* he got it, right? What did I care? I figured the old man would be happy to get his stuff back—I'd make some heavy coin—it'd be a wash, right?"

"You ever see this 'Smith' character again?"

"He didn't show up at my trial, that's for fucking sure."

"Mr. Burke, think back now. Is there *anything* about this guy that would help us find him?"

"You got pictures I could look through? Maybe he's one of your own. . . ."

"He's not," snapped the lawyer.

"Yeah, I guess you're right," I acknowledged. "He was like one of those buffs, you know? A real whacko."

"A 'buff'?"

"Yeah, like those guys who carry around PBA cards and pretend they're fucking off-duty cops and shit. You know what I mean."

His eyes flickered, just for a second, but I'd been watching for it. "Why do you think this individual was in that category?"

"Well," I said slowly, "two things, really. Besides the shoulder holster, he had another gun strapped to his ankle. And when he reached in his wallet to come up with the front money I wanted . . . for the supplies . . . I saw a gold shield. I guess it was one of those complimentary badges the cops give you if you make some contribution."

The lawyer screwed around for another hour or so, but his heart wasn't in it. I read in the *Daily News* three weeks later how an undercover narcotics officer was killed in East Harlem. Shot four times in the face, but they left his money alone. Only his gold shield was missing.

## 17

BUT THAT WAS YEARS AGO. Today I left seven grand with Mama. Max would know that five was for him and he should hold the rest for me.

There was no time for Mama's endless nonsense about Max, but I did have time to eat before I went back to the office to change. I had a court appearance for the afternoon, and I wanted to look my best.

Even though it was just a preliminary hearing, I normally wouldn't go into a criminal court. There wasn't any point pretending I had a private investigator's license, and even a flyweight defense attorney would have a ball asking me where I'd spent twelve years of my life. I testify a lot in civil court, though—matrimonials and crap like that. And I'm a lot more honest than the lawyers: I charge a flat rate for perjury, not so much an hour. But this was a special case.

It really started in Family Court, where this woman came in to get an Order of Protection against her husband. Seems they were showing a film about child sexual abuse in school and one of her daughters started crying and the whole sleazy story came out. Anyway, she gets this Order, and he's supposed to leave the house, but he comes right back in and starts screaming at the kid how the whole thing is her fault and how she's going to go to an orphanage and stuff like that. And the poor little kid just plain snaps out—she was only ten years old—and they take her to this psychiatric hospital and she's still up there. The slimeball naturally takes off, and the woman hired me to find him. It only took a couple of days. I threw a quarter into a pay phone and the Warrant Squad picked him up.

Most of the time the D.A.'s office wouldn't even think about prosecuting a guy like this. They got more excuses than Richard Nixon: the guy's the family breadwinner, the trial would be too tough on the kid, all that crap. The bottom line is that they don't want to mess with their sacred conviction rates—most of these family-style sex cases only get prosecuted when the perpetrator confesses, and even then the D.A.'s office doesn't get too worked up about it. After all, the family unit is the bedrock of America.

But they finally formed this new unit—City-Wide Special Victims Bureau. It's supposed to cover all crimes against children, in all courts. I heard the D.A. in this case was really going to go for it, and I wanted to see for myself.

I walked in all dressed up: dark-blue pinstripe, white shirt, dark-red tie, polished black shoes—even an attaché case. I wasn't carrying a piece—in the Supreme Court, they use metal detectors at the entrance because some politically wired judge complained about the dangerous radicals who might invade his courtroom and shoot it out with the guards. This happens in the Supreme Court about every other century, but you can't be too careful. On the other hand, right across the street in the Family Court, the average litigant carries some kind of weapon and violence is an everyday thing, but there's no metal detectors. That's New York—even the *names* of the courts are total bullshit—the lowest trial court is the "Supreme" Court, and the place where we turn abused kids into monsters is the "Family" Court. In this city, the name means more than the game.

The Assistant District Attorney was one I hadn't seen before—a tall brunette with a white streak in her thick mane of swept-back hair, wearing a gray silk dress and a string of pearls. She had a sweet face, but her eyes were cold. She wasn't from the Manhattan office—I guess they sent her over because she was handling another case against the same guy over in Queens or something. The court officers all seemed to know her, though, so I guess she was a trial veteran—those are the only ones they remember.

I sat in the front row—the one reserved for attorneys only. Nobody asked any questions—they never do.

The defense attorney was a real piece of work. His haircut cost more than my suit, and diamonds flashed from everywhere. It looked like it was only going to be a hearing on bail, and the lawyer had a long list of reasons why his man should be let back out on the street—the defendant was employed, sole support of his family, active in Little League . . . and that stuff. He looked like a weasel. His eyes darted around the courtoom—caught mine, and dropped. His wife wasn't even there.

The only person I recognized was the court reporter—the guy who takes down everything they say on one of those machines that don't make any noise. He was a tall guy with big hands, slumped over his machine. He'd gone to Vietnam about the same time I last went to prison, and it burned him out. I'd watched him a lot of times and he never changed expression, no matter what went down. I asked him about that once and he told me the courtroom was the same as 'Nam—only here they did it with words instead of with bullets.

The argument went on and on, and then the defense attorney made a mistake. He put his client on the stand, figuring the guy's long list of social contacts would get over on the judge. And it might have too, until the D.A. took her shot.

She stood up at her table and began questioning the creep in a soft voice, just background questions about his job, and where he'd be staying while waiting for trial—crap like that. She shuffled through some papers at the table as if she couldn't think of the next question to ask; then she took a step closer to him.

"Sir, on April twenty-fifth, did you enter your wife's home?"

"It's *my* home," the creep smirked, "I paid for it . . . I'm *still* paying the mortgage on it."

"Objection, Your Honor," said the defense attorney. "What does this have to do with a bail application?"

"It has to do with credibility," shot back the D.A. Then she gave a little bow of her head to the defense attorney, and told the court, "I promise to connect it up to the issue before this court, Your Honor, and I will not oppose a defense motion to strike the testimony if I fail to do so."

The judge tried to look like he was thinking it over, glanced over at his assistant (they call them "law secretaries" in New York—they're all political appointees and they make more money than the judges in the "lower" courts), caught the sign, and said, "Proceed, counsel," just like they do on television.

"Will you answer my question, sir?" the D.A. asked.

Then he went into his rap. "Yes, I entered *my* home, with *my* key. Of course I did."

"And did you have a conversation with your child Marcy at that time, sir?"

"It wasn't a conversation. I just said she had caused a lot of trouble with all these lies. You see, if it hadn't been for that stupid movie they showed at her school . . ."

"No further questions," snapped out the D.A., leaving everyone in the courtroom puzzled.

"You may step down," said the judge to the creep. Then he turned to the D.A.

"Young lady, I don't understand your line of questioning. If you can't connect this up . . ."

"My name is Ms. Wolfe, Judge, or you may refer to me as the Assistant District Attorney," she said in a gentle voice.

The judge smiled, humoring her, and the defense attorney rubbed his hands together. They weren't good listeners—the lady was being quiet, not soft. You could see she was a pro. There was steel inside, but she wasn't going to waste her time showing it when there was no jury around.

"Very well, *Ms.* Wolfe," said the judge, hitting the accent so the low-lifes hanging around the bench wouldn't miss his sharp wit, "the court is *still* waiting for you to connect it up."

"Yes, Your Honor," she said, her voice hardening, "I have here a certified copy of an Order of Protection, signed by Judge Berkowitz of the Family Court. Among its terms and conditions are that this defendant remain away from the home and person of the victim."

"Bring that up to me," the judge said to one of the court officers.

He scanned the two sheets of paper, looking even more puzzled than ever. He couldn't see where the D.A. was going, and neither could the defense. The creep's lawyer barked out, "Relevance, Your Honor?" The judge looked down at the D.A., no longer smiling, waiting for her to respond.

"Your Honor, the defendant has just admitted, under oath, that he violated an Order of the Family Court. He has further acknowledged that said violation was willful, that he intended to act as he did, and that he was without just cause. Thus, pursuant to the Family Court Act, section 1072, subsection B, he may be ordered to jail for a term not to exceed six months."

The defense attorney finally woke up—and it wasn't the coffee he smelled. "Your Honor, this has nothing whatever to do with the question of bail in a criminal proceeding. Counsel is referring to a *Family*

Court matter—that court has nothing to do with bail over here."

The lady D.A. went on speaking as if she hadn't heard the interruption. "The court has already heard evidence that this defendant fled when initially charged in the Family Court. In fact, he was located living under an assumed name in a hotel here in the city. The purpose of bail is to ensure the defendant's presence at trial. In this case, given the defendant's past actions, and the indisputable fact that he is facing a jail sentence in another court, the People respectfully request that any bail application be denied and the defendant summarily remanded until trial."

The creep looked like he'd been body-punched—a remand meant he'd sit in jail for a few months no matter how the criminal trial turned out. But his lawyer wasn't finished.

"Your Honor, the District Attorney is asking for a *remand!* That would be a travesty of justice for an individual with no criminal record, significant roots in the community, and, I might add, every anticipation of prevailing on the merits when we come to trial. It's not as though he were being charged with murder. . . ."

The D.A.'s head snapped back—an old trial-lawyer's trick—pulling every eye in the courtroom toward her.

"He *is* charged with rape, sodomy, incest, and sexual abuse, Your Honor. He *did* flee the jurisdiction of the court. And he *did* confess before this very court that he violated an existing Order of Protection."

"Judge, that was the *Family* Court!" yelled the defense attorney, firing his best shot.

It wasn't good enough. The D.A. let a dark undertone into her soft voice—it carried to the back of the room. "Surely Your Honor is not ruling that an order of one court is entitled to more respect than the order of another? A defendant who will spit on the lawful order of one court has displayed his true character and his utter disregard for the law. Indeed, if this court grants bail to this defendant, it will be providing him with a *motive* to flee. He is only *charged* in this court—he stands all-but-convicted in another. The People respectfully request a remand, not only for the protection of the victim herein, and for the protection of the community at large, but to give the Family Court the opportunity to impose such sentence as it deems appropriate for the violation. If bail is granted, and the defendant flees," and there she paused, holding it for a long count, "the child will certainly be in danger. This court should not provide such an opportunity."

"This is ridiculous, Your Honor," shot back the defense attorney. "Ms. Wolfe cannot know what is in my client's mind!"

"I don't *need* to, do I?" asked Wolfe. The message was clear.

The judge was caught. He scanned the courtroom quickly, looking for some help. I thought I'd give him some—I whipped out a reporter's notebook and started scribbling away. He looked closely, trying to figure out who I was, or what paper I worked for—and then he decided he couldn't take the chance.

"Defendant is remanded for transportation to the Family Court. If sentence is not imposed by that court, he shall be returned before me for additional bail arguments."

The creep looked wiped out. He looked to his lawyer for reassurance, listened while the lawyer told him he'd go right over to the Family Court, and then got shakily to his feet. The court officers moved to take him into custody, passing right by the court reporter's stand. The court reporter looked up from his machine. His combat-deadened eyes caught those of the freak. Making no effort to keep his voice down, the court reporter gave the officers some advice.

"Don't take away his belt," he said, getting off his stool and walking toward the back before the defense attorney had a chance to protest.

They took the creep away. The defense attorney went over to the D.A.'s table, preparing himself to play Let's Make a Deal.

"Ms. Wolfe?"

"Yes?"

"Ah . . . I assume you'll be going to Family Court on this personally?"

"Yes—and right now."

"Well, so am I. Could I give you a ride?"

"No, thank you," she told him in the same calm voice, stuffing papers into her briefcase.

"You've got no win on this one, you know," he told her.

Wolfe stood up, hands on hips, and stared him down. She'd been through this before. "You mean I can't *lose* this one, don't you, counselor? This is a fifteen-round fight, and your guy has to win every round. You win this trial—he'll do it again, and I'll get another shot. Sooner or later I'll drop him for the count. And when he goes down, he's going down hard."

The defense attorney's mouth opened, but nothing came out. She walked past him to the gate which separates the front of the court from the spectators, nodded to the officer who swung it open for her, and walked toward the exit. Her body swayed gently in the silk dress, and her high heels tapped the floor. I could smell her perfume in the air. A rare jewel, she was—never more beautiful than when she was doing her work. Like Flood.

# 18

I GOT DOWNSTAIRS BEFORE Wolfe did. I knew where she'd be parked, and I waited. The tapping of her heels echoed down the corridor just before she stepped into the sunlight on Baxter Street, behind the courthouse. I didn't want to spook her, so I made sure she had me in her sights before I said anything.

"Ms. Wolfe?"

"Yes," she responded, in exactly the same neutral tone she'd used with the defense attorney.

Now that I had her attention, I didn't know what to say. "I . . . just wanted to tell you that I admire the way you handled yourself in the courtroom."

"Thank you," she said, dismissing me and turning to go.

I wanted to talk to her again, make some contact with her—let her know we were on the same side—but nothing came out. I don't have many friends in law enforcement.

"Can I walk you to your car?" I asked her.

She gave me a brief flash of her smile. "That won't be necessary—it's only a short distance."

"Well," I shrugged, "this neighborhood . . ."

"It's not a problem," she said, and I caught the dull sheen of the thick silver band on her left hand. I knew what it was—a twine-cutter's ring, the kind with a hooked razor on the other side. The guys in the twine factories run the string through their hands and just flick the ring against the cord when they want to cut it. You put one of those things against a guy's face and you come away with his nose.

"You think that ring's going to keep the skells away?" I asked her.

She looked at me closely for the first time, seemed to be making up her mind about something.

"I appreciate your concern, Mr. . . . ?"

"Burke," I told her.

"Oh, yes. I've heard about you. . . ."

"Was it a good reference?"

"Good enough—Toby Ringer said you pull your own weight. And that you helped him on some cases."

"Maybe I could help you."

"I don't think so, Mr. Burke. Toby also said you work the other side of the street too often."

"Not when it comes to freaks," I told her.

"I know," Wolfe said, giving me just the hint of what I knew could be a beautiful smile—for someone else.

"It was me who found that dirtbag you just dropped inside, right? You think the Warrant Squad would've turned him up?"

"No," she admitted, "but this case is finished."

We were slowly walking toward her car—a dull, faded blue Audi sedan. The parking lot was bathed in sunlight, but the watchers were there. A pro wouldn't try to strong-arm anyone in the D.A.'s parking lot, but a junkie would.

"That's my car," Wolfe said, reaching in her pocketbook for the keys. I stepped ahead of her like I was going to hold the door—and a massive dark form shot up from the back seat. Its huge head was a black slab laced with gleaming shark's teeth. A Rottweiler—a good lapdog if you were King Kong. They look as if some mad scientist took a Doberman, injected it with anabolic steroids, and bashed its face in with a sledge-hammer. I froze where I was—this was one lady who didn't need an escort.

Wolfe opened the door and the Rottweiler lunged forward. "Bruiser! Down!" she snapped, and the beast reluctantly moved back to let her in. She turned to me over her shoulder. "Mr. Burke, if you ever get a case that I'd be interested in, give me a call, okay?"

It was a dismissal. I bowed to her and the Rottweiler, touched the brim of my hat, and moved back where I belonged. The huge beast pinned me with his killer's eyes out the back window as the Audi moved off.

# 19

I MADE MY WAY BACK through the dirty marble corridors of the Criminal Court, thinking my thoughts. Wolfe reminded me of Flood—so did the Rottweiler.

It was late March, but the sun was already blasting the front steps of the court. Maybe a real summer this year, not like the whore's promise we d been getting for the past weeks—the sun would shine but the cold would be right there too. Only city people really hate the cold. In the city, it gets inside your bones and it freezes your guts. In the country, people sit around their fireplaces and look at the white stuff outside—saying how pretty it is, how clean it looks. The snow is never clean in the city. Here, people die when the Hawk comes down—if the cold doesn't get them, the fires they start to keep warm will.

I reached in my pocket for a smoke, looking out over the parking lot across the street where I'd stashed my Plymouth. A black guy with a shaved head, resplendent in a neon-orange muscle shirt with matching sweatband, caught my eye. "Got a cigarette, pal?" he asked.

At least he didn't call me "brother." When I got out of prison in the late 1960s, that bullshit was all over the street. Being an ex-con was never too valuable a credential, but back then at least it was a guaranteed introduction to girls. And the Village was full of them—

promiscuously sucking up every shred of revolutionary rhetoric like marijuana-powered vacuum cleaners.

I made a good living then. All you needed was some genuine Third World people for props and you could raise funds faster than Reverend Ike—telling hippie jerkoffs that you were financing some revolutionary act, like a bank robbery. It was open season in the Village. Better than the Lower East Side. The hippies who lived over there believed they were making a contribution with their plotting and planning and their halfass bombs and letters to the editor. They were too busy organizing the oppressed to see the value of cash transactions, but they never knew where to buy explosives, so I did business with them too. Good thing they never tried to take out the Bank of America with the baking soda I sold them.

That's how I got started finding missing kids. It may have been Peace & Love in the streets, but the back alleys were full of wolves. The worst of the animals didn't just eat to survive—they did it for fun. So I'd run some of the kids down and drag them home. For the money. Once in a while one of the wolves would try and hold on to his prey. So I made some money and I made some enemies. I used up the money a long time ago.

When the revolution died—when BMWs replaced jeeps and the hippies turned perfectly good lofts a human could rent for a little money into co-ops with six-figure down payments—I stopped being relevant. I was ready for it. Some of the Third World wasn't, and they took my place in the jailhouses. Those that didn't go quietly got the key to Forest Lawn instead.

When things got nasty in New York, I rolled the dice on Biafra. I figured I'd do the same thing over there I was doing in New York, only on a grand scale—save a bunch of kids and make myself a fortune in the process. I didn't do either one, but I beat the odds anyway—I walked away from it. It's what I do best.

That was then. The black muscleman asking me if I had a cigarette was now.

"You taking a survey?" I asked him.

Our eyes locked. He shrugged, shifted his position, and went back to scanning the street. He probably didn't even smoke—just keeping in practice. His act needed work.

## 20

THE PLYMOUTH WAS IN the parking lot across the street. Even on a warm day, that lot's always cold. The three courthouses surrounding it make a perfect wind tunnel. The car's fresh coat of primer made it look like it had been painted with rust—the Mole always changes the color after the car is used on a job and we hadn't decided on what to use next. It looks like a piece of junk, but it's anything but, with its independent rear suspension, fifty-gallon tank, fuel injection, heavy-duty cooling and shocks, bullet-proof glass, rhino-style bumpers—all that stuff. It wasn't fast, but you couldn't break it no matter what you did. It was going to be the Ultimate Taxicab, but it didn't work out that way.

The woman was standing in front of the Plymouth, tapping her foot impatiently like her date was late. All I could make out was that she was female. She was wearing a tan summer trenchcoat over dark slacks, her head covered with a black scarf and her face hidden behind sunglasses with big lenses. Nobody I knew, but I put my hand in my pocket anyway—some people subcontract their revenge.

Her eyes were on me all the way up to the Plymouth, so I walked past it like it meant nothing to me. But when I heard "Mr. Burke?" I knew there wasn't much point.

I don't like problems out in public—especially when half the public is cops.

"What?" I snapped out at her.

"I want to talk to you," she said. Her voice was shaky but determined. Trouble.

"You got me confused with someone else, lady."

"No, I don't. I have to talk with you," she said.

"Give me a name or get lost," I told her. If she knew my face from the courthouse but didn't have a referral from someone I knew, I was gone.

"Julio Crunini," she offered, her face close to mine now.

"I don't know anybody named Julio, lady. Whatever you're selling, I'm not buying, okay?" And I reached past her to open the Plymouth's door and get the hell away from her and whatever she wanted. Julio's been out of prison too long, I was thinking—his mouth was getting loose.

She put her hand on my arm. Her hand was shaking—I could see the wedding ring on her finger, and the diamond sparkling in the sun next to it. "You know me," she said.

I looked into her face, and drew a blank. She must have seen what I was thinking—one hand went to her face and the sunglasses disappeared. Her face meant nothing to me. Her mouth went hard, and she pulled away the scarf—her flaming red hair fired in the sun.

"You know me now?" she asked bitterly.

It was the jogger from Forest Park.

## 21

NOTHING CHANGED IN MY face—I was raised in places where it isn't a good idea to let people know what you're thinking—but she wasn't looking for recognition.

"I don't know you, lady," I told her, "and I don't want to."

"You don't like my looks?" she challenged me. A real Mafia princess all right—she was used to this.

"I don't like your smell, lady. You stink of trouble, and I got enough of my own."

I pushed past her like I had someplace else to go. Her hand reached out and grabbed my forearm—I gave her the same look I'd given Julio in the garage, but she didn't have enough sense to know what it meant. Her hand was aristocratic—dark-red polish over manicured nails.

"If you don't talk to me here, I'll just come to Murray Street, Mr. Burke—to your hotel."

It was a good, hard shot—she thought. Julio must have opened up like the Red Sea. Only a few people knew I lived at the Deacon Hotel. Of course, those people were all wrong. The front desk would take a message for me from force of habit—the only force any junkie recognizes—but I hadn't lived there for years, ever since I got off parole. It didn't matter now—this broad was making word sounds from her mouth, but all I heard was "tick, tick, tick . . ."

Her face had the smug look of a woman with lots more cards to put on the table. Uncle Julio's halfass *omertà* was the modern version—rock-solid until it got a better offer.

"Get in the car," I told her, holding the Plymouth's door for her to slip past me.

"My car's right over there," she told me, gesturing toward the inevitable BMW sedan. "It'll be more comfortable—it's air conditioned."

"I don't care if it's got a waterbed, lady. You get in here, or you get in the wind."

She hesitated for just a second—the script wasn't going like she'd planned. Then the same tight-set look she had on her face when she'd started jogging around Forest Park appeared—she'd made up her mind.

Her reconstructed nose turned up at the Plymouth's interior but she slid across the vinyl bench seat without another word. I pulled out of the parking lot and headed toward the West Side Highway. I needed to find out what she knew, but I wasn't doing any talking until I was sure she was the only one listening.

I grabbed the highway at Chambers Street and turned uptown. The environmentalists had lost the first round—the old elevated structure was gone and along with it the shadows that provided the cover for the working whores. Michelle wouldn't be on the piers this time of day, and I needed her help. The new construction site on Eleventh Avenue a few blocks south of Times Square was my best bet.

The redhead opened her purse and started to rummage around. "Is it all right if I smoke?" she asked, still in that nasty-edged voice.

"As long as it's cigarettes," I told her.

"You have some religious convictions against marijuana, Mr. Burke?"

"Marijuana is against the law, lady," I told her, my voice toneless so the audience could get the sarcasm without the evidence to go with it. "If you have any illegal substances or objects on your person, I insist you remove them from this vehicle."

"Who're you trying to kid? After what you did in the . . ."

"Shut your fucking mouth!" I snapped at her. "You really want to talk, you'll get your chance, okay? You want to make some tapes for the *federales*, you make them someplace else. Got it?"

She got it. Her face got hard again, like I'd insulted her, but she didn't say another word. Two hard dots of red stood out on her cheeks—not her makeup.

The big Plymouth worked the city streets the way it was created to do . . . passing through traffic as anonymously as a rat in a garbage dump, eating the potholes, smoothing the bumps, quiet and careful. The tinted windows were up on both sides, the air conditioner whisper-quiet, watching the streets.

I spotted the first bunch of working girls on 37th. Business was always slow this time of day, but the girls who worked the trucks and cabs for a living had to try harder than their sisters across town. On Lexington Avenue, the girls wore little shorts-and-tops outfits—over on the West Side, they worked the streets in bathing suits and heels. Even that was more subtle than you'd find elsewhere in the city—over in Hunts Point, they work in raincoats with nothing underneath.

Nothing but hard-core pros over here—black women who hadn't been girls since they were twelve, white ladies too old or too out of shape for the indoor work. The pimps kept the baby-faces for the middle-class trade farther east—the runaways worked Delancey and the Bowery or strictly indoors. I love the words some of the jerkoff journalists use in this town . . . like "call girls." The only thing these ladies ever used a phone for was to call a bail bondsman.

I slid the Plymouth to the curb. A tall black woman with a silky wig swivel-hipped over to the window, wearing one of those spandex suits, the green metallic threads shimmering in the sun. Her bright smile never got near her eyes.

"Looking for something, honey?"

"For some*one*. Michelle. She around?"

"You her man, baby?" the whore wanted to know, casting a sly glance at the Plymouth—it wasn't exactly your standard pimpmobile.

"Only if someone gets stupid with her," I told her, just so she'd know.

"Honey, I'm out here in this heat about some *money*, you understand?"

"You find her and bring her back over here, I'll pay one trick's worth—deal?"

"I don't work blind, man," she said, all business now.

"Tell her Burke needs to talk with her."

She seemed to be thinking it over—looked past me to where the princess was sitting, nodding her head like she understood what was going on. Traffic was slow—her sisters strolled the sidelines, bored but watchful. It had been a long time since they'd seen anything new—or anything good. Finally, she made up her mind. "I get a half-yard for a trick, baby. That's the price for bringing Michelle around, okay?"

There was no trick in the world this woman could get fifty bucks for, but insulting her wasn't going to get the job done.

"I'll pay you *your* piece, okay? Let your manager go look for his commission someplace else. Fifty-fifty, right?"

She flashed me a quick smile and swivel-hipped her way back to the other girls. No car-trick whore splits fifty-fifty with a pimp, but letting her think I believed that myth was worth the discount—for both of us. It's a sweet life out on the stroll in this city—every street-whore has a guaranteed time-share in the jailhouse. And the emergency ward is her only pension plan.

I pulled the Plymouth through a wide U-turn into the mouth of the construction site, reached in my pocket for a smoke, and got ready to do some waiting.

# 22

THE REDHEAD WASN'T GOOD at waiting like I was—I could tell her life hadn't been like that. Too fucking bad.

I let my eyes roam around the flatlands, watching the whores work, checking for any backup the redhead might have brought along. It's easy to tail a car in the city, but anyone following us would have to be some distance away or I'd have spotted them by now.

She shifted her hips on the bench seat, recrossed her legs. The silk-on-silk sound was smooth and dry to my ears. Like a gun being cocked. "I've never been here before," she said. "What do you call this neighborhood?"

"After you talk to my friend, I'll talk to you, okay?"

"All I asked . . ."

"Don't ask me anything. Don't talk to me. When I know it's just me you're talking to, I'll answer, you understand? I'm not going to tell you again."

I was watching her face when I spoke to her. If she was wired and the backups were out of eyesight, she'd want our location to go out over the air—and I wasn't having any. Her face told me nothing—nothing except that she wasn't used to being talked to like that and she didn't like it. Well, I didn't like any of this, but if Julio was turning into a public-address system, I had to find out why. Everybody has rules they live by. Mine were: I wasn't going to die. I wasn't going to go back to prison. And I wasn't going to work a citizen's job for a living. In that order.

I spotted my bird-dog whore before I saw Michelle. She walked quickly over to the Plymouth, holding the wiggle to a minimum. She wanted to collect from me before a new customer took her for a ride.

"She'll be here in a minute, honey. You got my quarter like you said?"

"Right here," I told her, holding a twenty and a five in my left hand where she could see it.

The whore said nothing. I believed her that Michelle was coming—I'd had too good a look at her face for her to pull a Murphy game on me. That is, if she had any sense. But if she had any sense, she wouldn't be out here tricking.

Then I saw Michelle. The tall, willowy brunette was wearing pencil-leg red pants that stopped halfway up her calves—spike heels with ankle straps—a white parachute-silk blouse, the huge sleeves billowing as she moved. A long string of black beads around her neck and a man's black felt fedora on the back of her head. Like all her outfits, it would have looked ridiculous on anyone but her. That was the point, she told me once.

I released my hold on the bills and the whore flashed me a quick smile and moved back to her post. The redhead wasn't missing any of this, but she kept her mouth shut. I got out of the Plymouth and moved over to Michelle, my back blocking the redhead's view. I didn't have to watch her—Michelle would do that—she always knew what to do.

She put her left hand on my shoulder, reached up to kiss me on the cheek while her right hand snaked inside my jacket to the back of my belt. If there was a gun in there, she'd know the person inside the car was bad news. If I stepped to the side, the passenger would be looking at my pistol in Michelle's hand.

Michelle patted my back, whispered in my ear, "What's on, baby?"

"I'm not sure," I told her. "The redhead in the car braced me outside the courthouse. She's related to that old alligator—Julio. She wants something—I don't know what yet. The old bastard gave her some information about how to find me. She made it clear she was going to stay on my case until I talked to her."

"So talk to her, honey. You didn't drag me away from my lucrative profession to be your translator."

"I want to see if she's wired, Michelle."

Michelle's impossibly long lashes made shadows against her model's cheekbones; her fresh dark lipstick framed her mouth into a tiny circle.

"Oh," is all she said. Michelle's life must have been hell when she was supposed to have been a man.

"I'll pull over around the corner behind the trucks, okay? You get in the back with her—make sure she's clean. I'll check her purse."

"That's all?"

"For now."

"Baby, you know I started the treatments . . . but they didn't do the chop yet. Just the shots. And the psychiatrist—once a week. It's not cheap."

"You definitely going through with it?"

"If I was gay, I could *come* out, you know? But like I am, I have to *break* out. You know."

I knew. None of us had ever asked about Michelle, but she gradually told us. And the Mole had explained what a transsexual was . . . a woman trapped in a man's body. Even before she started getting the hormone injections and the breast implants, she looked like a woman—walked like a woman, talked like a woman. The big thing was, she had the heart of a woman. When you go to prison, the only people you could count on to visit you were your mother or your sister. I didn't have those people—it was Michelle who rode the bus for twelve hours one way and then walked through the ugly stares and evil whispering to visit me upstate when I was down the last time. She still worked the same car tricks—all she needed was her mouth. I knew what was in her purse—a little bottle of cognac she used for a mouthwash after each time. And the tiny canister of CN gas the Mole made for her.

"I don't have a price for this job, Michelle. It may not be a job at all, okay? But if she's got anything in her purse, we'll see about a donation."

"Close enough," she said, "but if she's got no cash, you take me to the Omega to hear Tom Baxter before he leaves town. Deal?"

"Deal," I told her, and she climbed into the back seat behind the redhead.

I found the dark spot in the shadow of the trucks and pulled in.

"Get in the back seat," I told the redhead.

"Why?" she snapped.

"Here's why," I told her. "I don't know you—I don't know what you want. My secretary back there is going to search you. If you're wearing a wire, out you go. It's that simple. She's here because I can't search you myself."

"I still don't see why . . ."

"Look, lady, you asked *me* to talk to you, okay? This is the way we do it. You don't like it, you take whatever business you have and you shake it on down the road."

The redhead softly scratched her long nails across one knee, thinking. I didn't have time for her to think.

"Besides," I told her, "haven't you had enough experience with men telling you to take your clothes off?"

Her eyes flashed at me, hard with anger, but she didn't say a word. I looked straight ahead, heard the door open, slam, open and slam again. She was in the back seat with Michelle.

"Toss your purse over the seat," I told her.

"What?"

"You heard me. My secretary's going to check your body; I'm going to check your purse . . . for the same thing."

The lizard-skin purse came sailing over the back seat and bounced off the windshield. I picked it up, unsnapped the gold clasp. Sounds from the back seat: zippers, the rustle of fabric. The purse had a pack of Marlboros, a gold Dunhill lighter, a little silver pillbox with six five-milligram Valiums inside, a tightly folded black silk handkerchief, a soft leather purse with a bunch of credit cards and a checkbook—joint account with her husband—and three hundred or so in cash. In a flap on the side I found thirty hundred-dollar bills—they looked fresh and new, but the serial numbers weren't in sequence. No tape recorder. Not even a pencil.

"She's clean," said Michelle from the back seat. I heard the door open and slam again, and the redhead was next to me.

"So . . . ?" I asked Michelle.

"All quality stuff. Bendel's, Bergdorf's, like that. The pearls are real. *Very* nice shoes. But that underwear is just *tacky*, honey.

Nobody wears a garter belt outside a motel room . . . didn't your mother tell you that? And that perfume . . . honey, you need some heavy lessons in *subtle.*"

The redhead snapped her head around to the back seat.

"From you?" she asked, trying for sarcasm.

"Who better?" Michelle wanted to know, genuinely surprised at such a stupid question.

"How much do I owe you?" the redhead asked Michelle in the same voice she would have used on the man who tuned her BMW.

"For what?"

"Well, you are a *prostitute*, aren't you? I know how valuable your time is."

"I see. Okay, Ms. Bitch—the hand job was on the house, but you can give me a hundred for the fashion advice."

The redhead reached in her purse. She never touched the new bills. She put together a hundred from the other supply and tossed it into the back seat. Michelle was dismissed.

She floated around to the redhead's open window, winked at me to say goodbye. Then she spoke in a soft voice to the redhead. "Honey, I may be a whore, but I'm not a cunt. Think about it." And she was gone.

## 23

"WHAT NEXT?" THE REDHEAD wanted to know, in a voice meant to tell me she was just about out of patience.

"Now we drive someplace else, and you tell me your story," I said, throwing the Plymouth into gear. We drove over to the West Side Highway in silence. I turned south, looking for a safe parking place near one of the abandoned piers on the Hudson River. I wheeled the car off the highway, pulled up to the pier, and backed in. From that spot, I could see every piece of traffic except the boats. If the redhead had friends with her, I'd know soon enough.

I hit a switch on the dash and both front windows opened.

Another switch locked her door, just in case.

I lit a cigarette, leaned way back in my seat so I could watch her and watch the street too. "Okay, lady, what is it you want?"

The redhead shifted her hips so she was facing me on the seat, her back to the window. "I want you to find a picture for me."

"A picture . . . like a painting?"

"A photograph—a photograph of a kid."

"Lady, will you just tell me the whole story? I don't have time to drag it out of you piece by piece, okay?"

"This isn't an easy thing to talk about."

"Then *don't* talk about it," I told her. "I didn't ask you to show up. I'll drive you back to your car and you find somebody else, okay?"

"No! It's *not* okay. Can't you give me a fucking minute to get myself together? It took me a long time to find you."

"Yeah. But you *did* find me, right? When you see Julio, tell him I'll remember this."

"Don't blame Julio. All he gave me was that phone number . . . the one the Chinese lady answers."

"I got your messages."

"So why didn't you call me?"

"Because I don't know you. I don't speak to strangers on the phone."

"That's why I had to find your car. Vinnie told me what you looked like—and your car. One of Julio's crew saw you at the courthouse this morning and he called me."

"Vinnie?" I said, thinking that I'd have to get the car painted and some new license plates.

"The guy who delivered the money to you from Julio."

"I don't know what you're talking about, lady."

"I told Julio why I needed to talk to you. He said it was none of his business—not family. He probably knew you'd never return my calls. So I told Vinnie to ask you for me."

"Nobody asked me anything."

"I know. He told me you wouldn't talk to him."

"I don't know what he told you. I don't care. I don't like people threatening me."

"Vinnie threatened you?"

"I don't know any Vinnie. *You* threatened me. In the parking lot, right? Either I talk to you or you keep hounding me."

"I didn't mean to threaten you."

"You're threatening me with this whole conversation. Julio's got his people on the street looking for me? Very fucking nice."

"Julio doesn't know anything about this. Vinnie did me a personal favor—and so did the guy who spotted you this morning."

"People like to do you these favors?"

She moved her lips in something between a smile and a sneer. "*Men* like to do me favors. You find that very surprising?"

"If this Vinnie is your idea of a man, no."

"You don't like any of us, do you?"

"Who's this 'us' you're talking about? An old man with a loose mouth? A punk kid? A woman who threatens me?"

"Us Italians."

"I don't like people who don't mean me any good, okay?"

"Okay," she said in a quiet voice, "but now that I went to all this trouble—now that we're here—will you listen to me and see if you're interested?"

"And if I'm not?"

"Then that's your decision. I won't bother you anymore."

"On your word of honor, right?"

Her eyes narrowed in on me. I thought I saw a tiny red dot in each one—it must have been the reflection from her hair. "You don't know me," she said.

"I don't *want* to know you," I told her.

She reached in her purse, fumbled around with her hand. Her eyes never left my face. "I'll pay you five hundred dollars to listen to what I have to say—why I want you to work for me. You don't take the case, you still keep the money. Okay?"

I took a minute to think about it. If I listened to her story and told her I wasn't interested, there was at least the chance that she'd go someplace else. And there was a filly pacer running at Yonkers that night that I just knew was going to break her maiden with a big win. She was due to snap a long string of losses. So was I.

"Okay," I told her.

The redhead ran her fingers through her hair in an absent-minded gesture. The diamond flashed on her hand. "My best friend has a . . ."

"Hold it," I told her. "Where's the money?"

"You listen to me first."

"No way."

"I thought only lawyers got money up front. You're only a private detective."

"Lady, you don't have the slightest idea what I am," I said, "but I'll give you a hint. I'm a man who's going to listen to your story—*after* you put five hundred dollars on the table."

Her hand darted into her purse. Out came five new century notes. She fanned them out—held them up. "Is this what you want?" she snapped.

"It's half of what I want."

"You mean you want a thousand?"

"I mean I want you to tell me your story and then get out of my life—like we agreed," I told her.

She released her grip on the money. It dropped to the seat between us. The street was still quiet—plenty of people around, but no problems. I picked up the money and pocketed it.

"So?" I asked her.

"My best friend, Ann-Marie. She has a little boy, only two years older than my daughter. He was in like a nursery-school thing during the day. Someone there did something to him. A sex thing. And they took pictures of him. We didn't even know about the pictures until the therapist explained it to us. But the boy, Scotty, he keeps saying they have his picture. Like they have his soul."

"This picture . . . he's doing something in it?"

"I think he must have been doing something . . . but he won't tell us. The therapist is working on it. I think if he got that picture, and we tore it up right in front of him . . . then maybe he'd be okay again."

"Just one picture?"

"That's what he said—he saw the flash."

"Lady, that picture's either in some freak's private collection or it's out on the street. For sale, you understand? It's just about impossible to come up with the stuff you want. And even if I found one print, the people who do the marketing make thousands of copies. It's a better business than cocaine: as long as you have the negative, you can make as many copies as you want."

"All we want is *one* picture . . . he's too young to know about making copies. I want to be there when we tear it up in front of him."

"It's a real long shot, you understand?"

"Yes. But it has to be done."

I looked directly at her—the little gangster princess wasn't going to take no for an answer. She wasn't used to it. "Why come to me?" I asked.

She had the answer ready. "Because you're friends with the Nazis."

## 24

I LOOKED STRAIGHT AHEAD through the windshield, trying to get a grip on what she just said. If she knew about the Nazis, then she knew about some of the scores I'd pulled over the past few years—home-grown Nazis are a con man's delight. Knowing an old hotel address was nothing, it wasn't the trump card she thought it was. But the Nazi thing—she could hurt me. A cold wind blew through my chest. She held better cards than I thought.

Nothing moved in my face. I lit a cigarette, throwing the question at her out of the side of my mouth. "What're you talking about, lady?"

"Julio said you were friends with them. In prison. He saw it himself."

The weight came off my chest. *Those* Nazis were a different breed.

"Julio's got a lot of medical problems, doesn't he?" I asked.

"What medical problems? He's in perfect health, specially for an old man."

"No, he's not," I told her, my voice quiet and calm now. "His eyesight hasn't been good for a long time. He's losing his memory. And his mouth is out of control."

She understood what I was saying. I wouldn't have to do anything to the old man myself—if some of his bloody brothers got the word that Julio was writing his memoirs, he was gone.

"He only told me," said the redhead, her voice tight with tension, trying to convince me. "He wouldn't tell anyone else."

"Sure."

"I *mean* it. I *made* him tell me. I was desperate, okay?"

It wasn't okay. I took a close look at her. I might have to describe her someday and I didn't think she'd pose for a picture. The red hair framed a small, heart-shaped face. Her eyes were big and set far apart, the color of factory smoke. Her makeup looked like it was done by an expert: dark-red lipstick outlined in black, eye shadow that went from blue to black as it flowed from her eyebrows to the lashes, blended blusher on her cheeks, breaking right at the cheekbones for emphasis. Her teeth were tiny pearls—they looked too small for a grown woman, and too perfect to be real. Her nose was small and sharply bridged, slightly turned up at the tip. Piece by piece, she wasn't beautiful, but the combination worked. It was hard to think of that red slash of a mouth kissing anyone. Her hands were small, but the fingers were long, capped with long, manicured nails in the same shade as her lipstick. The redhead's eyes followed mine as they traveled over her—she was used to this.

"And you're *still* desperate, right?"

"Right," she said, as if that settled everything.

It didn't settle anything for me. I turned the ignition key, listened to the motor catch, and moved the lever into Drive. The Plymouth rolled off the pier, headed back to the courts.

"Where are we going?" the redhead wanted to know.

"*We're* not going anywhere. *You're* going back to your car."

"What about this job?"

"I said I'd listen to you. I listened to you. We're square—that's all there is."

She sat in silence for a couple of minutes. I could feel her eyes on my face. She cleared her throat a couple of times, but nothing came out. As we pulled onto Centre Street near the courthouse parking lot, she reached across the seat and put her hand on my forearm. I turned to look at her. Her big eyes were even bigger, as if tears were only a second away. It was a good trick.

"All this for a lousy picture?" I asked her.

"Yes."

"It doesn't add up for me."

She pulled at my arm so I'd look at her. "I gave my word!" she said, each syllable spaced and heavy.

Now it made sense. The redhead's ego was on the line. So what? Better her ego than my body. I wheeled next to her BMW and waited for her to get out. But she wasn't ready to give up. She shifted her hips, pulled her long legs up underneath her so she was kneeling on the seat facing me.

"What can I do to make you change your mind?"

"I haven't made up my mind, okay? Write your phone number down and I'll call you when I know."

"How do I know you'll call?"

"You don't."

Her face darkened under the makeup. "You call me. I know what you did in the park. One phone call . . ."

She let it hang there as she shifted position again and got out. Before I could pull away she was standing in front of the Plymouth, looking through the windshield. Then she came around to my side of the car, leaned in, and whispered to me: "I am very serious about this."

I locked eyes with her, spoke quietly. "I'm serious too, lady. Threats make me nervous. I'm likely to do something stupid when I'm nervous."

She didn't bat an eye. "I'm used to getting what I want. I'm spoiled—more than you'll ever know. I pay for what I want. You just tell me the price."

"Not everything has a price."

"That's a cliché," she whispered, her face close to mine. She put her head inside the car, kissed me lightly on the cheek, and quickly moved away. I watched her snake-hip her way back to the BMW. She looked back once before she pulled away.

"So are you, bitch," I thought to myself. As it turned out, I was half right.

## 25

THAT WAS THE END of it, I thought. The little princess wouldn't get what she wanted for once in her life and she'd get over it. And I had five hundred bucks. It wouldn't balance the scales, but it would do for today.

I parked behind Mama's apartment, opened the back door, and stepped inside. The door's never locked, but when you open it some kind of bell goes off in the kitchen. When I stepped through the doorway, the short, squat Chinese Mama calls a cook was smiling at me, a butcher knife in one hand. He was ready to chop something—when he saw it was me, he settled for a slab of beef on the counter. I didn't bother to say hello to him—he never answered.

The restaurant was about half filled. Mama was in her usual perch by the cash register near the front door. I caught her eye and made a motion like dialing a telephone. She bowed her head—all clear. I stepped back inside the kitchen, went down a corridor to my right, and found the pay phone.

My call went to another pay phone, the one in Julio's social club.

"Yeah?" barked the receptionist.

"Put Julio on, okay?"

"Who?"

"Julio, pal. You know the name. Tell him he's got a call."

"From who?"

"This is private business, okay? Just tell Julio. He don't want to talk to me, that's his business."

I heard a thunk at the other end, telling me the receiver was swinging against the wall in the club. Julio came on the line.

"Who's this?"

"It's me. You know my voice?"

"Yes," he said, clipped, but not cold.

"I need to talk with you."

"So?"

"Face to face."

"About . . . ?"

"About three o'clock tomorrow afternoon. At the Eastern District."

Julio didn't answer, just hung up. Anybody listening to the conversation would think Eastern District meant the federal courthouse in Brooklyn. What it meant to Julio was the pier at the end of Jay Street, only a few blocks from the courthouse, but in another world. And tomorrow meant in one hour. If I wanted two hours, I would have told him the day after tomorrow. It was a good place to meet, open on all sides—Julio wouldn't be coming by himself.

I dialed another number, let it ring until it was picked up by my broker.

"What?" Maurice snapped into the receiver.

"Burke. Yonkers, tonight, in the seventh. Two yards to win on Flower Jewel."

"Flower Jewel, two on the nose in the seventh at Yonkers, that right?"

"Right."

"Bring the cash by closing time tomorrow."

"What if I win?"

"Come on," he sneered, "you've already had your quota for this year."

"I haven't hit one fucking race yet this year," I told him.

"I know," said Maurice, and hung up.

I went back inside the restaurant, took the booth at the rear, the one I always use. I wrote Julio's name on a napkin, folded it around the money for Maurice, and waited. Mama spotted me. She left her post and walked back to the booth. I stood up until she was seated.

"So, Burke. You have soup, okay?"

"Yes, Mama. But not too much—I've got work to do."

"Good thing, work. Max work with you?"

"Uh . . . not on this, I don't think. But take this money and give it to him, okay? Tell him to give it to Maurice tomorrow if he doesn't hear from me." I handed her the napkin wrapped around two hundreds and a twenty. Max would keep the twenty for himself if he made the delivery. And he'd go see Julio if I didn't come back.

Mama didn't make a move, but one of the so-called waiters came over, listened to her rapid-fire Cantonese, and vanished. He came back in a couple of minutes with a tureen of hot-and-sour soup. Mama served me first, like she always does.

"I may have a new case," I told her.

Mama lifted her eyebrows, the soup spoon poised near her mouth.

"I haven't decided yet," I said in answer to her unspoken question.

"Good case?" Mama wanted to know—meaning was I going to get paid.

"Sure. Good case, bad people."

"That woman who call you here last week?"

"Yes."

"You say you not call her back, right? When I tell you who . . ."

"She found me, Mama."

"Oh. At your office?"

"No. She doesn't know about that place. But she looked all over and got lucky."

"That girl very angry."

"Angry? Why? At who?"

"I not know this. But very angry. You feel in her voice."

"She didn't seem angry to me."

"Angry," said Mama. "And dangerous."

"To me?" I asked her.

"Oh, yes," she said. She didn't say anything else while I finished my soup. When I got up to leave, Mama asked, "You take Max with you?"

"Not today."

"When you do work for this girl?"

"I don't know if I'm going to work for her yet."

"Yes, you know," said Mama, a little sadness in her voice. She bowed her head in dismissal and I went out the back to meet Julio.

## 26

I GRABBED THE BROOKLYN BRIDGE on the Manhattan side and drove across, staying in the right lane. I took the first off-ramp and kept bearing right until I hit the light under the overpass. To the right was the federal courthouse. It's a good spot to meet someone like Julio—nice and private, but too close to the *federales* for anyone to start shooting. I turned left onto Jay Street and kept rolling my way through the side streets until I was just past John Street, in the shadow of the Manhattan Bridge. I turned the Plymouth parallel to the water on the passenger side, dropped my window, and lit a smoke. The deserted slips hadn't seen a boat in years. I was about fifteen minutes early.

I only had a couple of drags on the cigarette when the white Caddy pulled up. It pulled up to the Plymouth, stopping only when it was nose to nose. The passenger door opened and Julio got out. I opened my door and started to walk away from the cars, my back to the Caddy. I heard one man's footsteps crunching on the gravel behind me. When I got to the railing, I turned so I could see both cars, looking past Julio to see if he was going to be stupid.

The old man had both hands in his overcoat pockets, collar turned up, hat pulled down over his eyes. Maybe he was cold.

"What's so important?" he wanted to know.

"Your friend's daughter—you told her where to find me?"

"Yeah."

"She wants me to do something for her."

"So you do it. You get paid. What's the problem?"

"What if I don't want the job?"

Julio turned away from me, looking out over the water. "Times have changed, Burke. Things aren't like they used to be. It's different inside too, you know?"

"I know," I told the old man. And I did: When I was a kid, it was always "Do the right thing." You couldn't go wrong if you did the right thing. When the new cons roll up on a new kid inside the walls today, they still tell him to "Do the right thing." But they mean get on his knees or roll over. Even the words don't mean the same things.

The old man just nodded, watching me.

"You told her about the Nazis too?" I asked him.

The old man went on like he hadn't heard me. "Remember how it used to be? If you was a rat in there, guys would shank you right on the yard . . . just to be doing it. You knew where you stood. Now guys come in *bragging* how they sold their partners for a better deal."

"What's that got to do with me, Julio?"

The old man was wasting away. His cashmere overcoat looked three sizes too large. Even his hat was too big for his head. But his alligator's eyes were still the same—a man on chemotherapy can still tell someone else to pull the trigger.

He looked me full in the face. "I always thought it was you that did the hijacking," he said.

I moved closer to him, my right hand on the handle of the ice pick I kept in my overcoat pocket. The tip was covered with a piece of cork, but it would come right off if I pulled it out. Julio had spent more time in prison than on the streets—he knew what it meant for me to stand so close. You spend enough time inside, you don't even think about getting shot—there's no guns behind the walls. It takes a different kind of man to stab someone—you have to be close to do it—you have to bring some to get some.

"You thought wrong," I told him, holding his eyes.

He looked right at me, as cold as the Parole Board. "It don't matter anymore. People do things . . . maybe it's the right thing to do when you do it . . . who knows? It don't matter to me."

"So why bring it up?" I asked him, my hand still on the ice pick, eyes flicking over to the white Caddy.

"I want you to understand that some debts get paid, okay? Whatever you did years ago, you always been a standup guy, right? Enough years go by, *anybody* should be off the hook."

I knew what he wanted me to say, but not why. "Yeah," I told him, "we all got a life sentence."

He gave me a chilly smile—he was lying about something and I was swearing to it.

"You told her about the Nazis?" I asked him again.

"Yeah," he answered again. His voice was dead.

"Why?"

"She's like my blood to me, you understand? I can't refuse her anything." He moved his shoulders in a "What can you do?" gesture.

"I can," I told him.

The old man didn't say anything for a while. He lit one of his foul cigars, expertly cupping his hand around the wooden match. He blew a stream of blue-edged smoke out toward the water. I just waited—he was getting ready to tell me something.

"When I was a young man, the worst thing you could be was an informer. The lowest thing. That's all over now—you can't count on anything," he said.

"You said that already. When I was a kid, it used to be 'Don't do the crime if you can't do the time.' Now it's 'Don't do the crime if you can't drop a dime.'"

The old man made a dry sound in his throat—it was supposed to be a laugh. "Only now it's a quarter," he said. The laugh never reached his belly, like the smile never reached his eyes.

"I still want to know what this has to do with me, Julio. It's your family, not mine."

"Yeah. My family." He took a breath, turned his flat eyes on my face. "Gina *is* my family," he said, as if that settled it.

"Whose idea was it to send that clown with my money?"

"Okay, it was wrong. I know. She wanted him to do it—I didn't see the harm. There was no disrespect. You got your money, right?"

I just nodded.

"Did Vinnie get stupid?" he wanted to know.

"Vinnie *is* stupid," I told him.

Julio didn't say anything. Being stupid wouldn't disqualify Vinnie from employment.

"The girl threatened me," I said. "Like I do her work or else . . ."

"She don't know no better, okay? When she wants something, she's like a crazy person. I'll talk to her."

"Do that. I'd appreciate it."

"It's done," he said. The old man put his hand in his pocket, came out with a roll of bills wrapped in a rubber band. He handed it to me. I pocketed the money, waiting.

"For your trouble," he said.

"My past trouble or my future trouble?"

"For the past. I apologize. I never thought she'd go all the way on this."

"You know what it is?"

The old man took a breath. The smoke came out his nose in two faint wisps. He took too long to think about the answer. "Yeah," he said. "That picture."

Now it was my turn to just nod. The jackpot question was still on the table.

"I just walk away? No problems?" I wanted to know.

"Burke, you want to walk, you walk. But if you did this thing . . . for the girl . . . if you did it, I would be grateful. You would have my gratitude, understand?"

I nodded again. A hundred feet away the two cars stood in silence. They looked like two giant dogs, nosing each other to see who was in control. It was a good question.

The old man walked over to the Caddy. He never looked back. His door closed; the Caddy backed away from the Plymouth and pulled out with a chirp of tires on the pavement. I was alone.

# 27

I SAT IN THE front seat for a minute, lighting a cigarette and looking around. The pier was empty. I didn't expect anything else. There was no need for Julio to have me followed—I don't advertise in the Yellow Pages, but people know where to find me if they want to bad enough.

The bridge was quiet too, that time of day. I drove slowly back to Manhattan, thinking my thoughts, trying to put it together. I was making the turn onto Allen Street when this old fool stepped right in front of the Plymouth. I hit the brakes just in time. Instead of apologizing, the old bastard gets red in the face and screams, "Why didn't you blow your horn?" A real New Yorker. "If I'd known you were fucking blind, I would've!" I shouted back. I live here too.

I pulled into the alley behind the old industrial building near the Hudson where I have my office. It's all been converted to "living lofts" and the landlord is making a bundle. Except on me. I unlocked the garage and drove the Plymouth inside. The back stairs go all the way up to the top floor, where I have the office. Steel doors block the stairway at the top and bottom. There's a sign that says the doors have to be kept unlocked in case of fire, but it's always too dark to read it. The top floor has a door near the front stairs and another near the back. The one near the back is sealed from the inside—I haven't tried to use it in years. The other door has a fat cylinder set into the middle—when you turn the key, a bolt drives into both sides of the doorframe and into the floor too. I never use it unless both Pansy and I are out. I don't carry the key with me either—I leave it in the garage.

I took the door-handle key out and twisted it hard to the left before I turned it to the right to make it open. I heard a low rumbling from Pansy as I stepped inside. "It's me, stupid," I told her as I stepped over the threshold. If I hadn't twisted the key to the left first, a whole bar of lights aimed at the door would blast off, and whoever entered would get a few thousand watts in their face and

Pansy at their groin. She wasn't supposed to move unless the lights went on or if I came into the office with my hands up, but I didn't want to get careless with her—like I seemed to be with everyone else lately.

Pansy goes through personality splits whenever I walk into the office alone. She's glad to see me, but she's disappointed that there's nobody to bite. She followed me through to the back of the office. There's a door back there that would open out to the fire escape if this building still had one. The metal stairs go up to the roof. Pansy knew the way—she'd been dumping her loads up there for years, and I guess she still had room to spare. I keep telling myself that one day I'm going to go up there and clean up the whole damn mess. One day I'm going to get a pardon from the governor too.

The office is small and dark, but it never makes me depressed. It's safe there. A lot of guys I know, when they get out of jail after a long time, the first thing they do is find themselves some kind of studio apartment—anything with one room, so it feels like what they're used to. I did that too when I first hit the bricks, but that was because even one room was a strain on my budget. I was on parole at first, so my income was limited.

The office looks like it has two rooms, with a secretary's office on the left as you walk in. But there's nothing there—it's just a tapestry on the wall, cut so it looks like there's a way through. That's okay—there's no secretary either. Michelle made me up a bunch of tapes so I can have her voice buzz someone in from downstairs if I have to. I can even have her voice come over the phony intercom on my desk in case some client has to be reassured that I run a professional operation. To the right, it looks like a flat wall, but there's a door to another little room with a stall shower, a toilet, and a cot. Just like jail, except for the shower. It was supposed to be for when I had a big case running and I'd have to spend a lot of time in the office. I stopped kidding myself about stuff like that when Flood left. I stopped kidding myself about a lot of things—it's dangerous to lie to yourself, especially when you're as good at it as I am. I live in the office. I have a good relationship with the hippies who live downstairs. I don't know what they do for a living, and they don't know I use their phone.

The whole floor is covered in Astroturf. It's easy to keep clean, and the price was right. I can lock the front door with a switch on the desk in case I want to keep someone from leaving too quick. And the steel grate on the window makes it real tough for anyone to just drop in unless they bring along a cutting torch. Michelle always says it reminds her of a prison cell, but she's never been in prison. It's not a prison when you have the keys.

I left the back door open so Pansy could let herself back in when she finished on the roof. She lumbered over to me, growling expectantly. She was just looking for a handout, but it sounded like a death threat. Neapolitans were never meant to be pets. I checked the tiny refrigerator: I still had a thick slab of top round and a few slices of Swiss cheese. There's only a hot plate—I can't cook anything except soup. I cut a few strips from the steak, wrapped each one in a slice of cheese, and snapped my fingers for Pansy to come. She sat next to me like a stone lion—her cold gray eyes never blinked, but the drool flowed in rivers through her pendulous jowls. She wouldn't take the food until she heard the magic word from me—I didn't want some freak throwing a piece of poison-laced meat at her. I tossed one of the cheese-wrapped pieces of steak in the air in front of her. It made a gentle arc before it slapped against her massive snout, but her glance never flickered. Satisfied that she was in no danger of backsliding, I tossed her another piece, saying "Speak!" at the same time. The food disappeared like a junkie's dreams when he comes out of the nod. Her jaws didn't move but I could see the lump slip down her throat as she swallowed. "Can't you ever *chew* the damned food?" I asked her, but I knew better. The only way to make her chew was to give her something too big to swallow in one piece.

I sat there for a few minutes, patting her huge head and feeding her the rest of the steak and cheese. Pansy wasn't a food-freak like a lot of dogs. Most dogs will eat until they kill themselves if you let them. It's left over from being wild—wild things never know where their next meal is coming from, so they pack it in when they get the chance. When Pansy was a puppy, I got four fifty-pound sacks of the dry food she was raised on and lugged them up the stairs. I opened them all, dumped all the dog food in one corner of the office, and let her loose. She loved the stuff, but no matter how much she ate, there was always a big pile left. She ate until she passed out a couple of times, but once she got it that there would always be food for her, she lost interest. I always keep a washtub full of the dry food against the back wall of the office, near the door. And I have a piece of hose hooked up to the shower so her water dish refills itself every time the level drops. Now she eats only when she gets hungry, but she's still a maniac for treats, especially cheese.

The phone on my desk rang but I didn't move—it couldn't be for me. The Mole had hooked up an extension to the hippies' phones downstairs. I could make calls out when they weren't on the line, but that was all. I only had it ring to let me know if the line was in use, and to let clients think I was connected to the outside world. My clients never asked to use the phone—I don't validate parking either. The hippies didn't know I lived up here, and they couldn't care less anyway. All they cared about was their inner space, not who was sitting on top of their cave. It was my kind of relationship.

I glanced through the pile of mail left over from the last time I went to the drop and picked it up. It was the usual stuff, mostly responses to my series of ads promising information about opportunities for would-be mercenaries. When I get a legitimate response—one with the ten-dollar money order inside and a self-addressed stamped envelope—I send them whatever crap I happen to have lying around at the time. Usually it's a photocopied sheet of names and phone numbers in places like London or Lisbon. It's the real stuff, like "Go to the Bodega Diablo Bar between 2200 and 2300 hours, order a vodka tonic, and tell the bartender you want to speak to Luis." Sometimes I throw in a Rhodesian Army recruiting poster or a *National Geographic* map of what used to be Angola.

Don't get me wrong, I'm not in this just for the ten bucks—I keep a nice sucker list of anyone who replies to my ads. I've had a lot of careers, and as I get older I play it safer and safer. Stinging suckers and scamming freaks won't make me rich, but it won't make me dead either. And I'm much too old to go back to prison.

I used to sell other things, like handguns, but I stopped. I have to move between the cracks if I want to keep on being self-employed. Robbing citizens got me sent to prison, and the heroin hijacking almost put me down for the count. In the wild, when a wolf gets too old and slow to work with the pack, he has to go off on his own to die. If he's lucky, he gets captured and they put him in a cage to prolong his life. I already had that chance, and it wasn't for me. The way I figure it, I can always keep feeding myself if I work easier and easier game—prey without teeth. So what if the disturbos and petty crooks and outpatients don't ever add up to a retirement-level score? They might get mad, but they don't get even.

## 28

NONE OF THIS WAS getting me any closer to the answers I needed. I pulled out the roll of bills Julio had handed me at the pier. There was a century note on the outside, and it was no Chicago bankroll—every bill was the same, fifty of them, all used. Five thousand bucks. Too big to be a tip for the Forest Park job and not enough for the work the girl wanted me to do—but just the right amount for a warning. In case I missed the message, the last piece of paper inside the roll wasn't green—it had a phone number and the name "Gina" in a spidery, old-man's handwriting.

I went back into the other room and got a piece of mirror glass with a small red dot painted in the middle. I set it up so I was comfortable and sucked a deep breath in through my nose and down into my stomach, expanding my chest when I exhaled. I kept working on this, taking the air deeper and deeper each time, forcing it down to my lower stomach and then to my groin. I kept watching the dot, waiting to go inside, setting my mind to take this problem with me. The dot got bigger and bigger, filling the surface of the mirror. I concentrated on the sound of my own breathing, picturing the breath moving inside my body, waiting for it to happen. Images floated in: all gray tones—the prison yard, Julio's lizard eyes, a pool of dark water, a street in the rain. I came out of it slowly, feeling the cold spot between my shoulder blades. My hands were shaking.

I lit a cigarette, blew the smoke at the ceiling. The old man was trying to tell me something, and him wanting me to do the job for the girl was only part of it. I didn't need the dough, for a change. The girl wasn't going to lay off, and the old man wouldn't call her off. I should never have taken any work from Julio. My parole officer used to have a sign in his office: "Today Is the First Day of the Rest of Your Life." Sure. The trick is to make sure the first day isn't the last day.

I wanted to sleep for a while, but I knew what that meant. I wasn't tired, just depressed. And scared. It was safe in my office, so I wanted to stay. Some guys tried to sleep through their whole bit in prison. You could get all the medication you wanted from the unlicensed reject that passed for a doctor, and they let you have a TV in your cell too. But when they finally open the door, you could get killed while you were blinking at the light.

I always know what the right thing to do is—the hard thing. So I gave Pansy a pat, told her I'd bring her back a treat, and hit the street to buy some time.

## 29

I PULLED OUT OF the garage thinking about what I'd need to cover my trail. The Plymouth is legally registered—to Juan Rodriguez, who lives in an abandoned building in the South Bronx. I wasn't worried about it being traced to me: in the South Bronx, every abandoned building has dozens of registered voters—they never miss an election.

You have to change with the times—using Juan Rodriguez as an alias today was like using John Smith thirty years ago.

The name "Burke" was legally registered too—I took some of the cash from a decent score a few years ago and invested fifteen grand in a piece of a junkyard in Corona, a Queens neighborhood that's Italian to the south and black to the north, with an expanding seam of Puerto Ricans down the middle. I'm on the books as a tow-truck driver. Every two weeks, the owner mails a check for my salary to the post-office box I keep at the main station, across from Madison Square Garden. I cash the checks at this bar near the junkyard and give everything but fifty bucks back to the junkyard owner. It's a good deal for both of us: he gets a business deduction for paying an employee and I get a W-2 form and a legit source of income in case anyone asks. The owner even throws in a set of dealer plates I can legally slap on any car when I do salvage work for him. I give the desk clerk at the hotel where I used to live ten bucks a week for insurance, and I'm covered all the way around. If I get arrested, the desk clerk verifies that I'm a permanent guest and the pay stubs do the rest—I'm a citizen.

I use money orders to pay the yearly registration on the Plymouth. Juan Rodriguez is a straighter shooter: he pays his bills, never gets a parking ticket, and he's never in an accident. He insures the Plymouth through this outfit in the Bronx which specializes in cheap coverage. He even votes regularly. Not only that, he lends me his car whenever I ask him, and he's in no hurry to get it back.

When I have to use the Plymouth on a job, I get the Mole to strip off the paint. The cops are used to seeing old cars in the process of getting painted, especially in the neighborhoods I work. I also have some vinyl sheets in different colors I can just press right over the paint. That kind of cover doesn't last long, but I only use it for a few hours and then pull it off. The Mole has thousands of license plates in his joint—he takes a couple of them and splits them in half, then welds two halves together to make a new set of plates that won't come up on any computer.

Julio wasn't the only reason I had to see the redhead—I had to find out what she knew about me and then go back and erase the tapes.

As I drove through Chinatown, afternoon was fading into evening. The streets were clogged with women making their way home from the sweatshops—their eyes were down and their shoulders slumped, the only hope in their hearts that their children would have a better life. And as they walked from the blackout-curtained rooms, where a straw boss watched their half-paralyzed fingers fly over the sewing machines, to their walk-up apartments with toilets in the hall, other children took over the streets. But these children had no dreams. The Blood Shadows—they took their name from the chalk outline the police coroner draws around a body on the sidewalk. Wearing their trademark black leather coats, silk shirts, and glistening black shoes, they were living proof that hell is cold. The newspapers called them a "street gang," but they were nothing like the bopping gangs from East Harlem or the South Bronx. No cut-off dungaree jackets with their colors on the back for these boys. And no social workers either. Every year Hong Kong disgorges more of them, nobody knows how they get here, but they keep on coming. And America tolerates it like any toxic-waste dump as long as there's money in it for somebody. The Blood Shadows disdain common street mugging—they don't do their gang fighting with knives and chains. Chinatown runs on gambling and dope—organized extortion of these industries forms the Holy Triad, and the Blood Shadows were the sole survivors of a territorial war with other cliques for vulture's rights. The other gangs either merged with the Blood Shadows or got very dead. That left the old guard—what was left of the Tongs.

The old men had first tried to recruit the Hong Kong boys to their own use, but that wasn't working anymore. The old men retreated deeper and deeper into the networks they had spent years developing—but all their political contacts were useless against young boys with flat eyes and hungry guns, kids who didn't play by the rules. The old folks didn't have a chance. They had to import muscle while the kids were growing their own.

I nosed the Plymouth through the alley in back of the warehouse. Clotheslines stretched across the alley, and children ran past, shrieking at each other in a mixture of English and Cantonese. The kids were like birds in a jungle—everything was safe as long as they were making noise. When they went silent, a predator was walking the trails.

I pulled around the front and into the garage. I left the engine running while I pulled the door closed behind me. The Mole had once offered to wire the door so a light would blink and tell Max someone was around, but Max bowed his thanks and said he didn't need it.

I wasn't going to call the redhead from anyplace that could be traced—with cocaine accounting for half the gross national product of the city, half the pay phones in town have been tapped by one agency or another. I'd have to wait for an hour or two anyway. When Max didn't materialize on the landing at the back of the garage, I made a pillow out of my jacket, put it against the passenger door, and stretched out. I put on a Judy Henske tape and listened to her raw-silk voice sing "If That Isn't Love" while I smoked a cigarette in the soft darkness of the garage.

Max might be back in five minutes or five hours. In my life, time isn't important—so long as you're not doing it inside.

## 30

SOMETHING DROPPED ONTO the Plymouth's hood from upstairs, waking me up. I glanced through the windshield—it was a new deck of playing cards, still in the original box. Max was telling me he wanted a rematch of our last game of gin, and warning me not to cheat.

I pocketed the cards and went through the downstairs door all the way to the back. We had a little table back there and a couple of chairs. The table held a big glass ashtray and a chrome ghetto-blaster some would-be mugger had donated to Max. A true liberal, Max never called the police, realizing that the young man needed rehabilitative services instead. He left that task to the emergency ward.

Max floated in the side door, bowed to me, and made a motion like he was dealing the cards. I opened the new deck and riffled them between my hands, getting the feel. Max reached into one of the cabinets and pulled out one of those thick telephone message pads they use in government offices—we used the back for a score sheet. We play three-column gin: 150 points a game, twenty-five for a box, double for a schneid in any column, and double again for a triple. The stakes are a penny a point—first man to a million bucks wins the whole thing. I looked through our stack of tapes, asked Max which one he wanted me to put on. He pointed to Judy Henske. I slammed the cassette home and put the volume on real low. I know Max can't hear. I used to think he listened to music by feeling the bass line in his body or something, but Henske's voice doesn't get real low. One time I slipped a Marie Osmond tape on the player. Max listened for a minute, pointed to me, made a face to say "You *like* that shit?" and hit the "stop" button. He reached in, pulled out the cassette, and crushed it in one hand. He threw the mess into a bucket we use for a garbage pail, folded his arms, and waited for me to display some better taste. I still don't think he can hear the music, but maybe he can feel how I react to it. Lucky there's no bluffing in gin.

We were about an hour into the game, with Max ahead for a change, when Immaculata came into the room from behind Max. Her long black hair was pulled back into a severe bun and her face was scrubbed clean of makeup. She was wearing a white jersey sweatshirt that must have belonged to Max—it was big enough for two of her. She bowed to me in greeting as she put one hand on Max's shoulder. Her long nails were lacquered a shade of purple so dark it was almost black. Max reached up to touch her hand, but he never took his eyes from the cards. The first time Immaculata had walked into our clubhouse like she belonged there, I felt a stab of something—but it passed. She did belong there.

"Hey, Mac," I greeted her, "we're almost done."

Max reached across the table and snatched the score sheet from in front of me. His score was under "X" and mine was under "O"—we'd started playing tic-tac-toe first, years ago, and Max wanted to keep the same identifications just because he won the last time—Orientals are superstitious people. He handed her the sheet. His meaning was obvious—it was me who was almost done.

That did it—being ahead was bad enough, but bragging about it was gross. I immediately knocked, going down with two aces and a deuce—four points. Max spread his cards: three queens, three fives, and three tens. The only other card was my missing ace—an underknock—worth four boxes and fifty points . . . and the fucking third column too. The miserable thug couldn't keep the smile off his face as he handed me the pencil to total things up. Mac went to the hot plate in the corner to make some tea for her and Max—there was apple juice in the refrigerator for me. Max had cut deeply into his ongoing deficit with that last score.

I made the sign of a man rolling dice with his eyes closed to show that it was pure dumb luck, and Max made the sign of a man playing the violin to show how sorry he felt for me and my dismal lack of skill.

Max stashed the score sheet and lit a cigarette. He used to light up whenever he needed only one more card for gin. As soon as he realized I'd caught on to it, he just plain stopped smoking while we were playing—a typical fanatic. Immaculata brought the tea and the apple juice on a little tray and lit a cigarette of her own. I made the sign of talking into a telephone, telling Max I needed to plug into the phone system of the architects who had the building next door. I started to get up and Max held out his palm in a "stop" gesture. He turned to Immaculata, pointed to me, and waved his hands in front of his chest, fingers curling back toward his face. He was telling her to get on with it—whatever it was.

"Burke," she said, "I'm having a problem with my work. Max insists you could help me with it," she said, in a doubtful voice.

"I'll do what I can," I told her.

"I'm not sure there's anything you *can* do," she said. Her English was perfect, the mixture of French and Vietnamese in her voice sounding exotic but not foreign. "When I interview abused children . . . about what happened to them . . . like you saw with the dolls?"

I just nodded, listening.

"Well, if they're old enough to really talk, what I have to do is get it all on tape. You can't take notes . . . you just distract them if you do . . . they want to know what you're writing down. And we may have to use the tapes in court. You understand so far?"

"Sure," I said.

"Anyway, for these children, what we're working on is something we call 'empowerment.' It just means that sexually abused children have no sense of power over their own lives . . . these children are always in fear—they never feel really safe. The goal is for them to eventually be able to confront their abusers, and feel safe while they do it, okay?"

"Okay."

"So they have to feel in control. They have to believe that they're on top of the situation—even when they're working with the therapist."

"How come they don't feel in control when the freak isn't in the room with them anymore?" I asked her.

Immaculata looked at me, two long dark fingernails against her cheek, thinking. "Wait here, okay? I want to show you something."

She patted Max on the shoulder a couple of times, probably their signal that she was coming right back, and went out the way she came in. Max leaned back in his chair, looked over at me, and moved his fingers on the table top to make the sign of a trotting horse. He looked a question at me. I nodded in agreement. Sure, I was still betting on the horses—what was I supposed to do, open a fucking IRA? Max made the sign of opening a newspaper and glancing through it, and looked another question at me. He wanted to know which horse was the latest object of my interest. I shrugged—I didn't have a paper with me. The bastard moved his two fists like he was holding a steering wheel—didn't I have one in the car? Okay. I trudged out to the Plymouth, snatched the *Daily News* off the front seat, and went back to our clubhouse. I sat down and opened it to the right page as Max drifted around behind me. I ran my finger down the page until I came to the seventh race, showed him Flower Jewel, and waited. The line of Flower Jewel showed 8-4-3 reading across from her name—she had finished dead last a week ago, fourth the time before that, and third before that. Max pointed to the "8," put four fingers on the table, and moved them like a pacer would run, the two outside legs forward, then those on the inside—that's why they call them sidewinders. He paced halfway across the table, then broke into a gallop—the two front legs moving together. He looked a question at me. Yeah, I told him, the horse had broken stride in the last race. I held up my right fist to indicate my horse, started to move it across the table in a circle. Then I had my left fist cut in front, with the right veering off to the side. My horse had broken stride, but she had been interfered with by another—not her fault.

Max smiled knowingly. He rubbed the first two fingers and his thumb together in the sign for money, shrugged his shoulders, and spread his hands to ask how much I'd invested. I held up two fingers. Max reached over and pulled one toward him—he wanted to take half my action. The last time he'd done that was the first time he'd ever bet on a horse—back when Flood was here. And we'd won. I hadn't hit a horse since—maybe my luck was changing. But it was probably just that Max was standing up with me. He knew I'd been blue, and his own good fortune in finding Immaculata made him feel even worse for me.

When I wrapped up my sentence for the heroin scam, Max took me over to the warehouse and handed me an old airline carry-on bag. It was stuffed with money—almost forty thousand bucks. He took a paper packet of sugar out of his pocket, tore it open, and dumped the sugar on the table. He spread it flat, then divided it precisely in half with one fingernail. He swept half off the table into his hand, and pointed to the other half, and then to me. I got it—from the day I got arrested, he'd put away half of every score he'd made and saved it for me so I wouldn't have to start all over when I got out.

I didn't know what to say. Max cupped one hand on the table and used two fingers to burrow through it. The Mole. He put one hand on his chest, and spread the other wide in a gesture of impassioned oration. The Prof. The bag was half of everything they'd all made while I was inside. Then he touched his heart with his fist, and extended an open hand to me. Telling me that money didn't square the debt—he would always owe me.

### DOWN HERE

I've done time with a lot of gangsters over the years. The cream of the crop, the real elite, were the "made men," the guys who get to cut their fingers and swear undying loyalty to some boss. They keep their mouths shut and do their time, just like the movies say. When they finally make it back to the streets, they get a kiss on both cheeks and a few bucks from their boss. And they call themselves "wiseguys."

## 31

IT WAS ANOTHER FEW minutes until Immaculata came back. She had an armful of paper with her. "Look at this," she told me, and sat down next to Max.

They were kids' drawings: stick figures, crude crayons—they didn't mean anything to me.

"So?" I asked.

"Look at them again, Burke. Look closely."

I lit a cigarette and went through them again. "How come the pictures of the kids have no arms?" I asked her.

"That's it. Now you see. The children have no arms. And see how small they are next to the big figures? Look at this one. . . ."

It was a picture of a little child looking at a giant penis pointed at her face. The child had no arms—her mouth was a straight line.

"She's trapped," I said.

"Yes. She is without power, you understand? She is small, her abuser is huge. The penis is her whole world. She has no arms to fend it off. She has no legs to run. She's in a cage."

"How do you break her out?" I wanted to know.

Immaculata took a deep breath. "Some of them never do break out. We have to give them back a sense of control before that happens. If we start too late, they look for control with drugs, or they try suicide. Or they surrender."

"Surrender?"

"To the feelings. It's not just the loss of power. Children have sexual feelings too. If you awaken them too early, they get out of control, and the kids themselves look for sex . . . it's what they think is love."

"Fucking maggots."

Immaculata didn't say anything. Max reached across and took a couple of the wooden matches I used for my smokes. He broke one until it was about a third the size of the rest, and put it next to a full-size match. Then he took the big match and snapped it off until it was even smaller than the first one. He looked at Immaculata.

"It won't work. To the child, the abuser is always all-powerful. You can't make him small—you have to make the child big."

I took the tiny piece of match that was supposed to be the parent, lit another match, and touched it to the little piece. It went up in flames.

"That won't work either, Burke. You can make the perpetrator disappear from the earth, but not from inside the child's mind."

I didn't say anything. Immaculata's face was calm, her eyes watchful but showing nothing. I looked at Max—his face was a concrete mask. He wasn't buying this any more than I was.

"What's this got to do with the tape recorder, Mac?" I asked her.

"In my office, the child has to not just *be* safe, she has to *feel* safe. She has to learn she can control parts of her life. She has to learn she has the right to say 'No!' Okay?"

"Okay."

"Most of the kids have been involved in a conspiracy of silence. The offenders make them promise not to tell—keep it a secret. Or they make the kids believe something terrible will happen if they do. So I tell them if there's something they don't want to go on the tape recorder, all they have to do is reach over and turn it off. So *they* are in control."

"And they turn it off when they get to the stuff you need for court?"

"Sometimes they do," she said.

I lit another smoke and closed my eyes, buying some time to think. When it came to me, it was so simple I was sure they'd already thought of it.

"Use two tape recorders," I told Mac.

"Two tape recorders?"

"Sure. The one on top of the table—the one the kids can turn off if they want, right? And you keep another one out of sight, maybe under the table or something. And you let that one run all the time. So even when they turn off the first one, you still have everything on tape."

Immaculata put the two fingernails back against her cheek, thinking it over. "That would be dishonest," she told me.

"Better to let some scumbag walk away laughing?" I asked.

She waited a second or two. "No," she said. And a smile broke across her lovely face. "That's what we'll do."

Max made an "I told you so" gesture to his woman, now smiling himself. Immaculata reached over and squeezed my hand, and Max's smile broadened.

Immaculata was the first woman ever to come into our clubhouse. She'd be the last. Like all truly dangerous beasts, Max would mate for life.

I left them with each other and went in the back to make my call.

# 32

IT WAS JUST GETTING dark as I walked through the catacombs behind the warehouse. The cellar was one of many that ran under all the buildings on the block. The City Planning Office sold me a set of the plans years ago, and the Mole figured out how we could make all the basements connect to each other by drilling a few holes. It took almost a month for us to finish, but once you got to the warehouse basement, you could get out a dozen different ways. We originally did it just in case we had to leave quickly, but once we were under there, the Mole showed me how we could tap into the telephone lines in the other buildings. The warehouse is owned by some corporation Mama Wong set up, but it belongs to Max. His temple is upstairs, and the rest of the space is for whatever we need. For Mama, it's a warehouse. For me, it's the post office.

I found the metal footlocker, rooted through it past the stuff we kept there—coats, hats, glasses, anything to make you look different. I found the field telephone and the set of alligator clips. I walked through our cellar into the next basement. Above us was a firm of Chinese architects, and they never worked late. I clipped the field phone onto the junction points the Mole had shown me and I got a dial tone right away. I used the little box that looked like the face of a calculator and punched out the number Julio had written down, lit a cigarette, and waited.

I didn't have long to wait—she must have been sitting by the phone.

"Hello." It was the redhead.

"Hey, baby," I leered into the mouthpiece, "you free tomorrow night?"

She got it right away. "Sure. What time will you pick me up?"

"I'm going to be working late. I'll meet you, okay?"

"Where?"

"Same place—nine o clock," I told her, and unplugged the phone.

I put everything back where it was supposed to be and walked back through the cellar. Our clubhouse was empty. I fired up the Plymouth, hit the garage-door switch, and backed out into the alley. I got out to go back inside and close up, but I saw the garage door slide down. Max was on the job.

I drove over to Mama's. I needed some food for Pansy and an alibi for tomorrow night.

# 33

IT WAS PAST MIDNIGHT before I was ready to go back to the office. If Mama didn't hear from me by the same time tomorrow, she'd know the meeting had been a bust. Mama would tell Max, and call Blumberg to get a bondsman over to Arraignments in Queens. If I wasn't in jail, Max would go see Julio.

One more call to make and I could bring Pansy her Chinese food. I found a pay phone off Atlantic Avenue.

A young woman with a sweet West Indian accent answered. "A & R Wholesalers. We never close."

"Is Jacques around?" I asked her.

"Please hold one moment, sir."

It was cold in the phone booth, but the man's voice was as sunny as the Islands.

"Yes, my friend. May we be of service?"

"Jacques, this weather is really turning ugly out here, you know? I think I can move some of those portable electric heaters if I can get a good price."

"We may have some in stock, mahn—I'll have to check the inventory. And the price . . . it depends on how many you want, like always."

"If I can get some tonight, I'll take a dozen and try them out."

"That's not a big order, my friend. The more you take, the less they cost."

"I understand. But I'm not ready to risk a lot of capital—I have to see how they move this year, okay?"

"Whatever you want, mahn—we are here to serve. You are familiar with our line?"

"Sure. Now, look, I only want new merchandise, still in the original cartons."

"Of course, of course. You understand this too affects the price."

"I understand."

"Now, we have a good supply of the new automatic models—the ones which shut off by themselves if they tip over?"

"No, I only want the old-style. They throw plenty of heat."

"Yes, my friend," said Jacques, "but many customers prefer the advanced safety features."

"The new ones are too complicated for me. I want a product I can trust."

"We have just what you want, mahn," he assured me. "Do you at least want the ones that run on both twelve hundred and fifteen hundred watts?"

"Yeah, that's a good feature. Can I pick them up tonight?"

"We never close, my friend," he said. We both hung up.

I drove down Atlantic toward Queens. Soon it turned into a West Indian neighborhood. I turned left on Buffalo Avenue, past the abandoned bar on the corner, until I saw the storefront restaurant. There was a sign for Tower Isle Jamaican Meat Patties in the window, a pair of black Cadillacs parked in front. I turned into the driveway and pulled around the back. When I had the Plymouth's headlights aimed at the back door, I flashed the lights three times and turned them off.

The door opened and a man came out, both hands in the pockets of a big leather apron. I had the window down and my hands on the sill by the time he got close enough to see me.

"Jacques is expecting me," I told him.

The man said nothing. He backed away, still facing me, until he was inside the door. I lit a cigarette and got ready to do some waiting.

I was just lighting another when the door opened again. The leather apron came out first and walked over to me again. He said nothing. From behind him I could see another man—tall, with a little snap-brim hat. The other man was carrying a shopping bag in one hand.

I kept my eyes on the leather apron. The other man disappeared from view. I heard the Plymouth's door open and someone climbed inside.

"Is that you, Burke?" asked Jacques.

"It's me," I told him, turning to face him, my back to the leather apron like it was supposed to be.

Jacques hands me the shopping bag. Inside was a blue box. And inside that was a Smith & Wesson .357 magnum snub-nosed revolver. The blue steel even smelled new.

I popped the cylinder open, held my thumb in front of the barrel, and sighted down. The rifling was new too. Not a very accurate piece, but the best man-stopper at close range. It would take either .38 Special or .357 magnum slugs, and it had no safety. A lot better than the 9mm automatic Jacques had been pushing over the phone.

I nodded my head in agreement. Jacques held up his hand, palm out, fingers spread. I raised my eyebrows. He just shrugged.

It's good to deal with professionals—even if I was wired like a

Christmas tree, nothing would go on the tape. Five hundred bucks of Julio's money changed hands. I slipped the pistol into my coat pocket, put the box it came in back into the shopping bag, and waited. The West Indian took out a box of shells, holding them in his palm. I shook my head—I had all the bullets I needed. Jacques touched a forefinger to his brow. I turned to face Leather Apron again. I heard the car open and close, but I didn't move until I saw the bodyguard start to back away toward the restaurant door. Then I got out of there.

I drove down Atlantic, one hand on the wheel, the other pulling up the rubber floor mat and groping around until I found the panel next to the hump for the transmission. I had loosened the ratchets before I drove to the restaurant. The magnum slipped inside and the rubber mat went back in place. There was nothing in plain view. I couldn't do anything about a cop stopping me, but if he found the piece it wouldn't stand up in court.

The magnum was a heavy-duty piece. Just looking at the business end would scare most people. But guns aren't for scaring people, they're for people who are scared. I was—I just didn't know of what.

# 34

I DROVE BACK CAREFULLY, speeding up so I blended in with the late-night traffic. The streets were quiet, but if you looked close, you could see things. Two guys standing against the wall of a darkened gas station—the wool caps on their heads would turn into ski masks when they pulled them down, hands in their pockets. A lonely whore in a fake-fur coat with a white mini-skirt underneath, looking to turn one last trick before she called it a night. A van with blacked-out windows driving by slowly, watching the whore while the two men in the shadows watched the van. In New York, the vultures work close to the ground.

Back in the garage, I unscrewed the plate and took out the magnum. I needed to test the piece and I didn't have time to run over to the Bronx and ask the Mole. I broke the gun and loaded it with some

.38 Specials I keep in a jar full of nuts and bolts. The door to the basement is set into the garage floor, like a manhole cover. I pried it loose and backed down the stairs, reaching for the light switch with my hand. I heard the rats running across the floor even before the light went on. Some of the bolder bastards just looked at me—it was their place, not mine.

The walls are lined with sandbags donated from a construction site—about four bags deep all around the wall and up to the ceiling. I don't keep anything else down in the basement; there's no other way out except for the tunnels the rats use. It's good for nothing but testing things that make a big bang—you couldn't hear a cannon from the street.

There's a little workbench on the floor down there with a heavy-duty vise attached and a reel of two-hundred-pound-test fishing line. I wrapped the butt of the magnum in the vise, wedged it tight, and tied some of the fishing line around the trigger. I aimed it at the far wall, cocked the hammer, and ran the line back to the stairs. I climbed halfway up and gave it a hard pull. There was a sharp *crack!* sound and a puff of dust from one of the sandbags. I went over to look—just a nice round entrance hole—the other side would be wide open, but I wasn't going to pull the whole thing apart just to take a look.

I pulled the magnum out of the vise, held it two-handed, and emptied it into the wall. It kicked a bit, but not as much as I expected from the short barrel. I broke the gun and dropped the empties into my hand. Jacques was still selling quality merchandise.

The rats were back doing business before I had the trapdoor closed.

## 35

I WOKE UP THE next morning and just stayed there on the couch for a bit, watching Pansy growl in her sleep at a patch of sunlight on her face. I'd been dreaming of Flood—I do it all the time since she left. When I was a kid in reform school I used to dream about getting out—staying out—being somebody important, like a major-league gangster. Now I just replay the tapes of my past inside my head—I can't erase them but I do enough editing to keep me sane.

I took my time getting ready to go out and get some breakfast. I wasn't in any screaming hurry to check out the race results.

The bakery was a couple of blocks away, still standing despite the invasion of yuppies. Newspaper columnists who never rode a subway still call my neighborhood the "mean streets," but the only danger out there is maybe getting hit by a flying croissant.

There was a new girl working in the bakery, about sixteen years old, with black hair and dark eyes. From the way the guy who runs the place was watching her, she had to be his daughter. I make sure I don't buy there too often—the owner thinks I make the trip all the way from Brooklyn just for his bread. If too many people know where you live, sooner or later you get visitors.

I picked out a semolina loaf for Pansy and a couple of hard rolls for me. Next door in the deli I got some pineapple juice and seltzer plus a slab of cream cheese. A lot of guys I did time with said when they got out they'd always start the day off with a real breakfast—bacon and eggs, steak, hash-browns, coffee, all that. I never did that—I'm particular about who I eat with.

I grabbed a *Daily News* off the stand. The newsdealer is blind. I handed him a five, telling him what it was. He put the bill face down on this machine he has, moving his hand so it forced the bill over some lights. "Five dollars," the machine said in a robot voice. The paper costs thirty-five cents now. The price of everything except human life has gone up a lot in New York.

Upstairs I tore open the semolina loaf and scooped out the guts. Most of the slab of cream cheese went inside. I looked over at Pansy. She was sitting like a stone, drooling. I tossed her the loaf, saying the magic word at the same time. As usual, she bit right through the middle so that the piece on each side of her jaws fell to the floor. It was gone before I had a chance to make my own breakfast. "You've got the table manners of an animal," I told her. Pansy never looked up—nobody respects my social criticism.

I mixed the seltzer and pineapple juice, opened the hard rolls, and put the last of the cheese inside. Finally, I turned to the race results. Sure enough, Flower Jewel was the first horse listed in the seventh race. But before I had even a split-second's worth of pleasure out of it, I saw the tiny "dq" next to her name. Disqualified. I went over the charts, trying to see how I was robbed this time. My horse tried to get to the top but was parked by another animal all the way to the half before she was shuffled back to fourth against the rail. Then she pulled out and was flying in the stretch when she broke stride. When she crossed the wire first she wasn't pacing like she was supposed to, she was galloping. Flower Jewel was out of an Armbro Nesbit mare by Flower Child, a trotting stallion. She had her grandfather's heart, but not her father's perfect stride. What the hell: *she* probably didn't know she didn't win the race. My love for the animal was unchanged—she did the right thing—much better to get there first by cheating than play by the rules and finish back in the pack. At least she'd get another shot next week.

It was still early enough for the hippies downstairs to be asleep. I picked up the phone and called over to the restaurant.

"Poontang Gardens," answered Mama Wong. Some soldier had suggested the name to her years ago and she's too superstitious to change it.

"It's me," I said. "Any calls?"

"Same girl. She say you be there."

"What?"

"She call, okay? I say you not here. She say, 'You tell him be there,' and she hang up."

"Thanks, Mama."

"Hey!" she snapped, just as I was about to hang up, "People tell you what to do now?"

"No," I said and hung up.

I called Pansy back from the roof and went into the other room. I got the little TV set and went back to the couch. I asked Pansy what she wanted to watch but she didn't say. All she likes are shows about dogs and professional wrestling. I found a rerun of "Leave It to Beaver" and kicked back on the couch. I was asleep before it was over.

# 36

WHEN I CAME TO, there was some western on the screen. Two guys had just finished bashing each other's heads in and were getting ready to shake hands. Politicians do that too, but it comes natural to them—they're all dogs from the same litter.

I let Pansy out to the roof again and started to put together what I'd need for my date. If this was a regular case, I would have had her come to the office, where it's safer for me, but she was pushing too hard and I wasn't going to give her any more information about me than she already had. I set the magnum aside—I could put it back into the cavity next to the transmission hump just in case, but I didn't think I was walking into a shoot-out. Hell, I *wouldn't* walk into a shoot-out. The redhead wasn't really working together with Julio—if the old man wanted me put down he would have tried it already. He was just pushing on me the same way the redhead was, but not for the same reason.

I dressed like I was going to be arrested—when nothing feels right, you make plans for things going wrong. An old leather sportcoat; plain white cotton shirt, button cuffs; a black knit tie. All that camouflage wouldn't stop me from being rolled in, but it might stop the cops from being too forceful about it. If they only took me as far as the precinct, I still might be able to do something about it. But if they actually made an arrest, I'd be around for a while—my fingerprints would fall and they'd know I wasn't a citizen. Figuring the worst, I made sure I wasn't carrying anything that would make a problem for me. The ankle-high boots had zippers up the insides. They also had steel toes and one hollow heel. I folded five ten-dollar bills tightly to get them inside the heel. Soft money is the best contraband to have when you're locked up. A ten-dollar bill is just about right for a jailhouse transaction—more than enough to get me moved to another tier or for a supply of smokes and magazines. Twenty bucks would get me some private time on the phone and tap me into the rest of my money if it came to that. In jail they let you keep most of your streetside clothes. They don't take everything away until you get sentenced.

I took a shower and shaved carefully, listening to the radio say how warm it was for that time of the year. I've got a good watch, a gold Rolex some rich guy lost in his hotel room, but I didn't put it on. Times have changed—I was just a kid years ago, sitting in the holding cell, watching the cops bring a full-race pimp up to the booking desk. I was still handcuffed but they'd hooked me in front so I could smoke. I was splitting one of my last matches—you put your thumbnails carefully into the cardboard at the base of the match, then you pull up slowly until you have two matches with half a striking-head on each piece. The Puerto Rican kid next to me was holding the matchbook so we could get a light. When he leaned over for some fire he nudged me in the ribs so I'd look up. The pimp was raising hell, mouthing off about how the cops should be careful of his jewelry and how much it cost. The fat old sergeant at the booking desk acted like the pimp wasn't in the room. He picked up all the jewelry one piece at a time, read aloud what it was, and marked it down on the voucher sheet. They'd give it all back to the pimp when he paid his fine. It was all a dance. The sergeant made his list like a guy taking inventory: "One diamond bracelet, gold clasp. One signet ring, onyx and gold, initial 'J,' one pinky ring . . . " The pimp kept up a running fire about how much all that stuff cost. I think that was when I first got the idea that it was stupid to steal from citizens. The sergeant picked up the pimp's wristwatch. It was thin as a dime, with a dark-blue face and little diamonds all around the rim—a thing of beauty. He looked down at the pimp, who said, "Hey, my man, you best be careful with that watch. It cost more than you make in a year!" The cop looked thoughtfully at the watch for a minute, like he was trying to figure out how it could cost all that cash. Then he slammed it face down on the desk counter. The crystal cracked and little pieces went flying all over the place. The pimp screamed "Hey man!" like it was his head that got cracked. The sergeant looked at the pimp, said, "One man's watch—broken," and wrote it down on his sheet. His expression never changed. I wasn't worried about them doing that to my Rolex. Like I said, times have changed. Now they'd probably steal it.

It was almost six by the time I was ready to leave. The meeting was for nine, so the timing was just about right. I brought Pansy back downstairs and fixed things so she'd have food and water for at least a couple of weeks if I didn't come right back. I left the back door open a crack so she could get to the roof herself. The open door wouldn't help a burglar much—he'd have to be a human fly to get in the door, and a magician to get out.

I stopped at four different self-serve gas stations along Atlantic Avenue. The Plymouth has a fifty-gallon tank—if I filled it up at one place, they might remember me. Just before I made the turn onto the Inter-Boro I saw a gray stone building on my right. The windows were barred and there was barbed wire on the roof. The door looked like the entrance to Attica. The sign on the front said it was a Day Care Center.

It took less than an hour for me to finally get to the old spot in Forest Park. It was still light enough for the joggers and dog-walkers. I drove through the entire park a couple of times, looking for some other spots to park—and for people looking for me. I finally parked the Plymouth just off the road, opened the trunk, and put on the old raincoat and leather gloves I always keep in there. Then I changed the rear tire closest to the road, taking my time. It was a while before I was finished. I put everything back into the trunk except for the tire iron and the gloves, which I tossed into the back seat.

By the time I settled down to wait, the only thing that didn't belong in all that greenery was me.

## 37

WHAT WAS LEFT OF the weak sun filtered through the thick trees, making patterns of light and dark all around the Plymouth. By the time the shadows won the war I had stopped listening to my tapes. Headlights shot through the park, cars motored by. Once in a while

I'd see a bicycle or even a late jogger wearing reflective foil on his warmup suit. I ground each cigarette out against the car door, putting the butts inside a plastic bag. No point in telling the cops how long I'd been waiting, if it came to that.

It was almost nine when I heard the whine of a car kept too long in a lower gear. The little BMW tore around the far curve and headed right at me. The redhead was running a pair of driving lights on the front bumper—the white light blasted into my windshield as she slammed on the brakes and skidded to a stop almost on top of me. As soon as I heard her engine shut off, I started the Plymouth. I heard her door slam and I watched her walk the way women do in high heels on a tricky surface. She was close enough for me to see her face when I pulled the lever into gear and started to creep forward. Her legs were spread wide, anchored to the ground, hands on hips. Her mouth was open to say something, but I pulled past the BMW and stopped, foot on the brake. She walked toward me again, and I pulled forward some more.

She got it. The redhead walked back to her car. I waited until she started it again; then I pulled out slowly so she could follow, heading for the better spot I'd found before. The Plymouth calmly drove through the park; the BMW stuck to my bumper, her damned driving lights flooding the rearview mirrors. I turned the inside mirror backward and made two tours through the park, just in case she brought some friends. I could hear the angry roar of the BMW in the night—she was so close I could have merged with her front end if I hit the brakes.

I found the spot I wanted and pulled all the way in, leaving the Plymouth with its nose pointing back out to the road. The redhead was right behind me, but she didn't have room to turn around—like I wanted it.

I killed the engine.

Her door slammed hard enough to rattle the glass. She stalked over to where I was sitting, her little fox face set and hard.

"You all through playing games?" she snapped.

I got out of the Plymouth, reaching for the flashlight I keep in the door panel. I walked past her to the BMW, opened the door, and shone the light inside. Empty.

"Open the trunk," I told her.

The redhead made a hissing sound, but she turned and reached inside her car for the keys. I shined the light on her to help. She was wearing what looked like half a normal skirt, reaching over to the middle of her thighs. It had vertical black and white stripes and was topped by a wide black belt. Her stockings had dark seams down the back of her legs. She bent inside the car to get the keys—it was taking too long.

"Having trouble?" I asked her.

She looked back over her shoulder. "Just wanted to make sure you got a good look," she said, a bright smile on her face.

"Just get the keys," I told her, an edge to my voice.

She gave her hips a sharp little wiggle, then turned around with the keys in her hand. She walked back to the trunk, opened it, and stood aside. I shined the light inside. Lots of junk, but no humans. I pulled up the carpet, looked inside the spare-tire well. Nothing there either.

I gave her back the keys. "Follow me to the street," I told her. "We'll find a place to park your car and you can come with me."

"No way!" she snarled. "Go with you *where?*"

"Someplace where we can talk, okay?"

"We can talk right here."

"*You* can talk here if you want. You want me in on the conversation, you come with me."

"And if I don't?"

"Then we don't talk."

She ran her fingers through her fiery hair, front to back, thinking.

"Julio . . . " she started to say.

"Julio's not here," I said.

The redhead gave me one of those "You better not be fucking around with me" looks, but that was her last shot. She climbed back into the BMW and started the engine. I pulled the Plymouth away and headed out of the park.

# 38

I FOUND an empty spot on Metropolitan Avenue, pulled past it, and waited. She wrestled the BMW into the space, put a big piece of cardboard in the side window, and walked over to me. I got out and went over to look at what she left. It was a hand-lettered sign—"No Radio." I thought all BMWs came with those signs straight from the factory.

She slammed the Plymouth's door closed with all her strength. I made a U-turn on Metropolitan back toward the Inter-Boro eastbound. We pulled onto the highway, following the signs to the Triboro.

"We're going into the city?" she asked.

"Just keep quiet," I told her. "We'll talk when we get there."

She didn't say anything else. I checked the mirror. It was a relief not to have her driving lights burning in my eyes. Just before the turnoff to the Long Island Expressway, I pulled off into Flushing Meadow Park. She opened her mouth to say something, but I held my finger to my lips. Nobody was following us, but I didn't want her saying where we were going in case Michelle's search had given her some ideas.

"How come you use those driving lights even when there's traffic in front of you?" I asked her.

"They look nice," she said, as if that settled things.

I circled the park slowly until I came to the parking lot on the east side. A few cars were already pulled in, facing the sewage the politicians named Flushing Bay. The cars were spaced well apart, the windows dark. The cops used to make a circuit through here, flashing their lights. If they saw two heads in the window they kept on going. They stopped when the merchants on Main Street complained they needed more coverage of their stores.

Couples used to park back in the bushes too, but a gun-carrying rapist working the area stopped all that. Wolfe had tried the case against the dirtbag when they finally caught him. She dropped him for twenty-five to fifty, but people still stuck close to the water's edge.

I pulled in between an old Chevy with a jacked-up rear end, "José and Juanita" painted on the trunk in flowing script, and a white Seville with fake wire wheels. Lights from the incoming planes to LaGuardia reflected off the black water.

I cracked my window and lit a cigarette. By the time I turned to the redhead, she was already unbuttoning her blouse.

# 39

"WHAT THE HELL ARE you doing?" I snapped at her, my voice louder than it should have been.

"What does it look like?" she asked. "I'm showing you I'm not wearing a wire." She smiled in the darkness, her teeth so white they looked false. "Unless you have your little whore-friend with you in the back seat . . ." she said, looking over her shoulder.

"There's nobody here," I told her.

She kept unbuttoning the blouse like she hadn't heard me. She wore a black half-bra underneath, the lace barely covering her nipples. The clasp was in front. She snapped it open and her breasts came free, small and hard like a young girl's, the dark nipples pointed at me in the cool air. I didn't say anything, watching her. When I felt the cigarette burn my fingers I pushed it out my window without looking back.

The redhead reached behind her and pulled the wide belt loose. "I have to unzip this. I've got a big ass for such a small girl and the skirt won't go up. I'm sure you noticed."

I wanted to tell her to stop but . . . maybe it was a bluff . . . maybe she was wired and this was a game. I kept quiet.

The zipper made a ripping sound. She wiggled in her seat until the skirt was down past her knees. Her panties were a tiny black wisp, the dark stockings held up by wide black hands across her thighs. If she was wired it had to be inside her body.

"Yes?" she asked.

I just nodded—I'd seen enough. But she took it the other way. She hooked her thumbs inside the waistband of her underpants and pulled them down too. There wasn't enough light to see if her flaming hair was natural.

"Look out the window—smoke another cigarette," she hissed at me. I heard her struggling with her clothes, muttering something to herself. A tap on my shoulder. "Okay, now," she whispered, and I turned around.

"You have another cigarette for me?"

I gave her one and struck a wooden match. She came close to catch the fire. She didn't move her face, but her eyes rolled up to look at me.

I reached over and took her purse from her. She didn't protest while I went through it. She had her own cigarettes, a matchbook from a midtown restaurant, a few hundred in cash, and some credit cards. And a metal tube that looked like lipstick. I pulled off the top. Inside was a nozzle of some kind and a button on the base. I looked a question at her.

"Perfume," she said.

I pointed it outside the window and pressed the button. I heard the thin hiss of spray and smelled lilacs. Okay.

"I'm listening," I told her.

The redhead shifted in her seat so her hips were wedged into a corner, her back against her door, legs crossed, facing me.

"I already told you what this was about. I want you to do something for me—what else do you need to know?"

"Is this a joke? You're nothing to me—I don't owe you anything."

"It's not a joke. I'm not a joker." She drew in hard on her cigarette, lighting her face for a second. "You don't owe me . . . but you owe Julio, right?"

"Wrong."

"Then why did you do that other thing?"

"What other thing?" I asked her.

"In the park . . ."

"You're riding a dead horse, lady. I don't know anything about a park. You got me confused with someone else."

"Then why did you come out here at all?"

"Because you're pushing me. You're playing some silly rich-girl's game. I want you to get off my case, and I wanted to tell you to your face so you'd get it."

"I *don't* get it," she snarled at me. "And I *won't* get it. You work for money—like everyone else—I've got money. And I need you to do this."

"Get someone else," I told her.

"No!" she snapped. "You don't tell me what to do. Nobody tells me what to do. You think I *want* to use you for this? I told you, Julio said you know the Nazis."

"What's this about Nazis? It sounds like Julio lost it during his last stretch."

"Julio never loses anything," said the redhead, "and you know it. It's got to be you, and that's it."

"Because of these 'Nazis'?"

"Yes. And because they're the only lead I have."

I lit another cigarette. The air in the car felt charged, like just after a hard rain. The redhead sounded like she wasn't playing with a full deck, but what she had left were all wild cards.

I got out of the Plymouth and walked down toward the water's edge, not looking back. Before I got more than a few feet I heard the car door slam angrily behind me. I heard the tap of her high heels on the pavement and then felt her hand on my arm.

"Where do you think you're going?" she said, trying to pull me around to look at her.

"To the water," I told her, as if that explained everything.

She kept pace with me, tottering on the heels when we hit the grassy area, but hanging on.

"I want to talk to you!" she snarled.

The moon was out—almost full. Maybe it was making her crazy, but I didn't think so. Maybe she just didn't know how to act. I stopped at the water and grabbed her tiny chin in my right hand, holding her face so she couldn't move. I put my face close to her. "I don't give a flying fuck *what* you want, understand? You're not my boss. Julio's not my boss. You and me are square, okay? You think I'm some senile old uncle like Julio, you make a big mistake."

She squirmed in my hand, twisting her face but keeping her hands down. Her eyes slashed at me, but she didn't open her mouth.

"And if you think I'm some halfwit cock-hound like Vinnie, you're even stupider than you've been acting, understand?" I said, giving her face a quick shake. Her eyes flashed—I knew it hadn't been Julio's idea to send the Cheech with my money.

"Let. Go. Of. Me," she whispered, every word a separate sentence.

I pushed her face away from me, hard. She went sprawling away from me, lost her balance, and hit the ground. I walked away from her until I found one of the vandalized benches and sat down. Looked at the water. Tried to think my way out of the box I was in.

It was another couple of minutes before she sat down next to me, fumbling in her bag for a cigarette. I didn't light this one for her.

"You get your kicks shoving women around?"

"I wasn't shoving you around, princess—I was shoving you *away*."

"Don't do that," she whispered, her face close to mine again. "Don't do that—I can make it all right, just give me a chance, okay?"

I didn't say anything, waiting.

"I want this so bad," said the redhead. "I don't have much to go on. If I go to some private detective agency they'll just rip me off. I know that. I know the whole thing's a long shot."

I kept staring at the water, waiting.

"Let me just sit here with you. Like I'm your girlfriend or something—let me tell you the whole story. If you don't agree to help me when I'm done, we're quits. You take me back to my car and that's the end."

I lit another cigarette, still quiet. She put her hand on my arm—a fat diamond sparkled in the moonlight—cold fire.

"You swear?" I asked her.

"I swear," she said, her eyes big and glowing and full of lies.

I looked down at the diamond. "Tell me," I said.

## 40

SHE GOT OFF THE bench and walked around behind me. She leaned over against my back, her elbows on my shoulders, her lips near my ear. Like she'd been doing it all her life. Her voice was breathy, but she wasn't trying to be sexy now—she just wanted to get it all out.

"This is about Scott. He's my friend's little boy, like I told you. He's the sweetest little boy in the world—blond hair, blue eyes. He's a perfect little boy, always has a smile for everyone. Nobody's spoiled him yet—he loves everyone. He loves my Mia the most.

"My friend took him to a kids' party at the mall—where all the stores have clowns and singers and storytellers and all that, you know? Scott was having a great time until one of the clowns came up to him. All of a sudden he starts to scream and he runs away. His mother has to run and catch him. He won't tell her anything—he just wants to go home.

"He seems okay after that—like he just had a bad day or something. But a couple of weeks later, one of his father's friends comes over to the house. He has a Polaroid camera with him and he's taking pictures. When Scott comes downstairs, he sees the camera, and he goes rigid . . . like catatonic . . . he just freezes up. They take him upstairs and soon he's like okay again, but by then my friend figures something's really wrong and she takes him to a therapist.

"But he won't talk to the therapist. I mean, he won't talk about what's wrong. It's like he's himself most of the time, but something's really eating at him. He doesn't want to do things like he did before—he doesn't want to play, doesn't want to watch TV . . . nothing. The poor little guy is so sad.

"Anyway, my friend brings him over. She figures . . . he just *adores* my little Mia . . . maybe he'll play with her. But he doesn't want to do that either. And now Mia gets all upset too. 'Fix it, Mommy,' she says to me. What was I supposed to do? Mia . . . I *had* to fix it."

The redhead turns her face, gives me an absent-minded kiss like she's telling me "Don't move." She walks back around to the front of the bench and climbs into my lap—snuggles in to me like she's cold. Like I'm a piece of furniture. Her face is against my chest but I can still hear her when she talks.

"I tell my friend to stay in my house and I take Mia and we go out and buy a Polaroid. I come back to the house and I get this big hammer from the garage. I bring everything out to the patio and then I take Scott by the hand and bring him outside with me. I open the box and show him the camera and he starts to pull away from me. Then I take the hammer and pound that fucking camera until it's just a bunch of little parts all over the patio. I must have gone crazy for a minute . . . I'm screaming something at the camera . . . I don't even know what. And little Scott . . . he comes over to me. I give him the hammer and he smashes the camera too. And then he starts to cry—like he's never going to stop. I hold him and Mia too—all together.

"Finally he stops. I ask him, 'Is it all okay now, baby?,' and he says, 'Zia Peppina, they still have the *picture!*,' and he cries until I tell him I'll get the picture for him. I *promise* him. I *swear* to him on my daughter. On Mia, I swear to him I'll get this picture for him.

"And then he stops. He smiles at me. The little guy's got heart for days—he knows that if I swear that, it's done—it's done. He has trust in me."

She was quiet against my chest. I reached in my pocket, took out a smoke for myself, and lit it. She pushed her face between my hand and my mouth, took a drag from my hand. Waited.

"You know what's in the picture?" I asked her.

"Yeah. I know," she said.

"Because he told you or . . . ?"

"I just know."

"You did something to find out, right?"

She nodded against my chest.

"What?" I asked her.

"He used to go to this day-care center. Out in Fresh Meadows.

One day they took him someplace—he says out in the country—in the school-bus they use. There was a guy dressed in a clown suit and some other stuff. He can't tell me. He had to take his clothes off and do something—he won't tell me that either. And someone took pictures of him."

"Where was this place?" I asked her.

"I don't *know!*" she said, fighting not to start crying, biting her lower lip like a kid.

I patted her back in a careful rhythm, waiting until it matched her breathing. "What else did you find out?"

"A woman came there. An old woman, he said. She had two men with her. Big, scary men. One had a little bag—like a doctor's bag? With money in it. The old woman took the pictures and the clown got some of the money."

"And . . . ?" I prompted her.

"Scott couldn't tell me what the men looked like, but he saw the hands of the man who carried the little bag. There was a dark-blue mark on one of them. Scott drew it for me." She fumbled in her purse and pulled out a piece of paper. It was covered with all kinds of crosses and lines, drawn in crayon like a kid did it. Down in one corner was something in blue, with a red circle around it. I held the match closer. It was a swastika.

"This was on the man's hand?" I asked her.

"Yes."

"Back of his hand?"

"Yes."

"What did you do?" I asked her.

The redhead took a breath. "I showed the drawing to Julio. He took one look and said, 'Jailhouse tattoo.' I asked him if there were Nazis in prison. He said he really didn't know too much about it. I pressured him—I made him tell me. And that's when I got your name—he said you knew them."

# 41

IT WAS COLD OUT there by the water, especially along my spine. We had a deal—I had listened to her story and now I could walk away. But I wanted to buy some insurance—make her understand that I wasn't the man for the job anyway.

"Julio's full of shit," I told her in a flat voice.

"I know," she said, quiet and soft.

"I mean about the Nazis. I don't know them—they were in prison with all of us—nobody knows them—they keep to themselves, you understand?"

The redhead twisted in my lap until she was facing me. She grabbed the lower half of my face like I had done to her. I could smell the perfume on her hand. She put her little face right up against me, grabbing my eyes with hers.

"You're lying to me," she whispered. "I know all about men—I know more about men than you'll ever know. I know when a man is lying to me."

I met her stare with no problem, even though the moon was dancing in her crazy eyes.

"I'm telling you the truth," I said.

She leaned against me, shoving her lips hard against mine. I could feel her teeth. Then her tongue. She stayed like that for a solid minute, her hands somewhere on my chest. "Please?" she whispered.

She pulled her face away. "No," I said. I started to get up but she was still sitting on my lap. She put her face against me again, opened her mouth, and bit into my lower lip with all her strength. The pain-jolt shot through me like electricity—I stiffened two fingers and a thumb and drove them into her ribs. She grunted and pulled away from me, blood on her mouth.

The redhead rolled off my lap and bent double at the waist. I thought she was going to throw up, but she got herself under control. Her head came up. She was chewing on something—a piece of my lip.

"Mmmmm," she said, "it's so *good*." I watched her swallow a part of me. Her smile had red in it, like smeared lipstick.

I got up from the bench and walked back to the Plymouth, leaving her where she was. She didn't move until she heard the engine kick over. Then she walked to the car, taking her time.

She got in the passenger side, opened her window, and looked out—away from me. She didn't say another word until we pulled up next to her BMW.

# 42

METROPOLITAN AVENUE was quiet. The BMW was sitting there undisturbed. It was that kind of neighborhood.

The redhead turned to me. "Can I say one thing to you before you go?"

I just nodded, tensing my right arm in case she decided she was still hungry.

"One hundred thousand dollars. In cash. For you."

She had my attention, but I didn't say anything.

"One hundred thousand dollars," she said again, like she was promising me the most erotic thing in the world. Maybe she was.

"Where?" I asked her.

"I have it," she said. "And it's yours if you find me that picture."

"And if I don't? I mean, if I look and come up empty?"

"How long will you look?"

"*If* I look, I'll look four, five weeks. After that, there's no point. You could run some ads, shake some trees . . . but if it's around, still local, that's all the time there is."

"How do I know you'll really look?" she asked.

"You don't," I said, "and *that's* the fucking truth."

"Five thousand a week?"

"Plus expenses."

"For a hundred grand, you can pay your own expenses."

"If I find the picture," I said, "the hundred grand covers it all, okay? But if I don't, you pay five grand a week for a max of five weeks, plus expenses."

The redhead stroked her own face, soothing herself, thinking. Finally she said, "Ten grand up front and you start tonight."

"Twenty-five up front and I start tonight," I shot back.

"Fifteen," she offered.

"Take a walk, lady," I said. "I shouldn't have started this in the first place."

"You walk with me," the redhead said. "Back to my house. I'll give you the twenty-five."

"And a picture of the kid?"

"Yes. And all the other stuff I put together."

"And then you're out of it? I do my work and I let you know the result?"

"Yes."

"And then you forget you ever saw me?"

"Oh, I'll do that," she said, "but you'll never forget you saw *me*."

Even in the car I was still cold. "You have the money at your house? Your husband . . . ?"

"Don't worry about it. He won't be home tonight. Is it a deal?"

"No promises," I told her. "I'll take my best shot. I come up empty . . . that's all, right?"

"Yes," she said again. "Follow me."

She got out of the Plymouth and into her car. I let the engine idle while she started up. She pulled out and I followed her taillights into the night.

## 43

THE REDHEAD DROVE BADLY, taking the BMW too high in the lower gears, backing it off through the mufflers when she came to a corner, torturing the tires. The Plymouth was built for strength, not speed—I drove at my own pace, watching to see if she attracted attention with her driving.

The BMW ducked into the entrance for Forest Park. I lost sight of her around a curve, but I could hear tires howling ahead. I just motored along—there was no place for her to go.

She turned out of the park and into a section of mini-estates—not much land around the houses, but they were all big bastards, set far back from the street, mostly colonials. The redhead took a series of tight, twisting turns and stopped at a flagstone-front house with a wrought-iron fence. She got out and walked to the entrance, never looking back. Something from her purse unlocked the gate. She waved me around her car and I pulled into the drive. I heard the gate close again behind me and then the BMW's lights blinded me as she shot past me, following the curve of the driveway around to the back of the house—it opened as we approached—it must have had some kind of electronic eye. The light came on inside the garage. Only one stall was occupied—a Mercedes sedan.

I watched her slam the BMW into the middle space. I brought my car to a stop, and reversed so the Plymouth's rear bumper was against the opening of the garage. She motioned for me to pull all the way inside. I shook my head, turned off the engine. She shrugged the way you do at an idiot who doesn't understand the program and pointed for me to follow her inside.

The redhead pushed a button against the garage wall and the big door descended from the ceiling and closed behind us. She opened a side door and started to climb some stairs, flicking her wrist at me in a gesture to follow her.

The stairs made a gentle curve to the next floor. Soft light came from someplace but I couldn't see any bulbs. The redhead's hips switched almost from wall to wall on the narrow staircase. I thought about the magnum I'd left in the Plymouth.

She took me into a long, narrow room on the next floor. One whole wall was glass, facing the backyard. Floodlights bathed the grounds—there was a rock garden around a patio in the back; the rest faded into the shadows.

"Wait here," she said, and moved into another room.

She hadn't turned on a light in the big room but I could see well enough. It looked as if her interior decorator had a degree in hospital administration. The whole room was white—a low leather couch in front of a slab of white marble, a recliner in the same white leather. There was a floor lamp extending over the recliner—a sharp black stalk with a fluted wing at the top. A black glass ashtray was on the marble slab. Against the far wall was a single black shelf running the full length, the lacquer gleaming in the reflected light. I saw four floor-standing black stereo speakers but no components—probably in another part of the house. The floor was black quarry tile and there were two parallel strips of track lighting on the ceiling—holding a series of tiny black-coned spots. The room was a reptile's eye—flat and hard and cold.

I sat down in the recliner and lit a cigarette. My mouth burned with the first drag. I pulled the butt away—there was blood on the filter. I wiped my mouth on my handkerchief and sat there waiting. I heard the tap of her heels on the tile, turned my head without moving. I tasted the blood on my lip again. She was wearing a black silk camisole over a pair of matching tap pants. The whole outfit was held up with a pair of spaghetti-straps—they made a hard line against her slim shoulders. The redhead had a pair of black pumps on her feet—no stockings that I could see. She was all black and white, like the room.

"You want a drink?" she asked.

"No."

"Nothing? We have everything here."

"I don't drink," I told her.

"A joint? Some coke?" she asked me, an airline stewardess on a flight to hell.

"Nothing," I told her again.

She crossed in front of me, like a model on a runway for the first time, nervous but vain. She sat down on the couch, crossed her long legs, folded her hands over one knee. "We have a deal?" she asked.

"Where's the money?" I said in reply.

"Yeah," she said absently, almost to herself, "where's the money?"

She flowed off the couch and walked out of the room again, leaving me to my thoughts. I wondered where her kid was.

The redhead was back in a minute, a slim black attaché case in one hand. She looked like she was going to work. In a whorehouse. She dropped to her knees next to the recliner in a graceful move, crossing her ankles behind her on the floor, and put the attaché case on my lap. "Count it," she said.

It was all in fifties and hundreds—crisp bills but not new. The serial numbers weren't in sequence. The count was right on the nose. "Okay," I told her.

She got to her feet. "Wait here. I'll get you the pictures," she said, turning to go. "Play with your money.

As soon as she was out of the room I got up and took off my coat. I transferred the money from the attaché case to a few different pockets, closed the case, and tossed it on the couch. Lit another cigarette.

She was back quickly, her hands full of paper. She came over to the same place she'd been before, kneeled down again, and started putting the papers in my lap, one piece at a time, as if she was dealing cards.

"This is Scotty like he looks today. I took this last week. This is Scotty like he was a few months ago—when it happened. This is the drawing he did—see the swastika? This is me and Scotty together—so you can tell how big he is, okay?"

"Okay," I told her.

She handed me one more piece of paper, covered with typed numbers. "These are the phone numbers where you can reach me . . . and when you can call. Just ask for me—you don't have to say anything else."

"Any of these answering machines?"

"No. They're all people, don't worry."

I took a last drag of my smoke, leaning past her to snub it out in the ashtray, ready to leave. The redhead put her face next to mine again, whispering in a babyish voice, more breath than tone, "You think I'm a tease, don't you?"

I didn't say anything, frozen there, my hand mechanically grinding the cigarette butt into tobacco flakes.

"You think I'm just teasing you, don't you?" she whispered again. "Dressing like this . . ."

I pulled back to look at her but she hung on, coming with me. "You do what you want," I told her.

"I will if you close your eyes," she said in my ear. "Close your eyes!" she said, a baby demanding you play a game with her.

I was still so cold. Maybe it was the room. I closed my eyes, leaned back. Felt her stroke me, making a noise in her throat. "Sssh, ssh," she murmured. She was talking to herself. I felt her hands at my belt, heard the zipper move, felt myself strain against her hand. I opened my eyes a narrow slit; her red hair was in my lap. "You promised!" she said in the baby voice. I closed my eyes again. She tugged at the waistband on my shorts, but I didn't move—she was rough and clumsy pulling me through the fly, still making those baby noises in her throat. I felt her mouth around me, felt the warmth, her tiny teeth against me, gently pulling. I put my hands in her soft hair, and she pulled her mouth off me, her teeth scraping the shaft, hurting me. "You don't touch me!" she whispered, the voice of a little girl.

I put my hands behind my head so they wouldn't move. And she came back to me with her mouth, sucking hard now, moving her mouth up and down until I was slick with her juices. My eyes opened again—I couldn't help it. She didn't say anything this time. I opened them wider. The redhead's face was buried in my lap, her hands clasped tightly behind her back. My eyes closed again.

I felt it coming. I pushed my hips back in the chair, giving her a chance to pull her mouth away, but she was glued to me. "Just this!" she mumbled, her mouth full, a little girl talking, a stubborn little girl who made up her mind and wasn't giving in. My mind flashed to a girl I met once when I was on the run from reform school. This was all she'd do too—she didn't want to get pregnant again. Somehow I knew this wasn't the same.

It was her choice. She shook her head from side to side, keeping me with her. I felt the explosion all the way to the base of my spine, but she never took her face away—never reached for a handkerchief—I could feel the muscles in her cheeks work as she took it all.

I slumped back in the chair and she let me slide out of her mouth but kept her head in my lap. Her little-girl's whisper was clear in the quiet room. "I'm a good girl," she said, calm and smug. "Pat me. Pat my head."

My eyes opened again as I brought my hand forward, stroking her red hair, watching her hands twist behind her in the handcuffs she'd made for herself.

Her head came up. She was licking her lips and her eyes were wet and gleaming. Her hands came forward, taking one of my cigarettes and lighting it while I pulled myself in and zipped up. She handed me the lit cigarette. "For you," she said.

I took a deep drag. It tasted of blood.

"I have you in me now," she said, in her own voice. "Get me that picture."

I had to get out of there. She knew it too. I put on my coat, patting the pockets, putting the pictures and the other stuff she gave me inside.

"Come," she said, taking my hand, leading me back to the garage.

The Mercedes had a regular license, but the one on the BMW said JINA. "Is that the way you spell your name?" I asked her. "I thought it was Gina—G-I-N-A."

"They named me Gina. I didn't like it. When I have something I don't like, I change it."

"Who's Zia Peppina?" I wanted to know.

"Me. Auntie Pepper, you *capisce*? When I was a little girl, I was a chubby, happy child—always running, getting into mischief. With my red hair, they used to call me Peppina. Little Pepper. But when I got older, when I got to be myself, they stopped calling me that baby name. I only let Scotty call me that because he's special to me."

"People call you Jina now?"

"No," the redhead said, "now they call me Strega."

The side door slammed behind me and I was alone.

I drove too fast getting out of her neighborhood, cold speed inside me, rushing around like cocaine. Even the twenty-five grand in my coat couldn't keep out the chill. *Strega.* I knew what the word meant—a witch-bitch you could lust after or run from. You could be in the middle of a desert and her shadow would make you cold. And I had taken her money.

## 44

I SLOWED THE PLYMOUTH into a quiet, mechanical cruise when I hit the Inter-Boro. A dark, twisting piece of highway, paved with potholes. Abandoned cars lined the roadside, stripped to the bone. I lit a smoke, watched the tiny red dot in the windshield, feeling the tremor in my hands on the wheel. Not knowing if I was sad or scared.

The blues make a rough blanket, like the ones they give you in the orphanage. But they keep out the cold. I shoved a cassette into the tape player without looking, waiting for the dark streets to take hold of me and pull me in, waiting to get back to myself. When I heard the guitar intro I recognized the next song, but I sat and listened to the first call-and-answer of "Married Woman Blues" like the fool I was.

> Did you ever love a married woman?
> The kind so good that she just has to be true.
> Did you ever love a married woman?
> The kind so good that she just has to be true.
> That means true to her husband, boy,
> And not a damn thing left for you.

That wasn't Strega. She wasn't good and she wasn't true—at least not to her husband. I popped the cassette, played with the radio until I got some oldies station. Ron Holden and the Thunderbirds singing "Love You So." I hated that song from the first time I'd heard it. When I was in reform school a girl I thought I knew wrote me a letter with the lyrics to that song. She told me it was a poem she wrote for me. I never showed it to anyone—I burned the letter so nobody would find it, but I memorized the words. One day I heard it on the radio while we were out in the yard and I knew the truth.

I never had to explain things like that to Flood. She knew—she was raised in the same places I was.

There was too much prison in this case—too much past.

I tried another cassette—Robert Johnson's "Hellhound on My Trail" came through the speakers. Chasing me down the road.

## 45

BUT THE NEXT MORNING, the magnum was back in my office and all but five thousand of the money was stashed with Max. I told him most of what happened the night before—enough so he could find the redhead if things didn't work out. I couldn't take Max with me on this trip—he was the wrong color.

I took Atlantic Avenue east through Brooklyn, but this time I rolled right on past the Inter-Boro entrance, past the neighborhood called City Line and into South Ozone Park. In this part of Queens, everybody's got territory marked off—the gangsters have their social clubs, the Haitians have their restaurants, and the illegal aliens have their basements. When you get near J.F.K. Airport, you move into the free-fire zone—the airport is too rich a prize for anyone to hold it all.

I pulled into the open front of a double-width garage. A faded sign over the door said "Ajax Speed Shop." A fat guy sat on a cut-down oil drum just inside the door, a magazine on his lap. His hair was motorcycle-club-length; he had a red bandanna tied around his forehead. He was wearing a denim jacket with the arms cut off, jeans, and heavy work boots. His arms bulged, not all from fat. He'd been a body-builder once; now he was slightly gone to seed.

A candy-apple-red Camaro stood over to my right, its monster rear tires filling the rear tubs under the fenders. The garage specialized in outlaw street racers—guys who made a living drag racing away from the legal strips. The back of the joint was dark.

I didn't wait for the fat guy. "Bobby around?" I asked.

"What do you need, man?" he wanted to know, his voice still neutral.

"I want to try a nitrous bottle. Bobby told me he could fix me up."

"For this?" he wanted to know, looking at the Plymouth's faded four doors. Street racers use nitrous oxide—laughing gas—for short power-bursts. You need a pressurized tank, a switch to kick it in, and enough *cojones* to pull the trigger. They're not illegal, but you want to fix things up so your opponent won't know you're carrying extra horses. The Plymouth didn't look like his idea of a good candidate—or maybe it was the driver.

I pulled the lever under the dash and the hood was released—it popped forward, pivoting at the front end. The fat guy went around to the passenger side as I got out, and we lifted the entire front end forward together. The whole front-end assembly was Fiberglas—you could move it with two fingers.

The fat guy looked into the engine bay, nodding his head.

"Three eighty-three?" he wanted to know.

"Four forty," I told him, "with another sixty over."

He nodded sagely. It was making sense to him now. "One four barrel?" he asked—meaning, Why just one carburetor for so many cubic inches?

"It's built for torque—got to idle nice and quiet."

"Yeah," he said, still nodding. The Plymouth wasn't for show—just the opposite. He walked around the car, peering underneath, noting that the dual exhausts never reached the bumper. The rear undercarriage puzzled him for a minute. "It looks like an I.R.S. Jag?"

"Home-built," I told him. Independent rear suspension was better for handling, but it wouldn't stand up to tire-burning starts—drag racers never used it.

And that was his next question. "Whatta you run with this . . . thirty-tromp?"

You can race from a standing start or side-by-side at a steady speed and then take off on the signal. Thirty-tromp is when each driver carries a passenger—you reach thirty miles an hour, make sure the front ends are lined up, and the passenger in the left-hand car screams "Go!" out the window and both cars stomp the gas. First car to the spot you marked off is the winner.

"Twenty's okay," I told him. "It hooks up okay once you're rolling."

"You want the nitrous bottle in the trunk?"

"Where else?" I asked him. I opened the trunk to let him look inside.

"Motherfucker! Is that a fuel cell?"

"Fifty-gallon, dual electric pumps," I told him. The kid who built it would have been proud.

The fat guy's suspicions were gone—he was in heaven. "Man, you couldn't run this more than one time—it's a fake-out *supreme!* Where do you race?"

"Wherever," I said, "as long as they have the money."

"What do you duel for?"

"A grand—minimum," I said.

The fat guy scratched his head. He was used to guys spending thousands and thousands to build a car and then racing for fifty-dollar bills. Guys who put a good piece of their money into the outside of their cars—like the Camaro sitting there. He'd heard about guys who treated the whole thing like a business—no ego, all for the bucks—but he'd never seen one before. "I'll get Bobby for you," he said, "wait here."

I lit a smoke, leaning against the side of the Plymouth. I let my eyes wander around the garage but kept my feet where they were. I knew what was in thc back.

## 46

I HEARD A DOOR slam somewhere and Bobby came out of the darkness, hands in the pockets of his coveralls. A big, husky kid—with his long hair and mustache, he looked like an ex-college football player. He came on slowly, not hesitating, just careful. The fat guy was saying something about the Plymouth, but Bobby wasn't listening.

He got close enough to see. "Burke! That you?" he yelled.

"It's me," I said in a quiet voice, knowing what was coming.

The kid crushed me in a bear hug, almost lifting me off my feet. "Brother!" he yelled. "My brother from hell!" I hate that stuff, but I hugged him back, mumbling some words to make it okay.

Bobby turned to the fat guy. "This is my man. Burke, say hello to Cannonball."

"We met," I told him.

"Yeah . . . right. What's *happening*, man?"

"He wants some nitrous . . ." the fat guy said.

"My brother don't want no nitrous . . . do you, Burke?" Bobby said in a superior tone.

"No," I said, watching the fat guy. Bobby's eyes dropped to my right hand. It was balled into a fist, the thumb extended, rubbing a tiny circle on the Plymouth's fender. The jailhouse sign to get lost.

"Take a walk, Cannonball," Bobby told him.

"You oughta get the nitrous, man," Cannonball said by way of goodbye. He went off into the darkness in the back.

Bobby reached into my coat, patting around like he was doing a search. I didn't move. He pulled out my pack of cigarettes, lit one for himself. A prison-yard move—okay if you were tight, a spit in your face if you weren't.

"You want to move cars?" Bobby asked. The back of his garage was a chop shop. He took stolen cars and turned them into parts in a couple of hours. A good business, but it takes a lot of people to make it work.

"I'm looking for a couple of your brothers, Bobby," I told him.

The garage got quiet. "You got a beef?" he asked.

"No beef. I'm looking for somebody they might have done some work for. That's all."

"They're not in it?"

"They're not in it," I assured him.

"What *is* in it?" he wanted to know.

"Money," I told him.

"Same old Burke," the kid said, smiling.

I didn't say anything, waited. "You got names?" the kid asked.

"All I got is this, Bobby. One of them had the lightning bolt on his hand. Big guy. And they did some work for a woman. Older woman. Delivering money."

"With her?"

"Yeah. Bodyguard work."

"We do that . . ." he mused, thinking. Bobby rubbed his forehead—saw my eyes on his hand. The hand with the twisted lightning bolts—twisted into something that looked like a swastika.

"You never joined us," he said, no accusation in his voice. Just stating a fact.

"I joined *you*," I reminded him.

# 47

BOBBY'S FIRST DAY ON the Big Yard, he was just off Fish Row, where they lock all the new prisoners. A happy kid despite the sentence he was just starting. Not state-raised—he didn't know how to act. Virgil and I were standing in the shadow of the wall, waiting for some of our customers who had miscalculated the results of the World Series. Bobby walked in our direction, but he was cut off at the pass by a group of blacks. They started some conversation we couldn't hear, but we knew the words. Virgil shook his head sadly—the stupid kid even let a couple of the blacks walk around behind him. It was every new kid's problem—they test you quick and there's only one right answer. The next time he hit the yard he'd better be packing a shank—or spend the rest of his bit on his knees.

The whole yard was watching, but the kid couldn't know that. "Take my back," said Virgil, and started over to the group. Virgil was a fool—he didn't belong in prison.

Virgil strolled over to the group, taking slow, deliberate strides, not in a hurry, keeping his hands where you could see them. I was two steps behind—he was my partner.

"Hey, homeboy!" Virgil shouted out. The blacks turned to face us. Their eyes were hot, but they kept their hands empty. The kid looked at Virgil, a blank, scared look on his face.

Virgil shouldered in next to the kid, put his arm on the kid's back, guiding him out of the circle. One of the blacks stepped in his way. "This is your man?" he asked.

"He surely is," said Virgil, his West Virginia accent like the coal he used to mine—soft around the edges but hard enough to burn inside.

"This your *homeboy* too?" the black guy asked me, sarcasm dripping from his lips. One of his boys chuckled. The yard was quiet—we all listened for the sound of a rifle bolt slamming a shell home, but even the guards were just watching.

"That's my partner," I told him, nodding at Virgil.

"You sure he's not your jockey?" the black guy sneered, forcing it.

"Find out," I invited him, stepping back, hearing footsteps behind me, unable to look for myself.

But the black guy could—right over my shoulder.

"Not today," he said, and walked off, his boys right behind.

I shot a glance behind me—a gang of warrior-whites were rolling up. They didn't give a flying fuck about me personally, but even the off-chance of a race war got them excited. When they saw the black guys walk away they stopped. Stood there with arms folded. They knew, but the kid didn't. He came back over to the wall with me and Virgil and we started to school him right then about what he had to do.

## 48

BOBBY TOOK A SEAT on the hood of the Plymouth. "I remember," he said. "You calling in the marker?"

"There *is* no marker, Bobby. I'm asking an old friend for a favor, that's all."

"The guys you want to meet—you know who they are?"

"Yeah," I told him.

"Say the name," Bobby shot at me, a lot of memories in his eyes.

I put it on the table. "The Real Brotherhood," I said, my voice quiet in the empty garage.

"You didn't say it right, Burke. It's the *Real* Brotherhood."

"That's how *you* say it, Bobby."

"That *is* how I say it. That's how it is."

"I told you I got no beef with them. I just want to talk."

I let it hang there—it was his play. He reached into my pocket and helped himself to another smoke. I saw the pack of Marlboros in the breast pocket of his coveralls—we were still friends. Bobby took the fired wood match I handed him, lit up. He slid off the fender until he was sitting on the garage floor, his back against the Plymouth. The way you sat in prison. He blew smoke at the ceiling, waiting. I hunkered down next to him, lit one of my own smokes.

When Bobby started to talk his voice was hushed, like in church. He bent one leg, resting his elbow on the knee, his chin in his hands. He looked straight ahead.

"I got out of the joint way before you did. Remember I left all my stuff for you and Virgil when they cut me loose? I got a job in a machine shop, did my parole, just waiting, you know? A couple of guys I know were going to the Coast. See the sights—fuck some of those blondes out there—check out the motors, right? I get out there and everybody's doing weed—like it's legal or something. I fall in with these hippies. Nice folks—easygoing, sweet music. Better than this shit here. You see it, Burke?"

"I see it," I told him. And I did.

"I get busted with a van full of weed. Two hundred keys. Hawaiian. And a pistol. I was making a run down to L.A. and the cops stopped me. Some bullshit about a busted taillight."

He took a drag of the smoke, let it out with a sigh. "I never made a statement, never copped a plea. The hippies got me a good lawyer, but he lost the motion to suppress the weed and they found me guilty. Possession with intent. Ex-con with a handgun. And I wouldn't give anybody up. They dropped me for one to fucking life—do a pound before I see the Board."

Bobby locked his hands behind his head, resting from the pain. "When I hit the yard I knew what to do—not like when you and Virgil had to pull me up. I remembered what you told me. When the niggers rolled up on me, I acted like I didn't know what they were talking about—like I was scared. They told me to pull commissary the next day and turn it over." Bobby smiled, thinking about it. The smile would have scared a cop. "I turn over my commissary—I might as well turn over my body so they could fuck me in the ass. I get a shank for two cartons—just a file with some tape on the end for a grip. I work on the thing all night long, getting it sharp. In the morning, I pull my commissary. I put the shank in the paper bag with the tape sticking up. I walk out to the yard with the bag against my chest—like a fucking broad with the groceries. The same niggers move on me—tell me to hand it over. I pull the shank and plant it in the first guy's chest—a good underhand shot. It comes out of him when he goes down. I run to get room. Turn around . . . and I'm alone . . . the niggers took off. I hear a shot and the dirt flies up right near me. I drop the shank and the screws come for me."

"You should of dropped the shank when you ran," I said.

"I know that *now*—didn't know it then. Things are different out there." Bobby ground out his cigarette on the garage floor, took one of his own, and lit it. "They put me in the hole. Out there, the fucking hole is like a regular prison—it's *full* of guys—guys spend fucking *years* in the hole. Only they call it the 'Adjustment Center.' Nice name, huh? There's three tiers on each side. Little tiny dark cells. The noise was unbelievable—screaming all the time. Not from the guards doing work on any of the guys—screaming just to be screaming.

"I was sitting in my cell, thinking about how much more time I'd get behind this, even if the nigger didn't rat me out. I mean, they caught me with the shank and all. Then it started. The niggers. 'You a dead white motherfucker!' 'You gonna suck every black dick in the joint, boy!' All that shit. I yelled back at the first one, but they kept it up, like they was working in shifts or something. And then one of them yelled out that the guy I stabbed was his main man—he was gonna cut off my balls and make me eat them. They were fucking *animals*, Burke. They never stopped—day and night, calling my name, telling me they were gonna throw gasoline in my cell and fire me up, poison my food, gang-fuck me until I was dead."

Bobby was quiet for a minute. His voice was hard but his hands were shaking. He looked at his hands—curled them into fists. "After a couple of days, I didn't have the strength to yell back at them. It sounded like there were hundreds of them. Even the trustee—the scumbag who brought the coffee cart around—he spit in my coffee, *dared* me to tell the Man.

"They pulled me out to see the Disciplinary Committee. They knew the score—even asked me if the niggers had hit on me. I didn't say a word. The Lieutenant told me stabbing the nigger was no big deal, but I'd have to take a lockup—go into P.C. for the rest of my bit. You know what that means?"

"Yeah," I said. "P.C." is supposed to stand for "protective custody." For guys who can't be on the main yard—informers, obvious homosexuals, guys who didn't pay a gambling debt—targets. To the cons, "P.C." means Punk City. You go in, you never get to walk the yard. You carry the jacket the rest of your life.

"They kept me locked down two weeks—no cigarettes, nothing to read, no radio—nothing. Just those niggers working on me every day. They never got tired, Burke—like they fucking *loved* that evil shit. Screaming about cutting pregnant white women open and pulling out the baby. One day it got real quiet. I couldn't figure it out. The trustee came with the coffee. He had a note for me—folded piece of paper. I opened it up—there was a big thick glob of white stuff inside. Nigger cum. I got sick but I was afraid to throw up—afraid they'd hear me. Then one of them whispered to me—it was so quiet it sounded like it was in the next cell. 'Lick it up, white boy! Lick it all up, pussy! We got yard tomorrow, punk. The Man letting us all out, you understand me? You lick it all up, tell me how good it was!' He was saying all this to me and all I could think of was, there was no way to kill myself in that lousy little cell. All I wanted was to die. I pissed on myself—I thought they could all smell it."

Bobby was shaking hard now. I put my hand on his shoulder, but he was lost in the fear. "I got on my knees. I prayed with everything I had. I prayed for Jesus—stuff I hadn't thought of since I was a kid. If I didn't say anything, I was dead—worse than dead. I looked at that paper with that nigger's cum on it. I went into myself—I thought about how it had to be. And I found a way to die like a man—all I wanted.

"I got to my feet. I stood up. My voice was all fucked up from not saying anything for so long, but it came out good and steady. It was so quiet everybody heard me. 'Tell me your name, nigger,' I said to him. 'I don't want to kill the wrong nigger when we go on the yard, and all you monkeys look alike to me.' As soon as the words came out of my mouth I felt different—like God came into me—just like I'd been praying for.

"Then they went fucking *crazy*—screaming like a pack of apes. But it was like they were screaming on some upper register . . . and underneath it was this heavy bass line, like in music. A chant, something. It was from the white guys in the other cells—some of them right next to me. They hadn't made a sound through all this shit, just waiting to see how I'd stand up. I couldn't hear them too good at first—just this heavy, low rumbling. But then it came through all the other stuff. 'R.B.! R.B.! R.B.!'"

Bobby was chanting the way he'd heard it back in his cell, hitting the second letter for emphasis . . . "R.*B.!* R.*B.!*" . . . pumping strength back into himself.

"They kept it up. I couldn't see them, but I knew they were there. There for *me*. They didn't say anything else. I started to say it too. First to myself. Then out loud. *Real* loud. Like prayer words.

"When they racked the bars for us to hit the exercise yard—one at a time—I walked out. The sunlight hit me in the face—I almost couldn't see. I heard a voice. 'Stand with us, brother,' it said."

Bobby looked at me. His eyes were wet but his hands were steady and his mouth was cold. "I've been standing with them ever since, Burke," he said in the quiet garage. "If you got a beef with them, you got one with me."

# 49

I GOT TO MY feet. Bobby stayed where he was. "I already told you—I got no beef with your brothers. I want to ask some questions, that's all. I'll pay my own way."

Bobby pushed himself off the floor. "You think you could find the Brotherhood without me?"

"Yeah," I told him, "I could. And if I was looking for them like you think, I wouldn't come here, right?"

He was thinking it over, leaning against the car, making up his mind. Bobby made a circuit around the Plymouth, peering into the engine compartment, bouncing the rear end like he was checking the shocks. "When's the last time this beast got a real tune-up, Burke?"

"A year ago—maybe a year and a half—I don't know," I said.

"Tell you what," he said, his voice soft and friendly, "you leave the car here, okay? I'll put in some points and plugs, time the engine for you. Change the fluids and filters, align the front end. Take about a week or so, okay? No charge."

"I need the car," I said, my voice as soft and even as his.

"So I'll lend you a car, all right? You come back in a few days—a week at the most—your car will be like new." I didn't say anything, watching him. "And while I'm working on your car, I'll make some phone calls. Check some things out, see what's happening with my brothers. . . ."

I got the picture. The Plymouth could be a lot of things—a gypsy cab, an anonymous fish in the slimy streets—whatever I needed. This was the first time it would be a hostage.

"You got a car with clean papers, clean plates?"

"Sure," he smiled, "one hundred percent legit. You want the Camaro?"

"No way, Bobby. I'm not planning to cruise the drive-ins. You got something a little quieter?"

"Come with me," he said, walking to the back of the garage. I followed him to a door set into the back wall, watched him push a buzzer three times. The door opened and we were in the chop shop—bumpers and grilles against one wall, engines on stands against another. Three men were working with cutting torches, another with a power wrench. The pieces would all come together on other cars, building a live car from dead ones, Frankenstein monsters that looked like clean one-owners. I followed Bobby through the shop. He opened another door and we stepped into a backyard surrounded with a steel-mesh fence. Razor-ribbon circled the top, winding itself around barbed wire rising another two feet off the top. "Reminds you of home, don't it?" he asked.

In the backyard there were three cars—a dark-blue Caddy sedan, a white Mustang coupe, and a black Lincoln Continental. Bobby made an offhand gesture in their direction. "Pick one," he said.

I passed over the Caddy without a second glance. The Mustang had a shift lever as thick as a man's wrist growing out of the floor, topped with a knob the size of a baseball. Another dragster. The Lincoln looked okay. I nodded.

Bobby opened the door, reached in the glove compartment, and pulled out some papers. He handed them over—the registration was in his name.

"You get stopped, you borrowed the car from me. I'll stand up on it. I got all the insurance, recent inspection. You're clean on this one."

Sure I was—if Bobby told the cops he lent me the car. If he said it was stolen.

"Is it a deal?" he wanted to know.

"One week. I make those phone calls. Then we'll see," he said.

"What do you get for a stolen-car rap these days?" I asked him.

"Figure maybe a year—two at the outside."

"Yeah," I said, looking at him. He had me in a box, but not one that would hold me for long. "I'll show you the security systems on the Plymouth," I said, holding out my hand for him to shake.

"You won't know your own car when you come back, Burke," Bobby said, his hand on my shoulder, leading me back to the front garage.

"I always know what's mine," I reminded him.

We had a deal.

# 50

THE LINCOLN WAS A fat boat. Driving it was all by eyesight—you couldn't feel anything through the wheel—like they used Novocain instead of power-steering fluid. The odometer had less than six thousand miles showing. Even the leather smelled new.

I stopped next to a pushcart restaurant, loading up on hot dogs for lunch. There wasn't any point hiding the car—even if Bobby had called it in stolen, the plates wouldn't bounce unless they pulled me in for something else. I was in his hands—for now. He could make the Plymouth disappear easily enough—but if he fucked me around I could make him disappear too. I get real angry if someone makes a move on me when I'm playing it square. The way I have to live, I don't get angry too often.

When Pansy came back downstairs I gave her four of the six hot dogs, chewing on two of them myself, washing them down with some ice water from the fridge. Putting it together in my head—finding the little boy's picture would be like finding a landlord who gives too much heat in the winter. I had to have an angle, and Bobby was my best shot.

I keep my files in the little room next to the office. Six cabinets, four drawers high, gray steel, no locks. There's nothing in there that would get me in real trouble—no names or addresses of clients, no personal records. It's all stuff I pick up as I go along—stuff that could help me at some point. Gun-runners, mercenaries (and chumps who want to be), heavy-duty pimps, kiddie-porn dealers, con artists, crooked ministers. I don't keep files on crooked politicians—I don't have enough space, especially since I have to sleep in that same room.

But I do keep files on the flesh-peddlers—they can't run to the cops when they get stung, it's not in their program. Those merchants sell two products: people and pictures. I checked the magazine file—the kiddie-porn rags were all the same, mostly kids doing things to other kids, smiling for the camera, playing with fire that would burn their souls. Occasionally an adult would intrude on the fantasies of the freaks who bought this stuff—an anonymous cock in a little kid's mouth, a thick hand holding a kid's head down in a dark lap. The pictures were all the same—recycled endlessly behind different covers. The kids in those pictures would all be at least teenagers by now. Recruiting other kids.

The underground newsletters kept the pictures pretty clean. Lots of arty photography—nude kids posing, playing volleyball, wrestling with each other. Plenty of contact information—post-office boxes, mail drops, like that. But every Vice Squad cop in the country was probably on the mailing list and it would take months to work my way through the maze and actually make a decent buy. They'd try me out first—tame stuff, semilegal—with a ton of rhetoric about "man-boy love" for me to wade through.

I looked through my list of overseas addresses. Almost all kiddie porn used to come from places like Brussels and Amsterdam. The European countries are still a safer harbor for pedophiles, but the real heavy production was all home-grown now. Kiddie porn is a cottage industry. You can walk into a video store and come out with enough electronic crap to make a major motion picture. I didn't need the expensive stuff—a Polaroid was all the kid told Strega about. That was all I needed, and a lot more than I had.

Crime follows dollars—that's the way of the world. No buyers—no sellers. The professionals in the hard-core business have the technology to supply the huge amounts of filth humans want to buy, but the professionals were too big a target for me. Too spread out, too detached. The organized-crime guys were into kiddie porn for the money—if I wanted to find one lousy Polaroid, I'd have to go to someone who was in it for love.

# 51

IT WAS JUST PAST MIDDAY, probably early enough to risk using the hippies' phone, but I was going out anyway. Pansy was sprawled out on the Astroturf, an expectant look on her ugly face. "You can come with me later," I told her. I was going to see the Mole, and I couldn't risk turning my beast loose near the junkyard—if she didn't get into mortal combat with the dogs the Mole keeps around she might just decide to stay.

I called the Mole from a pay phone a few blocks from the office. No point in wasting a trip if he wasn't around, and only God knew the Mole's hours.

He answered on the first ring the way he always does—he picks up the phone but he doesn't say anything.

"Can I come up and talk with you?" I said into the mouthpiece.

"Okay," came the Mole's voice, rusty from lack of use. He broke the connection—there was nothing else to say.

The Lincoln drove itself north on the East Side Drive. I set the cruise control to fifty and motored up to the Triboro Bridge. A decent suit on my back, no gun in my pocket, and a set of clean papers for a car that wasn't stolen—I hadn't been this much of a citizen since I was ten.

I met the Mole when I was doing a job for an Israeli guy, but I didn't really get to know him until I did another job, much later. Another one of those anonymous Israeli guys came to my office one day. He wasn't the same guy I'd met the first time, when they wanted me to find some ex-Nazi, a slimeball who'd worked as a concentration-camp guard. I did that job, and now they wanted a gun-runner. The Israeli said he wanted to buy weapons and needed me to set up the meet. Somehow I thought there was a bit more to it. The man he wanted to meet sold heavy-duty stuff—shoulder-fired missiles, anti-tank cannons, stuff like that. And he sold them to Libya.

I told the Israeli I wouldn't meet with the guy myself—I didn't do business with him and I didn't want any part of someone else's beef. When I said I didn't trade with the gun-runner, the Israeli asked me if I was Jewish. He's the only guy I ever met who asked me that.

It was the Israeli who took me to the junkyard the first time. They left me alone in the car, the dog pack cruising around me in the night like sharks lapping against a rubber raft. I don't know what they talked about, but the Israeli got back into my car carrying a little suitcase.

The Mole has no politics—he doesn't consider blowing up Nazis political. After the second job, I was a friend to Israel. And after a lot of years, I was the Mole's friend too. After I took the weight down in the subway tunnel, I was his brother.

I threw a token into the Exact Change basket, hooking a left and then a right to Route 95. But I ducked into the warehouse district off Bruckner Boulevard, finding my way to the Mole's junkyard. Hunts Point—New York's badlands. Topless bars. Diesel-fuel stations. Whores too raunchy to work Manhattan stalked the streets and waved at the truckers, flashing open their coats to show their naked bodies, then closed them quickly before the customers got a good look. I heard pistol shots, spaced a couple of seconds apart. Over to my right, two men were standing a few feet away from an abandoned old Chrysler, pumping shots into the body. Glass flew out of the windows; the old wreck's body rocked with each shot. It wasn't a homicide going down—just a seller demonstrating his goods for a prospective buyer. Hunts Point is a dead zone for police patrols—no citizens allowed.

I turned the corner near the entrance to the Mole's joint, driving slowly, scanning the street with my eyes. I heard a horn beep. The Mole's head popped up in the front seat of a burnt-out Volvo sitting at the side of the road. He climbed out, wearing his dirt-colored jumpsuit, a tool belt around his waist and a satchel in his hand. He looked like another part of the wrecked car.

He walked over to the Lincoln and climbed into the front seat. "Mole!" I greeted him. He nodded, confirming my diagnosis. We drove around to the side entrance, a rusting old gate secured by a dime-store lock. It wouldn't keep a self-respecting thief out for ten seconds. The Mole jumped out, selected a key from the several dozen he had on a saucer-sized ring, and popped the lock. I pulled the Lincoln inside while he locked up behind me. I kept the windows up as we pulled deeper into the junkyard—I couldn't hear them, but I knew they were around. I glanced in the rearview mirror—the ground around the gate was already covered by a thick blanket of dogs. More of them loomed up from the dark depths of the yard, padding forward slowly, all the time in the world. The gate wouldn't keep a thief from getting in, but no power on earth was going to get him out.

The dogs were all sizes and shapes. I remembered the old Great Dane—a black-and-white Harlequin monster, now missing an ear. A matched set that looked like boxers approached from the front with something that might have once been a collie on their flank. But the real pack bounded up on my side of the car—lupine heads closer to wolves than German shepherds, alert, intelligent black faces over broad chests, thick tails curled up on their backs. Their coats looked like brown fur dipped in transmission fluid, matted and heavy. Only their teeth looked clean, flashing white in the dim sunlight. The pack had been working and making puppies in the South Bronx jungle for so many years that they had evolved into a separate breed—the American junkyard dog. They never saw a can of dog food. Or a vet. The strongest survived, the others didn't.

There were safer places to walk around than the Mole's junkyard—like Lebanon in the busy season.

The Mole jumped out of the Lincoln, shifting his head for me to follow. I slid over and got out his side. The Mole blundered through the dog pack like a farmer walking through a herd of cows, me right on his tail.

The dogs nosed my legs experimentally, wondering how I'd taste. One of the pack growled a threat, but the Mole ignored it like he does everything else they do. The Mole's underground bunker was on the other side of the junkyard—we weren't going there.

A red Ford station wagon was sitting in a patch of sunlight ahead of us, its entire front end smashed all the way into the front seat—a head-on hit. The back seat had been removed, propped up against the rear bumper. A cut-down oil drum was on one side, a thick book with a plain blue cover on top. The Mole's reading room.

A dog was asleep on the Mole's couch—a massive version of the others in the pack, his neck a corded mass of muscle. He watched us approach, not moving a muscle. Only his tail flicking back and forth showed he was alive.

"Simba-witz!" I called to him. "How's by you?" The huge beast's head came up, watching me. His ears shot forward, but his tail kept the same rhythmic flicking—back and forth, like a leopard in a tree. A bone-chilling snarl came from his throat, but it wasn't meant for us. The pack stopped dead.

The Mole walked over to his couch, sat down, half on top of Simba-witz. The beast slipped out behind him, sniffed me once, and sat down on the ground. I sat down next to the Mole, reaching for a cigarette, glad it was over.

The Mole reached in his jumpsuit, came out with a slab of fatty meat, and tossed it to the dog. Simba-witz tossed it in the air, caught it, and burst into a run, holding his prize aloft. The pack swung in behind him, yipping like puppies. We sat quietly until they disappeared. They wouldn't go far.

"Mole," I told the pasty-faced genius, "I need your help on something."

I paused, giving him a chance to ask what I needed his help for—it was a waste of time.

"I got a job," I said. "This little boy—he was in a day-care center or something, and someone took a picture of him. With a Polaroid. I need to get the picture back."

"Who has it?" the Mole asked.

"I don't know."

The Mole shrugged. He was good at fixing things, or making them work. And especially at blowing them up. But he didn't know how to find things.

"It's a sex picture, Mole."

"What?" he asked. It didn't make sense to him.

"Mole, these people forced the kid to do a sex thing with a grown man, okay? And they took a picture of it. To sell."

The Mole's little eyes did something behind the Coke-bottle lenses he wore. Or maybe it was the sunlight.

"Who does this kind of thing? Nazis?"

To the Mole, every evil thing on the planet was the work of the Nazis. If Bobby did get me a meeting with the Real Brotherhood, I'd have to go without the Mole.

"Kind of," I said, "kind of the same thing. People who go on power trips, right? In the kid's mind, as long as they have the picture, they have his soul."

"If you find the people . . ."

"I know, Mole. That's not the problem now. I need to find the picture."

He shrugged again—what did I want from him?

"I have to find the picture. It's like a scientific problem, right?" I asked, reaching for a way into his megawatt brain, probing for the switch to turn on the light.

"Scientific problem?"

"You once told me that to solve a problem in science you take all the known facts, then you work out some possible outcomes, right? And you keep testing until you prove . . . whatever you said."

"Prove the hypothesis?" the Mole asked.

"Yeah," I said, "the hypothesis."

The Mole sat slumped on his couch, watching the smoke curl from my cigarette. Quiet as concrete.

"You need a scenario," he finally said.

"What are you talking about, Mole?"

"A way something *could* happen. You take the result—what you already know—and you reason backward. You eliminate whatever wouldn't work until you are left with what the past had to have been."

The Mole took a breath—it was a long speech for him.

"I don't get it, Mole," I said. "You mean, if you have a problem, you reason backward and see how the problem started?"

"Yes."

"Could you figure out where cancer came from like that?"

"Yes," he said, again.

"So where did it come from?" I asked him.

"It would be too complicated for me to explain it to you," the Mole said.

"You mean I'm not smart enough?" I asked him.

The Mole turned his face slightly toward me, trying to explain. "You're smart enough. You don't have the background—the scientific knowledge. If it was in your world, you could do it."

"This picture is in my world," I told him.

"I know," he said.

I lit another cigarette, looking around the junkyard.

"Mole, show me how to do it."

The Mole sighed. "You understand—it only works if you have enough data."

I nodded.

"You know the Socratic method?" he asked.

"Where you ask questions to get at the truth?"

"Yes," he said, barely able to keep the surprise from his voice. You spend enough time in prison, you read more than comic books.

"Can we try it?"

"Yes. But not on cancer. Let me think."

I stubbed out my cigarette in the dirt next to the couch, waiting.

"You know about AIDS?" the Mole asked suddenly.

"Yeah, I guess. A superkiller."

"Where does it come from?"

"Nobody knows," I told him.

"I know," said the Mole.

I sat bolt upright on the couch. If he knew where AIDS came from, we could all be rich. "Tell me," I said.

The Mole held up his fist, index finger extended. He grabbed the finger with his other hand. Point number one.

"Did AIDS come from God? Is it God's punishment for something?"

"No," I said.

"How do you know?" he asked.

"God's been on vacation for fifty years from New York," I said. "You try Dial-a-Prayer here, all you get is a busy signal."

The Mole didn't say anything, still waiting for a Socratic answer.

"Okay," I said. "It's not God's punishment because little kids have it too. If God is punishing babies, we should have new elections."

The Mole nodded. It was good enough for him. He didn't hate the Nazis out of any religious conviction. The Mole worshiped the same god I did: revenge.

"How do people get this disease?" he asked.

"Sexual contact, blood transfusions, dirty needles," I said.

"If it comes from sex," he asked, "how did the first person get it?"

"It's something in the blood, right? Something where the blood doesn't make immunities like it's supposed to. . . ."

"Yes!" he said. "There has been some interference in the chromosomes to create the first cases. But how did that interference take place?"

"Nuclear testing?" I asked.

"No," he came back. "If that were so, far more people would have been affected. Especially people near the site of the tests."

"But what about if some people are . . . susceptible to radiation. You know . . . if it has a different effect on them than on other people."

"That is better—a better hypothesis. But it is too broad, too weak. Think of more experiments—experiments on people."

"Like they used to do on prisoners—like with malaria and yellow fever and stuff?"

"Yes!" he barked. "Experiments on people."

"Like the Nazis did in the camps?"

The Mole's eyes changed shape, like there was a different fuel in his reactor. "They experimented on us like we were laboratory rats. To make twins from the same egg . . . eliminate what they called genetic defects . . . test it on us before they used it on themselves."

"AIDS came from Nazi experiments?"

"No. They didn't have the scientific knowledge. Sadistic amateurs. They just wanted to torture people. They called it science. When doctors help the torturers . . ."

I had to get the Mole off that topic. When he thought too much about the Nazis, the blood lust blocked everything else.

"So some other experiments?" I asked. "Something going on now?"

"Maybe . . ." he said.

"They don't let prisoners volunteer for that stuff anymore. They let us test some crap that was supposed to grow hair on bald people when I was down the last time . . . but no real heavy stuff."

"Where would the drug companies test?" he asked.

"Well, they test in Latin America, right? That fucking formula they wanted mothers to use instead of breast-feeding . . ."

The Mole was coming around again. "Yes. Yes, now you are working. What else do we know about AIDS?"

"Haitians, hemophiliacs, heroin addicts, and homosexuals . . . the 4-H Club, right?"

"And why do the drug companies test in foreign countries?" the Mole asked.

"It's illegal here, right? But some countries—they let you do what you want as long as you got the bucks."

"In democratic countries?"

"Okay, Mole, I get it. The best country would be some outrageous dictatorship where the people do what they're told or they get themselves iced."

"Like . . ."

"Like . . . I don't know . . . Iran, Cuba, Russia."

"Haiti?" the Mole wanted to know.

"Hell, yes, Haiti. I did time with a guy from Haiti. He told me this Papa Doc was the devil, straight up. And that his kid was the devil's son."

"Close to the United States?" said the Mole.

"Yes."

"Need money?"

"Sure."

"Dictatorship?"

"Yeah!"

"Would the leader care if some of his people were exposed to the grave risk of biochemical experiments?"

"No fucking way," I said. The Haitians who try and cross the ocean on rafts aren't looking for better social opportunities.

"Who goes to prison in Haiti?" asked the Mole.

"Anybody Baby Doc wants to put there," I said, thinking. "And dope fiends. Sure!"

"Homosexuals?"

"You better believe it, Mole. Damn!"

The Mole smiled his smile. It wouldn't charm little children. "The drug companies seek a cure for cancer . . . or any other great disease. The cure will make them rich beyond our imagination. This is the fuel that drives their engine. The scientists want to experiment, and they don't have the patience to test rats. And rats are not people."

I lit another smoke, saying nothing. The Mole was on a roll.

"So they make arrangements in Haiti to test their new drugs. On prisoners. Many of them in prison because of heroin addiction or homosexuality, yes? And they alter the genetic components of the blood with their experiments. The homosexuals do what they do inside the prisons. When they become obviously ill, the government disposes of some of them. But the drug companies don't want them all killed. Like when the government let those black men with syphilis go untreated years ago—they never treated them because they wanted to study the long-term effects. Some of the infected Haitians come to America. And when they have sex with others, the drug companies lose control of the experiment."

"And we have AIDS?" I asked him.

"It's one scenario," the Mole said, still thinking it over.

"Son of a bitch," I said, almost to myself.

Simba-witz rolled back into the clearing—we'd been there a long time. He saw us both sitting quietly, flicked his tail over his back, and faded away again.

"Mole," I said, "I've got a scenario about this picture I need to find. The way it was taken . . . Polaroid camera and all . . . it was for sale. If it goes in a magazine, then it's in the stream of commerce and there's nothing I can do about it."

The Mole looked up, listening.

"But I don't think that's the deal," I told him. "I think it was taken for a collector—a private thing. If they put it in a magazine, someone could see it. Cause a lot of problems. I need some freak who gets off looking at this stuff. Not some money-makers. You understand? Someone who's got shoeboxes full of pictures like that."

The Mole nodded. It made sense—at least so far.

"So I need to talk to a collector—a serious, hard-core pedophile. Someone with the money to buy things like this. This is a no-consent picture, right? The freaks might trade copies back and forth, but I don't think it will get commercially produced."

"I don't know anyone like that," he said.

"Mole," I said, keeping my voice level, "you have friends . . . associates, anyway . . . people I did some work for a couple of times . . . when we first met." No point mentioning the name the man from Israel had given me—whichever branch of the Israeli Secret Service made contact with the Mole was likely to be a pure wet-work group anyway.

The Mole turned so he was facing me. "So?" he said.

I was talking fast now, trying to get this all out, get the Mole to agree. "So they have to keep files on freaks like that. Blackmail, whatever. They have to know what's going down on the international scene—know who the players are. I know they don't do law-enforcement or vice-squad shit, but *information* . . . that's something they always want. Anything to give you a leg up . . . a handle."

"So?" he said again, waiting.

"Mole, I want you to ask your friends to give you the name of such a person." I held up my hand before he could speak. "*If* they know . . . okay? Just a name and an address. I want to talk to this person. It's a real long shot he would have the picture, but he sure as hell could put me into the pipeline of people who might."

I was done talking.

The Mole got off the couch, hands in his pockets, and walked toward the Lincoln. I followed him. The pack followed me, materializing out of the shadows.

"Is the little boy Jewish?" the Mole asked.

"He wants his soul back," I said.

I opened the door of the Lincoln, climbed inside. I hit the power window switch, looking at the Mole.

"All I can do is ask," he said. "I'll call you at the restaurant."

The Mole turned and walked back into his junkyard.

## 52

DARKNESS WAS DROPPING ITS blanket over the city by the time I crossed back over the bridge into Manhattan. I got off at 96th Street and worked my way through Central Park, heading for the West Side. It was still too early for the yuppies to start their mating rituals, but the neon was already flashing by the time I got into the West Fifties—humans who buy their sex in New York expect twenty-four-hour service.

The Lincoln cruised Broadway, hugging the curb. A block-long video-game parlor washed the sidewalk with flashing strobe-lights. Electronic war-sounds poured through its doors, a harsh wave dividing the kids lurking on the sidewalk. Black teenagers were standing to one side in little groups, their pockets emptied of quarters by the machines inside, alert for another penny-ante score so they could go back inside. The white boys on the other side of the doors were younger—they cruised quietly, hawk eyes watching the cars for a customer. The groups never mixed. The black rough-off artists knew better than to move on the little stud-hustlers—a kid peddling his under-age ass and telling himself he's not really homosexual will be happy to stab you to prove it.

Hookers don't work the main drags in the Square after dark—they have the massage parlors for that. Lexington Avenue was their turf. The customers know where to go.

I cut off from Broadway over to Ninth Avenue, kept heading downtown. The fast-food joint I was looking for stood next to a theatre specializing in kung-fu films, a heavy streamer of red and blue lights making a banner over its canopy. I slid the Lincoln to the curb behind a dark Mercedes stretch limo, waiting my turn.

It didn't take long. Three little kids bounded up to the passenger window, arranging their faces into smiles. The Hispanic kid was working with a partner, a blond boy a little taller but even thinner. The dark-haired boy had eyes like dinner plates; his curly hair glistened in the neon. He probably told the johns his name was Angel. Wearing a red T-shirt over a pair of jeans with a designer label on the back pocket. He turned like he was talking to his partner to show me. I couldn't read the designer's name but I knew what the label said: "For Rent." The blond kept his hands in his pockets, eyes down, heavy shock of hair falling in his eyes. They looked about twelve years old.

I pushed the power window switch and slid over to talk to them. The third kid was a redhead, freckles on his round face, a trace of colorless lip gloss on his mouth. He was wearing a white sweatshirt with a "Terry" in script on the front, black pants. New white leather sneakers on his feet. His skin was already a pasty color from a steady diet of junk food and freak-sperm.

I nodded my head to the redhead and the two other boys didn't waste another minute fading back to the front of the fast-food joint. They weren't there for conversation.

"You want to go for a ride, Terry?" I asked him.

The kid didn't blink, his eyes shifting to the back seat and up again to my face, smelling for trouble, the mechanical smile still in place.

He knew the code. "I have to ask my uncle," he said. "Will you buy me something nice if I go with you?"

"Sure," I said, "where's your uncle?"

"I'll get him," the kid said, his soft white hands on the windowsill of the Lincoln. "Don't talk to any of the other boys while I'm gone, okay?"

"Okay," I told him, lighting a cigarette like I was prepared to wait.

It didn't take long. The redhead disappeared inside the joint, emerged in another minute with a man in tow. The man was in his early twenties, wearing a white sportcoat with the sleeves pushed up to display heavy forearms and a jeweled watch. He had an orange silk T-shirt on underneath, wide flowing white pants, the cuffs billowing over his shoes. The new look for kiddie-pimps—Miami Lice.

The man's hair was so short on the sides it almost looked shaved, but the top was grown out and flowed down his back. As he rolled up on the Lincoln, he grabbed the redhead by the waistband on his jeans and hoisted him onto the front fender with one hand. The waistband of the pimp's pants was wide, like a cummerbund. He hooked his thumbs inside the band, pressing his hands together to force the blood into his arms and chest. He wasn't a power-lifter: his waist was too small for that. He could lift the little redhead with one hand, but he was built for show, not go.

The pimp leaned into the Lincoln, his chiseled face filling the open window, sending me a message. "Terry says you want to take him out for some pizza?"

I let a tremor of fear into my face, mumbling, "Uh . . . yes, I just wanted to . . ."

He cut me off. "I know what you want. I'm responsible for the boy, see? You leave a deposit with me—just to make sure you bring him back on time, okay? Then you go and buy him that pizza."

"A deposit?"

"A hundred dollars," the pimp said. He wasn't going to discuss it.

I put my hand in my pocket like I was reaching for my wallet. Hesitated, watching his eyes. "What I *really* want . . ." I started to say.

"None of my business," he said, holding out his hand, turning his head casually to watch the street around us.

I cast my eyes down, looking at his open hand. "Pictures," I said.

The young man was getting impatient. "You want pictures, you take pictures, okay?"

"I want to *buy* some pictures," I said. "I'm a collector," as if that explained everything.

It did. "We got pictures of Terry. Candid shots. He's a beautiful boy," the young man said. He could have been describing a Chevy.

"How old is he?"

"Terry is"—thinking how low he could pitch this—"he's ten." The young man must have thought I looked dubious. "He's just tall for his age."

"You have pictures of . . . younger boys?"

"Pictures? Look, man. Take the boy here out for some pizza, okay? Take your own pictures. Anything you want."

"I just want the pictures," I said. "I . . . can't take them myself."

The young man rolled his eyes up, silently bemoaning the difficulties of his business. "I might be able to get you some pictures. It's a lot of work. Could be pretty expensive."

"I don't care," I assured him.

"Tell you what. You take Terry for his pizza, right? Bring him back to the big ships—you know the West Side Highway, near Forty-fifth? Where they have those navy ships you can walk around on?"

I nodded, eager to please.

"I got a red Corvette. A new one. Drive down to the pier, say around midnight? Look for my car. You bring back Terry—I'll have some pictures for you."

"How many?" I asked.

"How many you want, friend? They're expensive, like I told you."

"How many could I buy for . . . say, a thousand dollars?"

The young man's eyes flared for a split-second. Only a Class A chump would bargain like I was. "You want action photos or just poses?"

"Action," I whispered, my eyes downcast.

"That's four for a thousand," he said.

"Four different boys?"

"Four different. Action shots. Color."

"I have to go home and get the money," I said.

"Take Terry with you," the young man said. "After you buy him some pizza."

I just nodded, moving my Adam's apple in my throat like I was gulping it all down.

The pimp put his hand on the back of the redhead's neck. The little kid's face contorted in pain, but he didn't say anything. "You be a good boy, now," said the pimp in a dead-flat voice. The kid nodded.

The young man opened the door of the Lincoln, shoved the boy inside. He held out his hand for the hundred dollars.

I handed it over. Making my voice brave, I said, "How do I know you'll be there?"

"You've got my merchandise," the pimp said, pocketing the hundred and walking away in the same motion.

## 53

I PULLED OUT INTO TRAFFIC, grabbing a quick look at the boy sitting next to me. He was huddled against the passenger door, head down. The digital clock on the dash said seven-fifty-six—about four hours until I got to meet the man with the pictures.

I hit the power-door lock button—the boy jumped when he heard it click home. He looked at me, twisting his hands together in his lap. "Are you going to hurt me?" he asked in a calm voice. He wasn't looking to talk me out of it, just asking what was going to happen to him.

"I'm not going to hurt you, kid," I told him in my own voice.

His face shot up. "Are you a cop?"

"No, I'm not a cop. I'm a man doing a job. And I want you to help me."

"Help you?"

"Yeah, Terry. Help me. That's all."

The boy was scanning my face, looking for the truth—probably wouldn't recognize it if he saw it.

"What do I have to do?"

"I'm looking for someone. Out here. I'm going to drive around the streets, looking. I want you to look too, okay?"

"Really?"

"Really."

"Who are you looking for?"

"You know the little black guy with no legs—the one on the skateboard . . . pushes himself along with his hands?"

His face brightened up. "Yeah! Yeah, I know him. I talked to him once. He asked me if I wanted to run away."

"What did you tell him?" I asked.

"I was still talking to him when Rod came along."

"Is Rod the guy who I was talking to?"

"Yeah, that's him. He kicked the little black guy right off the skateboard. He has legs, you know," the kid said, his voice serious.

"I know," I told him. "You keep your eyes peeled now—we want to find him."

"How come?" he asked.

"He's going to help me do something tonight," I said.

"You're not going to hurt me?" he asked again.

"No, kid. I'm not going to hurt you," I promised him again, keeping my distance.

I made a couple of slow circuits through the cesspool, cruising between Sixth and Ninth on the cross streets, my eyes passing over the action, searching for the Prof. A police car pulled next to us; the cop's eyes were bored. Almost all the people on the street were male—dream-buyers looking for sellers, wolfpacks looking for prey. Hell eats its tourists.

I looped around at 39th, heading back uptown on Eighth. We were across 44th when the boy shouted, "I see him!," pointing excitedly at the front of a gay movie house. The Prof was on his cart, working the traffic, begging for coins with his cup, watching from ground zero like the cops never could. I ran the Lincoln into the curb, pulled the ignition key, and locked the door behind me, leaving the boy inside. The Prof heard my footsteps pounding toward him and looked up, his hand inside his long ragged coat. When he saw it was me, he grabbed some sidewalk and gave himself a heroic shove in my direction. In our world, when someone moves fast, there's trouble behind.

"Prof, come on," I told him, "we got work to do."

"If you're singing my song, please don't take long," he bopped out, ready for whatever, telling me to get on with it.

I grabbed his outstretched hand and pulled him along on his cart to the Lincoln. I opened the trunk. The Prof climbed off his cart and we tossed it inside. I opened the passenger door and the Prof jumped in. He pulled his own door shut as I went around to the driver's side. We were back into the uptown traffic in a minute.

"Terry," I said to the boy, "this is the Prof."

"The Prof?" the kid asked.

"Prof is short for Prophet, my man," said the little black man, pulling off his misshapen felt hat, his spiky Afro shooting up out of control. "I never fall because I see it all."

The kid's eyes were wide, but he wasn't afraid. Good.

"What's on?" the Prof wanted to know. He didn't use my name.

"Tell you soon, Prof. First we need Michelle. You know where she might be working?"

"Avenue C ain't the place to be."

(The Lower East Side was a dangerous place to work.)

"Working the docks is only for jocks."

(The gay hustlers had West Street sewn up.)

"So if you want sex, it's got to be on Lex."

I swung the Lincoln east, moving crosstown on 48th. I lit a cigarette, letting the big car drive itself. The whores wouldn't be working until we got into the Thirties.

"Can I have one?" asked the boy.

I handed him the pack. "How old you are, boy?" the Prof asked, not happy with my child-care techniques.

"I was smoking when I was his age," I told him.

"Yeah, and look how you turned out, bro'," came the response.

A smile flickered across the boy's face, as fleet as a memory. He handed the pack back to me.

The side streets crossing lower Lexington were so clogged with whores that the Lincoln had to creep its way through. I knew Michelle wouldn't be running up to a car—it wasn't the way she worked. The Prof knew it too. "A racehorse don't run with the mules," he said. "Racehorse" was the ultimate compliment for a working girl, reserved only for the very best.

It took us another half-hour to find her, lounging against a lamppost, a tiny pillbox hat on her head, a half-veil covering her face. She had a black-and-white-checked coat that came halfway down her hips over a black pencil-skirt. Ankle straps on her spike heels. Like a bad girl from World War II.

I pulled the Lincoln up to the lamppost, but Michelle never moved. She brought a cigarette lighter to her face, letting the tiny flame show off her perfect profile. If you wanted a ten-dollar slut, you were in the wrong neighborhood.

I hit the power window switch. "Michelle!" I called to her.

She sauntered over to the Lincoln. "Is that . . . ?"

"Don't say my name," I told her, before she could finish. "I've got company."

She kept coming, leaning into the car, kissing me on the cheek, looking past me to the front seat.

"Hello, Prof," she said, "who's your friend?"

"This is my man Terry," he said. The kid's eyes were round. Even for him, this wasn't a regular night.

"Get in the back, Michelle. We got work."

I climbed out, pulling the kid along with me by his wrist. I found the release lever and the driver's seat slid forward. I put the kid in the back, moving my hands so Michelle could follow him, like I was holding the door for a countess.

"Hi, baby," Michelle said to the kid.

"Hello," Terry said, not a trace of fear in his voice for the first time that night. I don't know how Michelle does it, and I'll never learn.

By the time the Lincoln was halfway to my part of town, they were whispering together in the back seat like the Prof and I weren't there.

# 54

I NEEDED TO SET THINGS up for later on. Michelle was the only babysitter I could trust. Someone had to watch the boy, and I didn't want him to see my office or anything else. I tooled down to the pier we always use for private conversations, off the Hudson just before the Battery Tunnel turns Manhattan into Brooklyn. I pulled over, cut the engine. A working girl detached herself from a small group and started to saunter over to the Lincoln. She stopped in her tracks when the Prof and I got out. Whatever we were, we weren't the customers she wanted.

"Be right back," I said to Michelle, motioning for the Prof to follow me.

I lit a smoke, handed the pack to the Prof, and looked at the dark water, thinking of the dark water in Flushing Meadow Park. Thinking of Strega. I was getting off the track.

"What's going down?" the Prof wanted to know.

"I'm looking for a picture. Kiddie porn. My client is concerned that a picture was taken of a certain kid. She wants it back."

"Why don't you just look for a fish out there?" he said, pointing at the silent Hudson.

"I know it's odds-against, Prof. I said I'd try, okay?"

"Where do I come in?"

"I hit the Square, asking around. The kid in the back seat with Michelle? He's hustling. I spoke to his pimp, told him I wanted to buy some pictures. He's going to meet me by the big ships around midnight. I'm supposed to bring a grand in cash, buy four pictures."

"Of who?"

"Who the fuck knows. The freak probably *has* some pictures. If he figures me for a customer, I'll buy the pictures, ask him for some more. Tell him what I'm looking for."

"And if he figures you for a tourist?" the Prof asked.

"That's where you come in. The Lincoln has one of those power trunk releases, okay? Michelle holds the kid in the front seat, keeps her head down. I climb out, she slides over where I was sitting. Any trouble—she pops the trunk and you come out. I got a scattergun you can use."

"I ain't dusting nobody, Burke," he said, trying to convince himself.

"I didn't say you had to take him out, Prof. Just keep me from getting stomped on, okay? Show him the piece, maybe break a cap in the air . . . that's all."

The Prof sucked cigarette smoke into his chest. "You going to play this one square?"

"If he's got real pictures, I'll buy and I'll ask him some questions. But if he moves on me and you have to brace him, we'll see what's he got on him. Okay?"

"What if he has backup?"

"He's driving a 'Vette. Easy to check. And Michelle will be keeping the peek from the car."

"It sounds like a job for Max," he said.

"It's a job for us, Prof. You in or out?"

"I may talk some jive, but I never took a dive," he snapped, insulted.

I patted him on the back. "We'll get Michelle to drop us off near my office. Get the stuff we need, hang out a bit. Okay?"

"Right on," said the little black man, "but if the hound is going to be around . . ."

"Pansy's cool, Prof. You just have to get to know her."

He looked dubious, but he wasn't arguing. We walked back to the Lincoln—Michelle and the kid were still rapping away in the back.

"Michelle, how about you drop me and the Prof off? Take the car and meet us back around eleven?"

"Terry and I need to get something to eat anyway," she said. "Give me some money."

I handed her two fifties. The way Michelle ate she probably wouldn't bring back any change.

I drove to within a couple of blocks of the office and pulled over to the curb. Michelle climbed out to stand next to me, leaving the Prof inside the car with the boy.

"Walk a bit with me," I told her. She took my arm and we strolled out of earshot.

"The kid's hustling . . ." I began.

"I know," she snapped. "We talked."

"I'm supposed to bring him back around midnight. Do a deal with his pimp. Cash for merchandise. The pimp might get stupid—the Prof's going to ride shotgun in the trunk. You handle the kid—keep him with you for a couple of hours till you pick us up. Okay?"

"Burke," she hissed, her eyes flaming, "you're not giving that boy back to a pimp!"

"Michelle, I'm not giving him back to anyone, okay? No matter what goes down tonight, you leave with the kid. Take him to the cops. Let him find his home."

"The only cop I'm dealing with is McGowan," she said. McGowan is a detective with the Runaway Squad. By me, most cops would have to step up in class to be garbage, but McGowan plays it fair. You could drop off a kid with him and he'd never put the deliveryman in his report.

"Any way you want, babe. It's up to you. Just make sure the little bastard doesn't take off while he's with you. He's the reason I'm sure the pimp is going to show."

"Any money in this?" she wanted to know.

"If the pimp plays it square, I'm going to pay him and that's all. If he gets stupid, we'll take what he has. Split it three ways. Deal?"

"You think I was standing under that streetlight because I lost something, honey?"

I threw up my hands in surrender, reaching for my shirt pocket.

"Honey, I have told you time and time again not to carry cash in your shirt pocket—only dice players do that. It's bad enough you dress like a bum."

"Hey!" I said. "This is a good suit."

"Burke, it *was* a good suit. It's yesterday's news, darling. Like your haircut," she said, a smile playing with her painted lips.

"We can't all be on the cutting edge of fashion, Michelle."

"Don't I know it," she retorted, taking the wad of bills and counting off a few fifties for herself. If I ever paid taxes, Michelle would be one hell of a deduction. She reached up to kiss me on the cheek. "Thanks, baby. That's one step closer to Denmark for me."

"Sure," I said. I'd heard it before.

Michelle climbed behind the wheel of the Lincoln as the Prof got out. She turned and said something to the boy. He scrambled over the back seat to sit next to her. She was saying something to him as they pulled away—probably telling him to keep his feet off the upholstery.

# 55

WHEN THE LINCOLN WHEELED around the corner, I was waiting. The kid was sitting next to Michelle on the front seat, eating an ice-cream cone. I climbed in and Michelle slid over, changing places with the kid so he was between us. I found the release lever, popped the trunk, and waited for traffic to pass.

As soon as it got quiet, I climbed out like I was getting something out of the trunk. "Okay," I hissed into the darkness. The Prof came out, dressed in one of those padded suits guys wear for working in meat lockers. He was carrying his own coat in one hand, the shotgun wrapped inside.

The light went on inside the trunk when I lifted it up. I took a roll of quarters out of my pocket and put it against the light. When I smacked it with the flat of my hand, the light went out. It wouldn't come on again.

The Prof checked out the interior—it was clean and new, covered with carpet. Even the spare tire was buried under the flooring. "I lived in worse places," he said, and climbed in without another word.

I worked my way back to the West Side Highway. Michelle sat with her arm around the boy, listening to me explain the deal.

"The kid sits straight up in the seat, okay? You lay down, below the windshield. When I get out, you slide over and put your hand on this release. You hear me raise my voice for *any* reason . . . no matter what I'm saying . . . you pop the lever."

"Terry is coming back with us," she said. Her voice was calm—just stating a fact. I glanced over at the kid—if this wasn't okay with him he was a hell of an actor.

"There won't be any problem," I told them both, the magnum heavy in my coat. "This guy doesn't try and hurt me, he won't get hurt."

"I hope he does try and hurt you," Michelle said, her voice soft.

I shot her a dirty look, but she wasn't paying attention. "Do you know what he did to Terry? You know what he makes . . ."

"I know," I told her.

When we crossed 14th Street I told Michelle to get down. "You just stay in the car no matter what happens," I told the kid.

"Terry knows what to do," Michelle snapped at me, sliding into position. The boy held her hand.

I nosed the Lincoln into a dark spot in the shadows cast by the big ships. No sign of the pimp. I hit the window switch, waiting.

It didn't take long. Headlights on high beam flashed behind me—the red Corvette. I climbed out of the car, walked around toward the trunk. Where I'd stash the pictures if I got any.

The Corvette hit the brakes, sending the machine into a controlled skid across the back of the Lincoln, blocking me in. The pimp revved his engine before he shut it down, climbing out in almost the same motion. The passenger seat looked empty. I walked over toward him to get a better look.

The pimp stood next to his car, hands balled into fists. I walked right up to him, stepping in his space, looking down like I was afraid. The inside of his car was empty. Good.

"The pictures?" I asked him.

He reached in a shirt pocket, coming out with a pair of sunglasses. He took his time adjusting them on his face, making me wait.

"The money?" he said.

I took out the thousand from my coat pocket, handed it to him. Put my hand back in the same pocket like I was guarding the rest of my money. Felt the magnum waiting there.

He handed me four Polaroids, watching me turn my back to him so I could catch some light. They were all of the boy. Terry. Three had him naked, sucking on another little boy who was doing the same thing to him. The last picture was a side view of a kid being penetrated in the rear—you couldn't see his face. My hands shook.

"You only take pictures of your own boys?" I asked him.

"That's the best way, man. From me to you—no problems and no complaints."

He took a leather notebook from his pocket. Flipped it open and pulled out a gold pen. Started writing.

"What are you doing?" I asked him.

"Writing down your license number, man. Just in case I want to get in touch with you again." His eyes were hidden behind the glasses.

I quickly looked around. Quiet as a graveyard. "Don't do that!" I yelled, and the trunk of the Lincoln popped open. The pimp grabbed a fistful of my coat, drawing back his other hand to shut me up. I hooked him deep in the belly with the hand holding the magnum, trying to drive it through him and scratch the finish of his red Corvette. He grunted and doubled over, catching a kick on the temple from my steel-toed shoe. The pimp's glasses flew off—he was reaching for something in his jacket when the Prof put the scattergun in his face.

The pimp just lay there while I checked his equipment. A little .32-caliber automatic, a pretty silver color. A diamond ring, a wafer-thin watch. A tiny leather address book. A key ring with a bunch of keys. A wad of bills in a wallet so thick it was almost a purse. A silver vial with a screw-on top. No identification. I pocketed it all.

He was gasping for breath by then, but watching me closely. Wondering what the game was.

I went around to the Corvette, shoved the lever into neutral, and put my shoulder to it. It moved forward a few feet—more than enough to get the Lincoln out. I pulled the keys from the ignition, walked back, and held them in front of the pimp's face.

"I'll leave these under the streetlight over there," I told him, pointing to my left. It was about a hundred yards away.

The pimp was still quiet—the shotgun was his whole world.

"You fucked with the wrong kid," I told him, and walked to the Lincoln. I started it up, backed it out, spun around so the passenger door was at the Prof's back. Michelle opened it from the inside and the Prof jumped in as I took off.

The Lincoln shot toward the streetlight. I hit the brakes hard. "He's still down," the Prof called out. I threw the vial out the window.

If the maggot remembered the license number of the Lincoln, he could ask the Real Brotherhood for his car keys.

# 56

I WANTED THE LINCOLN off the streets in case the pimp decided to make a phone call.

"Can you call McGowan from your place?" I asked Michelle.

"I'll handle it," she said from the back seat. The boy was quiet. I glanced in the mirror—he was trembling, Michelle's arm around him, his face in her chest.

I tossed the pimp's wallet into the back seat. "Have to throw the rest of his junk away," I said. The Prof nodded agreement.

The Lincoln rolled north on the highway, heading for 125th Street, where I'd make the sweep and head back to our part of town.

"Almost six thousand," Michelle said, a happy note in her voice. The wallet came sailing over the seat, landing on the dashboard.

"Take your cut," I told the Prof. The scattergun was stashed under the seat.

"Cash from trash," he said, sounding religious, "cash from trash."

He pulled a pair of cotton gloves from the freezer suit and started to work on the pimp's little gun, wiping it clean. He pulled out the clip, then jacked the slide, catching the unfired slug in his hand.

"One in the chamber," he said. The little automatic had been ready for work.

"One piece at a time," I said. The Prof nodded, hitting the switch to lower his window. First the bullets, then the clip. The silver gun was the last to go.

The Prof handed me my share of the pimp's money, softly clapping his hands together to say all the work was done. I let him off on Second Avenue in the Thirties, opening the trunk to let him take his cart and leave the freezer suit. The Prof strapped his cart to his back like it was a knapsack.

"Watch yourself, Prof," I told him.

"The street is my home, and that ain't no poem," he said. The pimp might see him again, but nothing would register. We pressed our palms together, chest high. The way you say goodbye in the visiting room in prison. Through the bullet-proof glass.

I rolled up outside Michelle's hotel, opened the door to let her out as if I was a chauffeur. The little boy was holding on to her hand like a lifeline. Maybe it was.

Michelle kissed me on the cheek. "Keep the change, honey," she said, and started up the steps.

I had the Lincoln back inside my garage in another fifteen minutes.

## 57

THE PIMP'S WATCH HAD some fancy engraving on the back. "L to R. All ways." Probably from the freak who turned him out the first time. No point trying to sell it. I opened it up, keeping only the timing mechanism—the Mole could always use something like that—pushing the rest to the side of my desk. The diamond ring was another story—a heavy white-gold base holding what looked like a two-carat stone. I screwed the loupe into my eye socket and took a closer look—no blemishes that I could see, nice fire. I pried the stone loose, pushing what was left of the ring over next to the wreckage of the watch.

The key ring was useless to me, but I took my time with the little leather address book. All first names or initials, with phone numbers next to them. In the right-hand column there was a single-digit number next to each name. Some kind of code for what the customer usually wanted? I copied everything from the book onto a yellow pad. I'd keep the book itself—it might turn into a poker chip sometime.

I went out to the metal stairs leading to the roof, calling for Pansy. The moon was a crescent, clear against the night sky. I lit a cigarette, watching the moon hang up there, a million miles from this junkyard we live in. I like to look at the moon—you never get to see it in prison.

Pansy lumbered downstairs. She saw me standing on the iron landing and put her paws on the railing. Standing like that, her face was almost level with mine. I scratched the back of her ears absently, trying to get a grip on my search for the picture. In the morning I'd see a guy who would get me the names and addresses to go with the phone numbers from the pimp's book, but it wasn't likely to give me anything. I had to wait on the Mole and Bobby, couldn't push them to move any faster. The only way to get more information was to talk to the kid myself.

I'd need Immaculata for that.

And Strega.

## 58

THE NEXT MORNING I went to work. First to Mama's, where I called Strega.

"It's me," I said, when she picked up the phone.

"You have what I want?" she asked.

"I'm still working. I have to talk with you—get some more information."

"What information?"

"Not on the phone," I told her. "You know the statue on Queens Boulevard, on the north side, just before the courthouse?"

"Yes," she said.

"Tonight. At six-thirty, okay?"

"Yes," she said again, tonelessly. And hung up.

I went back inside to the restaurant. Mama glided over to my table. "No serve breakfast," she said, smiling. I looked stricken. "But not too early for lunch," she told me. One of the alleged waiters materialized next to me, bowed to Mama. She said something in Cantonese to him. He just nodded.

"Hot-and-sour soup?" I asked.

"You speak Chinese now, Burke? Very good."

I didn't bother to answer her—Mama was only sarcastic when she was annoyed about something.

"You want me do something for you, Burke? Get Max over here?"

"Yeah, Mama. I want Max. But I could find him by myself, right?

I came here to give you something."

Her eyes opened slightly, looking a question at me. I put the diamond I took from the pimp on the table between us. Mama picked it up, held it to the light between her fingers.

"Man's stone," she said.

"Your stone," I told her. "A small gift to show my great respect."

A smile lit up her face. "Very nice stone," she said.

I bowed my head, saying the matter was closed. "Tell me about new case," Mama said.

"I'm looking for a picture," I said, and told her what kind of picture and why I was looking.

Mama put her hands in the sugar bowl, tossing a pinch of the white powder on the table top, using her fingers to push it into a long narrow column.

"Everybody do *something*," she told me, drawing her finger through the bottom of the column, drawing a line. "Some people do more things, okay?" Drawing another line, leaving more than half the column between us. "Gambling, funny money, jewels," she said, each time flicking more sugar off the column. "Guns, stealing . . . " More flicks of her finger—less sugar on the table. "Protection money, killing . . . " More sugar vanished. "Drugs," she said, and the last of the sugar was gone.

I got it. Everybody has to make a living. Everybody draws a line somewhere. The people who do kiddie porn are over the line no matter where you draw it. "I know," I told her.

"Business is business," said Mama, quoting her favorite psalm. "Everything has rules. Do the same way all the time. Reliable, okay?"

"Yes," I said, waiting.

"Even with war . . . rules," Mama said. I wasn't so sure—I'd been in one, but I let her go on.

"These people . . . " Mama shrugged, her face set and hard.

The soup came. Mama dished some out into my bowl. Gave some to herself. She bowed over the plates like she was saying grace.

Mama looked up. "No rules," she said.

"No rules," I agreed.

# 59

IMMACULATA CAME IN THE front door of the restaurant, made her way past the customers to our table.

"Hello, Mama," she said.

Mama smiled at her—a real smile, not the cat's grin she usually showed Max's woman. "You sit down with us, okay? Have some soup?"

Immaculata bowed. "Thank you, Mama. I have been told your soup is the finest of all."

That put the cap on it for Mama. "You help Burke on his case, yes? Very good. Very important case. Sit with me," she said, patting the seat next to her.

Immaculata shot her hips sideways and was next to Mama in a flash. She must have been working with Max—he'd been trying to teach me karate for a long time—I hoped he was having better luck with her. Mama gave her a generous helping of the soup, watching her bow over the food before eating, nodding her head in approval.

"Max coming?" she asked.

"Yes," Immaculata answered.

"Max good man. Fine warrior," Mama opened.

"Yes," said Immaculata, waiting.

"Good man. Make good father, yes?"

Immaculata's eyes were calm, but her golden skin flushed. She looked directly at Mama.

"You know? Even Max doesn't know."

"I know," said Mama, patting Immaculata's arm, her whole face smiling.

Immaculata watched Mama's face, then broke into a smile of her own. Without a word being said, she knew she wasn't a bar girl to Mama anymore.

# 60

MAX CAME OUT OF the kitchen, bowed to everyone at the table, then slammed into the booth next to me, almost driving me through the wall. He pulled out a tattered copy of the *Daily News*, spread it on the table, and pointed to the charts of Flower Jewel's race with a thick finger. He spread his hands to ask a question—what did this "dq" crap mean anyway?

I used the sugar bowl and the salt and pepper shakers to show him how it had happened. Max nodded, moving his right hand in the "hit me" gesture blackjack players use when they want another card. We were going to bet on Flower Jewel the next time she raced. It wasn't like I had any choice—I handed Max a hundred, ignoring Mama's broad grin and Immaculata's look of benign interest.

Max made the sign of a galloping horse, checked to see that all eyes were focused on him. Then he pounded his chest over his heart, balled his right hand into a fist, and laid his forearm on the table with the underside up. The veins looked like electrical cords. He touched a vein, touched his heart again. Made the sign of the horse.

I got it. Since the blood of Mongol warriors ran in his veins, he claimed to have a natural kinship with horses. I should listen to him.

Mama nodded in agreement. "Good blood," she said. Immaculata blushed again, but Max was too busy proving he knew more about horses than I did to pay attention.

Mama got to her feet as Immaculata stood to give her room to exit. She took Immaculata's hand, turned it over to see the underside of her forearm. She tapped the delicate veins there, nodded her head sharply. Smiled. "Good blood here too," Mama said, and kissed Immaculata on the cheek.

Max looked at me, puzzled. I didn't say anything—Mac would tell him when it was time for him to know.

I lit a cigarette as the waiter took away the soup bowls, and started to explain why I needed Immaculata.

# 61

BY THE TIME I was finished, it was mid-afternoon. Only the clock on the wall gave me a clue—daylight never reached the back booths in Mama's joint.

"You really think you can do it?" I asked her.

"It's not an interrogation, Burke. The little boy has information about what happened to him, but it's not so easy for him to talk about. He feels all sorts of things about the assault . . . guilt, fear, excitement. . . ."

"Excitement?" I asked her.

"Sure. Children are sexual beings, they respond to sexual stimulation. That's why, if we *don't* treat a child who has been sexually abused, he's likely to go on looking for the same experience."

"Even if it hurt him?"

"Even so," she said.

"What would make him talk?" I asked her.

"You don't *make* him talk. He *wants* to talk about it; he wants to get it outside of him . . . put down the pain. But first he has to feel safe."

"Like that nobody can hurt him anymore?"

"That's it. Exactly."

"So it's easier if he was assaulted by a stranger, right? So his family can protect him?"

"Yes, it is easier if the assault wasn't by a family member. If someone you trust hurts you, it changes the way you look at the whole world."

"I know," I told her. "If I can get the kid, where would I bring him?"

"Bring him to SAFE, the Safety and Fitness Exchange—where I work. I told you about it, remember? It's the best place for this—lots of other children around, and we know how to act around boys like this one. He'll know nobody can hurt him when he's with us."

"You think he'll come with me?" I asked her.

"Probably—I don't know. It would help if someone he trusted said it was okay for him to go—promised him he'd be all right.

Probably the best way would be for you to bring the child's parent, or anyone he trusted, with you. We work with relatives of abused children all the time."

"You wouldn't want to work with this one," I told her.

Max tapped his chest, folded his arms. The kid would sure as hell be safe with him, he was saying. I tapped my fist against his shoulder to thank him, bowed to Immaculata, and went back through the kitchen to Bobby's Lincoln.

# 62

I STASHED THE LINCOLN in my garage. Strega had already seen one car; that was enough. Pansy chomped on the heavy beef bones Mama had given me for her, snarling anytime she felt the slightest resistance. Her life would have been perfect right then if I could have gotten pro wrestling on the tube, but only the cable networks carry it during the day. The hippies downstairs must have cable—their lives wouldn't be complete without MTV. I'd have to get the Mole to make the necessary adjustments.

It was getting near time to leave. There's only two ways to ride the subways in New York: dress up like a carpenter or a plumber—anyone who routinely carries tools around with him—or carry a gun. I didn't handle tools like I knew what I was doing, and if I got dropped holding a piece I was looking at some serious time upstate. I put on a dark suit over a blue chambray shirt with a darker-blue knit tie. A hard-working architect. I pulled my new attaché case from under the couch. Its black fabric sides expand to hold a lot of stuff, but that's not why I wanted it. This attaché case is made of Kevlar—the same stuff cops use for bullet-proof vests. It looks like nylon, but it'll blunt a knife and stop a bullet—it even has a shoulder strap so you can keep your hands free.

I unzipped the case and threw in a pack of graph paper, some pencils, an old blueprint of a sewage plant, and a little calculator. I added a telescoping metal pointer, the kind architects use to point out features on their blueprints; it works just as well for keeping people from getting close enough to stab you. Then I hunted around until I found the clear plastic T-square the Mole made for me. It looks like the real thing, but if you wishbone the two ends in your hands and snap hard, you end up with a razor-edged knife. Perfect for stabbing and not illegal to carry. The CIA uses these knives to beat airport security machines, but their best feature is the way they break off inside a body—you can put a hell of an edge on plastic, but it stays very brittle.

I caught the E Train at Chambers Street, under the World Trade Center. That was the end of the line—the return would take me right out to my meeting with Strega without changing trains. And I got a seat.

The first thing I did was open my briefcase and take out my blueprints and T-square. I made a desk of the briefcase in my lap and sat there watching. During rush hour, the trains belong to the citizens. By the time we got into midtown, the car was packed with people. An Oriental man, his dark suit shiny from too many cleanings, face buried in a book on computers, shut out the train noises and concentrated. A dress-for-success black woman was reading some kind of leather-bound report—all I could read on the cover was "Proposal" stamped in gold letters. A pair of middle-aged women sat facing each other, arguing over whose boss was the biggest asshole.

The E Train has modern cars—blue-and-orange plastic seats set perpendicular to each other instead of lined up against the side like the older versions . . . subway maps set behind thick clear-plastic sheets . . . stainless-steel outer skins. Even the air conditioning works sometimes. By the time the train hit the long tunnel connecting Manhattan and Queens the car looked like a forest of newspapers and briefcases—gothic romances and crossword puzzles covered faces. A transit cop got on at Queens Plaza, a young guy with a mustache, carrying fifty pounds of equipment on his belt. His eyes swept the car for a second; then he started writing something in his memo book. The car was thick with people, but no skells—nobody smoking dope, no portable radio blasting. Working people going home from work. I felt like a tourist.

Roosevelt Avenue was the next stop on the express. The transit cop got off—Roosevelt Avenue was the Queens version of Times Square—the only thing free out on the streets was trouble. Next came Continental Avenue, where most of the yuppies made their exit. The train goes all the way out to Jamaica; by the time it got to the end of the line there wouldn't be too many white faces left.

I got off at Union Turnpike, stuffing the T-square back into my briefcase, checking my watch. I still had almost fifteen minutes to wait for Strega.

## 63

THE SUN WAS DROPPING into the west as I made my way across Queens Boulevard to the statue. The courthouse was to my right, a squat, dirty piece of undistinguished architecture that hadn't been put up by the lowest bidder—not in Queens County. Looming behind it, the House of Detention cast a shadow of its own, six stories of cross-hatched steel bars, cannon fodder for the processing system citizens call Justice. The guys inside—the ones who can't make bail—call it "just us." Wolfe's office was somewhere in the courthouse complex.

I found a seat at the base of the statue—some Greek god covered with tribute from the passing pigeons. I lit another smoke, watching my hands holding the wooden match. Citizens passed me without a glance—not minding their own business because it was the right thing to do, just in a hurry to get home to whatever treasures their VCRs had preserved for them. The statue was right behind a bus stop, just before the boulevard turned right into Union Turnpike. The human traffic was so thick I couldn't see the street, but I wasn't worried about missing Strega.

I was into my third cigarette when I felt the change in the air—like a cold wind without the breeze. A car horn was blasting its way through the noise of the traffic—sharper and more demanding than the others. A fog-colored BMW was standing right in the middle of the bus stop, leaning on its horn and flashing its lights.

I walked over to the passenger door. The window glass was too dark to see through. The door wasn't locked. I pulled it open and climbed inside. She had the BMW roaring into the traffic stream while I was still closing my door, the little car lurching as she forced it into second gear. We shot across to the left lane, horns protesting in our wake.

"You were late," she snapped, staring straight ahead.

"I was where I said I'd be," I told her, fumbling for my seat belt.

"Next time wait at the curb," she said. Telling the cleaning woman she missed a spot.

She was wearing a bottle-green silk dress, with a black mink jacket over her shoulders, leaving her bare arms free. A thin black chain was around her waist, one end dangling past the seat—it looked like wrought iron. Her face was set and hard behind the makeup mask.

I leaned back in my seat. Strega's skirt was hiked to mid-thigh. Her stockings were dark with some kind of pattern woven into them. Spike heels the same color as the dress. She wasn't wearing her seat belt.

"Where are you going?" I wanted to know.

"My house. You got a problem with that?"

"Only if it isn't empty," I said.

"I'm alone," said Strega. Maybe she was talking about the house.

She wrestled the BMW through the streets to her house, fighting the wheel, riding the clutch unmercifully. The car stalled on Austin Street when she didn't give it enough gas pulling away from the light. "God-damned fucking clutch!" she muttered, snapping the ignition key to get it started again. She was a lousy driver.

"Why don't you get a car with an automatic transmission?"

"My legs look so good when I change gears," she replied. "Don't they?"

I didn't say anything.

"Look at my legs!" she snarled at me. "Aren't they flashy?"

"I wouldn't get a car to go with my looks," I said, mildly.

"Neither would I—if I looked like you," she said, softening it only slightly with a smile. "And you didn't answer my question."

"What question?"

"*Don't* my legs look good?"

"That isn't a question," I told her. And this time I got a better smile.

# 64

SHE PULLED THE BMW around to the back of her house and hit the button on a box she had clipped to the sun visor to open the garage. I followed her up the stairs to the living room, watching her hips switch under the green dress—it looked like a slip in the soft light. She carried the black mink like a dishrag in one hand, tossing it in the general direction of the white couch as she went by.

Strega passed through the living room to another flight of stairs, and climbed toward a light at the top, not saying a word. The bedroom was huge, big enough for three rooms. The walls were a dusky-rose color, the wall-to-wall carpet a dark red. A Hollywood bed, the kind with a canopy over the top, was in the precise middle of the room, standing on a platform a few inches off the carpet. It was all in pink—pink gauze draped from the canopy almost to the floor. The spread was covered with giant stuffed animals—a panda, two teddy bears, a basset hound. A Raggedy Ann doll was propped against the pillows, its sociopath's eyes watching me. A bathroom door stood open to my right—pink shag carpet on the floor, a clear lucite tub dominating the room. A professional makeup mirror was against one wall, a string of tiny little bulbs all around its border. A walk-in closet had mirrored doors. It was half yuppie dream-scene, half little girl's room. I couldn't imagine another person sleeping there with her.

"His bedroom is on the other side of the house," she said, reading my mind. "This is just for me."

"Your husband works late hours?" I asked.

"My husband does what I tell him. I give him what he wants—he does what I want. You understand?"

"No," I told her.

"You wouldn't," she said. Case closed.

I patted my pockets, telling her I wanted to smoke. I couldn't see an ashtray anywhere.

"I don't smoke cigarettes in here," she said.

"So let's go somewhere else."

Strega looked at me like a carpenter checking if there was enough room for a bookcase.

"You don't like my room?"

"It's your room," I replied.

Strega slipped the straps of the green slip over her shoulders, pulling it down to her waist in one motion. I heard the silk tear. Her small breasts looked hard as rocks in the pink light. "You like my room better now?" she asked.

"The room is the same," I said.

She took a breath, making up her mind. "Sit over there," she said, pointing to a tube chair covered in a dark suede—it looked like something growing out of the carpet. I shrugged out of my coat, holding it in one hand, looking toward the bed. "Put it on the floor," she said over her shoulder as she walked out of the room.

She came back with a heavy piece of crystal, kneeling in front of me to put it on the carpet. Whatever it was supposed to be, it was an ashtray then. She was as self-conscious about being topless as two dogs mating—you wanted to look, that was your problem.

"You want something besides that cigarette?"

"I'm okay," I told her.

She was putting a smoke together for herself, loading a tiny white pipe—tiny brown pebbles mixed with the tobacco. "Crack," she said. Super-processed, free-based cocaine—too powerful to snort. She took a deep drag, her eyes on me. It should have lifted her right off the carpet, but she puffed away, bored.

"You wanted to talk to me?" she asked.

I watched her walk back and forth in front of me, the green slip now a tiny skirt just covering her hips, her heels blending into the carpet. The tube chair had a rounded back, forcing me to sit up very straight.

"I need the boy," I told her. "I need to have him talk to some people. Experts. He knows more than he told you—he might have the key in his head."

Strega nodded, thinking. "You're not going to use drugs on him?"

"You mean like sodium amytal—truth serum? No. It's too dangerous. It could get him to where it happened, but we might not be able to get him back."

"Hypnosis?" she asked.

"Not that either," I said. "There's people who know how to talk to kids who've been worked over by freaks. It doesn't hurt—might make him feel better."

"He's okay now," she said. "All he needs is that picture."

"He's not in therapy . . . not getting treatment from anyone?"

"He doesn't need any of that!"

"Yeah, he does. Or at least someone who knows what they're doing should make the decision."

"Not about this," she said, her voice flat.

"Look," I said, "you don't know anything about this, right? Treatment could make all the difference."

"I know about it," she said. Case closed again.

I took a deep drag of my smoke. "I need to have somebody talk to the boy, okay?"

"I'm going to be there when they do."

"No, you're not. That's not the way it's done. Nobody's going to be there."

She puffed on her little crack-laced pipe, flame-points in her eyes. "He wouldn't trust you."

"He would if you said it was okay, right?"

"Yeah. He'd do whatever I said."

"You bring him to a place, okay? I'll meet you there. I'll have the therapist with me. You hand him over—tell him to be a good boy, okay? I'll bring him back in a couple of hours."

"That's it?"

"That's it," I said.

Strega rubbed her eyes as if she didn't like what she was seeing.

"What if I don't do it?"

"You do what you want," I told her. "But you're paying me money to get something done—you don't bring the boy, it makes it harder. And it's tough enough already. It's up to you."

She took a last drag on her pipe, came over to me, and sat in my lap. She put one slim arm around my neck and leaned down to drop the pipe in the ashtray. "I'll think about it," she said, grinding her butt deep into my lap. Heat flashed below my waist but my shoulders stayed cold.

"When's your husband coming home?" I asked her.

"He can't come back here until after midnight."

"*Can't?*" I asked her, looking the question into her little face.

She buried her face in my chest, whispering so softly I could barely hear her. "We have a deal. I do him good. I'm what he needs. I know his mind. On his last birthday I brought a girlfriend of mine over for him—we did a threesome." She was wiggling frantically in my lap, whispering in that little-girl's voice. "All men are the same," she purred, reaching for my zipper, pulling it down, slipping her hand inside, stroking me, scraping a long thumbnail down the shaft. "A hard cock makes a soft brain."

The big house was quiet as a tomb. "Do I get the boy?" I asked her.

"Pull up my dress," she whispered, lifting her butt from my lap. It slid up to her waist as if it was oiled—the green silk made a thick band around her waist; only her dark stockings showed underneath.

She fit herself around me, never changing her position, her face still buried in my chest. She contracted the hard muscles in her hips, pushing back against me. "Say my name!" she whispered into my hair.

"Which name?" I asked her, my voice not as flat as I wanted.

"You know!" she cried, her voice years younger than her body.

"Strega," I said, holding one of her breasts gently in my hand, feeling myself empty into her. She ground herself hard against me, groaning like I was hurting her. In another couple of seconds she was quiet, still welded to me, leaning her head back, letting a long breath out with a sigh.

I rubbed my hand softly over her face. She took a finger in her mouth, bit down hard. I left my hand where it was. She shifted her hips. I popped out of her with a wet sound. She twisted in my lap, her face buried in my chest again. "I'm the best girl," she said. I patted her head, wondering why it was so cold in that pink room.

## 65

WE STAYED LIKE THAT for some time. I couldn't see my watch. "Have another cigarette," she said, climbing off my lap and walking into her bathroom. She closed the door. I could hear the tub filling.

She came out wrapped in a white terry robe, her red hair tousled above the thick collar. She looked thirteen years old. "Now you," she said.

When I came out of the bathroom the bedroom was empty. I heard music from downstairs. Barbra Streisand. Too bad.

Strega was sitting on the white couch, now dressed in a black pleated skirt and a white blouse. I walked past her to the steps. She came off the couch and held my arm, grabbing her mink with her free hand. I went down the steps first, feeling her behind me, not liking the feeling. We got into the BMW without a word.

She pulled into the bus stop, hitting the brakes too hard. "The boy?" I asked her, one more time.

"I'll do it," she said. "Give me one day's notice." Her eyes were somewhere else.

"Good," I told her, getting out of the car, looking back at her.

Strega made a kissing motion with her lips to say goodbye. It looked like a sneer.

## 66

IT WAS STILL A half-hour shy of midnight when I grabbed the subway heading back to Manhattan. The day-shift citizens were gone but the same rules applied—look down or look hard. I alternated between the two until the train screeched to its last stop under the World Trade Center. I stayed underground, following the tunnel a few blocks to Park Place, found the Lincoln just where I'd left it, and drove back to the office.

I let Pansy out to the roof, searching the tiny refrigerator for something to eat. Nothing but a jar of mustard, another of mayonnaise, and a frozen roll. I poured myself a glass of cold water, thinking of the mayonnaise sandwiches we used to make in prison, stuffing them inside our shirts to eat in the middle of the night. Sometimes it was hard to keep my mind from going back to doing time, but I could control my stomach anyway. I'd eat in the morning.

The pictures of Strega's boy Scotty were on my desk—a happy little kid. Like she had been, she said. There's a big slab of corkboard on one wall of my office, just over the couch. There was plenty of room for the boy's pictures. I tacked them up to help me memorize his face—I didn't want to carry them around with me. I lit a cigarette, my eyes sliding from the burning red tip to the boy's pictures.

Working on it. Drawing a blank.

The back door thumped—Pansy was tired of waiting for me to come up on the roof. I let her in, turned on the radio to get the news while I put some more food together for the monster. Then I lay back down on the couch. The radio was playing "You're a Thousand Miles Away" by the Heartbeats. A song from another time—it was supposed to make you think of a guy in the military, his girl waiting for him back home. It was a real popular song with the guys doing time upstate. I thought of Flood in some temple in Japan as I drifted off.

## 67

I WOKE UP SLOWLY to the smell of dog food. Pansy's face was inches from mine, her cold-water eyes unblinking, waiting patiently. Something was floating around at the top of my brain—where I couldn't reach it. Something about the boy's pictures. I lay there, ignoring Pansy, trying to get it to come back to me. No good. Lots of dreams never come to you again.

I took a shower and went out to get some breakfast, still trying to figure out what was bothering me. Whatever it was would have to get in line.

Pansy ate her share of the cupcakes I brought back. It wasn't until I put down the paper that I realized I hadn't even looked at the race results. Depression was coming down as surely as the Hawk—what people around here call the winter. They call it that because it kills. I had to get word to Immaculata that I was going to have the boy for her to interview. And after that, I had to wait.

I stopped at a light at the corner of the Bowery and Delancey. A big black guy with a dirty bandage over half his face offered to clean my windshield for a quarter. A used-up white woman with a cheap wig riding over her tired face offered to clean my tubes for ten bucks. I paid the black guy—V.D. isn't one of my hobbies.

The alley behind Mama's joint was empty, like it always is.

I slumped down at my table in the back, catching Mama's eye. One of the waiters came out of the kitchen with a tureen of soup. I waved him away—I wasn't hungry. He put the tureen down in front of me anyway. Bowed. If Mama told him to bring soup, he was bringing soup.

Mama came back in a few minutes, hands in the side pockets of her long dress. "You no serve soup?" she asked.

"I'm not hungry, Mama," I told her.

"Soup not for hunger. Not food—medicine, okay?" she said, sitting across from me. I watched her work the ladle, giving us each a generous helping. Women don't listen to me.

"I have to call Mac," I said.

"I do that. You want her to come here?"

I just nodded. "Good," said Mama. "I want to talk to baby."

"Mama, she won't have a baby for months yet."

"Too late—talk to baby now—prepare baby for everything, okay?"

"Whatever you say," I muttered. I wasn't in the mood for her voodoo that morning.

I ate my soup, keeping quiet as Mama loaded the bowl again,

smiling her approval. I lit a cigarette, looking at Mama. "You going to call Mac today?" I asked.

"Call soon," she said. "You get call here. Last night."

I looked at her, waiting. "Man say he has name for you. Say to call the Bronx."

The Mole. "Thanks, Mama," I threw over my shoulder, heading for the phones in the back. I dialed the junkyard—he picked up on the first ring.

"You have a name for me?"

"Yes."

"Can I come up?"

"I'll meet you. At the pad."

"When?"

"Day after tomorrow," the Mole said, and cut the connection.

I walked back inside the restaurant. The Mole would be at the helicopter pad just off the East Side Drive past Waterside Towers in two hours. With a name. It was a stupid place to meet, but there was no point arguing. The Mole loved helicopters.

Mama was still at the table. "I get Immaculata now?" she asked.

"Sure. Thanks, Mama."

"You feel better, Burke?"

"Yeah," I told her. And I did.

## 68

I WAS HALFWAY THROUGH a platter of roast duck, spare ribs, and fried rice when Immaculata came in. I got up from my seat, bowed to her, and indicated she should sit down and have something to eat. I was piling some of the fried rice onto her plate when Mama appeared over her shoulder. She shoved in next to Immaculata, pushing the plate away from her, barking something in Chinese. Another of the waiters came on the run. I don't know what Mama said to him, but he immediately started taking all the food off the table except for the plate in front of me. He was back in another minute, carrying a couple of plates with metal covers on top. Mama served Immaculata ceremoniously, arranging the food on her plate like an interior decorator.

"What was wrong with my food?" I asked her.

"Okay for you, Burke. You not mother, right?"

Immaculata smiled, not arguing. "Thank you, Mama," she said.

"Only eat best food now. For baby. To be strong, okay? No sugar, okay? Plenty milk."

I polished off the rest of my food, pushed the plate away, lit a cigarette.

"Smoke bad for baby too," Mama said, glaring at me.

"Mama," I told her, "the kid isn't here yet."

"Be here soon enough," Mama replied, "yes, baby?" she said, patting Immaculata's flat stomach.

I ground out the cigarette. "You think it will bother the baby if I *talk* to Mac?" I asked Mama.

"Talk in soft voice," Mama said. "And pay baby respect when you talk, okay?"

"What?"

"You talk to mother—first you tell baby hello, right? You finish talk, you tell baby goodbye. Very easy—even for you, Burke."

I rolled my eyes to the ceiling, looking back at Immaculata for sympathy. She looked back, her eyes clear. It apparently made sense to her too.

I bowed slightly to Mac. "Good morning, honorable infant," I said. "I have to speak to your beautiful mother, who is going to help me with something very important. You are the most fortunate of babies to have a mother and father so committed to you. I am certain you will have your mother's beauty and intelligence and your father's strength and courage. May all your days on this earth be blessed with love. I am Burke, your father's brother."

Mama nodded approval. Immaculata bowed slightly, the faintest of smiles playing about her lips.

"Mac, you know the kid I told you about? I figure he saw a lot of things when they took that picture of him. If you speak with him, maybe he'll tell you things he hasn't told anybody yet."

"He might," she said. "But it sometimes takes a while. The safer the child feels, the more he can tell us. His own therapist would be in the best position to get this information."

"He's not in therapy."

"Why is this?"

"His mother . . . other relatives . . . they feel the best thing is for him to forget it . . . go on with his life."

"That doesn't work," she said. "Kids who have been sexually abused have a lot of issues to work through. Guilt, fear, anger. Especially the anger. It's abusive not to give the child this opportunity."

I was thinking of prison again. If a kid was raped inside the walls, he had a shortage of choices: Keep on getting fucked by anyone who asked. Escape. Take a P.C. for the rest of his bit. Kill himself. Or kill the guy who did it to him. Only the last choice made any sense—the only way to get back to being treated like a human being. Instant therapy.

"Could you treat this kid?" I asked her.

"The interview you want me to do—that is the beginning of treatment. It would be unethical for me to simply work with the child to get some facts and then abandon him. It doesn't have to be me that works with him, but *someone* has to."

"I'll make that part of the deal," I told her. I glanced at my watch—time to get on the road and meet the Mole. "When can we do this?" I asked.

"Tomorrow afternoon I have some time free. Can you bring the child to SAFE around three o'clock?"

"Can we make it the day after, Mac? The kid's people need a day's notice."

"Okay. Thursday, then. But make it four instead."

"You got it." I stood up to leave, bowed to Mama and Mac. Mama's eyes were hard on me. "Goodbye, baby," I said to Mac's belly. "It has been a pleasure to be in your company once again."

Mama smiled. By the time I was halfway to the kitchen, she was deep into a discussion with Mac about cribs. I couldn't wait for Max to show up—Mama would probably want him to open a bank account for the kid's college education.

## 69

I TOOK THE EAST SIDE Drive to the 23rd Street exit, appreciating my cigarette even more than usual thanks to Mama's new edict. A guy on the radio was blubbering something about a political scandal in Queens—in the Parking Violations Bureau this time. Political corruption in New York isn't news, but they keep reporting it the same way they keep telling you the weather. People like to know about things they can't do anything about.

There's a big outdoor parking lot near the pad where the helicopters land and take off. The attendant was a ferret-faced little hustler. "You need a ticket, man?" he asked.

"I don't know," I said to him. "Do I?"

"Give me five and park it over there," he said, pointing to an empty corner of the lot. "Keep your keys." The sign on the lot said seven dollars for the first half-hour. A New York transaction—a little bit for you, a little bit for me, and fuck the guy who's not there when the deal is made.

I walked over to the edge of the helicopter pad. A blue-and-white copter sat there waiting for passengers—mostly tourists who wanted a different view of Manhattan than you get from the Circle Line boats which berthed on the West Side. I was into my second smoke when the Mole materialized from behind one of the cars. He was wearing a filthy white set of coveralls, with a tool belt around his waist, the usual satchel in his grubby paw. He didn't look dangerous.

"Mole," I said by way of greeting. When he didn't reply, I asked him, "You have that name and address for me?"

The Mole nodded his head in the direction of the highway, turned, and started to walk away. I followed him, wondering why he didn't want to talk by the launch pad. He led me to a South Bronx special—a battered old Ford, half primer and half rust, sagging on broken springs, no hubcaps, a hole already punched in its trunk from the last burglary attempt. The Mole climbed inside without unlocking the door. I followed him. He started the engine, put the car in gear, and pulled off.

"You think it's safe enough to give me that name now?" I asked.

"I have to go with you," he said.

"How come?"

"You can't hurt this person," the Mole said. "My friends, the ones who set this up—they make the rules. You can't hurt him. I have to go with you—make sure."

"Is he going to talk to me, Mole?"

"It is all arranged. He will talk to you, but only about his . . . thing, in general. You understand? Not about what *he* does, about what *they* do. 'Deep background,' my friends call it."

Great. "Can I threaten him?" I asked.

"He will know you can't hurt him. It won't do any good."

I lit another smoke, saying nothing. But the Mole read my thoughts. "You will know his address. He wanted the meeting to be where he lives. But if anything happens to him, my people will blame you. He is important to us."

"Slime like that is important?"

The Mole's eyes flashed behind his thick glasses. "We have a saying—the tree which bears fruit does not care about the fertilizer. And we must grow food in the desert. Okay?"

"Okay," I said. My one option.

The Mole drove the way he walked through his junkyard—like he wasn't paying attention, just blundering along. But he handled the Ford well, negotiating the traffic, paying no attention to the angry horns when he cut someone off, just being himself. We found a parking spot on 9th Street on the West Side. The Mole shut down the engine, looked over at me. "You have anything with you?" he asked.

"I'm clean," I told him.

"The cigarette lighter I made for you?"

I didn't say anything—he meant the throwaway butane lighter he had filled with napalm.

"Leave it here," the Mole said. I opened the glove compartment, tossed it inside.

"You going to leave your satchel in the car too?" I asked him. The Mole looked at me as if I should be on medication.

# 70

THE MOLE stopped in front of a limestone-front townhouse just off Fifth Avenue. It was three stories high, level with the rest of the buildings on the block. Maybe thirty-five feet wide. A seven-figure piece of property in that neighborhood. Four steps took us to a teak door, set behind a wrought-iron grating that looked custom-made. The Mole's stubby finger found the mother-of-pearl button, pushed it once.

We didn't have long to wait. The teak door opened—a man was standing there, waiting. You don't need a peephole when you have a couple of hundred pounds of iron between you and whoever's at the door. I couldn't see into the dark interior. The guy at the door was tall and slender, both hands in the pockets of what looked like a silk bathrobe.

"Yes?" he asked.

"Moishe," the Mole said.

"Please step back," said the man. He had a British accent.

The Mole and I went back to the sidewalk so the iron grate could swing out. We walked past the man inside, waited while he bolted the iron grate shut and closed the door. We were in a rectangular room, much longer than it was wide. The floor was highly polished dark wood, setting off overstuffed Victorian furniture, upholstered in a blue-and-white floral pattern. Only one light burned off to the side, flickering like it was gas instead of electricity.

"May I take your coats?" the man said, opening a closet just past the entranceway.

I shook my head "no"—the Mole wasn't wearing anything over his coveralls.

"Please . . ." the man said, languidly waving his hand to say we should go up the stairs before him. I went first, the Mole right behind me. We were breaking all the rules for this human.

"To your right," his voice came from behind me. I turned into a big room that looked smaller because it was so stuffed with things. A huge desk dominated the room, set on thick carved stubs at each corner. They looked like lion's paws. An Oriental rug covered most of the floor—it had a royal-blue background with a red-and-white design running from the center and blending into the borders. A fireplace was against one wall, birch logs crackling in a marble cage. The windows were covered with heavy velvet drapes the same royal blue as the rug. Everything was out of the past—except for a glowing video terminal on a butcher-block table parallel to the desk.

"Please sit anywhere," the man said, waving one arm to display the options in the room as he seated himself behind the big desk. I took a heavy armchair upholstered in dark tufted leather. A bronze-and-glass ashtray was on a metal stand next to the chair. The Mole stood near the door, his eyes sweeping the room. Then he sat on the floor, blocking the door with his bulk, putting his satchel on the ground. He looked from the man to where I was sitting, making it clear that we had an agreement. Then he pulled out a sheaf of papers and started to study some of his calculations—taking himself somewhere else.

"Now, then," said the man, folding his hands in front of him on the desk. "May I offer you some refreshment? Coffee? Some excellent sherry?"

I shook my head "no." The Mole never looked up.

"A beer perhaps?"

"No," I told him. I'd made a deal not to threaten him, but I didn't have to pretend I was his pal.

The man reached for a cut-glass decanter on his desk. Something that looked like a silver leaf dangled from just below the neck of the bottle, attached by a silver chain. He poured himself a wineglass of dark liquid from the bottle, held the glass up to the light from the fireplace, took a small sip. If he was any calmer he would have fallen asleep.

It was hard to make out his face in the dim light. I could see he was very thin, balding on top, with a thick pelt of dark hair around the sides of his head. Heavy eyebrows jutted from his skull, hooding his eyes. The face was wide at the top, narrowing down to a small chin—a triangular shape. His lips were thin—his fingers long and tapered, a faint sheen of clear polish on the nails.

"Now," he said, taking a sip from his glass, "how may I help you, Mr. . . . ?"

"I'm looking for a picture," I told him, ignoring the request for my name. "A picture of a kid."

"And you think I have this picture?" he asked, his heavy eyebrows lifting.

I shrugged. I should be so lucky. "Not necessarily. But I hope you can tell me about that kind of thing in general. Give me an idea where to look."

"I see. Tell me about this picture."

"A picture of a kid. Little chubby blond-haired boy. About six years old."

The man sat behind his desk, patiently waiting. I hadn't told him enough.

"A sex picture," I said.

"Um . . . " he mumbled. "Not such an unusual picture. Little boys in love do things like that."

Something burned inside my chest. I felt the Mole's eyes on me, got it under control, took another drag on the cigarette. "Who would have a picture like that?"

"Oh, just about *anyone*. It all depends on *why* the picture was taken."

"Why?"

The man made a tent of his fingers, his English accent making him sound like a teacher. "If the picture was taken by his mentor, then it wouldn't be circulated commercially, you understand?"

"His mentor?"

"A mentor, sir, is one who teaches you, guides you through life. Helps you with problems . . . that kind of thing."

I just looked at him, picturing a little dot of cancer inside his chest, keeping my hands still. I raised my own eyebrows—a question.

"Men who love boys are very special," the man said, his voice reverent. "As are the boys who love them. It is a most unique and special relationship. And very little understood by society."

"Tell me," I said, my voice flat.

"When a boy has a sexual preference for men, he is at grave risk. The world will not understand him—many doors will be closed to him. It is the task of a dedicated mentor to bring the tiny bud to full flower. To help nourish the growth of the boy into manhood."

"By taking pictures of the kid having sex?"

"Do not be so quick to judge, my friend. A true mentor would not take such a picture for commercial purposes, as I said before. The pictures are taken to preserve a unique and beautiful moment. Children grow up," he said, his voice laced with regret for the inevitable, "they lose their youth. Would not a loving parent take pictures of his child, to look upon in later years?"

I didn't answer him—I didn't know what loving parents did. Mine took a lot of pictures of me—they're called mug shots.

"It's capturing a moment in time," the man said. "It's a way of keeping perfect times always with you, even when the person is gone."

"You mean people . . . people like you . . . just want to *keep* the pictures? Not sell them or anything."

"People like me . . ." the man mused. "Do you know anything about 'people like me'?"

"No" I said. The deal was I couldn't hurt him—nobody said I had to tell him the truth.

"I am a pedophile," the man said. The same way an immigrant would one day say he was a citizen, pride and wonder at being so privileged blending in his voice. "My sexual orientation is toward children—young boys."

I watched him, waiting for the rest.

"I am *not* a 'child molester,' I am not a pervert. What I do is technically against your laws . . . as those laws now stand. But my relationship with my boys is pure and sweet. . . . I love boys who love me. Is anything wrong with that?"

I had no answer for him, so I lit another cigarette.

"Perhaps you think it's simple," he said, his thin mouth twisted in contempt for my lack of understanding. "I love boys—you probably assume I'm a homosexual, don't you?"

"No, I don't," I assured him. It was the truth—homosexuals were grown men who had sex with other grown men; some of them were standup guys, some of them were scumbags. Like the rest of us. This freak wasn't like the rest of us.

He watched my face, looking for a clue. "You believe my preferences to be unique? Let me say this to you: some of the highest-placed men in this city share my beliefs. Indeed, were it not for my knowledge of such things—of powerful men with powerful drive-forces in their lives—I would not have the protection of you people," he said, nodding his head in the Mole's direction.

The Mole looked straight at him, expressionless.

"Any boy I love . . . any boy who returns that love . . . benefits in ways you cannot understand. He grows to youth and then to manhood under my wing, if you will. He is educated, both intellectually and spiritually. Prepared for the world at large. To such a boy, I am a life-changing force, do you understand?"

"Yes," I said. It wasn't a lie this time.

"And I would . . . I *have* taken pictures of my boys. It gives us both pleasure in later years to look at this icon to our love, as it once was. A boy is a boy for such a short time," he said, sadness in his voice.

"And you wouldn't sell these pictures?"

"Certainly not. I have no need of money, but that is not the point. It would cheapen the love . . . almost immeasurably so. It would be a violation of the relationship . . . something I would never do."

"So nobody would ever see the pictures you have?" I asked him.

"Nobody outside my circle," he replied. "On some rare occasion, I might exchange pictures of my boys with others who share my preferences. But never for money."

"You mean you'd trade pictures? Like baseball cards?"

The man's eyes hooded again. "You have a crude way of putting things, sir. I know you do not mean to be offensive. . . ."

I nodded my head in agreement. I didn't want him to stop talking. The Mole's head was buried in his papers, but I could feel him telling me to watch my step.

"My boys *enjoy* knowing they give me pleasure. And it gives me pleasure to show their love for me to other men who believe as I do." He took another sip of his drink. "To be sure, there may be an element of egotism in exchanging photographs with others . . . I *am* proud of my success. But—and I'm sure you understand—one must be very discreet at all times."

I understood that all right . . . gave him another nod of agreement.

"There *are* those who produce pictures of children for purely commercial purposes. Not those who share my loves . . . my life style, if you will. But no true lover of boys would buy such pictures. They are so impersonal, so tasteless. One knows nothing of the boy in such a picture . . . not his name, his age, his little hobbies. Commercial photographs are so . . . *anonymous*. Sex is only a component of love. One brick in a foundation. Do you understand this?"

"I understand," I told him. It was true that the devil could quote the Scriptures, as the Prof was always saying. "Would a person ever destroy his pictures . . . like if he was afraid there was a search warrant coming down or something?"

"A true pedophile would never do that, my friend. I can assure you that, if the police were battering down my door at this very instant, I would not throw my memories into that fireplace."

"But the pictures are evidence. . . ."

"Yes. Evidence of *love*."

"People get convicted with evidence of love," I told him.

A smile played around his lips. "Prison is something we face all the time. A true believer in our way of life accepts this. Simply because something is against the law does not mean it is morally wrong."

"It's worth going to prison for?" I asked him.

"It's worth *anything*," he said.

"The people who . . . exchange . . . pictures of boys. You'd know how to get in touch with them?"

"We have a network," the man said. "A limited one, of course. You see the computer?" he asked, nodding his head toward the screen.

I nodded.

"The device next to it, with the telephone? It's called a modem. It's really quite complicated," the man said, "but we have something called an electronic bulletin board. You dial up the network, punch in the codes, and we can talk to each other without revealing our names."

I gave him a blank look.

"As I said, it's really quite complicated," he said smugly. I could feel the Mole's sneer clear across the room.

"Can you show me?" I asked.

"Very well," he sighed. He got up from behind the desk, bringing his glass with him. The man seated himself before the computer. He took the phone off the hook and placed it face down into a plastic bed. He punched some numbers into a keypad and waited impatiently, tapping his long fingers on the console. When the screen cleared, he rapidly tapped something on the keyboard—his password. "Greetings from Santa" came up on the screen in response, black letters against a white background.

"Santa is one of us," the man said, by way of explanation.

He typed in "Have you any new presents for us?" The man hit another key and his message disappeared.

In another minute, the screen blinked and a message from Santa came up. "Seven bags full," said the screen.

"His new boy is seven years old," said the man. "Are you following this?"

"Yes," I told him. Santa Claus.

The man went back to the screen. "This is Tutor. Do you think it's too early in the year to think about exchanging gifts?"

"Not gifts of love," came back the answer.

The man looked over his shoulder at me. I nodded again. Clear enough.

"Later," the man typed into the screen. He pushed a button and the screen cleared once more. He returned to his seat behind the desk. "Anything else?" he asked.

"If the boy's picture . . . the one I want . . . was taken for sale . . . not by a pedophile . . . I couldn't find it?"

"Not in a million years," the man said. "The commercial pictures . . . they sell them to just *anybody*. Besides, those pictures are not true originals, you see? They make hundreds and hundreds of copies. The only way to find an original is if it was in a private collection."

"Say I didn't give a damn if the picture was an original, okay? If I showed you a picture of the boy, would you ask around . . . see if you could find the picture I'm looking for?"

"No," he said. "I would never betray the trust of my friends." He looked at the Mole for reassurance. The Mole looked back, giving nothing away.

"And you don't deal with any of the commercial outlets?"

"Certainly not," he sniffed.

This freak couldn't help me. "I understand," I said, getting up to leave.

The man looked at me levelly. "You may show yourselves out."

The Mole lumbered to his feet, standing in the doorway to make sure I went out first.

"One more thing," the man said to me. "I sincerely hope you learned something here. I hope you learned some tolerance for our reality. Some respect for our love. I trust we can find *some* basis for agreement."

I didn't move, willing my hands not to clench into fists.

"I am a believer," the man said, "and I am ready to die for my beliefs."

"There's our basis for agreement," I told him, and turned my back to follow the Mole down the stairs.

# 71

I STOPPED AT A pay phone off the Drive to call Strega—tell her I would need the boy for the day after tomorrow. Her line was busy. I lit a smoke, took a couple of drags, and dialed her number again. She picked up on the first ring.

"Yes," she breathed into the receiver, her voice as hard and seamless as her body.

"It's me," I said. "Thursday afternoon, okay? Like we agreed? Bring him to the parking lot across from the courthouse in Manhattan, where we met the first time."

"What time?"

"Four o'clock. If the lot's too crowded, I'll be standing in front of the Family Court. The dark-gray building on Lafayette. You know what I'm talking about?"

"Make sure he understands that it's okay to be with me."

"He'll be all right," she said, in a mechanical tone.

"See you then," I said, getting ready to put the receiver back in its cradle.

"That's for then," Strega said. "What about tonight?"

"It's too soon. I need time to set this up."

"What about me?"

"What *about* you?"

"I'm here by myself tonight. All alone with myself. You want to come over and talk to me?"

"I can't come over. . . . I'm working."

"Maybe you just want to *come*," she whispered into the phone, playing with the last word. I could see the sneer on her painted lips, glowing in a dark room.

"Some other time," I told her.

"You can never be sure," said Strega. I heard the phone slam down at her end.

I headed back to the office, wondering where her sacred child was all the time.

# 72

I SPENT THE NEXT day taking care of business. American Express was threatening to sever the line of credit I maintain in several names unless they got some prompt payments. There's only one way to respond to such a legitimate request—I typed out some new applications, checking my list to make sure I didn't duplicate any of the old names. Then I placed some ads—my new mail-order company was offering the latest version of the Navy Seal Survival Knife for only twenty-five bucks. No CODs. My company doesn't take checks either—too many dishonest people out there. I checked my file of birth certificates for people who died within a year of their birth. I had some of them apply for Social Security numbers, others for driver's licenses. When I got back the paper, I'd move it into various productive activities—passports, disability payments, unemployment benefits. As long as you don't get too greedy, it goes on forever.

Finally, I checked my rent roll. I have a few apartments around the city—when a tenant in a rent-controlled building dies, the super calls me, money changes hands, and I'm the new tenant. Then I sublet the apartments to yuppies happy to pay several times the base rent, positive they're beating the system. Michelle works the phones for me. I split the rent each month with the super and everybody's happy. Sooner or later the landlord finds out what's going down and moves to evict the tenant. Then the yuppies are on their own. I don't collect any more rent from them. I don't return their security deposits either.

I took Pansy down to the piers on the Hudson, working her off-leash obedience to keep her tuned. Then I took her with me to Pop's poolroom, letting her watch in baleful disapproval as I dropped fifty bucks at the table in the back. The one right under the "No Gambling" sign.

Killing time. It's a lot easier when you're not in a cell.

# 73

AT FOUR O'CLOCK the next afternoon, I parked the Lincoln in the courthouse lot. Immaculata was next to me on the front seat, Max lying down in the back, hands clasped behind his head, staring at nothing.

"You want to go over it one more time?" I asked Mac.

"It's not necessary, Burke. I know what you want. But it's like I told you—disclosures often come slowly. I can't promise you the child will tell me everything on a first interview."

"How long does it take?"

"It depends on the child . . . and the extent of the trauma. Some children never tell the whole thing."

"Can't you put some pressure on him?"

Mac's eyes narrowed. "Of course I could do that. But I won't. That's not the way we work. This first interview—the one where we validate that the child has been sexually abused—it's not just to gain information—it's part of a process. The real goal is to treat the child."

"Yeah, okay," I said, lighting a cigarette.

"That is what we agreed," Mac said, tapping her long nails on the dash. She wasn't going to discuss it anymore.

"You told Max what he has to do?" I asked her.

Immaculata smiled. "He knew," she said.

The courthouse parking lot doesn't discriminate. Porsches stood next to Chevies—a limo took two spaces. So did a gypsy cab.

A Spanish guy walked by my open window. "Smoke?" he asked, looking past me. I didn't reply and he moved on, working the parking lot. If you had the cash, you could buy just about anything around the courthouse.

Immaculata and I got out of the Lincoln and walked over to the Family Court. A steady stream of humans walked out of the revolving doors—a fat Puerto Rican woman with tired eyes came out with a kid who looked about twelve years old, sporting a gang jacket and a black beret on his head. "You hear what the judge told you?" she said. "Fuck the judge," the boy replied, neatly dodging her feeble attempt to slap him, smiling a kid's smile. A guy dressed in a phone-company uniform was pulling at his lawyer's arm, mumbling something about "another goddamned adjournment." The lawyer shrugged. Another guy stormed out the front, a woman trailing him by a couple of feet, tentatively reaching out to touch his arm. He was slamming a clenched fist in his palm over and over, looking down.

I was watching for Strega's little BMW, so I didn't pay any attention to the beige Mercedes cruising back and forth through the parking lot until I heard the door slam. She was standing across the street, a black kerchief on her head, wearing a full-length black coat. She looked about sixteen years old. Her arms were extended to each side, a child holding each hand. A boy and a girl. She bent to say something to the little girl. The child waved merrily at me and they started to cross.

It wasn't that cold on the streets, but Strega's cheeks were flushed and glowing. "Hi!" she called out in a voice I hadn't heard before, holding out a gloved hand to me. I took it—she squeezed down hard.

"This is Scotty," she said, pulling a round-faced little blond boy close to her side. "And this is my Mia." She smiled. The little girl was wearing a black coat and scarf like her mother. Flaming red hair peeked out, a halo for a happy little face.

"What's your name?" she asked me.

"Burke," I told her.

"That's a funny name," she said, still smiling.

"So is Mia," I replied.

"It's a *special* name," the little girl said, a trace of a pout on her lips.

"It's a lovely name," said Immaculata, stepping forward.

"This is my friend, Immaculata," I told them all, spreading my hands to introduce her.

Immaculata gracefully dropped to her haunches, her eyes level with the children's faces.

"Hi, Scotty. Hi, Mia," she said to them, holding out her hands. Mia took her hand right away, babbling on like they were old friends. Scotty hung back. "It's okay," said Strega. He came slowly to Immaculata. "You smell good," he said.

Strega's eyes lashed at me. "This is your *friend?*"

"Immaculata is going to work with Scotty. Like we agreed," I said, nothing else in my voice.

Her big eyes never shifted. "I'm trusting you," she said.

I met her gaze. Our faces were a hundred miles above Immaculata and the children. "You got any time problems?"

"Just tell me where to meet you.

"How about right back here. About seven-thirty, eight o'clock?"

"Whatever you say."

I lit a cigarette while Strega patted Scotty on the head, telling him he was going with me and Immaculata and that she'd meet him later with Mia. They'd all go to McDonald's and then for ice cream.

"Okay, Zia Peppina," the boy said, holding Immaculata's hand. His eyes were still cloudy with worry but he was going to stand up.

"Say your name again," Mia asked Immaculata.

"It is Im-mac-u-lata," she said, "but my friends call me Mac."

"That's easier," said Mia.

"It is always easier to be friends," Mac told her gravely.

"I know," said the child.

It was time to go. "It was a pleasure to meet you," Strega said to Immaculata.

"And to meet you as well," Mac told her, bowing slightly. "You have a beautiful and charming daughter."

Strega's eyes lit up at this. She bowed back to Immaculata before she realized what she was doing. Mac had that effect on people.

"Let's go, Scotty!" Immaculata said, taking the boy's hand and starting across the street to the Lincoln.

"Are you Mommy's friend?" Mia asked me.

"What did your mother tell you?" I replied.

"She said you were."

"Does your mother ever lie to you?"

"Oh, no," said the child, her mouth rounded in an O of surprise.

"Then you know," I told her. I held out my hand to Strega again. She smiled at me, trying to crush my fingers into Jell-O. "Bye-bye," she said, turning her back on me, Mia in tow.

I lit a cigarette, watching the two little girls in their black coats cross the street to their Mercedes. Then I started across myself.

## 74

WHEN I GOT TO the Lincoln, Scotty was standing on the front seat looking at Max seated in the back. "Do it again!" he yelled, clapping his chubby little hands.

"Do *what* again?" I asked him, sliding behind the wheel.

"Max is a *protector*," Scotty said. "He's here to make me safe."

"That's right," I told him, watching Immaculata nod in approval.

"Max is the strongest man in the whole world!" Scotty practically shouted at me. "Do it again. *Please!*" he shouted at Max. I don't know what kind of father Max might be, but he sure as hell wouldn't get disturbed by the noise kids make.

Scotty was waving an old iron horseshoe in one hand. Max reached over the seat and took it from him. The Mongol held one end in each hand, breathed deeply through his nose with a clean, whistling sound, and pulled the horseshoe apart until it was just a straight piece of metal. He bowed his head, handed it back to the child.

"See?" Scotty asked.

"That's amazing," I told him.

"Max could lift this whole *car* if he wanted to, couldn't you, Max?" he said.

Max pressed his fingertips together, shooting his biceps full of the blood. The muscles leaped in his arms, more than a match for the thin casing of skin around them. Max pulled his hands to his chest, as if he was rocking a baby. He smiled. Then he flexed a bicep in a bodybuilder's pose, a vain look on his face. He shook his head "no."

"What is he saying?" Scott asked Immaculata.

"He is saying that great strength is only for protecting people, not for showing off."

"Oh." The kid thought for a minute. "Then why did he bend the horseshoe?" Whatever else they had done to Scotty, they hadn't made him stupid.

"Remember I told you that Max would be your protector?" Immaculata said, and watched the boy's solemn nod. "Well, I had to show you that Max was a *good* protector. We are friends, you and me. But you shouldn't trust new friends until they prove they are telling you the truth. Isn't that right?"

"Yes . . ." he said, a sad look on his face.

"I know," Immaculata said, patting his shoulders. "You are safe now. We're going to make it all better. Okay?"

The boy nodded dubiously. Max put his huge, scarred hand on the boy's shoulder. Just letting it lay there. And Scotty smiled as we drove through the city to the place on Broadway where we'd make it all better.

# 75

SAFE WAS IN THE VILLAGE, not far from the courthouse. I found a parking spot a few doors down and we all got out together, Immaculata leading the way, holding Scotty's hand. A tall black man was seated at a desk just inside the double glass doors. He got to his feet when he saw Max and me come in behind Immaculata. "They're with me," she said, smiling. The black guy sat down again.

We walked up a long flight of stairs to what must have been a factory loft years ago. A huge room, maybe forty by a hundred feet. Gym mats in the corner. A bunch of little kids working out, practicing some form of karate, screaming their lungs out with every move. Even younger kids were playing in a sandbox at one end of the room. Some were doing finger painting. One little boy was knitting something. It seemed like hundreds of kids, all hyperactive. Sounded like a happy subway tunnel.

A young woman detached herself from one of the groups of kids and walked over to us. She was maybe five feet tall with short dark hair flying around her face as she came over. Another pretty Italian lady—the other side of Strega's coin.

"Boss lady," Immaculata whispered to me. "Lily."

"Hi, Mac," the woman said. "And you must be Scotty," she said to the boy, coming down on her haunches the way Immaculata had in front of the Family Court. "My name is Lily," she said, holding out both hands. Scotty took her hands, but his eyes were riveted to the other kids. "You can play with the other kids later," Lily said, reading his mind. "First we're going to go to a special playroom. You have a *reservation.*" She made it like a big deal, and Scotty responded, feeling important.

She took Scotty by one hand. Immaculata took the other. On the way down the hall to the back office the two women lifted Scotty off his feet, swinging their arms. The kid giggled like he'd found heaven.

We turned into a small room stuffed full of kids' stuff—toy animals, a three-panel screen with puppies playing on its surface, dolls, coloring books. All the furniture was child-size.

"This is where you and Immaculata get to talk," Lily told Scotty.

"About the bad things?" he asked.

"If you want to, Scotty. We don't make you do anything you don't want to here, okay?"

He just nodded, subdued now.

"You go inside with Immaculata, and we'll all wait for you out here, okay?"

"Max too!" the boy said, tugging the Mongol forward.

Max picked the boy up by his belt and tossed him in the air. Scotty screamed in delight, never doubting for a minute that Max would catch him. Max caught the boy in his arms and carried him inside. Immaculata bowed to Lily and me and followed, closing the door behind her.

There was a long window in one wall. I could see the three of them inside. Scotty was sitting on Max's lap, Immaculata talking to him.

"One-way glass?" I asked Lily.

"Yes," she said. "We have graduate students observing all the time."

"You videotape the interviews?"

"We don't have the facilities to conceal the cameras here. And many of our children are phobic for video. You understand?"

"Sure," I told her. Kids who had been stars in porno movies could freak out if they saw a camera.

The boy was drawing something, holding the picture up for Immaculata and Max to see every couple of seconds.

"My name is Burke," I told her.

"I know who you are," she said, mixed feelings running through her words.

"You have a problem with me?"

She gave it some thought, looking directly into my eyes. "No . . . not a problem. In fact, a couple of our older girls said you pulled them off the streets. And McGowan says you're okay too."

"So?"

"Mr. Burke, when we work with children at SAFE we don't edit their disclosures."

I stood there, watching Scotty make word pictures with his hands for Max. Max's arms were folded on his chest, his eyes slitted in concentration. I was waiting for this woman to tell me what her beef was.

"You know a girl named Babette?"

I nodded. I was in a mess a few months ago and she ended up going off with McGowan. I guess she landed at SAFE. It was fucking sure she couldn't go back to the stepfather who paid me to find her.

"In group one day Babette told us how she happened to get free of her pimp," Lily said. "She said you shot the man."

"I thought he was reaching for a gun," I said lamely.

"Babette said your gun didn't make any noise," Lily told me, eyes level.

I didn't say anything. If I hadn't had the silencer, it might have been some uniformed cop coming to that hotel room instead of McGowan. Shooting a pimp should only be a petty misdemeanor anyway—like hunting without a license.

"Don't worry," she said. "Nobody's going to testify against you."

"I'm not worried," I told her. The Prof had visited the pimp in the hospital—given him the word.

"We don't allow guns at SAFE," Lily said, watching me.

"You want to search me," I grinned at her, opening my coat.

"No. I want your word."

"You got it."

We both turned back to the window. Scotty had his hands on his hips and was shouting something at Immaculata. Suddenly he struck out; his little fist pounded on her shoulder. Max didn't move.

"It's okay," Lily said. "It's probably a re-enactment."

I looked a question at her. "When the child relives the experience . . . some of them find it easier than talking about it at first. Or maybe he's already past it . . . maybe he told the secret. . . . Some of our kids fly into a rage when the truth is out . . . they have so much anger."

"So why's he hitting on Immaculata?"

"We encourage them to do it. At first. Then they progress to the self-defense classes. It all has to come out—first the secrets, then the anger."

"The secret is what happened to them—what people did to them?"

"No. That's what they call the 'bad stuff' or the 'scary stuff.' The secret is that the offender told them never to tell anybody about what happened. They usually make it so that if the child tells, something horrible will happen."

"To the kid?"

"Usually not. To their parent, or a puppy . . . even to some character on TV the child loves."

"The kid believes it?" I asked. When I was Scotty's age, I didn't believe anything.

"Of course. The offender is all-powerful. He can do anything. And the secret is helped by the guilt too."

"Why should a kid feel guilty if somebody did that to him?"

"Because they *like* some of it . . . it arouses new feelings in them. And, for some of them, they believe the person who is doing these things actually loves them. A parent will tell a child that if the secret comes out the parent may go to jail . . . and it will be the child's fault. You see?"

"Yeah, they make the kid take the weight."

Scotty was crying, his face buried in his hands. Immaculata was bending over him, talking to him, patting his back.

"You know a D.A. named Wolfe? With the City-Wide Special Victims Bureau?"

"Sure," said Lily. "She's the best. I do a lot of work for her office."

"You think you might be willing to put in a good word for me?"

"Are you looking for a job as an investigator?"

"No. I just want to talk with her about this case, maybe get some help. And I don't know too many people on her side of the fence."

"I could tell her what I know about you—that's all."

"Hey!" I said. "I brought the kid out safely, didn't I?"

"Yes, you did. Your methods left a bit to be desired, didn't they?"

"I don't know," I told her. "Why don't you ask Babette?"

Lily smiled. "I'll talk to Wolfe," she said, and we shook hands.

Scotty wasn t crying anymore. His tear-streaked face was turned to Max, his little hands flying. Max took some picture from Scotty's hands—it looked like crayon scribbles to me. Then he pulled the round wooden top off one of the tables, held it so the edge was facing the floor, and wedged it into a corner of the room. Max tested it with his hands to be sure it was solid. He wet his thumb and pasted the picture against the round surface. He bowed to Scotty, spun his wrists so the palms were facing outward, and flicked his fingers to his side. Telling them to stand back.

Lily was standing next to me at the window. "I never saw this one before," she said.

Max glided forward onto his left foot, twisting as it hit the ground. His right foot came around in a blur, shattering the wooden table like it was glass. He walked to the corner, pulled Scotty's drawing out of the wreckage, and turned to face the boy. Max tore the picture in half, throwing a piece to each side like it was garbage. The little boy's smile was wider than his face.

The door opened. Max stepped out first. He rubbed two fingers and a thumb together, pointing at me. "How much for the table?" I asked Lily.

"It's on the house," she said, a smile on her face too.

Immaculata came out with Scotty holding her hand. "I got the bad stuff out," he told Lily proudly.

"That's wonderful!" she said. "Would you like to play with the other children outside while we talk?"

"Can Max come?" Scotty asked.

Nobody answered him. "Come *on*, Max," he said, tugging at the Mongol's hand.

Immaculata nodded almost imperceptibly. Max and Scotty walked down the hall together to play.

## 76

LILY TOOK US TO her office, at the end of the corridor. It looked like a kid's playroom except for the computer screen on the desk. I looked at the keyboard—there was no lock-out device. "How do you keep someone from getting into your records?" I asked her.

She laughed, tapping some keys. "Want to play a fast game of Zork before we get down to business?" The screen had some kind of mazes-and-monsters game on it.

"That's all you have it for?"

"Sure," she said, looking at Immaculata as if I was an idiot.

I lit a cigarette, looking around for an ashtray. "Use this," Lily said, handing me an empty water glass.

Immaculata sat behind the desk; Lily perched on a corner. I stood against the wall and listened.

"Scotty was going to a day-care center every day after school. He'd get there around one in the afternoon and his mother would pick him up when she got out of work. Around six o'clock. One day a woman came to the center. Scotty said she was an 'old lady,' but that could mean anyone older than his mother. She had a van and a driver—a big, fat man with a beard. She told the kids she was going to take them to see the clowns and who wanted to go? Scotty went with some other kids. It took what he said was 'a long, long time' to get there. A big house with a high fence around it. There was a clown there—a big, fat clown, like the driver. His face was all made up like a clown, and he had presents for all the kids. The clown and the old lady took Scotty out of the group where he was playing with the other kids. They took him into the basement, where they had a puppy. They told him he could have the puppy if he would be a 'good little scout.'

"To be a good scout you have to take your pants off. They let him keep his shirt on. It was red and black stripes. He has it in his closet at home," Mac said, answering one of the questions I'd told her to ask.

"The clown took off his pants too. His penis was very large. It scared the boy. They asked him if he wanted ice cream. They rubbed some on the clown's penis and told Scotty to lick it off. He started to cry. The old lady told him if he didn't do what he was told, they would hurt the puppy. He still refused. The clown strangled the puppy in front of him. Scotty didn't want to watch but he had to. He has bad dreams about the puppy. He's always scared."

The cigarette burned into my fingers. I threw it on the floor, stepped on it. Immaculata's face was closed—a soldier doing her job.

"The man put his penis in Scotty's mouth—told him to suck very hard. The woman took a picture with a Polaroid and a flash. White stuff came out. Scotty cried. The old woman told him if he ever told anyone about this his mother would get very sick and die. They took him back upstairs and put him into the van with the other kids. The other kids all had a great time."

"How does he know it was a Polaroid?" I asked.

"He doesn't know the name, but he said a camera where the picture comes out the front."

"Did he see the picture?"

"I think so. At least the fact that there *was* a picture." She took a breath. "Scotty never told anybody—he was scared something would happen. But his mother took him to a therapist, and he told the therapist about bad dreams. That's all. He was afraid of the therapist—he had a beard like the big, fat clown.

"Later he told some of it to the redheaded woman who brought him to the parking lot today—he calls her 'Zia.' He told her that the old lady came to the day-care center with a big, strong man who had a leather bag. The man took money from the leather bag and gave it to the lady who runs the day-care center. And there was some strange mark on the big man's hand. That's it," she said.

"He's going to need help with the dreams," Lily said.

"I know," Immaculata replied.

"He's not still afraid of anything happening to his mother?" I asked her.

"No," she said, smiling faintly, "Max told Scotty he would guard his mother."

"What was that bit with the table, Mac?" Lily wanted to know.

"Scotty drew a picture of the big, fat clown. Max told him he was going to find the clown and break him in little pieces. He was showing Scotty what he meant."

I lit another cigarette. "Does he have any idea at all where the big house is? You think he could find it if we went over the route?"

"Not a chance," Mac said. "He wasn't paying attention on the drive out there—and he was too scared on the way back to the center."

"If this woman is running a big operation, maybe Wolfe would know about her," I said, looking at Lily.

"I'll talk to her," Lily replied.

I felt a tap on my shoulder. Max. He held one hand to his eye, tapped his finger against the hand. Taking a picture. He pointed at me, made binoculars of his fists around his eyes.

"Yeah, I'm looking for that picture," I told him.

Max tapped his chest, dealing himself in.

We all left the office together to pick up the boy.

## 77

SCOTTY WAS IN THE middle of a group of kids, all trying to push a giant beach ball in different directions. "We have to go?" he asked Immaculata. Not so happy about it.

"We'll come back, Scotty. And we'll play some more and talk some more, okay?"

"And Max too?" the kid demanded.

Immaculata took his hand. "Max has to work sometimes, Scotty. But he's never too far away. And his work is very important."

"Like watching Mommy?"

"Yes, like that. Okay?"

Scotty smiled. Max smiled too—the way an undertaker does. The boy waved goodbye to his new friends. Lily gave him a hug. And we were out the door.

Scotty was cheerful on the drive back. It was almost eight by the time I pulled up right in front of the Family Court. The Mercedes was sitting there, smoke coming from its exhaust. The driver's door popped open and Strega climbed out, Mia in tow. I got out too, halfway between the cars.

"I have to talk to you for a minute," I said.

"Mia, take Scotty and wait in the car, okay, sweetheart? Mommy will be there soon."

The little girl looked at me. "You're not handsome," she said solemnly. "My daddy is very handsome."

"Good," I said.

"In the car, Mia," Strega told her. She took Scotty's hand and went off. Immaculata stayed in the Lincoln, looking straight ahead.

"What happened?" the redhead asked.

"It went well," I told her, picking my words carefully. "We got a lot of information. But the more he gets comfortable with these people, the more we find out, understand? He needs to come back, like once a week for the next few weeks at least."

"Not for therapy?" she asked, a warning note in her voice.

"For information," I told her, lying as smoothly as the rug on that pedophile's floor. "If you want the picture . . ."

"You got it," she snapped. "I want to talk to her"—pointing to the car.

I waved Immaculata over—no point in Strega seeing Max.

They didn't greet each other this time. "Is Scotty going to be all right?" Strega asked.

"In time, yes. He had an ugly experience. It's a process. You *are* going to bring him back?"

"Once a week, right?"

"Yes." Immaculata watched Strega's face, making up her mind about something. "You should not attempt to debrief this child," she said, her voice clear as crystal and just as hard.

"Debrief?"

"Ask him what he said, what we talked about. He will not want to do this now. In his own time, it will come. If you put pressure on the child now, you will set back his progress, yes?"

"If you say so," said Strega.

"I *do* say so. It is very important. Scotty is a strong child, but this whole thing was a severe trauma. You, as his mother . . ."

"I'm not his mother," Strega snapped.

"This is his aunt," I said to Immaculata. "Zia."

Immaculata smiled. "You must be very close with this little boy for him to have told you what he did. He loves you and he trusts you. When the time comes, we will need you to help us with the last stages of the healing. Will you do that?"

"I'll do whatever Scotty needs done," Strega said, a faint smile touching her lips. Responding to praise just like a kid.

I took Immaculata's arm to go back to our car. Strega plucked at Mac's sleeve.

"Is Burke your boyfriend?" she asked.

Immaculata smiled—a beautiful thing to see. "Good God, no," she said, and bowed to Strega.

We watched as the redhead climbed in her Mercedes and drove sedately off.

# 78

I LET IMMACULATA AND Max off at the warehouse and drove back uptown looking for Michelle. She wasn't working any of her usual stands. The Prof was off the streets too. Like a hard wind was coming down and they had enough sense to get out of the way.

I thought about catching some of the later races up in Yonkers, but the thought slid by. The digital clock on the Lincoln's dash said it was ten-fifteen—a couple of hours gone. I thought about Flood—like biting into your own lip to make sure your teeth are working. When I started to think about calling Strega, I realized I had to talk to someone.

Dr. Pablo Cintrone's clinic would be open until at least midnight. Pablo is a Harvard-educated psychiatrist, a Puerto Rican who battled his way through the stone walls of prejudice circling the miserable slum that liberals love to call *el barrio*. He is a man without illusions—the pieces of paper he got from Harvard would fly him out of the neighborhood, but he'd have to make the trip alone. The people in his community call him *"el doctor"* in reverent tones. And if they know he runs an organization called Una Gente Libre they don't discuss it with the law.

Una Gente Libre—A Free People—a very low-profile group as terrorists go. They didn't pull armored-car robberies, no bank jobs, no bullshit "communiqués" to the newspapers. UGL wasn't interested in symbolic bombings or ego politics either. What they did best was take people out—simple, direct homicides—no "trademark" assassinations, no revolutionary slogans left at the scene. Somehow, people always knew when it was a UGL hit, though the *federales* were never sure. They knew the group existed, but they could never get inside. Without informants, they couldn't catch Jesse James if he was still doing trains on horseback.

A few years ago a suspected UGL triggerman was busted for blowing away a dope dealer who took his business too near an elementary school. The *federales* offered him pure immunity—a walk-away if he'd testify about the organization. No sale.

The gunman's trial was no revolutionary showcase—very straightforward. He pleaded "not guilty," claimed the dealer had a gun too and was beaten to the draw. Pablo was just one of a dozen character witnesses, all neatly dressed, solid citizens. No revolutionary slogans, no picketing, no clenched fists in the air.

The defense attorney was good—a hard piece of work. A heavy-set, bearded guy from midtown, he pounded away at what a slime-ball the dead dealer had been, never compromising, fighting the prosecutor and the judge every step of the way. The gunman was tried for murder—the jury was out three days and finally came back with manslaughter. The judge gave the gunman five to fifteen.

Everybody walked over to congratulate the defense attorney. He'd done a hell of a job to pull this one out—if the gunman fell for murder, he was looking at twenty-five to life. The lawyer sat at the counsel table, tears in his eyes, bitter that he hadn't won the whole thing. Not too many lawyers like that left, and they're worth whatever they cost.

The gunman went upstate and did some *good* time—a man of respect. He never had a blank visiting day, his commissary account was always full to the brim. And his wife hit *bolita*—the Spanish numbers game—for a big piece of change. Just lucky, I guess, but it took good care of his family while he was down.

When he hit the bricks, they threw a block party for him that lasted four days. He's still on parole, a driver for the ambulance service that works out of Pablo's clinic. To the cops, he's another ex-con. To his people, he's a POW returned to his home country.

If it was business, I would have called first. From a safe phone. But I just wanted to talk. I pulled the Lincoln into the empty space that's always in front of the clinic. Before I could even turn off the ignition there was a tap on the window. The glass whispered down into the door with a push of the little button. The guy tapping on the window wasn't too tall, but his width matched his height. A head the size of a basketball grew out of massive shoulders without benefit of a neck. Half his face was covered with old razor scars surrounding a glass eye—and that was his good side. The guy was ugly enough to need an exorcist.

"No parking here, *hombre*," he snarled.

"I'm here to see Pablo . . . *el doctor?*"

"Who you?"

"Burke," I said.

The monster held out his hand, palm up. I pulled the keys from the ignition and handed them over. He growled something and left.

He was back in a couple of minutes, his lips twisted in what he probably thought was a smile—his teeth were broken stumps. He jerked a thumb in a hitchhiker's gesture. I climbed out of the Lincoln. A young guy in a bright-red shirt worn outside his pants came up. The monster handed him the keys and the young guy climbed inside. They'd leave the Lincoln someplace—I could pick it up when I left. UGL's version of valet parking.

The monster gently shoved me ahead of him, guiding me through the maze of cubicles inside the clinic. A Spanish woman in a white nurse's uniform sat at the reception desk, the hard lines in her face the price of survival, not marring her beauty. The monster nodded to her as he prodded me forward, paying no attention to the activity around him. Phones rang, people yelled at each other, doors slammed. The people in the waiting room looked subdued, but not dead the way they do in the city hospitals.

Pablo's office was all the way in the rear. He was typing something on an ancient IBM when we came in. His eyes sparkled behind the round glasses he wore as he jumped to his feet to greet me. Pablo's got to be damn near as old as I am, but he looks like a young man. With his clear brown skin and neatly cropped hair he could get by any Puerto Rican mother in the world. He has four children that I know about and he's financed more abortions than Planned Parenthood.

"*Hermano!*" he shouted, grabbing my right hand in both of his, then embracing me in a hug.

The monster smiled again. "*Gracias, chico,*" Pablo said, and the monster threw a salute and went back outside.

"I got to talk to you, Pablito," I told my brother.

"Not business?"

"Just in my head," I said.

Pablo pointed to a couch in a corner of his office, sitting back down behind his desk.

"Tell me," he said.

## 79

RED NEON FROM THE bar next door to the clinic banked its ugly light against the window behind Pablo's desk. It was a mark of pride for the clinic that no bars were on the windows.

"It started with a picture," I began.

Pablo looked a question at me.

"Kiddie porn," I answered.

Not all psychiatrists practice with poker faces—violence danced a storm in Pablo's eyes.

"Yeah," I said. "Like that. A little boy, six years old. They used him only the one time, but he knows they took the picture and it works on his mind."

"You took him to that place downtown . . . SAFE?"

"Sure. And he's going to get better—they know what they're doing. But it'll never really be square in the kid's mind—like they have a piece of his soul, you know?"

Pablo nodded patiently.

"Anyway, I'm looking for this picture, right? And I come across this freak. A collector. I figure I'll ask him what makes him tick—get a line on who might have the picture I'm looking for."

"He spoke freely with you?"

"Oh, yeah. He's protected—they had a guard in the room with me—I don't even know his name."

"Too bad," said Pablo.

"His time is coming," I said. "From the people who are protecting him now. But that's not the thing—he tells me he's going to keep doing what he does. Forever. It's what he *wants* to do. He says he loves the kids."

"And you don't understand?"

"Do you?"

"Yes . . . but what I understand is the rationalization, not the drive. The medical profession knows a good deal about the workings of the human body, but the study of the mind is essentially political."

I raised my eyebrows—Pablo thinks "No Parking" signs are political.

"It is true, *hermano*. We no longer treat physical diseases with leeches, but we still treat mental disorders as though they exist in a vacuum. This is not logical, but it is comforting to the citizens. If we say that mental illness is biochemical, then people believe that the correct medication is the answer to all questions."

"Like methadone?"

"Sure. You understand. Of course, heroin addiction is a product of many, many things . . . but heroin was first really introduced into this country by the United States government. After World War I, too many of our soldiers returned addicted to morphine. Heroin was the wonder drug that would make them all well again."

"It sure raised hell with the fighting gangs," I said.

"You remember the heroin monster, sweeping through our communities, turning young people into zombies? This was because the street gangs had begun to reach a kind of political awareness."

"Some political awareness," I said. "I came up in the fifties—all we ever wanted to do was keep other clubs off our turf, drink a little wine, play with the girls. Nobody even mentioned politics."

"Not then," Pablo said, "but soon after. The fighting gangs were in every part of the city. Independent units, yes? If they had ever *combined* . . ."

"Not a chance," I told him. "I don't think I ever knew a word for a black guy except 'nigger' until I was out of reform school."

"Racism is like heroin, Burke—it divides people from their true needs—it pacifies them with promises of foolishness."

I held up a hand like a traffic cop. "Hold it, brother. You're going too fast for me. What's this got to do with a baby-raper?"

"It's the same thing. Politics controls the reality which is presented to the public. Look, Freud taught that sex between children and adults was simply a fantasy—something in the minds of the children—something they imagined as a way of dealing with their own sexual feelings toward their parents. Now we know these feelings actually exist—the Oedipus complex, for example. But just because all children have such thoughts does not mean that reports of actual incest were a fantasy. It took us a long time to learn this truth. Politically, it was better that incest be thought of as a fantasy. This meant we gave treatment to the victim, but this 'treatment' was bogus—it made the children believe a lie and doubt the reality of their own senses."

"That would make them . . ."

"Crazy. Yes, that is what it *did* do. And those children who acted crazy were displayed as proof of the fact that they were crazy to *begin* with. *Comprende?*"

"But why? Who wants to protect people who fuck their own kids?"

Pablo sighed, disgusted as always with my political ignorance. "Look at it this way. Suppose a slave were to escape from the South and make it to New York. Suppose we put him into psychotherapy—suppose we convinced him that the whole experience of slavery was nothing more than a bad dream—do you not see the political value? We would not have to confront the slave-keepers——we could continue to practice trade and commerce with them, maintain our own self-interest economically. Yes?"

"But slaves . . ." I said, groping for the clincher to prove Pablo wrong, "they'd still have the scars . . ."

"You think an incest victim would not have scars?" he said.

I lit a cigarette, thinking of Flood and the scars she made on herself to replace the brand of a rapist—how she poured gasoline on herself over the tattoo the gang put on her, lit a match, and held on to her one friend in the world until the fire made them free. "What good would it do to trick a kid like that?" I asked.

"Children don't vote," he said.

"And Freud said there was no such thing as incest?"

"Freud did not make a conscious decision to accept the women's stories as fantasies—he lived within a political climate and he responded to it."

"But we *know* it happens."

"Now we know. But to truly *know* it then, you had to experience it."

"So if you thought the experience was all in your mind . . ."

"Yes," said Pablo, grateful that I was finally seeing the light that shone so brightly for him.

I got to my feet, pacing uncomfortably in the small room. "Forget politics for a minute," I said. "We know people do these things to kids, okay? Do we know *why*?"

Pablo tilted his head until he was gazing at the ceiling. "I will tell you everything we actually know—it won't take long. We know people have sex with children—the children of strangers and also their own. We know this has something to do with power—the power grown people have over children. In fact, sex with children is not sex as *you* would understand it, Burke. It is not, for example, the kind of adaptive mechanism which could cause a man to turn to other men when there are no women—like in prison. This is another dimension entirely. The pedophile—the one who has sex with children—he may be able to have sex with women, or with grown men. But he does not *prefer* to do this. The more intelligent the pedophile, the more skillfully he may rationalize his behavior, but the truth is really simple—he knows what he does is wrong and he does it anyway."

"I thought those freaks couldn't help themselves?"

"No! They can stop—they choose not to."

"It can't be that simple," I told him. "Who the fuck would *choose* to pass up women and force little kids to . . . ?"

"All that is within them is within you and me, my friend. If every man who felt sexual violence toward a woman acted on that feeling, New York would not be a city—it would be a graveyard."

"You mean it's not?"

"You joke when you do not understand. Just because some of the lower beasts walk our streets does not make our community into a jungle—not so long as people struggle against the beasts."

Pablo took a dark bottle down from a shelf and poured himself a glass of that jungle juice he drinks all the time. I passed up his offer with a shake of my head.

"To rehabilitation!" he said, tossing down half the glass.

"You ever try that with one of these freaks?" I asked him.

"One time. One time we did just that," he mused, his eyes somewhere else. "My people brought a man in here years ago. He had been molesting children in the neighborhood, and it was thought best to turn him over to our clinic."

"Why not the cops?"

"My people wanted justice, Burke. And they knew the man would probably never be prosecuted. His victims were not important."

"What did they expect *you* to do?"

"The man agreed to go into treatment with us. He made a specific contract that he would cease his activity while we tried to do something about his behavior."

"Behavior?"

"Only his *acts* were a danger to our community—his motivations are so deep inside him that it would take years of treatment for them to surface. And even then we could probably do nothing about them. We asked only that he stop."

"Did he?"

"No. We cannot know why he made his choice—what forces were within him. We can only assume that he tried to walk the line. One day he slipped and fell."

"What did you do then?"

"Nothing. At that point, it became a matter for the police."

"I thought you said the cops couldn't do anything."

"They could in this case, *compadre*. When he slipped and fell for the last time, he was on a rooftop." Pablo held his glass in a silent toast to the only rehabilitation that really works.

We sat in silence for a minute—each waiting for the other. Pablo took another sip of the jungle juice. "*Hermano*, in truth we have been talking about crime, not about psychiatry. And you know more about the behavior of such people than I do. Many times we have called upon you to predict the actions of such evil people—our paths originally crossed for that very reason, yes?"

I nodded—it was the truth.

"And you have become my brother, *verdad*? Do you think I call a man my brother and do not understand him?"

"No—I know you understand."

"Then maybe you should tell me why you have come to talk with me," Pablo said.

I took a last drag on my cigarette, feeling the cold wind eddying in the corners of his office, stirring the dust, making its own howling only I could hear. And I started to tell him about Strega.

# 80

I TOLD HIM EVERYTHING. It didn't take as long as I'd thought it would—maybe there wasn't so much to tell. Pablo took off his glasses, carefully rubbed them on the lapel of his white coat, waiting to be sure I was finished.

"What is so puzzling to you, my friend? A person with a task to do uses the weapons he has, no? This woman wants you to do something—she obviously believes the money is not strong enough to bind you to her will. The sex is nothing more than a chain she tosses over your neck—a leash you put on a dangerous dog."

"It doesn't work like that. If she was working me to make sure I did the job, the sex would be a *promise*, right? A reward. Something to look forward to when the job was done."

"A promise, then? Not a performance?"

"It always *seems* like a promise . . . but it's not."

"The woman promises nothing?"

"Nothing."

Pablo looked at the ceiling, thinking it through. "She has already paid you some of the money, yes? If you took the money and didn't do the job . . . what could she do?"

"Nothing. Maybe she thinks she could, but . . . nothing."

Pablo shrugged. "I cannot see what makes this so difficult for you. Perhaps the woman is just covering her bets—making sure your nose is open—that you keep coming back for more. Remember when we were young men . . . how much we would risk for a night of love with a woman?"

"I'm not young anymore," I said. I couldn't remember ever being that young.

"Listen to me, Burke. It is not reality which controls our lives, it is the perception of that reality."

"More politics?"

"You cannot dismiss truth by mocking it," Pablo said, his voice hardening. "So long as my people believe their life is acceptable, then it *is* acceptable. My people live on a slave island, but their chains are food stamps and welfare programs."

"This is getting away from me," I told him.

"Because you are ignoring your senses—because you will not listen to what you have already learned."

"I *am* listening. I told you everything, Pablo."

"You have told me nothing. You said only what you *saw*—and you have been precise in your reporting, like an investigator. But you have told me nothing of what you *feel, comprende?*"

"No," I lied.

"What does this woman make you feel—that is more important than the sum total of everything else. Close your eyes, Burke. Think her name into your mind. *Feel* it . . . let it come to you."

I closed my eyes, playing it square. Letting it come into me. Pablo floated away from me—I could feel him in the room, but we weren't alone.

"What?" he asked.

"A cold wind," I told him. "A chill . . ."

"All this sex, and no fire?"

"No fire. Dark sex. It happens like it's supposed to, everything works, but nobody smiles. Only part of her is with me . . . like she's standing somewhere else . . . a movie director. . . . She's someone else when she wants to be."

Pablo was quiet, waiting for me to say something else. But I was tapped out.

"Burke, when you make love with her—do you think of making a baby?"

"It can't be. I can't say why . . . but we couldn't make a baby with what we do. . . . She has the only child she wants. . . . It's like . . . if she wanted . . . she could make acid run inside her."

"Even her kiss is cold?"

"I never kissed her," I said.

Pablo watched as I lit another cigarette, his eyes playing over the pictures of his children sitting on his desk. "You know that Puerto Ricans are a special tribe, my friend? You know we are not 'Spanish' like some gringos think we are? And like some of us wish to be? Puerto Ricans are African, Indian, Spanish. . . . Our roots are in many continents, and the knowledge of our people is that mixture in our blood. We call it 'racial knowledge,' and it is deeper than you could ever imagine."

I looked at Pablo—at his dark skin and tightly curled hair. I thought back to when the cops would bust the fighting gangs when we were kids. The dark-skinned Puerto Ricans would never speak English—they didn't want to be taken for black. I thought of the black face of the soldier on São Tomé, talking to me in a bar just before we went over the water to Biafra. Showing me a picture of his wife, smiling. Saying "*Muy blanco, no?*" to get my approval. Liberals wanted to find their roots—survivors wanted to keep from getting strangled by them.

"When you first talked about this woman, I thought you were describing a Santeria priestess. You know them—they mix voodoo and Christianity the way a chemist mixes two drugs. But this woman, she is nothing like that. Her rituals are in her head—they are not handed down from another—they are her own creation."

"Yeah. But . . ."

"What does she call herself, my friend?"

"That's a funny thing—her name is Gina, the name her people gave her. But when she got older, they started to call her something else. Strega. You know what it means?"

"*Sí compadre.* But it means nothing . . . or everything. It depends on who is talking. On the tone of their voice—their relationship to the woman. We have the same word in Spanish. *Bruja.* It means . . . witch, perhaps. A woman with great powers, but maybe with evil in her heart. It can even be a term of affection . . . a bitch with fire in her eye and the devil in her hips, you understand?"

"Witch. Bitch. It doesn't help me.

"One is inside the other—but, remember, the witch includes all else. A woman who is a witch can be anything she wants to be—she can take many forms. An old woman, a child. A saint, a devil. And this is always her choice. We can never see such a woman—only the manifestation of herself she allows us to see. If ten men see her, they see ten different women. And each will believe he has seen the truth. A man cannot see a witch."

"Pablo, come on. You believe that shit?"

"I believe what is true," he said, his voice grave. "I believe this wisdom handed down to us over the years has survived for a reason. To ignore the truth is to fail to understand why the truth has survived."

Survival. My speciality—my birthday present from the state. "What does she want?" I asked him.

"Only she knows that, Burke. *Bruja* is a fire—she must have fuel."

I ground out my cigarette. "The best thing for me to do is make tracks, right?"

Pablo nodded.

"But I have this job to do," I told him.

"You will not always be this confused, Burke. When *Bruja* manifests herself to you, it will be clear. You will know the truth. She will not attempt to hold you without the truth—you cannot be tricked by such a woman—they disdain the wiles of normal women. All their slaves are volunteers."

"Who would volunteer to be a slave?"

"A man who fears freedom," Pablo said, getting to his feet to embrace me. It was a goodbye.

# 81

THE LINCOLN WAS STANDING out in front of the clinic as if it had never moved. The driver's door was open, the engine running. I can take a hint. I was off the block in seconds.

It was deep into the hours past midnight—still not too late to go to Mama's joint, but I wasn't hungry. The Lincoln turned itself north toward the Triboro—I was going to loop around and head back to the office. But I found myself on the long span heading for Queens instead. The bridge was quiet. I passed the Brooklyn-Queens Expressway, my last chance to head back downtown. But the Lincoln kept rolling, past LaGuardia. By then I knew where I was going.

Strega's house was still and dark as I let the Lincoln drift to the curb—maybe her husband and her daughter were allowed to return to the castle after midnight. I hit the power window switch, leaving the engine running. Lit a cigarette and watched the red tip in the darkness like it was a book I wanted to read, listening to the night sounds. A Yellow Cab rattled past—a late-arriving passenger from the airport going home to the wife and kids.

I threw my cigarette into the street, watching her house. A tiny light came on in an upstairs window, barely visible behind a gauzy curtain. I looked hard, trying to fix the exact location. The light went out.

I pushed the gas pedal down, letting the big car take me back to where I was safe. It felt as if she was playing with me in that upstairs room—letting me go. This time.

## 82

THE NEXT MORNING WAS no better. Strange days. The big part of staying off the floor is knowing how to wait. When you hit the floor in my neighborhood, there's no referee giving you time to get your brain back together. I knew how to stay off the floor, but this case was all bent and twisted. I had money in my pocket, nobody was looking for me—I should have been golden. Julio's weak threats wouldn't make me lose sleep. I could just wait a few weeks, keep my head down—tell Strega I came up empty. And walk away.

But when you spend your life lying to everyone from streetside suckers all the way to the Parole Board, you learn that lying to yourself is a self-inflicted wound.

I drove over to one of the post-office boxes I keep around the city in various names. The one in Westchester County is the one I use for kiddie-sex freaks. It's in Mount Vernon, just over the border from the Bronx, maybe forty-five minutes from the office. All I found were some "underground" newsletters and a magazine. The newsletter never quite crosses the line—just some pictures of kids mixed with whining about this repressive society. One even had a column supposedly written by a kid himself—bragging about how his life was enriched by his "meaningful association" with an older man. That dirtbag the Mole had brought me to would have approved. Most of it reminded me of the stuff the Klan puts out—who got arrested recently (and why he was innocent), what politicians are trying to make a name for themselves with "anti-kid" legislation . . . that kind of crap. Some freaks burn crosses, some burn kids. The feature story was about some priest in Louisiana doing time for sodomizing a bunch of altar boys—the newsletter said the real issue was freedom of religion.

It was a waste of time. I knew it would be. Someone once said people in hell want ice water. If that's all they want, maybe they deserve to stay there.

I pulled the car over on the West Side Highway, near 96th Street. It was peaceful there—a few guys working on their cars, one crazy bastard casting a fishing line into the oil slick, a young woman throwing a stick for her dog to fetch. The dog was an Irish setter. His coat gleamed coppery red in the sunlight as he dashed in and out of the water, chasing the stupid stick. The woman called to the dog—time to go. The dog stopped and shook himself, water flying from his coat in a fine spray. I threw away my cigarette. That was what I needed to do—shake off this witch-woman and get back to myself.

I spent the next two days asking soft questions in hard places. Marking time until the week was up and I could return Bobby's Lincoln. I called him from a pay phone on Twelfth Avenue, near Times Square.

"It's Burke. My car ready?"

"Yep. Running like a watch. When's the last time that thing had a decent tune-up?"

"I don't know—didn't think it needed one."

Bobby made a growling sound in his throat—abusing good machinery made him crazy.

"You have any luck with that other thing?" I asked him, heading off a lecture on auto mechanics.

"Sure. No problem. Pick up your car this afternoon. About four, okay? We'll talk then."

"I'll be there."

"By yourself," he reminded me.

"I'll be the only person in the car," I told him. Pansy was going to get a ride in a Lincoln.

# 83

THE MASTIFF SNIFFED THE Lincoln like it was an enemy dog—circling around a couple of times, pawing at the tires, burying her giant snout in the front seat.

"It's okay," I told her, but she took her time, getting it right. Finally, she climbed into the back seat, growled a couple of times, then flopped down. She was half asleep by the time I wheeled onto Atlantic Avenue.

It was just past four o'clock when I pulled up. This time it was Bobby himself sitting on the crate in front of the garage. He raised a fist in greeting, hitting a switch to open the door so I could pull the Lincoln all the way in. My Plymouth was parked just inside, nose aimed at the street.

"I could've painted it while it was here, but I figured you'd rather keep it the way it was," Bobby said.

"That's right, Bobby. Thanks."

But I wasn't getting off that easy. He insisted on taking me through everything he'd done to the car—piece by piece. "What you got here is a *complete* tune-up, Burke. Valves adjusted, points and plugs, carb cleaned and rejetted, timing reset. And we aligned the front end, rotated and balanced the tires. Changed all the fluids—power steering, transmission. Had to bleed the brake lines—you got silicon fluid in there now. Had to adjust the bands in the tranny too. It runs perfect now."

"What do I owe you, Bobby?"

Bobby waved my offer away.

"Let's hear how it sounds," I said with an enthusiasm I didn't feel.

Bobby twisted the key—it was so smooth it sounded like a turbine. Pansy recognized the sound—her monster's head appeared in the windshield of Bobby's Lincoln. He heard something, looked.

"What the fuck is *that?*" he asked me.

"It's just my dog, Bobby." I went over and opened the Lincoln's door, slapping my hip for Pansy to come to me.

"Jesus H. Fucking Christ!" Bobby said reverently. "How much does it weigh?"

"I don't know—maybe one forty or so."

Bobby made a full circuit around Pansy, checking her lines. He didn't try and kick the tires.

"Could I pat it?" he asked.

"Pansy, jump!" I snapped at her. She hit the deck, lying-prone, her murderer's eyes the color of the East River, watching Bobby the way she watches food. "Go ahead," I told him. "She won't do anything now."

Bobby had enough sense to squat down so Pansy wouldn't think he was trying to dominate her. He scratched behind her ears. "I never saw anything like this outside of a zoo," he said. Pansy made a gentle rumble in her throat—like a subway pulling into a station. "Is he mad?" Bobby asked, still scratching.

"No," I told him. "That's when she's happy."

"It's a girl?"

"Sure is," I said.

Bobby got to his feet. "The other guys are out back, Burke. Okay?"

"Okay. You want me to leave Pansy out here?"

"Fuck no," Bobby said. "She might eat one of the cars."

Bobby led the way, me following, Pansy taking the point position to my left and just slightly in front of each stride. She knew what to do now—she was working.

There was only one car in the back this time—the Mustang. And three men—two a few years older than Bobby, the other more like my age. They all had prison-faces. The older guy had a regular haircut and was wearing a dark sportcoat over a white shirt, sunglasses hiding his eyes. The other two were much bigger men, flanking the guy in the sunglasses like they were used to standing that way. One was blond, the other dark, both with longish hair, wearing white T-shirts over jeans and boots. The blond had tattoos on both arms—in case anyone could miss where he got them, he had chains tattooed on both wrists. Black leather gloves on his hands. The dark one had calm eyes; he stood with his hands in front of him, right hand holding his left wrist. On the back of his right hand were the crossed lightning bolts—the mark of the Real Brotherhood.

I stopped a few feet short of the triangle. Pansy immediately came to a sitting position just in front of me. Her eyes pinned the blond—she knew.

Bobby stepped into the space between us, speaking to the older guy in the middle.

"This is Burke. The guy I told you about."

The older guy nodded to me. I nodded back. He waved his hand back toward himself, telling me to come closer. I stepped forward. So did Pansy.

The blond rolled his shoulders, watching Pansy, talking to me.

"The dog do any tricks?" he asked.

The hair on the back of Pansy's neck stood up. I patted her head to keep her calm.

"Like what?" I asked him.

The blond had a nice voice—half snarl, half sneer. "I don't fucking know . . . like, shake hands?"

"She'll shake anything she gets in her mouth," I told him, a smile on my face to say I wasn't threatening him.

The older guy laughed. "My brother says you're okay. If we can help you, we will."

"I appreciate it," I said. "And I'm willing to pay my way."

"Good enough," he said. "What do you need?"

"I know you," the blond suddenly blurted out.

I looked at his face—I'd never seen him before.

"I don't know you," I said, my voice neutral.

"You were in Auburn, right? Nineteen seventy-five?"

I nodded agreement.

"I was there too. Saw you on the yard."

I shrugged. Auburn wasn't an exclusive club.

"You mixed with niggers," the blond said. It wasn't a question.

"I mixed with my friends," I said, voice quiet, measured. "Like you did."

"I said *niggers!*"

"I heard what you said," I told him. "You hear what I said?"

The blond rolled his shoulders again, cracking the knuckles of one gloved hand in the fist he made of the other.

"B.T., I told you what Burke did for me," Bobby put in, no anxiety in his voice, just setting the record straight.

The blond looked at me. "Maybe you just had a personal beef with *those* niggers?"

"Maybe I did. So what?"

"Maybe you *like* niggers?" It wasn't a question—an accusation.

No point keeping my voice neutral any longer—he'd take it for fear. "What's your problem?" I asked him. That wasn't a question either.

The blond looked at me, watching my face. "I lost money on you, he said.

"What?"

"I fucking lost money on you. I remember now. You was a fighter, right? You fought that nigger . . . I forget his name . . . the one that was a pro light-heavy?"

I remembered that fight. The black guy had been a real hammer in the ring before he beat a guy to death over a traffic accident. I don't remember how it got started, but it ended up with a bet that I couldn't go three rounds with him. I remember sitting on the stool in my corner waiting for the bell to start the first round, the Prof whispering in my ear. "Send the fool to school, Burke," he was saying, reminding me how we had it worked out. I was a good fifteen pounds lighter than the black guy, and quite a bit faster. Everybody betting on whether I could last the three rounds was expecting me to keep a jab in his face, bicycle backward, use the whole ring. Make him catch me. That's what he expected too.

When the bell sounded, he came off his stool like he was jet-propelled. I threw a pillow-soft jab in his general direction and started back-pedaling to the ropes. The black guy didn't waste any time countering my little jabs—he pulled his right hand all the way down to his hip, trying for one killer punch that would end it all. That was the opening. I stepped forward and fired a left hook—caught him flush on the chin coming in, and down he went.

But then the plan came unglued. He took an eight-count, shaking his head to clear it. He got to his feet so smoothly that I knew I hadn't really hurt him. The black guy waved me in and I charged, pinning him to the ropes, firing shot after shot at his head. But he wasn't just a tough guy—he was a pro. He blocked everything with his elbows, picking off my punches until I realized I was running out of gas. I leaned against him to get a breath—he buried his head in my chest to guard against an uppercut. I collapsed all my weight on his neck, stepping on his toes, not giving him an inch of room to punch. The guard in charge of the bell rang it early—he'd bet on me too.

I let him chase me through the second round, still a step faster than he was. He wasn't going to charge again—just taking his time, punching so hard my arms ached from blocking. He caught me good at the beginning of the third round—I felt a rib go from a right hook. He doubled up, catching me on the bridge of the nose with the same hand. "Grab him!" I heard the Prof scream, and I brought my gloves up over his elbows, pulling his hands under my armpits until the referee forced us apart. He butted me on the break, aiming for my nose. I staggered back, letting my knees wobble to get closer to the ground, letting him come in. I threw a Mexican left hook—so far south of the border that I connected squarely with his cup. The black guy dropped both hands to his crotch and I threw a haymaker at his exposed head—missed by a foot and fell down from the effort. The referee wiped off my gloves, calling it a slip, killing time.

He came at me again. I couldn't breathe through my nose, so I spit out the mouthpiece, catching a sharp right-hand lead a second later. I heard the Prof yell "Thirty seconds!" just before another shot dropped me to the canvas.

I was on my feet by the count of six, with just enough left to dodge his wild lunge. He went sailing past me into the ropes—I fired a rabbit punch to the back of his head, moved against him, pinning him to the ropes with his back to me. He whipped an elbow into my stomach and spun around, hooking with both hands, knowing he had to finish it. I grabbed his upper body, feeling the punches to my ribs, driving my forehead hard into his eyes, not giving him room to punch. If I'd had to let go of him I would have fallen for good.

I was out on my feet when I heard the bell. It took four men to pull him off me. We won almost six hundred cartons of cigarettes that day. The prison even threw in a free bridge for my missing teeth.

"If you lost money that day, you bet on the other guy," I told him. "The bet was that I couldn't last the three rounds."

"I bet on you to *win*," the blond said.

I shrugged my shoulders—it wasn't my problem that some true-believer couldn't get with the program.

"You didn't even try and beat that nigger," the blond said, like he was accusing me of treason.

"I was trying to survive," I told him reasonably. Just the way I was trying to do now. "Look, pal, it's not a big deal. How much did you lose?"

"Three fucking cartons," he said. Like it was his sister's virginity.

"Tell you what I'll do. It was a few years ago, right? Figure the price has gone up a bit—how about a half-yard for each carton? A hundred and fifty bucks, and we'll call it square?"

The blond stared at me, still not sure if I was laughing at him.

"You serious?"

"Dead serious," I told him, slipping my hand into my coat pocket.

The blond couldn't make up his mind, his eyes shifting from Pansy to me. The guy with the sunglasses finally closed the books. "Let it rest, B.T.," he said. The blond let out a breath. "Okay," he said.

The blond started over to me for the money—Pansy went rigid. Her teeth ground together with a sound like a cement truck shifting into gear.

"I'll give it to you when I leave," I told the blond. Even a genius like him understood. He stepped back against the fence, still flexing the muscles in his arms. Pansy was real impressed.

"Can we do business?" I asked the guy with the sunglasses.

He waved me over to the side, against the fence by the Mustang. I flatted my hand against Pansy's snout, telling her to stay where she was, and followed him over. I lit a cigarette, feeling Bobby against my back.

"One of your guys did some bodyguard work. Delivered some money to a day-care center—money was in a little satchel—like a doctor's bag."

I couldn't see the guy's eyes behind the sunglasses; he had his hands in his pockets—waiting for me to finish.

"There was a woman with the bodyguard. Maybe he was protecting her, maybe he was guarding the cash—I don't know."

"Anything else?" he asked.

"The woman, she's no youngster. Maybe my age, maybe older. And she has a house somewhere outside the city. Big house—nice grounds. Has a guy who works with her—a big, fat guy. And maybe a schoolbus-type vehicle."

"That's it?"

"That's it," I told him.

"And you want to know what?"

"All I want to know is who this woman is—where I can find her."

"You got a beef with her?"

I thought about it—didn't know if the bodyguard work was a one-shot deal or if the Real Brotherhood had a contract with her. "She has something I want," I told him, measuring out the words as carefully as a dealer putting cocaine on a scale.

He didn't say anything.

"If you've got a contract with her . . . then I'd like to ask you to get this thing I want from her. I'll pay for it."

"And if there's no contract?"

"Then I just want her name and address."

He smiled. It might have made a citizen relax; I kept my hands in my pockets. "And for us to get out of the way?" he asked.

"Yeah," I told him. "Exactly."

The blond moved away from the guy in the sunglasses, his back to the fence. Pansy's huge head tracked his movement as if she was the center of a big clock and he was the second hand.

"B.T.!" Bobby said, a warning in his voice. The blond stopped where he was—a slow learner.

"What is this thing you want?" the leader asked.

"That means you have a contract?"

"No. And I don't know where her stash is either."

"It's not dope I'm after," I told him.

The leader took off his sunglasses, looked at them in his hands as though they held the answer to something. He looked up at me. His eyes had that soft, wet glaze only born killers get—after they've fulfilled their destiny a few times. "You're a hijacker, right? That's what you do?"

I held my hands together and turned my palms out to him—cards on the table. "I'm looking for a picture—a photograph."

"Who's in the picture?"

"A kid," I told him.

He looked a question at me.

"A little kid—a sex picture, okay?"

The leader looked at the dark-haired guy standing next to him. "I thought it was powder," he said.

The dark-haired guy kept his face flat. "I never asked," he replied.

The leader nodded absently, thinking it through. "Yeah," he said, "who asks?"

I lit a cigarette, cupping my hands around the flame, watching the leader from a corner of my eye. He was scratching at his face with one finger, his eyes behind the sunglasses again.

"Bobby, you mind taking your friend inside for a couple of minutes? We've got something to talk over out here, okay?"

Bobby put his hand on my shoulder, gently tugging me toward the garage. I slapped my hand against my side, telling Pansy to come along. She didn't move, still watching the blond, memorizing his body. "Pansy!" I snapped at her. She gave the blond one last look and trotted over to my side.

Inside the garage, I opened both front doors of the Plymouth and told Pansy to climb inside.

"B.T.'s okay, Burke," Bobby said. "He's just a little nuts on the subject of niggers, you know?"

"I know," I said. "No big deal."

We waited in silence. Pansy's dark-gray fur merged into the dim interior of the garage—only her eyes glowed. She missed the blond.

The back door opened and they came inside. The leader sat on the Plymouth's hood, leaving his boys standing off to one side.

"The woman told us she had to deliver money to various places—serious cash, okay? She was worried about somebody moving on the money—taking it away from her. Victor"—he nodded his head in the direction of the dark-haired guy—"he picked up a grand for every delivery. He carried the cash. We thought it was a regular series of payoffs—she never took anything back when she turned over the money."

I didn't say anything—I had a lot of questions but it wasn't my turn to talk.

"She told Victor no weapons—if someone made a move on them with a gun, he was supposed to turn over the bag he was carrying. He was just muscle, okay?"

I nodded. The woman wasn't worried about a hijack—Victor was there to intimidate the people who supplied the kids. He could do that just by being himself.

"You're sure she has this picture?" he asked.

"No question," I told him.

"This means she has others—that she does this all the time?"

"It's what she does," I told him.

The leader was wearing his sunglasses even inside the garage, but I could feel his eyes behind the dark lenses. "I'm a thief," he said, "just like you are. We don't fuck kids."

"I know that," I said.

"Some of our guys . . . they're a little crazy . . . like B.T. He'd stab a nigger just to stay in practice, you know?"

"I know."

"But none of us would do little kids. Our brotherhood . . ."

I bowed my head slightly. "You have everyone's respect," I told him.

"We do *now,*" he said, his voice soft. "If word got out that we were involved with kids like this . . ."

"It won't," I said.

He went on like he hadn't heard me. "If that word got out, we'd have to do something serious, you understand? We can't have anything hurt our name—people would get stupid with us."

I kept quiet, waiting.

"We give you the information you want—you going to try and buy this picture from her?"

"If she'll sell it."

"And if she won't?"

I shrugged.

"Victor made a lot of those cash runs for her," he said. "A couple of day-care centers, private houses . . . even a church. There has to be a fucking lot of those pictures around."

"Like I said—she's in the business."

The leader ran his fingers through his hair—I could see the tattoo on his hand. His voice was still soft. "Her name is Bonnie. The house is on Cheshire Drive in Little Neck, just this side of the Nassau County border. A big white house at the end of a dead-end street. There's a white wall all around the property—electronic gate to the driveway. Big, deep backyard, trees and shrubs all around. Two stories, full basement, maybe some room in the attic too."

"Anything else?" I asked him.

"She has that schoolbus you talked about—a little one, maybe a dozen seats in the back. She uses the big, fat guy as the driver."

"Any security in the house?"

"I don't know," he said. "The Real Brotherhood—we play it straight—we weren't even thinking about taking her off."

I handed him two grand, all in hundreds. "That square us?" I asked him.

He smiled. "I'll take B.T.'s money out of this," he said.

I held out my hand. He took it—his grip was firm, but not a bone-crusher. I wouldn't give B.T. the same opportunity.

"I'm going to move fast now," I told him.

"Do what you want," he said. "Take your time. She put down our name, you understand?"

I nodded—someday soon, B.T. was going to get the idea the

woman was a front for the NAACP.

I slammed the door in Pansy's face, waved a clenched fist to Bobby to thank him, and drove the Plymouth out of the garage.

## 84

EVEN PANSY FELT THE difference in the Plymouth as it purred along, heading back to the office. Bobby had done a beautiful job. I rolled to a stop at a red light on Atlantic near the Brooklyn-Queens border. An orange G.T.O. screeched to a stop next to me—two kids in their street racer. The passenger rolled down his window, smiling at me while his partner revved the engine, waiting for the light. I raised my eyebrows in respect for their dragster, and stomped the gas just as the light changed. I heard the G.T.O.'s tires squeal, hunting for traction on the rough road, but the Plymouth leaped ahead as though their orange machine was tied to a stake. The speedometer needle flicked at seventy before I backed it off for the next red light. I heard the G.T.O. roaring behind me, letting up on the gas while still in gear to make his exhaust pipes crackle. Very impressive. This time, they pulled up on the passenger side. I hit the power window switch just in time to hear the driver shout the street racer's time-honored question, "What you got in that, man?"

Pansy popped her head up from the front seat, snarling at all the noise. I heard another squeal from the G.T.O.'s tires and it was gone. The light was still red.

It was getting dark. Time to start making the phone calls, checking my traps. I wanted to drop Pansy off at the office, but I was short of time. The leader of the Real Brotherhood seemed like a patient man, but he was raised the same places I was—places where if your name went down, your body wouldn't be far behind.

I pulled up behind Mama's, opening Pansy's door to let her out. She prowled the walls of the narrow alley, finally relieving herself against both of them. She sniffed the air, a soft growl coming from her throat. I don't know if it was the smells from Mama's kitchen or whether she missed old B.T.

I let her back in the car and went inside through the kitchen. My table in the back was empty like it always was—Mama's heavy dinner crowd didn't fill half the joint—she kept the prices high and the ambience foul to discourage yuppies.

"Trouble?" she asked, approaching my table, her voice soft.

"No trouble, Mama. But I have to make a bunch of phone calls—and I have Pansy with me. Out in the car."

"This new puppy, Burke?" She knew my old Doberman, Devil.

"She's not really a puppy anymore, Mama."

"Big dog?"

"Big dog," I assured her.

"Maybe keep puppy in basement, okay?"

"Perfect, Mama. Just for a little while, right?"

"Sure," she said, doubtfully. "I tell cooks everything okay. Come."

I followed her back to the kitchen; she fired some Cantonese at the collection of thugs.

"Go get puppy," she told me.

I snapped Pansy's leash on. She lifted her head, wondering what was going on. She only got the leash when she was going to be around citizens.

When we walked through the back door, one of the cooks made a sound like "Eigh!" and backed all the way into the stove. They all started talking at once—arguing about something. Pansy sat at my side, drooling. They couldn't be sure it was the food. Two of them were pointing at the beast's head, standing chest to chest, screaming at each other. I couldn't make out a word. I had started to the basement with Pansy when Mama held up her hand.

"Burke, what country this dog from—don't say word, okay?"

I should have known—all the screaming and yelling was about some dumb bet—and Mama was looking for the edge. Mama's alleged cooks would stab you in the stomach and then bet you how long it would take you to die.

"Pizza," I told her, under my breath.

Mama charged into the argument, adding her own voice to the

din. Finally, she pointed to one of the cooks.

"Germany?" she asked me.

"No," I said.

She pointed to another.

"England?"

I said "No" again, watching their faces.

"China?" she asked, pointing to a young man in the corner.

"No," I told her again. "The dog is from Italy."

A smile broke out on Mama's face. She made me say it again, so everyone in the room would get the benefit of her wisdom. Everybody bowed to her. I didn't see money change hands, but I figured their pay envelopes would be a little short that week.

Pansy snarled her way down the steps to the basement, threatening the darkness. Mama switched on the lights—the place was filled floor-to-ceiling with boxes, some wood, some cardboard. Drums of rice stood to one side. There was still another basement below this one—I remember one time when the cops were looking for Max and they thought he was down there. They waited two days to find me to ask him to come out quietly.

"Puppy want food, Burke?"

"Sure, Mama. Whatever you think is best."

She bowed. "I come back soon," she said, and went back up the stairs. More screaming and yelling in Chinese erupted—I think the cooks wanted a rematch. She came back down with a volunteer helper; he was carrying one of those giant stainless-steel pots they use to keep the rice freshly steamed all day long. He put it on the floor, watching Pansy warily.

"This puppy good guard dog, Burke?" she asked.

"She's the best, Mama."

"She . . . this girl puppy?"

"Women the best warriors," Mama said, then translated it for the cook, who nodded dubiously. "Puppy guard down here?"

"If you want her to," I said. "Watch—and tell your man to keep his hands in sight, okay?"

She nodded. I slapped my side for Pansy to follow me, walking her so her back was in a corner formed by some of the stacked cartons. I took down a few cartons to make a little wall in front of her, about as high as her chest. Her face loomed above the barrier, watching. I knew just what trick Mama would love. "Pansy!" I said, my voice sharp to get her attention. "Friends!" I motioned Mama forward. "Go ahead and pat her," I said.

Mama hadn't gotten where she was by showing fear. She walked right up to Pansy, patting her head, saying "Good puppy!" a few times. Pansy stood still, her eyes on the cook.

"Okay, now step back, Mama." When she did, I got Pansy's attention again. "Guard!" I told her.

"Tell your man to approach like he's going to pat her too, Mama. But tell him not to reach over the barrier, you got it?"

She said something to the cook. His face stayed flat, but you didn't need a translator to see he was suspicious as hell. The poor bastard had gotten about five feet from the barrier when Pansy lunged at him, a blood-chilling snarl flowing between her teeth. He leaped back about twenty feet—the snap of Pansy's jaws was like a thick branch breaking.

"Pansy, out!" I yelled at her. She sat back down, her head swiveling to watch the entire room.

Mama clapped her hands. "Good trick, Burke!" she said. The cook went back upstairs. I rolled the pot of steaming food over to Pansy. "What's in this?" I asked her.

Mama looked insulted. "Beef, pork, lobster, shrimp, good vegetables, plenty rice. All best stuff."

"She'll love it," I assured Mama.

"How come she not eat, then?"

"She'll only eat when she's alone with me, Mama. Let me get her started and I'll come up and make those calls, okay?"

"Okay, Burke," she said.

I waited a minute or two before saying "Speak!" to my dog. A good survivor never shares all his secrets.

# 85

THE FIRST CALL WAS to SAFE. Lily was in a session—they asked if I could leave a number. I told them I couldn't and got a time to call back. They didn't seem surprised.

I got lucky with McGowan—he was in his office for a change.

"You know my voice?" I asked him.

"Sure do, pal." McGowan had a magnificent Irish baritone—he used it for sweet-talking little girls away from their pimps.

"I need a favor. You know Wolfe, the D.A. in charge of City-Wide?"

"Pal, that woman is aces with me, understand? Cases the other prosecutors won't touch—she grabs 'em up. You better not be having a problem with her."

"No problem. I just want you to put in a good word for me, okay? I need to talk with her—I figure she might do it if she knew I was all right."

"My friend, you are *not* all right if you're looking to sting that woman."

"McGowan, come *on*. You know what I do—it's part of that, okay?"

"*What* part?"

I took a breath, thinking it through. McGowan knew his phones could be tapped—he had every honest cop's fear of Internal Affairs.

"Look, all I want is for you to tell her I play the game straight. I'll tell her what I need—she can make up her own mind."

Another silence on the line. Finally his voice came back. "You got it," he said.

I started to ask him to do it tomorrow, but I was talking to a dead line.

Strega answered her phone on the first ring. "I was waiting for you," she said, her voice soft.

"How could you know it was me calling?"

"I know," she said. "I told you before—I always know."

"There's been some progress."

"Tell me," she said, her voice going throaty, playing with the words, stroking them.

"Not on the phone," I said.

"I know what you want—come to my house—come tonight—late, after midnight—come tonight—I'll have what you want."

"I just want . . ." and I was talking into another dead line.

I went back inside the restaurant, killing some time until Lily would be available. One of the waiters brought me some soup and a plate of fried rice and beef, green pea pods lancing through the mixture. Mama walked by, smiling. She tossed the *News* on the table in front of me. I scanned the headlines. Half of Queens County was getting indicted. Politicians were grabbing their lawyers in one hand and their guts in the other and dashing to the courthouse, offering everyone they knew in exchange for immunity from the deals they'd done together. That's why they call it the rat race.

The sports pages read like the front pages—one role model was using cocaine, another was going into an alcoholism rehab program. Another claimed he threw a prize fight.

But on the racing page I saw my horse again. Flower Jewel, running in the eighth race against the same collection she had faced last week. I checked my watch—not even nine-thirty yet.

Maurice didn't answer until the sixth ring—probably a lot of late action coming in.

"It's Burke," I told him.

"No kidding?" he said. Maurice didn't have the manners of a pig, but he was taking lessons and hoped to be right up there soon.

"The eighth closed yet?"

"Not until ten—where've you been, fucking Idaho?"

"Flower Jewel," I told him. "Three to win."

"Flower Jewel, eighth race. Three to win. That right?"

"Right," I said.

"Send your man around tomorrow with the money," Maurice said, slamming down the phone.

I went back to my dinner, wondering if even Pansy could eat all the food Mama had left down in the basement for her.

I lit a cigarette as the dishes were cleared away. Flood's face drifted up from nowhere, floating in the smoke—I ground it out in the ashtray, but it didn't help.

Lily herself answered when I called SAFE.

"It's Burke," I told her. "Did you speak with Wolfe?"

"Yes, I did."

"And?"

"And she gave me a number for you to call—anytime between eight and nine in the morning."

"She'll talk to me?"

"She just gave me the number to give to you."

I hadn't expected Lily to get over with Wolfe so easily—McGowan had been my backup plan. If he did get around to calling tomorrow, it wouldn't hurt. I sure as hell wasn't going to call him back and tell him to forget it—he'd be sure I was up to no good.

"Okay," I said. "The kid's been coming for treatment?"

"Right on time. But his mother doesn't want to be involved."

"The redhead?"

"Yes."

"She's not his mother."

"Oh. Will his mother . . . ?"

"I don't know. I'll see about it, okay?"

"Just so long as they keep bringing the child."

"I'll talk to his people. And thanks, Lily."

"Be careful," she said, hanging up.

I said goodbye to Mama and collected Pansy from the basement. She was still behind the barrier, but the steel container was as clean as if it had been washed. I could see her teethmarks on the rim.

Pansy was happy to be home, insisting on visiting the roof for old times' sake. I had a couple of hours before I had to meet Strega. I found a pro wrestling match on television and lay back on the couch to watch with Pansy. She growled in contentment—if she could have nailed B.T. it would have been a perfect day.

# 86

THE MOON'S cold light never penetrated to the dark streets, but I felt it deep in my spine as I wheeled the Plymouth past the burnt-out buildings on Atlantic. The radio was talking about Marcos settling down in Hawaii. He split the Philippines a few weeks ago, traveling light—a couple of loyal subjects, and the gross national product of his entire country for the last dozen years. A major-league scumbag.

I cut the engine, letting the Plymouth coast around to the garage in back. The door was standing open. Only the BMW was there. I backed the Plymouth inside, found the button, and closed the door. Waiting in the darkness.

A door opened. I could see her back-lighted silhouette standing there, weaving slightly—a candle flame in a gentle breeze.

I climbed out of the Plymouth. When I looked up again, the doorway was empty. I went through the opening and saw her gently floating up the stairs. Her body was wrapped in some gauzy black fabric, blending into the shadows under her red hair. When I got to the top of the stairs, she was gone again.

No lights were on in the house. I found my way into her white living room and took off my coat. I took out a cigarette, scraped the wooden match into life. As I touched the tip of the cigarette to the flame, I heard her voice. "Me too," she whispered, floating into the dark room, bending her face forward to the flame. A lollipop stick of marijuana was in her mouth.

I held the light for her, watched her puff to get the joint going and then suck in a massive breath. She floated away from me to the couch—the tip of the joint was a glowing pinpoint in the dark room.

"You having a séance?" I asked her.

"You afraid of the dark?" she retorted.

"I'm afraid of a lot of things," I told her.

"I know," she said, dragging on the joint again, holding her breath, expelling it in a hiss.

"It'll be over soon," I said. "I'm getting close."

"To the picture?"

"To the person who took the picture. I can't be sure the picture is still around—like I told you. But I think I can get some answers soon."

"You want me to do something?"

"I just want an answer to something. I have a couple of more things to do—then I'm going to the people who took the picture, okay? But the picture may be with a whole bunch of other pictures. I may not have time to look through them all—you understand?"

"So?"

"So what if I just destroy *all* the pictures? Make sure there aren't any pictures left. Of anybody."

Another drag on the joint, red tip blazing, sharp intake of breath, hiss when it came out. "I want to see the picture," she said.

"I'll do my best. But I'm not hanging around if things go bad, see? Scotty wasn't the only one—I'm sure of that now. The people who took the picture, they're in the business, understand?"

"Yes."

"I don't know how much time I'll have once I get inside."

She took a last drag and the joint went out; maybe she just pinched off the tip—I couldn't tell.

"You want to get inside now?" Strega said, coming off the couch toward me.

"No," I told her.

"Yes, you do," she said, standing next to me. She dropped to her knees, the black gauze fluttering behind me. Bat's wings. Her face was in my lap, her hands at my belt. My hand dropped onto her back, feeling the fabric—and the chill.

"Don't touch me," she whispered.

I watched my hands grip the arms of the chair; the veins stood out. A picture formed on the back of my hands—below the waist I was somewhere else—the picture formed and I could see my passport into the woman's house.

I felt myself go off, but her mouth stayed locked to me for a long time. She reached back one hand, pulled off the gauzy wrapper—her body was a gleam of white.

Strega took her mouth from me, wrapping the gauze around me, cleaning me off, tossing the fabric to the floor.

"You didn't even have to ask—I know what to do," she whispered against my chest.

I stroked her back. It felt too smooth to be a person.

"I'm a good girl," she said, her voice certain and sure of itself, the way a kid gets sometimes.

I kept stroking her.

"Yes?" she whispered.

"Yeah," I said.

We stayed like that for a long time.

"I'LL BE RIGHT BACK," she said, her voice strong and hard again. "I have to get something for you." She got to her feet and padded away.

The downstairs bathroom had two matching sinks; a telephone was built into a niche near the tub. I caught my reflection in the mirror—it looked like a mug shot.

When she came back downstairs, I was standing next to the wall-size window in the living room, watching the lights in the yard. She was wearing a white terrycloth robe; her hair was wet, copper-colored in the soft light.

"This is for you," she said, opening her hand for me to see.

It was a thick gold chain the size of my wrist—each link must have weighed a couple of ounces. I held it in my hand, feeling the weight. It was solid enough to be a collar for Pansy.

"It's beautiful," I said, slipping it into my pocket.

"Put it on," Strega said, reaching into my pocket to pull it out again.

I thought of the tattoos on B.T.'s wrists. "I don't wear chains," I told her.

"You'll wear mine," she said, fire-points in her eyes.

"No, I won't," I told her, my voice quiet.

She stood on her toes, reached behind me to pull at my neck—she was so close I couldn't focus on her eyes. "I'll keep this for you—I'll sleep with it next to my body. When you come back to me—when you come back with the picture—you'll put it on."

I put my lips against her—she pulled her face away.

"Bring me that picture," she said, turning her face to the window.

I left her standing there, looking like a little girl waiting for her father to come home from work.

## 87

THE PLYMOUTH TOOK ITSELF back to the office. I had to call Wolfe in a couple of hours; no point in trying to sleep.

I kicked my feet up on my desk, a yellow pad in my hand, and jotted down notes of what I knew, telling myself I was putting it together. When I opened my eyes, it was almost eight in the morning. Somebody had written Bruja on the pad and crossed it out—I could read the word through the scratches.

I took a shower, waiting for Pansy to come down from the roof. Checked the phone—clear to call. The number Lily gave me for Wolfe rang a couple of times.

"City-Wide."

"Ms. Wolfe, please."

"This is she."

"It's Burke. I'd like to talk to you about something."

"Yes?"

"In your office—if that's okay."

I could feel her hesitate.

"I have something to give you—something that will be of value in your work."

"What?" she asked.

"I'd prefer to show you."

Another silence. Then:

"You know where my office is?"

"Yes."

"Make it nine o'clock. Give your name to the desk man."

"There isn't much time," I told her. "I live all the way up in Westchester County—the traffic and all . . ."

"Nine o'clock *tonight,* Mr. Burke."

She hung up. I went back to sleep.

# 88

THE DAY came up bleak—dirty skies, a cold wind hovering over the city, waiting its turn. I blocked it all out, walking through the case inside my head, looking for a handle to grip. I didn't walk around while I was thinking—one of the first things you learn in prison is not to pace, it just underlines that you're in a cage. If you stay inside your head, you can go over the walls.

I'd been playing this all wrong—not paying attention to all the tuition payments I'd made in jails and hospitals over the years. Something about this case was making me afraid, but that wasn't so strange. I'm scared most of the time—it keeps me from getting stupid. But I'm used to being scared of the usual things—like being shot or doing more time . . . not this *bruja* nonsense Pablo told me about. You ever watch a fighter who slugged his way into a championship bout decide he's a fucking *boxer* and blow his big chance? You have to go with what got you there. I smoked a couple of cigarettes, thinking it over. Crime had never made me rich, but it kept me free. And it was what I knew best.

I didn't get started until late afternoon, taking my time about getting ready. I picked over my clothes, looking for something that wouldn't make the people in Wolfe's building nervous. I found a black wool suit with a faint chalk stripe hanging in the closet. It was brand-new, but a bit rumpled from storage—car trunks do that. I matched it with a white shirt—genuine Hong Kong silk, which is like saying "virgin vinyl." And a plain black tie. I washed my hair and combed it the best I could. Shaved carefully. Polished the black half-boots. I checked myself out in the mirror. Clothes do make the man—instead of looking like a thug who worked the docks, I looked like a pilot fish for a loan shark.

I folded some money into one pocket, took a couple of other things I needed out of the desk, and shut the place down. Pansy raised one eyebrow, still near comatose from the cubic ton of Chinese food. I told her I'd be back late and took the back stairs to the garage.

I checked my watch. A little past six. Plenty of time to have something to eat, get my mind right for the meeting.

When I first rolled past the restaurant, the blue dragon tapestry was in the window. Cops inside. I kept going all the way down to Division Street to the warehouse. Nobody was around. I checked the desk in the back room to see if any mail had circled around the loops I set up and come in for a landing. Flood knew how to work the loop, but she'd never written. The desk was empty.

When I drove back, the white tapestry was in place. All clear. I parked around the back. A couple of the cooks looked suspiciously at me—maybe the ones who lost the bet on Pansy's nationality. I took my table in the back. Mama sat down with me, handing over a copy of the *News*.

"You had the law here, Mama?"

"Yes. Police very worried about this place. The gangs—stores have to pay for protection. They ask me if it happen to me."

You could see Mama thought the whole idea was ridiculous—the gangs only tried their shakedown racket on legitimate businesses.

"What did you tell them?"

"I tell them the truth. Nobody bother me. You want soup?"

"Sure," I told her, opening the paper as she went back to her business.

I'd almost forgotten about Flower Jewel. I flipped to the back of the paper, looking for her name. I found it, but it didn't cheer me up. She'd left early, but some other nag parked her to the first quarter in 28:4. Too fast. She was shuffled back into the pack. Then she make a big brush at the three-quarter pole, going three-wide on the paddock turn. She actually had the lead at the top of the stretch, but the little "1x" told me the story—she broke stride, looking for more speed. Finished fourth. It looked like a lousy drive to me, but Maurice would want his money, not an autopsy.

I finished my soup, ate a few of the dim sum the waiter brought, smoked a couple of cigarettes. I went up to the front desk and slipped Mama the three hundred for Maurice with another thirty for Max.

"You not such good gambler, Burke," she said, a little smile on her face.

"I don't get many chances to bet on a sure thing," I told her. "Like where dogs come from."

Mama wasn't insulted. "Only way to bet," she said.

It was time to visit Wolfe.

## 89

TRAFFIC WAS LIGHT ON the way to the courthouse. I turned off Queens Boulevard and nosed past the D.A.'s parking lot, saw Wolfe's Audi near the door. The lot was half empty, but I didn't want to leave the Plymouth there. They have municipal parking a half-block away. It looked like a graveyard for the few cars still remaining. Dark and deserted—a mugger's paradise. I hit the switch to disable the ignition, not worrying about even the lowest-grade thief breaking in for the radio. I don't use a car alarm—they're a waste of time unless you're close by.

It was eight-forty-five when I pushed open the glass doors to the D.A.'s office. The guy at the desk looked up from his crossword puzzle. His eyes never reached my face.

"The jail's next door," he said.

"I know," I told him. "I have an appointment with A.D.A. Wolfe."

Still not looking at me, he picked up a black phone on the desk, punched in a couple of numbers.

"There's a lawyer here—says he's got an appointment with Wolfe."

He listened for a second, looked up again. "Name?" he asked.

"Burke."

He spoke my name into the phone, then put it down.

"Turn right past the divider, last door at the end of the corridor."

"Thanks," I said to the top of his head.

I found the place easy enough. Wolfe was sitting behind a big desk. The top was swept clean—a white orchid floated in a brandy snifter in one corner. Two monster piles of paper were on a shelf behind her. I guess she knew most cons can read upside down.

She was wearing a white wool jacket over a burnt-orange dress, a string of pearls around her neck. Her nails were a few shades darker than her lipstick—both red. Wolfe had a soft, pale face—one look and you could see it wasn't from fear, it was her natural color. The silver wings gleamed in her lustrous hair. When I came in the room she stood up, reached across the desk to shake hands.

"Thank you for seeing me," I said.

"I can't promise you much privacy," she replied. "There's a lot of people still working in the other offices."

I couldn't tell if it was a warning—it didn't matter.

"I've been working on something for a while," I said. "And I ran across some stuff I thought you'd be interested in."

She lit a cigarette with a cheap plastic lighter, pushing an ashtray with some hotel's name on it in my general direction. She was good at waiting.

"Anyway," I said, "I got to the point where I need some more information—another piece of the puzzle. . . ."

"And you believe I have this piece?"

"I'm sure you do," I said.

A tall black woman stalked into the office, ignoring me as if I was a lump of furniture. Her mouth was a grim line.

"It was an acquittal," she told Wolfe.

Wolfe's face didn't change. "It figured to be," she said. "Did you stand up?"

"Stand up?" the black woman asked.

I knew what she meant even if the black woman didn't. Baby-rapers have a way of smirking when the jury refuses to believe their victims—as if the jury said it was okay, what they did. A good prosecutor looks them in the eye, memorizing their faces.

"What did you do when the foreman read the verdict?" Wolfe asked the question another way.

"I went over to the defendant—I told him I'd see him again," the black woman said.

"You stood up," Wolfe told her. "Round one, remember?"

"I remember," the black woman said. "He'll be back. And I'll be ready for him."

Wolfe smiled—I could feel the heat coming off the black woman standing behind me. She knew what the smile meant.

"Want to take tomorrow off?" Wolfe asked.

"I'll take a day off when Jefferson goes down," the black woman snapped.

"We all will," Wolfe said. It was a dismissal.

I lit another cigarette. Wolfe hadn't hung around just for a meeting with me. Time to get to it.

"I'm playing it straight down the line on this. Did Lily talk to you?"

"Lily did. McGowan called me too."

"And?"

"And I still don't know what you want, Mr. Burke."

"I want . . ." I started to say. A guy about five and a half feet tall and four feet wide walked in, stepping between me and Wolfe. His hair was cropped close to his scalp—he had a round face but cop's eyes. He was wearing a black knit shirt over some gray slacks. The shirt didn't have an alligator on the front, but it did feature a shoulder holster. The .38 was only a small dot on his broad chest. He looked like a retired wrestler or a bouncer in a waterfront bar.

"How's it going?" he asked Wolfe, never taking his eyes from me.

"Jefferson was acquitted," she said.

"Jefferson is a miserable fucking piece of slime," the big guy said, chewing on each word like it was raw meat.

Wolfe smiled at him. "This isn't Jefferson's lawyer," she said.

The big guy shrugged. It was like watching an earthquake. "You want the mutt?" he asked.

"Sure, bring him over," Wolfe told him.

The big guy walked out, light on his feet. Maybe he'd been a boxer instead of a wrestler.

Wolfe lit another smoke for herself and held up her hand, telling me to wait.

The big guy was back in a minute, holding Wolfe's Rottweiler on a short leather leash.

"Hi, Bruise!" Wolfe said. The beast walked right past me, put his paws on the desk, and tried to lick her face. She slapped him away good-naturedly. "Bruiser, go to place!" she said.

The big guy unsnapped the leash. The Rottweiler walked to a corner of the room and flopped down on the carpet. He watched me like a junkie watching a mailbox on welfare-check day.

"I'll be around," the big guy said. I got the message—as if the Rottweiler wasn't enough.

"I'm listening," Wolfe said.

"I'm looking for a picture. Of a kid. A picture of a kid having sex with a man. I talked to a lot of people, went a lot of places. I think I know where the picture is. I think you know the people who have the picture. All I want is for you to give me a name and address."

"You said you had something for me?" she asked. One look at Wolfe and you knew she wasn't talking about money—even in Queens County.

I tossed the little leather address book I took from the pimp on her desk. She didn't make a move to touch it.

"It's from a guy who sells little boys. In Times Square. First names. Initials. Phone numbers. And some kind of code."

"How did you come by this?"

"I was taking up a collection—he donated it."

Wolfe took a drag of her cigarette, put it in the overflowing ashtray, picked up the book. She turned the pages slowly, nodding to herself.

"Did he get hurt making this donation?"

"Not badly," I told her. "If you want to ask him yourself, his name's Rodney. He works out of that fast-food chicken joint on Forty-sixth off Eighth."

Wolfe nodded. "And you want to trade this book for the information?"

I took a gamble. "It's yours," I told her. "No matter what you decide."

"You have a copy?"

"No," I lied.

Wolfe tapped her nails on the desk. It wasn't a nervous gesture—something she did when she was thinking. A phone rang someplace down the hall. It rang twice, then stopped.

A tiny little woman burst into the office, her face flushed, waving a bunch of papers in her hand. "We got the printout!" she yelled, the words sticking in her throat when she saw Wolfe had a visitor. The Rottweiler snarled at the intrusion. The woman had her hair all piled on top of her head; a giant diamond sparkled on her finger. She put her hands on her hips. "Bruiser, *please!*" she said.

The big dog subsided. Wolfe laughed. "I'll look at it later, okay?"

"Okay!" the other woman shouted, running out of the office as if she was going to a fire sale.

"Are all your people so worked up?" I asked her.

"We don't have draftees in this unit," she said, her eyes watching me closely.

"Not even the dog?"

"Not even him." She fingered her string of pearls. "What do you need?"

"I know the woman I'm looking for is named Bonnie. I know she lives on Cheshire Drive in Little Neck. Maybe with a fat guy."

"That's it?"

"That's it. She's running a kiddie-porn ring—I figure you have your eye on her."

Wolfe said nothing, waiting for me.

"And if you don't," I told her, "then I just gave you some more information, right?"

Wolfe took a breath. "What is it you really want, Mr. Burke? You obviously already know how to find this person."

I lit a cigarette for myself—it was time to tell her.

"I have to go in there—I have to get that picture. If I can buy it, I will."

"And if you can't . . ."

I shrugged.

Wolfe reached behind her and pulled a bunch of papers onto her desk. Some of the sheets were long and yellow—I knew what they were.

"Mr. Burke, Lily did call me, as I said. But I did a little checking on my own before I agreed to this meeting."

"So?"

"So you are not exactly unknown to law enforcement, are you?" She ran her finger down one of the yellow sheets, reading aloud, lifting her eyes to my face every once in a while. "Armed robbery, assault one, armed robbery *and* assault. Attempted murder, two counts. Possession of illegal weapons . . . Should I go on?"

"If you want to," I told her. "I was a lot younger then."

Wolfe smiled. "You're rehabilitated?"

"I'm a coward," I told her.

"We have twenty-seven arrests, two felony convictions, three placements in juvenile facilities, one youthful-offender adjudication."

"Sounds about right to me," I told her.

"How did you beat the attempted-murder case? It says you were acquitted at trial."

"It was a gunfight," I told her. "The cops arrested the winner. The other guys testified it was somebody else who shot them."

"I see."

"Anything on that sheet tell you I don't keep my word?" I asked her.

Wolfe smiled again. "Rap sheets don't tell you much, Mr. Burke. Take this one—it doesn't even give your first name."

"Sure it does," I told her.

"Mr. Burke, this shows a different first name for every single time you were arrested. Maxwell Burke, John Burke, Samuel Burke, Leonard Burke, Juan Burke . . ." She stopped, smiling again. "*Juan?*"

*"Dónde está el dinero?"* I said.

This time she laughed. It was a sweet chuckle, the kind only a grown woman can do. It made my heart hurt for Flood.

"Do you have a true first name, Mr. Burke?"

"No."

Wolfe's smile was ironic. "What does it say on your birth certificate?"

"Baby Boy Burke," I told her, my voice flat.

"Oh," Wolfe said. She'd seen enough birth certificates to know I'd never have to worry about buying a present on Mother's Day. I shrugged again, showing her it didn't mean anything to me. Now.

Wolfe took another piece of paper off her desk—this one wasn't yellow.

"The FBI has a sheet on you too," she said.

"I never took a federal fall."

"I see that. But you *are* listed as a suspect in several deals involving military weapons. And a CIA cross-reference shows you were out of the country for almost a year."

"I like to travel," I told her.

"You don't have a passport," she said.

"I didn't come here to ask you for a date," I said. "I'm not applying for a job either. I admire what you do—I respect your work. I thought I could help you—that you could help me too."

"And if we can't work this out?"

"I'm going into that house," I told her, looking her full in her lovely face like the crazy bastard this case had turned me into.

Wolfe picked up the phone, punched a number. "Nothing's wrong," she said. "Come in here." She hung up. "I want to be sure you're not wearing a wire, okay? Then we'll talk."

"Whatever you say," I told her.

The bouncer came back in, the .38 almost lost in his meaty hand.

"I told you nothing was wrong," Wolfe said.

"That was a few seconds ago," he snapped. The Rottweiler growled at him. "Good boy," he said.

"Would you please take this gentleman with you and see if he has anything on him he shouldn't have," Wolfe told him.

The big guy put his hand on my shoulder—it felt like an anvil.

"There's no problem," Wolfe said to him, a warning note in her voice.

We went past a couple of offices—the tall black woman was reading something and making notes, the little lady with the piled-up hair was talking a mile a minute on the phone, a handsome black man was studying a hand-drawn chart on the wall. I heard a teletype machine clatter—bad news for somebody.

"Doesn't anybody go home around here?" I asked the big guy.

"Yeah, pal—some people go home. Some people should *stay* home."

I didn't try any more conversation-starters. He took me into a bare office and did the whole search number, working at it like a prison guard you forgot to bribe. He took me back to Wolfe.

"Nothing," he said, disappointed. He left us alone.

The Rottweiler was sitting next to Wolfe, watching the door as she patted his head. She pointed to his corner again and he went back, as reluctant as the big guy was.

"Mr. Burke, this is the situation. The woman you intend to visit is Bonnie Browne, with an 'e.' She sometimes uses the name Young as well—it's her maiden name. The man she lives with is her husband. George Browne. He has two arrests for child molesting—one dismissal, one plea to an endangering count. Served ninety days in California. She's never been arrested."

I put my hand in my pocket, reaching for a smoke.

"Don't write any of this down," Wolfe said.

"I'm not," I told her, lighting the smoke.

"We believe this woman to be the principal in a great number of corporations—holding companies, really. But she doesn't operate the way most of the kiddie-porn merchants do. You understand what I mean?"

"Yeah," I told her. "You want the pictures—videotapes, whatever—you send a money order to a drop-box in Brussels. When the money clears, you get a shipment in the mail from Denmark, or England, or any other place they're established. Then the money orders get mailed to an offshore bank—maybe the Cayman Islands—and the bank makes a loan to some phony corporation set up in the States."

Wolfe looked at me thoughtfully. "You've been at this quite a while."

"I do a lot of work—you get bits and pieces here and there—you put it together."

"Okay. But this woman doesn't work like that. Her product is special. She guarantees all her stuff is so-called collector's items. No reproduction—every picture is one of a kind."

"What's to stop some freak from copying the pictures?"

"She puts some kind of mark on every picture she takes—like this." Wolfe showed me a tiny drawing of a standing man, his hand on the shoulder of a little boy. It looked like it was hand-drawn with one of those needlepoint pens architects use. Only it was in a soft blue color. "The mark won't survive a copy—she uses something called chroma-blue ink. She puts every mark on herself—by hand."

"What's the point?"

"There's two points, Mr. Burke. The first is that she gets a minimum of five thousand dollars a picture, so she can achieve huge profits without a lot of volume."

I took a drag on my cigarette, waiting.

"The other point is more significant. She produces pictures to order."

"You mean some freak calls her and says he wants to see a certain thing go down . . . ?"

"Yes. If you want a blond boy wearing a snowsuit, you got it."

"You going to drop her?" I asked.

"We *are* going to drop her—but not soon. We're just beginning to trace pictures back to her. We don't have a prayer of getting a search warrant now."

"And if you ask for one, it might get back to her?"

Wolfe raised her eyebrows. "You are a cynical man, Mr. Burke."

"Those black robes the judges wear," I told her, "they don't change you inside."

Wolfe didn't say anything for a minute, fingering her pearls. "Do you know anything about search warrants?" she finally asked.

Now I knew why she wanted to make sure I wasn't wired. "I know if a citizen breaks in a house and finds dope or whatever, the evidence won't be suppressed unless the citizen is an agent of law enforcement."

"Um . . ." Wolfe said, encouraging me. I hadn't told her what she wanted. Yet.

"I also know that if the police are called to a location . . . say because there's a burglary in progress . . . and they find something bad, they can take it."

"And use it in court."

"And use it in court," I agreed.

Wolfe's face was flat and hard. "This woman wouldn't report a burglary," she said.

I lit a last cigarette. "You have her house under surveillance?"

"We might—starting tomorrow."

"Round the clock?"

"Yes."

I took a drag of my smoke.

"Any citizen has an obligation to rescue people when there's a fire," I said.

Wolfe held her hand across the desk. I brought it quickly to my lips before she could do anything and walked out of her office.

# 90

I TOOK A COUPLE OF days to sort things out, telling myself that I didn't want to hit the filth factory in Little Neck the very first night Wolfe's people were on the job. The truth was that I wanted to get back to myself—get cautious, work the angles, find some way to get the job done with the least possible risk.

But it all jammed together in my head. I'd start to work out some scam—maybe have the Mole take out the phones in the house, walk in dressed up like a repairman, look around. Or maybe just a gentle breaking-and-entering while the two of them were out of the house in their little schoolbus. No matter what I tried on, it wouldn't fit. You can't scam humans who produce custom-tailored kiddie porn.

I thought about how out of control the whole lousy thing was. I could never have a woman like Wolfe. Flood wasn't coming back. I could live with not having the woman I wanted; I had a lot of practice at not having choices. But I couldn't live with Strega. I had to burn the *bruja*-woman out of my life before she took me down with her.

The Prof reported in. He had made a couple of runs past the target. Then he'd knocked on the door, asking if they wanted any yard work done. The woman answered the door herself—told him to get lost. No sign of security people.

I got the blueprints of the house from the city. Checked through the back files—the house was jointly owned by the woman and her husband. Purchased for $345,000 about four years ago. Conventional bank mortgage. Fifty bucks got me a look at the papers—she put down a little more than a hundred grand. Listed her occupation as "private investor." Declared an income of almost $250,000 a year.

The phone-company employees who sell information charge more—they still think of themselves as a monopoly. Two phones in the house—both numbers unlisted. Their combined bill ran about five hundred dollars a month, most of it toll calls. Just for the hell of it, I checked the numbers against the ones I'd copied from the pimp's address book I gave to Wolfe. None of them matched—they were in a different league.

It was time to be myself again.

## 91

I ROUNDED UP MOST OF the crew with no problems, but I couldn't find Michelle at any of her usual spots. Finally, I dropped in to The

Very Idea, a transsexual bar where she hangs out when she isn't working.

"She's getting her hair cut, darling," her friend Kathy told me.

I made a face—her favorite "salon" reminded me of a parakeet's cage, feathers flying, shrill shrieking, and shit all over the floor.

"Oh, Burke, don't look like that. Nobody goes *there* anymore. Daniel has opened a fabulous new place on Fifth—here's a card."

"Thanks, Kathy," I said, throwing a twenty on the bar to cover her tab.

"See you around, handsome," she replied. I don't think it was the twenty bucks—transsexuals just have more empathy.

La Dolce Vita was a couple of flights up. It had a tiny little elevator but I took the stairs. I wasn't worried about running into anything, but if I was going to get back to myself, it was time to get started.

The joint was all pastel colors and mirrors. The waiting room was decorated with people reading the Italian edition of *Vogue* and drinking coffee from glass cups. The receptionist was inside a little island in the middle, watching the fun.

"Can I help you, sir?" she asked.

"Is Daniel here?"

"He's with a customer."

"It's the customer I want—which way?"

She pointed straight ahead. I followed her finger into a room overlooking Fifth Avenue—the windows sloped at an angle, flowers covering the broad base. Michelle was getting combed out by a slim man wearing a white sweater over blue jeans—white running shoes on his feet. She was in the middle of a heated exchange with the woman in the next chair.

"Honey, please don't go on about the Holy Coast. The only thing Los Angeles ever contributed to culture is the drive-by homicide!"

I stepped between them before it got bloody.

"Burke!" she called out. "You're just in time."

"For what?" I asked her.

"For *Daniel*," she said, like I was from another planet. "He just got a cancellation—and you need a haircut."

Daniel and I shook hands—he had a strong grip, an ironic smile on his face.

"Burke," he said. "What's your first name?"

"I'm not paying by check," I told him.

"Will you *stop* it?" Michelle snapped, turning in her chair to slap at my arm. "This isn't a poolroom."

"Can I talk to you for a minute?" I said.

"Talk."

"Not here."

Michelle sighed. "Oh, really—it's always such a big deal. Just give me a few minutes—sit down," she said, pointing to the chair next to her.

"This has to stay a few minutes anyway, Michelle," Daniel told her, patting her hairdo.

"Don't rush yourself, baby. Anyway, you have to cut my friend's hair too."

Daniel looked a question at me. I shrugged—what the hell.

"You have to get shampooed first," he said.

"Can't you just cut it?"

"It has to be wet," he said with a sideways glance at Michelle.

"He was raised in a barn," Michelle sighed.

I let some little girl lead me to another room, where she put the shampoo in my hair, rinsed it out, did it all over again. Daniel was still playing with Michelle's hair when I came back.

"How would you like this cut?" he asked.

"Just do whatever you do," I told him. I saw him glance at Michelle again. "Don't get stupid," I warned him.

He walked out of the room to get something he needed.

"Michelle, we got something on for tonight, okay?"

"A phone job for me?"

"And something with the Mole too," I told her. For once, she didn't make a crack about the Mole.

"What time?"

"We'll meet around five, five-thirty. Mama's basement, okay?"

"I'll be there, baby," she told me, giving me a quick kiss and walking out.

Daniel finished cutting my hair. With the room quiet, it was like a real barbershop—he even knew something about prize-fighting. When he was finished, I looked the same—Daniel told me it was an art.

I went out to the receptionist, asking for Michelle.

"Oh, she left a few minutes ago. She said you'd be taking care of her bill with yours."

What was I going to do? "Okay, how much for the whole thing?"

"Let's see . . ." she told me brightly, "with tax, that's a hundred and seventy dollars and fifty-six cents."

"What!"

"Michelle had a styling, a color consult, a manicure, and a pedicure," she said, as if that explained everything.

I didn't leave a tip for Daniel—if he owned that joint he had a license to steal.

# 92

"HOLD STILL!" MICHELLE ORDERED. She was sitting next to me, my right hand spread out on a board she held in her lap, working carefully with a rapidograph, inking in the crossed lightning bolts of the Real Brotherhood.

The Prof peeked over my shoulder—he knew what the real thing looked like better than most.

"You should have been an artist, babe," he complimented her.

"Honey," Michelle said, "I *am* an artist—I give a whole new meaning to the term 'satisfied customer.'"

Max sat in the lotus position against the wall in Mama's basement. He was dressed all in black—not the ceremonial silk he usually wore for combat—some dull matte material. He fitted a hood of the same stuff over his face. It covered the back of his neck, blending into the jacket—only his eyes were visible. He was working with some black paste, rubbing it into his hands.

"Mole, you got the car?"

He nodded. We wouldn't use the Plymouth to approach the house. Michelle was going to stash it a few blocks away—if anyone was following us, we'd switch cars, leaving the Mole's untraceable junker behind.

"The phones go down at eleven-thirty?" I asked him.

He nodded again. There was no burglar alarm, no direct connection to the local police station either. There wouldn't be.

We didn't have to go over it again. Michelle would call, act like she was a telephone solicitor, ask to speak to the man of the house. If the husband answered, she'd do her best to keep him on the phone while I was ringing the front-door bell. Max would go over the back fence, penetrate the house. He'd take out anyone he found, except the woman—I needed to talk to her. If the woman answered the door, I'd brace her right there, take her inside, and get the pictures. If the wrong person answered the door, I'd show them the pistol, play it from there while Max worked his way through the rest of the house.

And if I didn't like the look of the front of the house, I'd find my own way inside.

The Prof and I each had a little radio transmitter the Mole hooked up. When I hit the switch, the Prof would climb behind the wheel of the crash-car and start the engine. I'd come busting out the front door. And the Mole would turn the house into an incinerator. Then he and Max would go back over the fence to where Michelle would be waiting.

It should all be over by midnight.

Michelle was finished with my hand and started on my face. The heavy pancake makeup made me a few shades darker, and the black mustache changed the shape of my face even more. I'd have a hat on my head and dark glasses over my eyes.

"What did McGowan say when you brought him the kid . . . Terry?" I asked her.

She didn't answer—I saw something in her face, her mouth set and hard.

"Michelle?"

"I didn't bring him to McGowan," she said.

"What did you do with him?" I asked her, keeping my voice level.

"Burke, he couldn't go home. His father's an evil pig—he's the one who started him off."

"That's why he ran away?"

"He didn't run away—his father sold him to that pimp."

And people think it's going to be air pollution that kills us all someday.

"What did you do with him?" I asked her again.

"He's my child now," she said. "I'll take care of him."

"Michelle," I said, my voice patient but my mind screaming *trouble!*, you can't keep that kid in your hotel. Sooner or later somebody's going to . . ."

"He's with me," the Mole said.

"In the junkyard?"

"I fixed up a place for him," the Mole said, a hurt tone in his voice.

"The Mole's teaching him, Burke," Michelle said. "He's learning all about electronics and stuff. He's real smart. You wouldn't believe how much . . ."

"Jesus Christ!"

"Burke, he's *my* boy, okay? We take him to SAFE. Lily's working with him. He's going to be fine."

"What if someone comes looking for him?"

"What if they do?" she challenged.

"Michelle, listen for a minute. You're in the life, baby. What kind of a mother could you be?"

"Better than the mother you had," she said, her voice quiet.

I lit a cigarette. Maybe the kid would never get to prep school, but the state makes the worst mother of them all.

"He's one of us," the Mole said, looking at Michelle.

I gave it up. "Just don't expect me to be his goddamned uncle," I said.

Michelle gave me a kiss on the cheek. "When I have my operation, I'm going to adopt him, Burke. He can go to college and everything . . . you can scam up some papers for him . . . I started to put money aside already. . . ."

"I know," I said. "And the Mole's going to buy him a puppy, right?"

"He has lots of dogs," the Mole said in a serious tone.

My fingers twisted into the sign for "Okay," aiming at Max. He was gone. I peered into the corner where he had been working with the black paste, wondering how he did that—and then I saw him. He hadn't moved at all—the black cloth ate the light until he was nothing but a puddle of shadow. They'd never see him coming.

The Prof came over and stood beside me. "Burke, if that old woman doesn't talk, you going to walk?"

I thought of what Mama said not so long ago. No rules. "I'm coming out with that picture, Prof," I told him. "It's the jailhouse or the graveyard. If it goes sour, do what you have to do."

"I know what I have to do," he said.

I took one last look around.

"Let's do it," I told them.

## 93

I LED THE TWO-CAR convoy carefully through Manhattan, me in the maroon Cadillac sedan the Mole had welded back together, Michelle following in the Plymouth. The Prof was crouched down under the dash on the passenger side of the Cadillac, keeping up a steady stream of chatter. He didn't look uncomfortable—for a guy who spent half his life pretending to have no legs, hiding under the dash was no big thing. The Mole rode next to Michelle in the front of the Plymouth. Max was in the trunk.

The City Planning map showed the cul-de-sac at the end of Cheshire Drive, but I'd gone over the ground in person a couple of times to be sure of the layout. The back of the house was separated from a little park by the same wall that went around to the front. I brought the Cadillac to a stop, checking the mirrors. Michelle pulled in behind me, getting out to pop open the Plymouth's hood as if she was having engine trouble. I took out the jumper cables, preparing to hook them up in case anyone watching got to wondering what we were all doing.

All clear. I opened the trunk of the Plymouth and Max flowed out. He was a black blot against the white wall for a second; then he was gone.

"You remember where the phone booth is?" I asked Michelle.

Her disgusted look was all the answer I was going to get.

A black rope flew over the wall. The Mole shouldered the strap of his satchel, got a grip, and heaved himself up. The Prof and I each grabbed a leg and shoved too—the Mole isn't exactly agile. Max would probably throw him over the wall on the way out.

"You make the call—you hang up—you cruise *slowly* back here and wait for Max and the Mole to come over the wall, okay? If there's trouble, it'll be at the front of the house."

"I'll be here," Michelle said.

The Prof and I got back in the Cadillac and motored quietly away, Michelle right on our tail. I drove her past the phone booth just to be sure, waiting until I saw her brake lights flash. I checked my watch—eleven-twenty-five.

The Cadillac turned into Cheshire Drive, cruising past a black Ford with two men inside. Wolfe's people were real subtle. I thought how easy it would be for anyone to block off the street on our way back, checking the manicured front lawns of the expensive houses on each side. Plenty of room.

I used the short driveway in front of the big house to turn around, leaving the Cadillac's nose pointing back out.

"It's time," I whispered to the Prof.

I closed the door of the Cadillac quietly. The front gate was locked. I jumped up and grabbed the top, pulled myself up in a second, dropped down on the other side. I covered the path to the front door quickly, my ears hurting from listening for sirens.

The door was black—a dramatic counterpoint to the fieldstone front of the house. I couldn't see a knocker or a bell. Soft light flowed from a large bay window, but the house was quiet. I eased away from the door, peering into the front window. It was a living room that nobody ever lived in—plastic covering the furniture, every piece sharply aligned, not a cigarette butt or an old newspaper in sight. Ringing the front-door bell would be a mistake. Maybe they were all asleep, maybe even sleeping right through Michelle's phone call.

I slipped off the front step and around to the side of the house, checking through each window for humans. Nothing. The joint was as quiet as a Russian civil-rights meeting.

A double-wide driveway continued from the front around the side, sweeping in a gentle curve to someplace behind the house. I followed it along, feeling the smooth pavement under my feet, checking the string of floodlights angling from the house. They were dark now, but there had to be a switch somewhere inside. The driveway ended in a teardrop-shaped slab of concrete behind the house—a schoolbus-yellow van sat next to a dark, anonymous sedan. A sloping extension had been built off the house. It looked like a garage, but it had to be the entrance to the basement.

I did another slow circuit before I returned to the most likely prospect—the window at the back corner of the house where it was pitch-dark. There was no alarm tape around the border—I couldn't see any wires either. I put on a pair of gloves before I tried to raise the window. The wood looked pretty old—I didn't want to get splinters. It was latched. I took a roll of heavy masking tape from my coat and carefully covered the pane nearest the latch. I used three layers of tape, leaving the ends free, smoothing it down from corner to corner. Then the little rubber mallet, softly tapping, working from the corners toward the middle of the pane. My heart was beating hard, like it always does when I work, but I breathed slowly through my nose, keeping it under control. You get too impatient doing one of these jobs, you get a lot of time to think about it in a place where the windows don't have glass.

I put my hand flat against the windowpane, working the cracked glass carefully, easing it away from the frame. It made a tiny crackle, like when you crumple the cellophane wrapper from a pack of smokes. I slipped my hand inside and pushed against the tape; the broken glass clung to its other side. I found the latch. Gently withdrew my hand and started to work the window up. Every couple of inches or so I sprayed some liquid silicon into the channel to smooth the way.

When the window got to the top, I took a couple of deep breaths to steady myself. Then I put my head inside and risked a quick spray from the flashlight. It looked like a man's den, the kind you see in magazines. Big leather easy chair, television set in one corner, some kind of plaques on the walls. The room felt musty and dead, like it was never used.

I climbed over the sill and dropped into the room, pulling the window closed behind me, adding up the crimes in my head. Breaking and entering. Burglary of an occupied dwelling. So far, not so bad. I pulled the dark nylon stocking mask over my head, adjusting it so the slits matched up with my eyes. When it felt right, I took the pistol from an inside pocket. From now on, it was going to be Felony City.

I stepped out into a long hallway running down one side of the house. To my right was an eat-in kitchen, windows on two sides. To my left was the foyer, with that plastic-covered living room off to one side. Still quiet. The whole place was covered with thick wall-to-wall carpet the same color as dirt. I think they call it "earth tones." I padded down the hall toward the front door, looking for the staircase. The stairs were carpet-covered too, but I eased my weight onto each one just the same.

Halfway up the stairs I heard the music. Some kind of orchestra stuff, but real light—all strings and flutes. I reached the top, waited, listening hard now. The music was coming from a room at the rear of the house, the only room with a light on—I couldn't see inside. I slipped around the newel post at the top of the stairs, heading in the opposite direction. The second floor wasn't anywhere near as big as the first—just two rooms that looked like bedrooms, windows looking out toward the street. Each had its own bathroom attached. I didn't risk the flash to look closely, just checked to make sure nobody was sleeping there. The rooms were all dark. Empty.

I walked toward the open door at the other end, toward the music and I didn't know what else. When I got close, I could see the door was at the far corner of the room; everything else was off to the left. I took the pistol in both hands, holding it high above my head over my right shoulder; my back was against the wall. Then I stepped inside with my left foot, pivoting and bringing the pistol down and across my chest, sweeping the room.

A short, stocky woman was sitting on a stool at a white drafting table, peering at something under an architect's lamp. The light came from behind her—I couldn't make out her face. She was wearing a pink quilted bathrobe, orthopedic shoes on her feet. She didn't even look up, concentrating on something. I was almost on top of her before she looked up.

"Don't scream," I told her, my voice calm, showing her the pistol.

She opened her mouth wide, gulped in a ton of air instead, her eyes bulging. "Oh my god!" she said, like she'd been expecting this.

"Just keep quiet and you won't get hurt," I said, still calm and quiet, gently reaching out toward her.

"What is this?" she asked, her voice shaking.

"It's about a picture, bitch," I told her, grabbing the front of her robe with one gloved hand, my voice filtered through the nylon mask. "I want a picture you have. Understand?"

She tried to pull away from me, plucking at my arm in a feeble gesture. I slapped her lightly across the face with the pistol. I put my face as close to hers as I could. "I got my orders—I bring the picture or your fucking head!"

The woman's eyes rolled up and she slumped against me—I jerked her face up again—she was breathing in gasps but she wasn't going to faint.

I grabbed her by the back of the neck, holding the pistol in front of her face with the other hand, pulling her off the stool, dragging her toward a chair near a butcher-block desk in the corner. A goose-neck lamp was shining on some papers. I shoved the woman into an oxblood leather chair and stepped back.

"Who are you?" she asked.

"I'm a man with a job, understand? I don't have a lot of time."

I tossed the picture Strega gave me on the table in front of her. Her eyes flicked over to it but she didn't make a move.

"That's the kid," I told her. "You got a picture of him somewhere in this house. I want it."

"Why would I have a picture . . ."

I stepped forward and backhanded her across the face, not too hard—just enough to make her focus on what she had to do.

I started pulling things out of my pocket—a small coil of piano wire, a little glass bottle of clear fluid, a strip of leather. And a straight razor. The woman's eyes were huge.

I stepped to her again—she cowered, covering her face with her hands. No rings on her fingers—no polish on her nails. I slipped the leather strip past her clawing fingers, fastening the gag in her mouth. She jumped forward—I jammed the heel of my hand into her chest—she let out a burst of air and fell forward from the waist. It only took me another minute to lash her wrists to the arms of the chair with the piano wire.

Her mouth was silent but her eyes were screaming. "You got two choices," I told her. "You see this bottle? It's ether. To knock you out. If I have to do that, I'm going to chop off the fingers on your hand. One by one. And I'm going to wait for you to wake up, bitch. You'll wake up screaming, understand?"

Her face was coming apart behind the gag.

"You understand!" I snarled at her.

She nodded her head hard enough to make it fall off her neck.

"I'm going to take the gag out now—you don't tell me what I want to know, you bleed to death right in that chair. Through the fucking stumps."

I pulled the gag from her mouth—she struggled for a breath, panting as if she'd run a mile.

I watched her face. "Don't even think about screaming," I told her.

She was more under control now. "I'm not alone in the house," she gasped.

"Yeah, you are," I said. "It's me that's not alone here."

Her eyes were on me, trying to figure out what I meant. Hard, flat doll's eyes—nobody home behind them. A thin, ugly smell came off her. Her breathing was under control. "I have no money here," she said, as if that settled everything.

I leaned close again, letting her look into my eyes. "I want the picture," I told her. "Last chance."

"Just the one picture?"

"Don't bargain with me, you fucking slime. I got my orders."

She was watching me, thinking. No good. I picked up the leather gag.

"In the safe!" she said. "Please, don't . . ."

"Where's the safe?"

"In the floor—under the work table."

I took a look—the floor under the table was all parquet squares. Four of them came away when I pulled. The combination lock was set so it was facing the ceiling.

"Give it to me," I said.

She knew what I meant. "Six left, twenty-four right, twelve left."

The safe was a deep one, maybe three feet into the floor. Video cassettes to the right, 35mm cartridges in plastic containers. And Polaroids—hundreds of them, each one in a separate plastic jacket.

"You got an index?" I asked her.

"No," she said, lifeless. She was probably lying, but I didn't have the time to find out. I knew what I was looking for. It only took a couple of minutes—a couple of minutes of looking through the worst thing on this slop basin of a planet—a little baby peacefully sleeping, a man's erect penis in his mouth as a pacifier—kids from a few days old to maybe ten or eleven, penetrated with every blunt object freakish minds could think of—smiling kids, playing with each other—a little boy, maybe six years old, his screaming face adjusted by the camera so you could see him being sodomized from behind, two strands of barbed wire drawn across his little chest to make a bloody "X." All the pictures had the tiny blue image of a man and a boy in one corner—her mark.

The picture of Scotty was just what he told Immaculata—wearing his little striped T-shirt and nude from the waist down. Sucking on a man wearing a clown suit. I put it in my pocket.

I went back to the woman. "You got what you wanted?" she asked. Her voice hard and confident now, back to something she understood.

"Yeah. I got it. And I'm going to give you something for it too." I held the razor to her throat, whispering in her ear. "You're dead, bitch. You took a picture of the wrong kid this time. I were you, I'd call the D.A. and surrender—cooperate with the Man. You know how it's done. Find yourself a nice, safe cell for a few years. But get someone to taste your food for you."

I poured the whole bottle of ether over the white cloth—the smell made me dizzy.

"You promised not to hurt me!" she screamed.

"You promised those kids a day in the country," I told her, slapping the sopping wet cloth over her mouth and nose, holding it there while she struggled, making sure she could get enough air to mix with the ether and take her down. The Mole had warned me I could kill her if I used too much. Accidents happen.

Her head lolled forward, unconscious. I unwrapped her wrists, slapping them to bring the color back. I dragged her out of the chair by the front of her robe to one of the bedrooms. Tossed her on the bed. Moved her around until she was lying face up. She looked asleep—I wasn't going to put my face close enough to her to find out.

Max and the Mole were somewhere in the house. I'd told them to give me fifteen minutes and then make tracks, but I knew they weren't going anywhere until they knew I was safe. Just like I knew the Prof would sit outside the front door with the motor running even if a SWAT team was coming up the street. I hit the stairs running. Every second in the house was a big risk now. The first floor was empty—even the kitchen looked like nobody ever ate a meal there. It was all for the neighbors, like a window display of a typical American home. The neighbors would never look in the basement.

I opened the door to the cellar stairs off the foyer and stepped through. Found myself in another small room, set up to resemble a cloakroom—coats hanging on hooks, umbrella stand in one corner. It took another minute to find the door behind the coats. Locked from the inside. I took out a credit card and slipped it between the door and the frame, working it gently, telling myself if there was a deadbolt on the other side I'd have to try another way in. But the loid worked, and the door popped open. Another couple of steps and I was at the top of a curving wrought-iron staircase. I tested my weight against the first step and then I heard a man's voice, high and shaky, like he was near the edge of something.

"Look, you guys are making a mistake, okay? I mean . . . I *know* people, understand? Whatever problem you got, I can take care of it. Just sitting here *looking* at me isn't doing you any good, right?"

I followed the staircase toward the voice. Halfway down, the darkness faded. Indirect lighting bathed the basement floor, coming from some concealed panels. A fat man was sitting in one of those huge beanbag chairs, one hand on each side for balance, staring into a dark corner like it held all life's secrets. The Mole was hunkered down against one wall at the side of the chair, his satchel open in front of him. His big head swiveled to cover the room, a stocking mask stretched over his thick glasses. He looked like a malignant frog.

The man's eyes rolled over to me as I came down the stairs. He watched me approach, relief coming into his face.

"Hey, are *you* in charge? These guys . . ."

"Don't talk," I told him.

It didn't have any effect. "What difference does it make, man? This whole place is soundproofed, okay? I mean . . . take a look around."

I did. The walls were lined with dark-brown cork, the ceiling covered with acoustic tile. Even the rug on the floor felt like it was covering a thick rubber mat.

"So nobody can hear the kids scream?" I asked him.

"Hey! What is this?" he yelled at me, trying for a hard edge to his voice.

I cocked the pistol. He winced at the sound. I stuck the gun into his fat face, depressing the skin under his right eye. "I. Don't. Have. Time," I told him, pushing at his face with every word.

"Whaaat?" he moaned. "Just tell me . . ."

"I want the *pictures*. I want the *film*. I want the *lists*. I want the *money*."

The fat man wasn t going to bargain like his wife. "It's upstairs. All upstairs. I swear . . . down here there's just some money . . . in the workbench . . . just walk-around cash. . . . It's all in the bank. . . . Tomorrow morning, when the banks open, I . . ."

"Shut up!" I told him, backing away. The workbench drawer had three short stacks of bills. I tossed the money to the Mole. It went into his satchel. The basement looked like a kid's playroom—stuffed animals, dolls, a hobbyhorse, electric trains in one corner. I checked behind the only door, but there was nothing except the oil burner and a hot-water heater. A back door opened into the extension to the house. I walked through it quickly. No windows to the outside, and the floor was concrete like the driveway. All designed so they could pull the van inside and discharge its cargo. And take pictures of kids.

It was time to disappear.

"Your wife is upstairs," I told him. "She's okay—just sleeping. I'm going to give you a shot too. When you wake up, the police will be here. You say whatever you want to say—make the best deal for yourself you can. You mention me or my people, I'll find you again, wherever you are. Understand?"

He nodded, still trying to talk. "Look . . . you don't need the shot. . . . I mean, I got a bad heart, you know? I'm on medication. Tomorrow I can get you all the money you want. . . ."

The Mole took a hypo out of his satchel, pushed the plunger, watched the thin spray, nodded to me. A shadow moved from a corner of the basement, flowed behind the fat man. He was jerked to his feet, one arm braced in front of him, veins clearly visible.

"We'll do it upstairs," I told the Mole, gesturing to Max to bring the fat man along.

I took the curving staircase first, listening. Nothing. Then came the Mole, with Max last. We stopped at the landing; the fat man stood against one wall, breathing much too fast.

"We need the fire now," I said to the Mole. "Something that started in the boiler."

He nodded, returned the hypo to his satchel, and went back downstairs.

The fat man was still having trouble with his breathing, sucking in gulps of air and trying to talk at the same time. I pulled off one glove to scratch at the mask, letting him see the tattoo.

"You guys! I know your boss . . . I mean, we have a contract, right? We got no problem. . . ."

I put the glove back on as if I hadn't noticed what set him off. "Shut up," I said, talking the way a machine talks.

The fat man never tried to make a move—combat wasn't his game. But it seemed like he had to find out mine—he couldn't keep quiet.

"What would it take?" he asked.

"I'm just doing a job," I told him, in the same mechanical voice.

"Look, you don't get it, okay? It's not like anyone got *hurt,* all right? Kids . . . they get over it. It's just a business."

I could feel the heat coming off Max, but I was empty inside. All maggots have a story to tell, and I'd heard most of them by then.

The Mole walked up the staircase, satchel in one hand. A day at the office. He held up a palm, fingers spread wide. Five minutes to ignition.

I took Scotty's picture from my pocket, held it up to the fat man's face. I was really showing Max that we'd rescued the kid, but the fat man decided I wanted an explanation.

"Hey! I remember him. Is that what this is all about? Hey, *look*, man . . . that is one sexy little kid, you better believe . . . I mean, he *loved* lapping it up. . . . It's not like I started him off or anything. . . ."

I saw red dots in front of my eyes where his face should have been. I gripped the pistol handle so hard my hand throbbed, hearing the sound of the shot in my mind, willing myself not to pull the trigger.

"Don't!" the fat man screamed, clasping his hands in front of his chest like he was praying. I heard a sharp hiss from the darkness where Max was standing, and then a sound like a meat ax driving into bone. The fat man's neck snapped to the left—and stayed there. Max released him and the body slumped to the ground.

The Mole dropped to his knees, doing his job even though we all knew it was over. "Gone," he said.

"The jailhouse or the graveyard," I'd told the Prof. Now it really didn't matter if the old lady upstairs was dead. I gestured Max to pick up the fat man's body and we all went back downstairs. I could feel the clock ticking in my head—the boiler was going to go. "He tried to escape the flames—ran up the stairs. Slipped and fell. Broke his neck," I said to myself. We hauled the fat man halfway up the stairs, to the place where they started to curve. Leaned him across the railing and pushed him over, face first. The silent basement swallowed the sound of his fall.

"Go!" I said to the Mole, pointing to the back of the house. Max's shadow followed him back into the basement.

I pushed the button on the radio transmitter, telling the Prof I'd be hitting the front gate any minute. I still had a little piece of time left to finish what I had to do—even when the boiler went off it wouldn't reach the first floor for a while. I ran back upstairs to the big office room, grabbing handfuls of the filth, throwing it all around the hallway, dusting every room with pictures and film. I pushed a few of the cassettes back in the safe and slammed it closed, thankful for the gloves I was wearing—no time to wipe everything down.

I checked the bedroom. The woman was still lying on the bed, like she hadn't moved. Maybe she never would.

I charged down the stairs, the gun in front of me, my ears sucking in every sound, waiting for the sirens. I heard a crackling sound from someplace in the basement.

I opened the front door a narrow slit, poked my head out. The street was quiet. I made sure the door wasn't going to lock behind me, patted my pockets to check I had everything, and charged for the fence. I dropped down on the other side—the driver's door was hanging open. I dove inside and the Prof leaped out of the way—he had the car in gear, holding the brake pedal down with his hand.

I looked over my shoulder—the basement windows were full of flame. I heard an engine jump into life somewhere down the street. Wolfe's surveillance team shot straight past us, heading toward the house. I kept rolling smoothly, flipping on the headlights when I turned the corner.

The Plymouth was waiting where it was supposed to be. Nobody was following, so I flashed the lights and Michelle pulled in behind me. We took the Throgs Neck Bridge over to the Bronx, pulling off the road just past the tolls, doing the same number with the jumper cables just in case.

I left the Prof to watch the cars, pulling everyone else into the shadows.

"I got it," I told Michelle. "Anybody answer when you called?"

"Sure did," she replied. "It was a man.

"No, it wasn't," I told her, lighting a cigarette for the first time since we got out. "Any trouble?" I asked the others.

"Just the fence," said the Mole, rubbing his side. He and Michelle went back to the cars.

Max was still in the dark cloth, but the hood was off his head. He watched the Prof approach us, made the gesture of a man taking a picture, moved his hand in a "come here" sign. He wanted the Prof to see the picture. I held it out to him. The mercury-vapor lamps they use on the bridge threw a cold orange light down on all of us. Max held the picture in both hands, waiting for the Prof to look and see what he wanted. He tapped his finger against the picture of the man in the clown suit—then his head suddenly twisted to one side.

"You understand?" I asked the Prof. He had been with us—he had a right to know.

The little man nodded his head. "It means the clown went down."

## 94

THE MOLE TOOK THE Cadillac back to the Bronx. Max got back in the trunk—explaining his night-stalker getup to a passing cop would be too much trouble. We found a turnaround and headed home.

"I'll have the money in a couple of days," I said to the Prof. "Where should I drop you?"

"It's too late for the Men's Shelter—let me try Grand Central."

"Michelle?"

"Home, baby."

I drove the Plymouth into the warehouse. Immaculata appeared while I was opening the trunk for Max to get out.

"It's done," I told her.

Immaculata examined Max like he was a piece of jewelry she was going to buy someday—her eyes going over every inch. She touched his chest, feeling his body, making sure. Max suffered in silence, his face stony. But his eyes were soft.

I bowed to them both. As I backed out of the warehouse, I could see Immaculata patting her stomach, gesturing to Max—the life-taker was a life-maker too.

## 95

IT WAS ALL OVER the midday papers. I liked the *Post*'s version best.

FIRE REVEALS KIDDIE PORN RING!

A fire late last night that killed a Queens man and hospitalized his wife led startled firefighters to discover the couple was operating a "major kiddie-porn ring" from the comfort of their Little Neck mansion, police said.

Killed in the blaze was George Browne, 44, who lived in the

house at 71 Cheshire Drive with his wife Bonnie. Mrs. Browne, 41, was taken to nearby Deepdale General Hospital suffering from smoke inhalation.

Firemen, alerted by a telephone call to the emergency 911 number, arrived shortly after the fire ignited at about 10:00 p.m., and had the blaze under control by 10:45.

It was while they were examining the damage, which a Fire Department spokesman called "moderate," that firemen made the shocking discovery of "literally hundreds of kiddie-porn photographs," the spokesman said. The firemen immediately notified the police, she added.

Captain Louis DeStefano of the 111th Precinct said that in addition to the Polaroid photographs, a "substantial amount" of undeveloped film and "several videotape cassettes" were also seized.

"I'm shocked. I'm absolutely shocked," a stunned neighbor, Elsie Lipschitz, told the Post. "They kept to themselves a lot, but they were always very polite when you saw them on the street. I can't believe it," she said.

Although the Fire Department and the couple's neighbors were caught off guard, the Post has learned that the $450,000 house at the end of the quiet cul-de-sac has been under police surveillance and that George Browne was arrested twice for child molesting in recent years.

In 1978 Browne, who listed his occupation as "entertainer," was arrested on felony molestation charges that were eventually dropped. Two years later, he was arrested again, and ultimately pleaded guilty to endangering the welfare of a minor—a five-year-old boy from upstate, according to police sources.

Browne's charred body was discovered at the bottom of the basement stairway. An apparent broken neck has led cops to theorize he was trying to escape the fire—which may have begun with an explosion in the boiler, according to firemen—when he was overcome by smoke and fell down the stairway. An autopsy is pending.

Among the first cops to arrive on the scene were detectives conducting round-the-clock surveillance for the City-Wide Special Victims Bureau. Assistant District Attorney Eva Wolfe, who heads the bureau, would only say that the surveillance was "part of an ongoing investigation." She declined to say when the investigation began.

Mrs. Browne has not yet been arrested, A.D.A. Wolfe said, adding that charges are expected to be filed "soon."

A hospital spokesman said the woman's condition is satisfactory.

The Prof was reading over my shoulder. "When people can't learn, they're bound to burn," he said.

The blues are the truth.

## 96

I MADE THE CALL the next morning.

"You have my money?" I asked her when she answered the phone.

"Was that you . . . ?"

"You have my money?" I asked her again, cutting her short.

"I'll have it tonight. Do you have . . ."

"Tonight. Midnight, right?"

"Yes. I'll . . ."

I hung up on her. A dry run.

## 97

I WAS THERE ON TIME. Fear was strong in me; I couldn't put a name to it. Nobody wants surgery, but when the disease is fatal, even the knife looks good.

The back of the house was soft, sly darkness. Shadows played their games. There was no music.

"I have you in me now," Strega said once. I called to Flood in my mind, telling her Strega had lied. Telling myself.

I had Scotty's picture in my pocket. It was enough to get me into the house—I wasn't sure it was enough to get me out.

The garage was standing open, a space ready for my Plymouth. I left it outside, nose pointing toward the drive.

I walked up the stairs to the living room. It was empty. I fired a wooden match, looking for a light switch. I couldn't find one—settled for a lamp that flowed gracefully over the couch. I bit into a cigarette, watching the match flare with the first drag, waving my hand to put it out. I put the match in my pocket, waiting.

She came into the room wearing a red slip, her feet bare. Her face was scrubbed and clean. Sat down next to me on the couch, tucking her feet underneath her. She looked like a young girl.

I took the picture from my pocket, gave it one last look, and put it in her lap. An offering—take this from me and go haunt someone else. She ran her finger lightly over the surface of the picture. "This is the one,' she whispered.

I didn't want a ceremony. "You have my money?" I asked her.

"I'm going to burn this in front of Scotty," she said like she hadn't heard me. "And it will all be gone."

"It won't be gone—only the people at SAFE can do that," I told her.

"You know what I mean," she said.

She had her magic words—I had mine. "Where's the money?" I asked her again.

"It's upstairs," she said, flowing to her feet. "Come on."

A woman's hatbox was in the middle of her bed. I could see it through the canopy. A diamond floating on quicksand. She pointed to it, one hand on her hip.

I reached through the lacy fabric and pulled it out. The top came off—inside was the money, all neatly stacked. And the thick gold chain on top of the pile.

"Touch it," she whispered against me. "It's warm. Just before you came, I took a nap. I slept with it inside my body—it's warm from me."

"I don't want it," I said.

"Don't be afraid . . . take it."

"I don't want it," I said again, hearing my voice go hollow, holding on.

She pushed me to the chair in the corner. I stood hard against her, not moving. "It has to be in a chair," she whispered. "It's the only place I can do it. You have to be sitting down."

"I just want the money," I told her.

She grabbed the front of my coat with both hands, pulling at it with all her weight, her devil eyes firing both barrels at me. "You're mine," she said.

I met her eyes—something danced in there—something that would never have a partner. "I did my work," I told her, staying where I was safe. "I'm done."

"You can't walk away from me," she whispered, holding on.

"Forget it, Strega."

"You call my name—you think you know me. You don't know me."

"I know you. And don't waste your time running to Julio—there's nothing he can do."

Strega knew an exit line when she heard one. She let go of my coat, turned her back to me, one hand holding a bedpost.

"Yes, Julio," she said. "My precious uncle Julio—the great and good friend of my father."

She turned to face me. "Who do you think taught me to make nice while he sat in a chair—be a good little girl?"

"What?" I said. I've had a lifetime of keeping my thoughts off my face, but it didn't work with Strega. She answered the question I never asked.

"Julio. I was Peppina then. I loved everybody. Especially Julio—he was so good to me. When he started with me, I told my father on him," she said, her voice that of a little child.

"What did he do?"

"What did he do? He beat me with a strap for telling evil tales about Julio. Julio the Saint. He was a saint to my father . . . because of the money and the fear. And I went back to Julio."

I just looked at her, watching her eyes. Cold fire. Hate.

"They taught me—money and fear. They taught me good. One day I wasn't little stupid happy Peppina anymore."

I saw Julio in my mind, the last time we talked. I knew why he looked like that now. "That's why Julio wanted me to do this . . . get the picture for you?"

"Julio does what I want now. They all do what I want. Money and fear."

"Jina . . ."

"Strega. To you, Strega. And when you come back to me, Strega still."

"I'm not coming back," I said, putting the hatbox under one arm, holding the money against the cold.

One tear escaped her eye, ran down her cheek. "I have my Mia," she said, her voice as dead as the clown in the big white house, "and I have myself. I will always have myself."

"I've got more than that," I thought, walking out, the cold wind swirling at my back. Guarding its child.

# Blue Belle

For Abe, who I never met but have always known.
And for Nathan, who I knew.
Two pieces of the root.
Watching me from someplace above the junkyard.

TECHNICAL ASSISTANCE:
R. Winslow Dennis
Dr. Loretta French
Dr. Richard Pitz
Jeffi Rochelle Powell
Larry Smyj
Dr. Walter Stewart
Woody Vachss
Roosevelt 10X Yamamoto
Anne T. Zaroff

# 1

SPRING COMES HARD down here.

The switchman was in the lotus position—serenely posed on an army blanket he had neatly folded into quarters before he assembled his tools and took up his post for the day. A black man with glowing bronze skin, hair falling straight and glossy down either side of his head like a helmet, framing a face that was mostly skull.

He held a thick pad of graph paper open on his lap, carefully filling a page with finely shaded symbols—a covert calligraphy all his own. He didn't bother to hide his work from passing citizens. His half-smile said it all—the simple slugs thought him insane; they could never understand the difference between the messenger and the message.

A pale-blue quilt covered his shoulders. He placed three identical blue china bowls on the blanket around him. To his right, the bowl sported a generous supply of fine-point felt-tip pens in different colors. The bowl on his left held a heavy Zippo cigarette lighter and some loose cigarettes—various brands. Directly in front was a bowl with some coins, encouraging the passing citizens to make a contribution to his mystical cause.

He had long tapering fingers, clean and smooth, the nails manicured and covered with clear polish. I got a good look at his hands yesterday when I stopped to look over his shoulder and watch him work. He filled a quarter of the page with symbols, never using the same one twice, working in five separate colors, not acknowledging my presence. I helped myself to one of his cigarettes, lit it with his lighter. He never moved. I tossed some coins into his china bowl and moved on, smoking his cigarette. It tasted like it was about my age.

I didn't need the polished nails to tell me he was the switchman. The neighborhood is full of halfway houses for discharged mental patients—they disgorge their cargo into the streets each morning, but this guy wasn't part of that herd. He wasn't talking to himself and he hadn't tried to tell me his story. And he didn't look afraid.

The little piece of winter chill still hanging around in April didn't seem to bother him. He worked the same post every day—starting around eleven in the morning and staying on the job until about three. The switchman had a choice spot, always setting up his shop at the edge of a tiny triangle of dirt on West Broadway, between Reade and Chambers. The slab of dirt had a couple of broken backless benches and a runty tree that had been bonsai'ed by years of attention from pigeons, dogs, squirrels, and winos. An alley without walls. Down in this part of the city, they call it a park.

At eleven, he would still be in shadow, but the sun would make its move from the East River over to the Hudson past noon, and things would warm up. The switchman never took the quilt from his shoulders.

His patch of dirt was a border town: Wall Street was expanding its way up from the tip of Manhattan, on a collision course with the loft-dwelling yuppies from SoHo. Every square inch of space was worth something to somebody—and more to somebody else a few months later. The small factories were all being converted into co-ops. Even the river was disappearing as land-greed took builders farther and farther offshore; Battery Park City was spreading its branches into the void left when they tore down the overpass for the West Side Highway. Riverfront joints surrendered to nouvelle-cuisine bistros. The electronics stores that would sell you what you needed to build your own ham radio or tap your neighbor's phone gave way to sushi bars. Antique shops and storefront-sized art galleries shouldered in next to places that would sell you some vitamins or rent you a videotape.

People have always lived down here. The neighborhood used to be a goddamned art colony—it produced more pottery than the whole Navajo nation. The hippies and the artists thought the winos added just the right touch of realism to their lives. But the new occupants are the kind who get preorgasmic when you whisper "investment banking," and they didn't much care for local color. Locksmiths were riding the crest of a growth industry.

The Superior Hotel entrance was around the corner on Chambers Street, with rooms extending all along West Broadway. Mine was on the top floor, facing out over the park. Seventy-five bucks a week bought me a swaybacked single bed on an iron frame, a ratty old easy chair worn down to the cotton padding on the arms, and a metal closet standing against the wall. The room was painted in some neutral-colored stuff that was about half disinfectant. A heavy length of vinyl-wrapped chain stood against the wall, anchored at one end to U-bolts driven into the floor. The other end stood open, padlocked to nothing, waiting patiently. I hadn't gone for the optional TV at only two bucks a day.

Someone who had never lived in one might say the room looked like a prison cell. It didn't come close.

Almost one in the afternoon. Into my third hour of watching, I shifted position in the chair, scanning the street with the wide-angle binoculars, watching the human traffic flow around the switchman. A young woman strolled by with her boyfriend. Her hair was dyed four different colors, standing up in stiff spikes, stabbing the air every time she moved her head. Her hand was in the back pocket of her boyfriend's jeans. He looked straight ahead, not saying a word. A biker rolled up to a tobacco-colored Mercedes parked at the corner. The car's window slid down and the biker put his head and hands inside. He wasn't there long. The Mercedes and the biker went their separate ways. A young woman about the same age as the one with the spiked hair tapped her business-length heel impatiently on the curb, holding a leather briefcase that doubled as a purse, wearing a pin-striped skirt and jacket over a white blouse with a dark-red bow for a tie. Winos stretched out in the sun, sprawled across the benches—passengers on a cruise ship in permanent drydock. A diesel dyke cruised into view, her arm braced around the neck of a slender, long-haired girl, her bicep flexed to display a bold tattoo. I was too far away to read it, but I knew what it said: hard to the core.

Still no sign of the target. I had followed him for three weeks straight, charting every step of his lunchtime route. The calligrapher on the blanket had to be the switchman—it was the only stop the target always made. I rotated my head gently on the column of my neck, working out the stiffness, keeping my eyes on the street. Invisible inside the shadows of my room, I lit another cigarette, cupping the wooden match to hide the flare, and went back to waiting. It's what I do best.

## 2

I WAS WORKING IN A dead-end hotel, but I'd gotten the job in the back seat of a limousine. The customer was a Wall Street lawyer. He dressed the part to perfection, but he didn't have enough mileage on his clock to make it seem like sitting in a hundred-thousand-dollar taxi was an everyday thing for him.

"It took quite a while for you to get back to me, Mr. Burke," he said, trying for a tone that would tell me he wasn't a man used to waiting for what he wanted. "I reached out for you yesterday morning."

I didn't say anything. I'm not in the phone book. You have to have a phone of your own to qualify for that. The lawyer had called one of the pay phones in the back of Mama Wong's restaurant. Mama always answers the same way: "Mr. Burke not here, okay? You leave message, okay?" If the caller says anything else, asks more questions—whatever—Mama just runs through the same cycle. She says it enough times, the caller gets the message: If it's *not* okay with you, it's too fucking bad.

The lawyer tried another ice-breaker. "My firm has a problem, Mr. Burke, and I was told you might be the ideal individual to assist us."

I shrugged my shoulders slightly, telling him to get on with it. He wasn't in a hurry—that's the problem with paying guys by the hour.

"Is there any particular reason why we had to meet out here?" he wanted to know, gesturing toward the Hudson River with an impatient sweep of his hand. He had a nice watch. Pretty cuff links.

"Who gave you my number?" I asked, stepping on his question.

The lawyer swallowed his annoyance, reminding himself he wasn't speaking with an equal. Time to put me in my place. "Do I have to say anything more than 'Mr. C.'?" he asked, smiling.

"Yes," I said.

He looked honestly puzzled. Since he was a lawyer, only part of that could be accurate. "I thought that would be enough. I was given to understand that a recommendation from Mr. C. would be all that you would require."

"Give the understanding back, pal. And tell me who gave you my number."

"I *told* you."

"You saying Mr. C. spoke to *you*?" I asked him, watching his face.

"The number came from him," he said, answering questions the way a lawyer does.

"Have a nice day," I said, reaching behind me for the door handle.

"Wait a minute!" he snapped, putting his hand on my sleeve.

"You don't want to do that," I told him.

He jerked his hand away, sliding into his speech. "I can explain whatever is necessary, Mr. Burke. Please don't be impatient." He shifted position on the soft gray leather seat, pushed a button, and watched proudly as the padded wall between us and the driver opened to reveal a well-stocked bar. "Can I get you a drink?"

"No," I told him, taking a single cigarette from my jacket. I put it in my mouth, reached the same hand back inside for a match. I kept the other hand in my pocket, where it had been since I climbed in the limo. The gesture was wasted on him.

"Would you mind opening the window if you're going to smoke? . . . I'm allergic."

I pushed the switch and the window whispered down, letting in the traffic noise from the West Side Highway. We were parked in the pocket between Vestry Street and where the highway forks near 14th. Cars went by, but not people. The limo had picked me up on Wall Street; I told the lawyer where I wanted to go, and he told the driver.

I lit the cigarette, inhaled deeply, watching the lawyer.

"Those things will kill you," he said. A concerned citizen.

"No, they won't," I promised.

He shrugged, using the gesture to say that some people are beyond educating. He was right, but not about me. He tried one more time. "Mr. C. is a client of our firm. In the course of discussing . . . uh . . . other matters, he indicated that you might be better suited to our immediate purposes than a more . . . *traditional* private investigator." He glanced at my face, waiting for a reaction. When he realized he'd have a long time to wait, he shifted gears and rolled ahead. "Mr. C. gave us certain . . . uh . . . *assurances* concerning your sense of discretion, Mr. Burke." His tone of voice made it into a question.

I drew on my cigarette. The breeze from the open window at my back pushed the smoke toward his allergic face.

The lawyer slid a leather portfolio onto his lap, deftly opened it into a mini-desk, tapped a yellow legal pad with the tip of a gold ballpoint to get my attention. "Why don't I write a figure down, Mr. Burke. You take a quick look, tell me if you're interested." Without waiting for an answer, he slowly wrote "10,000" in large numbers. Reverently, like he was engraving a stone tablet. He raised his eyebrows in another question.

"For what?" I asked him.

"Our firm has a . . . uh . . . *confidentiality* problem, Mr. Burke. We occupy a rather unique position, interfacing, as we say, between the business, financial, and legal arenas. Necessarily, information crosses our desk, so to speak. Information that has a short but exceedingly valuable life. Are you following me?"

I nodded, but the lawyer wasn't going to take my word for it. "You're certain?"

"Yeah," I replied, bored with this. Yuppies didn't invent insider trading—information is always worth something to somebody. I was scamming along the tightrope between prison and the emergency ward while this guy was still kissing ass to get into law school.

The lawyer stroked his chin. Another gesture. Telling me he was making a decision. The decision never had been his to make, and we both knew it.

"Somebody in our firm has been . . . profiting from information. Information that has come to us in our fiduciary capacity. Are you following me?"

I just nodded, waiting.

"We know who this person is. And we've retained the very best professionals to look into the matter for us. Specialists in industrial espionage. People who are capable of checking things we wouldn't want to use a subpoena for. Still with me?"

"Sure."

"We know who it is, like I said. But we have been unable to establish a case against him. We don't know how he moves the information. And we don't know to whom he passes it."

"You checked his bank accounts, opened his mail, tapped his phones . . . all that, right?"

Now it was the lawyer's turn to nod, moving his head a reluctant two inches.

"Telegrams, visitors to the office, carrier pigeons . . . ?"

He nodded again, unsmiling.

"How much time would he have between getting the information and making use of it?"

"Ah, you *do* understand, Mr. Burke. That's exactly the problem. We deal with extremely sensitive issues. Nothing on paper. In a normal insider-trading situation, a profiteer would have a minimum of several days to make his move. But in our situation, he would have to act within a few hours—no longer than close of business on the same day the information comes in."

"And you've had him under surveillance every day for a while?"

He nodded.

"Drawing a blank?"

He nodded again.

"You call in the *federales*?"

"That wouldn't be our chosen scenario for this situation. The firm itself has its own interests, as well as the obligation to protect our clients. Perhaps you don't understand some of the complexities of our profession. . . ."

I gave him the closest thing to a smile I ever give citizens. I'd never heard the laundry business called a profession before.

"Why don't you just fire him?"

"We can't do that. He's a very well connected young man. Besides, our clients will demand some actual proof of his guilt before taking any action. They were very insistent on that, for some reason."

Sure. The "clients" wanted to make damn sure the problem was going to get solved for good. The only time humans like that are interested in the truth is when a mistake will cost them money.

"What do you want from me?"

"We want you to find out how this individual gets the information out. And we want *proof*. Something we can show our clients."

"And the only time he could possibly pass this along is during business hours?"

"Yes. Without question. After that . . . it wouldn't be of value to him or anyone else."

I lit another cigarette, thinking it through. It sounded like they had the wrong guy. Maybe the "clients" were setting them up. Maybe this lawyer was the one doing the stealing. It wasn't my problem. Money was. Always is.

"The only time I could watch him would be when he leaves the building, right?"

"Yes. Inside the building, he's completely covered."

"A grand a day. Until I find out how he does it or you call me off. Another ten if I get the proof for you."

"Mr. Burke, with all due respect, that's triple the rate charged by the finest security firms. And you'll only be working a couple of hours each day."

"In cash. In front. Nothing bigger than fifties. No consecutive serial numbers. No new bills," I told him. "You know how it's done."

The lawyer looked at me, watching my face for the first time since I'd climbed into the limo. "What makes you worth so much?"

"Ask Mr. C.," I suggested.

He dropped his eyes. "We won't need you every day. Just those days when something comes in. We'll call as soon as . . ."

"No."

"I don't understand."

"I need to work this guy *every* day, okay? I need to know him. I need to know when he's changed his pattern. You don't need to call me when the information comes in. I watch this guy long enough, *I'll* know."

"That could take weeks. . . ."

I nodded agreement. "Maybe longer. Who knows? I probably won't get him the first time he moves anyway. Depends on when you get something for him to trade."

"And you may not get him at all?"

"And I may not get him at all."

The lawyer pretended to think it over. Maybe he was better at pretending to be honest. "We need to get started on this. This is Friday; could you be on the job Monday?"

"Sure."

"All right, Mr. Burke. I am prepared to pay you one thousand dollars in cash right now. For Monday's work. In advance, as you requested. We will meet each evening—you'll give me your report and we will decide if you are to continue."

I just shook my head. Why they sent this fool to do business with me was a mystery: he was a pin-striped shark, but he couldn't bite people who never went near the water.

"You have another suggestion?"

"Yeah, pal. Here's my suggestion. You hand me twenty thousand dollars, like we agreed. Okay? That buys you twenty days, unless I pull it off quicker. I pull it off *before* ten days, you get a refund. Nothing jumps off in twenty days, we meet and see what you want to do. Got it?"

"That's outrageous," the lawyer said, his face a half-step out of sync with his words. "You expect me to just . . . "

"I'm tired of this. I'm tired of you. If Mr. C. really sent you out here to do business, you've got at least twenty large in that pretty briefcase of yours. And if you're a fucking little errand boy, go back and tell your boss that he sent the wrong messenger."

He sat there, staring. I lit another cigarette. "When this smoke is finished, so am I," I told him, waiting.

The lawyer tried to smile. "I'm no errand boy," he said, holding his head stiff. He opened another compartment in the briefcase. The money was neatly stacked, a paper band around the fifty-dollar bills. He counted off twenty little stacks, tossing them contemptuously on the broad seat between us, making sure I could see there was plenty left in the briefcase.

Telling me they would have paid more. That he had the last laugh.

"Can I drop you someplace?" he smirked.

I threw an empty pack of cigarettes back over my shoulder, out the window. "Thanks anyway," I told the lawyer, shoving the cash into different pockets of my coat, "I'll call a cab."

A battered gypsy cab rolled up next to the limo. The rusty old hulk was so filthy you couldn't even see through the windows. The lawyer's mouth dropped open. I nodded to him, backed out of the limo and into the gypsy. The driver dropped the hammer, and we moved out in a cloud of black smoke.

# 3

I SPOTTED THE INSIDER when he was still a half-block away. Watching him for days tuned me in—I could pick him up in a crowd just by the way he moved. Heading for the switchman, like always. I zoomed the binoculars in on the switchman's hands. He was still working on his charts, face bent over in concentration. When the insider got close, I focused in on the three bowls, flicking past the one that held the pens to the second one—the one with the cigarettes. I locked into the last bowl in the triangle—the one with the coins. There was nothing else in my vision. I breathed gently through my nose, my elbows pressed into my chest.

Silver dropped into the switchman's bowl. Some coins. And a flat-folded piece of aluminum foil. I reached one hand up to the window shade and pulled it straight down. I dropped to the floor and raised the shade an inch at the bottom, so I could peek out without the binoculars.

A kid in a striped T-shirt shot around the corner on a skateboard. He lost control and spun out; the skateboard took off by itself and crashed into a parked car. The kid was ready for the crash: gloves on his hands, thick pads covering his elbows and knees. His head was hidden under a white plastic mask—the kind hockey goalies wear. He shook himself off, dazed.

Then he charged right at the switchman, snatched the coin bowl in both hands, and flew up the block, the bowl tight against his chest. The switchman started to come off his blanket when one of the winos stumbled into him from behind. The wino's long floppy raincoat blocked most of my view, but I could see the switchman whip an elbow into his chest, knocking him backward. The wino grabbed at the switchman to break his fall; they fell to the ground together. The switchman wrenched himself loose, stopping for a second to kick the helpless wino in the chest.

When he turned around, the kid was gone. I saw the gypsy cab pull away, heading for the river.

The switchman did a full circle, knowing he was too late. The wino crawled away, his hands wrapped around his ribs. The switchman pulled the corners of his blanket together, held it in two hands, and spun it around a couple of times to form a sack. He threw the sack over his shoulder and ducked into the subway.

It took me less than a minute to throw everything I had with me into the battered suitcase and head out the door.

I went out the side door on Chambers, and walked back through the park. The street was the way it was before the crash. Even the kid's skateboard was gone.

## 4

MY PLYMOUTH WAS PARKED on West Street, near one of the construction sites. The guy who built it years ago was trying to create the ultimate New York taxicab, but he died before he got it done. I threw my suitcase in the trunk and started the engine. The two-and-a-half-ton dull gray machine started right up, the way it always does. I hit the switch and my window slid down. Lit a cigarette and pulled away, heading for the pier.

I was there first. I backed in until the bumper tapped the base of the pier, shoved a Judy Henske tape into the slot, listened to "If That Isn't Love" for the thousandth time. Waiting again. If Linda Ronstadt is a torch singer, Henske's a flame thrower.

A couple of guys walked by, hand in hand, talking just to each other. An overmuscled beach boy posed against a burned-out abandoned car. A black man was adding a few touches to an oil painting of the riverfront. A man with a teenager's body cruised the scene on roller skates, wearing mirror sunglasses to hide the truth. The whores don't work this pier. Some zoning regulation the City Council would never understand reserved it for gays.

Nobody came near the Plymouth. I was into my third smoke, and

Henske was breaking chops with both hands on "Good Old Wagon" by the time the gypsy cab pulled in at an angle next to me, its nose aimed at the Plymouth's trunk. The kid jumped out first, the goalie's mask gone, his baby face glowing with pride.

"Hey, Burke!"

"Keep it down," I told him, climbing out of the car.

"Did you see it? It went *perfect!*" He was bouncing up and down like he just hit a home run in Little League. Snatching money off the street was as close as Terry would ever get.

The Mole slowly emerged from the darkness of the gypsy cab. He was wearing a greasy pair of coveralls, a heavy tool belt around his waist, with another strap running over his shoulder. Something glinted off his Coke-bottle lenses—I couldn't tell if it was the sun. He walked into the shadow where our two cars touched and squatted on the ground, fumbling in his leather satchel. Terry hunkered down beside him, his hand on the Mole's shoulder, trying to peer inside the satchel. The Mole's pasty-white hands with their stubby fingers looked too awkward to open the clasp, but he had a touch like a brain surgeon. He pulled out the foil disk and dropped it in my palm, looking up at me with a question.

"Let's see," I told him, unwrapping it carefully.

In a neat, almost prim handwriting were the words "Maltrom, Ltd." Nothing else. I didn't need anything else.

"Nice work, Mole," I told him.

The Mole grunted.

"You drop Max off?"

He grunted again. Max the Silent didn't get his name because he moved so quietly. A Mongolian free-lance warrior who never spoke, Max made his living as a courier, moving things around the city for a price. His collateral was his life. He was as reliable as cancer, and not nearly as safe to play with. The wino who stumbled into the switchman had been Max. He'd taken the kicks to the ribs, even though he could have snapped the switchman like a matchstick. A professional.

The Mole was still hunkered down in the shadows. The kid was next to him. Waiting quietly now, like he'd been taught.

"I got about an hour," I told the Mole.

His face moved—the Mole's idea of a smile. "You don't want to call your broker first?"

I don't have a broker. I don't get mail and I don't have a phone. Maybe it's true that you can't beat them—you don't have to join them either.

"I have to see Michelle," the kid piped up.

I caught the Mole's eye, nodded okay.

"Give her my share," he said.

## 5

I WHEELED THE PLYMOUTH across the highway and started to work my way through the back streets of SoHo. Carefully, like I do everything.

Lily runs a special joint that works with abused kids. They do individual and group therapy, and they teach self-defense. Maybe it's all the same thing.

Max's woman works there. Immaculata. It wasn't so long ago that she tried to stop three punks from attacking what she thought was an old man on the subway. The old man was Max. He went through the punks like a chain saw through Kleenex, left them broken and bleeding on the subway floor, and held out his hand to the woman who stood up for him. Their baby was born a few months ago—two warriors' blood in her veins.

Terry watched me without turning his head, working on what we'd been teaching him. But he was doing it for practice—he wasn't scared anymore. The first time I took him away in a car, he was a rental from a pimp. We were working a deep con, looking for a picture of another kid. We picked up Michelle on the street so she could watch Terry while we got ready to deal with his pimp.

I lit a cigarette, thinking back to that night. "Want one?" I asked him.

"Michelle doesn't want me to smoke."

"I won't tell her."

The kid knew better than to use the dashboard lighter in the Plymouth. I snapped a wooden match into life, held it across to him. He took a deep drag. We had a deal.

I watched him scan the passing streets with his eyes, not moving his head.

I was in Biafra during the war. It got bad near the end. Staying alive was all there was. No food, landlocked, soldiers pinching all four corners, planes spitting death—low enough in the sky to hit with a rifle. If you had a rifle. Too many ways to die. Some screamed, some ran. Nobody won. I saw kids lying like litter all through the jungle, their faces already dead, waiting. I had a 9mm pistol with three bullets left in the clip, half a pack of cigarettes, a pocketful of diamonds, and almost a hundred grand in Swiss francs. I left a sack of Biafran pounds back in the jungle. About a million face value, if Biafra won the war. It wasn't going to, and carrying a sack of money from a defeated country while you're running for your life is what they mean by "dead weight." I didn't even bury it—I wasn't coming back. Another big score gone to dirt. The gunfire stopped, and the jungle got dead quiet. Waiting. A young woman ran past me on my right, wearing only a pair of tattered men's shorts way too big for her, every breath a moan. I heard a grunting sound and hit the ground, the pistol up in front of me. A wounded soldier? If he had a rifle, maybe I could trade up. It was a little boy, about three years old, a tiny head on a stick body, his belly already swollen, naked. Alone. Past being scared. The woman never broke stride; she scooped the baby up on the run, shoving him up toward her slender neck, holding him with one hand. If she made it, the baby would have a new mother.

That's what Michelle did with Terry.

# 6

I PARKED A COUPLE OF blocks away. Terry and I walked over to Lily's, not talking. The black guy at the front desk was reading a thick book through horn-rimmed glasses.

"Hey, Terry!"

"Hey, Sidney!" the kid greeted him. "Sidney's going to law school," he told me.

Somehow I didn't think Sidney would end up making deals with guys like me in the back of limos. "Is this your father?" he asked Terry. "The one who teaches you all that electronic stuff?"

That cracked the kid up. "Burke?" It was the Mole's thought, but the laugh was Michelle's. It's not just chromosomes that make blood.

Sidney waved us past. We walked down a long corridor to the back offices. The right-hand wall was all glass. On the other side, groups of kids were running, jumping, screaming their lungs out. Everything from disciplined martial-arts classes in one corner to some crazy game with kids taking turns trying to dive over a mound of pillows. Business as usual.

Immaculata burst out of one of the back offices, her long glossy hair flying behind her, a clipboard in one hand.

"Lily!" she yelled out.

"We're all back here," echoed a voice.

Immaculata saw us and spun in a graceful arc, her long nails flowing together as she pyramided her hands at the waist. She bowed gently to us.

"Burke. Terry."

"Mac." I bowed back.

Terry tried to bow too, but he was too excited to get it right. "Is Max here?"

"Max is working, honey."

"But is he *coming*? Maybe later?"

Immaculata's smile ignited the highlights in her eyes. "Who knows?"

"Max is the strongest man in the world!" the kid said, not inviting a dispute.

Immaculata bowed again. "Is strength so important? Do you remember what you have been taught?"

"Yes. Strength of character. Strength of spirit."

"Very good," the beautiful woman proclaimed, bending at the waist to give Terry a kiss. "And so . . . is Michelle strong?"

"She's so brave."

"And the Mole?"

"Michelle says he's the smartest man on the earth. That's what she says."

"And Burke?"

The kid looked doubtful, waiting.

"Burke is not strong like Max?"

The kid shook his head.

"Or brave like Michelle? Smart like the Mole?"

"No . . . " Terry said, reaching for it.

"So how does he survive?"

The kid knew all about survival. "He has strength too, right?"

"Right!" said Immaculata, giving him another kiss.

The kid was in heaven. Maybe he'd never see the inside of a prep school unless he went along on a burglary, but how many kids get to work a major-league scam, hang out with a lunatic, and get kissed by a lovely lady all on the same day?

"Come on," said Immaculata, reaching out her hand. I followed them down the hall to Lily's office.

# 7

LILY WAS SEATED AT THE screen of her so-called computer, playing some electronic game with the keyboard, a baby on her lap, balanced between her elbows. She was wearing a painter's smock over pink jeans; her hair was tied back. Her scrubbed face looked like a teenager's, animated with attention as she bounced the baby on her lap in time with a man running through a maze on the screen. Michelle sat on the desk, her flashy legs crossed, smoking a cigarette in a red lacquer holder. Her outfit was all black-and-white triangles. Even her nail polish was black. On a straight lady, it would have looked whorish. On Michelle, it was fashion.

"Mom!" Terry yelled, charging over to her.

Michelle pulled him close, hugging him, looking over his shoulder. "You spend a few minutes with Burke and you leave your manners in the street?"

Terry gave her a kiss, smiling, knowing she wasn't mad at him. "I greeted Immaculata," he said.

"And . . . "

The kid turned to Lily. "Hello, Lily."

"Hi, Terry!"

"Hello, baby," he said to the infant on her lap.

"Baby has a name," Immaculata reminded him gently.

"Hello, Flower," the kid said, taking her tiny hand and kissing it.

Immaculata clapped. "See! He learns his good manners from Burke."

Michelle laughed. "He'd be the first."

"Can I hold Flower?" Terry asked Mac.

"As I showed you," she warned him. Every female eye in the room was riveted on the kid, but he tucked the baby into the crook of his arm, sat down next to Michelle, and started cooing to Flower like he'd been doing it all his life. Like nobody ever did to him.

I gave Michelle the high sign. She tousled Terry's hair and slid off the desk. We left them in the office and walked down the hall, looking for an empty room.

## 8

WE DUCKED INTO A cubicle a few doors down. I didn't have much time.

"The Mole and I just did some work. He said for you to hold his share."

I handed her the cash. She snapped open her purse, divided the money into two piles, stowed it away.

"A little closer to Denmark, baby—to the real me," she said, blowing a soft kiss at the cash. Michelle had been talking about the operation ever since I'd known her. She'd been through the full-body electrolysis, the hormone injections, even the silicone implants in her breasts. But she had balked at the psychological counseling American hospitals required before they'd do a full sex-change operation.

"You'll take Terry back to the Mole?"

I nodded, checking my watch. "You go get him," I told her.

I dialed a number while I was waiting for her. The lawyer with the limo answered on the first ring.

"It's done," I told him. He started to babble. I cut him off. "You know Vesey Street, where it runs past the World Trade Center? Take it all the way west, right to the river. I'll meet you there in forty-five minutes." I hung up on him.

Michelle came down the hall, holding Terry's hand, calling good-bye to Lily and Immaculata over her shoulder.

## 9

TERRY SAT BETWEEN US on the front seat. I lit a cigarette. "Want one?" I asked him.

"Michelle doesn't want me to smoke," the kid said, his angelic face giving nothing away. Michelle gave him a kiss. The Mole was teaching him science; I was teaching him art.

"I got to meet a guy, Terry," I told him. "You'll have to ride the trunk, okay?"

"Sure!"

"And when I'm finished, I'll take you back to the Mole."

"I can't go right back," he said.

I looked over at Michelle. "Why not?" I asked him, watching her eyes.

"Mole says he has work to do. Someplace else. He says for you not to bring me back until after six."

"How about if I bring you back to Lily's? I'll roll by in a few hours."

"Why can't I hang out with you?"

Michelle patted him. "Burke has work to do, baby."

The kid was hurt. "I do work too. I help Mole. Lots of times."

"I know you do, baby," she said. I shot the kid a warning glance. If Michelle wanted to think the kid helped out by holding the Mole's soldering iron, that was fine with me.

We rolled into the Wall Street canyon, following Michelle's directions. She had customers down there too. I pulled over to the curb.

She gave Terry another kiss and flowed from the car. We watched her make her way into the building. Watched men turn to look at her, thinking they had never seen a woman with so much style. I used to wonder what men would think if they knew the truth, but I don't anymore. The man waiting for her knew the truth.

## 10

I WHEELED THE PLYMOUTH around the corner and slid along until I found an empty spot, just past the little park where they assemble crowds who want to visit the Statue of Liberty. A lot of people bring their cars down to the river to work on them. Guys were changing the oil, draining radiators, doing tune-ups. I pulled over and popped the trunk. The inside was lined with the padding that furniture movers use. A steel box in one corner covered the battery; a fifty-gallon fuel cell took about half the storage space, but there was plenty of room for a man to wait comfortably. A neat row of quarter-inch holes was punched through the tip of the trunk. I pulled the piece of duct tape away so air would circulate. "You know where everything is?" I asked the kid.

He looked at me the way the Mole does sometimes, his eyes shifting to the cable that would open the trunk from the inside and let him out. He knew he could also get out through the back seat if he had to. Two plastic quart bottles were bolted to the side of the trunk, one full of a water-and-glucose solution, the other empty. A man could stay there for a couple of days if he had to.

I pulled a thick roll of neon-red tape from the trunk, peeled off a precut piece, and handed the end to Terry. He pulled it taut, and we walked it over to the hood. It fit perfectly. Another piece went over the roof. One more for the trunk, and we had a distinctive racing stripe from front to back. Terry took the rubber block I handed him and smoothed out the little bubbles under the tape while I attached a foxtail to the antenna and snapped some blue plastic covers over the parking lights in the grille. I pulled another set of license plates out of the trunk and screwed them on over the ones I'd been using. In ten minutes we had a different car. With untraceable plates.

Terry patted himself down, making sure he had his butane cigarette lighter. Michelle didn't mind him carrying the lighter. It was a gift from the Mole. Loaded with napalm. The tiny Jewish star the kid wore on a chain around his neck gleamed dull against his pale skin. It was made of steel. "They took gold from our people's mouths to make their evil ornaments," the Mole once said, explaining it to me.

The kid made himself comfortable. I closed the lid and climbed back inside. On schedule.

## 11

THE LIMO WAS ALREADY there when I pulled up. I left the Plymouth a half-block away and walked toward the blacked-out passenger windows, hands in my pockets. He must have been watching my approach. The door swung open.

I handed him the foil-wrapped disk. Watched as he carefully opened it, smearing any fingerprints that would have been on it if I had left any. He held the paper away from me so I wouldn't get a look at the magic name. His hands shook. His tongue ran around his lips. He was looking at his ticket up the ladder.

"This is it," he said. Reverent.

"Good. Give me the money."

"Sure. Sure . . ." he said, almost absently, reaching in his briefcase, counting it out, not making a ceremony of it this time. Handing it over to me, not even watching as I buried it in my coat pocket.

I reached for the door handle. "Wait a minute," he said.

I waited, my hand wrapped around a roll of quarters in my pocket, measuring the distance to the spot just below his sternum, breathing through my nose, calm.

"How did you get this?"

"That wasn't our deal."

"I'm just curious."

I looked at his face until his eyes came up to mine.

"Ask Mr. C.," I advised him.

The limo was pulling away before I took three steps back to the Plymouth.

## 12

I DIDN'T KNOW IF THE lawyer had other eyes around, so I drove away slow, sliding through the maze of streets parallel to the river until we got back to the open piers a few blocks uptown. I stripped the tape off the car, pulled the foxtail, and popped off the parking-light covers. I tossed everything inside the trunk, reaching inside to get a screwdriver for the plates. Terry never moved, lost inside the darkness. "Want to get something to eat at Mama's?" I asked softly. His little fist tapped against the fuel cell once. Yes.

## 13

THE PLYMOUTH PUSHED its anonymous nose past the entrance to Mama's restaurant, giving me a chance to read the messages. Mama used three identical dragon tapestries for a window display: one red, one white, one blue. Tourists thought it was patriotic. Only the white dragon stood in the window. No cops inside—no other trouble either.

I pulled around to the alley in the back. The alley walls were whitewashed, garbage cans neatly stacked, tightly capped. A calico cat the size of a beagle sat on top of one of the cans, marking his territory. A short set of Chinese characters in foot-high black letters stood stark against the white wall. Max's message to anyone who might have stupid ideas about asking Mama for a contribution to their favorite charity.

I popped the trunk and Terry climbed out, shaking himself like a dog coming out of water. The back door was steel, painted the same color as the building. You had to look close to see it. There was no doorknob. I pushed against it, and Terry followed me inside. We were in the kitchen. Half a dozen young Oriental men were scattered around. Two of them were tossing handfuls of meat and vegetables into a set of giant woks while a third man stirred, a flat wooden tool in each hand. He rapped sharply on the rim of one of the woks. Another man came forward, his hands wrapped in rags. He grabbed the wok by the rim, dumped the contents into a metal pot, and dropped the wok onto another burner. He tossed in a glassful of water, swirled it around, dumped out the water, and put the clean wok back in front of the cook. Handfuls of pea pods, water chestnuts, and some red stuff I didn't recognize flew into the empty wok. A vat of rice steamed against one wall. None of the workers gave us a glance. A fat man sat at the door connecting the kitchen to the restaurant, a tapestry the size of a tablecloth covering his lap. The tapestry rested on a wood frame, like a small table, the cloth reaching almost to the floor. The fat man's eyes were lost in folds of flesh, no more visible than his hands. I stopped in front of him, one hand on Terry's shoulder to show he was with me. The fat man's head held solid, drawing a bead. I didn't rush him. I knew what he was holding under the tapestry frame. Finally, he tilted his head a fraction of an inch. Okay. We went into the restaurant.

Terry and I took my table at the back. The place was empty except for a young woman and her date. She was wearing tinted aviator glasses, a string of pearls over a black silk T-shirt. A skinny, mean-faced woman with capped teeth. Her date had a neat, short haircut. The kind of tan you can buy without getting near the beach. He looked like a sheep that worked out a lot—taut lines, stupid eyes. She was asking the waiter a series of intricate questions about how the food was prepared. He answered every question with the same Cantonese phrase, reading her like a menu with only one dish on it. This went on for a couple of minutes, until Mama climbed off her stool by the cash register at the front and came over to them. She wore a bottle-green silk dress cut tight all the way up to the high mandarin collar and flowing loose from the waist down. Her hair was pulled back in a glossy bun, her broad face unlined. Only a fool would try to guess her age; only a fool with a death wish would ask her.

The waiter stood aside as she approached. She bowed gently to the woman and her companion.

"You have questions?"

"I certainly do. I have been *asking* this gentleman if you use MSG in the preparation of your food. Our diet doesn't permit . . . "

Mama stepped on the rest of the sentence. "Oh, yes. Plenty MSG. No problem."

"You don't understand. We don't *want* any flavor enhancers in our food. MSG causes . . . "

"MSG in everything here. Soup, vegetables, meat. Special stuff. Plenty MSG."

The woman gave an exasperated sigh. "Don't you have provision for preparing meals *without* MSG?"

"Why you want that? MSG in everything. Good for you. Make blood nice and thin."

The woman looked over at her date, a pained expression on her pinched face. I lit a cigarette, blowing the smoke in her direction.

"You have a No Smoking section, I presume?"

"You want cigarettes?" Mama asked, innocently.

"No. We don't want cigarettes. And we don't want MSG. Is that so hard to understand?"

Her date looked uncomfortable, but he kept quiet.

"Everybody smoke here. Even cooks smoke, okay? Plenty MSG. No American Express." Mama looked at her, smiling. "Not for you, right?"

"It certainly is not," said the woman, pushing her chair back. "Come on, Robbie," she said to the sheep.

"Have a nice day," Mama told her. She watched the woman and the sheep walk out the front door, giving their table a quick wipe. She looked around her empty restaurant and smiled. Business was good.

I slid out of the booth, bowed to Mama as she approached. Terry bounded over to her, his arms open. Mama clasped her hands at her waist, bowed to the kid. It stopped him like he ran into a wall, confusion overflowing his face.

"Easy. Move slow, okay?" She smiled down at him.

"I was just going to . . . "

"You going to kiss Mama?"

"Sure!"

"You see Burke kiss Mama?"

"No . . . "

Mama's face was calm. Set. "Mama kiss babies, okay? Not kiss man."

Terry stared at her face, figuring it out. Knowing by her tone not to be afraid. "I'm not a man," he said.

"What, then?"

He looked at me for help. I blew smoke out my nose. I didn't know the answer. He took a shot on his own. "A kid?"

"Only two pieces," Mama said. "Baby or man. No more baby, time to be a man."

"I won't be a man until I'm thirteen."

"Who says this?"

"Mole."

Mama glanced over at me. "Bar Mitzvah," I told her. "Jewish ceremony."

"Good. Not *official* man until thirteen, right?"

"Right," Terry told her.

"Start now," Mama said, bowing to him again. Case closed.

Terry bowed.

Mama sat down across from me. Terry waited, saw there wasn't going to be any more instruction, sat down too. Mama said something to the waiter. He disappeared.

"Soup first, okay?"

"Can I have fried rice?" the kid wanted to know.

"Soup first," Mama said.

The waiter brought a steaming tureen of Mama's hot-and-sour soup. Three small porcelain bowls. Mama served Terry first, then me. Then herself. I pressed my spoon against the vegetables floating in the dark broth, taking the liquid in first, holding it above the bowl, letting it cool. I took a sip. "Perfect," I said. It was the minimal acceptable response.

Terry pushed his spoon in too deeply, covering it with vegetables. He carefully turned the spoon over, emptying it back into the bowl. Tried it again. Got it right. He swallowed the spoonful, tears shooting into his eyes. His little face turned a bright red. "It's good," he said, his voice a squeak.

Mama smiled. "Special soup. Not for babies."

I took another spoonful, swallowed it slowly. Let it slide down, breathing through my nose. Terry watched me. Tried it again. Smaller sips this time.

I threw a handful of hard noodles into my bowl. Terry did the same. He watched as I spooned off the top layer of liquid, mixing the last spoonfuls with the vegetables, not chewing any of it, gently breathing through my nose. The kid went right along.

When my bowl was empty, Mama spooned it full again. Terry was right behind me. Mama called for the waiter. He took the tureen away. Came back with a heaping plate of fried rice for Terry. The plate was beautiful—big chunks of roast pork, egg yolk, scallions—each grain of rice floating on top of another into a perfect pyramid. The kid's eyes lit up. He dug in without another word. I helped myself to a few forkfuls, bowing my acknowledgment of perfection to Mama.

Terry was halfway through the giant mountain when he looked up at Mama.

"What's MSG?" he wanted to know.

"Bad stuff. Special salt. Make weak food taste strong, okay? Chemical. Fake. No good for you."

Terry smiled at her, putting it together. "No MSG here, right?"

Mama smiled back at him. "Right."

I lit another cigarette. "How's business?" I asked her.

"Always same."

I put the money from the lawyer on the table. Split it into two piles. "For Max," I told Mama, touching one pile. "For the bank," I said, touching the other. Mama would hold the money for me. Her bank didn't pay interest. In fact, she took a piece for a storage fee. But her bank was open twenty-four hours a day and it didn't file federal paper every time you made a deposit.

Mama's long fingers flashed over the money, faster than a blackjack dealer's. The two piles became four. She pointed at each in turn.

"For Max. For the bank. For Mama. For baby."

I nodded agreement. I knew the pile marked for Flower had some of my money and some of Mama's. Max knew nothing about it—it wasn't his business. Whenever Mama saw Immaculata, she would have a pink silk purse in her hand. "For baby," is all she ever said.

Down where we live, every day is a rainy day.

## 14

WE WERE IN THE BACK room, the one between the restaurant and the kitchen, waiting for the cook to finish chopping up a pile of thick marrow bones, putting together a food package for me. Terry was in the kitchen, watching everything. Staying out of the way.

Three pay phones stood in a bank against the wall. The one at the end rang. Mama looked at me. I nodded. She picked up the receiver.

"Mr. Burke not here. You leave message, okay?"

I couldn't hear the other end of the conversation. It didn't matter what they said—Mama never went past the script.

"Not here, okay? Don't know. Maybe today. Maybe next week. You leave message?"

Mama listened. Wrote something on a scrap of paper. Hung up.

She handed me the paper. A phone number I didn't recognize.

"Woman. Young woman. Say you call this number before nine tonight."

"She say what she wanted?"

"A job for you."

"Anybody we know?"

"I never hear the voice before. Woman say her name is Belle."

"I don't know her."

Mama shrugged. Bowed goodbye to me and Terry. The steel door closed behind us. I turned the Plymouth north to the Bronx.

# 15

TERRY WAS QUIET ON the ride back. I let him have his silence—it's something a man has to learn. As he got older, I'd teach him not to give things away with his face.

I didn't fill the silence with the radio or my tapes. The radio works, but the faceplate is really just to disguise the police-band scanner built into the dash.

And all my tapes are the blues.

Kids can't sing the blues; when they try, it sounds wrong. They have the pain, but not the range.

We rolled over the Triboro to the Bronx. The kid watched as I tossed a token into the basket in the Exact Change lane. Learning. Don't call attention to yourself. When we pulled up to the junkyard, Terry made a circle with his finger. Go around to the back.

The back fence was heavy-gauge cyclone mesh, with three twisted bands of razor wire running across the top. Everything was two-tone: pollution-gray and rust.

A big dog the same color as the fence was basking in a patch of late-afternoon sunlight. His lupine face was impassive as we approached, but his ears stood straight up. Yellow eyes tracked the car, locking onto the target like a heat-seeking missile. An American Junkyard Dog. Best of a breed the American Kennel Club never imagined. City wolf.

I pulled the car parallel to the fence, Terry's door closest to the dog. The beast growled deep in his chest. Dark shapes moved behind the fence. Dots of light and flashes of white. Eyes and teeth, both ready.

"Tell the Mole Michelle has his money."

"Okay, Burke."

Terry climbed out of the Plymouth, flipped the door closed behind him. Walked over to the dog, talking in a low voice. The beast walked over to meet him. Terry scratched the dog behind his ear, standing next to him. I knew the dog wouldn't move until I did, so I wheeled the car in a tight circle, heading back the way I came. When I looked back, Terry was down on all fours, following the dog through a cut-out section of the fence. He had to twist sideways to get in.

# 16

IT WAS DARK BY THE time l turned into the narrow street behind the old paper-tube factory where I have my office. The garage is set into the building just past the sidewalk. When the landlord converted the joint into living lofts, he bricked up the old loading bay, where the trucks used to pull in, to make room for storefronts. The garage only has room for one car, right at the end of a row of little shops. I pulled in, hit the switch; the door rattled down, leaving me in darkness. I locked the car, took the steel steps up four flights, walking quietly past the entrance to each hallway. The doors lock from the outside and I keep them that way. There's another flight of stairs at the far end of each floor. If there's a fire, the tenants know which way to go.

When I got to the top floor, I let myself into the hall. I closed the door behind me. It looked like a blank wall.

There's no sign on my door. My name's not on the directory downstairs. As far as the tenants know, the fifth floor is sealed off. Most of it is.

I don't have a lease. I don't pay rent. The landlord's son did something very stupid a few years ago. The landlord is a rich man, and he spent the right money in the right places. The kid has a new name, a new face, and a new life. Home free. Until I found him. I wasn't looking for the little weasel, but I knew who was. They still are.

It's not a home, it's where I live for now. When the time comes I have to leave, I won't look back. I'll take everything I need with me.

And when I walk away, there won't even be a fingerprint left for them to play with.

# 17

I TURNED THE KEY, listening to the bolts snap back. Three dead bolts: one into the steel frame on the side, another at the top, the final one directly into the floor. The hall's too narrow for a battering ram. By the time anyone broke in, I'd have long enough to do anything I needed to do.

Another key for the doorknob. I turned it twice to the right and once to the left, and stepped inside.

"It's me, Pansy," I said to the monster sitting in the middle of the dark room.

The monster made a noise somewhere between a snarl and a growl. A Neapolitan mastiff, maybe 140 pounds of muscle and bone, topped with a head the size of a cannonball and just about as thick. So dark she was almost black, Pansy blended into the room like a malevolent shadow, teeth shielded, cold-water eyes unflickering. Pansy can't handle complex thoughts. She wasn't sure if she was glad to see me or sorry she wasn't going to get to tear some flesh. Then she smelled the Chinese food and the issue was settled. The snarl changed to a whine, and slobber poured from her jaws. I threw her the hand signal for "Stay!" and hit the light switch.

The office is one small room. Desk facing the door, one chair behind, one in front. No windows. Couch against one wall. To the left, there's another door, leading to the office where my secretary works. The door's a fake. So's the secretary. The other wall is covered with a Persian rug that never got closer to Iran than 14th Street. The floor is covered with Astroturf. I told my decorator I wanted low-maintenance modern.

I pulled the rug aside and stepped into another room, even smaller than the office. Tiny stand-up shower I installed myself, sink and toilet in one corner. Hot plate and refrigerator in another. A cot between them. The back door opens out to a landing. The fire escape rusted off years ago.

I opened the back door, calling for Pansy, and stepped out to the landing. Watched the Hudson River slime-flow to the west, patting my dog's head as she stood next to me. Three rooms, with view.

Pansy ambled past me, taking the stairs to the roof. She's been lumping her loads up there for years. There's stuff growing on the roof I don't even want to think about.

Pansy came back downstairs as I was putting away the food Mama packed for me. I pulled a big slab of roast pork from a container, held it in front of her. Every fiber of her dim brain focused on that pork. An icicle of drool formed in one corner of her gaping mouth, but she didn't move. She wouldn't take the food until she heard the magic word. It's called poison-proofing.

"Speak!" I yelled at her, tossing the slab of pork in a gentle arc toward her face. It didn't last as long as a politician's promise. I tried a big fat egg roll. One chomp, and Pansy was swallowing in ecstasy, pieces of egg roll all over the floor. "You're a slob," I told her. She nodded happily.

Pansy's food-supply system is against the wall. A pair of hollowed-out cement cinder blocks with a forty-pound sack of dry dog food suspended above one and a tube connected to the sink above the other. When either bowl is empty, she pushes against the tube with her snout and it fills again.

I filled a big ceramic bowl with three quarts of Mama's cooking and told her to make a pig of herself. She buried her face up to the eyes in the steaming mess, making noises Stephen King never dreamed of. I threw some of the marrow bones into a pot and put them on the hot plate to boil.

I went inside to my desk. It was almost seven-thirty, and the woman Mama had spoken to said to call before nine. There was a phone on my desk. It never rang, and I never got a bill from Ma Bell—the Mole had it connected to the trust-fund hippies who lived downstairs. I could use it early in the morning, when the sensitive artists were still recovering from trying to find the light at the end of the marijuana tunnel they'd explored the night before, but not otherwise.

I'd had the phone for years. No problems. I never used it for long-distance calls. That's why God made other people's credit cards.

The office looked the same way it always does. I don't get clients coming here much. The last one was Flood. The day I let her in, she came in too deep. I lit a cigarette, not wanting to think about the chubby little blonde head-hunter. She came into my life, got what she came for, and left me empty.

I didn't want to think about Flood. She came too often in my sleep. "I'm for you, Burke," I can still hear her saying. The way only a woman can say. And only say it once, if it's the truth.

It was.

Part of the full bloom I was still waiting for.

I went out to make my phone call.

## 18

ALMOST EIGHT BY THE time I found the pay phone I wanted. Near the river, just a couple of blocks from the Yuppietown the developers had built by reclaiming a piece of the Hudson. Within eyeshot of the bullshit "security lights" flanking the high-rise but safe in a pool of darkness.

Like I was.

I don't like cold calls. My phone number's circulated all over this city. The phone's listed to Juan Rodriguez, and the address is the back end of a junkyard I own. The old man who runs it draws me a paycheck every two weeks. I cash it and give him back the money. It makes me a citizen—I pay my taxes, build up my Social Security, all that. Having a citizen's name is important. The name opens the door to all the goodies: legit address, driver's license, Social Security card. I don't lose any sleep worrying about the FBI, but the IRS is another game. I have a birth certificate too. It's so phony it even has a father's name on it.

My credit with Ma Bell is excellent. Never miss a payment. Never make any toll calls. I never make any calls at all. Anyone who calls the junkyard number activates the call diverter I have set up. The signal bounces over to one of the phones at Mama's.

I unscrewed the mouthpiece of the pay phone and slipped in the flat disk the Mole gave me. It changes my voice just enough to throw off the machines, in case anyone's listening. I pulled the tiny tape recorder from my coat and hit the switch; the booth was flooded with the background noise from a bowling alley. The number had a 718 area code. Brooklyn or Queens. I dropped a quarter and dialed the number.

She answered on the third ring. A young girl's voice, with the hard twang that sounds Southern unless you've spent some time in Detroit.

"Hello?"

"Belle?"

"Who's this?"

"Burke. Returning your call."

"Oh. I didn't think it would be so fast. I'm doing a favor for someone. Someone who wants to talk to you."

"Who?"

"I'd rather tell you in person."

"I'd rather you tell me over the phone."

"I can't do that. I promised."

"What's in it for me?"

"Money."

"How much money?"

"That depends. You'd have to work it out with him. I just said I'd talk to you. Tell you about it. See if you're interested in getting together."

"You get paid win or lose?"

"Yes."

"Tell him I said no, and collect your money."

"You have to hear me out. Tell me to my face. That's the deal."

"That's not *my* deal."

Her voice shifted, dropped a note. "What *is* your deal?"

"Time is money. My time is your money, okay?"

"How much money?"

"How much time?"

"Fifteen minutes."

"Five yards."

"That's a lot of money."

I didn't say anything, listening to the silence at her end, the sound of pins falling at mine.

"Can you meet me? Tonight?"

"Is he there with you?"

"No."

"How do you know he'll go for the cash?"

"I don't. I have to make some calls. I work at . . . "

"I don't care where you work," I said, cutting her off. "Do what you have to do. Speak to the man. I'll call you tomorrow morning."

"Not before eleven, okay? I get in late."

"You have a car?"

"Yes."

"I'll call you tomorrow. Tell you where to come and meet me. You bring the money—we'll talk."

"Thank you," the young girl's voice said, and she broke the connection.

## 19

WHEN I CALLED HER the next morning, her voice sounded the same. Not breathy, or trying to be sexy. Short-winded.

"I got the go-ahead."

"And the money?"

"Yes."

"What kind of car do you drive?"

"A Camaro. A red one. With a T-top."

"You know Metropolitan Avenue?"

"In Queens? By the cemeteries?"

"Yeah. Take it west. Like you're going to the city, okay? Just keep going until it crosses over into Brooklyn. You'll come to a little drawbridge. Go over the bridge and look for a gas station on your right. Just pull up to the pumps—I'll meet you there."

"What time?"

"Three."

"How will I know you?"

"I'll be the man asking for the money."

## 20

I TOOK THE DELANCEY Street Bridge out of Manhattan, hooked back around to Metropolitan Avenue. I cruised past the gas station. At two in the afternoon, it looked the way it always does—a wino asleep in the sun, a dead bottle of T-bird half out of a paper bag next to him. A pair of red-brown dogs that had never been pets swept the empty concrete, all legs and ribs, looking for food. A black guy wearing a winter coat, tattered cowboy hat on his head, pushing a supermarket basket full of cans and bottles, checking the alleys for more nuggets. Grayish dust from the concrete plant on the other side of the drawbridge settled over everything. The sun hit hard. The wino was half in shadow—he'd been sleeping a long time.

I parked the Plymouth a few blocks away, backed in against the metallic strip of water that carried the ore barges under the drawbridge. It took me less than five minutes to get back to the gas station. I found myself a comfortable spot against the wall and sat down to wait.

The skinny dogs circled, watchful. I reached into the paper bag next to me and took out a piece of cheese. I unwrapped it slowly, watching them from beneath the brim of my battered felt hat. I tossed the cheese in their direction, arcing it gently so they'd know it was no threat. The bigger dog moved in, sniffed it quickly, and took it into his mouth. He moved away, chewing slowly. I unwrapped another piece, tossed it the same way. The big dog's partner dashed in, snatched it, and moved back to where the other one was standing.

I lit a cigarette, watching the dogs sniff the air, trying to do the same. From where I sat, there was no way to approach the gas station without me seeing it. I wasn't worried about customers—the only gas in the place was in the plastic bottle in my paper bag.

Almost an hour passed. I'd gone through several smokes, and the dogs had exhausted my supply of cheese. They wouldn't come close enough for me to touch, but the big guy sat about ten feet away, watching me; his partner stretched out next to him.

I was completely in shadow when the red Camaro pulled up to the pumps. The windows were down. A woman in the front seat. She turned off the engine. The dogs left me, ambling over to the car. Trucks rumbled by on Metropolitan.

She got out of the car. A big woman. Honey-taffy hair, hacked off near her shoulders, bangs covering her forehead almost to her eyes. She was wearing a peach-colored sweatshirt over a pair of loose white pants. Hands on hips, she turned one complete circle, sweeping the area.

I came to my feet quietly, moved to her. She saw me coming, a wino with a paper bag in one hand. She stood her ground.

"Hello, Belle," I said.

"You're Burke?"

I nodded, watching her eyes to see if she was expecting company of her own. Her eyes were small, dark, set close together. Her face was round, smooth—unformed except for a tiny pointed chin. She was as tall as I was, wider through the shoulders and hips. I glanced at her feet. White running shoes, small, like her hands. No watch. No rings.

The back seat of the Camaro was empty. "Would you open the trunk?" I asked her.

"Why?"

"I want to see if you've got a spare."

She bobbed her head like she understood. Bent inside the car to pull the keys from the ignition. Her hips flexed under the loose white pants. She handed me the keys. The trunk held only a blue overnight case.

I motioned her to get in the car, climbed behind the wheel, and started it up. She walked around the front of the car, opened the passenger door, turned her back to me, swung her butt inside, and dropped it into the seat. Pulled her legs in and closed the door. She filled the seat. Sat there, tiny hands in her lap. Waiting.

I drove aimlessly around the area for a few minutes. Nothing out of place. The second time I passed the spot where I'd parked the Plymouth, I pulled in next to it, nose toward the water. I got out, walked around to the back of the car, leaned against the trunk. Belle followed me. Stood next to me. Put her hands behind her, palms against the trunk. Hoisted herself up. The trunk bounced a few times with her weight. If the hot metal was burning into her backside, she didn't show it.

"The man who wants to meet you . . . "

I held up my hand like a traffic cop. "We had a deal."

She pulled up her sweatshirt. A bunch of bills was folded into the waistband of her pants. Green on milk. She pulled the sheaf of bills out, handed it to me. All fifties. Ten of them. Used. I slipped them into my shirt pocket.

"Fifteen minutes," I told her.

"There's a man who wants to meet with you. He doesn't want you to get the wrong idea."

"This man have a name?"

I watched her face in profile. Her nose was barely a bump—lost on her broad, round face. A bead of clear sweat ran down one cheek. "Marques Dupree," she said.

I took a drag on my cigarette. "I already have the wrong idea," I told her.

"You said you'd hear me out."

I took another drag.

"He has a problem. A big problem. He said you're the man to help him—you'd know what to do."

"I know what to do. Why should I do it?"

"He said this is something you'd want to do."

"You know what it is?"

"No."

"So what's there to talk about?"

"Marques wants to meet with you. He said you wouldn't come if he called."

"He's right."

"He sent me to show you he's on the square. It's a job, okay? That's all."

"I don't work for Marques."

"He said you'd say that too. All he wants is for you to meet with him."

I bit into the cigarette, thinking. Marques was doing this the right way. He wouldn't be stupid enough to just roll up on me—he didn't have the weight for that. If Marques Dupree was coming to me, he had to have real troubles.

"You one of his ladies?" I asked her.

Her tiny chin came up. She turned full-face to me. Her close-set eyes were almost black; I couldn't see the pupils. "I'm not a whore." She wasn't mad—just setting it straight.

"So why you doing this?"

She reached out a tiny hand, patted my shirt pocket. Where the money was.

"I'll think about it, okay? Where can I find you?"

"Me?"

"Yeah. You. I *know* how to find Marques."

"I work at The Satellite Dish. Out by JFK."

"That's a strip joint," I said.

Something must have shown in my face. Her tiny rosebud mouth made a quick kissing motion. "You think I'm overqualified?"

I shrugged.

"I work every night except Tuesday."

I put my hand on her wrist. Gently, holding her attention. "Tell Marques not to call me. If I want to meet him, I'll come and tell you first."

"What if you don't want to see him?"

"Then I won't," I told her, guiding her back into the driver's seat, motioning for her to take off.

I started walking in the opposite direction. The Camaro drove off. I watched over my shoulder as she turned the corner; then I went back to the Plymouth.

# 21

THE WAREHOUSE OFF Division Street in Chinatown looked like it always does. Empty. Deserted. I pulled in, turned off the engine. Waited. When I heard the door close behind me, I knew Max was home.

The warehouse was furnished with dim shadows. I followed Max up the back stairs to the second floor. He usually went to the back room, where we'd work on our life-sentence gin game. Something different today. Max stopped on the landing. His temple was upstairs. The dojo where he practiced, the teak floor marked with a white-pine border. The sacred ground where Flood met a freak who called himself the Cobra. The killing floor.

Immaculata was sitting in a low chair in a corner of the white room. A black lacquer table covered with books and papers at her elbow. The baby sat across from her, wearing only a diaper, her little face grave as she watched her mother work. A butcher-block table ran the length of one wall, with hardwood straight-back chairs at each end. Max gestured to one of the chairs. I sat down as Immaculata put her notes aside and rose to her feet.

"Hello, Burke."

"Hi, Mac. How's Flower?"

"She is a perfect child," Mac said, as though she'd carefully considered all the other possibilities. "Some tea?"

"Thank you," I said, knowing what she meant.

Mac started to walk into the next room. The baby made a sound, less than a cry, maybe a question. Mac knelt next to her child, speaking quietly, her voice steel-cored. "Mother will come back, baby. *Always* come back, yes? *Never* leave you." She kissed the infant gravely on the forehead. Waved a goodbye gesture to the child.

Again and again, patiently, until the child moved her hand too. "Smart baby!" Immaculata clapped.

I took out a cigarette, held it up for Max to see, asking if it was okay to smoke near the child.

Max pointed to an ashtray the size of a dinner plate, aluminum on the outside, glazed red ceramic on the inside. He lit a cigarette of his own, blowing the smoke toward the ceiling. Spreading his arms to say the whole world smoked and the baby wasn't going to spend the rest of her life in the house.

Immaculata came back inside. She had a pot of tea with two cups, a glass of iced ginger ale for me. "I have your mail," she said, handing me a stack of letters. I use a P.O. box over in Jersey. One of Mama's drivers empties it for me about every two weeks, leaves the letters in Mama's basement. Max picks them up when he has the chance and holds them for me. I shuffled through them. Nothing from Japan. Nothing from Flood. I put them in my coat.

Immaculata pulled up a chair, joined us, one eye on her baby. Flower was gurgling happily to herself. It sounded like singing.

Max held up one finger, catching my eye. Pay attention.

He moved off his chair without a sound, crouched behind the baby. Suddenly he slapped his hands together. It sounded like a gunshot. The baby jumped, trying to turn her head in the direction of the sound. Max scooped her up and held her against his chest, nuzzling her, his horn-callused hands now soft as a cloud. The baby's tiny hands searched—found one of his fingers, grabbed, and held.

Max carried the baby back to his chair, held her on his lap. Smiling.

Immaculata stood watching him, hands on hips. "Max!" she snapped, stamping her foot. He ignored her, watching me.

Immaculata sighed. "When I was pregnant, he'd do that all the time. He said the baby could hear him. When she came out of my body, he made everyone be quiet. He waited until she was nursing. . . . Then he clapped his hands like that. When she moved—when she *heard* him—I thought he was going to burst, he was so happy."

"She recognized his voice," I said.

"Sure. That's what *he* said."

"What else could it be?"

"I think"—she looked at her husband—"I think he was afraid our baby would be born deaf."

"Was Max born deaf?"

"I never asked him," she said, a slight warning tone in her voice.

He was my brother. I had earned the right to know. Earned it in a prison cell. I pointed at Max. Made a gesture as if I was rocking a baby. Pointed at him again. At my ear.

His face went hard, eyes slitted, mouth a straight line. He shook his head. No.

I opened my hands. "How?"

Max gently picked up his baby, carried her back over to the floor, put her down. Kissed her. He stood between Immaculata and me. Pointed to himself again. A fist flashed into his palm so quickly I only saw the vapor trail. A sharp crack. He pointed to his ear. Held his palm thigh-high. A little child. His hand became a claw, snatched something, lifted it off the ground. Threw it against the wall. Walked away. Pointed to himself again.

He wasn't born deaf.

I tapped my heart twice, bowed my head. My eyes felt funny.

Max pointed at Flower, playing by herself on the floor. Reached his hand across the table. Immaculata put her hand in his. He circled his thumb and forefinger. Okay. Okay, now.

Yeah. He was ahead of the game.

I took a sip of the ginger ale. Lit another smoke. I held my palms close together, not touching. A meeting.

Max did the same. The palms became fists.

I shrugged. Maybe. Who knows?

I pointed at him. At myself. Waved a pointing finger. A meeting outside. In the street.

He looked a question.

I rubbed my first two fingers and thumb together. Money. Maybe a job.

Max hissed an inhale through his nose.

I shook my head. Not cocaine. I made the sign of injecting something into my arm. Shook my head again. Not heroin. Held an imaginary joint in my mouth, triple-inhaled fast. Shook my head again. Not marijuana.

Max took a dollar from his pocket. Held up three fingers.

I shook my head again. Not funny-money.

Immaculata watched us, like a spectator at a tennis match. Waiting for the punch line.

Max pointed a finger, cocked his thumb. I told him no again. Not guns. I weaved my fingers in the air, making an hourglass. Women.

His face went hard again as he held his hand chest-high, asking.

I put my palm to my forehead, like a salute, measuring for him. Not kids. I made a gesture like I was talking to someone, negotiating. Showed money changing hands. I took some cash from my pocket, put it on the table. Made one big pile with a single bill off to the side. Pocketed the pile. Pushed the remaining bill across the table to my left. Made the hourglass sign again. Her share.

Max circled his hands around his head, tilted a hat brim forward.

I nodded. A pimp.

Max smiled. He made a gesture like he was pulling a wristwatch off. Pulled rings off fingers. Reached inside his shirt for a wallet.

I shook my head. Not a shakedown. Not a rough-off. I held my palms together again, not touching. Just a meeting. Okay?

He nodded.

I pointed at my watch. Made an "I don't know" gesture. I'd let him know when it was going down.

The baby cried. Immaculata went over to her, picked her up, and sat her down on her lap to nurse. I bowed to Max, to Immaculata, to my brother's baby.

I went down the stairs to my car, thinking of Flood. Back to being alone.

# 22

I WENT THROUGH THE mail back in the office. The usual stuff. Congenital defectives replying to my ad promising "south of the border" opportunities for "qualified adventurers." Most of the mercenary action is in Central America now; the Cubans have made it real clear that Africa isn't the promised land. The good scams concentrate on "training exercises." There's decent money in stinging maladroits who want to dress up in camouflage gear and run around the New Jersey swamps learning how to "survive." I don't run one of the camps—I don't want to meet any of my customers face to face. But, for a reasonable fee, I'm always happy to process their applications.

The pedophile letters always have P.O. boxes of their own for return addresses. One was neatly typed on creamy bond paper, the monogram "CX" engraved in one corner. "I'm always interested in the real thing. Especially discipline, golden showers, and snuff. I hope we can be friends." I put the letter aside. If it wasn't from a Postal Inspector, I had a genuine freak—the kind who expected to pay for his fun. Scumbags. They always manage to get what they pay for. Sometimes I get lucky; then they pay for what they get.

The rest of the mail was replies to our new series of personal ads. We run them everyplace—from literary journals to hard-core slime-sheets. Variations on the same theme: young girl, serving a prison sentence, getting out soon. Lonely, broke, needs a friend.

Honey Blaine is the sweet young girl's name. If any of the suckers bothered to write directly, they'd find an "H. Blaine, #86-B-9757," doing time at Bedford Hills. Just the way it said in the ad. Honey would set them straight right away. She'd explain that she couldn't write the kind of letter she'd *really* like to: the prison censors wouldn't permit it. Honey had a secret P.O. box, though, and if a sincere man was willing to be a little patient, well . . .

I screened the letters. Michelle answered them. We had a few dozen different photos we used. All Polaroids ("That's the only kind they let us take here, darling"). Whatever the suckers wanted, that's what they got. Honey could be a nineteen-year-old victimized by a cruel pimp. A lesbian whose lover informed on her in a drug deal. A car thief. Anything but a scam artist. She could be the answer to an old man's prayer or the bottom of a minister's ugly fantasy. A very flexible girl, this Honey. All it took was Michelle's never-miss instincts and some creative writing. Honey would play the sucker, work the hook in deep, turning up the heat to full boil. Then the poor girl would start to have problems: a bull dyke hitting on her, demanding her body or her life; a threatened transfer to another section of the prison, where she wouldn't be able to correspond. Overdue rent on the P.O. box. A nice piece of cash needed to bribe the Parole Board. Gate money. And the money orders would start to come in.

After a while, the sucker would get his last letter returned. Unopened. An official prison stamp on the outside. Black-bordered. "Return to sender. Inmate deceased." The suckers always bought it—if it was a scam, why wouldn't sweet Honey have cashed the last money order?

H. Blaine, #86-B-9757, wasn't allowed visitors. Good thing. The name and the number were legit, but Hortense Blaine is a fifty-five-year-old, three-hundred-pound black woman. She raised three generations of foster kids. From babies dropped down incinerators who didn't die, to kiddie prostitutes who never lived. She never had a kid of her own, but she was mother to dozens. Her boyfriend raped one of the kids. A twelve-year-old girl named Princess.

I have a copy of the trial transcript. I got it from the lawyer who's working on the appeal. A hard-blues lyric they'll never put to music.

DIRECT EXAMINATION
BY MR. DAVIDSON:

Q: What, if anything, did you do after Princess told you about the rape?

A: I told the child he was never going to hurt her again. I carried her into my room. Put her in my bed.

Q: The same bed you shared with Mr. Jackson?

A: He wasn't going to be using it no more.

Q: And then?

A: I waited for Jackson to come home. He was out gambling someplace. He comes in the door, sits at the kitchen table. Tells me to get him a beer.

Q: Did you get him a beer?

A: Yeah.

Q: Tell the jury what happened next.

A: I asked him why he did this. I said . . .

Q: Excuse me for interrupting you, Mrs. Blaine. You asked him *why* he raped the child? Not *if* he did it?

A: There was blood in the child's bed.

Q: I see. Please continue.

A: I asked him why he did what he did. He tells me Princess going to be a woman soon. Won't hurt her none. Get her ready for what life's all about, he said. He said she was walking around in her nightgown when I was out working. Said she asked for it.

Q: Did you see the expression on his face when he said this?

MR. HAYNES: Objection. Calls for a conclusion of the witness.

MR. DAVIDSON: An observation of demeanor is not a conclusion, Judge.

MR. HAYNES: Your Honor, counsel for the defense is trying to introduce blatant hearsay. This is an attempt to impugn the character of a dead man.

MR. DAVIDSON: This Court has already heard the testimony of the child Princess. The character of this rapist is already in evidence.

MR. HAYNES: Objection! Mr. Jackson is not on trial.

MR. DAVIDSON: That's right. He's already been tried.

THE COURT: Gentlemen, that will be quite enough. The objection is overruled.

Q: I ask you again, Mrs. Blame. Did you see the expression on his face when he admitted to you that he raped Princess?

A: Yeah. He was smiling. Like it was nothing.

MR. HAYNES: Objection.

THE COURT: Overruled.

Q: Did he say anything else?

A: He said the little bitch got what she deserved.

Q: What happened then?

A: I picked up the kitchen knife and I stabbed him in his heart.

Q: Did you mean to kill him?

A: Yes.

Q: Why?

A: So he'd never hurt my baby no more.

MR. DAVIDSON: Your witness.

Defending a murder charge wasn't a job for a courthouse gonif. Too many of our people had spent time with Hortense when we were coming up. Like the Prof. Short for "Professor." Or "Prophet." A tiny black omen-master who'd been on the hustle since before I was born, he talked rhyme and he walked crime. The Prof only stood as high as my chest, but he always stood up.

"Cutting up slime ain't no crime," was all he said, dealing himself in on whatever we had to do to raise the cash.

Davidson was the man for the job. A husky guy with a full beard, he plays the game hard. I first heard about him when he defended one of the UGL gunmen years ago. Davidson told us the only way to roll on this one was to do what he called a "psychiatric autopsy" on the dead man.

And he pulled it off. When he was finished, the jury knew Jackson had been a piece of living scum before he died. They came back with a verdict of Manslaughter, Second Degree. You could feel the weight lift—murder carries a twenty-five-to-life top in this state. But Davidson slammed his fist down on the defense table hard enough to break it. He never raised his eyes.

One of the jurors walked over to him. A fat guy in a brown suit. Said Davidson did a great job, asked him for his card. Davidson raised his face to look at the juror. His eyes were wet. "I'm particular about who I defend," he said, turning his back on the juror's outstretched hand.

The judge hit Hortense with two-to-six upstate. Only child molesters get probation in New York. One of her foster sons stood next to her when she got the sentence. All grown up now, he works in a bank, lives in the suburbs. When he heard she was going down, he started to cry. Hortense put a big hand on his shoulder. She had to reach up to do it.

"Be a man," she told him. Not giving an inch.

She gave Davidson a kiss on the cheek and held out her hands for the cuffs.

Davidson's working on the appeal. Working hard, the way he always does. While he's working on the appeal, we're working on putting together some cash for when Hortense walks out. Once a month, the Prof visits her at the prison, bringing a batch of money orders for her to sign. There's a check-cashing joint in the Bronx that doesn't ask a lot of questions. Hortense gets half the money; Michelle and I split the rest. It was supposed to be a four-way split, but the Prof gives his piece to Hortense. "Not *all* payback's a bitch," he said when we asked him.

Michelle doesn't work the streets anymore. I thought it was AIDS, but she said she couldn't risk a bust now. Now that she's a mother.

So she does phone jobs, suckers letting their credit cards run wild while she talks them over the top. Or she visits her clients indoors.

It was only right that she and Hortense would work a sting together. Walking different sides of the same one-way street.

## 23

I FELT BAD, AND I DIDN'T know why. I was some cash ahead, for a change. The last job went down like sweet syrup, and maybe there would be some more of that kind of work down the road. Nobody was looking for me.

I didn't spend time thinking about it. I used to do that. I used to do time. A couple of bad habits.

Pansy ambled over to where I was sitting, put her huge head on my lap. She made a noise that sounded like a growl, but I knew what she wanted.

"Not today, girl," I told her, scratching her head between her eyes. Max and I were training her to stay low when she hit. Most dogs leave their feet when they attack, some deep instinct forcing them to go for the throat. That doesn't work on people: human throats are too far off the ground. We take Pansy over to this vacant lot in Brooklyn. Pay some kid ten bucks and talk him into putting on the agitator's suit—leather covered with padded canvas. I hold Pansy on a snap leash, facing the agitator. Max stands to the side with a long bamboo pole. When I send Pansy, Max brings the pole down. Hard. If she stays low, about groin-height, she can nail the kid wearing the suit. If she leaves her feet, Max cracks her in the head. Lately she's been getting through most of the time. I call her off as soon as she gets a good bite.

I have to get a different kid each time. The suit feels like it's armor-plated, but Pansy can turn a leg into liquid right through it.

I flipped the channels on the TV until I found a pro wrestling match. Pansy's favorite. I gave her one of the marrow bones and stretched out on the couch, opening the racing sheet. Maybe I'd find a horse I liked. Make my own kind of investment.

The last thing I remember before I fell asleep was Pansy grinding the marrow bone into powder.

# 24

IT WAS PAST TEN WHEN I woke up. On the TV, a private detective was getting hit over the head with a tire iron. I lit a smoke. Opened the back door for Pansy. When I walked back inside, the private eye was wide awake and looking for clues.

I took a shower. Looked at my face in the mirror. Deep, past the image. Looked into myself, breathing through my nose, expanding my stomach, exhaling as my chest went out.

When I came out of it, I felt clear. Centered. Ready to go to work.

I shaved carefully. Combed my hair. I put on a pair of dark-gray slacks and a white silk shirt. Alligator boots. Custom-made, but they were a pretty good fit on me anyway. I moved aside some shirts in the bottom drawer of my dresser. Looked at a whole pile of rings, watches, bracelets, gold chains. The spoils of war.

I held a smuggler's necklace in my hand. Each link is a one-ounce gold ingot; it comes apart one piece at a time. Too classy for this job. I pawed through the stuff until I found the right combination: a thick gold neck chain, a gold bracelet, and a gold ring set with a blue star sapphire.

Checked myself in the full-length mirror on the door of the closet. Something missing. I found some gel in the bathroom. Ran it through my hair until it looked thicker and a bit greasy. White hair shot through the black just past my temples. It didn't bother me—the only thing I ever posed for was mug shots.

I slopped some cologne all over my face and neck. To throw the dogs off the scent.

A few hundred bucks in my pocket, one of the Mole's butane lighters, a wallet I stripped of bogus credit cards, and I was ready to visit a strip joint.

# 25

JFK AIRPORT SITS AT THE end of Queens, near the Long Island border, sticking out into the bay. The surrounding swampland is slashed with two-lane side roads running off the expressway. Warehouses, light industry, short-stay motels.

The Highway Department keeps the roads in good shape, but they don't waste any money on streetlights. A bandit's paradise.

I found The Satellite Dish easily enough. A one-story blue stucco building, standing alone on a slab of blacktop. Two long, narrow windows framing a set of double doors, the dark glass covered with fluorescent promises: Go-Go Girls. Topless. Bottomless. Exotic Dancers.

I nosed the Plymouth through the parking lot. General Motors must have held a white-on-white sale: Eldorados, Buick Regals, Oldsmobiles. Vinyl tops, tinted glass, hand-painted monograms on the doors. I left the Plymouth at the edge of the blacktop, dull paint fading into the shadows. It looked abandoned.

I stepped through the double doors into a square foyer. White walls, red carpet. Hawk-faced guy in a powder-blue double-knit suit sitting at a little table to one side. The joint wasn't classy enough to have a hat-check girl—and not hard-core enough to shake you down for weapons.

"Ten bucks cover, pal. And worth every penny," the hawk-faced guy said. His heart wasn't in it.

I paid, went through the next set of doors. The place was bigger than it looked from the outside, so dark I couldn't see the walls. A T-shaped bar ran the entire width of the room, with a long perpendicular runway almost to the door. Small round tables were spread all over the room. Two giant screens, like the ones they use for projection TV, stood in the corners at each end of the long bar. The screens were blank.

The tables were empty. Every man in the place was seated at the bar, most of them along the runway. Hard-rock music circled from hidden speakers. Three girls were on top of the bar. Two blondes and a redhead. All wearing bikini bottoms, high heels, and sparkle dust. Each girl worked her own piece of the bar, bouncing around, talking to the customers. The redhead went to her knees in front of a guido with a high-rise haircut and diamonds on his fingers. She spun on the bar, dropped her shoulders. The guido pulled down her panties, stuffed some bills between her thighs, patted her butt. She gave him a trembly wiggle, reached back and pulled up the panties, spun around again, ran her tongue over her lips. Danced away.

It was somewhere between the South Bronx shacks where the girls would blow you in the back booths and the steak-and-silicone joints in midtown where they called you "sir" but wouldn't screw you out of anything more than your money.

I found an empty stool near the left side of the T. A brunette wearing a red push-up bra under a transparent white blouse leaned over the bar toward me. She raised her eyebrows, smiling the smile they all use.

"Gin-and-tonic," I told her, putting a fifty on the bar. "Plenty of ice. Don't mix them."

She winked. I was obviously a with-it guy. No watered drinks for this stud.

She brought me a tall glass of tonic, jigger of gin on the side. Put four ten-dollar bills back in front of me. Class costs.

"My name is Laura," she cooed. "I go on after the last set. You going to be here?"

I nodded. She took one of the ten-spots off the bar, looked a question at me. I nodded. She stuffed it between her breasts, winked at me, and went back to work. I left the money on the bar.

I sipped my tonic, waiting.

The music stopped. A short, stocky guy in a pink sport coat over a billowy pair of white slacks stepped to the intersection of the T. The lights went down. The house man hit the stocky guy with a baby spot. He had a wireless microphone in one hand.

"Here's what you've been waiting for . . . the fabulous . . . Debbie, and the Dance of Domination!"

The bar went dark again. Most of the men moved to the back tables. A door at the right of the T opened, and two dim shapes walked to the intersection. The music started. No words, heavy bass-lines and drums. One of the shapes went off the stage.

A hard white spot burned the center of the T, making it into an isolated island. A black straight-back chair stood by itself, thick high posts on each side. The giant TV screens flickered into life. The camera zoomed in on the chair, filling the picture.

A blonde in a black sheath came into the light. Black spikes on her feet, black gloves up to her elbows. A black pillbox hat on her head, a black veil covering her face. She sat down on the chair, crossed her legs. She tilted her chin up, waiting.

I could hear the humans breathing under the music, but there was no conversation. Topless waitresses were working the darkness, stopping at the little tables, taking orders for drinks. Business was booming.

It was like no strip act I'd ever seen. No playing to the audience—they were all watching through a window. Quiet. Lost and alone in their ugliness.

The stage went dark. The music stopped. Herd sounds from the crowd.

Nobody moved.

When the spot came on again, the blonde was on her knees, facing the crowd. She ran her hand across her thighs, into her crotch, as the music built. Then she lifted the veil slowly. The pillbox hat came off. The camera came in on her face. She licked her lips, her eyes wide. As she opened her mouth, the stage went dark again.

It stayed dark for a couple of minutes. Cigarette lighters snapped in the crowd. Tiny red flares.

Flood came into my mind. I saw her struggling to work skin-tight pants over her hips, shifting from toe to toe, flexing her legs. Bending over another chair, in another place, the fire-scar on her rump dark against the white skin. I put the image down—those bodies were buried.

The lights came up again, blaring rock music came back through the speakers, the TV screens went dark. Three different girls were working the top of the bar, gesturing for the men to come away from the little tables and get closer.

I poured the gin into the empty tonic glass, mixing it with the ice. The bargirl came back to where I was sitting, bringing me another set; she put my empty glasses on a little tray.

"You like that stuff?"

"Not my taste," I said.

"Maybe later you'll tell me what you like," she whispered, sweeping the rest of my money off the bar, doubling her tip.

I reached in my pocket for another fifty. Waiting for Belle wasn't a cheap job.

## 26

I FIGURED BELLE MUST work as one of the back-table waitresses, but I didn't want to ask for her by name. The tables stayed empty while the girls worked the top of the bar, so I'd have to wait for the next number, move into the darkness by myself, look around. I sipped my tonic, lit another smoke.

I watched the girls spread themselves on the long bar, as turned-on as a gynecologist.

It was a good twenty minutes and another half-century note before the guy in the pink jacket took center stage again. "Cassandra," was all he said. The stage went dark again. I could see shapes moving around, setting things up. This time I went back to a table near the back wall. I took the tonic, left the gin.

When the spot hit the stage, a girl was seated on a padded chair, looking into a mirror. The camera came in on her face. Belle. A mask of makeup making the soft lines hard, a white bathrobe around her shoulders, a white ribbon around her hair.

The speakers fired into life. Nasty music, zombie-swamp blues, voodoo drums.

Belle was taking off the makeup, patting her face with cream. She shrugged her shoulders and the robe dropped to her waist. Her breasts were enormous, standing out straight, defying gravity in a white D-cup bra. The camera watched them in the mirror.

She rose to her feet, holding the robe in one hand at her waist like a skirt. The spotlight widened: she was in a bedroom, white ruffled bedspread, white shag rug on the floor. Belle stalked the white room, a young girl getting ready for bed. Running a brush through her thick hair, maybe humming to herself. She opened her hand and the robe dropped to the floor. Belle hooked it with one foot, delicately tossed it onto the bed.

With the robe off, it was a different Belle on the screen. She faced the crowd in the white bra and plain matching panties, bending slightly forward, as if she was looking out into the night. The big woman wasn't fat; she was wasp-waisted. When she turned sideways, the stinger was a beauty, standing out by itself, straining against the fabric.

The music came harder. Her hips wiggled, like they had a mind of their own. She paced the room, stretching the way a cat does, bending to touch her toes, working off the restlessness, too wired to sleep.

The speakers spit out the music, sliding from the voodoo drums into words. Words I'd never heard before. A man's voice, gospel-tinted blues now. Warning. Blood moon rising. Slide guitar climbing on top of the drums, picking high notes, bending them against the black fabric of the bass. The words came through at the bottom of my brain; my eyes were locked on Belle.

*The swamp gets mean at night.*
*Bloody shadows eat the light,*
*Things that snarl,*
*Things that bite,*
*Things no man can fight.*

The music stayed dense, but the tempo picked up. Belle cocked her head, listening. She unsnapped the bra, carefully hung it on the bedpost. Her huge breasts didn't sag an inch. She raised her hands high above her head, touching them together, standing on her toes. She made a complete turn that way, a tiny smile on her face. Not a muscle twitched in the smooth skin. Her body was as seamless as an airbrushed photograph. Her shoes were gone. She stalked the little room again, listening to the throbbing music, rolling her head on the column of her neck, working out the kinks. A nurse, tired from a hard day's work? A waitress, finished with her shift?

The camera ran the length of her body. Only the white panties on her hips, a thin gold chain around her neck, a gold cross resting between her breasts. Some kind of blue mark on the front of one thigh. Even with the camera zooming in, I couldn't make it out.

She rolled the panties over her hips, down past her butt. It took a long time, but not because she was teasing the audience—the panties had a long way to travel. Belle picked them off the floor, fluffed them out, went over to the bed, and hung them on the bedpost. On top of the white bra.

The music drove harder.

Belle dropped to her knees in front of the low bed. She clasped her hands. A little girl praying. The camera moved from her broad shoulders, past her tiny waist, down to the giant globes of her butt. The seamless skin was sweaty in the burning spotlight.

The words pushed back the music.

*Yes, boy, you better beware,*
*You better walk with care.*
*You can carry a cross,*
*You can carry a gun,*
*But when you hear the call, you better run.*

*There's worse things than gators out there.*
*Worse things than gators out there.*

Belle's whole body was shaking now. Trembling as the spotlight blended from white to blood-red and back to white. She got to her feet and turned to face the crowd. She pulled back the covers, slid into the bed. She fluffed the pillow, pulled the covers to her shoulders, lying on her side. The mound of her hip was as high as her shoulders. The music faded down. The lights dimmed.

The music wouldn't let her sleep. Her body thrashed under the covers. Drums working her hips, guitar plucking her soft breasts. A blue spot burned down on her face buried in the pillow, turning her taffy-honey hair a ghostly white. The spot turned a softer blue, widening to cover the whole bed. The warning voice came back, soft, demanding. Telling the truth, the way the blues always does.

*There's worse things than gators out there, boy.*
*Much worse things than gators out there.*

Belle threw back the covers, the music pulling her from the bed. She looked out into the night, shook herself. She reached for her robe, put one arm into a sleeve. Then she dropped the robe to the floor.

The blue spot played over her body as she walked into the darkness.

# 27

WHEN THE LIGHTS CAME up, I saw I had two more drinks in front of me. I hadn't touched them. The pile of ten-spots in front of me was lighter.

I went back to my spot at the end of the bar, no closer to talking with Belle than I'd been. Laura came over to me, her little tray loaded with another gin-and-tonic in separate glasses. She leaned over the bar.

"You like that act better?"

I felt a hand on my shoulder. "He sure does," said a little girl's voice.

I didn't turn around. I knew who it was.

"Is this yours?" Laura asked Belle.

"All mine," Belle said.

"I thought you didn't like men," Laura said, a nasty little smile on her face.

"I don't like boys."

Laura looked past me. She reached her hand over to my pile of tens. Took one. Stuffed it in her cleavage, looking over my shoulder.

"Take two," Belle told her, razor tips on her breathy voice.

Laura shrugged, pretending she was thinking about it. She pulled another bill off the bar and walked away.

I felt Belle's face close to mine in the darkness. Smelled her little-girl sweat.

"Where's your car?" she whispered in my ear.

I told her.

"Finish your tonic. I'll meet you outside in ten minutes."

I felt her move away.

## 28

I WAS STILL ON MY first smoke when I saw the floating white shape moving through the parking lot toward the car. Belle. In a white shift a little smaller than a pup tent.

She opened the door and slid into the front seat. "Got a cigarette, big boy?" she asked, her voice a parody.

I gave her one. Snapped off a wooden match, watching her face in the glare. It was scrubbed clean again. She inhaled the way you take a hit off an oxygen tank. Her breasts moved under the shift. Her thighs gleamed in the night. The blue mark was a tattoo. A tiny snake, coiled in an S shape.

She saw me looking. "You like my legs?"

"They look like, if you squeezed them, you'd get juice."

"Want to try?"

I put my hand on her thigh, fitting the snake tattoo in the web between my thumb and finger.

"Not that one," she said.

I moved my hand. Squeezed. Felt the baby skin on top, the long, hard muscles beneath. I watched her face.

"No juice."

"Not there," she said, shifting her hips on the car seat.

I took my hand away. Lit another smoke.

"How long were you watching?" I asked her.

"How'd you know?"

"You knew where to find me in the dark."

"Maybe I worked my way through the joint."

"You knew I wasn't drinking the gin."

Belle took another deep drag. "Maybe you *are* a detective," she said, a little smile playing around her lips. "There's a strip of one-way glass that runs all around the place. So we can see who comes in."

I didn't say anything, watching the snake tattoo.

"You know why it's set up like that?"

"That joint can't be making money. The strip acts cost a lot to package. The projection TV, the music system, all that. You're running a low cover charge. You don't sell sex. Even with the guidos paying grope-money and the watered drinks, the boss couldn't break even."

"And . . . "

"And the building's a hell of a lot bigger than the bar."

Belle took a last drag. Threw her cigarette out the open window. "What's that tell you?"

"Who knows? You got space enough back there for trucks to pull in?"

"Sure."

"The airport's real close."

My pack of smokes was sitting on top of the dashboard. Belle helped herself to one. I lit it for her.

"Marques *said* you were a hijacker."

"Marques is a pimp."

"I know. Not *my* pimp. I work for me. That's why that bitch made that crack about me not liking men. I don't sell sex."

"If you did, you'd be rich."

That bought me another smile. Then, "You came out here to tell me you're going to meet with him?"

"Tuesday night."

"Why Tuesday?"

"That's your night off, right?"

"So?"

"So you're coming along."

"Says who?"

"That's the deal, Belle. Tuesday night. Pier 47. Marques knows where it is. Eleven o'clock. Tell him to bring two grand. Tell him that's mine. For the talk."

"That's a lot of money for talk."

"You get paid for your work—I get paid for mine."

Belle took another drag. "What time will you pick me up?"

"I won't. Tell Marques it's gunfighters' rules—we each bring one person with us. He gets to bring you."

"I don't use guns."

"Neither does the guy I'm bringing with me. Tell Marques what I said. He'll get it."

"I don't want Marques knowing where I live."

"Tell him to meet you someplace."

"And after . . ."

"I'll take you home," I told her.

"Should I call you and tell you if he . . . ?"

"Don't call me. I'll be at the pier. Just tell him if he doesn't show not to call me again."

"You take me home anyway."

"Yes."

Belle leaned against me. A big, sweet-smelling girl with a snake tattoo on her thigh. She pushed her hand against my chest, holding me against the seat. Kissed me hard on the mouth, saying, "See you Tuesday," at the same time.

I watched the white shift dance in the dark parking lot until it disappeared behind the blue building.

## 29

MAX WAS ALREADY DEALT in on the meeting with Marques. I could get a message to the Mole easy enough, even if he didn't answer his phone. That still left me a few days to find the Prof.

It might take that long. The little man could be sleeping in doorways or prowling hotel corridors. He could be working the subway tunnels or the after-hours joints. He never had an address, but you couldn't call him "homeless." I asked him once why he didn't find himself a crib somewhere—why he lived in the street. "I got the balls, and I don't like walls," he told me. He didn't have to explain any more than that—we'd met in prison.

I think "Prof" was once short for "Professor," because he always seemed so much older and smarter than the rest of us. But somewhere along the line, he started telling the kind of truth they never write down in books, and now it stands for "Prophet."

A citizen couldn't find the Prof, but I knew where he picked up his paycheck. A few years ago, I'd fixed him up with SSI. Psychiatric disability. His official diagnosis was "Schizophrenia. Chronic, undifferentiated." The resident at Bellevue noted the Prof's grossly disorganized thought pattern, his grandiose pronouncements, his delusion that he was getting his marching orders from the dead spirit of Marcus Garvey. A typical microwave case. They tried medication and it did what it usually does—the Prof got sleepy. It was worth the thirty-day investment. When they discharged the Prof, they gave him a one-week supply of medication, a standing appointment at the clinic, and what the little man called his "crazy papers."

Once a year, the *federales* would send a letter to the Prof demanding a "face to face." He had to make a personal appearance at the clinic. Not to prove that he was still crazy, just that he was still alive. Uncle Sam likes to keep a close watch on his money.

It was a two-sided scam. Not only did the Prof get a disability check every month, but the diagnosis was a Get Out of Jail Free card in case he ever went down for something major. Nothing like putting an insanity defense together before you commit the crime. The government mails him the check to General Delivery, at the giant post office on Eighth Avenue, right across from Madison Square Garden. There are so many homeless people in New York that the General Delivery window does more business than most small towns.

I addressed a postcard to the Prof. Wrote "Call home" on the back, and dropped it in the box.

# 30

BY LATE TUESDAY EVENING, I had everything in place. I ate dinner at Mama's, working over my copy of *Harness Lines*, looking for a horse that would make me rich. Max came in, carrying his baby, Immaculata at his side. Mama snatched the baby from Max and pushed him toward my booth. She took Immaculata into a corner of her own. I saw a flash of pink as the purse changed hands.

I explained to Max that there'd be five hundred apiece for us no matter what Marques wanted. We weren't going to rough off any extras unless the pimp got stupid. He pointed at the racing sheet I had spread out in front of me, looked a question. I shook my head—there was nothing worth an investment.

Max held up five fingers, looked a question. He knew Marques was paying four times that—where was the rest of the money going? It wasn't like Max to ask. Maybe a baby changes everything. I held one hand chest-high, waving the other in sweeping gestures. The Prof. Then I made goggles of my hands, held them over my eyes. Max looked a question. I made the sign of pushing a plunger with both hands, setting off an explosion. The Mole. He looked another question—why all these people for a meeting? I spilled salt on the table, drew a circle. I put two coins inside the circle. Marques plus one coin. He was bringing somebody with him. I put down two more. Me and Max. Then I added the Prof, tapping the side of my head. I didn't know what Marques wanted and I might have to give him an answer right there. The Prof knew the hustling scene—he'd be more on top of Marques than I would.

I picked up one more coin, gesturing that it was the Mole. Put it on the table, deliberately outside the circle. Patted my back. Insurance policy. Max nodded.

Immaculata came over to the table, put her hand on Max's shoulder.

"Burke, is this dangerous?"

"Not a chance, Mac," I said, making the sign of steering a car. "You think I'm going to let Max drive?"

She laughed. Max looked burned. He thought he could drive the same way he walked: with people stepping aside when they saw him coming. But weasels who wouldn't meet his eyes on the street get big balls when they're behind the wheel. Driving a car, he was a rhino on angel dust.

Max kissed Flower goodbye. Mac held the baby's little hand at the wrist, helping her wave goodbye to her father.

## 31

WE FOUND THE PROF WHERE he said he'd be, standing by a bench at the east end of the park in Union Square. When he saw the Plymouth pull up, he hoisted a canvas sack over one shoulder and walked to us. The Prof was wearing a formal black tuxedo, complete with a white carnation in the lapel. The shiny coat reached almost to his feet, like a cattleman's duster. Some chump was going to be poorly dressed for his senior prom.

"Yo, bro', what you know?" he greeted us, climbing in the back of the Plymouth like it was the limo he'd been waiting for.

I turned west on 14th, heading for the river. The Prof poked his head between me and Max, linking our shoulders with his hands. "What's down, Burke?"

"Like I told you, Prof. Marques Dupree wants a meet. He went to a lot of trouble to get to me—walking around the edges. He's supposed to bring two G's with him. Four-way split. All we have to do is listen to his pitch."

"Who's the fourth?"

"The Mole will be there. Off to the side."

"You want me to ride the trunk?"

"No, we go in square. I don't know what he wants, okay? I may need a translator."

"The street is my beat," said the Prof.

Max looked straight ahead.

We got to the pier around ten-thirty. I pulled the Plymouth against the railing, parked it parallel. The pier was deserted except for a dark, boxy sedan parked about a hundred feet behind us.

We all got out. Max was dressed in flowing black parachute pants and a black sweatshirt. Thin-soled black leather shoes on his feet. He disappeared into the shadows. The Prof stood next to him. I leaned against the railing a few feet away. We waited. Max and the Prof took turns smoking, Max bending forward every time he took a drag when it was his turn. A watcher would see the little red dots, murky shapes. Two people.

Headlights hit the pier. A big old Rolls-Royce, plum-colored, with black fenders. I could see two heads behind the windshield. The Rolls parked at right angles to the Plymouth. Two doors opened. The Prof and I stepped into the outer fringe of the headlights, letting whoever was in the car see us.

Two people came toward us. Belle was a shapeless hulk in a gray sweatsuit. Even with sneakers on her feet, she was as tall as the man next to her.

Marques Dupree. A chesty mahogany man with a smooth, round face. He was wearing a dove-gray silk suit with a metallic pinstripe. Deep-slashed lapels over a peach-colored shirt. Sprayed in diamonds. He and Belle stopped in front of me.

"You're Burke?"

"Yeah."

"Who's this?" Indicating the Prof.

"My brother."

"You don't look like brothers."

"We had the same father."

Marques smiled. I caught the flash of a diamond in his mouth. "I never did time, myself."

I didn't want to swap life stories. "You want to do business?" I asked him.

Marques put his hand in his pocket, pulled out a roll of bills. A car door slammed. He didn't turn around. "What's that?"

"Just checking your car. Making sure you didn't bring friends."

"You said one friend apiece."

"You said you never did time."

Another door slammed. I lit a cigarette. Two more slamming doors. A bright burning dot of light fired where the dark sedan was parked. Okay.

"Your trunk is locked," I said. "I don't need to open it. Let's walk over this way."

I moved to my left, farther away from the parked cars. Marques kept his cash in his fist.

"Here it is," I said. "If anyone opens your trunk, there's a big bang. Okay? Everything goes right here tonight, goes like it's supposed to, my friend takes the package off your trunk. Understand?"

"No problem. You said two large?"

I nodded.

Marques peeled hundreds off his roll, letting me see the two thousand was nothing. I pocketed the cash.

Marques turned to Belle. "Go sit in the car."

She turned to go, nothing on her face. "Stay where you are," I said.

Marques shrugged, his face showing nothing. I knew what was in his mind—if Belle was a hostage, she was a worthless one.

I lit a cigarette. Max materialized out of the night. Marques jumped, his hands flying to his face. Max reached out one hand, picked up the Prof by the back of his jacket, and hoisted him to the railing.

Marques slowly dropped his hands. "You got a lot of friends, huh?"

"A lot of friends," I assured him.

He adjusted his cuffs, letting me see the diamond watch, getting his rap down smooth before he laid it out. Pimps don't like talking on their feet. "I paid for some time."

"Here it is."

Marques took a breath through his nose. It sounded hollow. Cocaine does that. His voice had that hard-sweet pimp sound, promise and threat twisting together like snakes in a basket. "We never met, but we know each other. I know what you do—you know what I do. I have a problem. A business problem."

I watched his face. His eyes were narrow slits in folds of hard flesh. I backed up so the Prof could put his hand on my shoulder.

"I'm listening."

"I am a player. A major player. I got a stable of racehorses, you follow me? All my girls are stars. All white, and all right."

The Prof laughed. "You got nothing but tire-biters and street-scarfers, my man. One of your beasts sees the front seat of a car, she thinks it's the Hilton."

Marques looked at me. "Who's this, man? Your designated hitter?"

"No, pal. He's a polygraph machine."

"You know my action or not?"

I felt the Prof's hand on my shoulder. A quick squeeze.

"Yes," I said.

"Then you know I don't run no jail bait, right? No kiddie pross in my string?"

Another squeeze from the Prof. I nodded agreement.

"I am an *elevated* player, you understand? That ride cost me over a hundred grand, and I got a better one back at my crib. I wear the best, I eat the best, and I live the best. I don't associate with these half-ass simps who think they can run on the fast track. I don't hang around the Port Authority snatching runaways. I don't wear no leopard-skin hats, I don't flash no zircons, and that ain't no Kansas City bankroll in my pocket. My ladies are clean machines, and they're all of righteous age. I got lawyers, I got a bondsman, and I got my act together, all right? I don't *make* trouble, and I don't *take* trouble."

The Prof spoke up, his voice a near-perfect imitation of the pimp's. "Okay, Jim, you ain't Iceberg Slim. We got the beat, get to the meat."

Marques smiled. "You got some rhythm, man. The little nigger does the rapping, you just stand there."

"I talk the talk, Burke walks the walk," the Prof told him.

Marques wasn't a good listener. "What's the chink do, man? You going to send out for Chinese food?"

The Prof's voice went soft. "This is Max the Silent, pimp. You hear the name, you should know the game."

Recognition flashed in the pimp's eyes. "He's the one . . ."

"That's right, fool," said the Prof, cutting him off. "Max ain't Chinese, but he sure as hell does take-out work."

"You done with the dozens?" I asked.

"Yeah, man, let's drop the games. I know you're a hijacker, I now you run guns, I know you do work on people. I need some work done."

"I don't work for pimps."

"I *know* that, man. You think everybody on the street don't know who shot Merlin?"

"I don't know any Merlin."

"Yeah, right. 'Course you don't. But I know Merlin was no player, man. He was a stone rapist—that's what he was. Jumping on those little girls like an animal. Whoever shot him did all the real players a favor."

"So?"

"So you got no beef with me, man. I know you used to rough off trollers in Times Square—take them down right in the bus station. I know you chase runaways. See what I'm saying? I *know* you. That's why I didn't call myself. Didn't want you to get the wrong idea." He waved his hand at Belle. "I paid this bitch real money just to put you and me together."

"That lady don't look like no bitch to me," the Prof said. "Don't look like one of yours either."

Belle stepped slightly to the side, flashing a tiny smile at the Prof.

"She don't need to be mine to be a bitch, man. They all sell their time."

"I didn't know you were a philosopher, Marques," I told him. "And I don't give a fuck. The only time you bought here is mine. And you've about used it up."

Marques locked eyes with me. "You know the Ghost Van?" he asked.

The Prof's hand bit into my shoulder.

I nodded.

The pimp went on as though I'd said no. "Big smoke-colored van. No windows. A few weeks ago, it comes off the river on Twenty-ninth. I got ladies working that block. Van pulls past the pack. Stops. One of the baby girls, not mine, she trots over. The doors swing open and she drops in the street. Nobody heard a shot. The other girls get in the wind. Papers say the little girl was fourteen. Shot in the chest. Dead."

I lit another smoke. Beads of sweat on the pimp's smooth face, his hands working like he didn't know where to put them.

"The next week, two more shootings. Two dead girls. One fifteen, one nineteen. I move my girls over to the East Side, but the pickings too slim there. This van must come off the river. The girls say it's like a ghost. One minute everything's cool; the next this gray thing is on the street. Taking life.

"Last week, one of the little girls gets in a blue Caddy. The Caddy goes up the street. One of my ladies gets curious; she pokes her head around the corner. Two guys get out of the Caddy, holding the girl. She's kicking and screaming. They throw her into the Ghost Van. The Caddy drives off and the van just fucking disappears.

"My ladies don't want to work. The street's like a church social, man. I move the girls again. Way downtown. Brooklyn. The Bronx. Everyplace, man. Three more girls been shot, one more snatched. All near the river. But even out of the city, working girls be saying they seen the van. Like a hawk coming down. The girls see the shadow, they run."

"What do you want from me?"

"Cops is all over the street. My ladies got to work someplace. If they can't work near the river, I got a serious deficit, you follow me? Between the Man and the van, I'm up against it. Until they take that van off, my girls are running scared, jumping at shadows. That hurts me, man."

"In the pocket."

"Yeah, okay, Burke. You a good citizen, right? You look down on me—that's your business. But this is your business too, the way I hear it."

"How's that?"

"The van is full of shooters and snatchers, man. And babies is what they hit. Right up your alley, right?"

"Wrong."

"Look, man, let's all be telling the truth here. The word's been out a long time—you got a kiddie problem, you call Burke. I know you ain't no social worker. You an outlaw, like me. You just work a different side of the street."

"I work for money."

"You think I'm here for myself? The players got together. This is bad for *everyone*, not just Marques Dupree. We put up a kitty."

"Pussy put up the kitty," said the Prof.

"Call it like *you* see it, it make you feel better. I call it what it is."

I waited.

"A bounty. Fifty thousand bucks. Dead or alive. The van's got to go. Goes to Attica, goes to Forest Lawn, makes no difference to us."

"Hire a private eye."

"I said a bounty, man. I look like a fucking trick to you? We not paying anyone by the hour."

"Put the money out on the street."

"Can't do that."

"Why?"

"We can't wait for some faggot to drop a dime. And we can't be sure the Man will do the work anyway."

"Why not?"

"We heard the van's *protected*. That's all I know. But the word is out, all over the street. Uptown, downtown. The van has to have a parking place, you got it?"

The Prof's hand worked on my shoulder again. "Yeah," I said.

"It's good money, Burke. I'll work out any collateral you want."

"You're carrying your collateral."

Marques looked puzzled. "My jewelry?"

"Your head," I told him.

He took another deep breath. "You'll do it?"

"I'll think about it."

"You need to know anything else?" he asked.

"When the van goes down, we'll be around," said the Prof.

"Let's go, bitch," Marques said to Belle.

"She'll go with me," I said.

Marques Dupree smiled. "You like cows?"

"Go home and play with your coat hangers," I told him, waving to the Mole. So Marques could open his trunk later without losing his collateral.

# 32

THE ROLLS MOVED OFF. "Wait in the car," I told Belle. She waggled her fingers at the Prof in a goodbye. "Good night, pretty lady," he said. Max stood stone-still.

I watched her walk away.

"Prof, you know what he was running down?"

"The van's for real, Burke. It's been all over the street for weeks."

"You know something?"

"Something. When I know it all, I'll give you the call."

I gave Max his five hundred, a thousand to the Prof. "Take care of the Mole—he'll drop you off."

Max bowed. I shook hands with the Prof. "Watch yourself," I told him.

I got into the Plymouth. Belle was sitting against the passenger door, looking out at the river through the open window.

"Where to?" I asked her, watching the dark sedan pull away.

## 33

BELLE REACHED INTO THE waistband of her sweatsuit, pulled out a pack of smokes. I handed her my little box of wooden matches, waiting. She inhaled deeply. It was like watching the Alps shift.

"You know Broad Channel?"

"Sure."

"I'll show you once we get on to Cross Bay Boulevard."

I pointed the Plymouth downtown, heading for the Battery Tunnel.

"How'd you meet Marques?"

"When I first came to New York. I was working at Rosie's Show Bar."

"Dancing?"

"I was a barmaid."

"He try and turn you out?"

"He thinks I'm a lesbian. Okay?"

She knew the score. Plenty of lesbians turn tricks, but a smart pimp doesn't want one in his stable. One day he turns around and he's missing two girls.

"They think the same thing at that joint you work at?"

"The boss doesn't care one way or the other."

"So why did Marques pick you for a messenger?"

"It's one of the things I do. I carry stuff, drive a car, deliver a message . . . like that, you know?"

"You carry powder?"

"No."

"That's where the money is."

"The fall's too far."

"You ever been down?"

"Just overnight a couple of times. Once for a week. In West Virginia."

"What for?"

"The cops thought I drove on a bank job. They didn't want me—I was just a kid—they wanted the gunman."

"They only held you a week?"

She caught something in my tone. "I stood up, Burke. The P.D. got bail for me and I caught a bus north. I know how to do it—if I go to jail, I go by myself."

"You never did time—where'd you learn the rules?"

Belle smiled in the dark. Slapped the side of one thigh. "Maybe I'm too heavy to roll over."

I looped the Plymouth onto the Belt Parkway, heading east to Queens. A red panel truck ahead of me changed lanes suddenly, cutting me off. I tapped the brakes, flicked the wheel to the right, touched the gas. The Plymouth flowed around the panel truck like a shark passing a rowboat. Belle wiggled her hips deep into the seat, testing her balance.

"This car's a lot more than it looks."

"So are you."

Her smile flashed again. A prim smile, showing just the tips of her teeth.

I wheeled the Plymouth off the Belt, picking my way through Ozone Park. No reason for Marques to have the car followed, but Belle said she played by our rules—she wouldn't want the pimp knowing where she lived. We stopped at a light. An abandoned factory stood to the side, waiting for a developer to finish the job a fire started years ago. It was wallpapered with graffiti except for a broad rectangle in the center that somebody had carefully whitewashed. On that white canvas was a message, lovingly slash-scripted by a gifted graffiti-writer. Day-Glo orange letters, shadowed in black so they screamed off the wall.

DISS AT YOUR OWN RISK!

Belle read the message, fascinated, going over every word, biting her lower lip. "What does it mean. 'Diss'?"

"It's short for 'disrespect.' This is a border town. Black and white."

She didn't say another word until we turned onto the Boulevard. I followed her directions into Broad Channel. Mostly little bungalows, set close together, right on the water. Years ago they were summer shacks, but most of them had been fixed up now, and people lived there year-round.

The cottage was at the end of a short block. White with blue trim around the one window, the dark roof almost flat across the top. Her red Camaro was parked in front.

"This is me," she said.

## 34

I SLID THE PLYMOUTH to the curb, killed the engine. The block was quiet, every house dark.

"Come in with me?" Belle asked.

The cottage was set close to the sidewalk, the path to her front door only a few feet long. She turned her key in the door, pushed it open, stepped aside. The inside of the house was in shadow; a soft light coming from the back. Belle motioned me to go ahead of her.

"You first," I said.

A little smile. "You being polite? Or scared?"

"Scared."

She walked in ahead of me. I watched from the doorway, gently pushing the door back and forth with my left hand, feeling for resistance. Belle bent from the waist in the shadows. I heard a click. A lamp came to life. She moved a few feet. Another.

"Close the door behind you," she said.

The cottage was one big room. A long modular couch took up one wall, side tables with lamps on either end. The kitchen was strung out along the opposite wall, Hollywood-style, everything half-size. The side walls were blank, no windows.

"You want coffee?"

"No, thanks."

I lit a cigarette, walking toward the couch. The back of the house was still dark. I could see a triple-width window next to a door on the far left, a bed on the right.

Belle pulled the top of the sweatsuit over her head, tossing it into a white plastic basket next to the refrigerator. Her black bra was some kind of jersey material, the straps crossing behind her back so her shoulders were bare. She stepped out of the sweatpants. Underneath she had what looked like a pair of men's white boxer shorts.

She took her coffee cup in one hand, a pack of cigarettes in the other. Walked to the back door.

I opened it for her, followed her outside. A wood deck stretched out in the black water, a waist-high railing on both sides. The other cottages had decks too. I saw a small sailboat tied to one, a rowboat with an outboard to another. Belle walked out to the end, carefully balancing her coffee cup.

"Hold this," she said, handing the coffee and cigarettes to me. She turned her back to the water, one palm out to each side, and vaulted herself onto the railing. I put the coffee cup on one side of her perch, handed her back the smokes. She kicked one out, leaned forward, one hand on my shoulder for balance. I lit it for her.

I could feel the night air's chill through my jacket. Belle didn't seem to notice. I leaned my elbows on the railing next to her, watching the harbor lights a half-mile away. I felt her hand on my shoulder again.

"Did you really do all that stuff?" A soft voice, loaded with her breath. A girl's voice. The twisted snake tattoo stood out sharply on her thigh, inches from my face.

"What stuff?"

"What that guy said tonight."

"No."

She giggled the way kids do when they know you're playing with them.

"Yes, you did," she said.

I shrugged.

"I have something you might be interested in," she said, her voice quiet.

"You got something *anybody'd* be interested in."

She giggled. "I didn't mean *that*. Business. Can I tell you about it?"

"Not here."

"Why?"

"Sound carries over water."

She put an arm around my neck, pulling her face close to mine. Whispering. "You think I don't know that? I was raised on the water. Inside."

"Okay."

I turned toward the house, slipping an arm around her waist. She slid off the railing against me, her legs pointing straight out. I threw up my other arm instinctively, grabbing her thighs. Belle nestled into my arms. "Carry me," she said, soft-voiced.

"I'll get a double hernia," I growled at her, leaning against the railing for support.

"Please."

I would have shrugged again, but I needed all my strength.

She ducked her head into my chest as we went through the door, pushing it closed with her toe. I tried to put her down on the couch gently, but I dropped her the last couple of feet.

I flopped down next to her. "I love to be carried," she said, leaning over and kissing my cheek.

"Don't get used to it."

Belle bounced off the couch. She came back in a minute. Put her coffee cup in the sink, lit two cigarettes off the gas burner, walked over, and handed one to me.

"You first," she said.

I dragged deep on the cigarette, wondering how she knew.

"That music . . ."

"In my act?"

"Yeah. Swamp blues. I never heard it before. Louisiana?"

"Florida. It's an old record. I don't even know the singer. I found it in a store in the city."

"How do you know it's from Florida?"

Belle got off the couch. Walked over to the darkened bed. She hit a light switch. The bed was low, covered in white, a white rug on the floor. It was the bed in her act.

She came back to the couch, pulling her bra over her head as she walked. Turned off the two lamps on the end tables, one by one. She stretched out full-length on the couch, her head in my lap, facing up at me, eyes closed. Even with her arms at her sides, her breasts stood straight up at me, carved in flesh.

Her face was indistinct in the soft light, her eyes lost in the sheaf of taffy-honey hair. No lipstick on her mouth. Only the tiny chin with its sharp point moving.

"I'm from Florida. When I heard that song, I knew it was a home call. Understand?"

"Yeah."

She took my hand, pressed it to where her breast covered her heart. I could feel the beat. Strong, slow, steady.

"What did you think of my act?"

"I never saw anything like it before."

"Each girl gets to design her own. As long as our clothes come off before the lights go out."

"It's a psychiatric mirror."

"A what?"

"A psychiatric mirror. You do your act—people watch it—they all see something different—if you knew what they were thinking, you'd know them."

"Like that inkblot test?"

"*Just* like that."

Belle sighed. A tiny slash of white across her face where she chewed her lower lip. "It's true. Men send notes backstage."

"You ever answer them?"

"No. I'm like you."

"What does that mean?"

"I don't work for pimps either."

"You could work for yourself."

"I do work for myself—I'm not for sale."

She reached for my cigarette, ignoring her own. Put it in her mouth, took a deep drag. The smoke shot out her nose. I watched her stomach muscles flex.

"Did it work on you?"

"What?"

"My act—did you think of something?"

I bit into the cigarette filter. "I saw it like a play. Young girl coming into herself. Things pulling at her. Evil calling."

"Tell the truth—you saw a play?"

"*Like* a play. It all meant something."

"Not what you think."

"Yeah, *exactly* what I think. That's the way the mirror works."

Belle pulled herself into a sitting position, her back to me. She got to her feet, took my hand. "Come on," she said.

She walked over to the bed. Put a hand against my chest. "Stay here," she said. She hooked her thumbs into the waistband of the shorts, pulling them over her hips, dropping them to her feet. She stepped out of the shorts and padded to the bed. She fell to her knees, bent forward onto the bed, her hands clasped in front of her.

"Tell the truth," she said again, her little-girl voice almost hissing. Demanding. "What did you see?"

I looked at the shadows play over her body. "I saw a young girl. Praying."

"What did it make you want to do?" she whispered, looking back at me over one shoulder, wiggling her butt.

I took a breath. Telling the truth. "Answer your prayers," I told her.

Her little chin came up, smile flashing.

"Come on," she said.

# 35

SHE STAYED ON HER KNEES, watching me over her shoulder. She cocked her head to one side, listening as my clothes hit the floor.

"Where's your gun?"

"I don't have one."

"Marques did."

"I know—in his left-hand pocket," I said, standing next to her, my hand on her shoulder.

She came to her feet, facing me. Without the heels, she was maybe a half-inch shorter than me. Her eyes were set so close together it was hard to look into them. I ran two fingers along her jawline, feeling for bone lost in the soft flesh, cupping her little chin. I kissed her softly, feeling her lips swell. Her teeth clicked against mine.

"How'd you know he had a gun?" she asked, her tongue darting out, whispering into my mouth.

I moved my hands to her waist, and down to her sculptured butt, feeling the soft skin, squeezing the hard muscles beneath the surface. She locked her hands behind my head and fell backward, pulling me down with her.

The bed was hard. No springs squeaked when our weight came down. I landed on top of her, but she slid out from underneath me slick as an otter leaving a rock in the water. She snuggled into my chest, nudging me onto my back with her shoulder, one hand trailing across my stomach, throwing a thigh over mine. She burrowed her face into my neck, her whole body quivering.

"You have to tell me," she whispered. "I have to know those things."

"Why?"

She reached her free hand between my legs, wrapping it around me, rubbing the tip with the pad of her thumb. "You think this is the answer to my prayers?"

"I had hopes," I said.

"Come on, honey. How'd you know?"

"When you walked up with him, he didn't want you on his left side. When you moved away, he was more relaxed."

"So?"

"So either he was carrying on his left side or you were holding a piece for him."

"How'd you know I wasn't?"

"You kept your hands free. The clothes you had on—that sweat-suit—you couldn't get to it in time. Besides, you weren't his woman."

"Because I said so?"

"The way you carried yourself."

She stroked me gently, her mind somewhere else. Mine wasn't.

"What if you were wrong?"

"Huh?"

"What if I *was* carrying?"

"You're not fast enough to make it work."

"Not fast enough for you?"

"For Max."

"Which one was Max?"

"The guy that didn't speak."

"He was ten feet away from me."

I shrugged.

She shifted her weight, holding her head in one hand, her elbow cocked against the bed. Her breast was an inch from my face. The dark nipple looked tiny against the white globe. I kissed it. Her hand pulled against me in response.

"He's really that fast?"

"Faster."

Belle moved her head into my chest again. Her hand slid down the shaft, cupping my balls, lifting them gently, like she was trying to guess their weight. Her voice was all soft curves, hardness flexing underneath, the same as her body. "Tell the truth. When you saw me in the club—in the play—and you wanted to answer my prayers?"

"Yeah?"

"What did you want to do?"

"I'm not sure. . . ."

"Tell me!" she whispered hard against my chest, her hand closing on me.

"I wanted to rescue you," I said.

She moved her hand back to the shaft, shifting her body on top of mine, fitting me inside her. She was wet—I slid in like a bullet being chambered. Her hands were on either side of me, taking her weight, her breasts brushing my face. I moved my hands to her butt as she started to grind against me.

Her mouth came down to mine. "Rescue me," she said.

## 36

WHEN I WOKE UP A while later, Belle's face was on the pillow next to mine, her body still covering me. I couldn't see my watch. I flexed my shoulders to see if I could slide from under her without waking her up.

"You want a cigarette, baby?"

"I didn't know you were awake," I said.

"I never went to sleep. I've been here all along."

"How come you didn't get up?"

"I was guarding you," she said, her face close to mine. "I knew the only way you'd sleep is if I didn't move."

She padded over to the kitchen, opened a door next to the refrigerator. I heard water running. Belle came back with a big glass ashtray, cigarettes and matches inside, a washcloth over one shoulder. She bent over me, set the ashtray on the far side. She put a cigarette in her mouth, fired it up, handed it to me. Lit one for herself.

She smiled down at me in the darkness. "Are you my boyfriend now?"

I thought I was going to laugh—it came out kind of a snort. "Your boyfriend?"

"Yes, my boyfriend."

"What does that mean?"

"I don't know. I never had a boyfriend. But if you rescued me, you have to be my boyfriend, right?"

"If that's what it takes to rescue you, there must have been a thousand applicants for the job."

She bent to kiss me. "You're a sweet man. But that was a down payment. I'm not rescued yet."

She ground out her cigarette, pulled the washcloth off her shoulder. Started to clean me off, not being that gentle about it. The washcloth was wet, warm. I felt myself growing in her hands.

I finished my cigarette. Belle was still scrubbing me like she was going to use my cock for surgery, kneeling on the floor, her body at right angles to mine. I lit another. She tossed the washcloth aside, climbed on the bed, her knees next to my chest. She bent forward and took me in her mouth, her butt in the air, blocking my view of the rest of the world.

She took her mouth from me, peeking back over one shoulder, licking her lips. "Put out your cigarette."

"Why?"

"I don't want you to burn me."

"I wouldn't burn you."

She caught the warning in my voice. "I didn't mean on *purpose*, honey," she whispered. "I know you're not like that."

I held the cigarette in my left hand, took a deep drag, my right hand stroking her outside thigh.

"Just don't keep it in your mouth," she said, bending forward again, nibbling at my cock. She swallowed the engorged tip, sucking hard. I put the cigarette in my mouth, dragging deep, letting the smoke bubble out my nose, lost in the feeling.

Belle moved her inside foot against me, sliding it onto my chest. I shifted the cigarette to my left hand as she threw her leg over, straddling me, her butt still in the air, now squarely in front of me. She wiggled her rear, sucking, working her tongue. I took another drag. Her butt came down, moving toward my face. I flashed my right hand hard against her cheek, a sharp crack in the quiet room.

She pointed her butt in the air again, pulling her mouth off me. "Was that a message—or did you just want to see what it felt like?"

"A message," I told her.

"Why didn't you just tell me?"

"There wasn't time."

She pivoted on her knees so her face was close to mine. "You don't want to taste me?"

"No."

"Why not, honey? Don't you think I'd be sweet?"

"It's not that."

"You think a man doesn't do stuff like that?"

I snubbed out the cigarette. "I don't think that. It's just not me."

"Prison?"

"It's not that simple. There's no code against it." I laughed. "The only cons who swear they've never eaten a woman are pimps."

Belle rubbed her face against my chest. "Wouldn't you do something to make me happy?"

"Some. Things. You understand?"

"I'd do whatever you want."

"The only way it works is if you do what *you* want, Belle. That's the only thing that goes the distance."

She lit a cigarette for herself.

"Do you have a woman?"

"Yes."

"With you?"

"No."

"Where is she?"

"I don't know."

The tip of her cigarette flared. "But you love her—you're waiting for her?"

"Yes."

"She's coming back?"

"I don't know."

She ran her hands through her hair, holding it in a bun on top of her head, looking down at me.

"Will you love me?"

"I never thought I would love her," I said.

She held the cigarette to my mouth. Her face was intent in the light it threw. She didn't have to ask me to tell the truth—she knew it when she heard it.

"I'm going to love you, Burke. And you're going to rescue me." She moved her hand away from my face, leaving the cigarette in my mouth.

"If I try to sit on your face again, you going to give me another smack?"

"You want me to tell you another way?"

She spun on her knees again, bending her face down again. She looked back over her shoulder. "No, send me another message. I like the way you did it."

Her mouth locked onto me again. I went hard in her mouth. She rubbed her thighs together. My hand stroked her butt. Her thighs opened. I stroked my fingers against the back of her knees. A liquid drop fell into my hand. I felt the pinpricks of pressure in my balls, tightening into a thick mass. I hooked my hand around the front of her thigh, pulling her toward me. She wouldn't move, sucking harder now. Strega flashed into my mind—Strega and her witch games. I jerked her thigh hard, trying to pull her face off me. It was rigid as a cell bar.

"Belle," I whispered. "Come here."

She didn't move. I cracked her hard against the same cheek I'd hit before. She made a humming noise but stayed where she was. I hit her twice more, feeling the sting in my palm, wondering what she felt.

Her mouth came off my cock. She crawled forward on the bed, throwing a leg over me. She pushed her butt between my legs until I was smoothly inside her, moved to her knees, straddling my body, her back to me.

"Come on!" she said, her voice hard, bucking until we both got there.

## 37

SHE SLEPT THEN. ON HER stomach, one arm flung across my chest. I slipped under it, found the bathroom. It was small-scale, like the kitchen. Cheap black-and-white tile covered the floor and ran halfway up the wall from the tub. The hot water came up right away; the pressure was good that time of night. I took a quick shower, used some of her Brand-X shampoo, toweled myself off. The little medicine cabinet was empty except for a toothbrush and a bottle of aspirin. A plastic hairbrush and a bottle of green mouthwash stood on the sink. I wondered where she kept all her makeup . . . maybe on the dressing table near her bed.

The bathroom was full of steam, the mirror cloudy. I wiped it off, looked at my face. Whatever she wanted, she hadn't seen it there.

My foot hit something under the sink. A black metal box with a latch on the front, carry-handle on top. I popped it open. Sterile bandages, individually wrapped. A roll of gauze. Elastic tape. Three scalpels with different-sized blades. A pair of surgical scissors. A bottle of iodine. Two more of sulfa powder. A pair of matching plastic vials, both full, unlabeled. I opened them. Penicillin. Percodan. There was no tag on the metal box, but I knew what it was. Bullet-wound kit.

The refrigerator had a half-empty carton of milk, a lump of cream cheese, and a head of lettuce under a plastic wrap. I found some ice cubes, filled a glass, let it get cold while I got dressed.

I sipped the water in the easy chair near her bed, smoking, trying to think it through. A Ghost Van in my mind.

Belle rolled over on her side as her eyes came open.

"This time you guarded me," she said.

"I've got to go," I told her.

"Let me take a shower first." She didn't wait for an answer, shoving past me to the bathroom. It was still dark outside—my watch said it was almost four-thirty.

She came out of the bathroom brushing her hair, her body gleaming wet.

"Why do you have to go?" she wanted to know, stepping close to where I was sitting.

"There's something I have to take care of."

"What's her name?" she asked, a mock-growl in her voice.

"Pansy."

She pulled back. "You better be kidding."

"Pansy's a dog. My dog."

She giggled. "You have a dog named Pansy? You tie ribbons in her hair and all that?"

"She's about your size."

"I'd like to see that."

"You will."

"Can I come with you?"

"Not this time," I said, getting to my feet.

She put her arms around my neck, pushing her nose so close to mine that my eyes went out of focus. "You'll be back here tonight?"

"I thought you had to work."

"I'll call in sick. Most of the girls do that after their night off— it's no big deal."

"Okay," I said, running my hands down her smooth back to the swelling of her rear.

"What are you thinking?"

"I was thinking if I pressed a quarter against your back and let it go it would fly off your ass like it was a ski slope."

She slipped her hand between us, patting my crotch. "You got a quarter in there someplace?"

"No," I said, pushing gently against her. "I have to go—no joke."

She put her hand in mine, walking me toward her door. "Burke, you know when you didn't want to taste me? You said that wasn't you, right?"

I made a yes noise, walking with her.

"That's okay. You can be you. It's okay that I keep dancing?"

"If that's what you want to do."

"I'm telling the truth now, Burke. I'm going to love you. And you're going to love me too, when you see how I am. But I have to be me while I do it, understand?"

"I'm not arguing with you, Belle."

She put her mouth on my ear, whispering in that little-girl breathy voice, holding my hand tight. "I'm me. You don't change for me—I don't change for you. But I wouldn't let you dance."

"That means what?"

Her voice was pure and sad in my ear. "If Pansy's a dog, like you said, I'm going to pat her. If she's a woman, I'll kill her."

She kissed me on the cheek, pushed me away, stood to the side while I stepped out the door.

I looked back at the cottage as I climbed into my car. It was dark.

## 38

THE PLYMOUTH TRACKED its way back to the office, its monster motor barely turning over. The all-news station was talking about Kuwaiti ships flying the American flag in the Persian Gulf, minesweepers guarding the point. I flipped to the oldies station. Screamin' Jay Hawkins. "I Put a Spell on You." Growling his love-threats to his woman and to the world.

> *I don't care if you don't want me, I'm yours*
> *Right now.*

Belle would know he was telling the truth.

Most of the traffic was trucks, highballing it toward the city. A customized van passed on my right. Big glass doors cut into the side, a plastic bubble on its roof. As it went by, I saw a narrow metal ladder running from the bumper up to the roof. A mural was painted on the back—some religious scene.

I lit a smoke. The van I was looking for was a custom job too. I knew that meant something, but I couldn't lock in on it. It would come.

If Marques was right, the van had been working for a few weeks now. Time enough for the police to be on the job. I flicked my cigarette out the window, wondering if McGowan was working nights.

Bob Seger came through the radio. "Still the Same." Motor City blues. Somebody once said it was about a guy catching up with his old girlfriend, but it never sounded like that to me.

It sounded like a kid catching up with his father.

## 39

I LET PANSY OUT to her roof. Picked up the phone on my desk, checked for hippies. All quiet.

I dialed a number.

"Runaway Squad, Officer Thompson speaking." A young woman's voice.

"Is McGowan around?"

"Hold on."

I lit a smoke, waiting. Any other detective bureau in the city, they ask you who's calling. The Runaway Squad knows most of the callers won't give their names.

"McGowan," said the voice on the phone. The same hard-sweet voice pimps use, but McGowan did it different, giving you your choice.

"It's Burke. We're working the same case. Got a few minutes to meet with me?"

"I'm off at eight. Breakfast at Dino's? Eight-fifteen, eight-thirty?"

"I'll be there," I told him, and put down the phone.

Pansy ambled in, rested her head in my lap. I patted her. "You're always glad to see me, aren't you, girl?"

She didn't answer me.

I pushed her head off my lap, helped myself to a drink of ice water from the refrigerator. I took out two hard-boiled eggs, cracked them against the wall, peeled off the shells.

"Wake me in an hour," I told Pansy, handing her the eggs.

I closed my eyes so I wouldn't see the mess she made.

## 40

WHEN I OPENED MY eyes, it was seven-thirty. I took another shower, changed my clothes. I let Pansy out again, watching her run around while I took a deep slug of Pepto-Bismol. Eating at Dino's on an empty stomach was dangerous.

I drove north on the West Side Highway, moving against the snarled rush-hour traffic. Dino's was on Twelfth Avenue, about ten blocks south of Times Square. Yuppies in New York are heavy into diner food now, but Dino's wasn't going to make the list.

McGowan's unmarked cruiser was parked right out front, empty slots on either side. I pulled in, not wasting my time trying to spot him through the greasy windows.

He was sitting in a booth near the back corner, hat tipped back on his long Irish face, cigar in his mouth. Wearing a dark suit, a shirt that had once been white, a blue tie that had never been silk. I sat across from him, my back to the door. We'd known each other a long time.

He shook his head sharply before I could open my mouth, tilting his chin up. Somebody coming.

It was only three hours into her shift, but the waitress was already tired, her broad face lined with strain. Still, she had a smile for McGowan. They all did.

"Good morning, lovely Belinda," he greeted her. "How's the play coming?"

"It comes about like I do, McGowan. Not too often."

"Nothing good comes easy, my little darling," he said, turning aside gloom like a bullfighter. He took one of her hands, holding it in his, patting her.

"Belinda, it was your choice. A lovely young girl like you, the boys would be all over you and they had a chance. But it's not the life of a housewife for my girl, is it now? Your play will come. Your day will come."

"Ah, McGowan . . ." she said, trying to sneer at his blarney. But the smile came out, like they both knew it would.

"Give me two of your finest eggs, sunny-side up. Bacon, toast, and some Sanka, will you, girl?"

She wrote it down, turned to me.

"Two eggs, fried over hard, break the yolks. Ham, rye toast, apple juice. Burn everything."

"You got it," the waitress said, moving away, the bounce back in her walk.

McGowan puffed on his cigar, knowing we wouldn't talk until the food came.

"How's Max?"

"The same."

"I heard he was a proud papa."

"That's on the street?"

"Sure," he said, watching me closely. "Any problem with it?"

I shrugged. No point asking McGowan where he got it—maybe from one of the little girls he brought to Lily's program, maybe . . .

The food came and we ate.

It didn't take either of us long. Swallowing it wasn't as bad as looking at it. The Senator's Motto.

Belinda cleared our plates. McGowan settled down over his second cup of Sanka, relighting his mangy cigar.

"So?"

"The Ghost Van—you know it?"

"Everybody knows it."

"Any more than what's been in the papers?"

"A bit. What's your interest?"

"Some people want me to find it."

"And take it off the street?"

"It's just an investigation. The people who want me to do this job don't have anything personal at stake. For all they care, I find it, I could call the cops."

McGowan leaned across the table, his Irish blues going cop-hard. "It's personal to me, Burke. The swine shot one of my girls."

"When?"

"The second shooting. Little girl named Darla James. Fifteen years old, and on the stroll for the last two. I was close to taking her off the track. Real close, Burke. They put two into her chest at twenty feet—she never had a prayer."

I lit a smoke, watching his face. McGowan had been working the cesspool for twenty years and he'd never fired his gun. He won some and he lost a hell of a lot more, but he always kept coming. He played the game square, and we all respected him.

"You want me out of it—I'm out of it," I told him.

"I want you *in* it, pal. In fact, I was going to put it out on the wire last week for you to come around. These are bad, bad people, Burke."

"How do you make it?"

He puffed on the cigar, his eyes still hard, but not looking my way. "Has to be a vigilante trip. One of those sicko cults. They're shooting the poor little girls to fight the devil. Or maybe they're sacrificing bodies to Satan. It all comes out the same."

"You sure?"

"I'm not sure of anything. I'll tell you what we have—it's precious little enough."

I kept my hands on the table, where he could see them. McGowan would know I don't write things down, but he looked upset enough to forget.

"Tell me," I said.

"There's been five girls shot, not the three the papers reported. And two snatched—not just the one everybody knows about. Ballistics says they were all shot with the same piece. Military hardware, probably an M-16, or one of those Russian jobs. High-speed ammo. Ballistics says the slugs were twenty-two-caliber."

"They mean 5.56-millimeter. About the same thing."

"Whatever," McGowan snarled. He wasn't a forensics man. "The girls were all torn up inside— ripped to pieces. Dead before they hit the ground."

"You ever find either of the girls who were snatched?"

"Not a trace."

"Were all the girls underage?"

"Either that or they looked it."

"You sure it's random?"

"We thought of that. Questioned half the pimps in Times Square. We can't make a connection."

"Who's 'we'? The Commissioner got a task force working on this?"

McGowan's laugh was too ugly to be cynical. "Task force? Sure, and why would they be doing that? It's not like it was citizens getting killed."

I sipped my apple juice, thinking out loud to draw him in. "Seems like a strange piece to use. . . ."

McGowan's eyes snapped into focus. "Why?"

"It's not an assassin's weapon. Doesn't have the shock power of a heavier slug. That high speed's a waste at such close range. The bullets fly so fast that they tumble around as soon as they hit something. That's why the girls were so torn up inside. And it makes a hell of a bang—real hard to silence."

I took another drag, thinking it through. I wasn't playing with McGowan: it really didn't make sense. "Automatics jam," I told him. "You know that—that's why they don't let you guys carry the nine-millimeters you want. So why risk an automatic when you're only going to fire off a couple of shots? And if it was so random, why didn't they just sweep the street? With an M-16, they could chop down a dozen girls just as easy as one. You check with ATF?"

"They're too busy looking for Uzis. The guy I talked with said what you said. Doesn't even have to be a military piece—there's all kinds of semi-auto stuff floating around—AK-47s, AR-15s. Takes ten minutes to convert them to full auto, he said."

"It's still the wrong gun for killing at close range. A heavier piece, even if you hit someone in the arm, you'd blow it right off. They'd be dead before the ambulance got there."

"Maybe it's all they have?"

"Doesn't add up. This is an expensive deal, McGowan. And for what?"

His honey voice turned sour. "Couple of bullets and gas money—it don't sound so expensive to me."

"You ever find the van?"

"No. So?"

"So they didn't dump it after the shootings. So they have to have a place to stash it. They got to have at least a driver, a shooter, and another guy to fling open the doors. And the snatch . . . they had a switch-car for that, right?"

"Where'd you hear that?"

"Out there," I said, pointing vaguely out the greasy window.

"Yeah. We found the switch-car. Took it apart, piece by piece. We got some decent prints, but no match."

"Anything else?"

"There's no pattern. No thread. The girls didn't know each other. Two were on the runaway list, but that doesn't mean anything. Half the little hookers out there were on the list one time or another."

"Any mail?"

He knew what I meant. Some serial killers have to tell the cops how clever they are.

"No letters. No phone calls. Blank fucking zero. It's so bad the pimps aren't even afraid to be seen talking to us—they want these guys off the street too. I even heard talk about a bounty. . . . " His eyes locked on mine. "You hear anything about a bounty, Burke?"

I met his stare. "No."

It didn't impress the cop. He knew where I'd been raised.

"People like that . . . who knows what could happen if they were arrested. A smart lawyer . . . maybe some kind of NGI deal . . . drop a few dimes. Maybe they'd make it a goddamned miniseries."

NGI. Not Guilty, Insanity. "Better they don't get arrested," I said quietly.

His eyes were ball bearings.

## 41

I HEADED BACK TO MY office, weaving through the West Side blocks, checking the action. It looked the same to me. If the Ghost Van was trying to keep baby pross off the street, it wasn't working. I couldn't pick up the scent—you have to work close to the ground to do that. If it was out there, the Prof would find it.

Called Mama from a pay phone. Nothing.

Back at the office, I let Pansy out to her roof. I had a few more calls to make, but they'd have to wait until the afternoon.

Pansy ambled over to the desk, where I was working on the racing form, making that snarling noise she does when she's trying to tell me something. I knew what she wanted. "I was at Dino's," I told her, explaining why I hadn't bought her a present.

There was a trotter I fancied in the fourth race at Yonkers. Mystery Mary, a five-year-old mare, moving down from Canada. She'd been running in Open company at Greenwood, finishing pretty consistently in the money, but no wins. She had a lot of early speed, which is unusual for a mare, but she kept getting run down in the deep stretch. Greenwood is a five-eighths-of-a-mile track—a long run from the three-quarter pole to the finish line. Yonkers was a half-miler—a longer launch and a shorter way home. She was moving up to higher purses in New York, but I thought she had a shot if she could get away clean. I checked the last eight races. Mystery Mary was a sure-footed little trotter—no breaks on her card. The morning line had her at 6-1. Most of the OTB bettors would use the *Daily News* as a handicapping form. All that would show is her last three outs: two thirds and a fifth-place finish. I made a mental note to call my broker before the close of business, flipped on the TV, and kicked back on the couch. The last thing I remember before falling asleep was Abbott telling Costello that paying back rent was like betting on a dead horse.

It wasn't a good sleep. Dark, fleshy dreams. Flood facing the Cobra, the snake on his arm turning into the tattoo on Belle's thigh. Strega licking her bloody lips, crazy eyes full of ugly promises. The Ghost Van zoomed up a narrow street, a silent gray shark. Max at the end of the block, waiting, shielding Flower in one arm.

I woke up before the crash, sweating like when I'd had malaria. Sergeant Bilko was on the TV. A little past three o'clock.

I took a shower, changed my clothes. Pansy jumped on the couch as I was walking out the door.

Mama still had nothing for me. I dropped another quarter, called Maurice. He answered in his usual breezy style.

"Yeah?"

"It's Burke."

"This a social call, or what?"

"Yonkers. Give me the two horse, fourth race. A deuce to win."

"At Yonkers. Horse number two, race number four. Two on the nose, is that right?"

"Right. How you doing, Maurice?"

"You want conversation, play fucking Lotto," he said, hanging up.

I changed phones, fed another quarter. I don't know why they make dimes anymore. I rang the direct-line number of a reporter I know.

"Morelli."

"It's Burke. You got anything outside the clips on this Ghost Van?"

"Bullshit gossip. Cop talk. Nothing good."

"The cops think they're close?"

"They're waiting for the van to get a parking ticket."

"Can you pull the clips for me?"

"You looking?"

"Looking *around*, anyway."

"You'll clue me in front?"

"If I can."

"I'll pull the clips, leave them downstairs by six. Okay?"

"Yeah. Could you do a NEXIS spin too? See if there's any more van jobs around the country?"

"You think it's a group?"

"No, but check anyway."

"You got it."

One more call. Belle answered on the first ring, sounding like she ran a hundred yards to snatch it off the hook.

"Hello?"

"It's me. Want to get some dinner?"

"Oh, I'm *starved*. There's nothing in the house."

"I know. Why didn't you go out?"

"I knew you were going to call."

"I said . . . never mind. I'll pick you up in an hour, okay?"

"Hurry up," she said.

I put the phone down, moving fast to beat the charge out of the city.

## 42

I PULLED IN BEHIND THE red Camaro a little after five. The door opened as my fist came down to knock. A hand came around my neck, pulling me inside. Belle mashed her face against mine, kissing me hard, firing her hip at the door to close it.

She pulled her face back a couple of inches, still holding on to me.

"That was a cold kiss. Didn't you miss me?"

"I was working, Belle."

Her mouth went down at the corners. "I'm sorry," she said. "I didn't mean to push you."

I put my hand on the back of her neck, working the tight muscles, keeping my voice quiet.

"You're not pushing me. You don't know me, okay? I don't show a lot on the surface—it's not my way."

"You *did* miss me?"

"I did miss you."

She twirled away, flashing a smile. Her face was all made up, the blue eye shadow making her eyes look bigger, bright lipstick smeared on her teeth. She was wearing a fire-engine-red T-shirt big enough for a linebacker. It fell to mid-thigh, just covering the tattoo.

"I'm just about ready, baby. Give me a minute. I have to find my shoes."

She scooped a pair of glasses from the dressing table. Big round lenses with a light-blue tint, sitting in a thin black plastic frame. "Here they are," she said happily, dragging a pair of red spike-heeled shoes from under the bed.

"Belle."

She was bending forward, slipping on the shoes. Black panties that didn't have a prayer of covering her rump peeked out as the T-shirt rose. "What, honey?"

"You're going out like that?"

Her face fell. "You don't like it?"

Damn. "It's not that," I said quietly, walking over to her, taking her chin in my hand. With the spikes on, she was taller than me—I had to look up into her eyes.

"You go on the street like that, every man that's not brain-dead is going to remember you."

"So?"

"So it's not my game to attract attention, girl. The places I have to go—I don't make reservations, understand?"

"You like me better when I'm all covered? When I look like a big fat cow?"

"I like you the same. It's *you* I like, yes?"

"Yes?"

"Yes!" I said, slapping her rear.

She grabbed my hand, pulled it around to her butt. Held it there. "You like this big fat thing?"

I looked deep into her eyes, watching a tear run down her cheek. Keeping my voice quiet: "Belle," I told her, "it works on me like a hormone shot."

She never took her eyes off mine. "Burke, I'd do anything for you."

"Will you put on a pair of pants?"

"Sure, baby. I've got just the thing."

She rummaged through a chest of drawers, throwing clothes on the bed. Finally, she pulled out a pair of white overalls, the kind with suspender straps. She kicked off the high heels and stepped into the overalls, pulling the straps over her breasts. She wouldn't disappear in a crowd, but at least she wasn't flashing a hundred yards of skin.

"You look beautiful," I said.

She threw me a smile, lacing up a pair of dirty white sneakers. "I'm ready," she announced, bouncing off the bed to me. She wasn't the only thing bouncing.

"Belle . . ."

"What now?"

"Could you put on a bra too?"

She took off her glasses, unsnapped the suspenders, pulled the red T-shirt over her head. She found a white bra with heavy shoulder straps. Slipped into it, hooked it in front.

"I didn't know they made them that big," I said, watching her.

"Boobs?"

"Bras."

She slapped me on the arm, smiling, pushing me to the door with her hip.

## 43

I HELD THE CAR DOOR open for her. She slid across and flicked the inside handle to let me in. I wheeled the Plymouth in a tight U-turn and headed back to the city. When we hit the highway, I shoved a cassette into the dash. Belle sat with her back against the door, feet on the seat between us, hands clasped around her knees. Smoking and listening. Charley Musselwhite's harp barking its challenge on "Stranger in a Strange Land." Buddy Guy driving his mojo north to

Chicago, Junior Wells riding shotgun. Lightning Hopkins being sly about grown-up schoolgirls and John Lee Hooker threatening anyone with an eye for his woman. Paul Butterfield riding the mystery train.

The tape looped over to the Brooklyn Blues. One group after another slipped through the speakers and surrounded us. The Jacks, the Chantels, the Passions. When I heard Rosie and the Originals, the clear, high voice of the girl singer hitting "Angel Baby" like no one else ever could, I kicked out the cassette.

I felt Belle's eyes on my face. "Remind you of something?"

"Yeah," I said. Dancing with Flood in the warehouse garage, helping her pull it back together before her last fight. I should have erased the fucking thing.

We were heading toward the Midtown Tunnel. I pulled into the Exact Change lane, tossed a two-dollar token into the basket, and slid into the right lane. When we pulled up outside the magazine on Second Avenue, it was already past six.

"Go inside and tell the guard you're there to pick up a package from Mr. Morelli," I said.

She didn't ask any questions. She was back in a minute, tossing a thick manila envelope on the seat between us.

"Where're we going, honey?"

"You wanted to meet Pansy," I said, pointing the car downtown.

# 44

I TUCKED THE PLYMOUTH into the garage, showed Belle the back stairs, motioning her to go ahead. Her swaying hips narrowed the staircase.

She knew how to act—didn't make a sound on the way up. When we got to the office door, I gently pushed her to one side while I worked the locks. I went in first, saying "Pansy, jump!" as soon as I did. She hit the floor, paws out in front, her monster's head tilted up to watch Belle.

I made the hand motion that said everything was okay, and told Belle to come in.

"This is Pansy," I said.

Belle stood on the threshold of the office like she was rooted. "Good sweet Jesus! That's a *dog*? He looks like a swamp panther. What kind is it?"

"*She's* a Neapolitan mastiff. The most beautiful Neapolitan mastiff in the world, aren't you, girl?" I asked Pansy, rubbing her head. Pansy growled agreement, her tongue lolling in happiness. Belle hadn't moved.

"Go sit on the couch," I told her. "It's okay."

Belle obediently went to the couch, sat down like she was in church, knees pressed together, hands in her lap. I spread my arms wide, telling Pansy she was released. The beast plodded over to Belle, sat in front of the couch, cocked her head.

Belle didn't move. Pansy rammed her head into Belle's lap, shoving at her hands, demanding a pat. Or else.

"She won't hurt you," I said.

Belle gave Pansy a halfhearted pat on the head. The beast made a rumbling noise in her chest. Belle jerked her hand away. Pansy shoved her head back in Belle's lap.

"She just wants to be friends."

"Burke, I swear to God, she's scaring me to death."

"That's her happy noise," I assured her.

"How much does she weigh?"

"About the same as you."

"I'd kiss you for that if I wasn't scared to move off this couch."

I went into the next room, pulled a couple of strips of steaks out of the refrigerator, tossed one at Pansy, saying "Speak!" as I did. The steak disappeared. I threw the other piece on the floor and watched Pansy drool over it.

"Why won't she eat it?"

"She's waiting for the word."

"What you just said?"

"Yep."

Belle looked at Pansy, said "Speak!" in the same tone I'd used. Pansy ignored her. "It only works when you say it?"

"That's right."

"Well, *say* it, then. The poor dog's dying for the meat."

Pansy flashed Belle a grateful look as I gave her the word. As soon as she polished off the steak, she came back to the couch. Belle patted her with a bit more confidence. "I think she likes me, Burke. Does she do any more tricks?"

"Those aren't tricks," I told her. "Pansy works. Just like you and me."

I threw Pansy the signal and she came over to the door. I opened it and she disappeared into the dusk.

"Where's she going?"

"To the roof."

"It must be beautiful—can we go up there?"

"Belle," I said, "trust me. That roof's one place you never want to go."

"Can I get up?"

"Sure. It's okay—Pansy understands."

I showed Belle the rest of the office. I let her poke around by herself while I laid out the clips Morelli got for me on the desk, thinking I should have heard from the Prof by then.

Belle walked in, put a hand on my shoulder. "Pansy will know me from now on?"

"Sure."

"So if I came here by myself . . . if I had a key . . . she'd let me in?"

"She'd rip you to pieces, Belle."

"Oh," she said in her little-girl's voice, watching as Pansy came back inside and curled up in a corner.

I stubbed out my cigarette, anxious to get in the street, see if the Prof had called in.

"Want some dinner?"

"If you do, baby."

"I thought you were starving."

"I can wait for what I want," she said, her voice still too small for her body. "I waited for you."

So she went through a lot of résumés looking for the ideal hijacker. Big deal. "Let's go," I told her.

Belle was still rubbing my shoulder, watching the dog. "Will she get jealous if I kiss you?"

"She couldn't care less."

"That's my kind of girl," Belle said, and kissed the side of my mouth.

## 45

THE JOINT I TOOK HER to just says "Bar" over the green metal door. A hustlers' hangout off West Street, it serves decent food in the back room, all the tables set aside in booths so people can do business.

I left Belle in the booth to call Mama from one of the pay phones in the bar. I dialed the number that rings at her desk, in the front of the restaurant. She said something in Cantonese.

"Anything?" I asked.

"No calls," she said, recognizing my voice.

I hung up, went back inside. A redheaded waitress was talking to Belle. I recognized her as I got close. MaryEllen. She'd been working there for years. It was a nice quiet joint, no grab-ass drunks, all business.

"What'll it be?" she asked, like she'd never seen me before. My kind of place.

"You order?" I asked Belle, watching her settle into the booth. Sitting down, she was shorter than me—I guess most of her height was legs.

"I waited for you, honey."

I looked up at MaryEllen. There's no menu, but the food doesn't vary much.

"We have some real nice shell steaks."

I looked a question at Belle. She nodded. "One medium and one . . . " I looked at Belle again. "Rare," she said. I ordered a ginger ale. "You have beer on tap?" Belle asked. MaryEllen shook her head no.

"What brand?"

"Cold," Belle said, smiling at her.

Maybe she had been starving—Belle TKO'd her steak in the first round. She had two more beers and half my potatoes before I was halfway through. "You want another one?" I asked her, joking. She nodded happily. Even with the head start, we finished about the same time.

MaryEllen cleared the plates off. I lit a smoke.

"Don't they have dessert?" Belle asked.

"Not here," I told her. "You want coffee?"

"Can I have ice cream later?"

"Sure."

I was smoking my cigarette, thinking about the Prof. Belle sipped her coffee, watching me quietly. I felt a hand on my shoulder, a lilac-and-jasmine smell. Michelle. Wearing a wine-colored silk sheath, a black scarf at her throat. She looked a question at me. I moved over so she could sit down next to me. She gave me a quick kiss as she slid in, turned to look at Belle, talking to me out of the side of her mouth.

"Hi, baby. Who's your friend?"

"Michelle, this is Belle."

Michelle held out a manicured hand. "Hi, honey."

"Hello," Belle said, shaking her hand. Holding on to it too long, watching my face.

Michelle took her hand back, figuring it all out in a split second. "Don't look at me like that, girl. This ugly thug's my brother, not my lover."

Belle's mouth twitched into a half-smile. "He's not so ugly."

"Honey, *please!*"

Belle laughed. "He's got other fine qualities."

"I know," Michelle said.

Belle's face went hard. "Do you?"

Michelle stiffened, her claws coming out. "Look, country girl, I say what I mean. And I mean what I say. Let's put it all out, okay? I never had a brother until Burke came along. I love him—I don't sleep with him. Wherever you go with him, I don't want to go. And where I go with him, you *can't* go. Get it?"

"I get it."

"Get this too. You want to be my friend, you come with the best recommendation," Michelle said, patting my forearm. "You want to be a bitch, you came to the right place. I'll be here after you're gone, girl."

"I'm not going anywhere," Belle said.

"Then let's be friends, yes?" Michelle said, her sculptured face flashing a deadly smile.

"Yes," Belle said, reaching over and taking my hand.

Michelle took one of her long black cigarettes from a thin lacquer case and tapped the filter, waiting for a light. I cracked a wooden match. She cupped my hand around the fire, gently pulling in the smoke. Belle watched Michelle as if she had the answer to all her questions.

Michelle fumbled in her huge black patent-leather purse. She pulled out a sheaf of photographs. Terry. In a blue blazer with gold buttons, wearing a white shirt and a striped tie, his hair slicked down. "Isn't he handsome?" she asked me.

"A living doll," I assured her.

Michelle jabbed me in the ribs with her elbow. "Pig," she snapped. She held the photos out to Belle. "My boy."

Belle took the pictures. "He *is* handsome. Does he go to boarding school?"

I laughed. Michelle jabbed me again. "He most certainly does, honey. One of the most exclusive in the country, I might add. And if it wasn't for certain people teaching him bad habits . . . "

"Don't look at me," I said.

"The Mole does not smoke," Michelle said, ending the discussion.

"How old is he?" Belle asked.

"He's almost twelve."

"He's going to be a heartbreaker when he gets older."

"Just like his mother," Michelle said, ready to talk about her favorite subject for the next few days.

"I can't find the Prof," I told her, bringing her back to the real world.

"Well, honey, you know the Prof. He could be anywhere."

"He was supposed to call in, Michelle. We're working on something."

"Oh."

"Yeah. Will you . . . ?"

"I run on a different track now, baby. But I still have my associates in the right spots. I'll throw out some lines, okay?"

"Tonight?"

"I have a late date—I'll make some calls before I start. If you don't hear by tomorrow, give me a call and I'll take a look myself."

"Thanks, Michelle."

She waved it off.

I got up to call Mama again. She answered the same way.

"Anything at all?"

"Nothing. You worried?"

"Yes."

"Call later. Leave number, okay?"

"Okay."

When I got back to the booth, Michelle and Belle were yakking it up like old pals. Michelle had Belle's face in her hand, twisting it different ways to catch the light. The big girl didn't seem to mind. I sat down, lit another smoke, listening to Michelle rattle on.

"You draw the eyeliner *away* from the center, honey. *Separate* those eyes. And we use a sharper line *here*"—drawing her fingernail across Belle's cheekbone—"for an accent. Are you with me so far?"

Belle nodded vigorously, not trying to talk while Michelle was grabbing her face.

"Now the mouth . . . we use a brush, yes? We paint a *thin* line just past the lips, then we fill it in with a nice dark shade. Widen that mouth a bit. Then we . . . Oh, come on," Michelle said, standing up, dragging Belle by the hand. "We'll be back in a minute," she said to me.

I ignored her. I knew what a minute meant to Michelle. I knew what it meant when the Prof didn't call in.

It was two ginger ales and a half-dozen cigarettes before they came out of the ladies' room, Michelle still leading Belle by the hand. They both sat across from me. I had to look twice. Belle's soft face was sharpened, different. Her eyes looked set farther apart, bigger. Her cheekbones stood out, her tiny mouth was more generous. And her hair was pulled over to one side, tied with Michelle's scarf.

"You look beautiful," I said.

"You really like it?" she asked.

"Honey, face it, you're a traffic-stopper," Michelle told her. "All it takes is a little work."

"Michelle, you're a doll," Belle said.

"They all say that." Michelle smiled. "Don't they, Burke?"

"Among other things."

Michelle was in too good a mood to pay attention to me. "Stripes," she said to Belle. "Vertical stripes. You're big enough to be *two* showgirls, sweetie. And watch the waist—you cinch it too tight, your hips look huge."

"He likes my hips," Belle said, smiling at me.

"All lower-class men like big hips, honey. Don't pay attention to him."

Belle looked at me. "You've got some family. A little black brother and a big Chinese one. And a gorgeous sister."

Michelle flashed her perfect smile. "It's the truth, girl."

She gave each of us a kiss. "I've got to go to work—my baby needs violin lessons."

Belle kissed her back. "Thanks, Michelle. For everything."

"Fry their brain cells, honey," she said, "and watch the walk."

A quick over-the-shoulder wave and she was gone.

# 46

I WAS STOPPED AT a light at 43rd and Ninth when Belle's baby voice poked through the mist in my brain.

"Honey . . ."

"What?"

"We've been driving around for two hours. Around and around. You haven't said a word to me—you mad at me for something?"

I took a breath, glanced at my watch; it was past eleven. I was just going to make one quick sweep of the city, see if I could spot the Prof. I replayed the path in my head: both sides of the river, Christopher Street to Sheridan Square, across Sixth Avenue to 8th Street, back downtown to Houston, across to First, through the Lower East Side to Tompkins Square Park, outside the poolroom on 14th up to Union Square, across to Eighth Avenue and up into Times Square, working river to river into midtown. And back again. Driving through the marketplace, somebody selling something every time the Plymouth rolled to a stop. Crack, smoke, gravity knives, cheap handguns, watches with Rolex faces and Taiwan guts, little boys, girls, women, men dressed like women. Cheap promises—high prices. Murphy Men selling the New York version of safe sex—the hotel-room key they sold you wouldn't open the door, and they wouldn't be standing on the same corner when you went back to ask for better directions. Islands of light where flesh waited to take your money—pools of darkness where wolf packs waited to take your life. And vultures to pick your bones.

Something else out there too. Something that would make the wolves step aside when it walked.

I looked over at Belle. She was facing out the windshield as though she didn't want to see my face, twisting her hands together in her lap. It hurt my heart to watch her—it wasn't her fault. "You're a good, sweet girl," I told her. "It has nothing to do with you; I'm looking for my friend."

"The little black guy?"

"Yeah."

"I've been looking too," she said, her voice serious. "You think we should get out? Ask around?"

I patted her thigh. She was down for whatever it took—knew I had to do this. I couldn't explain how it worked to her. Asking around for the Prof could get him in deeper than he already was.

I drove back to the river, turned downtown until I saw a pay phone. Mama still had nothing for me. If the Prof had been swept up by the cops, he'd get a call out sooner or later. Nothing to do but wait.

I sat on the hood of the Plymouth, feeling the warmth of the engine through my clothes, watching the Jersey lights across the river. I felt compressed. Things were moving too fast—not like they were supposed to. Belle was inside my life without the preliminaries. We'd made some deals without talking them over—she'd been in my office, Michelle was showing her baby pictures and giving her make-up advice. I was going to help her hijack some hijackers. All too fast.

The Prof was lost somewhere in the freak pipeline under the city, and I couldn't go after him without spooking the shadows.

I got back into the car, started the engine.

"I'll take you home," I said.

"Will you stay with me?"

"I have to leave a phone number. Where I can be reached tonight."

"Why don't we go to your house?"

"There's no phone there," I told her. She hadn't put it together that I live in my office.

She lit a smoke, watching me, her voice soft. Not pushing. "What if I don't want my number given out?"

"It's okay. I'll drop you off. See you soon, all right?"

"No!" It sounded like she'd start crying in a minute. "You can leave my phone number. I know it's important, Burke. I'm sorry, okay?"

"Yeah."

"Can't we go to your house first?"

I looked a question at her.

"So you can pack a suitcase."

I tried to smile at her, not knowing if I pulled it off. "I can't stay with you, Belle. Not while this is going down."

"But when it's over . . . ?"

"Let's see what happens."

She moved close to me, gave me a quick kiss. "*Whatever* happens," she said.

I pointed the Plymouth out of the city.

## 47

IT WAS PAST TWO WHEN I called Mama from Belle's phone. I gave her the number where I'd be, told her I'd call when I went on the move again. She didn't tie up the phone lines telling me not to worry.

"Where's the nearest pay phone?" I asked Belle.

"About four blocks down. Outside the grocery store on the right."

"I'll be back in a few minutes," I told her.

"Honey, why don't you use this phone? If it's none of my business, I can step outside on the deck until you're finished."

"It's you I'll be calling. Make sure your phone works, okay?"

She watched my face. "Whatever you say."

I found the pay phone, called Belle's number, listened to her answer, hung up.

The walk back didn't help—I could work it out in my head easy enough, but the answers were no good. The Prof was dead reliable. If he hadn't called in, he was in trouble, or he was dead. Either way, I had a debt.

Belle let me back in. I checked the phone; the cord was long enough to reach anyplace in the little cottage, even out onto the deck. I asked Belle for a fingernail file. Then I flipped the phone over, opened it up, checked the contact points, making sure the bell would work. I closed it back up, turned the dial on the underside to the loudest setting. I put the phone back on the end table near the couch, watched it.

Belle's voice came through the fog. "You can do everything to phones but make them ring, huh?"

The room came back into focus. Her face was scrubbed clean, but the glow was gone. "What is it, Belle? You look like you're afraid of me."

"I'm afraid of you shutting me out."

"This isn't yours," I told her, my voice flat.

Belle's hands went to her hips. Her little chin tilted up, eyes glistening. "What kind of a woman do you think I am?" she demanded.

I shrugged, knowing it was cruel, locked into my own course.

She moved closer, taking up all the space between us. "I said I was going to love you, Burke. You think I'd make you tell the truth and not do it myself?"

"No."

"You think I told you the truth?"

"Yes."

"You know what I want?"

"Sure."

She bent down to where I was sitting, pulled the cigarette out of my mouth, pressed her nose against mine.

"Tell me what I want."

I didn't move, didn't change expression. "The back of the joint where you work—it's like a suitcase with a false bottom. Plenty of room back there. Armored car gets hit at the airport—the hijackers take off running. But they don't go far, right? They pull in the back of the joint, stash the getaway car, and walk into the club. When the cops come looking, they've been there for hours. An alibi and a hideout all in one. Easy to come back in a few weeks. Move the cash out." I took the cigarette out of her hand, leaned back, took a deep drag. "How do they get rid of the getaway car—chop it down? repaint it back there? drive it into the back of a moving van, dump it in the swamp one night?"

She didn't answer me. Just watched.

"All that money just sitting there. Clean, unmarked bills. Probably two or three good jobs stashed in one place. Couple of hundred grand, minimum. Wouldn't be the first time somebody turned around and hit the syndicate. Hijackers aren't like numbers runners—that's why they don't make good employees."

I took a last drag, stubbed out the butt. Feeling her eyes burn on my skin.

"Whoever set this up, it's a big operation. Costs a lot of cash to front. The syndicate probably takes a piece from every hijacking at the airport. That's the way they'd do it. I know how things work. All the young mob guys want to do today is move product. They leave the armored cars and the banks to the independents."

I lit another cigarette, thinking back to the way I used to be. Telling the truth, the way she wanted it.

"A good thief, he can't stand to see a big lump of cash sitting around. Just a matter of time before some crew takes a shot."

Belle took the cigarette away from me again, put it to her lips. A red dot glowed in front of my face. Two more in her eyes.

"You didn't answer me, Burke. Tell me what I want. Tell me the truth."

"You want me to hijack the cash."

I saw her right shoulder drop, but I kept my eyes on her face. Her hand came around in a blur, her little clenched fist catching me high on the cheekbone just under the eye. She drew back her fist again. "That's enough," I said.

Her mouth trembled. The firelights went out of her eyes. She pulled away from me, fell face-down on her big white bed. Cried softly to herself as I pulled some ice cubes from the refrigerator. I wrapped the ice cubes in a towel and held it to my face. Sat by the phone.

## 48

WHEN I WOKE UP, it was past four o'clock in the morning. My jacket was soaking wet on the left side. I snatched the phone. Dial tone.

"It didn't ring." A soft voice from the bed. "I've been listening since you fell asleep."

"Thanks."

"I'll stay by the phone now. When you get where you're going, you can call me. If you don't get your call by then, you can switch the numbers, okay?"

"Yeah."

"I've got an electric heater: it gets cold by the water in the winter. You can dry your clothes first."

I pulled off my jacket, unbuttoned my shirt. Belle came off the bed. I handed them to her. "Your face is swollen," she said, her voice a breathy whisper, the way you tell a secret.

"It's no big deal. Nothing's broken."

"My heart is broken," she said. Like she was saying it was Wednesday morning.

"Belle . . ."

"Don't say anything. It's my fault. I made a mistake. I wanted a hard man. A hard man, not a cold man."

I lit a smoke. She came back over to me, her voice sad now. Sad for all of us. "Not a cold man, Burke. Not a man who wouldn't take my love."

"I just . . ."

"Yeah, I know. You think telling the truth's not a game for a woman to play."

"That's not it."

"No?" she challenged, her little-girl's voice laced with acid. "You think I couldn't find a cowboy to stick up a liquor store for me? You don't think I could pussy-whip some guido into picking up a gun? Sweet-talk some cockhound into showing me what a big man he is?"

"I know you could."

Belle stalked the room, unsnapping the suspender straps, pulling the T-shirt over her head, unhooking the bra. She worked the zipper, pulled the white pants over her hips. She sat down on the bed. Unlaced her sneakers, threw them into a corner. She went over to the kitchen corner, where my shirt and jacket were stretched on coat hangers, baking in the glow from the electric heater. She picked up my shirt. "It'll dry better this way," she said, slipping into it. She tried to button it; it wouldn't close over her breasts.

She fell to her knees beside me, hands on my thigh, looking up at my face.

"Can we have another chance?"

"Who's 'we'?"

"You and me."

"To do what?"

"To tell the truth. Let me tell you the truth. The real truth. I swear on my mother," she whispered, one hand making an X on her breast. "That's my sacred oath."

"Belle . . ."

"Don't hurt me like this, Burke. I'd never hurt you. You don't know what I want. You don't have any idea. Let me say what I have to say."

She got to her feet, held out her hand.

I took it.

She pulled me to her bed. "Sit down," she said. She took a fat black candle, grounded it in a glass ashtray, positioned it on top of the headboard of the bed. "Light it," she said.

I fired a wooden match. I heard a click—the electric heater snapping off. Belle laid back on the bed, her hands behind her head. I sat next to her, watching the tiny candle flame.

"This is the truth," she began. "I grew up in a little place you never heard of. In South Florida. Just me, my father, and my big sister. Sissy. We lived on the edge of the swamp in a tiny house. Not much bigger than this one. My father did a little bit of this, a little bit of that. Like everyone there. Grew some vegetables out back. Made some liquor. There was a mill nearby—he'd work when they had work. Shoot him some gator for the hides. Fix boats. We lived poor, but nice. When my father would make a good score, he'd always buy something for the house. Had a big old freezer, nice color TV. Good boat too. Mercury outboard." Her voice trailed off, remembering. I lit a cigarette, handed it to her.

"I was always told my mother died giving birth to me. Sissy really raised me—took care of me—my father never paid me any attention."

She took a drag on the cigarette, looking at the dark ceiling.

"I was a big, tall girl, even when I was real young. And skinny too—you believe that?"

"Sure."

"I was. Like a board. Ugly old skinny girl with no kind of face at all. Sissy was pretty once. You could tell by looking at her in the morning light. Sissy was hard on me. I had to do my chores *sharp,* or she'd let me know it. Homework too. We had a school, all the kids together in one class. Sissy made sure I did my homework. Always sent me to school clean, no matter how things were at home. She never had a new dress in all the time I knew her. Said it didn't matter to her. She had nice nightgowns, though. She caught me trying one on once and she took a switch to me so hard I didn't want to sit down for a couple of days. Anything she had, she'd give to me. Except those nightgowns. Or her perfume."

She took another drag.

"My father never much bothered with me. Once in a while, I'd do something to make him notice me. Pay some attention to me. He didn't care if I did my homework, but he had to have his coffee just so: dark coffee with a big dollop of cream across the top; he never mixed it.

"I talked back to him once. He grabbed my arm, pulled off his belt to give it to me. Sissy jumped in between us, kitchen knife in her hand. The devil was in her face—you could see it. You never put a hand on that child, she told him.

"He backed off. Told her I had it coming, but he wouldn't look her in the face. Sissy said if I had something coming *she'd* be the one to give it to me. Go ahead, my father said, give it to her.

"Sissy ripped the belt out of his hands, dragged me outside to the back. You better yell now, she told me. *Loud!* She whipped me something fierce that time. Brought me back inside by the hand, told me to get to work on my chores and keep my mouth shut. My father was watching us when we came in. Sissy went back in the bedroom. I saw her taking one of her nightgowns out of her drawer. My father went back there too."

She drew on the cigarette again, the flame close to her hand.

"My father was real drunk one day. Late in the afternoon, swamp shadows across the back of the house. I heard him fighting with Sissy when I came back home. I swear I'll kill you, Sissy told him. He just laughed at her. Slapped her hard across the face. I went after him. He threw me off, but I got up again. Sissy and me fought him until he was out of wind. He just lay there on the floor, looking up at us. I'll be back tonight, he told Sissy, I'll be back, and I'll take what's mine.

"He staggered out the door. Sissy grabbed me, took me to the back of the house. Your time has come, she told me. She took out a suitcase. I didn't even know she had one. Put all your clothes in this, she told me. Don't argue. I helped her fill it up. I thought we were going to run away together. We snuck out the back, into the swamp. Sissy showed me a marker on a cypress tree, where she'd cut it with her knife. She gave me a shovel and told me to dig. Deep. I found an old mason jar, wax-sealed. Found two more. Sissy broke the jars open. There was near a thousand dollars in the jars."

Belle yelped—the cigarette had burned into her fingers. I held out the ashtray and she dropped it in, put her fingers in her mouth for a second to suck on them.

"Sissy sat me down at the table. He'll be back in a couple of hours, she said. You take that suitcase and get into the swamp. I'll fix the boat so he can't go after you. You take the back trail all the way through, to where it catches the highway. The late bus to town comes past there about nine— you got plenty of time to make it."

Belle's face was wet with tears, but her voice was the same quiet whisper.

"Where am I going? I asked her.

"You go to the bus station. Take a Greyhound north, and don't stop until you're out of this state. Go north and keep going, Belle, she told me. You're going to be on your own.

"I didn't want to go—I didn't understand. Sissy wouldn't listen to me. You're grown now, she said. Almost fifteen years old. I held him back as long as I could, baby, but now your time has come. You got to mind me, Belle, she said. This one last time. You got to mind me—do what I say. She took her nightgowns out of the drawer, threw them in the suitcase too. Your nightgowns . . . I said. I won't be needing them anymore, she told me. I think I knew then. For the first time."

Belle was crying now, working hard to keep her voice steady.

"I grabbed on to her. Hugged her tight. Don't make me go, Sissy, I begged her. She pushed me away. Looked at me like she was memorizing me. Then she slapped me across the face. Hard.

"Why'd you slap me, Sissy? I asked her. Why'd you slap me? You never slapped me in the face in all my life."

Belle took a deep breath, looking straight at me in the dark.

"I slapped you so you'll never forget my name, baby. Don't you ever call me Sissy again, not even in your dreams.

"I was standing there, crying. Sissy rubbed my face where she'd slapped me. So tender and sweet. She kissed me to take away the pain, like she used to do when I was little.

"We heard my father's car pull in. Sissy was calm. I'm not just your sister, Belle. I'm not Sissy. I'm your mother.

"I couldn't move. Go! Sissy said. Go, little girl. I'm your mother. I kept you safe. Now run!

"I ran into the swamp, but I didn't go far. I hid down in a grove, so scared I couldn't make my legs work. I heard my father yell something at Sissy. Then I heard this explosion; flames shot up. The boat. You stay right there, bitch! I heard my father yell. Then I heard his gator-gun blast off. Once. Twice. He yelled my name. Screamed it out into the night. I ran through that swamp. My mother wasn't lying there dead by the boat—she was inside me—running with me—keeping me strong. She's always inside me."

Belle grabbed me, holding me tight, her arms locked around my back.

Crying the truth.

# 49

I DON'T KNOW HOW LONG we were like that. Belle loosened her hold. She drew back from me, reaching out a hand to touch my face.

"Does it hurt?"

"No."

"I didn't mean to hurt you. I just wanted you to remember my name," she whispered.

"I do."

"Will you get in bed with me, honey? Lie down with me?"

"Sure."

She propped herself on one elbow, reached across my chest for the cigarettes. "I have to tell you the rest," she said.

"You don't . . ."

"Yes. Yes, I do. You still don't know what I want from you."

I fired a match for her and watched the smoke drift out her pug nose, not pushing her.

"How old do you think I am?" she asked.

"Twenty, twenty-two?"

"I'm almost twenty-nine years old," she said. "It was fourteen years ago when my mother saved me. I went running. Even when I was a young girl, they only looked at my chest, not my face. There's always young folks running in this country. I found them—they found me. I made some rules for myself, promises to my mother. I never turned a trick, but I let my tits hang over plenty of bars. I could always make men buy drinks. I never let a man beat me—there's some who wanted to try—big girl like me makes them feel small, I guess. I drove cars too—I'm real good at it. Getaway cars sometimes. I ran 'shine over the mountains in Kentucky. Drove stolen cars from Chicago to Vegas. I thought I was going to be a showgirl there. I've got the size and the body for it, but my face . . ."

"You have a beautiful face, Belle."

"No, I don't. But I know it's the truth to you. Just listen to me, don't talk."

I nodded, rubbing her shoulder.

"I saved my money. I read a lot of books, teaching myself. I'm an incest child. You know what that means? I have my father's blood and my sister's too. That's why my face is so . . . like it is. My eyes close together and all. I have bad blood, Burke. Bad blood. Only the Lord knows what's gone on in my family before I was born. Or what happened to Sissy's mother. My grandmother, I guess. I saw a doctor. At New York University. I told him the truth. He did some tests, but he couldn't tell me anything without testing my father too. I'm all messed up inside. I'm missing a rib here"—she pressed my hand under her heart—"and one leg's a bit shorter than the other. The doctor wouldn't tell me that much, but I made him say the truth."

She smoked in the dark while I waited.

"I can never have a child. Never have a baby of my own, you understand? My father's bloodline has to stop with me."

She felt the question.

"He's down to Raiford State Prison. In that drawer over there, I have all the papers. I was busted once with a station wagon full of machine guns. I rolled over on the people who hired me," she said, watching my face. "They told me it was stolen watches when they asked me to drive."

"They didn't tell the truth," I said.

"Yeah, you understand. They didn't tell the truth. I got a free pass out of it—no testimony, just the names. And one of the feds, he looked up my father for me. He's doing a ten-year jolt for manslaughter; he gets out this Christmas."

"How come he's still in on a ten-year hit if it happened fourteen years ago?"

Belle's face twisted—I saw her teeth flash, but it wasn't a smile. "He never did a day for killing my mother. He shot a man in a dispute over some gator hides."

She pointed her toe in the air, flexing her thigh, drawing my eyes to the tattoo.

"Look close," she whispered. "Look real close. What do you see?"

"A snake."

"When I was running through the swamp that first night, I stopped in a clearing. A snake hissed at me. Cottonmouth, maybe. I couldn't see him in the dark. He had me rooted—too scared to move. Then my mother's spirit came into me and I knew I had to go. No matter what. I threw a branch at the noise and it stopped. A gator wouldn't stop. I was dancing in this club in Jersey. All of the girls had tattoos. Butterfly tattoos. Their boyfriends' names. A rose on their butt. They told me where they got it done. I had the man do a snake. Right on my thigh, pointing at my cunt. A poison snake—that's all the men saw."

I looked hard at the tattoo, knowing there was more. Seeing it. "The snake, it's the letter 'S'."

"Yes. For 'Sissy.' For my mother. It's the only gravestone she'll ever have."

I lit a cigarette. "That's where your dance comes from."

"Tell me," she whispered. "Tell me you see it."

"I see it. There's worse things than gators out there," I told her. "But not as bad as what's in the house."

She kissed my chest. "That's what I wanted," she said, talking fast now, like I'd cut her off before she finished. "That's what I wanted from you. Marques told me he wouldn't meet you without a cut-out. He told me you were a dangerous, crazy man. Said you used to be a hijacker and now you're a hired killer."

"Marques doesn't . . ."

"Ssssh . . ." she said, putting her finger to my mouth. "He said you killed a pimp just because he had a little girl on the street. He said everyone knows you lose your mind when people fuck kids. He said you took money to bring back some runaway girl. You got her away from the pimp, then you shot him anyway."

"And you wanted . . ."

"I wanted you to *rescue* me. I told you the truth, honey. I told you the truth. It's my soul that's lost. My spirit. My mother saved my life—I need someone to save the rest."

"The hijacking . . ."

"I deserve to have my ass beat for that. I played it wrong. I wanted a hard man. I knew I couldn't hold you with sex. I wanted you to rescue me—I wanted to be your partner. I thought if I brought you a solid-gold score, handed it to you on a platter . . . you'd know I was worth something. I didn't want the money."

"Damn."

"Burke. I don't care if you take off the back room. You want to do it, I'll drive the car. And I'll leave the engine running until you come out the door, I swear it."

"And if I don't?"

"I'll go inside and pull you out."

I took a deep drag. "I mean, if I don't want to pull the robbery?"

"I just want you to want me," she said, her voice grave. "I never meant anything more in my life."

I took another drag, feeling so tired.

"I can't rescue you, Belle."

"You let me help you. Help you with your friend. Find that van. Then decide."

I sat quietly, watching the shadows.

"Please, honey."

"Go to sleep, Belle," I said, stroking her back. "If the Prof's okay, you can help."

She closed her eyes on the promise.

## 50

SHE SLEPT WITH HER face against my chest. I brought the Prof's face into my mind, keeping him alive. Seeing the Prof made me see prison. Where we met. I never knew what sent him down that time. Any time the subject came up, the little man made it clear what he was about. "I didn't use the phone, and I came here alone," is all he'd say. It was enough.

The first time I went down, I was a kid. In New York, sixteen years old, you're too far gone for another bit in reform school. I came in with a good jacket: attempted murder. But it wasn't enough. One thing good about all that time in reform school—I knew the rules. I did the thirty days on Fish Row by myself. The Prof rolled up on my cell one day—he was the runner. Said, "This is from a friend," and tossed a couple of packs of smokes and an old magazine in my cell. I wanted a smoke bad, but I left everything on my bunk, waiting for him to come around again. I grabbed him through the bars, pulling him close.

"Take this stuff back where you got it," I said to him, nice and quiet. "I got no friends here."

The little man looked up at me. His eyes had a yellowish cast. No fear in them.

"Here's the slant on the plant, son. Don't play it hard when you not holding no cards."

"I'm holding *myself*," I told him. "You tell whoever gave you this stuff for me that I'm sending it back, okay? And if he don't like it, tell him I'll send it back with interest when I hit the yard."

The little man smiled, not even trying to pull away. "Jump back, Jack! I ain't no wolf, and that's the truth."

I looked over at the cigarettes. "From you?"

"From me, fool. You never heard of the Welcome Wagon?"

"I thought . . ."

"I know what you thought, youngblood. Here's a clue—don't play the fool."

"I can't pay you back," I told him. "I got no money on the books."

"Look here, rookie. I've got more time behind the Wall than you've got on the earth. In prison, first you learn, *then* you earn."

"Learn what?"

"Here's your first case, Ace. Don't smoke the butts. Don't read the magazine. Let it all sit. Don't trust me. When you get into Population, keep your ear to the ground, ask around. People call me the Prophet. I don't stand tall, but I stand up. Take a look before you book."

I let go of him. The little man made his way down the tier, rhyming the time away.

When I got into Population, I moved slow. Asked around, like the man said. The Prophet had some rep. Guys knew him going back twenty years—this was at least his fifth time behind bars. He once did four years straight in solitary for smuggling a gun inside. He hooked up with a guy doing three life sentences, running wild. They took a guard hostage. Got all the way to the front gate when they ran out of room. The guy with him got blown away. The hacks broke half the bones in the Prof's body.

In solitary, they kept at him. Every day, every night. He kept telling them the gun came to him in a vision. Every con in the joint knew where the gun came from . . . where it *had* to come from. A guard. And the Prof was too much of a man to give up even one of them.

It took a few weeks, but I finally saw the Prof on the yard. I rolled up on him, keeping both hands where he could see them. The group of men around him pulled up close. The Prof made a motion with his head and they peeled off, giving me room.

"What's the word, rookie?" he challenged me.

I took the two packs of smokes and the magazine from under my shirt.

"You handing them back?" he asked.

"No. I wanted you to see for yourself," I said, opening a pack, taking out my first cigarette in seven weeks. "Smoke?" I asked him, holding out the pack.

"Much obliged, Clyde," the little man replied, a smile shining.

I hunkered down against the wall with him, my back to the yard, watching. Speaking out of the side of my mouth, looking straight ahead.

"I'm sorry for what I thought."

"That's okay, gunfighter. You just a schoolboy in here."

I wasn't looking at him, but he must have felt the question.

"I glommed your jacket."

"How'd you pull that off?"

"You don't have to pay if you know the way," the little man said.

I did three years on that bit. Not a day went by that the Prof didn't teach me something. When it was near my time to leave, he schooled me about how to act in front of the Parole Board. When the Board set a release date for me, he gave me the hard stuff. Straight.

"You're short now, schoolboy. You know what that means? Thirty days to wait, and you walk out the gate. They'll come at you now. Punks you backed down before, they'll get bold, knowing you don't want to fuck up the go-home. You got two plays: hide or slide."

"Break it down."

"First guy fucks with you, you can go to the Man. Take a PC for the rest of your bit."

"No."

"Yeah, that only works for the citizens. The guys who're never coming back here. That ain't you. So we got to slide. I got people here—leave it to me."

"Which means?"

"Which means young blood is hot blood. You got to be cold if you want to grow old. Someone moves on you, tell them 'later' with your eyes, but don't do nothing right away, okay?"

"Okay, Prof."

By the end of the week, it happened. A big fat jocker named Moore who'd moved on me early in my bit. I showed him a shank and he backed off. Went looking for easier game—there was a lot of it around. I was sitting at my table during chow when I felt him looking down at me.

"You lost four crates on the Series, Burke. When you planning on paying?"

"You're dreaming, pal. I never bet with you."

"I say you did. You got till Monday. Then I want my four crates or I take it out in trade."

I pushed my chair back, knowing everyone was watching. The Prof made a growling noise in his throat. I looked up at Moore.

"I'll see you before Monday," I promised him, my voice under control.

He walked away, slapping five with one of his buddies.

Late that afternoon, we were on the yard. A pair of bikers broke from their group and came our way. Monster bodybuilders both, their arms were so choked with muscle they had to cock their elbows to walk. I reached for my sock. A bluff—I wasn't carrying so close to parole, but I wanted to give the Prof time to run. He chuckled. "Take a hike, Mike," he said.

I wouldn't disrespect him by arguing. When I glanced back over my shoulder, he was deep in conversation with the gorillas.

Sunday morning, the cafeteria was buzzing when I came in. A black guy I knew slightly from boxing walked by my table. "Right on, man," he whispered. I lit a cigarette to mask my face.

Bongo pulled up a chair across from me, an old buddy from reform school. His trick was using his head as a battering ram in a fight. He'd done it too many times.

"Burke, you hear what happened in the weight room last night?"

I shook my head no.

"You know Moore? That big fat faggot? He decides he's going to bench-press four hundred and fifty pounds, can you dig it?"

"That's a lot of weight."

Bongo giggled his crazy laugh. "Too *much* fucking weight, man. His spotters musta been bigger punks than he was—they dropped the weight right on his chest."

"What?"

"Yeah, man. Square business. The hacks found him on the bench. Crushed his chest like it was cardboard."

When the Prof finally walked out the gate, I was there.

# 51

I LIT ANOTHER SMOKE, keeping the Prof alive in my mind. Belle stirred in her sleep. I patted her, saying, "Ssssh, little girl," but it was no good.

"I can't sleep, honey. What time is it?"

"About five."

She pulled her body away from me, shifting her hips so they were against the headboard, her face still on my chest.

"Help me go to sleep," she whispered, rubbing her face on my stomach.

"Belle . . ."

She squirmed lower, gently licking my cock, taking me in her mouth, making soft sounds to herself. I felt myself stir, but it was like someone else.

"Pull my pants down," she said, taking her mouth off me.

I got them past her butt, but that was as far as they could go. A black ribbon across her thighs. I went semihard in her mouth.

"I don't . . ."

"Don't do anything, honey. Please. I'm lonely for you—you're far away. Let me just hold you till I fall asleep."

She put her mouth back on me. In a minute, she was asleep again.

## 52

I PATTED HER RUMP, drifting in and out. At least it was a hell of a lot more than time on my hands. Time. Back to prison, where time is the enemy and you kill it any way you can. It was the Prof who got me into reading books. The first time he laid it on mc, I laughed at him.

"They don't write down everything in those books," I said.

"Just because you locked in a dump, you don't have to be no chump, bro'. Pay attention. Hear the word. What you going to do when you hit the bricks, get a job?"

"Who'd hire me?"

"You gonna hook up with a mob—kiss some old asshole's pinky ring?"

"No way."

"That's the true clue. You ain't Italian anyway, right?"

"I don't know."

The Prof's face flashed sad for just a second. "You really don't?"

"No. I did the State Shuffle. Orphanage to foster homes to the gladiator schools. To here."

"And you always knew you were coming."

"I always knew."

"Okay, bro', then know *this*. You can't score if you don't learn more, got it? One way or another, you got to steal to be real. And I know what's in your schoolboy head: pick up the gun and have some fun. Right?"

I smiled at the little man, thinking about guns. And banks.

He grabbed my arm, hard. I was always surprised at the Prof's powerful grip.

"You got to go on the hustle, schoolboy. There ain't no fame in the gun game—play it tame, the money's the same."

"I'm no hustler. I don't have the rap."

"Man, I'm not talking about no Murphy Man shit. Or pimping off some little girl either. The magic word is 'scam,' my man. *Use* this time. Study the freaks in here. Watch them close. Learn. How. Things. Work. That's the key to the money tree."

I started reading books just to show the Prof respect. It was his advice—it had to stand for something. I read it all. Everything I could get my hands on. When the prison library ran low, I joined the Book-of-the-Month Club. I scored a couple of dozen books before they threatened to garnishee my salary. I wrote to religious organizations—they sent me books too. I covered hundreds of pages with notes, calculations. Figuring the odds.

When I got out, things didn't work like I planned. It took me another couple of falls to get things down to where I have them now. But I always kept reading, listening. Watching for the crack in the wall.

It was during my second bit that I started reading psychology. I never knew they had sweet words for some of the freakish things people did. The Prof said, if I read the books enough, one day they'd talk to me. I knew what I wanted to be, just not what to call it.

Ice-cold.

Stone-hard.

And I worked at that too.

One day, I was reading a psychology book and a word jumped out at me. "Sociopath." It called to me. I read it over and over. "Sociopath. The essential characteristic of this disorder is a lack of remorse, even for violent or criminal behavior. The sociopath lacks the fundamental quality of empathy."

I ran to the battered old dictionary I kept in my cell. "Empathy: the intellectual identification with or vicarious experiencing of the feelings, thoughts, or attitudes of another." I puzzled it out. A sociopath thinks only his own thoughts, walks his own road. Feels only his own pain. Yeah. Wasn't that the right way to live in this junkyard? Do your own time, keep your face flat. Don't let them see your heart.

A couple of weeks later, I watched the hacks carry an informant out on a stretcher, a white towel over his face. A shank was sticking out of his chest. "That's a nice way for a rat to check out of this hotel," I said to the guys around me. They nodded. I knew what they'd say—Burke is a cold dude.

I kept my face flat. I never raised my voice, never argued with anybody. Practiced letting my eyes go slightly out of focus so I could look in a man's face for minutes without turning away.

Sometimes, alone in my cell at night, I'd say the word softly to myself. "Sociopath." Calling on the ice god to come into my soul. Willing to be anything but afraid all the time.

I listened to the freaks. Listened to Lester tell us how he broke in a house, found some woman taking a bath. Put his gun to her head, made her suck him off. Then he plugged in her hair dryer, tossed it in the water. I kept my face flat, walking away.

Lester grabbed a young boy who'd just come in. "Shit on my dick or blood on my knife," he told the kid, smiling his smile. I took him off the count the next night. He never saw me coming. I hooked him underhand in the gut with a sharpened file, ripped it upward all the way to his chest. I dropped the file on his body, walked away. A few guys saw it—nobody said anything. I let them think it was over a gambling debt.

I read the psychology books again and again. They have some of us pegged. Michelle is a transsexual. A woman trapped in a man's body. *The Diagnostic and Statistical Manual of Mental Disorders* even has a special coded number for it—302.50.

But I never got it to feel right for me—never found the name for what I was. And the number they gave me upstate didn't tell me a thing.

## 53

THE PHONE WOKE ME. I snatched it off the hook on the first ring.

"Yeah?"

"Your friend call," Mama said. "He say come to Saint Vincent's Hospital. Room 909. Visiting hour at nine o'clock. You ask for Melvin, okay?"

"Thanks, Mama."

Belle was awake, still twisted like she was when she fell asleep, looking up at me.

"He called?"

"Sure did." I got up. "I'm going to take a shower, okay?"

"Let me use the bathroom for a minute first."

She padded off. I lit a smoke. Melvin was the Prof's brother, a semi-legitimate dude who worked the post office. He must be in the hospital for something or other. If we had to meet in the daytime, Saint Vincent's was as good a place as any.

"All yours," Belle said, giving me a kiss.

I didn't sing in the shower, but I felt like it. Pansy's the only one who likes my singing.

I slipped into my shirt. It smelled of Belle. She was bustling around the little house, a smile on her face. "You're going?" she asked.

"Yeah. I got to be downtown at nine."

"It's not quite six, honey."

"I got to hit my office, grab a shave, change my clothes."

Belle went over to the bed, bent from the waist, looking back at me, her big beautiful butt trembling just a little bit. "You've got some time," she said.

I went over to her.

"This has got to make you think of *something*," she said, her voice soft and sweet.

I slid into her smooth. She dropped her shoulders to the bed, pushed against me. "Come on."

Belle locked her elbows tight as I slammed into her from behind, my hands on her waist. I was lost in her.

"I'm coming," she said, her voice calm.

"Try not to get so excited about it," I told her.

She giggled. Her whole body shook. "I mean I'm coming *with* you. To the hospital . . . oh!"

I blasted off inside her, fell on top of her on the bed. I lay there, catching my breath until I got soft and slipped out of her. "You want a smoke?" I asked her, lighting one for myself.

"No, I have to get dressed," she said, bouncing off the bed.

I didn't argue with her.

# 54

THE MORNING WAS BRIGHT and clear. Like I felt. We pulled off the West Side Highway just past the Battery Tunnel. I motored quietly up Reade Street, heading for the river and my office. A mixed crew of blacks and Orientals were taking a break from unloading a truck. The black guys were eating bowls of steaming noodles, working with chopsticks like they'd been doing it all their lives. One of the Orientals yelled something in Chinese to a guy standing in the doorway with a clipboard in his hand. The only word I caught was "motherfucker."

Pansy was glad to see me. She always is, no matter what's in my hands. I love my dog. Guys doing time promise themselves a lot of things for when they hit the bricks. Big cars. Wall-to-wall broads. Fine clothes. Who knows? I promised myself I'd have a dog. I had one when I was a kid and they took him away from me when they sent me upstate. I'll never go to prison again over anything money can buy. Wherever I have to run, I can take Pansy.

The beast took my signal and let Belle inside. I gave her a couple of the bagels we'd brought with us and went inside to shave. When I came out, Belle was sitting on the couch, holding her paper cup of coffee with both hands, her arms stiff as steel. Pansy was lying on the couch, happily slurping from the cup, spilling coffee all over Belle.

"Pansy, jump!" I yelled at her. She hit the floor, spilling the rest of the coffee in the process. "You miserable gorilla," I told the dog.

Belle looked at me, appealing. "I didn't know what to do—I was afraid to push her away."

"It's not your fault—she's a goddamned extortionist."

Pansy growled agreement, always eager for praise.

Belle's white sweatshirt was soaked. She pulled it over her head. "I'll wear something of yours," she said, smiling.

I knew none of my shirts would fit her, but I kept my mouth shut. I found a black turtleneck sweater in a drawer, tossed it to her.

I pulled out a dark suit, nice conservative blue shirt, black knit tie. A pair of black-rimmed glasses and an attaché case and I was set.

Belle looked me over. "I didn't know you wore glasses."

"They're just plain glass—they change the shape of your face."

"That's what I wish *I* could do," she said bitterly.

"I like your face," I told her.

"It doesn't look like his," she said. "But I still see him in the mirror sometimes."

"If it hurts you, maybe you should fix it."

"You mean like plastic surgery?"

"No."

"Oh. You think . . . ?"

"Now's not the time, little girl."

She nodded. A trusting child's face watching me. Listening.

Just about time to go. I let Pansy out to the roof, blanking my mind. No point speculating—the Prof would have something for me and I'd find out when I saw him.

Pansy strolled downstairs and flopped down in a corner. She wasn't into exercise.

"You want a beer?" I asked Belle.

"Who drinks beer at this hour?"

I pulled the last bottle of Bud from the refrigerator, uncapped it, and poured it into a bowl. Pansy charged over—made it disappear.

## 55

SAINT VINCENT'S IS IN the West Village, not far from my office. "Just act like you know where you're going," I told Belle.

The information desk gave us a visitor's pass and we took the elevator. Room 909 was at the end of the corridor. I walked in first, not looking forward to shooting the breeze with Melvin, hoping the Prof was already on the scene.

He was. In the hospital bed, both legs in heavy casts, suspended by steel wires. A pair of IV tubes ran into his arm. His face was charcoal-ash, eyes closed. He looked smaller than ever—a hundred years old.

My eyes swept the room. Empty except for a chair in the corner. I came to the bed quietly, images jamming my brain.

The Prof didn't move, didn't open his eyes. I bent close to him.

"Burke?" His voice was calm. Drugged?

"It's me, brother."

"You got my message?"

"Yeah. What happened?"

His eyes flicked open. They were bloodshot but clear, focused on my face. His voice was soft, barely a whisper. "I was poking around. On my cart. Scoping the scene, you know? I was working Thirty-sixth and Tenth. By the Lincoln Tunnel."

The Prof does this routine where he folds his legs under him and pulls himself along on a board with roller skates bolted to the bottom. It looks like he has no legs at all. Sometimes he carries a sign and a metal cup. Working close to the ground.

"You want to wait on this? Get some rest?"

His eyes hardened. "They gave me pain, but I'm still in the game.

The nurse'll be around in a few minutes to give me another shot. You need to know now."

I put my hand on his forearm, next to the IV tubes. "Run it," I said, my voice as quiet as his.

"You ever hear of this freak karate-man they call Mortay?"

"The one who's hitting all the dojos? Challenging every sensei?"

"That's him. You know Kuo? Kung-fu man?"

"He teaches dragon-style, right? Over on Amsterdam?"

"He's dead, Burke. This Mortay hits the dojo, slaps Kuo in front of his own students. Kuo clears the floor and they go at it. Mortay left him right there."

I let out a breath. "Kuo's good."

"He's good and dead, bro'. It's been going on for a while. This Mortay's been selling tickets—says he's the world's deadliest human. The word is that he was kicked off the tournament circuit—he wouldn't pull his shots. Hurt a lot of people. He fought a death-match about a year ago. In the basement under Sin City."

"I heard about it."

"Every player on the scene was there. They put up a twenty-grand purse, side bets all over the place. He fought this Japanese guy from the Coast. The way I heard it, Mortay just played with him before he took him out. Now he's hooked on it. Death. He finds a dojo, walks in the door. The sensei has to fight him or walk off the floor."

"He's got to be crazy. Sooner or later . . ."

"Yeah. That's what everybody's been saying. But he's still out there."

The Prof took a deep breath. "He does work too."

"For hire?"

"That's the word."

"He did this to you?"

"I'm on my cart, talking to a couple of the working girls, handing out my religious rap. Like I'm the man to deal with the van, you know?"

"Yeah."

"Car pulls up. Station wagon. Spanish guy gets out. Short, heavy-built dude. Big diamond hanging from his ear. Tells me he has someone wants to talk to me. I tell him that I bring the Word to the people, so the people got to come to me. The Spanish guy don't blink an eye. Pulls a piece right there in the street. Tells me he has to bring me, don't matter what condition I arrive in. I tell him not to get crazy—how am I supposed to go, walk? He calls to another guy. They each grab one end of my cart, put me in the back of the wagon. The girls just faded. They're hijacking me off the street, nobody's paying attention."

The Prof's voice was the same quiet flow, his eyes focused on someplace else.

"They take me to one of the piers. Past where they have the big ships. I'm not blindfolded or anything. They haul me inside this old building at the end of the pier. Place is falling apart: big holes in the roof, smells like a garbage dump.

"Guy's waiting for us. Tall, maybe six two, six three. Couldn't weigh more than one and a quarter."

"That thin?"

"Skinny as a razor blade, man. Arms like matchsticks. You'd look like a weightlifter next to him."

"Mortay?"

"Oh, yeah. Mortay. No mystery—he *tells* me who he is. Like his name is supposed to stand for something. He got this weird voice. Real thin, high-pitched. He says that he heard I been asking around. About the Ghost Van. He says that's a bad thing to do. Could make him mad, I keep doing that.

"I rap to him. Try my crazy act. He don't go for it. He says he knows me too. Calls my name—the Prophet. Asks, if I know the Word, why I can't cure myself. Fix my own legs.

"I tell him no man can change the will of the Lord. He comes over to me, kneels down, starts on me with his hands, pressing spots on my face, watching me. Then he says, You lie. Just like that. You lie. He slaps me right off the cart, tells me to stand up. For a minute, I thought my legs stopped working for real . . . but I got to my feet.

"He says he's going to have to show me it's a mistake to ask questions. I know bodywork's coming up. I got no place to go. I fucked up, brother," the little man said, his voice shaking. "I was scared. You know I don't spook easy, but this freak . . . It was like he was sending out waves. Hurting me inside, and he wasn't even touching me."

I felt Belle behind me. "Wait outside," I told her. I didn't know what was coming, but it wasn't for her to hear.

"It's all right, Prof," I said to my brother, squeezing his arm.

His voice went sad. Shamed. "No, it ain't all right. I lost control, Burke. I put Max's name out. I told this freak the Silent One was my brother. I ran the whole rap. Told him the widow-making wind would tear down his house if he messed with me. I figured if he knew I was hooked up with Max . . ."

"It's the truth. And he's not the only one."

The Prof's face was deep-down sad. "You know what he did? He *smiled*, man. He said he *wanted* Max. In a match. Said he made me walk, he could make Max talk. The freak said he had word out for months that he wanted to meet Max—that Max was dog-yellow.

"I went dumb. It wasn't no act. It was the devil talking to me, standing right there. He said he's been looking for Max's dojo. When he finds it, he's going to take it for himself.

"And then he asked me where it was. Smiling at me. Saying since Max was my *brother* and all, I *had* to know.

"I told him I didn't. I know when a man is lying, he says. Looks at me. Right through me.

"The Spanish guy says something. Mortay flicks his wrist at the Spanish guy's face like he's brushing away a fly. Blood jumps out on the Spanish guy's face.

"Then the freak says to me he sees I don't know where Max's dojo is. So he wants me to give him a message.

"I say okay—tell me the message. He takes this fucking machete from someplace. Hands it to me. Test the blade, he says. Big smile on his face. I touch the edge—it goes right into my hand, draws blood.

"Sharp enough? he asks me. For what? I say.

"I'm going to fix your legs, he says.

"I try and stall him. Put the blade down, take off my coat. Like I'm getting ready to duel with him. I pick up the blade, swing it in both hands. Like I'm testing it? I check the door where they brought me in. Spanish guy standing there, holding the gun. No place to go.

"I was scared, Burke. But shamed too. I knew I put Max's name out. Broke the rules. I'm a man. I never cried when they broke me up in the joint. I have a name too."

"Your name is gold, Prof."

The little man wasn't listening; tears on his face.

"I pulled it together. I called his name: Come on, pussy! He came at me. I hit the floor, flipped onto my back, flashing the blade up at him with both hands—hard. Going to cut his balls off."

The Prof's arm trembled in my hand.

"He *floated* right over me. Musta been six feet off the ground. He comes again. I step to him, blade going side to side, razor-circle. No way in for him. He comes *inside* the blade, chops me on the wrist. The blade goes flying.

"Fun's over, nigger, he says."

The Prof's eyes closed.

"I grab for his eyes. White mist comes. I hear a crack—I know it's my leg. I go down."

His eyes opened.

"When I come around, I'm in the back of the station wagon. Mortay—he's sitting like Max sits. Against the back door, facing me. Taking you to the hospital, he said. Put you in a nice private room—everything's on me. Tell Max *I* did this. Says his name real slow. Two pieces. Like More-Tay. Get it right, he said. Give him my message."

The Prof bit into his lip, reaching inside for what he needed. "You're the only one I called," he said.

"I know."

"I fucked up. Fucked up bad."

"You did the job, brother. This Mortay . . . he's got to be locked into the van somehow."

"But Max . . . ?"

"He *knew* about Max before he ever grabbed you, Prof. That's his own scene. You gave him nothing he didn't already have."

"Burke . . . I never saw nothing move so fast in all my life."

I patted his arm, feeling the little man's fear vibrate through to me.

"I need you on this one, brother," I told him.

"I won't be running no races for a while," he said, looking at his legs.

"It's your brain I need. Knife-fighters are a dime a dozen."

The ghost of the Prof's old smile showed. "If you got a plan, I'm your man."

"They still have the death-matches in the basement under Sin City?"

"They move them around, what I heard."

"Who'll know?"

The Prof thought a minute. "Got to be Lupe, brother. That dude's a battle-freak. Cockfighting, pit bulls, rope-dancing . . . it's a good bet he'll be on the set."

"Where's he hang?"

A bigger smile this time. "Your favorite place, Ace. Every weeknight, he's at the end grandstand at Yonkers."

"Which end?"

"Way past the finish line . . . where it looks like bleachers?"

"Yeah, I know it."

"Every night. He sets up matches. Takes a piece."

The little man's eyes moved into stronger focus. Working again. "Light me a smoke."

I fired one for him, held it to his lips. He took a deep drag.

"Lupe's about fifty. Greasy 'do, wears it in an old-style D.A. Pachuco cross on his hand. Short, fat dude. Bad teeth. Got him?"

"Yeah."

The Prof looked up at me, eyes clear. "All the faggot broke was my legs, Burke."

"I know."

"No rhyme this time. This is the true word: he'll be sorry."

"For breaking your legs?"

"For not killing me when he had the chance," the little man promised. Back to himself.

I heard loud voices in the corridor. Pushed open the door a crack. A big black nurse was trying to push her way past Belle and not having any luck.

"It's okay," I told Belle, holding open the door.

The nurse came in, pushing a cart with a metal tray on it. "Time for your medicine," she told the Prof, a West Indian tang to her voice.

The little man winked at her.

"You better hope that ain't no dope," he said, pointing his chin at the hypo on her tray.

"And why is that?" she said, a smile creeping onto her broad face.

"Dope makes me sexy, Mama. I couldn't trust myself around a fine cup of Jamaican coffee like you."

"Never mind with a smart mouth, mahn," she snapped, still smiling, loading the syringe.

The Prof looked at me and Belle. "Look here, fools, can't you see me and this lady want to be alone?"

I waved goodbye. Belle bent over and kissed him.

He was already deep into his rap with the nurse by the time we got the door closed.

## 56

BELLE RESTED HER HAND lightly on my arm as we waited for the elevator, not saying a word. She stayed quiet until we got in the car.

"What happened to him?"

"He was in an accident."

Her face went sulky. "I told you the truth. I told you my secrets. You don't have to tell me yours." She lit a cigarette. "But don't lie to me—I'm a big girl, not a baby. It's none of my business, just say that. Don't tell me stories, you want me to trust you."

"It's none of your business," I said.

She didn't say another word until I hit the highway and she saw where I was headed.

"No."

"No what?"

"No good. What happened to your friend—it's none of my business, okay. But you're going to do something now. I know you have to."

"And?"

"And *that's* my business. I'm in too."

"No, you're not."

"Yes, I *am*. Don't you tell me I'm not. I can do things. I can help."

"Look, Belle . . ."

"*You* look. You think I'm just a piece of ass with a sad story? I'm a woman. A woman who loves you. You don't want my love, you say so. Say so right now."

"I . . ."

"Just shut up. I don't sell my love. I never gave it away before. I said I was going to love you. That *means* something. My love is worth something—you have to give me a chance to show you."

"You'll get your chance."

"How? Coming to see you on visiting day?"

"If that's what it comes down to."

"No! I love you. I swear I love you. I pay attention when you talk. I learn things. You want to mistreat me, I'll still love you. I play for keeps. But you can't disrespect me. Like on that wall you showed me."

"I'm not disrespecting you."

"No? You've got work to do, I should stay at home, right? I'm too fat for an apron, and I don't know how to cook."

I lit a cigarette, blew smoke at the windshield, driving mechanically.

Belle moved in close to me, her hip against mine, both arms around my neck, talking softly into my ear. "You *have* to love me. And you won't . . . not *really* love me . . . unless you let me in. I won't get in the way—I'll just do my piece. You say what it is. But you have to let me in or you'll never see what I am . . . you'll never love me, Burke."

I took a deep breath. Let it out slow.

"You won't free-lance? You'll do what I tell you?"

"I swear."

"I'll pick you up tonight. Around seven."

"Where're we going?"

"The racetrack."

"I thought . . ."

"That's not the deal," I reminded her.

She gave me a kiss, nuzzled against me for a minute, moved back to the passenger side.

"You're the boss." She smiled.

Sure.

## 57

WHEN WE GOT TO HER house, Belle bounded out of the car like she was going to a fire sale on salvation. I wheeled the car around and shot back to the city. Lots of work to do.

I pulled in behind Mama's. Grabbed the *Daily News* from under the register and sat in my booth. The waiter brought me some hot-and-sour soup, not even pretending I had a choice. I read the paper, waiting for Mama. Nothing about any new Ghost Van murders. I flipped through to the back. The race results. Mystery Mary came out on top. Wired the field, trotting the mile in 2:00.3. She was three lengths up at the top of the stretch and held on by a neck. Paid $14.10. I was up almost a grand and a half. I couldn't remember the last time I figured a race so perfectly. I waited for the rush. It didn't come.

Mama moved into the booth. Greeted me, her eyes shifting to the newspaper.

"You win?"

"Yeah."

"I tell Max pick up the money?"

"Yeah. And tell him to lay low for a few days. Stay off the street, okay? I'm working on something—a nice sweet score. Let people think he's gone away for a while."

Mama looked at me, waiting.

"I got to go," I told her.

She didn't say anything.

## 58

I HIT THE POST OFFICE. Told Melvin where the Prof was, gave him the phone number of the private room. Anyone comes around asking for the Prof, he should call me at Mama's, leave the word.

The City Planning Office had the detailed grid maps I needed. I paid for them in cash.

I spent another couple of hours at the library, groping around, not sure what I was looking for.

I drove to the junkyard. Turned around before I got there. It wasn't time for the Mole yet.

I went back to the office. I put the grid maps of the city on the wall. Spread out the clips Morelli got for me. I couldn't make them work.

I went into myself, deep as I could go. I came back empty.

Pansy and I shared some roast beef.

When I looked at my watch, it was time to go.

## 59

THE DOOR OPENED BEFORE I could knock. "Close your eyes," Belle said. "Keep them closed."

She led me over to the couch, pushed me into it. "Just sit for a minute, honey—I'm not done yet."

I lit a smoke, looking around. The whole place was a mess—boxes and paper all over the floor, bed not made, ashtrays overflowing.

Belle came out of the bathroom, prancing on a pair of shiny black spikes. Her hair was swept to one side, held together with a black clip. Her face was so different I had to look twice: dark eye liner pulled her eyes apart, sharp lines over her cheekbones. Her mouth was a wide, dark slash. She was wearing a black silk top over a pair of skin-tight pants in a wide black-and-white stripe. Two heavy white ropes tied loosely around her waist. She twirled before me, as pretty-proud as a little girl in her first party dress.

"See. Just like Michelle said."

I stared at her.

"Burke. Say something!"

"Damn!"

"What does that *mean*?" she demanded, moving closer.

"I think my heart stopped. You want to try some mouth-to-mouth?"

The smile lit up her face. "Isn't it great? Michelle's so smart." She twirled again. Stood hip-shot, her back to me. "Vertical stripes," she boasted, patting her hip.

The black-and-white stripes were vertical all the way up her legs. But when they got to her butt, they stopped going parallel and ran for their lives in opposite directions. Flesh stomps fashion every time.

"You're the loveliest thing I've ever seen in my life," I told her, reaching out my hand.

She slapped it away. "No, you don't." She laughed. "I didn't put all this on for you to pull it off."

I got to my feet, reaching in my pocket for the car keys. Belle moved in close to me, holding the lapel of my jacket with one hand. Dark-red polish on her nails.

"Burke, I was only teasing. You want to stay here, it's okay."

I patted her on the rear. "I wish we *could* stay here. We're working, remember?"

"Then why'd you say . . . ?"

"I lost my head."

She gave me a quick kiss. "Wait till later," she promised.

# 60

I ROLLED ONTO THE Belt Parkway, taking it past the crossover for the airport, heading for the Whitestone Bridge. When I saw a break in traffic, I pulled over on the shoulder. Turned off the engine. Belle sat quietly, black-and-white-striped legs crossed, waiting patiently.

"Were you really a driver?" I asked her.

"Oh, yes," she said, her eyes opening wide, watching me close.

"Want to show me?"

She was behind the wheel in a flash, almost shoving me out the door. I went around to the other side, let myself in. Lit a smoke, watching her.

Belle kicked off the spike heels, wiggling her hips in the seat. She wasn't playing around, just getting the feel of the machine. "Can I move the seat back a bit?"

I showed her where the lever was. She took it back an inch or two, extending her arms toward the wheel, looking another question at me. I threw a toggle switch and the wheel dropped into her lap. "Move it to where you want it and I'll lock it in place."

She played with the wheel for a minute, getting it just the way she wanted it, squirming around in the seat, checking the mirrors, rolling her shoulders to get the stiffness out. "Anything I should know?" she asked.

"Like what?"

"Do the brakes grab? Does it pull to one side?"

"No. It tracks like a train. Stops straight. But watch the gas—it's a lot stronger than it looks."

She nodded. Turned the key. Blipped the throttle a couple of times. "No tach?" she asked.

"It's built for torque, not revs. You want to drop it down a gear, just kick the pedal. Or you can move the lever down one from D."

Belle gave herself plenty of room, waited until the traffic was quiet in the right lane. She came down hard on the gas, adjusting the wheel when the rear started to slide, and pulled out onto the highway hard and smooth. She merged with traffic and flowed along, getting the feel.

"Where's the flasher for the headlights?"

"Flick the turn signal toward you. But be careful—the high beams are real monsters."

"Horn?"

"There's two. The hub on the wheel is the regular one; the little button near the rim—see it?—that's for moving trucks out of the way."

She flicked a glance over her right shoulder. "Okay to play?"

"Go," I told her.

She spotted an opening, mashed the gas, shot all the way across to the far-left lane, blew past a dozen cars, backed off the gas, and rolled into the center lane. She pulled the Plymouth so close behind the car in front that it looked like we were going to hit. Kept it right there until the guy in front of us pulled over.

"Follow the signs to the Whitestone Bridge," I told her.

Belle handled the big car like it was part of her, cutting through traffic, moving from one clot of cars to another, staying in the pack each time. When we got to the bridge, she pulled into the Exact Change lane without me saying a word. I handed her a token. She flicked it into the basket without looking. We motored along the Hutchinson River Parkway, Belle still putting the Plymouth through its paces, not talking to me. We came to the last toll before the hook-turn to the Cross County. A guy in a white Corvette was in the lane next to us, coming out of the chute at the same time. Belle goosed the Plymouth, heading for the left lane. The 'Vette jumped out ahead of us. Belle kicked it down—both cars were flying to the same lane, the 'Vette a half-length in front. Belle kept coming. The gap got narrow. I heard the scream of rubber—the 'Vette's driver stood on the brakes as we shot through.

A minute later, the 'Vette steamed by in the right lane, cutting sharply in front of us as soon as he passed. Belle flicked the brights, punching the horn button at the same time. The sky lit up. The twin air horns under the horn blasted the warning call of a runaway semi. The 'Vette ducked out of the way as we went by. Belle slashed over into his lane. I heard the shriek of brakes again.

Belle brought it down to about seventy. We were in the right lane, heading for the hook-turn at Exit 13. Bright lights flooded the back window. Belle reached up, turned the rearview mirror to the side. She hit the hook-turn with the 'Vette boiling up behind us.

"Come on, sucker," she muttered as the 'Vette pulled into the outside lane behind us. She nailed it around the sweeping turn, holding the inside track. The 'Vette roared behind us, closing fast. Belle's mouth was a straight line. She slid the Plymouth into a piece of the outside lane, but this time the 'Vette was ready for her—he darted back to the inside. Belle slashed the wheel back to the right, carrying the 'Vette right off the road onto the grass. She pulled the Plymouth together for the straightaway, swept under the overpass, and slid into the new traffic stream as smoothly as a pickpocket working a crowd.

She patted the steering wheel hard—like you'd do a horse who'd run a strong race. "Good girl," she said.

"You took the words out of my mouth."

She flashed me her smile.

We exited the Cross County and hooked back to the racetrack. I showed her where to pull in: around the back, near the stable area. Nobody parks there except the horse vans—it's a long distance to the entrance. I gave Belle the buck and a half for the guy collecting the entrance fee, and we motored slowly through, stopping for grooms to walk their horses across the road.

"Park over there," I told her, pointing at a blacktop road that runs behind the paddock. "Leave the nose pointing out."

There are a couple of hundred acres of gravel behind the road. Pitch-dark. Belle turned off the road, stomped the gas, blasting straight into the darkness. She floored the brakes, feathering the gas at the same time, spinning the Plymouth into a perfect bootlegger's turn right into the spot I'd pointed to. She turned off the engine. A whirlwind of dirt and dust flew outside the windows, settling on the car.

"What'd you think, honey?"

"You're a natural," I told her.

Her face went sad. "No. No, I'm not."

I took her hand, squeezed it. "Don't disrespect your mother," I told her.

She gulped. Took a breath. "You always know what to say, Burke."

"I know what to do too," I promised her.

I walked her past the paddock, holding her hand. The black-and-white stripes swayed in the night. I bet some of the mares were jealous.

# 61

I PAID OUR WAY PAST the turnstiles. Stopped in the open area to toss a dollar at the guy selling programs from behind a little desk. There was a box of tiny pencils next to the stack of programs. Belle reached past me and took one.

"That's a quarter for the pencil, lady," the guy called out.

Belle looked at him like he was deranged. "For this little thing?" She tossed it back into the box.

"Behave yourself," I told her, taking her hand to lead her outside. A booth about the size of a one-bedroom apartment was set up outside, open along the sides, canvas across the top. Barbecue grill inside. "Want something?" I asked her.

Smart move. She ordered four hamburgers with everything, two beers. The guy behind the counter finally stopped staring and barked the order over his shoulder, not moving his eyes from her chest.

"What're you getting, pal?" the counter geek asked me.

"He gets it later," Belle assured him.

The guy's jaw went from gaping to unhinged.

I paid the money, carrying a beer in each hand, motioning for Belle to climb the stairs ahead of me, admiring the view. We found seats in the outside grandstand, right near the top of the stretch.

Belle put her hamburgers on one seat, took some napkins, and thoroughly cleaned off two more. She took a slug of beer, then handed it back to me to hold for her while she worked on the burgers.

"You see that guy's face?" she asked innocently. "Michelle was right about the makeup."

When she finished eating, I stowed the refuse under our seats, lit a smoke, and opened the program. Belle slouched against me, her head on my shoulder, holding the last beer in one hand.

"What do all those little numbers mean?"

"They all mean something different. You really want to know?"

"Yes," she said, sounding injured.

I went through it quickly, just once over lightly. Showed her how you could tell the horse's age, sex, color, breeding, all that kind of thing. I was up to the comparative speed ratings at the different tracks and she was still paying attention.

"What's the most important?" she wanted to know.

"What d'you mean?"

"Like, all that stuff. It can't all mean the same thing."

"Belle, that's the trick of it. It all means different things to different people. Some people like speed, some people like breeding, some people . . ."

She cut me off. "What about you? You think breeding is important?"

I looked at her face against my shoulder. "Class is what's important to me. Heart. Going the distance. Breeding don't mean a thing."

"But breeding has to count for something, right? Or they wouldn't put it there," she said, pointing to the program.

"They put *everything* on the program, girl. Because the gamblers want to know, see? What possible difference could a horse's color make? That's on there too."

"But it must . . ."

"It does mean something, Belle. I've been looking at horses since I was a kid—I'll tell you what it means—you want to tell if a horse has real class, you look at its mother."

She tilted her head up to me, a smile growing. "Truly?"

"That's the way nature made it, girl. You can never know for sure who the father of a baby is, but there's never a doubt about the mother."

"Never a doubt," she agreed, patting my thigh.

The P.A. system blared into life; the horses were on the track for the first race. Belle watched as they paraded in front of the grandstand behind the marshal. She lit a cigarette, watching everything, leaning forward in her seat, her hand on my knee.

The tote board said two minutes to post time. "Are you going to make a bet, honey?"

"Not this race," I told her, watching.

Belle sipped delicately at her second beer. The very image of a lady, about ten percent past life-size.

The race wasn't much. If I'd had binoculars, I would have looked for Lupe.

Belle finished her beer. "Who's going to win the next race?" she demanded.

I studied the program. Same class, same crop. Mostly older horses on the way down. But there was one four-year-old, a Warm Breeze mare; Hurricane was her name. I pointed her out on the program.

"This one's getting stronger all the time—maybe she's a late bloomer."

Belle lit a smoke. "I like this," she said, watching the horses come out for the post parade. "Which one is ours?"

"The five horse," I told her. "The one with the white blanket."

"She's pretty. Kind of small, though."

At five minutes to post, Hurricane was up to 15-1.

"Let's bet on her," Belle said.

"Okay. I'll be right back," I said, getting up.

"Can't I come too?"

"Come on," I said, ripping the front and back covers off the program and folding the pages into the rungs of our seats to mark them as ours.

She held my hand as we walked to the windows. A group of Latins were standing against a pole, arguing about the race in Spanish. One blurted out "*Mira, mira!*" as we walked by. Belle stiffened. "It just means 'Look at that!'" I said to her, squeezing her hand. "Must be those vertical stripes."

I threw a double-sawbuck down on the mare.

Back in our seats, Belle squirmed, swiveling her head so she wouldn't miss anything. I lit a smoke as they called the horses to the gate. As the car pulled off, the horses charged into the first turn, fighting for position. Hurricane didn't get off quickly—she was pushed to the outside, deep in the pack.

"Oh, she's losing!"

Hurricane moved wide on the paddock turn, gaining a little ground. The three horse was in front, the six next to him, Hurricane running behind the six.

Belle was pounding her fist on my knee, bouncing a little in her seat. "Come *on!*"

Hurricane fired on the back stretch, going three-wide around the horse in front of her, collaring the leader. But she couldn't pull ahead, and the three horse looked fresh. The two of them ran away from the pack into the final turn and pounded for home, not giving an inch.

"Don't quit, baby!" Belle yelled.

The three horse pulled a neck ahead, but the mare wouldn't give it up. She reached down and found something, shot forward again. The crowd roared—the three horse was the odds-on favorite. They crossed the finish line together—too far down the track for me to see who came out on top. "Photo" shot up on the board.

"Did she win?"

"I don't know, Belle. It was close—we have to wait for the photo."

"She didn't quit, though, did she?"

"Sure as hell didn't."

The crowd buzzed. The "Photo" came down and the numbers went up: "5-3-4."

Belle stood up, her hands on the railing, leaning out into the night. "Good girl!" she shouted to the mare. Heads turned toward the sound; the male heads stayed turned. I grabbed her hand, pulled her back into her seat.

Hurricane drove past us, heading for the stable. Belle stood up again, clapping her hands. "Oh, she's beautiful!" she said, happy as a kid at Christmas. The kind of Christmas the Cosby kids have.

I lit a smoke. Almost $350 to the good. With Mystery Mary last night, I was on the longest winning streak of my career.

"Burke, it's just like you said. Heart. She had heart—she went the distance."

# 62

"ANYTHING YOU WANT to bet in the next race?" I asked her, keeping my voice as neutral as possible under the circumstances.

"No, honey. I don't want to bet anymore. Let's just watch, okay?"

"I'll be right back," I said.

I cashed in the ticket. "Nice hit," the teller congratulated me. The money made a sweet roll.

I sat down next to Belle. "Now, listen—I have to go and see someone. On the other side of the track. You stay here. Don't get out of your seat. Okay?"

"Yes."

"The next race is going to start soon. I'll get up like I'm making a bet. I'll be back as soon as I can."

"Okay."

"Now, *listen*, Belle. And don't tell me anything. If I'm not back by the end of the seventh race, you get up and leave." I pressed the car keys into her hand. "Drive to your house. Call the number you called me at the first time. Ask for Mama. Tell her I met with a man named Lupe. Tell her everything you know."

"When will you be back?"

"I don't know. I'm going down a tunnel. If you don't hear from me in a couple of days, call Mama again. She'll tell you what to do."

"Burke . . ."

I held her face in my hand, grabbing her eyes. "You want to be my woman?"

She nodded.

"This is part of what it costs," I told her.

I didn't look back.

## 63

I WENT TO THE BETTING windows, put down ten to win on the six horse, slipped the ticket into my pocket. I hadn't looked at the program. I made my way through the track until I was past the finish line. Then I went downstairs, paid an extra buck, and went into the Clubhouse area. I stayed outside, climbing into the dark grandstand at the end, working my way to the top row.

I spotted Lupe in a couple of minutes, sitting by himself in the far corner, wearing a neon-green jacket with some writing on the back. I moved down until I was across from him, making sure. The Prof's description was right on the money.

I lit a smoke, stuck it in my mouth, and moved over to him, both hands in front of me.

"Lupe?"

"Who wants to know, man?"

"Name's Burke," I said, sitting down.

He grinned, showing me his lousy teeth. "I know you, man. I heard of you. You got that monster dog, right? You want to put her in the ring?"

"Only if you get in there with her," I said, keeping my voice even.

"I got no beef with you," he said quickly.

"I got no beef with you either. I heard you were the man to see about a match, that's all."

"What you got?"

"I got nothing. I want to get down on some action."

"You know Van Cortlandt Park?"

"I don't mean dogs, pal. Or roosters either."

"So?"

"I heard this guy Mortay—he's been doing some duels. Heavy action."

"*Mucho* action, man. But this motherfucker Mortay—he only had that one match."

"With the Jap?"

"Yeah! You saw it?"

"No, just heard about it."

His eyes glittered, crazy-cold eyes. "You got someone wants to meet Mortay, man?"

"Yeah. Me."

Lupe laughed. "With what, man? A machine gun?"

"I don't want to fight him—just have a talk. I figured you could set it up."

"No, man," he said, sadness in his voice. "I don't find him—he finds me. He's got this guy, Ramón. He's the one who makes the meets."

"How'd he find the Jap?"

"The Jap found *him*, man. Guy rolls in from the Coast, puts the word out. I hear this Mortay totaled his brother out there. He was looking for payback."

"Didn't have much luck, did he?"

"Man, Mortay don't take prisoners. He *earned* his name. Mortay, man. You get it? *Muerte*. Death. He deals death, man. Eats it alive."

"You don't know where to find him?"

"Man, I don't *want* to know where to find him."

"Yeah. Okay. This Ramón comes around, you tell him I'd like to meet Mortay. Public place, no problems. Just want to talk to him for a minute."

Lupe shrugged. "He comes, I ask him, man. Where you gonna be?"

"Just give him my name. I'm in the phone book," I told him, walking off.

## 64

I WAS BACK NEXT TO Belle before the start of the fifth race.

"Not so bad, huh?" I asked her.

"I waited here, just like you said."

"Good girl."

"But if you hadn't come back, I was going looking."

"That's not what I told you to do."

"I wasn't going to make trouble. Just poke around."

"Yeah, you got a great disguise all right. Nobody'd remember seeing you."

"Burke, I love you. I had to . . ."

"You had to *listen*. Like I told you to. Like you promised. Stupid bitch."

"Honey!"

"You don't want to listen, you can walk. We made a deal."

"I'm sorry, baby. I am. I just . . ."

"Just. Fucking. Nothing. I'm not going to tell you again."

She leaned into me, her hand near the inside of my thigh, whispering. "You want to take me home, beat my ass, teach me a lesson?"

"I thought you said no man ever hit you."

"It'd be worth it," she whispered. "You know why?"

"Why, dopey?"

"You'd have to be there to do it," she said.

I stood up, held out my hand. She took it, meek as a lamb, a little smile on her face.

## 65

I DROVE THE PLYMOUTH on the way back. Belle was quiet. "You mad at me?"

"I'm not mad at you—I'm not *going* to be mad at you. That's not the way I work. You want to be with me, I have to trust you. That's all there is."

I turned to look at her. A tear rolled down her cheek, tracking through the makeup.

"Okay?" I asked her.

"I swear," she promised, lying down on the front seat, curling up next to my leg. She didn't say another word all the way back to her house.

## 66

WHEN I PULLED IN BEHIND the red Camaro, Belle was still lying across the front seat, her head against my leg. She put her hand on my thigh, grabbed hard enough to hurt.

"You have to come in with me."

"Pretty bossy, aren't you?"

She looked up at me, her face wet, the lovely makeup ruined.

"Just come inside, honey. Come inside—you can be all the boss you want to be, but don't go away now."

I opened my door, got out. Walked around to her side of the car to let her out. I held my hand out to her. "Come on," I told her.

She piled out of the Plymouth faster than I thought she could move.

## 67

"DON'T TURN ON THE LIGHTS," she said, pushing me to the couch. She patted my pockets, found cigarettes and matches. Lit one for each of us. The little flame shot highlights into her hair.

"I don't know what to do," she said, sounding lost.

"About what?"

"I want to wash my face. Take these tears off. But if I do, the makeup won't stay."

"Wash your face."

"But you liked the way I looked. You *said* so."

"I like the way you look in those pants too—does that mean you'll never take them off while I'm around?"

"It's not the same thing," she sniffled.

"Yeah, it is," I told her. "Exactly the same thing. Underneath whatever you put on there's still you."

"But . . ."

"But what?"

"That's not the way it is, honey. All my life . . . it's been the same thing. I have to take off my clothes to make a man forget my face."

I held her against me, her face pressed into my chest, talking softly into her ear.

"Listen to me, Belle. You said you'd listen to me, yes?"

Her head nodded against me.

"*You're* the one who doesn't like your face. Because you don't understand it's your *own* face. I know whose face it is, okay?"

She nodded against me again.

"Go take off the makeup," I said, patting her gently.

While she was in the bathroom, I called the Prof. His voice sounded much stronger.

"I'm on the line with plenty of time."

"It's me."

"Back from the track?"

"Yeah. I spoke to the man."

"So we got a plan?"

"No. Not yet. I want to see the guy you talked with. Square the beef. Drop the case. Walk away."

"He's got to pay, but not today?"

"Right. And we don't want anyone else in the game—just you and me."

"He's not going to stop till he gets to the top."

"I'm not sure that's right, Prof. I think this dueling shit isn't the real story—he was riding shotgun on this other thing, and you stumbled into the line of fire."

"Could be, man. But . . ."

"No names, we'll talk later. I'll come and see you. On the first shift, okay?"

"I can't run, son."

I hung up.

# 68

BELLE CAME OUT OF THE bathroom wearing a black bra over the striped pants, a doubtful look on her freshly scrubbed face. She lit another of her fat black candles, propping it on the sink.

"I'm ugly again," she said.

I gave her a hard look but she didn't flinch. "I looked for myself," she said, her voice sad.

I took a drag of my cigarette. "You want me to fix it?"

"How? Put a bag over my head?"

"Come here," I said, keeping my voice even.

She walked over to the couch.

"Take off those pants."

She reached back to unhook her bra. "Just the pants," I told her.

She stepped out of her spike heels. Even with the zipper all the way down, getting the pants off was a struggle. She stood there in her bra and panties, hands on her hips. "You want these off too?" she asked, her thumbs hooked in the waistband.

"Yeah."

She did, watching me every second. "Now what?"

"Come with me," I said, taking her hand. I led her back to the bathroom, posing her in front of the sink. The candle's flickering glow carried through the open door.

"Lean forward," I told her, my hand on her shoulder. "Look into the mirror."

"I still think . . ."

"Shut up. Just do what I tell you, okay?"

"Okay."

"I'm going to ask you some questions," I said, sliding my hand down to her waist. "Soon as you get the right answer, I'll stop. Got it?"

"Yes."

"Look in the mirror—tell me what you see."

"An ugly old girl."

I slid my hand to her butt, took a plump cheek in my right hand, gave her a hard, sharp pinch.

"Ow!" she yelped.

"Wrong answer," I told her. "What do you see now?"

"The same thing," she snapped, her voice set and stubborn.

I pinched her harder.

She yelped again. "Take another look," I told her. She tried to rub herself—I slapped her hand away.

"I don't care if you pinch it right off, I'm not . . . Burke!" she squealed as I pinched her again. My hand was getting tired.

"I see a beautiful young girl," I whispered to her. "You *sure* I'm wrong?"

Tears rolled down her face. "You mean it? You swear you mean it?"

I squeezed her butt, gently this time. "I've got all night," I promised her.

"This isn't fair," she said, a smile peeking out from beneath the pout.

"Tell me what you see," I said, still holding her in the same place, tightening my hand. "Last chance."

"I see a beautiful young girl," she said. Like a robot.

I pinched the sweet flesh hard. She tried to push past me but I blocked her way.

"Okay!"

I stroked her butt gently. "Tell me."

"I see a beautiful young girl."

"Me too," I said, kissing her.

She came into my arms, baby-soft. I kissed her for a long time. "I'm going to be black and blue," she said against my chest.

"I'm sorry."

"I'm not," she said, pulling me toward the bed. "It's a lot better than being just blue."

# 69

SOMETHING FLICKED AT MY brain just before I drifted off to sleep. Something about a letter. I made a grab for it, but I went under before I could pull it close.

When I came around, it was still dark. Belle was lying crossways on the bed, her breasts flattened against my chest, her face buried in the pillow next to mine. She was awake too—I could tell from her breathing.

"What, baby?" I asked her.

She turned her head, propping herself on an elbow. "Baby . . . I'll never have a baby."

"Sure you will. Someday."

"No, I won't. I fixed it. I had a real ugly harelip—you know what that is?"

"Yeah."

"Well, I had a bad one. Pulled up so bad you could see my teeth all the time. I saved some money—went to a plastic surgeon. You know what, Burke? He told me he could fix the whole thing, give me a different face. A real nose instead of this little pig's snout, cheekbones, anything I wanted."

"So what happened?"

"I started on it. He did the harelip first. Did it real good too. But then I went on a job with a couple of boys. It got nasty right in the middle—the wheels came off and we had to fly. We got away, but one of the boys got himself shot up pretty bad. There's this old doctor, back in the hills. We went by his place, stayed there for damn near a month. Cost us every dime we had between us, but he pulled Rodney through."

She fumbled around the night table, looking for a cigarette. Her body gleamed in the flame from the match.

"This old doctor—he was an outlaw. Like us. I don't even know if he was a real doctor and all, but he had good hands. I was pregnant—maybe two, three months gone. I found out while we were holed up. I was just a big dumb old girl—never figured on getting pregnant. When the doc told me, I told him to go and get the baby. Take it.

"He wanted to know was I sure. So I told him. I told him the truth. He said I was right—I was doing the right thing. He said he saw a lot of babies like I was gonna have—said they never did too well. Trying to make it gentle for me, but I knew what he meant."

She took a deep drag off her cigarette.

"He said he could fix me up inside when he went to get the baby. Tie my tubes. I didn't have to think a minute."

Her voice was soft in the night. "I could love a baby—I know I could. But I figured, if I loved a baby, I'd never have one. You understand?"

"Yeah."

"How come you never worried about it?"

"About what?"

"Making me pregnant."

I laughed. "I can't make babies, Belle."

"You tried? With that woman . . ."

"No. I never tried. Never thought about it when I was young. Spent most of my time in places where you couldn't make a baby anyway. I got jumped once. Long time ago. It wasn't a personal thing—I was in the wrong place. Or maybe I was just the wrong color. Doesn't much matter. Anyway, they really did a number on me. When the ambulance dropped me at the hospital, the pain was so bad . . . there's no way for me to describe it to you."

"What'd they do?"

"Broke some ribs. Fractured my jaw. But the real hurt . . . they kicked me in the balls so many times I thought they were going to fall off. The doctor said it was a testicular torsion."

"A what?"

"A torsion . . . like a twist." I held my two fists together in front of her face, twisted one sideways. "Like that."

"Ugh!"

"Yeah. I looked down at myself—the whole sac was black. Before they put me out, the doctor said the blood supply was pinched off—they'd have to cut me open and stitch a new wall inside to hold the balls in place."

"God!"

"I remember telling them, could they do a vasectomy while they were at it. . . . The doctor thought it was funny—like, as long as they were in the neighborhood and all. But they did it. No babies from me either."

"Does that hurt you?"

"No. It's not for me. I don't think about it. But I never told anyone before."

Belle kissed me. "You can tell me anything," she said.

I reached past her. Lit a smoke for myself. My watch said it was past four in the morning.

"Go back to sleep," I said, rubbing her back, pushing against her shoulder.

"I have to sleep on my stomach," she said, a smile playing around her lips.

"You're breaking my heart—I didn't pinch you that hard."

"You *did!*"

"Give it a rest, Belle. I'd need a set of vise grips to do a job on all this," I said, patting her butt.

"I looked in the mirror. While you were asleep. You made a big mark."

"It'll be gone soon."

"I know," she whispered. "That's why I'm sleeping on my stomach. I want to see it again before it goes away."

She put her face in my chest. I felt the tears.

"What?"

"It'll fade away. You will too."

"I'm right here."

"For now."

I took a last long pull on the cigarette, tangling my hand in the hair at the back of her neck.

"It's like you said before, Belle. We're outlaws. Tomorrow's for citizens. For us, it's always now."

"I love you," she mumbled into my chest.

"Go to sleep, little girl," I told her, holding her, kissing her hair. Waiting for daylight.

# 70

I WAS BACK UP A couple of hours later. I lit a cigarette, walked out onto the deck. A big seagull sat on the railing. He didn't fly away as I walked closer to him, just shifted his head so he could watch me close. He knew he had the whole sky to run to.

I felt Belle behind me. "You better go back to sleep," I said.

"Why? I'm awake now."

"You already missed a couple of nights' work. You're going to be wiped out if you don't get some rest."

"I'm not going back. In that business, girls come and they go. It happens all the time."

"Yeah, but . . ."

"I'm in this with you, Burke. I know you could walk away from me anyway. When it's over. But I got to take this shot. Show you what I can do . . . so you'll want to be with me."

"Look, Belle . . ."

"You promised. Maybe you didn't say the words, but you promised. An outlaw's promise—I'm in on this. I've got some money put away. You won't have to take care of me."

"Hell, I'd have to rob a bank just to feed you."

She slapped me hard on the arm. "I *mean* it. Don't joke around."

She slipped her arms around my neck from behind, pressed against me, talking only for my ears. "I'm going to be with you. I don't want men looking at me anymore the way they do. You made it too late for that." Her grip tightened. "I want a man who looks at my face."

I let out a breath. "Get dressed," I told her.

# 71

WE WERE BACK IN MY office by seven-thirty. I let Pansy out to the roof, called Mama. No messages came in for me, but she got mine out to Max. One more quick call. The Prof was a little blurred on the phone—I guess they were still shooting him up.

"How you holding up, brother?" I asked him.

"If the Board don't call, it's time for the Wall."

One of his old sayings—if you can't scam the Parole Board, it's time to start working on an escape plan. I guess he was pretty sick of the hospital.

I spread out the street maps on the desk again, stared at them.

Belle's hand on my shoulder. "What're you looking for, honey?"

"I don't know yet."

Pansy came back downstairs. One glance told her the situation. I was working—no point in trying to extort food. Then her beast's brain came as close to an idea as she was ever likely to get. She butted her massive head against Belle's leg, pushing her back a few feet. Belle headed for the couch, but Pansy cut her off, butting at her again.

"What does she want?"

"Food," I said, not looking up.

I heard the refrigerator open. "Well, what suits you?" Belle asked. Pansy growled. "Can I give her some of this brown rice?"

"Heat it up first," I told her, keeping my eyes on the maps.

Belle came back inside. "Honey, is there a store around here?"

"What kind of store?"

"Like a supermarket or a grocery?"

"Not far. Why?"

"I need some stuff."

"Later, okay?"

"But I want . . ."

"Belle, I'm trying to figure something out. Just be quiet for a while, okay?"

She leaned over the desk, her breasts in my face, one hand slipping into my lap. "Maybe you should put something in my mouth . . . shut me up good."

I looked up at her, holding her eyes. "If you won't let me work with you here . . ."

Her eyes went soft and sad. "I was playing."

"Now's not the time."

She leaned closer, watching my eyes. "I know. I thought you'd give me a slap. Where you pinched me last night."

"What good would that do?"

"I have to feel you. You won't let me help. . . . I just wanted . . ."

"I *will* let you help. But if you don't shut up, I'll never figure out how."

I patted her rump. Gently. "Okay?"

"Okay."

# 72

WHEN I LOOKED AWAY from the map, she was curled up asleep on the couch, Pansy was lying parallel to her on the floor.

I snapped my fingers. Pansy's head swiveled. I pointed toward the far corner of the office. She moved with the speed of a runaway fire hydrant. As soon as she was at her post, I went over to the couch. I kissed Belle on the cheek. She came awake. "What is it, honey?"

"I got something for you to do—you awake?"

She rubbed her eyes. "Sure."

"When you spoke to Marques, he call you or did you call him?"

"Both."

"So you have a phone number for him?"

"Sure."

"I want you to call him. Tell him I came by the club and saw you. Asked you to get in touch with him—set up a meeting. Tell him I said any time, any place. About what we talked about the last time."

"What if he has to call me back—where do I tell him?"

"Don't tell him anything. If he can't give you a time and a place right then, tell him to call my number. The one he gave you the first time."

"The Chinese woman."

"Yeah."

"Burke, is she the one? The one you . . . ?"

I ruffled her hair, kissed the back of her neck. "Come on, Belle. We got a lot to do today."

## 73

ON THE WAY TO THE hospital, I asked her about Marques.

"You know the best time to call?"

"What difference does it make?"

"He's a pimp. He goes off the street before four, five in the morning, the other players will think he's losing a step. Best time to catch him at his crib is early afternoon."

"Sometimes, when I come off my shift, I can't sleep. Maybe I could try him now."

"Yeah, okay. When I go up to see the Prof, you take the car. Find a pay phone, take a shot." I looked at my watch. Almost ten-thirty. "I'll meet you in the parking lot around noon. If you haven't reached him by then, we'll try again."

I pulled up outside Saint Vincent's. "The registration papers are in the glove compartment. You get stopped by the cops, tell them you borrowed the car. It's not on any list."

I showed her the papers.

"Juan Rodriguez?"

"That's me. I met you at the club. Told you you could borrow the car any time you wanted. You've never been to my house. I told you I wouldn't need the car for a couple of weeks 'cause I'd be on vacation."

I gave her a slip of paper with a phone number on it. The phone would ring at the junkyard I own a piece of in the Bronx. The old man who made out my paycheck would tell anyone who called I was on vacation. In Puerto Rico someplace. Juan Rodriguez was the ideal employee—he never showed up for work, but he cashed his paycheck and gave the boss back the money. Fuck the IRS.

"Drive the car like it was hot. Don't call attention to yourself. But if you get pulled over, don't run. If you get a ticket, just take it. Don't say anything."

"All right, honey."

The Plymouth pulled away and disappeared in traffic. Smoother than I ever drove it.

## 74

THE PROF LOOKED stronger already. I pulled my chair to the head of the bed and we talked like we used to on the yard. Quiet, each looking in a different direction. The West Indian nurse came in.

"I smell smoke in here," she said, like she'd caught us stealing.

"Smoke don't have a prayer against your own sweet smell, Mama," the Prof sang out.

"There's no smoking in the patients' rooms. Now, you know that very well. I have told you before."

The Prof spread his hands to the heavens, seeking divine guidance. "Lord, what must I say to make this woman give me a play?"

The nurse's broad face creased as she fought off the smile. "You smart-mouth little man—I'd break the rest of your bones."

"You don't mean a word of it, a goddess like you."

The nurse had a pill and a plastic cup of dark liquid. "You going to take this medicine with no more of your speeches?"

The Prof regarded her, his fine head cocked to the side. "You know why a man climbs a mountain?"

She sighed, used to this by now.

"So, then. Why does a man climb a mountain?"

" 'Cause the air's so sweet when you get to the top," the Prof said, and popped the pill in his mouth, holding the glass like a toast. "You going to give a poor man a reason to live?"

"You keep messing with me, you *have* no reason to live," she warned him, then waited patiently for the Prof to finish drinking his medicine. Snatched the glass from his hand and stalked out.

"A little more time and she's all mine," the Prof said. He was right—all Mortay broke was his legs.

I lit another cigarette, pulling the half-filled water glass we used as an ashtray from under the bed.

"I went to the track. Saw the man. Like I told you."

"And?"

"He can't put me in touch. Says this Mortay's a death-dealer for real. That duel with the Jap—it really went down."

The Prof dragged deep on his cigarette. "Yeah. But he's no warrior. Not like Max. He's a junkie for it."

"It connects, Prof."

His eyes flashed. "Run it down, home."

"You weren't looking for this freak, right? Just poking around . . . asking about the van."

"Right."

"And this guy's no bodyguard. You must have stepped on his turf by accident."

"It's not enough. We need to know more if we going to score."

"I'm working on it. I told this Lupe . . . the guy who makes matches . . . I want to meet."

"You not going to bring Max?"

"Max is out of this one, Prof."

He reached his hand across the bed. I squeezed it.

"That seals the deal," he said.

"Right. You getting anything over the wire?"

"Not yet. It'll come, though. I got a lot of hooks floating."

I stood up to leave. "You need anything?" I asked.

"I need a nurse," he said.

# 75

BELLE WAS BEHIND THE wheel of the Plymouth as I came through the parking lot, reading a newspaper spread over the steering wheel. She had the car moving before I closed the door.

"Very nice," I told her.

"This is some lovely car."

"You're some lovely woman. You call Marques?"

"No answer. Can't we try him from your office?"

"That phone's no good past eight in the morning. You can't stay on the line more than a minute anyway. I'll show you where to pull over."

We found an open pay phone by the river. I handed Belle a quarter. She took one of those premoistened towelettes from her purse, ripped off the foil, wiped down the mouthpiece.

She dialed the number. Waited. Somebody picked up. I only heard her end of the conversation.

"Could I speak to Marques, please?"

. . .

"Belle."

We waited a couple of minutes. I opened my palm to show her I had another quarter ready.

"Hi. Remember that man you wanted me to call for you? Burke? He came by the club. Said he wanted to meet with you. About what you talked about the last time."

. . .

"He said it was up to you. Any time. Any place."

. . .

"No, he didn't seem mad at all. He just said he needed information about the scene, and you were the best person. . . . He didn't want to poke around without checking with you, he said."

. . .

"Okay. Wait, let me write this down," she said, signaling to me. I nodded. "Go ahead," she said into the phone.

. . .

"Junior's? Where's that? Oh, he'll know."

I nodded to her again.

"What time?"

. . .

"Eleven. Okay. And tell him not to bring his friends? Sure. Okay, thanks. I'll tell him—he said he'd call me before I go to work tonight."

She put down the phone.

"Good girl," I told her.

She tossed her head, smile flashing in the sun. "You just wait and see," she promised.

## 76

I TOOK THE WHEEL. As I pulled out, I noticed the back seat full of cartons. "What's all that stuff?" I asked her.

"Stuff I needed," she said. Case closed.

"You hungry?"

She made a noise like Pansy does when you ask her the same question.

I pulled in behind Mama's, taking Belle by the hand as we walked through the kitchen. Mama's collection of thugs watched us impassively—they'd seen stranger things come through the back room.

The joint had a few customers—no way to keep them all out at lunchtime—but my booth was empty, the way it always is.

The waiter came over to us, blocking Belle's side of the booth, looking a question at me with his eyes. I shook my head, telling him Belle wasn't trouble. He flicked his eyes toward the front of the room. I nodded—send Mama over.

Mama's dress was a deep shade of red. Opal earrings matched the ring on her hand. She returned my bow, face a mask.

"Mama, this is Belle," I said. "Belle, this is Mama." I said it carefully. Nice and even, same tone of voice. Mama was stone-solid reliable when it came down to a crunch, but she was funny about women.

She bowed. "Friend of Burke, friend of Mama."

Belle started to reach out her hand, thought better of it. Bowed gently. "Thank you, ma'am." Polite as a little girl in church.

Mama slid into the booth next to me, barking something in Cantonese over her shoulder.

The waiter brought the soup. Mama served me, then Belle, then herself. Watched carefully, smiling with approval as the bowl emptied. "You have more soup?"

"Yes, please. It's *delicious*."

Mama bowed again. "Very good soup—good for strength. Special for my people. Always here."

Belle looked a question.

"Burke my people," Mama said. No expression on her face, nothing in her tone. But a low-grade moron would have caught the warning.

Belle quietly worked her way through beef in oyster sauce, snow-pea pods, water chestnuts, fried rice, hard noodles, paying no attention to us.

Mama took a look at the empty plates, raised her eyebrows, called the waiter over again. Belle had a portion of lemon chicken, washing it all down with some Chinese beer. She patted her face with her napkin. "Oh, that was *good!*"

"You want more?" Mama asked.

Belle smiled. "No, thank you."

"You come back sometime. When no more trouble, okay? See my granddaughter, yes?"

"You have a granddaughter?"

"Why not?" Mama asked, her face hardening.

"You don't look old enough."

A smile flashed. Disappeared. "Plenty old enough. Burke explain to you sometime."

"Do you have pictures of her?"

Mama scanned Belle's face, taking her time. "Many pictures," she said, tapping her head. "All in here."

Belle walked past the warning like she hadn't heard it. "What's the baby's name?"

"Flower."

Belle sipped her tea, prim and proper. Her eyes were soft. "If I was a flower, I know what kind I'd be," she said, half to herself. "A bluebell."

Mama bowed, as though she understood. The way she always looks.

## 77

"I HAVE TO GO IN THE street for a while," I told Belle as we climbed in the Plymouth. "I'll call you when I'm done with Marques. Late, okay?"

"Can't I wait at your office?"

"It's only a little after two now—I'll be coming back there to change around eight. It's a long time to be cooped up."

"I won't be cooped up."

"Yeah, you would. I could leave you there with Pansy, but she wouldn't let you out."

"It's okay."

I drove back to the office, helping Belle carry her boxes up the back stairs.

"I'm not playing, girl. Pansy lets people in, but they're always there when I come back, understand?"

"Sure. Go ahead. I'll just take a nap."

"Don't use the phone. And don't open any of the file cabinets."

"O-*kay!* I got it."

I gave her a kiss.

# 78

I FOUND MICHELLE AT The Very Idea, a transsexual bar on the East Side. I walked through a jungle of hard looks until I got to her table, feeling them fall away when she kissed me on the cheek.

"Hi, handsome." She smiled. "Looking for me?"

I sat down next to her, lit a cigarette, waiting patiently for her two girlfriends to leave. Michelle didn't introduce me.

"The Prof's in the hospital," I told her.

"What's the rest of it?"

"His legs are broken. Somebody did it to him. For poking around, asking questions."

"You know who?"

"Guy named Mortay."

Her big eyes went quiet, two long dark fingernails flirting with her cheekbone, meaning she was thinking. "I don't know him . . . but it seems like I heard the name. . . ."

"It's Spanish for 'death.'"

"Honey, you know my language is French."

I didn't say anything, looking straight ahead. Michelle's hand grabbed my wrist. "Honey, I'm sorry. But it's business, right? The Prof was poking around, like you said. It's not the first time he stepped on a nail."

"The guy didn't have to do it, Michelle. It was a message. He's some kind of freak—wants to fight Max. That's why he worked the Prof over."

"He wants to fight *Max?*"

"That's what he said."

"He should change his name to 'death *wish*.'"

"Yeah, great. Thanks for your help." I got up to leave.

"Burke!"

"What? You think I came here to listen to your snappy dialogue? The Prof's my brother. Yours too. I know you're off the street—I didn't think we were off your list."

Michelle grabbed my arm, her talons biting deep. "Don't you ever say that!" she hissed, pulling me closer. She got to her feet, hooking her arm through mine. "Let's get out of here—too many ears."

We walked out into the daylight. I let her lead me down the street to another joint—a singles bar that wouldn't come alive for a couple of hours. We grabbed a pair of stools near a corner. Glass tinkled; a brittle edge to the juiceless, anorexic laughter of the patrons. The bartender brought Michelle her white wine and me my ginger ale.

"Tell me," she said, not playing now.

"You know the Ghost Van?"

"Just the rumors. The gossip off the street. But I know it's for real—somebody's shooting the working girls."

"There's a bounty on it. I talked with some people. Made a deal to track it down. The Prof was in on it. That's what he was looking for when he ran into this Mortay."

"So they're connected?"

"I don't know. When Mortay leaned hard, the Prof pulled out Max's name. Thinking to put some protection on himself. It backfired. Mortay *wants* Max—that's what he said. Wanted to know where his dojo was. The Prof didn't know. Mortay snapped his legs."

"How'd you find him?"

"They brought him right to the hospital. Like I said—a message."

"Where are you now?"

"I did some digging. There's this guy Lupe. Works out of the Bronx. Sets up matches. You know: cockfights, pit bulls, crap like that?"

"Yes?"

"He said this Mortay fought a duel. A bunch of the players got together, put up this purse. Twenty grand. Mortay killed the other guy in front of the whole crowd."

"I can see it. Regular prizefights are too tame for the freaks. Too much cocaine, too much filth . . . After a while, they have no nerve endings at all. It takes a superjolt to get their batteries started. They want the real thing."

"I told this Lupe I want to meet Mortay."

"Burke, that's not like you, that macho foolishness."

"Not fight him, Michelle. Meet him. Just to tell him I'm walking away. No hard feelings."

"Baby, I've known you forever. *All* your feelings are hard feelings."

"I have to turn him away from Max."

"It doesn't sound like . . ."

"I don't know what it sounds like. If he's free-lance, it doesn't matter. He can't find Max."

"So?"

"So, if he's tied up with this Ghost Van, maybe he's tied up with people who *could*."

The bartender brought us another round. I felt a flesh-padded hip bump my arm. A girl in a pink leather skirt, moving onto the stool next to me, talking to her girlfriend. Secretaries prolonging their lunch hour to look around.

Michelle sipped at her wine. "What do you want me to do?"

"Ask around. About the van. I'll check out this Mortay the best I can. See if it all catches up."

"I thought you were going to walk away."

"If I can, I will. I don't like any of this. If this guy's really fighting duels, he can't last forever. There's no old gunfighters."

Her big eyes pinned me over the rim of her glass. "I may be a sweet young thing, honey, but I go back a ways, remember?"

"Ex-gunfighter," I said, quietly.

"Yeah, we're all X-rated, aren't we, babe? I'm an ex-streetwalker, and you want me back on the stroll to listen to the beat. And you're ready to pick up the gun again—I can hear it in your voice."

"It'll be all right. I'll talk with him, square it up."

The girl in the pink skirt leaned into our conversation, her hard-pointed breasts brushing my arm. "Excuse me, honey," she said to

Michelle, "could I ask your boyfriend a question?"

Michelle gave her an icy smile. "He's not my boyfriend—he's my lawyer."

"Oh, perfect!" the girl said, pulling her pal into the scene. She looked at me, flicking her tongue over her lower lip. "Do you think prenuptial agreements take the romance out of marriage?"

I blew a jet of smoke across the bar. "Rubbers take some of the romance out of sex," I said, "but they beat the hell out of AIDS."

I tossed a couple of bills on the bar. Michelle followed me out.

## 79

I DROVE MICHELLE OVER to her hotel. She was quiet on the drive, her eyes on the street. I pulled up down the block from her place.

"I can't explain it to you," I told her. "I wish I could—it's somewhere inside my head—I have to work with it until it makes sense."

"Not everything makes sense."

I lit a smoke, shook my head. "It's just a feeling . . . but I know this whole thing is bad for us. For all of us. I'm not looking for trouble."

"Okay, honey. I'm with you."

"Thanks, Michelle."

She lit one of her long black cigarettes like she does everything else. Elegantly.

"You still with that big girl?"

"Yeah."

"That's a very fine woman, Burke. Believe me when I tell you. Nobody's ever been nice to her."

"I'm nice to her."

She smiled. "Are you?"

"Yeah, I am. She took your advice."

"Vertical stripes."

I laughed. "You should have seen them on her."

Michelle slapped my arm with unerring instinct in the same spot

Belle always used. "You work with what you have, baby. You're looking at the expert."

"I know."

"Okay. You got some cash on you?"

"Yeah."

"Then let's do some shopping."

"Shopping? For what?"

"For a *present*, you idiot. For your girl."

"I have to . . ."

"Drive down to the Village," she ordered me, not willing to discuss it further.

Michelle found what she wanted in a little basement dive on Sullivan Street. A necklace of small dark-blue stones. The old Turk who ran the place had been a chemist before he fled some border war a hundred years ago. He'd been one of the Mole's first teachers.

"How much for this old thing, Mahmud?" Michelle asked, holding the necklace up to the light.

"That is pure lapis lazuli, young lady. Very fine. Very special."

"Sure, sure. About a hundred bucks retail, right?"

"A hundred dollars? For Old World craftsmanship? The stones alone are worth many times that."

"Since when is Taiwan the Old World, Mahmud?"

The old man's eyes gleamed. "Lapis lazuli. The mineral is called 'lazulite.' Very rare. You will not find it in the Far East. This perfect crystal comes only from Madagascar."

"Does the geography lesson cost extra?"

Mahmud and I exchanged shrugs. "Even a hurricane eventually passes, leaving the calm," he said.

Michelle wasn't moved. "You take American Express?"

Mahmud laughed so hard, tears ran down his face. "From him?" he said, pointing at me.

Michelle moved in for the kill. "Okay, so how much of a discount for cash?"

Mahmud moved to center ring, gloves up. "This necklace is worth one thousand two hundred dollar."

"Get out of town! Do I look like I'm on medication?"

"You look lovely, as always, Michelle. One thousand two hundred dollar."

"Four hundred. And you don't have to gift-wrap it."

"For you, because you are so beautiful, because such a beautiful necklace should have a beautiful home . . . a thousand."

"It's not for me, you old bandit, it's for Burke. For his girlfriend."

"This is true?"

I nodded.

"He just brought me along for protection," Michelle said, smiling sweetly.

"Ah, I see. Eight hundred, then."

"Did you say five?"

"Seven hundred dollar, and only because I respect your good taste."

"Can we split the difference?"

"Seven hundred dollar," the old man said. He meant it.

"Give him the money," Michelle ordered me.

I handed it over. Mahmud slipped the necklace into a soft leather pouch, handed it to me. "You take this too," he said, rummaging around under the counter. He came up with a tiny round wood box. He unscrewed it, holding it out to me. It was filled with a fragrant paste, colorless in the dark wood.

"Jasmine," he said. "Just a touch on the lady's finger, then . . . here"—touching his chest. "The lapis takes its fire from the earth; it will blaze all the brighter if there is fire in the heart."

I bowed to Mahmud. Michelle gave him a kiss. When we hit the street, it was past six.

## 80

"WHERE TO?" I asked Michelle.

"Take me back to my hotel. I need to change my clothes before I get to work."

"Michelle . . . you'll look?"

"I'll do better than that, baby. There's plenty of those little girls out there that know me. Like the Prof would say, if they know me, they owe me."

"Debts."

"Debts all come due, Burke. You know I love you. And even if you were still nothing but a rough-off artist like you used to be, I'd still love you." She lit a smoke, her face dead serious. "I'd love you because you're right . . . sometimes you have to go down the tunnel even if you don't know what's at the other end."

She blew the smoke at the windshield. Reached over and squeezed my hand. "I don't know what you're doing half the time. I don't think you do either. You're a hard man trying to be a hustler, and you don't always make it. I don't know why you went into that house last year—all I did was make a phone call like you asked. I don't know why you started that whole mess."

"It doesn't matter now," I said. Thinking of the witch-woman, Strega. "It's all over now."

"It doesn't matter why you did it . . . but I know this. You brought me my son. And I'll never forget."

She leaned over to kiss me as the Plymouth pulled to the curb. "If it's out there, I'll find it," she said.

"Michelle . . ."

"What?"

"Use a telescope, okay?"

She just waved a goodbye and moved down the street. Heads turned. Her walk didn't make men want to bite into their palms like Belle's. It pulled at a different piece, but it pulled just as hard.

## 81

IT WAS ALMOST SEVEN-THIRTY by the time I got back to the office. I had the key in the lock when the smell hit me. A hard-sharp smell. I stepped inside. Pansy was at her post, tail wagging, even happier to see me than usual. All the furniture was against one wall. The fake Persian rug was off the wall. The smell was stronger inside.

Belle came in from the back room. Barefoot, wearing only a bra and pants, her hair tied on top of her hand, a rag in one hand.

"You came home too early."

"What in hell is this?"

"It's *almost* a clean office, honey. Lord, this place was dirty—I damn near had to use a chisel on the floor in the back."

"Belle . . ."

"I couldn't get that rug up. And you don't have a vacuum—I should've known. It's some kind of plastic, isn't it? I had to scrub it down. . . . It's still damp—watch where you put your feet."

I walked over to the couch. Sat down. Slowly. Pansy leaped onto the cushions, pressing against me. I patted her head.

Belle came over to me. "That old beast—she followed me around everywhere. Big busybody, poking her nose into everything. She wouldn't hardly let me work."

"I . . ."

"Honey, don't you like it?"

"Yeah. I mean, it's great. I just . . ."

"Take a look," she said, reaching out her hand to me. "Come on."

The bathroom sparkled, the back window gleamed. The floor glistened. The walls were a color I had never seen before. Even the hot plate looked new.

"Damn!"

"It's *good*, huh?"

"It's unbelievable."

"I thought there was another room. Behind the rug on the wall."

"That's what people are supposed to think," I said, half to myself. The surfaces of the file cabinets looked like someone had worked them over with a power sander. My old desk was oiled—you could even see the grain in the wood.

"How'd you do all this?"

"I'm a working fool—always have been. I was raised on work."

"I don't know what to say." It was the truth.

The big girl moved in against me, sharp sweat-smell blending with her natural juices into something way past sweet. "Say what I want to hear," she whispered.

I slipped both hands inside her pants, pulling her tight against me. "Go take a shower," I said.

She ground her hips against me. "That isn't it," she said.

"Trust me."

"I do."

"Well . . . ?"

She pulled back from me, walked toward the back room, shaking her butt like she was on the runway. Pansy shook her head in amazement. "You want out?" I asked her, opening the back door. The beast turned away in disgust—I guess she'd been on the roof a few times since I'd been gone.

I had most of the furniture back in place in a few minutes. I was rehooking the rug on the wall when Belle came out. Nude, beads of water covering yards of pink flesh. She had a towel around her head, holding it in place with her hands.

"I'm all clean."

"Come here," I said, reaching into my jacket pocket.

She came over to the desk, giving her hair one final rub with the towel, then tossing it over to the couch.

"Just stay there for a minute," I said, signaling Pansy to come with me. I dumped everything in the refrigerator into her giant bowl. I added some chocolate-chip cookies and a pint of vanilla ice cream. "Speak!" I told her. It would keep her occupied for a good five minutes.

I went back inside. Belle was standing by the desk, the soul of patience. I stood close to her, holding her face in my hands, looking into her dark eyes.

"Turn around," I said.

She turned her back to me, bent over so her elbows were on the desk, butt in the air.

I stepped in against her, grabbed her shoulders, pulled her back so she was standing up again. "Just do what I tell you," I said.

"I thought . . ."

"Sssh. Close your eyes."

"Okay, I . . ."

"And be quiet."

She stood with her back to me, hands at her sides. So quiet I could hear her breathing.

I took the necklace out of the leather pouch, unhooked the clasp, and slipped it around her neck. I hooked it closed. "Turn around," I told her.

Her eyes were still closed, but her mouth was trembling. The lapis was blue fire against her, falling down just to the top of her breasts. I kissed her on the lips. "Take a look," I whispered to her.

Belle kept her eyes closed, working the necklace with her fingers, feeling the heat. Her eyes came open; she lifted it in her hands, bent her head.

"It's the most pure-beautiful thing I've ever seen in my whole life," she said solemnly. Tears on her face.

"What're you crying about—you don't like it?"

"Don't be such a hard guy," she said, ignoring the tears; "you *know* why."

I kissed her. "Okay. Be a baby if you want to."

"It's your baby I want to be," she said, pushing me to the couch. She dropped into my lap, sprawling across me, covering me, knowing she wouldn't fit and not giving a damn. I snaked a hand around her hip and pulled out the jasmine box. Handed it to her.

"What's this?"

"Open it."

"Oh, it's perfume!"

"Paste, not spray. Here," I said, touching my finger to it, rubbing it between her breasts.

She pulled my head down to her. "How do I smell?" she asked.

"Like juicy flowers," I told her.

She rolled off my lap, pulling at my belt. "I've got some juice for you, baby. Come on, come on!"

# 82

IT WAS AFTER NINE when I looked at my watch. Belle was lying half on top of me on the couch. Pansy was spread out on the floor, looking glum. I rolled off, sliding away from Belle.

I took Pansy to the back door, jumped into the shower, dressed fast. Junior's at eleven, Marques had said.

I leaned over to kiss Belle on my way out. "You going to be okay here?"

"I do love you," is all she said.

The Plymouth hummed, a fast horse on a short rein. Maybe it missed the way Belle drove. Junior's was over the border. Uptown. A players' joint, it wouldn't even start to roll until past midnight. The bar was in shadow, Billie Holiday on the jukebox. "God Bless the Child."

I wasn't going to pull a house-to-house search through the booths. The bartender came over. Slash of white skin across his dark face like a scar.

"Can I help you, Officer?"

"I'm not the Man. I'm looking for Marques. Marques Dupree."

"Nobody by that name here, friend."

"Yeah, there is. He's expecting me. Ask him."

"What name should I call?"

"How many good-looking white men you see in this bar?" I asked him.

He looked me full in the face. "None," he said, moving away.

I lit a cigarette. Felt a tap on my shoulder. Slim blonde woman in a bottle-green sheath. "Burke?"

"Yeah."

"Marques is over this way," she said, moving off.

I followed her to a horseshoe-shaped red leather booth. Marques was sitting at the center, another blonde to his left. The one I had followed moved to his right. I sat facing him.

"My man!" Marques said, not offering his hand. "How's the hijacking business?"

I nodded to him, not answering.

"You come by yourself?" he asked, not looking around, sure of himself on home ground.

"Same way I came into this world," I assured him.

"You packing?"

I let out a breath, disgusted with his bullshit games. "Yeah, I got a machine gun in my pocket."

"Mind if Christina takes a look?"

"Whatever it takes to get on with this."

The blonde who had come over to the bar moved next to me, running her hands over my body. She reached into my crotch, squeezed. "Nobody home, huh?"

I didn't answer her, my eyes on Marques.

She slid back next to him. "He's got three packs of smokes, two lighters, bunch of keys, some folding cash. . . . He's empty."

I watched Marques's teeth flash. "Can't take chances with you gunslingers."

"Ready to talk now?"

"Fire away."

I looked deliberately at the blonde on his left. Turned my head, looked the same way at the one on his right.

"My ladies are cool—you can talk in front of them."

I shrugged, putting a pack of cigarettes and a butane lighter on the table in front of me. I lit another smoke, snapping off a wooden match. He didn't pay attention. That's why he was a pimp and I was what I was.

"You know a man named Mortay?"

"The fighter?"

"Yeah."

"I don't know him. Man, I don't *want* to know him. He's not on my list—I don't let my women mess with no freaks."

"What's that mean?"

"I saw him do his thing, man. It was unreal. He fought this other dude. . . ."

"The Japanese guy. In the basement under Sin City?"

"Right on. I didn't even know what the entertainment was going to be, but it was on the wire that it was a big thing, you know? I had to make the scene. Get down, be around. When you set the style, you got to show it off."

"Yeah, right. You saw the whole thing?"

"The whole thing. This Mortay, man, that's a scary dude. Moves like a fucking ghost."

"That may be the connect, Marques."

"I'm not reading you, man."

"Read this: One of my people was looking around. On that job you and me talked about?"

"Yeah?"

"And he met Mortay. I don't know if it was just a territory thing, wrong guy in the wrong place . . . maybe so. It happens to all of us."

"So?"

"So Mortay warned him off. Maybe he's front-ending the thing. Guarding the van."

Marques snapped his fingers. The blonde on the left pulled a vial from her purse, tapped out some white powder on a mirror. She cut it into four lines with a gold razor blade, put it in front of Marques. He rolled a bill into a tight straw, snorted a line up each nostril. Each of the blondes took a remaining line for herself. The pimp looked across at me, letting the coke rush around inside his head.

"I can't see it, man. You're off the wall."

"Could be. What if I'm not?"

"Look, man. We had a deal. You're working for *me*. I pay, you play my tune."

"Watch your back, Marques," I said, starting to get up.

"Hey! Hold up, I'm not downing you. Just lay it out, okay? Why you here?"

"I'm here because you know things I don't know. And you can find out things I can't. I don't want any more to do with this Mortay than you do. But if I'm going to do the job on the van, I need to know if he's in the play."

"How would I know?"

"I'll find that part out myself. What I need is whatever you can find out about Mortay. *Anything* could do some good—I won't know till I get it. He's out there—he has to live someplace, hang out someplace. I'm not asking you to walk the wire, just listen to what you hear, okay?"

"I don't know, man."

I felt like breaking his face. I lit another cigarette, centering myself, coming to what would work. I kept my voice quiet, letting another pitch take over, working the corners. "Marques, there isn't another player in this town with your weight. You want to take the Ghost Van off the streets, protect your women—I respect that. You know your game—I know mine. That's why we got together, right? We're partners on this thing. Now I need your help. That's why I came here. This Mortay, he had people with him. Guy named Ramón, for one. If they show anywhere on the set, somebody'll scope them out. All I want is for you to use your network—you don't have to get out of your Rolls-Royce—just let it come to you. And pass it along."

The pimp sat like he was considering, basking in the praise. "I'm the one that can get the lowdown, no question about it."

"None at all," I agreed.

"All right, hijacker. I don't promise nothing, but I'll get back to you if something comes up."

"Thanks," I said, getting up to go again. Putting the butane lighter back in my pocket. I don't use it to light cigarettes.

The blondes never said a word. Good bitches. Whores in their hearts. Renting out what they never owned.

## 83

I SLIPPED THE PLYMOUTH through Times Square on the way back. Sin City was a monster building squatting in the middle of a long block. It stood four neon-faced stories high, towering over the storefront-sized sleaze shops on either side. I stopped at the corner. A black stringbean sporting a red porkpie hat was hunched over a folding table covered with gold chains. Cesspool Specials: the chains were broken, so the suckers would think they'd been snatched on the subway. The hustler breaks the chains himself—nobody snatches gold-plated junk. "Check it out!" he called to the passing pack of slugs. He wouldn't be there tomorrow.

I motored slowly around the block—couldn't see the back of Sin City from the other side. The buildings were packed tighter than the crowd at a lynching.

The Prof felt the pain before Mortay ever touched him. That kind of power leaves a scent.

But only to those he marked.

Tenth Avenue was quiet. Eleventh was alive with working girls. The river was only a block away. A black woman in a blond wig strolled up to the Plymouth. Red spandex pants, a matching halter top, red heels. All yesterday's stuff, like she was.

"You want some action, baby?"

I let her come close, watching the other girls through the windshield, trying to get the feel of the street. It felt calm—didn't make sense. The Plymouth sat through the green light; the pross took it for a signal. She leaned into the window, folding her arms under her breasts to poke them forward.

"What you say, honey. Fifty takes you around the world."

I looked in her face, keeping my voice low.

"You got a room?"

"We just drive around the block, honey. Nice dark places to park—take all the time you need."

"Around here? Haven't you heard about the Ghost Van?"

She laughed. Hard and bitter. "The Ghost Van don't eat no dark meat, baby."

It started to hit me then. I feathered the gas pedal and the Plymouth moved off, leaving the whore alone in the street.

## 84

PAST MIDNIGHT. I FOUND a phone, rang Mama's.

"It's me."

"Nobody call."

"Okay."

"Max has your money."

"You keeping him close?"

"Yes. Keep close. Waiting for you."

"I'll call you tomorrow."

"Burke?"

"What?"

"Nice girl you bring here. Nice big girl."

"Yeah."

I put the phone down. Dialed the Mole. I heard the phone being picked up, nothing on the other end. The way he always answers.

"It's me. I need to come see you tomorrow night—talk something over. I'm bringing someone with me—someone you need to meet. Okay?"

"Eight o'clock," said the Mole, hanging up.

## 85

IT HIT ME AS SOON AS I stepped out of the back staircase into the hallway. The electricity started at the base of my spine. It shot upward in little jolts, forming a T-bar at my neck, firing out to my shoulders. My hands trembled. I knew what it was—an old friend. Fear.

I opened the door. The office was pitch-dark. Pansy was standing at her post, wire-tight, eyes glowing. The hair on the back of her neck was standing straight up. I closed the door behind me, hit the light switch.

Belle was on the couch—on her knees, a butcher knife in her hand.

"What happened?" I asked her.

"Somebody rang the bell downstairs. It buzzed up here. Maybe twenty minutes ago. I didn't answer it. I killed all the lights, turned off the radio. Then those strobes, the ones above the door, they started flashing."

"Somebody coming up the stairs."

"That's what it was. Pansy, she ran right over to where she is, making these ugly low sounds. Like a gator eating a pig. I got scared."

"Anybody try and get in?"

"No. They just pounded on the door. Real loud. I thought the dog would bark, but she just stayed where she was. Like she was waiting."

"She was."

"They rattled the doorknob—you know, just shaking it, like they were mad. There were at least two of them; I could hear the talking."

"You hear what they said?"

"No. I was scared to move from here—I didn't want to get in the dog's way—she looked crazy. But one had like this Mexican accent."

"How long'd they stay?"

"Just a minute, maybe—but it seemed longer. The strobes went off again. It's been quiet since then."

"And you're still on the couch?" I asked, as I walked over to her, put my hands on her shoulders.

She looked up at me. "Burke, I don't know much, but I know about men. You learn to tell. From little things. The guy talking—the Mexican—he was one of those nasty men you see in the club sometimes. The way they look at you—like screams would make them smile."

"I know. You did the right thing." I gave her a smile, my thumb under her chin. "What were you going to do with that knife?"

"I didn't know what to do . . . but I could see the dog knew. Where she was standing, they'd walk in right past her. I figured they come toward me, and Pansy'd just blind-side them."

"That's what she'd do all right. But she'd do the same thing if you hid in the back room."

"I was going to give her a hand," Belle said, her hands still shaking but no tremble in her voice.

I cupped a breast. It overflowed my hand. "There's a big heart under this big thing," I said.

"It's yours."

"Which?" I asked, squeezing her breast.

"Both. But only one's for playing with," the big girl said, eyes locked on mine.

I kissed the bridge of her nose, between her eyes. She put her face against my chest. I held her for a minute, making up my mind.

I let go of Belle, threw the signal to Pansy to pull her away from her post. Opened the back door to let her out to the roof.

"Get ready to go," I told Belle, opening drawers, filling my pockets.

# 86

IN THE GARAGE, SHE watched quietly as I lifted the rubber floor mat, spun the wing nuts, and put the pistol inside the hollowed-out space near the transmission hump.

"You remember how to get to your place from here?"

"Sure. I couldn't tell you how to do it, but I can take the car there."

I checked the back of the garage. The street was quiet. Belle backed the Plymouth out. I hit the switch and the door closed behind us.

The Plymouth tracked through the empty streets. Belle handled it like it was a baby carriage. I lit a cigarette, putting it together. Any fool could get into my building from the front—just press the hippics' bell in the middle of the night and they'd buzz you in. It wasn't a customer—they'd come in even when my bell hadn't been answered. Spanish accent. Pounding on the door, but they hadn't tried to break in. Lupe would have told them about my dog.

"Anybody with us?" I asked Belle, not looking around.

"No," she said, her eyes flicking to the mirrors. "Not since we pulled out."

## 87

AS SOON AS WE WALKED in the door, I grabbed the phone. Mama answered like it was noon.

"They called, right?"

"Yes. Man say playground, behind the Chelsea Projects. Midnight tomorrow."

"Spanish accent?"

"Yes. Nasty man. Whisper on phone, like those men who call women, you know?"

"Yeah, I know. You say anything to him?"

"Nothing to say. You want Max now?"

"No! Mama, this is a bad play. You keep him close, like we said."

"If . . ."

"Mama, listen. Listen to me. If Max comes in now, it could be trouble for the baby, okay?"

She said something in Chinese. I didn't need a translator. "Later, Mama," I told her, hanging up.

Belle came over to the phone as I was lighting a smoke. "Me too," she said, holding my hand, guiding the match. She was wearing a white T-shirt that came halfway down to her thighs, the blue necklace around her neck.

"I'll be right back," I told her, reaching for my car keys.

"Let me . . ."

"Stay here," I told her.

She dropped to her knees, holding her hands out in front of her, bent at the wrists like dog's paws.

"Don't be so fucking smart," I said. "I'll be back in a couple of minutes—I need a pay phone."

## 88

I THREW IN A QUARTER, listened to the woman say something in Spanish.

"Dr. Pablo Cintrone," I said. Waited patiently for a long rap about how the doctor wasn't in at that hour of the night, but if it was an emergency . . .

"*Attention!*" I barked into the receiver. "Dr. Cintrone. Burke. *Teléfono cuatro*. Ten o'clock tomorrow morning, *por favo*r. Okay?"

The voice never changed tone. "Burke. *Teléfono cuatro*. Ten o'clock tomorrow morning."

"*Gracias*."

She hung up.

When a citizen's scared, he calls the cops. Where I live, you call a terrorist.

## 89

THE FRONT DOOR WAS unlocked. I shut it behind me, walked through the cottage. Belle was out on the deck. I leaned on the railing, looking across the black water. Belle moved in next to me, fingering the necklace.

"You know why I danced in front of men?"

"Yes."

"I know you do. You're the first man who ever looked at my face after I took my clothes off." She pulled the cigarette from my mouth. Took a drag, handed it back.

"Nothing on this earth means anything all by itself. You know those orchids they sell in fancy flower shops? They grow wild in the swamp near where I was raised. And gator hide . . . It costs so much to make a little purse out of it, but the big old things are out there thick as mosquitoes. You know about gators?"

"Not much."

"Baby gators, they ain't got much of a chance. It's easy to find the eggs—the mama gators just bury 'em and they walk away. Most of them don't make it even if the eggs do hatch. When they're born, they're only a couple of inches long. The big birds grab them up. Bobcats, panthers, coons, damn near everything in the swamp feasts on them. Baby gators, they're not like puppies or kittens. You know the difference between a six-inch baby gator and a six-foot bull?"

"No," I said. Her face was turned in profile, tiny flat nose just a bump.

"Five and a half feet. They don't grow, they just get bigger, you understand?"

"Yeah."

"What they say about gators . . . Most of the little ones, they never get to be big ones, what with everything out there trying to eat them and all. The ones that do get their full growth—they spend the rest of their lives getting even."

"I know people like that."

"I thought I was like that too, once. But it's not the whole world I need to get square with."

"I know."

She moved against me, hip bumping gently. "There's things inside me. Bad things. In my blood and in my bones. I'll never have babies and I'll never get old. You're good with words, but there's things you don't like to say."

"I don't understand."

"Yeah, you do. Remember when I wanted you to taste me? When we first came together? I've met plenty of men good at romance, but I never met one any good at love. You're what I want, and you can't do things but one way. Your way."

"Belle, I . . ."

She pressed her fingers against my mouth. "Don't say anything. You already said all I need you to say. I'm with you to the end. Just make me one promise?"

"What?"

Tears rolled down her face, but her voice was steady. "I know you have people. I don't have anybody. If my time comes, you settle my debts. Pay them off."

"I will."

"One more thing. Just one more thing, and I'm going to give you my life, Burke. I'll never take my clothes off for another man again. And I'll never take this necklace off either. You see that I'm buried in it."

"Cut it out," I said, smacking her on the rump, trying for a smile.

She turned her face to me, holding my shirt with both hands. "Now's not the time for that. You can't change what's going to happen. You *promise* me. Promise me right now. I married the outlaw life—I've got a right to be buried in my wedding dress."

"I promise, Belle."

She pulled me close, her mouth butterfly-soft against mine. "My mother saved my heart for me. She died to do it. I waited a long time. I'm giving it to you now. And I'll die to do it too."

I held her against me in the dark. For that little piece of time, I didn't have to call on the ice god of hate to fight the fear.

# 90

BELLE FELL ASLEEP HOLDING me in her mouth. The bedside clock said four. I set it for six, stubbed out my last cigarette, and drifted off.

When the alarm went off, I was sleeping on my side. Belle was wrapped around my back. I slapped the clock to shut off the buzzer. The morning light was just coming through. Belle reached down for me, holding me in her hand, whispering in my ear.

"When I went shopping . . . to buy all that stuff to clean your office . . . I bought something else. A surprise for you. Something to give you nobody else has ever had. I was going to give it to you last night, when you came back. But you came back with my necklace. And all that other stuff happened. It's still here for you. Special. But not now," she said, stroking me, "not now. When your blood's up."

I felt myself grow in her hand. "Seems like it's up to me," I said.

She laughed, a rich laugh from her belly, moving against me. "When your *blood's* up, honey. I'll know. But as far as this other thing . . ." The big girl pushed against my shoulder, shoving me flat on my back, swinging one huge leg over me, her hand guiding me inside. "Come on, now," she whispered, her teeth in my shoulder.

## 91

AN HOUR LATER, WE WERE moving into the city. I had to be at the pay phone in the lobby of the Criminal Court before ten. The last phone in the long bank near the back wall. *Teléfono cuatro.*

There were only two places in the city I could go for what I needed. This freak I had to meet could call himself "death" if that's what got his rocks off, but I knew a guy who earned the title. A guy we did time with years ago. A guy who let the ice god into his soul like I'd wanted to. A guy named Wesley. Even saying his name in my mind made my hands shake. The other choice was the UGL.

Una Gente Libre—A Free People. Puerto Rican terrorists to the *federales*, hard-core *independentistas* to their people. The FBI had been trying to get a man inside for years—they'd have better luck getting Jimmy Hoffa to testify. The UGL didn't blow up buildings. They didn't write letters to the newspapers. Some of them fought in the mountains of their home, some in the city canyons of America. Their New York territory stretched from East Harlem to the Bronx. They kept their plate clean. You try to sell crack on their streets, you *get* cracked. You come back again, you get iced. The Colombians didn't like that much. One of their honchos sent a crew into UGL turf. Sprayed the streets with machine guns. Dropped five people, one of them a pregnant woman. The next day, the crack salesmen were back, stopping the BMWs and Mercedeses full of mobile slime on their way to the suburbs. Smiling. Three days later, the first salesman who showed up pushed his way through a crowd packed around a fire hydrant. The honcho's head was sitting on top of the fireplug like a bust in a museum display case. Whoever hacked it off hadn't been a surgeon. The last thing the salesman left on that street was his puke.

Dr. Pablo Cintrone was a psychiatrist. *New York* magazine did a profile on him once. Harvard Medical School graduate who returned to the mean streets to minister to his people. It made him sort of a hero to the upscale crowd for a couple of weeks. Not too many people in Spanish Harlem or the South Bronx read the magazine, but they knew El Jefe of the UGL.

# 92

INSIDE THE OFFICE, I LET Pansy out to the roof while I checked the security systems. Nobody'd made a move on the place last night.

I changed into a dark pin-striped suit, grabbed a leather attaché case. It wouldn't get anybody's attention if I stood by the pay phone in the Criminal Court waiting for it to ring.

When Pansy saw the leash, she spun in a circle, dancing for joy. I hooked her up and we all went down the back stairs.

First stop was the hospital. I left Pansy in the back seat, taking Belle's hand.

"Is she going to be all right back there?"

"What could happen to her?" I asked, reasonably enough.

The Prof was sitting up in bed, half a dozen pillows propped up behind him. His legs were still in casts, but lying flat on the bed. A metal bar ran between the casts. I looked a question.

"To make sure they stay straight until the casts come off," he said.

"How you doing?"

"Not as sweet as drinking wine, not as bad as doing time."

"We got something," I said, moving close to the bed.

The little man's eyes shifted to where Belle was standing against the wall. I held out my hand behind me, not turning my head. She came up and took it. "She's with us," I told him. "She's in this."

He flashed his smile at her. "This your man, little girl?"

Her smile blazed back. "He surely is."

"That makes me your brother-in-law, darlin'. Soon's we finish this fight, I'll show you the sights."

She leaned over and kissed him. "I'll be waiting."

Belle sat on the bed. It didn't shift more than half a foot. I pulled up the chair, keeping my voice down.

"Mortay called. We got a meet tonight."

"Where?"

"Playground back of the Chelsea Projects."

"Skinner heaven."

"I know."

"I don't like it. If he don't buy the play, how you gonna walk away?"

"I need a shooter. With a night scope. On the roof."

"The only one I know is . . ."

"Not Wesley. I'll get someone else—I got it covered." The Prof didn't know about my connect to UGL.

His voice dropped even lower. "You going to dust him?"

"No way. Just make sure he gets the word—I want to tell him we got no beef. Walk away. The shooter is in case he wants to try and send another of his freakish messages."

"Burke, I'm telling you, this Mortay . . ."

"I got it covered," I told him again. "You hear anything?"

"Got some promises, but no product."

"I'll see you tomorrow."

He put his hand on mine. "Burke, listen to me like you used to on the yard. You want to roll the dice, make it nice."

"I got it," I said, throwing him a salute.

## 93

I HELD THE DOOR FOR BELLE to get into the car. "He's really so much better, isn't he?"

"He's better, but he's not back to himself yet."

"You'd expected him to be dancing by now?"

"Not the physical thing. The Prof, he's like two people. Half is this rhyming-time, upbeat thing you see, okay? The other half is how he got his name. Like a religious thing—I don't have a name for it. He got his name because he can *see* things."

"Like what's going to happen?"

"Sort of. Like I said, I can't really explain it. But he can preach, square business. Talk that religion like he means it. Strong enough to make you buy a piece sometimes, when he really gets on a roll. That's what's missing now."

Belle tapped fingernails on one knee, paying attention, listening close. She turned to look at me. "Maybe he don't like what he sees comin'," she said, the Southern-swamp tang strong in her voice.

## 94

I PULLED THE PLYMOUTH into the parking lot across from the Criminal Court. The parking lot where I met Strega for the first time. The court where I first saw Wolfe in action. It was nine-forty-five—all the spaces were taken.

"Cruise around the lot like you're looking for a place to park," I told Belle. "You find one, pull in. Watch for me—I'll be coming down those steps," I said, pointing across Centre Street. "You see me coming, catch my eye. We may have to move out right away."

I gave Pansy the signal. She flopped down in the back seat, filling it to capacity.

I crossed the street, grabbed the phone I wanted. I picked up the receiver, holding down the hook, and acted like I was listening to someone on the other end, glancing at my watch.

I knew my watch was accurate, because it read ten o'clock just as the phone rang. I released the hook.

"Can I see you? Today?"

"*Muy importante*?"

"*Sí.*"

"Handball court closest to Metropolitan. One o'clock."

"Thanks."

I was talking to a dead line.

## 95

I CAME DOWN THE STEPS, spotted the Plymouth making a slow circuit. I caught it on the second pass, opened the door. Belle rolled out to Lafayette Street, turned south, in the direction of the office.

"I don't have to get moving until around noon," I told her. "But I need the car when I do."

"I'll go with you."

"No, you won't. And get that pout off your face."

She didn't. "Make a right," I told her as we came to Worth Street. "Head down to the river."

Pansy poked her head over the top of the front seat. "Want to run, girl?" I asked her. She growled.

I showed Belle where to pull in. There were only a few cars on the broad strip of concrete, the usual collection of humans minding other people's business. I opened the back door, hooked Pansy's leash, and we strolled along the river. Her snout wrinkled at the smells, but she held her position. On my left side, slightly ahead. Every time I stopped, she sat. When we got to the deserted pier, I let her off the lead, making a circle with my hand, telling her not to roam far. Freed of the restraint of the leash, she did what comes naturally to her. Lay down.

"You lazy old thing," Belle said. She looked around, her eyes sweeping the Jersey shore on the other side. "Sure doesn't smell like any water I ever saw."

"It's not water—just a liquid toxic-waste dump."

"You can't swim in it?"

"No. But on a good day, you could walk on it."

"Ugh!"

A sailboat went by, loaded with yuppies in yachting gear. Sailboats down here make about as much sense as No Smoking sections in L.A. restaurants, so you see a lot of them.

Belle pointed to one of the round beams that held up the pier. "Boost me up," she said, one foot in the air. I cupped my hands and she stepped in, reaching to the top of the beam. I heaved, and up she went. It wasn't as bad as loading trucks, and the view was a lot better. I lit a smoke, handed it up to her. The breeze pulled at her hair, pulling it off her face. She turned to the side, sucking in a deep breath. I took one of my own—no Viking ship ever had a prouder figurehead.

Two teenagers pulled up, riding those little motor scooters you see everyplace. They stopped a decent distance, watching Pansy.

"What kind of dog is that?" the taller one asked.

"One that bites," I told him.

"He looks like a giant pit bull."

"Close enough."

"Where could I get one?"

"You can't."

The shorter one piped up. "He looks like a big lump to me. That ain't no pit bull."

"Pansy, watch!" I snapped at her.

She came slowly to her feet and strolled toward the kids, making her noises. I never heard an alligator eat a pig, but I knew what Belle meant. She pinned the boys with her ice-water eyes, one skull-crusher of a paw pulling at the concrete.

"Jump!" I yelled at her. The kids took off before she hit the deck. She looked over at me, bored to death. I made a circle sign again. This time she took off, loping the length of the boards, peering over the edge into the water. She jogged back, stopping at the beam where Belle perched. The beast leaped up, her paws locking into the wood a foot below Belle. She reached down and patted her. "Does she want me to come down?"

"I think she wants to come up."

"There's no room."

"Maybe that's a message."

Belle jumped down from her perch, landing next to me. "What message?" she said, bunching a small fist.

"That they should make those beams bigger."

"Or these smaller?" she asked, smacking herself on the rear.

"Wouldn't be my choice," I assured her.

She took my arm and we walked around some more, Pansy hanging close.

"She's so beautiful. She really is like a panther, the way she moves. So smooth."

I lit a smoke, thinking it was the truth.

"Burke, how come you got a female dog?"

I shrugged.

"Well, she's for protection, right? A guard dog? I thought they were all males. I thought they were tougher, you know? A man I knew once, he had a German shepherd. Wouldn't have a female dog around him—said a bitch would turn tail and run from a fight."

"He's a moron. Male dogs, they smell a bitch in heat, you know what they want to do?"

"Sure."

"No, you don't. What they want to do is fight every other male dog around. In the wild, they run in packs. The way the pack stays alive, they only let the strongest bulls mate with the bitches. So the litters are strong too. The way they see who the strongest dog is they fight it out."

She put her head against my shoulder. "Maybe they're right."

"They're right for dogs. Not for people. I grew up like that. It took me a lot of years and a lot of scars before I snapped that a good woman won't make you fight over her."

"I worked with girls like that. Fire-starters. Blood makes them come."

She swayed against me, pulling me to a stop along the pier. "Is that why you have a girl dog? So she won't want to fight other dogs and all?"

"Males are just no good. Any kind of male. A man'll fuck a chain-link fence."

She patted my pockets, took out a cigarette. I cupped a wooden match against the wind for her. She sat on the bench. Pansy jumped up next to her. I sat on the other side.

Belle looked at the water. "The man who said a bitch would turn tail—that's what he wanted me to do. I never had much of my own. Things you buy . . . they're not really yours. But I own what I do. He found out too."

"What happened?"

"I cut him. Cut him good."

We walked back to the Plymouth. "You want to wait at the office for me?"

"Me and Pansy," she said.

## 96

BACK AT THE OFFICE, Belle looked at the street maps rolled up in a corner. "Can I tack these on the wall?"

"Sure. I was going to do it anyway. Why?"

"I want to learn the city."

"Okay. I'll be back in a couple of hours, maybe more."

I moved to the door.

"Honey?"

"What?"

"Come here for a minute. Sit with me."

I sat on the couch. She put her head in my lap, looked up at me. "Can I ask you something?"

"Sure."

"What I told you, about my mother and my father and all? Is that the worst thing you ever heard?"

I thought about kiddie porn. About selling little boys in Times Square. Rapists. Child molesters. Snuff films. The tape looped inside my head. I hit the stop button. "It's not close," I told her. "Everybody's pain is the worst thing in the world for them. Your mother really loved you. *Died* for you—you always have that."

"You think I'm . . . sick."

"No. I think you're hurt. And, one day, we'll fix that."

"I love you."

I bent to kiss her. "I've got to go," I said.

She pressed her head down against me. "Tell me something worse. Tell me something worse than what he did."

"It'd be worse for someone else, baby. Like I told you. Everybody has their own. Good and bad."

She came to her knees next to me. "Tell me the worst thing. The worst thing you know."

I looked in her face, talking quietly. I'd had enough of this crazy game. "People steal babies, Belle. Little tiny babies—they steal them from their parents. And they never bring them back."

"What do they do with them?"

"They sell most of them. Some of the pretty white kids, they sell them to nice rich folks who want a baby of their own. Black-market adoption."

"What about the others?"

"You know what a chop shop is?"

"Where they steal cars, break them down for parts?"

"Yeah. They have them for babies too. They sell the white babies. The other ones, they're not worth too much for adoption, so they cut them up for parts."

"Burke!"

"Rich baby needs a heart transplant, a new kidney, you think they care where the organs come from?"

"I don't believe you!"

"The world I live in, it's a lot deeper underground than any subway. It's a world where you can buy a baby's heart."

I held her against me. "Don't ask questions so much, little girl. I only got ugly answers."

She pulled back from me, dry-eyed. "You saw this? You saw this yourself?"

"Yeah. Guy's kid was in the hospital. Dying. Needed a transplant. It was in the papers, on TV. Looking for a donor. Baby only had a few days to live. He got a call. They promised him a baby's heart. Fresh. All packed and ready for transport to the hospital. Twenty-five thousand, they wanted. He made some calls—a lot of calls. A cop I know sent him to me. I went down the tunnel."

"What happened? Did they have the heart?"

"Just like they promised."

"You took it? The baby was saved?"

"Yeah."

She nodded. "Damn their souls to hell."

"I don't do souls," I told her. "Just bodies."

## 97

THE HANDBALL COURT WAS in the shadows of Metropolitan Hospital, just off 96th Street near the East River. Once the tip of Spanish Harlem, it was now liberated territory—the yuppie land-grab machine wouldn't be satisfied until gentrification ate the South Bronx. I liked it better the old way, when the human beings lived in the tenements and investment bankers lived in the suburbs. Now we got plenty of rehab apartments for tomorrow's leaders. And more people living in the streets than they have in Calcutta.

I parked under the East Side Drive overpass and walked over to the court. Ten minutes to one. I watched people playing: handball, paddleball, basketball. No stickball. People working too. Working the cars. Selling flowers, newspapers, clean windshields. Ninety-sixth Street was the DMZ when I was coming up. North was theirs, South was ours. Now it all belongs to someone else—they just let us play there while they're at work downtown.

"These chumps can't play no basketball." A voice behind me. Pablo. The lack of a single Puerto Rican in the NBA makes him crazy.

He was wearing his white doctor's coat over a black turtleneck, his round face looking the same way it did when he walked out of Harvard fifteen years ago.

"*Gracias, compadre*," I said, thanking him for coming.

He shook hands the way he always does, using both of his.

"Something bad?" he asked me, standing close.

"I have to meet a man. Tonight. He hurt one of my brothers. He said it was a message. I don't know what's on his mind. I want to walk away—tell him I got no beef with him. But he might not go for it."

"You have Max."

"Can't use him for this, Pablo. It may be Max he wants. He's a *karateka*. Been going around the city, challenging sensei in their own dojos. Max, I think his name may be in the street over this. You know Lupe? The guy who sets up the cockfights?"

Pablo spat on the ground. "I know him. *Mamao*. A punk. Tough talk—no *cojones*."

"He set up a match. Between this guy I have to meet and a Jap. Duel to the death."

"I heard about that. In Times Square?"

"Yeah. That's what I mean. Seems like everybody's heard about it. Max fights this guy, he's got no win. Probably have cops in the audience."

Pablo looked at me. "Max wouldn't walk away from a challenge."

"So he doesn't get to hear one."

"I see. You want your back covered when you meet this guy . . ."

"Mortay."

"*Muerte*?"

"Yeah. I don't know how he spells it, but it means the same thing."

"He's not a problem for us?"

"Not for you. Not now. I'm working on something, and I just bumped him accidentally. How he's tied in—*if* he's tied in—I don't know for sure."

"You chasing a missing kid?"

"Dead kids. The Ghost Van."

Pablo's round face went hard. His eyes were dark, flat buttons behind his round glasses. "Baby-killers. That van comes into our *barrio*, we'll *make* it a ghost."

"It just works off the river, near Times Square. I got a lot of threads, but no cloth."

"This Mortay . . . he knows?"

"I don't know. I'm not gonna ask him. He lets me walk, I'm gonna promise him I won't come his way again. He wants me off the van, I'm off the van."

"That's what you'll *tell* him."

"Yeah," I said, lighting a smoke.

"What time is your meet?"

"Midnight tonight. The playground behind the Chelsea Projects."

"How many people do you need?"

"Just one," I told him. "El Cañonero."

Pablo's lips moved. Just a tic. Nothing else showed in his face. "He only does our work."

"I don't want him to take anybody out. Just be around, break a couple of caps if he has to. He can do it from a distance. I figure maybe the roof . . ."

"He only does our work. He is not for hire. My people are soldiers, not gangsters."

"They do what you say."

"They follow me because they follow the truth. My personal friendship is with you, *hermano*. I can commit only myself."

I put my hand on his shoulder. "I understand what you say. I respect what you say. But there are two reasons why he should do this."

"Yes?"

"He does only your work. More than once, I have also done your work, this is true?"

"True."

"El Cañonero does this work tonight for UGL, it is UGL I owe. *Comprende*?"

He nodded. Rubbed the back of his neck like it was stiff. A young Hispanic woman in a blue jogging outfit stopped her slow circuit of the courts and trotted over. He took her aside, speaking in rapid-fire

Spanish. She took off, running hard now, heading for the street.

We watched the basketball game. It wasn't in the same league as the semipro action at the court on Sixth Avenue in the Village, but it was intense. I asked him about his kids. Pablo's got a lot of kids—the oldest one's in college, his baby girl's still in diapers. He's never been married. Takes care of all his children. He never seems to make anybody mad with all his tomcat stuff, not even the women who have his babies. Most of them know each other.

I met Pablo in prison. He wasn't doing time—he was doing his residency in psychiatry. His supervisor was a wet-brain who did five-minute interviews with the cons before they saw the Parole Board. And handed out heavyweight tranquilizers any time they shoved the Rx pad under his nose. I was the wet-brain's clerk—a scam artist's dream job. Five crates of cigarettes and you got the prescription of your choice, twenty crates bought you a "fully rehabilitated" write-up for the Board. It only took Pablo a month to read my act, but he never said a word. I was on to him faster than that. He wasn't studying mental illness among convicts—he was recruiting.

The woman in the jogging suit ran back to us, pulled Pablo aside. Pablo turned to me. "You parked close by?"

"Under the overpass," I said, pointing.

"Sit on the hood. Smoke one of your cigarettes. See you in ten minutes."

He walked off with the woman.

# 98

THREE SMOKES LATER, a black Lincoln sedan pulled up. Dark windows, M.D. plates. The front door popped open and I stepped inside. The woman was driving. I glanced in the back seat. Pablo. And El Cañonero.

"*Vete*," Pablo said. The Lincoln moved off.

Pablo's voice came from the back seat. "Turn around, *compadre*.

My *hermano* needs to memorize your face."

I turned full-face to the back. El Cañonero was a short, stocky Hispanic, not as dark as Pablo. He had straight, coal-black hair. Pablo once told me Puerto Ricans were a mixture of all the world's races. Looking at the two men in the back seat, I could see the African in Pablo, the Incan in El Cañonero. The shooter's face was featureless except for heavy cheekbones. But I'd seen his eyes before. On a tall, lanky man from West Virginia. Sniper's eyes—measuring distances.

The Lincoln worked its way downtown. We pulled to a stop across from the playground.

Kids were running everywhere. Little kids screaming, chasing each other, bigger kids in a stickball game. Teenagers against the fence, smoking dope, listening to a giant portable stereo. Pablo jerked his thumb. We got out, leaned against the car.

The gate to the park would be closed at midnight. Wire mesh—it wouldn't keep anybody out.

El Cañonero's eyes swept the scene. He said something in Spanish to Pablo, who just nodded.

I saw the man against the wire mesh. A medium-sized white man with a baseball cap on his head. Watching the kids play. He was wearing a yellow sweater, the sleeves pushed up almost to his elbows. I focused in on him, lighting a smoke. He had a heavy rubber band around one wrist. He pulled at it again and again with his other hand, snapping it against the inside of his wrist. I nudged Pablo, pointing at the man with a tilt of my head.

"Aversive therapy," I sneered.

His face went hard. "They should've tied the rubber band around his throat."

El Cañonero grunted a question. Pablo explained it to him. I couldn't follow the words, but I knew what he was saying. They have programs where they try "conditioning" on child molesters. The idea is to show them a lot of pictures of kids—then blast them with an electric jolt when the freaks get aroused. Nobody believes it works. When they discharge one of the freaks, they tell him to wear a rubber band around his wrist. When he feels himself getting excited over a kid, he's supposed to snap the band—reactivate his conditioning.

The shooter's eyes bored in on the man in the yellow sweater. "*Maricón!*" he snarled. Pablo launched into another speech. A child molester isn't a homosexual; most gays hate them too. El Cañonero listened, flat-faced. I heard my name. The shooter nodded. Then he held out his hand. I shook it. Pablo must have told him what I did.

Pablo leaned over to me. "We're going around the back, take a look. You stay here with Elena."

"I want to talk to the freak. Just take a minute."

"*Sí*" He gestured for the woman to move close. "Elena, that man over there, he is a molester of children. He is the wolf, stalking the baby chickens. My *compadre* wants to approach him, get a good look at his face, so *el gusano* will know he is known to us. Perhaps threaten him with violence, okay?"

She nodded. Pablo and El Cañonero moved off.

"Do you speak any English?" I asked the woman.

"I *teach* English," she said, nothing on her face.

"I didn't mean to offend you."

"You could not offend me. Just say what you want me to do."

I told her. I held out my hand. She took it, moving smoothly against me as we crossed the street.

Elena left me and moved off behind the freak. He stayed glued to the fence. I wrapped my hand around the roll of quarters in my pocket, moving my shoulder against the freak, slipping my left hand behind his back.

"Kids are cute, huh?"

He jumped like he'd been stabbed. "What?"

I snatched a handful of his sweater, locking his belt from behind, shoving my face into his, my voice cell-block hard. "When did they let you out, freak?"

"Hey! I didn't . . ."

I pushed him against the fence, my face jammed into his. "Don't come back to this playground, scumbag. We've been watching you. We know you. We know what you do. You do it again, you're dog meat. Got it?"

The freak twisted his head away from me. I looked where he was looking. At Elena. Standing three feet from us in her blue jogging suit, hands buried in the pockets of the sweatshirt. She took out her left hand, pulled up the waistband. A little black pistol was in her other hand. The freak whipped his head back to me. I pulled him away from the fence, bringing my right hand around in a short hook to his gut. He made a gagging sound, dropped to the ground. I went down on one knee next to him. His face was against the pavement, vomiting.

"We know your face, freak," I said quietly. "Next time we see you, you're done."

I stomped my heel hard into the side of his face; it made a squishy sound. Nobody gave us a look. When we climbed back inside the Lincoln, Pablo and El Cañonero were already in the back seat. Elena took the wheel and we moved off.

The rifleman tapped my shoulder. I turned around. He nodded his head once, a sharp, precise movement.

The Lincoln dropped me off at my car. Pablo got out with me. He handed me a strip of cloth, Day-Glo orange.

"Tie this around your head when you walk into the playground tonight. Bring a couple of bottles of beer. Pull your car into the playground, put the bottles on the hood. You raise your hand, one of the beer bottles blows up. This Mortay, he'll know you're covered."

"Thanks, Pablito. I owe you."

"El Cañonero said to tell you he'll be on the roof by eleven."

"Okay."

"He said to ask you something. . . . If it gets bad . . . if this guy won't be warned off . . . if he comes for you . . . you want El Cañonero to drop him or just fade?"

"Drop him."

"*Bueno*."

## 99

I HEADED BACK DOWNTOWN, stopped at Mama's. She took a long time to come to my booth. When she did, Immaculata was with her. They slid across from me. Mac didn't waste any time.

"Burke, is there trouble for Max?"

"I don't know. I'll know soon," I told her, stabbing Mama with my eyes. She stared right back. I shouldn't have mentioned the baby.

"You'll tell me as soon as you know?"

"Will you give me a fucking *chance* to head it off first?"

She reached across the table, took, my hand. "I will. And I'll keep Max close for a few more days. Don't blame Mama. She told him you were working on something and he keeps pushing her. He thinks it's you who's in trouble. She needed my help."

"No hard feelings," I told her, remembering Michelle's words. "Where's Max now?"

"He's home with Flower." She got up to leave. Kissed me. "Be careful," is all she said.

Mama gave me about thirty pounds of Chinese food to take with me. I bowed to her as I left. Her eyes asked if I understood.

"It's okay," I said.

## 100

"ANYBODY COME CALLING?" I asked Belle, stepping past Pansy.

"Been real quiet," she said, taking the cartons of food from me. Pansy followed her into the back room, ignoring me. The bitch.

Belle cleared off the desk so we could eat. "What's all that?" I asked her, pointing to yellow legal pads covered with scrawls.

"Just some charts I made. I have to see the streets for myself—the maps don't do it all. But I wrote down some ideas."

"Is it easier for you to memorize directions if you're driving or if you're a passenger?"

"Driving is best."

"Okay," I said, digging into the hot-and-sour soup, "you drive tonight."

"Where're we going?"

"To a place you might have to come back to by yourself someday. A safe place."

She nodded, her mouth full of food. I tossed an egg roll over my shoulder, saying "Speak!" as I did. It never hit the ground.

I smoked a cigarette while Belle put the dishes away, playing with the few pieces I had. I put the thoughts down—after tonight, I'd have more pieces.

Six o'clock. I let Pansy out to the roof, went to the back to put things together. Steel-toed boots with soft rubber soles. Black cotton pants. A black sweatshirt. I took a white jacket from the closet, checked the Velcro tearaways at the shoulders. Slipped the orange headband into a pocket. I put a clean set of papers together: driver's license, registration, Social Security card, all that crap. Six hundred bucks in used bills, nothing bigger than a fifty. A cheap black plastic digital wristwatch.

I let Pansy back inside. Took a shower. Put on a terry-cloth robe. When I came out, Belle was lying on the couch, her hands locked behind her head, long legs up on the backrest. Wearing one of my shirts over a pair of little red panties. She couldn't button the shirt.

I sat down. She dropped her legs across my lap.

"Burke, this is it, isn't it?"

"What're you talking about?"

"This place. This office. That's all there is, right? This is where you live."

"Yep."

She rolled over on her stomach, pushing her hands against the couch until her hips were across my lap. There's a new kind of stove they make. Induction coil, they call it. You don't have to turn it on—the burner stays cold until you touch it with a copper-bottom pot. I knew how the stove felt.

Belle leaned her head on her folded arms, talking back over her shoulder at me. "I thought you had a house. I thought you wouldn't take me there . . . wouldn't let me sleep in your bed. Because you had a woman there. The woman you talked about."

I lit a cigarette, watching my shirt move on Belle's rump every time she readjusted herself.

"But she's gone, isn't she? Like you said. You told me the truth."

"Yeah. I told you the truth."

"I'm a bitch. I know that's not all bad—it's what I am. But I should have believed you, there's no excuse."

"Outlaws only lie to citizens."

"No, I met plenty of outlaws who lie. But I know you don't. Not to me."

She wiggled her hips, snuggling tight against me, feeling the heat.

"Is she dead?"

"I don't know, Belle," I said, my voice hardening. "I told you all this before. There's no more to tell."

"Are you mad at me?"

"No."

"I'm sorry, honey."

"Forget it."

She pulled the shirt off her hips. "Why don't you give me a smack? You'll feel better."

"I feel fine," I said.

Belle wiggled again. "Come on, please."

I put my hand on her rump, patting her gently.

"Come on. Do it, just a couple of times. I swear you'll feel better."

I brought my hand down hard. A sharp crack. "Do it again," she whispered, "come on."

I smacked her twice more in the same place. She slid off my lap to her knees, looked up at me. "Feel better?" she asked.

"No."

"You will," she promised, taking me in her mouth.

## 101

WE WERE ON THE East Side Drive, heading for the Triboro Bridge. Belle took a drag of her cigarette, watching the road.

"How do I turn up the dashboard lights?"

I told her. She peered at the speedometer. "I can tell how fast we're going without it, but I need to know the mileage."

"There's a trip odometer."

"It's okay, I'm keeping count."

We motored over the bridge. I showed her the cutoff, led her through the twisting South Bronx streets, past the warehouses, past the burned-out buildings, into the flatlands. "Next corner, left," I told her. "That's the spot."

She pulled to the side of the road. No streetlights here—we were in darkness.

Belle turned to me. "You think I'm a freak?" she asked, her voice shaking a little bit.

"Why would I think that?"

"Don't play with me—you know why I asked you. I liked it when you pinched me so hard—when you made me say what I saw in the mirror. I liked it when you spanked me before. I like it when you do that. Makes me feel like you love me. Special." She took another drag. "You think that makes me a freak?"

I lit a smoke of my own. "You want the truth?"

"Tell me."

"I think *you* think you're a freak. I think you believe your life is a damn dice game. Genetic dice, rolling down the table, and all you can do is watch."

"My blood . . ."

"Your blood may have done something to your face. Your blood tells you not to have babies. But it doesn't tell you how to act. You still have your choices."

"You don't understand."

"You're the one who doesn't understand, girl. You see it but you don't get it. Remember what you told me about alligators—the difference between a six-inch gator and a six-foot one?"

"I remember."

"What's the difference between a puppy and a dog? The same thing? Just size?"

"Isn't it?"

"How you raise the puppy, how you treat it, what you feed it—it all makes a different dog when it grows up. Two puppies from the same litter, they could be real different dogs when they grow up."

"Okay."

"Don't give me that 'okay' bullshit. You don't get it, we'll sit right here until you do."

"I get it."

"Then explain it to me."

She started to cry, her face in her hands. "I *can't*," she sobbed.

"Come over here," I told her. "Come on."

She unbuckled her seat belt, slid over against me, still crying. "I'm sorry. . . ."

"Shut up. Just be quiet and listen, okay?"

"Okay," she gulped.

"Telling you about dogs and puppies wasn't the way to do it. You think blood will out, don't you?"

She nodded. "Yes." Still crying.

"You know about Dobermans . . . how they're supposed to turn on their owners?"

"Yes, I heard that."

"It's a lie, Belle. People get Dobermans, they're afraid of them. They've all heard the stories. So they beat the hell out of them when they're still puppies. Show them who's boss, right? One day, the dog gets his full growth, the owner goes to hit him, the dog says, 'Uh uh.

Not today, pal,' and he rips the guy up. So this fool, this creep who's been beating up on his own dog, mistreating him all this time, he says, 'Well, the son of a bitch *turned* on me.'"

Belle giggled. "He sowed his own crop."

"Sure did. There's nothing genetic about Dobermans' turning on their masters. What's genetic about them is that they don't take a whole lot of shit once they get their growth. That's the truth."

"I thought . . ."

"We're people, Belle. Not alligators. I know people so cold, so evil, you meet them, you'd swear they came out of their mothers' wombs like that. But that's not the way it is. All the human monsters have to be *made*—they can't be born that way. You can't be born bad, no matter what the fucking government thinks."

"But if he . . ."

I cut her off sharp—I knew who "he" was. "It was his choice, Belle. No matter how he was raised, no matter what was done to him. There's no law says he has to repeat the pattern. He's not off the hook. I came up with guys raised by monsters. Did time with them when I was a kid. They still had choices."

I lit a cigarette. "Hard choices. The only kind people like us get. But choices still . . . You understand?"

"I do. I swear I do this time." She nestled against me. "I knew you were going to rescue me."

She kissed me full on the mouth, stabbing me with her tongue. I pulled back from her, watching the lights dance in her dark eyes. "The man we're going to see, millions of his people died because some slimy little psychopath decided their blood was bad. The psychopath, he's in the ground. The maggots are eating his body, and if there's a god, his soul is burning. And there's a country called Israel where there used to be only desert."

I squeezed her gently. "Okay?"

She let the whole smile go this time. "Okay."

# 102

I SHOWED BELLE WHERE to pull in. "Flash the high beams three times, then shut the lights off."

"Something's coming," she said, peering into the darkness.

"Dogs," I told her. "Just be quiet."

They came in a pack. Simba didn't wait to make his entrance like he usually does. There was a tawny flash and a light thump as he landed on the hood of the Plymouth, baring his fangs as he looked through the windshield. Belle looked back at him. "Is that a wolf?"

"City wolf," I told her. "And that's his pack"—pointing to the river of beasts flowing around the car.

"What d'we do?"

"Wait."

The kid came through the crowd, bumping dogs out of his way like the Mole does. He called to Simba. The dog jumped off the hood, followed the kid around to the driver's side. "Switch places with me," I told Belle. I hit the switch. The window came down. Simba's lupine face popped into the opening.

"Simba-witz!" I greeted him.

Simba sniffed, poking his nose past me to look at Belle. A low growl came out of his throat. The pack went quiet. "It's okay, Terry," I told the boy. "This is Belle—she's with me."

The kid was wearing a dirty jumpsuit, a tool belt around his waist. A regular mini-Mole. Michelle would be thrilled.

"I'll open the gate," he said.

I drove the Plymouth a few feet into the yard, watching the gates close behind us. "I'm going to get out now," I told Belle. "I'll come around and let you out. The dogs will be with us, but they're okay. Don't be scared."

"Too late for that," she muttered.

When I let her out, she stepped to the ground. The dogs moved in close. "Should I pat them?" she asked.

Terry laughed. "Follow me," he said.

I took Belle's hand as we moved through the junkyard. Simba flashed ahead of us in a Z pattern, working the ground. The dogs came close, barking at each other, not paying much attention to us.

The Mole was sitting on a cut-down oil drum a few feet from his underground bunker. He got up when he saw us coming, pulling a slab of something white from his overalls. He threw it in a loping motion, like it was a grenade. The dogs chased off.

Before I could open my mouth, Terry took over. "Mole, this is Belle. Belle is Burke's friend. She came with him. I'm Terry," he said, holding out his hand. Belle shook it, gravely.

The Mole didn't offer to shake hands, pointing at more of the cut-down oil drums like they were deck chairs on his yacht.

"I should stay?" Terry asked.

The Mole looked at me. I nodded. The kid reached in his tool belt, pulled out a cigarette, lit it with a wooden match. He gets something from everyone in his family.

"Mole, I brought Belle here because she may need a place to run to. Soon. She's our people. She's mine, okay?"

"Okay."

"I wanted you to get a look at her. She has to come back in a hurry, you'll know her."

He nodded.

"Can Terry take her around—show her the other ways in?"

He nodded at the boy. Terry came over to Belle, holding out his hand. "Come on," he said. She went meekly as a child, towering over the kid.

I moved my oil-drum seat closer to the Mole. "I'm working on something. The Ghost Van. The Prof was nosing around. Guy named Mortay caught him. Broke both his legs. Told him to stay away."

The Mole nodded, waiting.

"I don't know if this Mortay is fronting off the van or he's got his own list. He told the Prof he wanted Max. In a duel. He's been moving on other *karateka* around the city. I can't bring Max into this until I know what the score is."

The Mole watched me as if I was one of his experiments. Waiting for something to happen.

"I'm meeting him. Tonight. Midnight. I've got backup. I'll call you when I get back. You don't hear from me, you call Davidson. The lawyer. You know him, right?"

"Yes."

"If I don't call you, I'll probably be locked up. Tell Davidson I'm good for the cash. Tell him to call Mama if he needs bail money."

"Okay."

"Thanks, Mole."

"There's more?" he asked. I couldn't see his eyes through the Coke-bottle lenses.

"Maybe. Maybe a lot more. I got pieces, but they may be two different puzzles. After tonight, I should know enough to come and ask you."

He nodded. Terry came back, leading Belle by the hand. "She knows the way," he said, standing by the Mole.

"Take them back to the car," the Mole told him. Nodding goodbye to me and Belle.

# 103

WHEN WE CROSSED THE Triboro, I told Belle to bear left.

"That's toward Queens."

"I know. You're going home. I need the car. I'll come back when it's over."

"I want . . ."

"I don't care what you want. It's way past nine and I'm meeting a man at midnight. You're not coming. And I'm not telling you again."

She drove in silence for a few minutes. "Burke, what's that orange cloth you put in your pocket?"

I lit a smoke. "A sign. So I'll be recognized."

"What's it mean?"

"Signs mean different things to different people, right? Middle-class kid, he's on his way to school. There's this bully waiting for him. Middle-class kid, he don't want to fight, but he don't want to look chicken. So he wraps his hand in bandages, says he cut himself. Understand?"

"Yes."

"You wear the same bandages in the places I was raised, just makes you an easier target. Different rules, okay?"

"Okay."

We pulled up outside her cottage. Ten o'clock. I followed her inside. She didn't turn on the lights.

"Burke, don't hate me for asking this . . ."

"What?"

"Are you scared?"

"Scared to death."

"Then . . ."

"I'm more scared not to go. I have to find out. Get some answers."

"Let's run," she said, standing close to me in the dark. "Let's just go. We can be in Chicago by tomorrow. Or anyplace you want to go. I've got money stashed. Right here in the house. We can . . ."

"No."

She turned away from me. "What scares you?"

"This guy I have to meet—he's a psychopath. Behind the walls, being a psychopath is like walking a high-wire. Guys are scared of a man with eyes like an alligator's. That's good—makes people keep their distance. But it's no good to scare people too much. Just the *possibility* you might get hurt, that keeps you away. But if there's no doubt about it, if you know the guy's coming for you, you take him first. If you can."

"And that's what you need to find out?"

"That's it."

She moved close to me again, whispering in the dark room. "Why take a chance?"

"It's not that simple. I can't do anything until I find out. I don't know what else's out there."

"Burke, you come back here. You come back here to me."

"I will. As best I can."

I lit a last cigarette, pulled her to me. "You don't see me by tomorrow morning, drive back to the junkyard. The Mole will know who to contact, what to do."

"You'll come back. I've got something for you."

"I know you do," I said, giving her a kiss.

## 104

ELEVEN-FIFTEEN. I WAS parked down the street from the playground. Breathing deep through my nose, sucking the air into my belly, expanding my chest as I let out each breath. Fear snapped around inside me. I gathered it together in a spot in my chest. Worked my mind, putting a fluid box around the fear. Testing the box, pushing it in different directions. I concentrated on the box, shooting clean, cold beams at it. Breaking it into little pieces. Smaller and smaller. *Seeing* the fear-blob break up into little liquid pieces inside me. Like tears. I held my hands out in front of me, willing the little pieces of fear to come out the ends of my fingers. Feeling them come. Some came out my eyes.

I felt so tired. Closed my eyes for a second. My watch said eleven-forty. Time.

I nosed the Plymouth up on the sidewalk, up to the playground gate. I jumped out, holding the heavy bolt-cutters in two hands. The chain around the fence gave way with one squeeze. I pulled the Plymouth inside the dark playground. Got out and closed the gate behind me. I made a slow circle of the yard, stopped when the Plymouth was pointed back at the street.

I got out, taking a six-pack of beer with me. Glass bottles. Lined them up on the trunk of the car, all in a row. Parallel to the building where the shooter would be waiting. I popped the top off one, held it to my lips. Lit a cigarette. Slouched against the car to wait.

The tip of my cigarette glowed. The streetlights didn't reach the corners of the buildings ringing the playground, but it was bright enough where I stood.

"You're early, punk." A voice from the shadows.

I dragged on my cigarette, keeping both hands in sight.

Two men walked toward me from the left. One more from the right. I watched them, not moving. Well-built Spanish guy in a short-sleeved white *guyabera* shirt. Dark-haired white man in a leather jacket. And a tall man in a white T-shirt and white pants. He looked like a stick figure moving toward me. Mortay.

"Step away from the car," he said. His voice was a whisper-hiss, snake-thin.

The Spanish guy came to meet me. I held my hands away from my body as he searched. A diamond glinted in his ear. A fat diamond, not a stud.

"Empty," he said, stepping back.

Mortay stopped four feet from me. His face was at the end of a long, thin neck, so small I could have covered it with my hand. Hair cropped close—I could see the shine of his scalp. A heavy shelf of bone linked his eyebrows, bulging forward, a visor over his eyes.

"I don't recognize the school," he said. Meaning the orange headband. "Do you fight?"

"I'm just a student."

"You wanted to meet me?"

"Thank you for coming," I said, my voice gentle and low. "You had a dispute with a friend of mine. A small black man. On a cart."

He stood stone-still, waiting.

"The dispute was our fault, and we apologize. He wasn't looking for you. We don't know anything about you. We don't want to know."

"What was hc looking for?"

"The Ghost Van."

"Don't look for the Ghost Van," Mortay hissed. "You wouldn't like it if you found it."

"I'm not looking for it. I'm off the case. I just wanted to tell you to your face. We have no quarrel with you—whatever you did, it was just business, okay?"

I turned to go.

"Stay where you are."

I faced him. He hadn't moved.

"I gave the little nigger a message. Didn't you get it?"

"I just told you we did."

"About *Max*. Max the Silent. Max the *warrior.* I called him out. I want to meet him."

"If I see him, I'll tell him."

"You know my name? You play with me, you play with death."

"I'm not playing."

"I know you. Burke. That's you, right?"

"Yeah."

"Max is your man. Everyone knows that—it's all over the street. Everyone says he's the best. He's not. It's me. Me. He wants to admit it, go down on one knee, he can live. Otherwise, we fight."

"You can't make him fight."

"I can make *anyone* fight. I spit on dojo floors. I killed a kendo master with his own sword. Everybody has a button." He opened his hands, a gambler fanning a handful of aces. "I push the buttons."

"Let it go," I said.

He moved in on top of me. Spit full in my face. I didn't move, watching his eyes.

"You're better than I thought," he whispered. "You're too old to jump if I call your mother a name. But you spit in an ex-con's face, he has to fight."

"I won't fight you."

"You *couldn't* fight me, pussy." I felt my face rock to the side, blood in the corner of my mouth. "Never saw that, did you?"

"No," I answered him, chewing on my lip, my mind back in an alley when I faced another man years ago. Wishing I had a gun, glad I didn't.

"I'm the fastest man there is. Max, he's nothing but a tough guy.

I'll kill him in a heartbeat—he'll never see what does it."

"You can't make him fight—he doesn't fight just 'cause you call his name."

"What if I snap your spine, leave you in a wheelchair the rest of your life? You think that'll bring him around to see me?"

"You can't do that either," I said, my voice soft. "I'm not alone here."

The Spanish guy laughed. "I don't see nobody," he said, pulling an automatic from his belt.

I raised my hands as though I was responding to the pistol. One of the beer bottles exploded. I took another step away from Mortay.

"There's a rifle squad on the roof. Night scopes and silencers."

Mortay was ice, watching me.

"Want to see it again?" I raised my hand. Another bottle exploded. El Cañonero was the truth.

"I don't want any beef with you. You scared me good. I don't want anything to do with you. This is a walk-away. You can't hurt me, and you can't make Max fight you. It's *over*, get it?"

Mortay's voice was so low I had to lean forward to catch it. "Tell Max. Tell him I know about the baby. Tell him I know about Flower. Tell him to come and see me. Come and see me, or the baby dies."

I threw myself at him, screaming. I felt a chop in the ribs and I was on the ground. A flash of white and Mortay was gone. Bullets whined all around the playground. The dark-haired white guy went down. His body jumped as more bullets hit. Pieces of the building flew away.

I crawled over to the car, pulled myself inside. I twisted the key, floored the gas, and blasted through the gate.

# 105

THE PLYMOUTH THUNDERED toward the river, running without lights. I grabbed the highway, sliding into the late-night traffic, willing myself to slow down. My shoulders were hunched into my neck, tensing for the shot that never came. No sirens.

A quick choice—my office or Belle's? My office was closer, but Mortay knew where it was. The Plymouth's license plates were smeared with dirt and Vaseline—nobody could call in an ID.

I slipped through the Battery Tunnel, staying with traffic, one eye locked to the rearview mirror. Clear. I pulled the sleeves off the jacket I was wearing. The Velcro made a tearing sound. One sleeve went out the window on the Belt Parkway, the other a few miles down the road. I slipped out of the body of the jacket, dumped that too. The orange headband was the last to go, slipping away in the wind.

Two blocks from Belle's. I stopped at a pay phone, pulling the pistol from under the floor mat. She answered on the first ring.

"Hello?"

"It's me. You okay?"

"I'm fine, honey."

"What's your favorite animal?"

She caught it. "An alligator. It's clear, baby."

I hung up, stepping back into the Plymouth. Her door opened as I was coming up the walk. I slipped into the darkness, the pistol in my hand.

## 106

I WENT TO THE COUCH, set the pistol down next to me, reached for the phone. Belle sat next to me, reaching out her hand.

"Honey . . ."

"Get away from me, Belle. I got work to do and I don't have much left."

I punched the numbers, cursing Ma Bell for having different area codes for Queens and Manhattan. Mama picked up.

"It's me. No time to talk. You get to Immaculata. Get her to come and see you, okay?"

"Okay."

"She has to go out of town for a while. With the baby, Mama.

That's the important thing. With the baby. Let her tell Max whatever she wants—visit friends, whatever. But get her out of here."

"Max too?"

"Can you do it?"

"Big problems for me. Business problems. In Boston, okay?"

"Okay. But keep him low to the ground. Work quiet."

"Tomorrow morning he goes."

"With the baby."

"With baby. Like you say. Come by, tell me soon."

"Soon."

"Plenty help here, okay? Nobody hurt baby."

"Get them out of here, Mama."

"All done," she said.

I took a deep breath. Belle was motionless next to me. I punched another number, taking the lighted cigarette she held out. The Mole's phone was picked up at his end.

"It's me. I'm okay."

He hung up.

I started to shake then. Couldn't get the cigarette into my mouth. Belle put her arms around me, pressing my head to her breasts.

"Let it go," I said, pushing her away. "Let it come out—I know what to do."

I let the fear snake its way through me, shaking my body, a terrier with a rat. I replayed the tape—back in the playground, down on the ground, a ribbon of killer bees death-darting between me and Mortay, El Cañonero on the high ground keeping me safe.

My body trembled in the terror seizure. Malaria flashes. Taking me back to the burned-out jungle in Biafra where fear grew thicker than the vines.

I couldn't make it stop—didn't even try. I stayed quiet and still. Careful as a man with broken ribs—the kind that puncture a lung if you cough.

Fear ran its race.

When it stopped, I was soaking wet, limp. Drained. I closed my eyes then, sliding my face into Belle's lap.

# 107

IT WAS STILL DARK WHEN I came around. I turned my head. My face slid across Belle's lap, her thighs slick with sweat. Or tears. I pulled myself up, next to her.

"Can you get a duffel bag out of the trunk of my car? I need to take a shower—I don't like the way I smell."

"You smell fine to me."

"Just do it, okay?"

She got up without another word. I took off my clothes. They felt heavy in my hands. I dropped them on the floor, stepped into the shower.

When I came back out, Belle had the duffel bag on the couch. I toweled myself off, put on a fresh set of clothes. Belle's clock said two-fifteen. I took a pillowcase from the duffel bag, stuffed everything I'd been wearing into it, even the cheap watch.

"I don't have a washing machine here," she said, watching my face.

"This stuff needs an incinerator," I said, tossing it near the front door.

"You want a drink?"

"Ice water."

She cracked some cubes in a glass, ran the tap, brought it over to me. I lit a cigarette, watching my hands on the matches. They didn't shake.

I propped myself against the arm of the couch, sipping the water, smoking my cigarette. Watching the smoke drift to the ceiling. Belle stood a few feet away, watching me, not saying a word.

"Come here, baby," I said.

She sat on the floor next to the couch. I put my hand on the back of her neck, holding her. It was quiet and safe in the dark. Belle took the ashtray from me, put it on the floor where I could reach it. Lit a smoke of her own.

"When I was a young man, just a kid really, I had a place of my own. A basement, but it was fixed up like an apartment. I was raised in other people's places: the orphanage, foster homes, reform school. Nothing belonged to me. I got to thinking that place was real important."

I dragged deep on the cigarette, watching the glow at the tip.

"A man wanted my basement. I didn't know how to act then—there was nobody to tell me what to do—nobody for me to listen to. I got a gun and I went to meet him. In an alley. I was scared. I thought if I couldn't keep my basement I could never keep anything. Never have anything of my own.

"I had to meet the man. Like tonight. I can still see it—like I was right back there. I got ready to go. Ran Vaseline through my hair so nobody could get a grip. Wrapped my body with layers of newspaper in case he had a knife. Taped the handle of the pistol. So I wouldn't leave fingerprints . . . but really because I was so scared I thought I'd drop it when I took it out. I looked around that basement one last time. My basement. Left the radio playing as I walked out the door. It was Doc Pomus. A great old blues singer. Walking the line just before rock 'n' roll came. 'Heartlessly.' That was the song. I still hear it.

"He was there, waiting for me with his boys. I tried to talk to him. He just laughed at me—called me a punk. I showed him the pistol. He said I wouldn't pull the trigger—said I was scared to death. He was half right. I shot him."

"Did you kill him?"

"No. I didn't know it at the time. I just pumped a slug into him. The other people with him—they saw me do it. I just walked away. Back to my basement. I thought the word would be on the street. Don't fuck with Burke. He's a man now. Not a kid."

"What happened?"

"They came for me. I went to prison. I paid attention in there—found people I could listen to. I never wanted to be a hijacker. I'm not a gunfighter in my heart, I'm a thief. I never wanted to be a citizen—knew I never could anyway. But I didn't want to stick up liquor stores. I wanted to walk the line. Use my head, not my hands."

I stubbed out the cigarette.

"I've been waiting for full bloom all my life, Belle. It never worked out for me, Belle. I run some scams for a while, make a few good scores. But it seems like I always end up going back into that alley."

I took another hit of the ice water, Belle's hand on my chest.

"I thought it was all about that damn basement. I swore I'd never fight over a *thing*, never again. No matter what, I'd walk away. Travel light."

I lit another smoke.

"I cut the crap out of my life. I don't drink, don't play with dope. I learned to be careful. Real, real careful. I've got cut-outs inside cut-outs. Boxes inside boxes. Background tapes when I make telephone calls, phony license plates on the car. I got passports, birth certificates, driver's licenses. I sting freaks who can't sting back. I just wanted what the little ones want—what your mother wanted for you."

"To be safe?"

"Yeah. To be safe. The pattern I made for myself—it was like a ritual. Something you pray to. To keep you safe from demons. I was so scared before, when I was shaking on the couch. It made me think. Like you're praying your ass off and the devil shows up instead of God. It makes you stop praying. It's not a world out here, it's a junkyard. I grabbed a little girl once, maybe fourteen years old. Working the street. She spent her nights with her eyes closed and her mouth full. Turned over all the money to some dirtbag who beat her up and sent her back for more. I was taking her to this place I know, where they'd keep her safe, and I asked her about being a runaway. I thought you ran away to get to a better place. She told me she *was* in a better place."

"I know."

"I know you do. I've been thinking about it. Lying here. I wanted to live off my wits. Not beat the system, just take my little piece off to the side. Play it extra-safe.

"But I see it now. It was a pattern. The one thing you don't want to do."

"What pattern?"

"In prison, a guy who's thinking about going over the Wall . . . you can tell. You watch him, he falls into a pattern. Does the same thing every day. Maybe he stays in his cell instead of falling out for the movie. 'Cause he's working on the bars. Little piece at a time, putting dirty soap into the cuts to hide them. Waiting. Or you see him on the yard, watching the guard towers. Making schedules in his head. *Any* pattern marks you after a while. This South American dictator, he always went everywhere in an armored limo. Bodyguards in front, bodyguards in back. Safe as a bank vault. The other side, they blew up the car with a fucking rocket. See? The pattern taught them what to do. They didn't waste time with hijack stuff. Just blew the problem away."

"But . . ."

"It's me too, Belle. I've been at it too long. I play it safe, but I don't play it alone. You understand what I'm saying?"

"No, honey."

"I can walk away from that office and never look back. They'll never nail me fighting over my home again. I don't have a home. Remember when you said we should run? I can't run. I don't have a home, but I have people. My people. The only thing that's mine. That's my pattern."

"The little black guy?"

"The Prof is one. There's others. I don't know how it happened. I didn't mean for it to happen. I have these dreams. I was going to be a gunfighter. Live hard until I died. But I found out I didn't want to die. Then I was going to be a scam artist. But I kept running into kids. And they keep pulling me into what I didn't want to be.

"I wanted to use my head, Belle, and they make me use my hands. I was going to be a lone wolf. I even liked the way the words *sound*, you know? But it's not me. All my life, I never found what I am . . . just what I'm not."

Belle shifted her weight on the floor, looking at me. "I know what you are," she said.

"No, you don't. You know what you want. I do that too. I think

I want something, I make what I have into whatever that is. It doesn't work."

She grabbed a handful of my shirt. "You better not be telling me a fancy goodbye, Burke."

"There's nothing fancy about it. There's not going to be any more basements in my life. I'm over the edge now. Past the line. This guy, the guy I met tonight—he wants my brother. And he knows how to make him come to fight. I can't let Max do it."

"If he's as good as you say . . ."

"It's not a duel, Belle. Max has a baby. He's an outlaw. Like us. But he walks his own road. He fights this freak, there's no win. It's like turning over a rock—you don't know what's underneath. This Mortay, he's started something. If they fight, maybe Mortay wins. And my brother is dead. Max wins, he won't win easy. And even if he does, he's out of the shadows and into the street. Don't you get it?"

"No!"

"Listen to me, little girl. Listen good. There's no more outlaw code. There's no rules for freaks. I've known this since I was a kid, but I never really dealt with it. When I went back to my basement, after I shot that guy?"

"Yeah . . ."

"The people who came for me, they weren't his friends. It was the cops."

"I . . ."

"Listen! It was the *cops*. I was a stupid fucking kid who thought he was going to be a gunfighter. I went back to my basement. I thought they'd come for me—we'd shoot it out. I didn't care if I lived or I died. If I couldn't have my basement, I didn't care. If they came for me and I won, I'd have a rep. Walk down the street, women would look at me, men would whisper my name. I thought they'd come with guns—they came with a warrant."

I lit a smoke. My hands were still steady.

"I'm telling you the truth now. Max can't win a fight with this freak. *Somebody's* coming for him after that. Sooner or later . . ."

"Burke . . ."

"I've got my debts too, Belle. You've never been a slut with your body; don't be one with your respect. But give me what's coming to me. I got no choice about this. I don't want to live here if I have to pay so high."

"You have to kill him," she said. It wasn't a question.

"I have to kill him. And I'm not good enough to do it and walk away."

"You've been to prison before. I said I'd wait for you. I'll wait for you even if you buy a life sentence."

"I'm doing a life sentence right now. It's time to stop playing with myself. I got a plan. I know how to take him out. But it'll never end up in court."

"Honey . . ."

"The Mole. The guy you met tonight? He's a genius. Like you wouldn't believe. I'll have him make me a jacket. Line it with the right stuff. I'll find Mortay. He'll do what he does. And when he hits, there's a big bang and it's over."

She was crying, her head on my chest. "No, no, no . . ."

"Don't take this from me," I said. "If I could figure out another way, I'd do it in a minute. But I looked in his eyes. There's nobody home there. I can't take a chance. If I try and I miss, my people will go down. And it'll be me who did it.

"I could live with jail again, Belle. But if I miss this freak, I couldn't live with myself. I'd have nothing to come back to."

"Why can't you . . . ?"

"What? Call the cops? Have us all move to the mountains? I'm going to *try*, okay? I don't want to die. I'm not good enough with my hands to take him out. For a minute, when I was in the shower, for just a minute, I let it run in my head. Thought the answer was there. There's a *reason* for this freak being connected to the Ghost Van. It's all patterns. If I could hook into his, maybe I'd have a handle to twist him with."

She pulled back, watching my face as if she could see past my eyes, big round tears on her face. Glass beads—they'd shatter if they hit the floor.

"You'll try?"

"I'll try, sure I'll try. I don't have much time. I have to put it together . . . but maybe it doesn't fit. Maybe there is no pattern."

"But you'll *try*? You swear?"

"I swear. But I'm cutting you out, Belle. Right now, nobody has you with me. You can be out of here in a few hours. I've got some money. I'll give you a number to call. It'll all be over in a few days, one way or another."

"Get some sleep, baby," she said, kissing me on the lips.

# 108

I FELT THE HEAT. My eyes snapped open. My head turned to the side. Belle stood naked in front of me, my eyes on a level with the triangle of her hips, the soft pelt between them.

"You think you're being a man?" she asked.

"I'm being myself. Trying to be myself."

"I won't stop you. I love you. But you can't stop me either."

"What're you talking about?"

"I'm in this. I'm with you. Whatever way it plays."

"I told you . . ."

"What're you going to do, big man? Beat my ass? I *like* that, remember?"

"Belle . . ."

"You know *why* I like it?" she whispered. "Yes. Yes, you do. I only let two people hit me in my life. Sissy. And you. She loved me, and I wanted you to love me too. Own me. Take care of me. Rescue me, like she did. You don't want to live in this world alone. I understand what you said. I listened to you. I'm not running away, make some fucking phone call, find out if you're dead."

"Do what I tell you."

"I'll take your orders. I'll take whatever you have. But only if I'm *yours*, understand? I'm in this."

"You're not."

"I'm *in* this, you bastard. You can't stop me. You let me in this, you let me help you, I'll obey you like a slave. I'll do whatever you say. But if you don't, I swear I'll go back to work tomorrow night. And I'll tell every man in the place that I'm your girlfriend. I'll tell my boss. I'll put it on the street. I'll take an ad in the fucking newspapers, I have to! You don't want me in the pattern, you have to let me in your life."

I propped myself on one elbow, looking straight ahead. "You big, stupid bitch." It was all I could say.

I wasn't watching her face, but I could feel the flash of her smile. "I'm a beautiful young girl," she whispered, "and you taught me that. I'm a woman. Your woman. And you're going to see just what a stand-up woman is all about."

I closed my eyes again.

## 109

WHEN I CAME AROUND again, Belle was standing in the same place, hands on her hips. "What time is it?" I asked her.

"Time to get up," she said, kneeling down next to the couch, pressing her mouth against me, hands fumbling at my belt. I stroked her back, smooth and moist, like she just stepped out of a bath. She smelled of jasmine.

She unbuttoned my shirt, her face against my chest. The necklace shone against her skin. She licked my chest, my belly. Then she took me in her mouth.

I knew what she was doing. I knew it wouldn't work. But I felt myself grow in her mouth. Swell to bursting. I looked at the ceiling. Shadows. I closed my eyes.

She took her mouth from me. "Almost ready," she whispered.

"I'm ready now."

"Not yet. Wait." She stroked me with something slippery in her hand, gently working it in from the root to the tip. She took my hand. "Come on," she said, pulling me from the couch, leading me to the bed.

She sat down on the bed, pulling me with her, pushing me onto my back again. She lit a cigarette, put it in my mouth. She lay down on her stomach, her face inches from mine.

"Will you do something for me?"

"What?"

"Never mind what—will you do it?"

"I . . ."

"Just listen to me, okay? Then decide. All right?"

"Yeah." I felt so tired. Like an old man starting another long sentence.

"Remember I told you about that man I was with once? That tough guy? The guy who wouldn't have a bitch dog?"

"Yeah."

"Remember I told you he said all bitches would turn tail? That's what he wanted me to do?"

I nodded, dragging on the cigarette.

"You know what he meant? He meant turn *my* tail. He wanted to fuck me in the ass."

"Uh."

"He said a real man could always find a piece of ass—said he'd been in prison and he even found some there." She reached over, took the cigarette from me, drew on it. Handed it back. "Did you ever do that?"

"What?"

"Fuck a man. In prison."

"No."

"What'd you do?"

"I went steady with my fist," I snorted. Close to a laugh, but not there yet.

"'Cause a real man doesn't do that?"

"I don't know what a real man does. It's like everything I know, Belle—I only know the dark side. I only know what a man doesn't do."

"Is that why you wouldn't taste me? The first time we made love?"

"I told you the truth then—it's the same truth. In prison . . . men do things. I don't put them down for it. Man wants to fuck another man, it doesn't say anything about him."

"What is it a man *doesn't* do, then?"

"He doesn't fuck someone who doesn't want to be fucked, okay? That's the only rule, the only real one. Fucking another man in the ass doesn't make you less of one. But *taking* it . . ."

"I know. It makes a man into a girl."

"That's bullshit. A kid who gets raped in prison, it says something about the guy who did it to him, that's all."

"But if the kid doesn't fight . . ."

"He *has* to fight. He doesn't have to win."

"What happens to a kid who's raped?"

"He can lock up, go into PC. Protective Custody. Or he can hang up. Take himself off the count. I guess he could even escape. But he can't walk the yard unless he squares it."

"How does he square it?"

"Kill the guy. Shank him, pipe him, poison him . . . it don't matter. Even it up. Get it back."

I sat up in the bed, lit another cigarette. "That's what I was trying to tell you. There's rules. For everything. They don't have to be fair ones. The first time I was in reform school, one of the bigger kids rolled on me. I never let him finish his pitch. We fought. He could beat me, but he knew he'd never turn me. The next time I went back inside, I was older. Smarter. They were running another game then. It was all gangs inside. They'd make one of the little kids run. Take off at night. Then they'd run out and catch him. Kick the shit out of him, drag him back. They used to get a go-home behind it. Just another way of being raped.

"When they came to me, I told this big guy I'd do it, but I wasn't doing it for nothing. He had to give me his radio. I watched his face—I could see he was thinking what a chump I was.

"He gave me his radio and I told him I'd run in a week. I spent a lot of time on the grounds. Looking around. Getting ready. When the night came, I took off. I told him I'd be waiting for him by this big tree. Made him promise not to hurt me when he brought me back. I kept watching his face—I knew he was lying.

"I took off. Climbed up in the tree with this cinder block I'd found. He came looking for me. Calling my name. Real quiet, so he'd be the one to bring me in. Get all the credit for himself."

I bit into the filter tip of the cigarette, feeling myself smile inside at the memory, my hand on Belle's hip.

"I dropped the cinder block right on his head. He went down. I jumped on top of him, stomped his face into the ground. I held the cinder block over my head and slammed it into his ribs a couple of times. Then I went back and told the Man that this guy had escaped and I'd stopped him, but he was too heavy for me to drag back.

"I got my parole. He went to the hospital."

"Good."

"Yeah, good. I know how things work. I had to pay for what I know, but I know."

"You can figure this out too, honey."

"I don't know."

"You're scared of this guy, but . . ."

"I'm always scared of *something*, Belle. The trick is not to let it get in the way. Like ego—ego gets in the way. I went there tonight to tell the guy I wasn't carrying a beef. Almost *begged* him to walk away, let it go. But it wasn't what he wanted."

Belle reached for me again. "How about what I want?"

"*What* do you want?"

She squirmed until she was next to me, one arm on my shoulder, still holding me in the other hand, slippery.

"I told you only two people hit me in my life. You and Sissy. I told you the truth—I told you why," she said, moving closer to me, whispering in the night. "I took my clothes off for men to watch. Everything I ever did with a man, I did with you. But special. From the very first time. I knew. Sometimes you just *know* something. I want you to do it to me. What he wanted. Nobody ever did."

Her voice dropped even lower, swamp-orchid soft. "I didn't know what I was saving it for, but I knew I had to save something. It's for you."

I kissed her cheek. "You saved it *all* for me, girl. Don't fuss about it."

"Burke, do it! Come *on*. I need you to do it. It's special. For you. Not for you to take . . . for me to give."

"Belle . . ."

Her mouth was against my ear, tongue darting inside. "Want me to get down on my knees and beg?"

I got off the bed, stood facing her. She was on her knees, taking me in her mouth. "Aagh!" she said, pulling her face away. "That stuff tastes awful."

"What is it?"

"K-Y Jelly. I bought it when I went shopping. It was supposed to be your surprise." She stroked me again, slathering the stuff on. "Yes?"

I nodded.

She turned, still on her knees, her backside to me. "Where's that stuff?" I asked her.

She handed it to me. I covered myself again. Patted her butt, squeezed a glob on my finger, worked it inside her. Softly, slowly. She wiggled her rear. "Uhmmmm . . ."

I put one hand on each side of her, gently pulling her apart. I felt the tip slide into her. Pushed forward.

"*Easy*, honey. A big house can have a little door."

I pulled out of her.

"Come on."

"I don't want to hurt you."

"I was just teasing, baby. Come on, now. Come on."

I slipped in her again, working the tip back and forth, a little bit at a time. She rammed herself back against me, grunting, maybe in pain. I looked at her in the dark, split by my cock, her palms flat on the bed, elbows locked. She looked back over her shoulder. "Nice and easy," she said, smiling. The blue beads swinging from her neck.

I found the rhythm. She moved with me, just a little, working me deeper into her. "Just for you," she whispered, as I shot off inside her.

# 110

WE WERE ON THE MOVE before it got light outside. I swung the Plymouth into the garage, led Belle up the stairs, the pistol cocked in my hand.

Everything was as I left it. I let Pansy out to her roof, poured some food into her bowl. Belle stood next to me.

"You're not worried he'll try this place?"

"I don't think he wants anything to do with rooftops after last night."

"What happened?"

"It doesn't matter," I said, popping open file cabinets, handing her papers to put on the desk.

Pansy strolled into the room. Belle patted her head. The beast ignored her, demolishing the food. I opened the floorboard in a corner of the back closet. Belle knelt next to me. "Take this stuff over there," I told her, filling her arms with death.

She dumped it all on the couch like it was laundry. A sawed-off .12-gauge holding three-inch magnum shells. Double-O buckshot in one barrel, a rifled deer slug in the other. A Sig Sauer .45—the closest thing to a jam-proof automatic they make. Six fragmentation grenades, little gray baseball-sized bombs. Four sticks of dynamite, wrapped together with duct tape. A heavy Ruger .357 magnum single-action revolver.

I went over to the desk, moved the papers to one side, reached for the phone. Belle was standing by the couch, watching.

"Come here," I said, watching her face. When she got close, I made one last try.

"I don't think he's coming here. But if he does, it'll take him a while to get through that door. He does, and this whole building's going up. You understand?"

"Yes."

"You *sure?* I can't use the guns. There's no way to shoot through that door, and if he gets inside, there's no room. No time. He's too fast. Mortay makes it inside here, there's no gunshots. Just one big boom."

"I know."

"You can work with me. I'll keep my promise. But I don't want you to stay here. You take the car, go back to your house. I'll call . . ."

"Forget it."

"I'll call you when I *need* you, okay? Not when it's over. Before that. When I need a driver," I said, trying my last hope.

She put her hands on her hips, her legs spread wide apart. "You want me to take Pansy with me?"

"No."

Her dark eyes were on fire. "One bitch is good enough to die with you, not the other, huh?"

"Belle . . . Pansy wouldn't go with you."

"That's bullshit. You could get her out of here. You just think she might do you some good."

I threw up my hands. "I give up," I told her.

"Burke, don't give up. I'm not asking you to give up. Let it play out, okay?"

"Okay," I said, reaching for her hand.

She sat on the corner of the desk, looking down at me. "Where do you think you go when you die? You think we all go to the same place?"

"I don't know."

"This guy comes here, we'll find out together," she said, holding my hand tight.

## 111

I STARTED GOING THROUGH the papers piled on my desk. Smoking and thinking. Belle put her hand on my shoulder. "You want some paper, write stuff down?"

"No. I'm not used to working like that. I have to do it in my head."

"Can I help?"

"Not yet."

I went back to the files, working over the clips on the Ghost Van, sorting what I had into little boxes inside my head. Stacking them in rows, building a foundation. You work from the ground up, brick by brick. When you reach out your hand for a brick and it's not there, you've found the door. Whatever's missing, that's where you have to look.

The man who played with death wanted Max. I wanted him. He had all the cards, but I had one edge. I knew something he never would. How to be afraid.

The edge burned at the corners of my guts.

Seven-thirty. I picked up the phone. All clear. Dialed Mama. She answered in the middle of the first ring.

"Gardens."

"It's me. What?"

"Gone."

"All of them?"

"All gone. Maybe three weeks, okay?"

"Perfect."

"You have two calls. Man called Marques, couple hours ago. And the cop. McGowan. Maybe ten minutes ago."

She gave me the numbers. McGowan was calling from the Runaway Squad; I didn't recognize the other one.

"I'm off, Mama."

"You come soon?"

"Soon."

I lit a smoke. Ten minutes ago . . . I dialed McGowan. He answered himself.

"You called me?"

"We got to meet, pal. *Now.*"

"I'm hot."

"Just say where."

"Battery Park. Where they park to go out to the Statue of Liberty. The benches facing the water."

"Thirty minutes?"

"I'll be there."

Belle was behind me, her hands on my shoulders. I told her the number Mama gave me for Marques.

"That the same one you have?"

She went into the back room, came out with her purse, fumbled around. Pulled out a little red leather book, thumbed through the pages. She looked up. "No."

I punched the number into the phone. A woman's voice came on the line.

"Mr. Dupree's office," she said, a coked-up giggle in her voice.

"Get Marques," I told her.

The pimp took the phone. "Yes?" Like an executive.

"You called me a couple of hours ago?"

"Who's this?"

"You called at the Chinese Embassy, okay?"

"Oh, yeah. I get you. Look, man, I got some dynamite stuff. This guy who hangs with him, he . . ."

"Hold up," I barked, listening hard. The phone didn't sound right. "Where you calling from?"

"From my ride, man. You ever see one of them car phones?"

"Yeah. It's a *radio* phone. It's not just me you're talking to now, get it?"

"It's cool."

"It's *not* cool. Give me a number to call you at."

"No way, José. I got business out here, won't be back to the crib for *hours*. Give me *your* number, I'll ring you in an hour."

I pulled a looseleaf book from the desk drawer. "East Side or West Side?"

"What?"

"Where you going to be in an hour? In your car. Where?"

"Oh. East Side, man."

I ran my finger down the list of numbers. "Make it nine o'clock, okay? Rush hour, nobody's paying attention. There's a pay phone in the gas station at Ninety-fourth and Second. Go there, fill up your ride, I'll ring you there."

"You'll call *me*? On a pay phone?"

"Yeah, don't worry about it. We set?"

"They got super-premium gas in that station, man?"

I hung up the phone.

## 112

PANSY PUT HER TWO front paws on the desk, making her noises. I scratched behind her ears. "Not now, girl." She licked my face. I'd have to use disinfectant for an after-shave.

One more call. The Mole. I heard the phone picked up.

"It's me. I need another car. Can I make the switch in a couple of hours, leave mine there?"

"Okay."

I pulled my first-aid kit out of the bottom drawer. "Belle, come over here."

She came over. Quiet and watchful. "I have to meet some people. Can you take a cab over to the hospital? See the Prof? Just stay there until I call—three, four hours?"

"Why can't I go with you?"

"There's a thin line between a brat and a bitch," I said, holding an aluminum splint against my forearm, measuring. "A little girl can't be a bitch, an old woman can't be a brat."

I pulled a three-inch-wide roll of elastic bandage from the kit, put it aside. Started cutting pieces off a roll of Velcro, working fast. "Woman your age, she can be either one. Or both. Big as you are, you can still act like a little brat sometimes. You want something, you put your hands on your hips. Pout, stamp your feet. It's cute, okay? Makes me want to give that big rump of yours a slap."

She smiled her smile.

"But when you try and go back on a deal, you're over the line.

Makes me want to dump you someplace. Not come back."

Her face went hard. "You better . . ."

"Shut up, Belle. We made a deal, right? You're in this, but you . . . Do. What. I. Tell. You. That's what you said—that's what you do."

"I'm sorry."

"Don't be sorry. I don't have time for sorry."

"Honey . . ."

"Get me one of the grenades."

"These?" she asked, holding one of the metal baseballs like it was an orange.

"Yeah."

She handed it to me. I put it down on the desk, rolled up my sleeve, fitted the aluminum splint into place. "Hold this," I told her, wrapping the tape around until I had a thick pad. I put the grenade in my hand, wrapped my fist around the blue lever. Pulled the pin.

"Burke."

"Yeah. That's right. I let go of this thing, everything blows up."

I wound the Velcro strips around my fist, leaving a loose tab at the end. It looked like I broke my hand punching a wall and drew a ham-fisted intern when they brought me to the emergency ward. I swung my hand back and forth, testing the tape. I relaxed my fist. The lever stayed tight.

I got to my feet. "Help me on with my jacket," I said to Belle. She took the surgical scissors, slit the left sleeve neatly. I slipped my arm through.

"Honey, why . . . ?"

"It's safe. Unless I pull this tab," I said, showing her how the Velcro worked to seal the lever. I put the pin in my pocket, handed her a spare. "Tape this to the inside of your wrist—we might need it in a hurry."

"I don't . . ."

I put my arm around her waist, pulling her close to me. "You go to the hospital, like I said. I'm out in the street, I could run into this freak. I'm *trying* to put it together. Like I promised you last night.

But if he comes for me before I'm ready . . ."

"It's crazy! If that thing comes loose . . ."

"Everything's already come loose," I said, holding her. Making her see it in my face.

## 113

IN THE GARAGE, I said goodbye. "I'm going out first. You wait a few minutes, then you slip out. Take a cab to the hospital. Wait for my call there. You won't see this car again until it's over."

She kissed me hard. "You be careful."

"That's what I do best."

She kissed me again, her hand rubbing my crotch. "Second-best," she whispered.

I backed out into the street, watching the garage door close through the windshield. I couldn't see Belle in the shadows.

## 114

I PARKED THE PLYMOUTH near the Vista Hotel and walked to where I said I'd meet McGowan. The grenade felt heavy swinging at the end of my arm—I'd have to rig up some kind of sling when I got the chance.

I found the bench, sat down. I one-handed a wooden match out of the little box, braced it between my taped-up hand and my knee, fired it up.

McGowan's car swung in. He popped out the passenger side, walking toward me fast. I heard tires on the pavement, flicked my eyes to the side. Another dark four-door sedan. Whip antenna, two guys in front. About as undercover as a blue-and-white with roof lights.

"You're here," he greeted me.

"Like I said I would be. And all by myself too."

His smile was hard. "Volunteers. Not your problem. What happened to your hand?"

"I grabbed something I shouldn't of."

"Not the first time, huh?"

"Nope. What'd you want, McGowan?"

He fired one of his stinking cigars. "You trust me?"

"So far."

"I'm not wired. The other guys, they're backup. Not for you. For me."

"Go."

He looked straight ahead, puffing on his cigar, keeping his voice low. "A man named Robert Morgan got himself killed last night."

"Never heard of him."

"Nine-one-one call came in around midnight. Uniforms found a dead man. In the playground by the Chelsea Projects."

"So?"

"He had seven slugs in him, maybe a four-inch group, all in the chest. High-tech stuff. Whoever smoked him was a pro."

"So?"

"Nobody heard a shot. This was no punk kid running around on the roof with a .22—it was a hit."

"So?"

"The ground was all chewed up. Pieces of concrete ripped right out. The shooter had more than one target."

"This is real interesting, McGowan. Give me a light, will you?" I leaned close to his lighter. His hands were steady.

"Where were you last night, Burke?"

"With someone. Far away."

"You're sure?"

"What's the big deal?"

McGowan's cigar steamed in the morning air. It smelled as bad as his story.

"The guy had ID. That's where we got the Robert Morgan handle. Since it looked like a pro hit, they ran his prints. Nothing. The lab guy's a good man—he was on the ball. I heard from him an hour ago."

"Heard what?"

"This Robert Morgan, his prints matched one we took off the switch-car. The one that snatched the baby hooker."

"Why tell me?"

He looked straight ahead. "You're good, Burke. I think they could wire you to a polygraph and you'd never bounce the needles." He tilted his head back, looking up at the sky. "This dead guy, he was in the Ghost Van. It's the first lead we got. I figure you left it there for us, but you didn't know it."

I dragged on my cigarette, waiting.

"I think you're already in the tunnel. We're coming from the other end. I don't want to meet you in the middle—somebody could get hurt."

I snapped my cigarette into the street. "Stay out of the tunnel," I told him, getting up to leave. "I'll call you."

I didn't look back.

## 115

NOBODY FOLLOWED ME to the Plymouth. I took the East Side Drive to 61st, hooked York Avenue, and kept on going uptown. I pulled over on 92nd, checking the clock in the window of a boutique that hadn't opened yet. Eight-thirty-five. Plenty of time.

I made a sling out of a loop of Ace bandage, holding one end in my teeth to tighten the knot. Smoked a couple of cigarettes. Mortay was tied into the Ghost Van now for sure. For dead sure. And maybe it wasn't just bodyguard work he was doing. I was in a box—I had to get him in there with me. And know where the back door was.

I watched the cigarette smoke puddle against the windshield, playing with it. I was in Family Court once, listening to Davidson sum up on a case, watching him for the UGL—they wanted to know what he was made of before they hired him for a homicide case. They had this baby in foster care for years. Kept him there while the social workers tried to make parents out of the slime who tortured the kid. In this city, a pit bull bites two people, they gas it. To protect the public. A human cripples his own kid, they give him another bite.

Davidson was representing the kid. They call it being a "law guardian." The parents had their own lawyers; the city's lawyers represent the social workers. I still remember what he said:

"Judge, this baby will only be a child for a little while. Then he's an adult. We only have a few years to help him. The parents, they've had their chance. More than one. But this baby's not in foster care, he's in limbo. What about *him?* Isn't he entitled to some end to this? All butterflies, no matter how beautiful, have to land sometime. Or they die. The parents started this mess. The social workers kept it going. It's up to you to stop it. Stop it now. Let this baby have a *real* family."

The judge went along with it. He let the butterfly land. The baby was released for adoption. The mother cried. For herself. Davidson makes a living keeping criminals out of jail, but that day he kept someone from going to jail years later. I know.

My thoughts floating like that butterfly, looking for a safe place to land, I got out of the Plymouth. The clock said eight-fifty-five.

I started walking to the pay phone on the corner, snapping away my cigarette.

# 116

MARQUES ANSWERED ON the first ring. "That you, Burke?"

"Yeah. I just wanted to make sure the phone was working at your end. I'll call you back in five minutes."

"Man, you think I got nothing better to do than to sit around here and . . ."

"Five minutes, Marques. No more. Then we'll talk. Be cool."

I hung up, started walking again.

I turned the corner, spotted the Rolls parked next to the pay phone. I came up to the driver's window from the back. It was open, a man's elbow resting on the sill. Diamonds on his wrist.

"Let's talk," I said.

Marques jumped. "What? How'd you . . . ?"

"Everything's cool. Just relax. I didn't want to talk on the phone. How about we go for a ride?"

"I ain't going *anywhere* with you, man," he said, eyes darting around.

"In *your* car, okay? Anywhere you want to go."

He got hold of himself. "In the back seat," he snapped to the blonde next to him.

I held the back door for her. One of the whores who'd been with him in Junior's. She didn't smile. I climbed in the front. Marques backed the car out of his spot, headed uptown, to Harlem. "What happened to your hand, man?"

"Nothing much."

"Yeah. Okay, look here, I . . ."

"You want to talk in front of Christina?" I asked him, tilting my head toward the back seat.

"I told you before, man. This is my bottom woman. Besides, she's the one got the dope."

I lit a smoke. The windows whispered up, sealing off the outside world. We stopped at a light. Two kids rolled up to the driver's side. Marques hit the switch. A black kid bent down. "You want your windows done, Mr. Dupree?"

"Later, baby," the pimp said, slapping a bill into the kid's hand.

We pulled away, cruising. I waited. If Christina wanted to listen to Marques, that was okay with me, but I wasn't adding to the conversation.

"Remember you asked about this guy with Mortay? Ramón?"

I nodded.

"He's a switch-hitter, man. Takes it up the chute from Mortay, hands it back the other way."

"To boys?"

"To girls, man. This Mortay, he pulls hard guys. Right off the street in Times Square. Takes the most macho guys he can find: rough-off boys, sluggers . . . you know what I mean?"

I nodded again.

"He's bent, man. Bent out of shape like you wouldn't believe. He takes the hard guys, makes them suck his cock. Turns them right around. Then he marks them. With that diamond in the ear. This Ramón, he's not the first. He had another boy. Guy they called Butcher. Mortay turns him over. One day this Butcher is shaking down street people, doing his thing—next day he's walking with Mortay, that diamond in his ear."

I opened my hand in a "What happened next?" gesture.

"He just disappears, man. Poof! He's off the street. And Ramón—he's wearing the diamond."

"And he's an evil freak too!" Christina snarled, leaning forward between me and Marques.

"Tell him, baby," Marques said.

The blonde's voice was ugly. "He was known before. He wasn't a player, but he'd grab some little girl, slap her around, take her money. Like Marques said, a rough-off artist. Always carried a gun, let you see it. Times Square trash."

"Tell him the rest."

"He does the massage parlors now. All the girls know him. He pays big, so he got a lot of play at first. But he's a pain-freak, man. He has to hurt a girl to get off. You know Sabrina? Big fat Sabrina?"

I shook my head no.

"She does pain-for-gain. Whips and chains. She used to work at Sadie's Sexsational? Just off Eighth?"

I nodded.

"This Ramón had a date with her. Goes in the back. Stays a long time. Manager comes back to see what's taking so long, Ramón's just walking out. Points a piece in the manager's face and just keeps going. Sabrina was a mess, man. He tied her up, put a ball-gag in her mouth, whipped her till she was nothing but blood. Left a whiskey bottle sticking out of her ass."

I bit into my cigarette. I'd seen it before. They start out mean, they end up evil.

Christina sat back in her seat. Marques snorted a fat line of coke off his wrist. "That's the story, man. Nobody knows where Mortay lives. This Ramón, he's on the street most every night. Meets Mortay different places and they go off together."

"You did good," I said, dragging on the smoke.

"I'm out of it now, man. These people are too heavy for me. I'm a lover, not a killer. That's why I came to you."

I didn't say anything.

"Drop you someplace, man?"

"Thirty-ninth, anywhere near the river."

"Man, that's only a block away."

"Downtown. Not a Hundred and thirty-ninth."

"Oh, yeah. Right," Marques said, flashing his pimp-smile. "I forgot you was white."

Marques rambled on during the drive downtown. It's expensive to keep good women working. The IRS just took a major player off the street for back taxes. Bail bondsmen and lawyers were eating him alive. Couldn't find a decent mechanic for the Rolls.

I mumbled just enough to keep him talking, my mind floating someplace else. Like a butterfly.

Hawks have to land too.

# 117

MARQUES DROPPED ME OFF where I asked him. "I'm out of it," he said again.

I leaned into the window, keeping my voice low. "You're out of it when the Ghost Van's off the streets. You did your piece. But if I need to talk to you again, I'm going to call."

He wouldn't meet my eyes. "Yeah, man. Right on. You know where to find me."

I watched Christina let herself into the front seat.

"I always will," I promised him.

I watched the Rolls pull into traffic.

## 118

HE ANSWERED THE PHONE like he always does.

"Morelli."

"It's Burke. I need to talk."

"Talk."

"Not on the phone."

I heard the groan in his voice. "And you won't come to the office, right?"

"Take a walk downstairs. I'll meet you on the benches in front of the UN. Right across from Forty-first."

"Now?"

"Now."

## 119

I HAD A GOOD TWENTY minutes to myself, waiting for Morelli. My mind was a rat, gnawing at the corner of a warehouse full of grain.

The UN towered behind me. Useless piece of junk. I wondered how long it would be before somebody turned it into a co-op.

I spotted Morelli across the street. Tall guy, looks ten years younger than he is. Never wears a hat, even in the winter. Dressing better now that he's married, but not much. He doesn't look like an investigative reporter. Hell, he doesn't look Italian. But he's the best of both.

He was twenty feet away when it hit me. Money. Where's the money? I filed the thought like a bitch-wolf hiding her cubs.

I shook hands with Morelli. "Let's walk," I said.

We found a place by the railing. Tourists flowed by. Security guards. People late for work. Morelli didn't waste time asking about my hand—it wasn't his way.

"What've you got?"

"I may have this fucking Ghost Van," I told him, watching his eyes light up. A hound on the scent.

"Tell me."

"There's a pattern. A karate-freak's been fighting duels all over the city. Challenging the leaders of every dojo. Killed at least a couple. He had a death-match. In the basement of Sin City. Every player made the scene. Big purse, side bets, the whole thing. Like a cockfight, only with people. I thought he was fronting off the van. Bodyguard work. He warned one of my people off. Broke his legs. Some other things happened, and now it's me he's looking for."

Morelli glanced at my left hand.

"Yeah," I said. "Like that. We're off the record now. Way off, okay?"

"Okay."

"A man got killed last night. The cops matched his prints to the switch-car for the Ghost Van."

"Yeah . . . ?"

"The guy that was killed, this karate-freak was with him when he bought it. It won't make the papers."

"Where do I come in?"

"We got two pieces left. Why the Ghost Van in the first place? What's it doing out there? That's my piece. Here's yours: where's the money?"

"What money?"

"There's always money. Somewhere, there's always money. This whole operation cost a bundle—somebody's scoring."

"I read the clips myself. It sounds like a sicko trip to me."

"You're reading it wrong. I know it. Let me do that bit, it's not for you."

"What's mine?"

"Sin City. Who owns it? Who's watching it? There's something about that place that ties it up. This karate-freak. Mortay. Nobody knows where he lives. But that's where he fought the duel. I'll work it through. I'm close now. I know it."

"I have to sit on the fingerprint story?"

"Yeah. But you're in on the kill when it all comes down. My word on it. No matter what happens, you'll get the whole story."

"First."

"From the horse's mouth."

"How much time I got?"

"Less than I got. And I got none."

He shook hands again, moved off.

I watched the street for a minute. Then I stepped on the up-town bus.

# 120

THE PLYMOUTH WAS WHERE I left it. In some neighborhoods, I worry about amateurs trying to strip it for parts—in Yuppieville, the only danger is that some citizen will want it towed away as an eyesore.

I headed for the Bronx on automatic pilot, still working the puzzle in my head. Pulling the pain into a laser point to burn through the haze.

The junkyard looks the same, day or night. Terry walked past the dogs, motioning me to shove over. He got behind the wheel. "I know the way," he said, steering carefully through the mine field until we pulled up outside a row of corrugated-iron sheds. The kid drove right in. I stood to the side, watching him jockey a couple of wrecks back and forth, filling up the area. In five minutes, the Plymouth had disappeared.

We walked through the yard, heading for the Mole's bunker. Terry bummed a cigarette. "Shouldn't you be going to school?" I asked him, handing it over.

"I am," the kid said.

The Mole was waiting for us. "What kind of car do you need?"

"Something that won't make people look twice."

"Big car? Fast?"

"Doesn't matter."

He turned to Terry. "Get the brown Pontiac."

The kid took off.

I sat down next to the Mole. If I waited for him to ask questions, I'd do a life sentence in the junkyard.

"Thanks for the car, Mole."

He grunted, disinterested.

The kid rolled up. The Pontiac was a couple of years old. A chocolate-brown four-door sedan. A nice, clean, boring commuter's car. It had New York plates, a fresh inspection sticker.

"Registration's in the glove compartment. Insurance card too," Terry said.

"Good work." If I got dropped, I'd tell the cops I borrowed the car from a guy I met in a bar. The owner would never show up to claim it, and the Pontiac wouldn't be on any hot-car list.

I lit a smoke. "Mole, I need to talk to you for a minute."

"Talk."

"The kid . . ."

"He has to learn," the Mole said.

"I'm working on something. The wheels came off last night. This guy's looking for me—I'm looking for him."

The Mole tapped my left hand. "What's that?"

"Grenade."

"I have better stuff."

"It's okay for now. That's not what I need."

The Mole waited. Terry opened his mouth to ask a question, caught the Mole looking at him, shut it down.

"There's a tie-in to this whole mess I told you about before. I think it's inside a building. Times Square, on Eighth. Maybe the basement. I'm having some things checked out now." I dragged deep on the smoke. The Mole and the kid sat like twin toads.

"Can you get inside the building for me?"

Terry laughed. It was like asking Sonny Liston if he could punch.

"I'm hot. This freak, Mortay, he's got the area wired. He sees me, I'm gone. I'm not ready for him yet. I can't go in with you."

The Mole shrugged.

"And you can't use Max for backup. He's out of this until it's over."

"Why?"

"I met the freak. Face to face. He wants Max, says he'll take out the baby to make Max fight. Mama sent him out of town for a few weeks."

"He knows?"

"No."

The Mole wiped his hands on his greasy jumpsuit. "You want something from inside?"

"Just a look around. A good look."

"When?"

"I'll get back to you. But soon, okay?"

"Okay."

I stomped out my cigarette. "You can't take out the electricity. It's right in the middle of the cesspool. Takes a lot of juice to run all that neon."

The Mole turned to Terry. "Get the master-blaster," he said.

I followed the Mole to the entrance of his bunker. There's a network of tunnels under the junkyard, shored up with I-beams. He led me down some steps. Bright light ahead. Terry came up behind us.

The Mole pointed ahead. "Streetlight," he said. "Like they have outside. Turns on at night—goes off in the daytime. You know how it works?"

"Con Edison?"

"No. Infrared sensor. When it gets light out, the sensor reads it. Shuts itself off."

"So?"

We turned the corner. Terry handed the Mole a portable spotlight. The kind you plug into the cigarette lighter in your car. The Mole aimed the spotlight, pressed the button. A flash of white-hot light. The streetlight went out. We stood in the pitch dark. I counted ninety seconds in my head. The streetlight came back on. I followed the Mole outside.

"Car headlights, maybe seventy-five thousand candlepower on

high beams. Cop's spotlights, maybe a hundred and fifty thousand. This throws a million. Tricks the streetlights—tricks motion sensors—anything."

"Damn! What happens if you blast somebody in the face with it?"

"They go blind for a few minutes. Too close, you burn the eyeballs."

"Mole, you amaze me."

"Let Terry drive the car out of the yard," he said.

## 121

BELLE WAS LYING ON HER stomach across the hospital bed, chin in her hands. Her legs were bent at the knee, feet twirling behind her. Like a teenage girl talking on the phone. The Prof was in an easy chair, the casts on his legs still separated by the bar, propped on a footstool. He looked sharp—clean-shaven, bright-red robe.

"It's quiet?" I asked, stepping into the room.

"This is a hospital, fool."

"I mean . . ."

"We *all* know what you mean. Everything's cool. Too bad you showed so soon, I was just getting ready to show the lady your baby pictures."

I pulled up another chair. "You got something?"

Belle climbed off the bed, sat down on the floor between us, her hand on my knee.

The little man was back to himself. All business, but working in circles. "You remember J.T.?"

"Yeah."

He turned to Belle. "This J.T. was a real country boy when he came up here. A stone rookie. Wouldn't know a hoe-down from a throw-down. Couldn't decide if he was gonna be a yutz or a clutz. You follow?"

Belle tilted her chin to look up at me. "What's a throw-down?"

"A challenge. Or a fight."

"How do you tell the difference?"

"One you do with your mouth, the other with your hands. Now shut up—let the man finish."

Her lips turned into a perfect pout, like she'd been practicing all her life.

The Prof patted her arm. "Don't pay attention to this thug, girl. You can school a fool, but you can't make him cool. J.T., he's not what you call a mental heavyweight, but he's good people. A few years ago, he got into this beef over a girl. Working girl. He thought he was in love. Shot the pimp right on Forty-fourth Street. Girl starts screaming, J.T. starts running. I'm on my cart, see him flying. I told him to toss the piece. Buried it in my coat. The cops grabbed him a couple of blocks away, but they never found the gun. The pimp didn't die. We put together a package for J.T. Michelle talked to the girl, Burke talked to the pimp. Visited him right in the hospital. They held J.T. a few months, waiting for somebody to testify. Finally, they cut him loose. He's still a dumb-ass cowboy. Too dumb to hustle, and he's not cold enough for stickups. He's always out there, picking up spare change. You understand?"

Belle nodded, a serious look on her face. Like there was going to be a test later.

"Anyway, old J.T. hears what happened. Out there. He comes to see me. Like I said, he's good people, but he ain't swift. Wants to square the beef for me—take care of the people who busted me up. I tell him to back off, it's been handled. He gets a look on his face like I just downed him, you know? Like I think he ain't worth shit. So I give him this *assignment*, okay? Just do what he does, but keep his eyes open. Don't ask nobody nothing. Just watch. Last night, he walks in here. Brought me that radio," the Prof said, pointing to a suitcase-sized boom box sitting in the corner. "And he brought me this too."

He put it in my hand. An eight-sided gold metal coin. Embossed on one side was a nude woman, one hand behind her head, spike heels on her feet. I turned it over. On the other side it said "Sin City."

"It looks like a subway token," Belle said.

"It works the peep-show machines. Costs a quarter."

"So what's the . . ."

I chopped a hand in the air to cut her off, holding the coin in my fingers. "He say anything else?" I asked the Prof.

"Said he followed the guy—not Mortay, the Spanish dude—into the railroad yards. On Forty-third, off Tenth. Spanish guy disappears. J.T. figures, the hell with it, he'll go watch a movie. He goes right to Sin City, goes in the front door. Now, that's the *only* door, babe. And who does he see when he gets to the bar? The Spanish guy. J.T. says there ain't no way in the world that the Spanish guy could've got there first."

"So there has to be another way in?"

"Has to be."

"What time was this?"

"Like eleven in the morning, man. Broad daylight."

I lit a smoke. "He did good, Prof."

"When you cast bread upon the waters . . ."

"Yeah. You got anything else?"

"Just one more little piece. I reached out for Tabitha, asked her to make the run up to see Hortense, explain to her I was laid up. Now, you know Tabitha; she owes Hortense too. So she did it. Anyway, she comes back to see me. Said Hortense said she'd whip her ass when she got out, Tabitha didn't do something for me now. So Tabitha, she's in the life, but she's straight, she tells me she saw the duel."

"Mortay and the Jap?"

"Right on. In the basement. So I put it together, ask her how she got *into* the basement, dig? She says she and her man, they go downstairs from the main floor. Big metal spiral staircase. Everybody goes down that way, everybody goes out that way. Get it?"

"Yeah."

"One more thing, she says. This Spanish guy, she knows him too. Her man, Earl, he won't let none of his women anywhere *near* the Spanish guy. Word is he uses blood the way some freaks use Vaseline."

"I heard that too. Just today."

The Prof went on like he hadn't heard me. "But Tabitha, man, she thought that was funny. The Spanish guy, he don't want nothing to do with nothing that ain't white. No Puerto Ricans, no Chinese . . . nothing that's out there but white meat."

I drew on my smoke, watching Belle's face half hidden under the thatch of honey-taffy hair. Coming together.

"I'm out of here, Prof. It's coming down. I may not be back for a while."

"*What's* coming down, home?"

"A hard wind, brother. Hold tight to your alibi."

"You going to work solo? That ain't the way."

I bent close to him, lowering my voice even more. "What am I gonna do, wait till you're out of the hospital? Max is out of this—he has to be. I'm working on something . . . but I don't have it yet."

He tapped the end of my bandage. "That ain't much of a plan, man."

"That's the backup, not the plan. It all connects. Everything. But I can't call the shots. This is just in case he moves first."

The little man's eyes were hard, the yellowish cast gone. He was the Prophet again, the man who could see the future. "This freak feels froggy, he's gonna leap—I know you can't wait. But use your head, schoolboy. Pearl Harbor. When it comes to Nazis, the Mole don't play the role."

I squeezed his hand—his grip was hard as his eyes. Nothing more to say.

Belle bent to kiss him goodbye. "Remember what I told you, lady. Outside hell, blood don't tell."

"I'll remember."

When I looked back, he was pushing the button to call his nurse.

## 122

I WALKED BELLE OVER TO the Pontiac, let her in the passenger side.

"What happened to the Plymouth?"

"On vacation."

"I'm glad you didn't have to dump it. That's one fine machine."

"Yeah."

"What d'we do now?"

"Wait. There's stuff out there—I have to wait for a bite."

I drove back to Queens. Stopped at a deli in Forest Hills, waited in the car while Belle picked up some food. It was the first time I'd been to her house in the middle of the day. The street was quiet. Working people at work, kids at school. Belle saw me sweeping the street with my eyes.

"It's real quiet here until the summer. Once they start coming out to the water with their boats and all, it fills up."

"It'll all be over way before then."

"You're sure?"

I didn't answer her. I parked the Pontiac behind her Camaro. "That car's been moved since the last time."

"I took it down to the gas station. Changed the oil, front-end alignment."

I looked a question at her. "Just in case," she said.

"I don't need a driver on this, Belle."

This time she didn't answer me.

We brought the food inside. I called Mama. Nothing. Nobody looking for me. On the phone, anyway.

Belle made some sandwiches. Roast beef, boiled ham, lettuce and mustard. Opened a bottle of beer for herself, ginger ale for me. I opened the *Daily News*, scanned it quickly for any news of the Ghost Van. Nothing. I flipped to the race results out of habit, but I couldn't concentrate.

"Is it good?" she asked.

"What?"

"The *food*."

"Oh. Yeah. Great."

Her face went sad. "I'm not a good cook. Sissy was a *fine* cook. She was going to teach me. . . ."

"Who cares?"

"I thought you would. Remember when I cleaned your place? I did a good job, didn't I?"

"Perfect."

"Well . . ."

"Let it go, Belle. It was so important to me, I would have learned how to do it myself."

She pulled her chair next to me. "You can't do everything for yourself."

"Where's this going?"

She got up, moved in little circles. Like she was lost. "You're walking around with that ugly thing in your hand. . . . Maybe we won't have a little house with a white picket fence and all that . . . but I'm not gonna sit around and make plans for a funeral."

I slipped my hand around her waist, pulled her against me. "I know. But you got it wrong. I'm back on track now, I can feel it. This is just in case, like I told you. It's coming together. There's a way to take him down and walk away too. I need a couple more bits and pieces . . ."

"And you'll know where to look?"

"Yeah. In my head. I have to keep feeding stuff in, work it around. I can't go in the street and look for him—I have to figure it out. Where he is. This thing in my hand is only if he finds me first."

"What if you don't get any more information?"

"I *have* to. What I got, it's not enough. There's pieces missing. Maybe only one piece. I don't know yet. But if you don't feed the fire, it goes out. You get trapped."

She sat next to me again, her hand on my arm, watching me close. "Trapped?"

"Patterns. Like I told you. I'm looking for a guy, right? I think he's holed up in a certain neighborhood. So I walk around, ask questions, leave notes. Sooner or later, he's looking for *me*."

## 123

LATE AFTERNOON. I called Morelli.

"Anything?"

"Yeah. I'm not finished. Can't talk now—I gotta work the phones before the record rooms shut down for the day."

"Can I call you later?"

"I'll be here till nine."

"Eight-thirty," I said, hanging up.

Mama said it was all quiet. Asked me when I was coming around. I told her soon.

I put the phone down. "I got to get out of here."

"Why, baby?"

"I wasn't kidding about inertia, Belle. If there's an answer, it's in my head. No matter what kind of bites I get out there, I have to put it together. I can't work here. I need my stuff."

"Stuff?"

"In my files. It's not that I can't think here. I can think in a cell. But that stuff I've collected—it's like having a conversation. . . . I ask it questions, sometimes it talks back. Okay?"

"Okay," she said, opening her bureau drawers. "As long as I'm around when you have that talk."

## 124

BELLE SAT IN THE FRONT bucket seat of the Pontiac, watching the road. She giggled to herself.

"What's so funny."

"The Prof. I told him. About me. Not the whole thing, but enough. That's what he meant about blood only tells in hell."

"What's funny about that?"

"He said when the Lord made people He made them all the same for starters. But life marks people. If you know the way, you can read them like maps. He said the Lord made you so ugly for a test."

"What?"

"That's what he said. I told him I thought you were real good-looking. He said that was the test—I wasn't deep in love with you, I couldn't say such an outrageous lie."

"He should fucking talk."

"Burke! He *is* a handsome little man. I thought that nurse was gonna claw my eyes, she saw me with him." She giggled again. "He told me God only made one mistake. He said, you see a red-haired, blue-eyed nigger, you're looking at a stone killer."

"Sure, everybody knows that."

"Don't be crazy. He was just playing."

"Hell if he was. Every one I ever saw was a life-taker."

"That's ridiculous."

I shrugged.

The highway slipped by. Battery Tunnel coming into view.

"Burke?"

"What?"

"Why would the Prof call somebody a nigger?"

"It's just a word. Anybody can use words. I can't really explain it. . . . You say some words—say them the right way—they lose their power to hurt. The Prof, he'll say, 'That's my nigger,' he means that's his main man. Somebody *else* says the word, he's ready to rumble."

"But why . . ."

"I told you the truth. I really can't explain it. Maybe the Prof can, I never asked him, not really."

"Maybe I will, someday."

## 125

THE OFFICE WAS QUIET. Pansy was her usual sluggish self. She brightened a bit when I rolled the extra roast beef and ham into a fat ball and tossed it in the air for her.

Belle curled up on the couch with the newspapers. Pansy jumped up there too, growling. "What does she want?"

"Television."

"She wants to watch television?"

"Yeah. See if you can find pro wrestling; that's her favorite. But leave the sound on low, okay?"

Belle gave me one of her looks, hauled the portable over to the end of the couch. Pansy sat up, tail wagging. I went back to my work.

"Honey," Belle's voice broke through to me.

"What?"

"It's eight-thirty. Don't you have to make a call?"

I looked at my watch—I'd been out of it for three hours. I snatched the phone, hoping the hippies weren't discussing their latest dope deal. The line was quiet.

"Morelli."

"It's me."

"Come over to Paulo's tonight. Eleven. We'll have some supper."

I hung up quick. Looked over at the couch. Belle and Pansy were both watching me.

"Good girl," I said. Pansy came off the couch, strolled over to me. "I meant her," I told the beast, pointing at Belle. Pansy slammed a paw on the desk. "You too," I told her. I let Pansy out to her roof. Walked over to the couch, turned off the TV set.

"That's one strange dog, honey. She really does like pro wrestling. I thought dogs couldn't see TV. Something about their eyes."

"I don't know if that's true or not. Maybe she just likes the sound."

I lit a smoke. "Was I asleep?"

"I don't think so—I think you were somewhere else. Your eyes were closed some of the time. But you smoked a lot of cigarettes."

I rubbed my face, trying to go back. I gave it up—it'd come when it was ready.

"Burke, could I ask you something?"

"Sure."

"You know about this?" she said, pointing to a headline in the paper. I knew the story—it had been running for weeks. High-school cheerleader, sixteen years old. Father started raping her when she was eleven years old. While her mother was dying of cancer in the hospital. She finally told her boyfriend, he told somebody else. Ended up she hired another kid to kill her father. For five hundred bucks. Drilled the old man right in his driveway. Everybody pleaded guilty. The kid who did the shooting got a jackpot sentence, seven to twenty-one years. The radio talk shows took calls from freaks who said the little girl should have told the social workers—that is, if it "really" happened. Some people thought the father got what was coming to him. Not many. The judge sentenced her to a year in jail.

"Yeah. I know about it."

Her eyes burned. A little girl asking a priest if there really was a god. "Burke, do you think the little girl did anything wrong?"

"Yeah."

Belle's face twisted. "What?"

"She hired an amateur."

"The lawyer . . . the one who pleaded her guilty?"

"Not the lawyer. The shooter."

Her face calmed, but she was still struggling with it. "But he killed the guy. . . ."

"He wasn't a pro, Belle. Left a trail Ray Charles could follow. Talked about it to everyone who'd listen. Kept the gun. And he opened up when they popped him. You hire a killer, you buy silence too."

She took the cigarette from my mouth, pulled on it. "I'd like to break her out of that jail."

"Forget it, Belle. She wouldn't go. The kid's no outlaw. She's a nice middle-class girl. It wasn't simple for her—she didn't work it through. She still feels guilty about the guy getting killed. Incest, you don't just walk away from it like if a stranger raped you. That was her father. He's dead. Her mother's dead. She's gonna need a lot of help—she can't go on the run."

Tears spilled down her face. "My mother saved me from that."

"I know," I said, holding her.

# 126

TEN-THIRTY. I PUT ON A dark-gray suit, black felt hat. I hated to rip the sleeve, but I had to make the sacrifice. Belle did a neat, clean job. "I'll sew it back together later," she said, concentrating, the tip of her tongue sticking out the corner of her mouth.

"I'll be back in a couple of hours."

"I'll be here."

I kissed her. Her lips were soft. I slipped my fingers around her neck, pulling at the necklace, making it bounce against her chest, coaxing a smile.

"Me and Pansy, we'll have a beer, watch some TV."

# 127

PAULO'S ISN'T ONE OF those new restaurants in Little Italy. It was built when they were working on the third chapter of the Bible. When Morelli started working the police beat as a reporter, he would eat there every day. His mother came over, made sure her son was eating the right food. Marched right into the kitchen, told them what was what. They still have a couple of dishes on the menu named after her.

He was there when I walked in at eleven, sitting in a far corner. I started over to him. Two guys with cement-mixer eyes got in my way. I nodded over to Morelli's corner. One of the guys stayed planted in front of me; the other turned, caught the signal. They moved aside.

Morelli had a thick sheaf of papers next to him, glass of red wine half empty. I sat down. The waiter came over, looking at me like I was his parole officer.

"What?"

"Veal milanese. Side of spaghetti. Meat sauce. No cheese."

"No cheese?"

"No cheese."

"No wine?"

"No."

He moved off, mumbling something in Italian. When he came back, he had my food. Morelli had linguini with white clam sauce. The waiter said something to Morelli, moved off again.

I cut into the veal. It was perfect, light and sweet. We ate quietly, talking about the magazine he worked for, his kids, the neighborhood.

The waiter cleared the plates. "You want a hot fudge sundae?" he asked me.

"Tortoni," I said.

He bowed. I never saw a guy do that and sneer at the same time before.

When we finished, I lit a smoke, waiting. Morelli leaned forward. "We have a deal?"

I nodded.

He spoke quietly, one hand protectively guarding his papers. "You want the whole package or just the bottom line?"

"Bottom line."

His finger traced a path through the bread crumbs the waiter left behind on the white tablecloth. "Sally Lou," he said.

"Yeah."

"Adds up?"

"I think so."

Morelli sipped his espresso. "Burke, explain something to me. I grew up with these guys, I got no illusions. That dog you got . . . the Neapolitan? I know one of the old boys, has one just like yours. Keeps him in the back of the house. Every day he sends one of the kids to the pet store. Comes back with a couple of live white rabbits. The old man, he throws the rabbits over the fence. The dog catches them in the air, crunches them like a trash compactor. The old man, he thinks it's the funniest thing he ever saw." He took another sip of his espresso. "I know they put up with Sally 'cause he's a good earner. What I don't understand . . . where's the market?"

"You know where it is."

"No. I really don't. This whole porno business, most of it's bullshit. They make this triple-X film, tell the world it grossed fifty million dollars—it's just a laundry for dope money."

"So?"

"So why mess with the heavy stuff? Kiddie porn, stuff like that? The penalties are stiffer, they're taking all kinds of risks. There can't be *that* many freaks out there?"

Morelli's face was tight. Maybe having your own kids raises the stakes.

"There don't need to be that many," I told him. "Every one of them is a bottomless pit. It's not like dope—too much dope and you die, right? But these freaks, they can never get enough. One little piece of videotape, they can sell it again and again."

"Sally Lou, he's bent that way?"

"I don't think so. That's the hell of it—the market's so good, the wise guys are getting into it. It used to be just the freaks, making their own stuff. Mostly with their own kids. Now it's a business. The Postal Inspectors, they nail the end users. That's all. It's like when the DEA busts a bunch of mules—the processing plant keeps making the coke."

I ground out my smoke. "I'll let you know," I said.

His eyes held me. "Where do they get the kids? For the videos?"

"Same way they get anything else. Some they buy, some they steal."

"You going after Sally Lou?"

"No. He's not on my list."

"He's on mine," Morelli said.

## 128

THE PONTIAC DIDN'T DRIVE itself the way the Plymouth did. I poked it carefully through Little Italy, heading for home. Salvatore

Lucastro. Sally Lou. A made man in one of the Manhattan families, but not a heavyweight. Years ago, he started moving in on the porno joints in Times Square. Nobody paid that much attention—he was operating with permission. It wasn't one mobster, it would be another. The sleaze-sellers paid off, the way they were supposed to. Then he went into business for himself, actually producing the peep-show loops, branching into full-length films, videos. Nobody had a good line on where his studio was. He was making so much money, the bosses let him run. The kiddie-porn stuff was recent, maybe last year. From what I heard around, it was his biggest grosser ever.

Sally Lou owned Sin City.

## 129

I SWUNG BY MAMA'S, parked in the back. I went into the kitchen, waited there while they brought her back. We went into the hall, near the entrance to the basement, standing by the bank of pay phones.

"I can't hang around, Mama."

"What is this with Flower?"

"Just give me a minute, okay? One call."

I dialed the Mole. Heard him pick up. "Go," I said. Hung up.

I turned to Mama. "It's complicated. There's a man wants to fight Max. Like a duel, understand?"

She watched my face, waiting.

"He made, like, this *public* challenge, okay? So it's all over the street. Max fights him, he has to kill him. And everybody knows. Big trouble."

Mama wasn't worried about Max killing someone. "Flower." It was all she had to say.

"This guy, he wanted to make *sure* Max would fight him. He said if Max didn't he'd kill the baby."

Mama's eyes were black marble. A fire flared; then it was gone. "Tell him Max here. Come any time."

"It won't work, Mama. It won't go down that easy. I've got it put together now. Just a few more days, maybe a little bit more. He couldn't find Max in Boston?"

She shook her head.

"I'll take care of it."

Mama bowed, showing respect. That I could bring it off. I turned to go, felt her hand on my arm.

"What name?"

"Mortay," I said. "Mor-tay."

"What that mean?"

"In Spanish, it means 'death.'"

Mama bowed again. "In Chinese, means 'dead man.'"

I bowed back. Goodbye.

## 130

THE BACK STAIRCASE was quiet. I checked the pieces of tape I left behind. Still in place. The trip-wires were still attached in the hall. I let myself in. Pansy was at her post. "Where's Belle?" I asked her. The beast let out a halfhearted snarl. I bent to give her a pat. Her breath smelled like formaldehyde.

Belle was in the next room. On her back on the gym mat I keep there. Nude, covered with a sheen of sweat. "Twenty more," she said, her hands locked behind her head. She was doing killer sit-ups, up fast, down slow. Muscles rippled under the soft skin.

"How many do you do?"

"Two hundred a day, six days a week. The only difference between me and a fat pig is a small waist. I damn near killed myself to get *this* light, I'm not gonna be backsliding."

I lit a smoke, went back into the office room. Pansy didn't want to go out.

Belle came back inside, toweling herself off. "Pansy was watching me work out for a while—I guess she got bored."

"She heard the door."

"Oh." She slapped the outside of a thigh. "Only way I can get these any smaller is plastic surgery."

"They're perfect just the way they are."

She moved next to me. "I'm glad you said that."

"Because you weren't getting plastic surgery no matter what, right?"

"No, because I would if you wanted."

I gave her a kiss. "Help me off with this," I said, taking the pin from my jacket pocket. Belle slowly peeled back the bandage, working her way to the Velcro tab. "When I pull the tab, you wrap your hand around mine while I slip in the pin; my hand may be cramped."

Her forehead furrowed in concentration—her hands were steady. I popped the tab, squeezing the lever as hard as I could. My hand felt dead. Belle wrapped both of her hands around mine. Her knuckles were white. I slipped in the pin. "Let go," I said.

Her face was sweaty. "I can't."

"Come on, Belle. It's okay. Come on. . . ."

I watched her hands unlock slowly. Suddenly she pulled them away, closing her eyes. I grabbed the grenade in my right hand, slipped it into the desk drawer. My left hand was a claw.

"Go in the bathroom. Get me the little jar of Tiger Balm, okay?"

She opened her eyes. Went off without a word. Came back with the jar of red ointment. "Rub it into my hand. All over, hard as you can."

She worked my hand like she was rubbing oil into leather. I couldn't feel a thing. "Does it burn?" she asked.

"It'll get warm, that's all. Once you're done, I need to wrap it."

I sat on the couch. Belle came back with a towel. Sat down next to me on my left side, squirmed against me so my right arm was around her. She twisted sideways, took my left hand, and put it between her breasts. She pressed them together. "Pull the blanket over me," she said. I did it. In a few minutes, I could feel the heat. I wiggled my fingers, working the cramps out. "That stuff won't burn you," I promised. "Don't care if it does," she said, making sweet little sounds in her throat.

"How many beers did you give Pansy?"

"Just three."

"Damn! That's the most she's ever had. No wonder she looks glazed."

"I wanted her to like me."

"You can't buy stuff like that."

"I wasn't *buying* it. I just wanted to do something nice for her."

"Okay."

"You sleepy?"

"A little bit."

"Go to sleep, baby," she said.

I closed my eyes, my hand between her breasts, warm.

# 131

PANSY'S GROWL WOKE ME up, her snout inches from my face. It wasn't an emergency; she just wanted to use her roof.

"All that beer, huh?" I asked her, disentangling myself from Belle.

When I came back inside, Belle was on the couch, the blanket pulled up to her chin.

"Where're we going to sleep?"

"You sleep right there. Go ahead, I got work to do."

"You going out?"

"No. I got to put things together," I said, working my left hand. It was fine. I stacked the news clips in a pile, started to sort through what I had so far. The street maps were still on the wall where Belle had tacked them. I started working. The Mole was going into the basement in Sin City—it had to be the last piece.

Pansy came downstairs, strolled to a corner, and closed her eyes. Belle threw off the blanket, came to where I was working at the desk.

"I want to help."

"You want to help, put some clothes on."

"Why?"

"Because you're distracting me. And because I told you to."

She leaned over the desk, her breasts against my face. "Do they smell like that Tiger stuff?"

"No."

"Take a deep breath," she said, pushing the back of my head to her.

"They smell like you."

"Still want me to put my clothes on?"

"Yeah."

She threw me a pout, switched her hips hard walking away. I heard the shower go on, went back to work.

I covered a yellow legal pad with scrawls, but the list was in my head. Ghost Van. Baby hookers. Mortay. Ramón. The dead man El Cañonero left in the Chelsea playground. Pain-for-gain. Ghost Van won't eat dark meat. Chilly menace like fog, working close to the ground. The peep-show token. Sin City. Church where they worship the ice god. Basement duel. And Sally Lou.

I felt a tap on my shoulder. Belle, a yellow sweatshirt covering her to her thighs. "You said I could help."

"Sit down," I said, patting the desk. "Listen to me play it out."

She planted herself on the desk, hands in her lap. Watchful.

"This all started with the Ghost Van, remember? Comes off the river, shoots some little girls. Marques doesn't care why; he just wants it off the streets. So he reaches out for me. I start looking around, and this Mortay shows up. Puts the Prof in the hospital. So he's linked to the van some kind of way."

She lit a cigarette, nodding to show me she was following along.

"Except that he's not just a bodyguard—he's a freak. Hitting dojos, challenging the leaders. We know he fought a duel with some Japanese *karateka*. In the Sin City basement. You ever work there?"

"No. You have to mix with the customers."

"Okay. The Ghost Van, it only hits young girls. And only white girls. The night I went out to meet Mortay, when I came back so scared? A guy got killed. The cops pulled his prints. One of them matched one they got from the switch-car for the Ghost Van. So this

Mortay, he's not just linked, he's connected too."

I lit a smoke for myself. It was good to use two hands. Belle was listening so hard her shoulders shook.

"Mortay's stooge, this Ramón guy. With the diamond in his ear. He's a pain-junkie. Likes to hurt women, gets off on it. He's the gunman—Mortay only uses his hands. And now I find out that Sin City's owned by this mob guy. Sally Lou. He's a sleaze-dealer. Hardcore stuff. Kiddie porn, snuff—you want it, he makes it."

"You think this Mortay works for the mob?"

"No. I looked in his eyes. He don't work for anyone. But that doesn't mean he wouldn't *do* stuff. . . ."

"Why would he . . . ?"

"I'm not sure. But it all adds up. Look at the maps. The Ghost Van has to have a place to land. Someplace close by where it hunts. Times Square. Sin City—the basement's big enough for hundreds of people to watch a duel. That's where it's got to be."

"I don't get it."

"Mortay has to be doing something for Sally Lou. If the Ghost Van's down there, then they're all hooked in. The reason the cops can't catch freaks, they don't know them. They don't ask people who do. Wasn't for informants, the *federales* couldn't find a donkey in Tijuana. Sex-death freaks, they love vans. I don't know why, but they do. And they feed each other—put two of them together, you got more than twice as much evil as two people could do on their own. Ramón loves pain, Mortay deals death. I don't know what the third guy was into. It doesn't matter. The Hillside Strangler—it was *two* freaks. That Green River Killer? The one who's been murdering all those street girls out in Washington State for years?"

She nodded.

"I think the cops are making a mistake. Looking for one guy. It sounds like a team to me. *Feels* that way."

Belle shuddered. I put my hand on her bare thigh. It was cold.

"People always think they know what to do," I told her. "Ever hear of chemical castration?"

"Arggh! It sounds disgusting."

"They get a chronic sex offender. One of those guys who's never going to stop, okay? Then they make him take these injections. Depo-Provera. Lowers the sex drive, so he won't be thinking about jumping on some little kid."

"Does it work?"

"Who knows? What's the difference? This one old freak, he was still raping little kids when he was seventy years old. Started on the shots years ago. He figured out how to beat the deal—got some bootleg doctor to shoot him up with hormones. And remember that baby-raper on the Coast? Instead of dumping him into prison, the judge made him post a sign on his house. Child Molester Inside—Kids Stay Away. Something like that."

"Yeah. Like a brand."

"Some brand. All the guy has to do is move to another neighborhood. Where they don't read English. Plenty of them around."

"It's so *sick*."

I grabbed her eyes. "You think your father was sick?"

"He's a dirty, evil man."

"They all are. It's their choice, Belle. Blood didn't make them that way. *You're* not that way."

"How do you know so much?"

"I never figured out what I was, but I figured out I was going to go the distance. Survive. Knowing is how you do it." I lit another smoke. "Mortay, he won't be living down there. Too risky. But Ramón, he'll lead me right to him."

"How you going to find out?"

"The Mole's going in. Tonight, tomorrow morning." I took a deep drag of my cigarette, thinking about the letters in my files from freaks. Always interested in the real thing. "I know what he's going to find."

"What?"

"I met this guy once. State senator. Spent so much time kissing ass, his face looked like it was split down the middle. But he told me something that was true. Where's the money? That's always the question. Where's the money? To the little whores on the street, the Ghost Van's a killer shark. But to Sally Lou, it's a money machine."

"How can he make money from shooting whores?"

"I got to wait for the Mole to be sure, but I think I see it. And if I'm right, I know how to do it."

My voice trailed off, tangled in my thoughts. Belle shifted her hips, sliding along the desk until she was right in front of me. "You're different now."

"How?"

"When you came to my house—shaking and all—you got past it. Whatever it was. And taping that grenade in your hand. Like you wanted to die. Just blow yourself up and go to a better place. But now . . . it's like you're getting cold inside. Like you're not scared anymore."

"I'm still scared. But I'm back to myself now. Whatever that is, that's where I am. It's true, I feel calm inside. But not dead. Just . . . centered, you know?"

"Yeah. It feels right."

"There's lot of things I can't do. I stopped feeling bad about them a long time ago."

"But you can do this?"

"I can do this."

## 132

BELLE CAME BACK INSIDE, a glass of ice water in her hand. "Want some?"

I took the glass from her, sipped it slowly. "It's late, Belle. Go to sleep."

She bumped a rounded hip against my shoulder. "Come with me."

"I'm still putting it together."

"But you told me . . ."

"I *think* I know what it is. I have to play with it some more. Get it straight. We're playing for keeps now."

"Just lie down with me. Let me hold you. In my mouth. Like I did before. Until I fall asleep." Her eyes were sadness. "I'm so cold, honey."

I took her hand, led her to the back room.

## 133

THE ROOM HAD A FAINT glow when I came around—the closest thing this joint gets to sunlight. Belle's head was against my chest, the gym mat hard against my back.

"I'm awake," she said, before I could ask her.

"How long?"

"I don't know. I've just been lying here. Thinking. Does Pansy always walk around at night?"

"Yeah."

"She's restless?"

"Pansy? She'd spend all her time sleeping and eating, it was up to her. She's just patrolling. Watching over me."

"I'm jealous of her."

"You're a dope."

She snuggled in against me, warm, smelling like soap. "Burke, can I ask you something?"

"Sure."

"Can you love two people? At the same time? Love them both?"

Flood came into my mind. Flash-images. Flood standing in a Times Square alley, facing three skells, her purse on the ground. Waving them in, daring them to come close enough. Blond hair flying. Chubby little hands that could chop or caress. The crosshatched scar on her face. Fire-scar on her butt. The duel to avenge her sister's baby. Flower. The name Max gave his child to honor the warrior-woman he'd never see again. I felt her spirit in me, sunburst smile covering my soul.

"I don't know," I said. "I don't know enough about love. It came so late to me."

"It's come again, darling. I asked the Prof."

"About what?"

"Love. He knows about love. Blood love. I remember what he said: Life ain't dice—they don't roll nice, you can roll 'em twice."

"What's that supposed to mean?"

"Nobody's stuck. Me and Sissy were walking back of the house one day. When I was just a little girl. This old coon was down by the water. Hunting. I saw he only had one front paw. Sissy told me he must have been caught in a trap. Bit his own paw off to get out. It costs something to be free." A tear welled, rolled down her cheek. "I didn't know what she meant then."

I kissed the tear track. She slid on top of me, reached down, fitted me inside. "The way people talk, it's not the truth," she whispered. "You can't *make* love. It's there or it isn't."

Her hips flicked against me, slow-sliding, one arm around my neck, her face buried against me. "I know it's there. You know it's there. Take it."

"Belle . . ."

"Take it!" Grinding hard, her teeth against my neck.

## 134

BELLE WAS GETTING DRESSED. I was watching television with Pansy. The late-morning news. Some people tried to escape the Dominican Republic in an overloaded wooden boat, heading for Puerto Rico. The boat went down in shark-infested water. Another boat came alongside. Somebody had a video camera. The TV showed some of the footage. Living color. Blood thick in the water, like pus from a wound. Screams. Chunks torn out of humans. Sharks hitting again and again. Sound of shots fired. Belle stood behind me, hand on my shoulder.

"God! How can people watch something like that?"

Right then I knew. Why the Ghost Van hunted.

# 135

WE WAITED UNTIL almost noon. "Ready to go?" I asked Belle. When she nodded, I took the grenade out of the drawer, rolled up my sleeve. "Come over here; give me a hand with this."

She took the grenade from the desk, bounced it up and down in her hand. "Let me hold it."

"Forget it."

"Listen to me . . . just for a minute?"

I said nothing, feeling the stone in my face.

"I'll carry it in my lap. Cover it with a scarf. You can carry your gun. If it happens . . . if he comes too soon . . . you get *two* chances."

"He's too fast, Belle. I'd probably never get a shot off. You want a gun, I'll give you one."

"I'm no good with a gun. Never shot one. I could stab him, but if he's too fast for you . . ."

"No."

"*Listen* to me! I'll get out of the way. He gets past the gun, puts his hands on you, I'll toss it."

"You'd toss it right at me? Blow me up too?"

"He gets to you, you're going to die anyway. I wouldn't let you go alone."

I watched her face. "You don't have the heart for it—you'd never pull the pin."

"I *would!*"

I lit a smoke. "Stay here, Belle. I'm going to the junkyard."

"I thought I was going with you."

"You *were* going with me. Not now. Stay here."

"You can't make me."

"Don't make me laugh."

"I'm telling the truth. You can't make me. You'd have to hurt me to do it. Really hurt me. And you can't do that."

I walked away from the desk. Belle stood, arms folded over her breasts. I snapped my fingers. Pansy's head came up. "Watch!" I said, pointing two fingers in front of me. I turned to the door. Belle stepped forward. Pansy bounded between us, an ugly snarl ripping from her throat, teeth snapping. "Pansy!" Belle said, like her feelings were hurt. "Don't try her," I warned.

The muscles stood out across Pansy's shoulders, hair rigid on the back of her neck. Belle snatched the grenade from the desk, cupped the blue handle, pulled the pin. She tossed the pin in a gentle arc over Pansy's head. I caught it in my hand. The beast never moved.

"I'll just hold this until you come back," she said, her voice quiet and steady.

I let out a breath, the pin in my hand.

"Pansy, jump!" She hit the ground. I snapped my fingers again, calling her to me. Gave her the command that everything was okay. She started to walk over to Belle. I held up my hand for her to stay.

I crossed the room, fast. "Hold it steady," I told her, slipping the pin back in. She put it on the desk, went in the back room, came out with a blue chiffon scarf. Wrapped it around the little metal bomb. "Let's go," she said.

I pushed her back against the desk, making her sit on it. Moved in so close her eyes were out of focus. "Swear on your mother," I said. "Swear on Sissy that you'll throw it if he gets to me."

"I swear."

I buried my hands in her thick hair, snatching a handful on either side of her face, pulling her nose against mine. "When we get back here . . ."

She licked my mouth, pushed her lips against me. I couldn't make out what she was saying.

## 136

BELLE FOLLOWED ME DOWN the stairs into the garage. I snapped her seat belt in place for her, arranged a shawl over her lap. I worked my way through Lower Manhattan, grabbing the East Side Drive off

Pearl Street. Belle was as good as gold, quiet and peaceful in the bucket seat, hands in her lap, little smile on her face. Like a kid who threw a successful tantrum—got her way and didn't want to brag about it.

"Call off the directions," I told her.

She was right on the money, every step of the way. I lit a smoke. "Me too," she said. I held the filter to her mouth.

"Don't get spoiled. It won't work every time."

"I know." Phony contrite tone in her voice, the Southern twang not softening it much.

"I'm not kidding."

"I *know*. Turn right up ahead."

I turned into Hunts Point, heading for the junkyard.

"You know something, Burke—you're not exactly what they call a well-rounded personality."

"Well-rounded's nice, long as you don't have to cut something."

She stuck out her tongue. A queen-sized brat. With a bomb in her lap.

I rolled the Pontiac up to the gates. "Will the dogs know it's a different car?" she asked.

"They won't care.

Simba made his move first. Sitting patiently while I rolled down the window. I talked to him, waiting for someone to come and let us through.

It was Terry, shoving his way through the pack just like the Mole. He saw who it was, stuck his head in the window.

"Hi, Belle!"

"Hi, good-looking. You gonna show this lug how to drive a car?"

The kid looked at me. I opened the door, climbed in the back seat. He piloted the Pontiac in an elaborate weave, showing off for Belle.

"Are you Burke's girlfriend?"

"Hey! The Mole teach you about asking questions?"

"I just . . ."

"Shut up, Burke. I sure am, sweetie. But if you were a few years older . . ."

"I'm *getting* older," the kid said, his voice squeaking, looking over at her.

She saw where he was looking. "I know you are, honey," she said, flashing a smile.

He pulled the car into a safe area. Jumped out, held the door for Belle. I lit a cigarette. The kid was so entranced he forgot to glom one off me.

"We don't need it here," I told Belle. "Hand it over."

She pulled the scarf from the grenade, put it in my hand. Terry paid no attention, chattering away, explaining all the features of the junkyard to Belle. I followed behind them.

The Mole was outside his bunker. He tilted his head. We all followed him downstairs, Belle's hand on my shoulder, Terry bringing up the rear. I hoped the view wouldn't stunt his growth.

The tunnel sloped, curved gently back and forth. Lights flicked on each time we came close to a curve. The Mole's living room was always the same. A thin concrete slab over hard-packed dirt, old throw-rugs on the floor. The walls are all bookshelves. Tables covered with electrical motors, lab beakers, other stuff I couldn't recognize. A tired old couch in the middle of the room, easy chairs from the same dump. All covered with white oilcloth. I caught the quiet whirr of the electric fans built into the ceiling, venting to the outside. It looked the same, but it felt different. The Mole built it to live underground—before Terry came along.

I sat on the couch, Belle next to me. The Mole pulled up a chair. Terry sat on the arm. Took his eyes off Belle long enough to ask me for a cigarette.

The Mole took off his glasses, rubbed them with a rag he pulled from his belt. No point asking him if he got into Sin City—he would have said so in front, if he hadn't.

"I found it," he said.

"You sure?"

His eyes were dim behind the heavy lenses, head solid on his stubby neck. "In the back, anchor holes. For a tripod. Video camera. Professional quality, heavy. Arc lights over the top.

Cross-bolted brace. Beanbag rest."

"For the shooter."

"For the killer. The back doors work off a hydraulic valve. One switch—open and close."

"You understand what it is, Mole?"

"I understand. Killing machine. They go past the girls, hit the switch. Doors pop open. Killer shoots. Door closes." He took a breath. "And the camera is rolling. Taking the pictures."

"Snuff films," I said. "Live and up close. The real thing."

"Who does this?" Belle asked, her voice shaking. "What kind of freaks?"

The Mole pinned her with his eyes. "Nazis," he said. "They took pictures of us going into the ovens. Pictures of their evil. Treasures of filth."

"You find anything else?"

"Three more cars. Dark sedans. Another room. More cameras, lights. Drain in the floor."

That's where the baby pross they snatched off the street went. Down the drain.

I bit into the cigarette. I'd been ready for it, but red dots danced behind my eyes. I waited for the calm. For the hate to push out the fear.

"They have to go down, Mole. Can you get back inside?"

He didn't bother to answer me. Waiting.

"Can you wire it so it all goes up?"

He still waited—I hadn't asked him a question yet.

"Off a radio transmitter? So you push a button and . . ."

"How far away?"

"You tell me."

"It's all steel and concrete, that part of the city. The basement is deep. No more than four, five blocks to be sure. Easier to wire it to the ignition. They start the van . . ."

"That's no good. There's two freaks left who work the van. The shooter, and the man who wants Max. I think the driver's already dead. The van could sit there for weeks."

"Okay."

I got to my feet, stalking the underground bunker. Like they must have done in the Resistance a lifetime ago. "I got a plan. The shooter's bent—I think I can bring him in. Make him tell me where the other one is. Soon as I know, you can blow the basement."

"How long?"

"Couple of days—couple of weeks. I need more people," I said, catching his eye.

He knew what I meant. Didn't want to say Michelle's name in front of the kid. The Mole nodded again.

"I'll call you soon as I'm ready."

The Mole grabbed Terry's arm, pulled him around so the kid was facing him.

"Remember what I told you? About the Nazis? About our people?"

"Yes."

"Tonight," said the Mole, holding the boy's arms. "Tonight is Bar Mitzvah."

## 137

I BANKED THE PONTIAC across the on-ramp for the Triboro. Belle was quiet, smoking one cigarette after another, staring straight out the windshield.

"Go ahead," I told her. "Say it."

She turned in her seat. "You never gave me the grenade back."

"I know."

"You don't trust me?"

"I do trust you. I have to get out of the car, I'll hand it back to you." I glanced her way. "Okay?"

"Okay."

"Don't sulk."

"I'm not."

"Then you're a hell of an actress."

She tapped her fingers against one knee, keeping it under control. I lit a smoke for myself.

"What's the rest of it?"

She didn't answer me. Manhattan high-rises flew by on our right, river to our left. Midafternoon traffic still light.

"Burke, he's going to take that boy inside with him? Wire up a bunch of bombs?"

"Yeah."

"He's just a kid."

"It's his time. Like it was yours once."

"I wish . . ."

"Don't wish. It's a poison inside you."

"You don't wish for things?"

"Not anymore."

We were in midtown, heading for the Times Square cutoff. I rolled on past. Belle craned her neck, looking through the Pontiac's moon roof at the luxury apartments, balconies overlooking the river, high above it all.

"You think it's true? That it's lonely at the top?"

"I've never been there. All I know, it can be lonely at the bottom."

"But not always," she said, her left hand resting on my right thigh.

I covered her hand with mine. "Not always."

We passed under the Manhattan Bridge. I ignored the exit, taking it all the way downtown.

"Was the Prof really a shotgun bandit?"

"Where'd you hear that?"

"From him."

"I don't know if it's true or not. Ever since I've known him, he's been on the hustle. Maybe when he was younger, a long time ago. . . . Why'd he tell you?"

"I was telling him about me. That I was a driver. He said he used to cowboy liquor stores."

"Old as he is, he probably robbed stage coaches."

Belle giggled. "He's not so old."

"Anyone older than me is old."

"You don't feel old to me," she said, her hand shifting into my lap.

I grabbed her wrist, pulled her off. "Cut it out. Pay attention."

"I am."

"We got bigger things to think about."

"Bigger than this?" Grabbing me again.

I snarled at her. She giggled again. I turned off at the Brooklyn Bridge exit, took Centre Street to Worth, skirting the edge of Chinatown. I needed to make some calls, and I couldn't use the basement under Max's warehouse. Not now.

# 138

I PULLED IN BEHIND Mama's. A black Buick sedan rolled across the entrance to the alley behind us, blocking us in. Its back doors opened. Three young Chinese jumped out. Long, shiny, swept-back black hair, red shirts under black leather jackets. They stepped into a triangle, using their car for cover. Two of them braced their elbows, locking their hands around automatics. The other crouched against the alley wall, an Uzi resting on one knee. No way out.

Belle caught it in the side mirror. "Burke!" she whispered.

"Don't move," I told her. I knew what it was.

The back door to the kitchen popped open. A monster walked out. He looked like a pair of sumo wrestlers. Shaved head, eyes buried in fat. He grabbed our car, shook it like a kid with a toy. He looked into my face.

"Mor-Tay?" It sounded like someone had taken his tonsils out with razor wire.

I put my hands on the dashboard, keeping my eyes on his face.

"Burke," is all I said.

He shook the car again. Mama came out into the alley, said something to the monster. He let go, stepped aside. I motioned to Belle to get out. We followed Mama inside. Took my booth in the back. I lit a smoke. A waiter came up, a tureen of soup in his hands. When he leaned over, I could see the magnum under his arm.

"Where'd you find 'Zilla, Mama?"

"Always around. Good friend."

"I see you taught him some English."

Mama bowed. "Teach him everything." Most Orientals are fatalists—Mama was fatal.

I sipped the soup. Mama was serene. Greeted Belle, reached over, held her hand for a second. I left them there, went in the back to make some calls.

"Runaway Squad."

"McGowan. It's me. I got something. Can you meet me at the end of Maiden Lane, by the pier?"

"I can roll now."

"Make it in an hour."

"Right."

I tossed in another quarter, rang the private number for the phone-sex joint where Michelle worked.

"Yeah?"

"Michelle?"

"We got no Michelle here, pal."

"I know. Tell her to call Mama."

A sleepy woman's voice answered the next call.

"Put Marques on."

"He's not here."

"Right. Tell him Burke's going to call him. In two hours. Tell him to be in his car. In two hours, you got it?"

"I'm not sure . . ."

"This is Christina, right? You *be* sure. Two hours, I'll call him. Tell him to be in the car."

I hung up, not waiting for a whore's promise.

Back inside, Mama and Belle were huddled together, talking. I sat down across from them. Mama spooned some meat-stuffed dumplings onto my plate, still talking to Belle.

"Dim sum. Burke's favorite."

"How do you make them?"

Mama shrugged her shoulders—she wasn't a cook.

I ate slowly, one eye on my watch. The Maiden Lane pier was just a few minutes away.

"Mama, Michelle's going to call here. If she doesn't do it before we leave, make sure you get a number where I can reach her. Tonight. Very, very important, okay?"

"She help you. On this?"

"We'll see."

Mama bowed. More food came. Belle ate like Pansy, only with better table manners. I never felt so safe.

Finally, I pushed the plates away. Belle was still eating. "You hear from Mac?" I asked Mama.

She smiled. Made a gesture with her hands like a flower opening to the sun.

"Boston quiet?"

"Quiet soon. Max working."

I bowed. Held out my hand to Belle. She looked unhappy, not wanting to leave the warmth any more than I did.

Mama walked us out to the back. "I'll call later—check on Michelle."

The monster was still standing by the door. The Buick was still across the alley mouth, no gunners in sight. I backed up the Pontiac slowly, watching the Buick move out of the way in the rearview mirror. Pointed the car toward the pier.

# 139

BELLE WAS FINISHING OFF a last egg roll. She delicately wiped her mouth with the chiffon scarf, tossed it into the back seat.

"How come you call her Mama?"

"It's what she calls herself."

"Where're we going?"

"Meet some cops."

"Cops?"

"They're okay. For this, they're okay. They want him too." I handed her the grenade. "You stay in the car."

"But . . ."

"Shut up. I let you have your grenade, took you for a nice drive to the Bronx, gave you a nice meal. That's all the babying you're going to get today."

She reached into the back seat, put the greasy scarf in her lap, covering the grenade. I turned in to the pier and backed the Pontiac into an empty space, watching for McGowan. We were early.

"Burke?"

"What?"

"That huge guy . . . the one who came out the back door?"

"Yeah?"

"If he's Chinese, how come he has an Italian name. 'Zilla'?"

"It's not his name, just what people call him. Short for 'Godzilla.'"

"Oh. Why'd he say that name? Mor-Tay?"

"He was asking a question. That pimp, Marques. He wants to know about putting a bounty out on someone, he should talk to Mama."

## 140

MCGOWAN'S CAR PULLED up. I got out of the Pontiac, making sure he could see me, walking toward him, both hands in sight. His partner reached behind him; the back door popped open. I climbed in. His partner closed it behind me—no door handles on the inside.

"You know Morales?" McGowan asked.

"Yeah."

"He's with me on this. Understand?"

"Yeah."

"You called me out here."

I lit a smoke. "You sure you want your partner to hear this?"

They looked at each other. Morales said, "I need some cigarettes. Be right back. You need anything?"

McGowan shook his head. Morales stepped out.

"I found the Ghost Van."

"Where?"

"It's underground. There's three men in on the front end. One's the dead guy you found in the Chelsea playground. Two more left. I got a plan to trap one, work him until he shows me where the other one is."

"You saw the van?"

"Not with my eyes. I know where it is."

"That's enough for a warrant."

"The guy who saw it, he's not coming in. Neither am I. I got a deal. You interested?"

"Go."

"I need some things from you. Everything works out, I take this guy who wants Max. And the Ghost Van goes boom."

"What's mine?"

"The shooter," I said. "And Sally Lou."

McGowan knew the name. He puffed furiously on his cigar. I could see where they got the idea for smoked glass. "What do you need?"

"A massage parlor. In Times Square. And for the cops to stay away. A week, maybe two."

"Where am I gonna get a massage parlor?"

"McGowan, don't negotiate. I got no slack in my rope. You already got a couple of them. Maybe not you personally, but the cops have. That joint just off Forty-sixth—that was yours, right?"

"That was a sting. The tax boys. And it's all closed down now."

"But you got more. You've been after Sally Lou for years."

"There is one. But it's not ours."

"The *federales?*"

"Yeah."

"Tell them you need it. Couple of weeks. I'll staff it myself."

"With what?"

"Marques Dupree. He'll lend me some girls."

"He's in this?"

"It started with him. Like I told you. I'll be calling him in an hour.

Get him over here. I want you to tell him it's okay."

"Now you want me to make a deal with a pimp."

"McGowan, you'd make a deal with the devil to drop Sally Lou."

"Spell it out—what do I get?"

"The shooter comes to the massage parlor. I talk to him. He turns over this other guy I want. We dump the shooter anyplace you say. The Ghost Van goes up in smoke. And you find everything you need to take Sally Lou down."

"This other guy . . . What if it doesn't work out?"

"I got one more deal. One more piece. You and me take a walk over to that brown Pontiac. The one I came out of. There's a girl sitting in the front seat. You take a good long look at her. Whatever happens, you make sure she walks away. In exchange, I leave you a letter. With everything in it. The Ghost Van, the shooter, this karate-freak, the shooting in the Chelsea playground, Sally Lou."

"And I let the girl walk?"

"She'll be the one mailing you the letter. Enough for a dozen cases."

"Let's take a look," he said.

# 141

WE STROLLED TO THE PONTIAC. I motioned for Belle to roll down her window.

"This is Detective McGowan, NYPD," I told her. She didn't take her hands out of her lap. "He's the one you're going to mail that letter to, okay?"

"Okay." No expression on her face.

We walked back to McGowan's car. Morales was halfway across the parking lot. McGowan waved him in.

"One more thing," I said.

"What now?"

"You know Morelli? The reporter?"

"Sure."

"He gets it first. Exclusive. He'll take care of you."

"And your people."

I nodded.

"Okay," he said.

Morales joined us. "Take a walk with me," McGowan said. "I'll fill you in."

I went back to the Pontiac, let myself in, watched McGowan and Morales standing by the pay phone on the pier.

"Good girl."

"What's in this letter I'm supposed to mail?"

"A free pass—I'll tell you later."

I watched McGowan pick up the phone. He talked for a couple of minutes. Stood where he was. Picked up the phone again. Talked some more. Waved.

"Be right back," I told Belle.

I walked up to McGowan. "Call the pimp," he said.

## 142

MARQUES WAS ON HIS car phone. Answered it himself.

"You know who this is?"

"Yeah, man. What . . ."

"The Maiden Lane pier. *Now*. It's coming down."

"I ain't walking into no . . ."

"This is a safe place, Marques. The *only* fucking safe place for you in the city, you don't show up."

I hung up.

McGowan stood on one side of me, Morales close on the other.

"You know Sadie's Sexsational?"

I laughed.

"What's so funny?"

"Girl got beat up there. Real bad, right? So bad the cops moved in, closed it down."

Morales turned to me. "You think *that's* funny?"

"I think *you're* funny," I said to McGowan. "You've been running the place ever since, right? That joint doesn't belong to the *federales*. You called One Police Plaza, not the FBI."

McGowan touched the brim of his hat. "What d'you care?"

"I don't. In fact, that joint is perfect."

"Why?"

"Good location," I told him, eyes flat.

Morales didn't like any of this. His eyes scanned the pier, waiting for the pimp.

"You guys know what to do?" I asked McGowan.

"We'll make it clear to him."

I lit a smoke.

"How you gonna get the shooter into this one massage parlor?" McGowan asked.

"I know what he wants."

# 143

THE ROLLS PURRED INTO the parking lot.

"That's him," I said.

"We know. Go and get him."

Marques was behind the wheel, Christina next to him.

"Thanks for showing."

"You didn't give me much motherfucking choice."

"Be cool, Marques. Be yourself—show your class. Walk over to the water with me."

"I don't like this."

I leaned in the window. "I wanted you off the count, you'd be in the morgue. You know it, I know it. This is legit. Come on."

He exchanged a look with Christina. Got out of the Rolls. We walked to the water. I couldn't see McGowan or his partner.

"I'm taking over a massage parlor," I said.

"You?"

"Me. And I need some girls. For a couple of weeks."

"You crazy, man."

"I got the van, Marques. I got it pinned to the wall. Start counting that bounty money; it'll be mine soon."

"What's that got to do with . . ."

"The van didn't move by itself. You wanted it off the street, you think I was gonna give it a flat tire?"

"Look, man . . ."

"I need the girls. Fill the joint up, make it look righteous. They can keep everything they score. The guy who did Sabrina? The pain-freak? He's the one—the lead to the van. I got to pull him in."

"My girls don't . . ."

"I *know* they don't. But you know some who do, right? I just need one. She takes the pain-tricks, your girls take the rest. You keep the cash. This one guy comes in, the show's over."

"My girls don't . . . Hey!"

McGowan stepped in behind me; I saw Morales roll up behind Marques.

"You know who this is?" I asked Marques.

"Yeah, man," he sneered. "Every player knows *Detective* McGowan."

"You don't want to know him better, you'll shut up and listen. He's here to tell you something."

McGowan leaned over my shoulder. "Nobody's going to bother Sadie's Sexsational for a couple of weeks, *Mister* Dupree. Nobody. Not the wise guys, not the heat. Got it?"

"I got it."

Morales pressed in against Marques. "Get *this*. You *go* along, you *get* along. You don't, I got a little girl. Says you tried to pull her. Says you had *mucho* coke in your ride. More than enough for a warrant. I toss your car, I find a couple of fucking kilos. Any fucking time I want."

Marques nodded. "I'm in. You got it."

McGowan spoke to him. "You got two days. Friday night, nine o'clock, you be there. With your girls."

"It's in the bank, man."

Morales pressed closer. "Or you're in the joint."

Marques walked back to his car alone. He didn't look back.

"I see your hand got better," McGowan said.

"I got more cards in it," I told him.

## 144

I WAITED UNTIL McGOWAN and his partner pulled off before I went back to the Pontiac.

"What's going on?" Belle asked.

"It's coming together, little girl."

I drove a few feet to the pay phone, left the engine running, dialed Mama.

"It's me. Michelle call?"

"Yes. Come here tonight. Eleven."

## 145

BACK IN THE OFFICE, I let Pansy out, told Belle to stay where she was. I went down to the basement, came back with a big metal box. Belle watched as I laid the stuff out. I lit a smoke, left it smoldering on the edge of the desk while I worked. My hands were moving on the equipment, but I was watching a different picture in my mind. Seeing it happen.

I picked up the cigarette, took a last drag.

"Belle, honey, would you take off your top?"

She pulled it over her head.

"The bra too, okay?"

She unsnapped it, waited. Her breasts made a joke of gravity, the blue necklace falling just to the cleft. It wouldn't work like that. "Wait here," I told her.

I came back with a white T-shirt of mine. "Try this."

She slipped into it. Her breasts fought the thin material, the cleavage gone. No good.

"You have any real thin tops? Gauzy, maybe? The kind you can see through?"

"Like a nightgown?"

"That might work . . . if you have a real short one."

"I have a couple. Some teddies too."

"No. I need something that kind of opens down the middle. So your breasts stay separated."

"Why, baby? I can go buy anything you want."

I held up a pistol. From the side, it looked exactly like a Colt Python .357 magnum, even down to the ventilated rib across the top of the barrel. "You know what this is?"

"A gun."

"It's not, though. It's a gas gun. Works off $CO_2$ cartridges. It shoots these things," I said, showing her a handful of red plastic balls.

"What are they?"

"Paint pellets. Sixty-two-caliber. The survival-freaks use them when they play their little war games. The pellet hits you, it leaves a red splat, so you know who got hit."

"Do they hurt?"

"They sting. Especially up close. And you can feel them smack into you."

"What'd you want with it?"

"I got a plan, Belle. And part of it, I got to pretend to shoot you. Up close. Real close."

She pulled the T-shirt over her head. "Go ahead. Let me see how it feels."

"No. When it happens, you've got to feel it for the first time. You know it doesn't hurt, you won't act nervous enough."

"Honey . . ."

"You don't want to do it, say so."

"There's nothing I wouldn't do for you."

"I know," I said, holding her against me. I gave her a kiss. "Let me work now. I have to see it."

"See what?"

"See it happen. Like in karate, when they train you to punch. You don't punch *at* something, you punch *through* it. You have to see it happening, see your fist go right through the board. You don't see it, it doesn't happen. Something goes wrong in your head and it stops your hands. Okay?"

She nodded, solemn-faced.

I went back to work. The paint gun would need something that looked like a silencer. I fitted a piece of aluminum tubing, trying it out. Coming to it.

## 146

WE PULLED INTO THE alley behind Mama's just before eleven. Instant replay: the Buick rolling in behind us, the monster coming out the door. At least this time he didn't rattle the car.

Michelle was already inside, sitting in my booth. She looked pristine and elegant in a white double-breasted wool jacket, black blouse underneath. I let Belle in first. Michelle took Belle's face in her hands, turning it to catch the light.

"*Much* better. I think we could go for a little stronger look around the eyes. And your hair . . ."

"Michelle, we don't have a lot of time."

"You drag me down to this godforsaken neighborhood—no offense, Mama—right in the middle of my working hours, and *you're* in a hurry." She flashed her smile at Belle. "Men are always in a hurry, but they never have that much to do. That's a beautiful necklace," she cooed. Belle leaned forward so Michelle could hold it. "Burke bought it for me."

"Unbelievable. It's a beautiful thing, perfect for you. Maybe he's learning some class."

Belle was throwing off more wattage than the lights. Clothes weren't the only thing Michelle did right.

I got out of the booth. Bowed to Mama. "We can use the basement? Talk?"

She bowed.

The women followed me downstairs. "Very chic," said Michelle, pointing at the wall of stainless-steel vats. "Is that high-tech?"

I ignored her. The basement is well lighted. The subbasement isn't. Max keeps things down there. I never asked what.

Mama bowed again, leaving us alone. Michelle perched on a wooden crate, crossed her silky legs. "You didn't bring me down here to talk about our stock investments."

"No. It's the Ghost Van. We're all in it now. All that's left. I have to pull a sting. Smoke out a freak. It's all worked out, but I need you to run it."

"Tell me."

"There's a massage parlor in Times Square. Sadie's Sexsational, it's called. You know it?"

"Nasty place."

"Yeah, it is. Our place, for the next couple of weeks. McGowan cleared out the trash—nobody'll bother us."

"Us?"

"Marques Dupree; we're going to run his girls out of the place. There's two guys left from the Ghost Van. The shooter, he's into pain. Other people's pain. He's the one that tortured that girl before the cops moved in to close the place. So we're opening up again. I want to pull him in."

"I know Marques. His girls . . ."

"He's going to get one more. A free-lancer. She'll do all the whip-jobs. The rest, we run it like a regular joint. Customers come in, say what they want, pick a girl, pay the money. Guy comes in, asks for some freak-fun, we turn him over to this other girl. I'll be there—it won't get out of hand. But when this other guy comes, this guy we're looking for, he gets Belle."

Michelle's eyes flicked to Belle, back to me. She took a long black cigarette from her purse, tapped it on a fingernail.

"Belle takes him to the back. We'll have a place fixed up."

"What then?"

"Then he tells me where to find the other guy. And I go find him."

"There's no other way?"

"No. He walks back with Belle, I'm ready for him. We'll have it all worked out. You see this guy go back with Belle, you're gone. Just walk out. The other girls too."

"Who else is in on it?"

"The Mole. He found the van. I can talk him into it, he'll work the front desk."

Michelle's lovely face was serious, not playing now. "I always wanted to be a madam. Of course, I envisioned nicer surroundings, but . . . this'll do. I'm in charge?"

"You're in charge. The girls get to keep what they make, but pull the money at the front desk to make it look correct."

"You have pictures?"

"Pictures?"

"Of the girls. We need a book of pictures, show the johns when they come in. Let them pick the ones they want."

"I don't know."

"I'll take the pictures once they get in there. The Mole has the stuff. When does it happen?"

"Friday night we start. McGowan will put the word out. Sadie's Sexsational is the spot, you want to beat up a girl. It'll get around. We got two weeks tops. I'll be staying there. Once I go in, I can't go out. Can't take a chance of getting spotted. You bring food in with you every day. I'll be there until it's over."

"What if the freak doesn't bite?"

I shrugged. "I'm not thinking that way."

"Okay."

"We're playing for everything on the table, Michelle."

"I know. What if we need some operating cash?"

"Take it out of my share of the last score."

She dragged on her cigarette. "You worked with the Mole. . . . You see my boy?"

"He's fine," I assured her.

"A real doll," Belle chipped in.

Michelle smiled. Gave me a kiss. Kissed Belle. "I'll get a cab," she said.

## 147

"TAKE EVERYTHING YOU'RE going to need," I told Belle. We were back in her cottage, two in the morning. She bustled around, filling two big suitcases.

"What about my car?"

"You follow me back to the city with it when we go in for the last time. Day after tomorrow. I'll stash the Pontiac on the street. We'll keep your car in the garage."

She was on her hands and knees, poking around in a corner near her bed. She came up with two handfuls of cash. "I've got about fifteen thousand here," she said.

"I'll show you where to hide it."

"You want . . . ?"

"No."

I walked out onto the deck, lighting a smoke. I felt Belle behind me. "How's this?"

I turned around. She was wearing a flimsy red wrapper, tied at the waist with a thin ribbon. Her breasts were barely veiled, slash of white skin down the middle.

"You'll freeze out here."

She moved into my arms. She was warm, soft. Her hips trembled against me. My hand slid to her butt.

"Doesn't this thing come with pants?"

"I'd just have to take them off," she said. "Come on."

## 148

IN THE CAR HEADING BACK, Belle fiddled with the radio. Full-throated, late-night blues. "I'm a stranger, and afraid"—the singer well within himself, coming to grips, looking it in the eye.

"He's telling the truth," Belle whispered. "I've been both all my life."

I found her hand in the darkness.

The disc jockey broke in. "That was Johnny Adams, out of New Orleans. Singing a new Doc Pomus tune, 'A World I Never Made.' You all remember Doc Pomus, the man who gave us 'Save the Last Dance for Me,' 'Little Sister,' and so many other monster hits. Doc's one of the world's great bluesmen. Now here's the flip side. Down and dirty. Like they don't do anymore."

Rattling soft piano, sinuous spiking guitar notes dancing on the top, teasing. Johnny Adams, making his promises, bragging his brag. "I'm your body and fender man, let me pound out your dents." In case anyone listening had maple syrup for brains, he spelled it out:

*I don't care if your body's brand new*
*Or it's been knocked around . . .*
*I swear they're all the same, babe,*
*When you turn them upside down.*

"He's off the mark there," Belle said.

"No, he's right. There's no such thing as a golden snapper—the difference is in here," I said, tapping my chest.

"Here," she said, pulling my hand to her breast.

I lit a smoke. Doc Pomus on the radio again. Like that night I left my basement. Full circle.

## 149

THE PONTIAC SLIPPED INTO the garage. I showed Belle the circuit-breaker panel in the back corner. "You know what this is?"

"Sure. Like a fuse box."

"Watch." I punched the switch marked Hall. Then Lobby. Then Second Floor. The box popped open, flat plate inside. I used a thumb-nail to open the setscrews. Behind it was a deep, lead-lined box. A revolver rested on a neat stack of bills. "Put your money in there."

"That's neat. It has wires running from it and everything."

"The wires run to the house current. Electromagnetic switches. Like a combination lock. You remember?"

"Hall, lobby, second floor."

I patted her butt. "Good girl."

"If I tell you again, will you pat me some more?"

"Upstairs."

## 150

"YOU READY TO GO over it again?"

"Honey, I got it down pat."

"One more time—it's got to be perfect."

"Okay," she sighed.

I took the handcuffs from the drawer, hooked one cuff to her right wrist, the other to the back of a chair. She took the long-handled speed key from the desk, holding it in her left hand.

"Go!"

She twisted her wrist, exposing the key slot, slammed the speed key home, twisted it, pulled free.

"Beautiful."

She stood up. "I am. A beautiful young girl. Like you taught me."

## 151

LATE THAT NIGHT. Belle on her knees in front of me, her head bent between my legs. Licking me like a cat cleans her kittens. Thick thatch of hair falling. I felt the beads of the necklace lapping against my thigh.

Her head came up. Whispering in the dark. "You think it's too much?"

"What?"

"This. The way I am. I'm just like this with you. I swear it."

"What're you talking about?"

"I want your hands on me—I want you inside me. All the time. Everyplace inside me. When you just pat me on the bottom, I get wet."

"It's your way of dealing with it. Everybody's lying but you and me, Belle. To each other. This all started out with a lie. Some punk lawyer, chumping me off, he thought. And Marques, with his fifty-grand bounty. He probably collected a hundred. Maybe made a side bet about taking the van off the street. I lied to Max to get him out of the way. Mama helped me. McGowan trying to tell me the *federales* had the massage parlor. Me telling him I'm going to give him the van, and Sally Lou too. There's no letter for him—there never will be. The Mole, he could never tell Michelle he's made a Nazi-hunter out of the boy. Morelli, he thinks there's a story in this for him. Mortay. He's the only one who told the truth."

His name hung over us in the dark. I could see it. Neon-red, dripping.

"I looked in his eyes. He wasn't lying. He's earned his name. Scared me *past* death. Till I came out the other side. My old friend's here. On the other side. Hate. It didn't save my basement, but it saved my life. Plenty of times. You got your way, I got mine."

"Will it stop? When it's over?"

"It might for you," I told her. "It won't for me."

## 152

I CALLED MAMA AT seven the next morning.

"Anything?"

"Nobody call."

"Good."

"Nobody come either," she said. "Too bad."

I left Belle a note, telling her I'd be back soon with something to eat. Took my time about it. Fresh rolls, big slab of cream cheese, two six-packs of beer, pineapple juice, seltzer. I grabbed a copy of the *Daily News*. Bob Herbert's column came out on Thursdays—he'd been pounding the cops about the Ghost Van, the only one writing about it.

When I got back to the office, Pansy let me in, a distracted look on her face. She sniffed the food. "You been out?" I asked her.

"She sure has." Belle's voice from the back room. "Come on back here, you nasty old thing, let's finish this."

Pansy loped off. Belle was on her hands and knees, wearing just a bra and pants. Pansy ran over to her, lowering her head like a charging bull. They butted each other back and forth, going nose to nose. Belle was bigger and heavier, but Pansy wouldn't budge an inch, snarling happily.

"Are you nuts? What if she snaps at you?"

"She won't do that—this is a fair fight."

They pushed at each other, faces pressed together, Belle making grunting sounds of her own. Finally she dropped to the floor, face-down. Pansy sniffed the back of her neck. "You win," Belle muttered.

I put the food together. "What was that all about?"

"I told her I didn't mind her threatening me before, but if she messed with me again, I was gonna kick her ass."

"You're out of your mind."

"It was fun. You want to try?"

"Not this year. With either of you."

Belle went into the shower. I mixed the pineapple juice and seltzer, added some ice. Then I stuffed a roll full of cream cheese and gave it to Pansy. Belle came out, wrapped in a towel. Helped herself to the food.

"Beer for breakfast?"

"Save it for later. And don't give Pansy any."

Belle dropped to her knees, hands in front of her like a dog's paws. "Just one?"

Pansy stood next to her, watching me closely.

"Yeah, all right. I give up."

Belle's laugh was sweetness on the morning.

# 153

PANSY PROWLED THE FLOOR, sniffing the corners, snarling at nothing in particular. Our last night in the cottage. Belle was stuffing another pair of suitcases.

"Why'd you bring that old dog anyway?"

"I wanted to get her used to sleeping outside the office—she's going to be at the massage parlor with us."

"In case somebody wants something special?"

I didn't answer her. I dialed the Runaway Squad. They told me McGowan was in the street—they'd take a message. I hung up. Mama had nothing to tell me. I had nothing to tell the Mole.

"Don't make it look like you moved out," I warned Belle.

"I'm just taking a few things. The rent's paid till the end of the month, and I got two months security down. I'll throw another money order in the mail to the landlord. People mind their own business out here."

I went out on the deck, minding mine. Pansy trotted along next to me. She jumped up on her hind legs, hooking her front paws to the railing. I scratched the back of her neck. "You want to see the junkyard, girl? Meet a few new guys?" She made a happy rumble in her throat. The sound rippled across the water. I smoked a couple of cigarettes, calm inside. Once you jump off the bridge, everything's smooth until you hit the water.

It was past midnight when we came back inside. Belle was wearing a gauzy blue nightgown, her face fresh-scrubbed and clean. Ready for bed. She took a bottle of beer from the refrigerator, poured herself a glass. Pansy made a pitiful moaning noise, brushing her head against Belle's thigh.

"Oh! *Now* you wanna be pals, huh?"

She found a cereal bowl, another bottle of beer. Took them both into a far corner. Bent from the waist and filled it up. Pansy got about half of it, the floor got the rest.

I lit a cigarette. "You taught me something."

"What, honey?"

"The poison-proofing I did with her . . . so she won't take food unless she hears the right word?"

"Yes?"

"I'm a jerk. I never thought about liquids. She'll drink any goddamned thing."

"Can't you . . . ?"

"Yeah. You take the time, the patience, you can train a dog like Pansy to do just about anything. I didn't do it. And I just figured out why."

Belle was next to me, my arm around her waist, listening like I was saying something important.

"There's no way to throw liquid under a door. She wouldn't take it anyway—not unless it was in a bowl, or in a pool. I never figured on anyone being *inside*, you understand?"

"I'm inside," she said softly.

"Yeah, you are. Let's go to sleep."

She gently twirled away from me. Turned off the lights. "Not yet, honey. Sit in the chair. This is our last night here. Until it's over. I want to say my prayers."

She knelt before the bed, hands clasped in front of her. Her skin glowed under the nightgown. Blue light.

Belle looked over her shoulder. She played with the sash at her waist. The nightgown floated to the floor.

"Rescue me," she whispered.

## 154

IT WAS STILL DARK WHEN I watched Belle slip the Camaro into my garage. I stashed the Pontiac a few blocks away, in a safe spot near the river.

I didn't like the walk back to the garage. Pinprick tingles all across my back. But it was quiet—my fear was just picking up long-distance signals.

The garage was dark when I stepped inside. I headed for the stairs, sending Pansy ahead, Belle right behind me. She pulled at my arm. "Wait."

She stood before the circuit-breaker box. Punched the three buttons in the right sequence, puffing out her chest like a proud little girl when the box popped open. If little girls looked like that when they got a question right, I might have stayed in school. She slipped off the necklace, holding the blue glow in her hands. I watched her, one foot on the first rung of the stairs.

"I can't do it," she said. Slamming the box closed. "It don't seem right to wear it inside a whorehouse, but . . ." She patted the front of her thigh. Where her mother's gravestone was etched in her flesh.

## 155

UPSTAIRS, I DIALED McGowan again. This time he was around.

"It's me. Everything okay?"

"It's empty right now. There's an alley running behind it. Room for three cars, four if they're packed tight. Chain-link fence, barbed wire on the top. They used to keep a German shepherd out there."

"Okay. I'm rolling."

"Wait. There's one more thing. The joint next to it. The video store. That's ours too. You can walk in, go down to the basement, and walk through. We punched a tunnel through. You can go in and out."

"Thanks, McGowan."

"I should've been straight with you." His honey-Irish voice was soft around the edges. "Square it up, now."

"For all of them," I promised, hanging up.

I called the Mole, gave him the word. Whoever was listening at the other end hung up when I was finished.

Belle was unpacking her clothes, laying them across the couch, bumping Pansy out of the way with her hip.

I called Mama.

"I'm going in. You know where everything is. Max knows the rest. I'm putting it all down. In a letter. To the Jersey box."

Mama said something in Cantonese.

"What was that?"

"If the letter come, I fix everything."

"I know. Goodbye, Mama."

She hung up. A sadness-shudder passed through me, leaving me chilled. I lit a cigarette and started to write.

## 156

FRIDAY NIGHT. EIGHT O'CLOCK. I followed Pansy down the back stairs, a heavy suitcase in each hand. Belle behind me, carrying two more. I left her in the garage with all the stuff, snapped the lead on Pansy, and went for a walk.

Electric fear-jolts danced through me. Pansy felt it. Her massive head swung back and forth, pinning everyone she saw. Her teeth snapped together in little clicks, kill noises slipping through. Her eyes were ice cubes.

A yuppie couple approached, her hand through his arm. They crossed the street. A wino was propped against the car right next to the Pontiac. I tightened the leash. Pansy lunged, snarling. He sobered up, moved off. I opened the door, put Pansy in the back seat.

Belle was ready when I pulled up in front of the garage. I popped the trunk; we threw the suitcases inside and moved off.

West Side Highway to Tenth Avenue. Across 30th down to Twelfth. And then a right turn back into what the tour guides would call the heart of Times Square.

The fear-jolts were spiking inside me. Pansy prowled the back seat, side to side; her face loomed at the windows.

"Jump!" I snapped at her. Nobody'd remember the Pontiac, but nobody'd forget Pansy. She went down, snarling her hate for whatever was frightening me.

I found the alley, nosed the car in, creeping forward, driving with my left hand, the pistol cocked in my right. The fenced-off section was where McGowan said it would be—huge padlock in place. I stopped the car, popped the door for Pansy, calling to her. "Watch!"

I walked to the fence, the gun in front, poking its way through the darkness.

A flashlight beam behind the fence. I hit the ground, leveling the pistol as Pansy charged past me, throwing herself at the chain links. "Don't shoot—it's me." The Mole's voice. I called Pansy off, met him at the fence. He reached through, opened the padlock, swung the gate open. I pulled the Pontiac inside, between a white panel truck with the name of some kosher butcher shop on the side and a dark station wagon. "All ours?" I asked the Mole.

"Sure," he said.

## 157

WE FOLLOWED HIM INSIDE. Big room, dim lights, cartons stacked against the walls, steel shelving loaded with video cassettes.

"Basement," the Mole said.

"You know about the video store next door? Like I told you over the phone?"

The Mole barely kept the sneer from his voice. "I was in last night." He held up a ring of keys. We could go visit the cops, but they couldn't come see us.

Upstairs, we walked through the place. The front door was between two windows, one a little square patch of glass, the other running down the length of the place. All the glass was blacked out except for the little square near the door. Lights flashed outside.

"One-way glass," the Mole explained.

The joint was a long hall, L-shaped at the far end. Rooms opened off the corridor. Tiny hook-and-eye locks inside. Vinyl massage tables set up for quick-change sheets. Wood benches in some, leather chairs in others. They all had tables in a corner, bottles of lotions, perfumes, air fresheners. Tiny sinks against the wall. Heavy mats on the walls. All class. The L-shaped area was much larger. Bathrooms off to the side. Big ones, complete with glassed-in stall showers. Partitions made a private office in one corner. Red leather executive's chair, blond wood desk, red leather couch, white two-line phone. Even had a view—dirt-streaked window, thick bars running the full width across.

I walked back through the place, the Mole behind me. Wall-to-wall industrial-grade carpeting that had once been pink covered every square inch of floor. Recessed lighting ran the length of the hall. A desk was set up against the wall right across from the door. A wood railing made two gates—one to the desk, one to the corridor. Huge blowup pictures covered the walls of the entryway. Only two chairs, both against the left-hand wall. No Waiting. A giant round mirror was in the upper right-hand corner, cocked at the angle formed by the wall and the ceiling. I sat at the desk, looked up. You could see the length of the corridor.

"We need a . . ."

"Periscope," the Mole stepped on my lines. "You stay in the back room, see every face that comes in."

"Okay. What's that?" I asked, pointing to a light on the desk.

"Switch in every room. Girl has trouble, she pushes it."

The phone on the desk rang. I picked it up. "Yeah?"

"It's me." McGowan's voice. "I'm next door. I see you managed to get in."

"We're in." I looked around. "One more thing. I can't work the bouncer job in here. Got to stay out of sight. I'm going to have some boys sent over."

"What kind of boys?"

"Chinese boys."

"No way! That's all I need. Can you rig up a buzzer? Between us? Your man hits it, we'll have someone through the basement in a minute."

I looked at the Mole. He nodded. Rigging a buzzer wasn't going to overload his brain cells.

"Okay, we'll take care of it right away."

"Hey, Burke?"

"What?"

"Tell your man to leave the door open, okay?"

I hung up on him.

## 158

MICHELLE SHOWED A LITTLE later. You could see her through the square piece of glass. The Mole buzzed her inside. She was wearing a scarlet pants suit over a white turtleneck sweater, black spikes on her feet. The Mole and I stayed out of her way as she stalked the length of the corridor. Me smoking, watching the door, the Mole starting to set up the periscope.

Michelle came back to the front room, hands on hips. "This place is the pits. Mole, I need everything out of the first room. That'll be my office. And put that disgusting tool belt someplace—you're supposed to be the manager, not the janitor."

"I have to fix things," the Mole said, mildly.

"Well, go ahead and *fix* things. I'll go out tomorrow, get you some decent clothes."

"Michelle . . ."

"Don't you *Michelle* me. I work my beautiful butt off to keep my kid in nice clothes, and every time I see him he looks more like *you*, God forbid."

"He's my boy too."

"Sure. Next thing, you'll want him Bar Mitzvahed."

The Mole said nothing—even a lunatic knows the limit.

I left them to fight over who was going to go back to the junkyard every morning to check on the kid.

# 159

BELLE AND PANSY WERE in the back. Pansy was stretched out on the couch, Belle in the chair. "You okay?" I asked her.

"I'm fine, baby."

I gave her a kiss. Heard the buzzer. Female noises, Michelle's voice cutting through the chatter. I heard someone coming back, stepped outside into the big room. It was Michelle.

"I have to have a meeting with my girls. And take some pictures. It's gonna be a while—you both just stay back here, keep it quiet."

I nodded, putting my finger to my lips. Pansy closed her eyes.

A couple of minutes later, I heard Michelle bossing the Mole, telling him where she wanted the light stands, not to get his greasy hands on the lens. One day she was going to push him over the edge.

The room filled with girls. Pansy's face wrinkled at the overpowering smells. Michelle's voice:

"Okay, now, I understand you ladies have not worked inside before. Which one of you is Christina?"

"Marques says Miss Bitch don't have to do this. Just us."

Murmur of voices.

"Well, girls, it seems to me that opportunity is knocking. Here's the way we work it: the trick pays thirty bucks—he gets fifteen minutes. Straight massage, that's a handshake. He wants something more, *anything* more, that's an extra, got it? The trick pays at the front desk; whatever he tips, that's up to you."

"How much for the extras?" one girl asked.

"You decide. Set your own list. And don't do anything you don't *want* to do, got it? You turn over your tips to Marques, you don't turn them over, it's not my problem."

"But Marques . . ."

"Marques isn't running this show. I am. And I run it my way. Now, which one of you turns the hard tricks?"

"That's me." A husky grown-woman's voice.

"What's your name, honey?"

"Bambi."

"Okay, Bambi. You set your prices, you keep the coin. And listen to me, girl. This is a no-risk gig, you follow me? There's a button in each of your rooms—I'll show you where it is. You hit the button, and we have some nasty men to take care of any problem."

"The guy with the tool belt?" one of them giggled.

Michelle's voice went from sweet cream to barbed wire without missing a beat. "That man with the tool belt, honey, he makes people *disappear*. You watch your smart mouth, bitch. Your idea of a hard guy's some half-ass nigger pimp with a coat hanger in his hands."

"Hey!"

"You want to get down, go for it. Right now."

The room went quiet.

Michelle let the silence hang. Then she sheathed her claws. "Honey, I've been around longer than this sweet young face shows. Now, I want to treat all of you like the *ladies* you are. Nobody's going to mistreat you while you work for me. Nobody's going to disrespect you. You work your shift, you mind your business, and you make some nice money. We're just moving the stroll indoors for a couple of weeks, that's all. But anyone gets the idea they can fuck with my friends, they go back to work without a face."

The room was quiet again.

"Okay?"

The girls stepped on themselves agreeing with her.

"Fine. Now, the next thing, we have to put together some portfolios for each of you."

"Like models?"

"Of *course*, like models. Isn't that what we are? Are we any different from those walking sticks in the magazines? A john comes in, he comes to the desk. We show him the book. Pictures of each of you. He picks the one he wants."

"We don't have to line up?"

"This isn't the precinct, honey. A trick wants to see live skin, he puts his money down. Now, there's five girls, we got nine rooms. The first one, the one near the desk, that's mine. Leave the last two empty, the ones right across from here. You divide the rest the way you want—Bambi, you take the one furthest back. And no fighting! Tomorrow I'll go out and get some decent furnishings. Okay? Now, we are *not* open for business tonight. You come back, one at a time, we'll put the portfolios together. When we're done, you can hang around or you can split. Be back tomorrow. Four o'clock. We'll work twelve-hour shifts; you leave at four in the morning. Any questions?"

Nobody said a word.

"One more thing. This place is under *heavy* protection. You'll never see a cop in here. You play this right, it's a working girl's dream."

## 160

"WHAT'S YOUR NAME, honey?" Michelle asked.

"MaryAnne."

"Let's lose the black stockings, honey. Your legs are already so nice and slim—the black won't show them off."

"Okay."

"And just a touch more rouge . . . there! Brings out your color. Now, sit straight in the chair. Cross your legs. *Elegant!*"

"Michelle?"

"Yes, honey?"

"The guy with the tool belt? The one out front? Boy, you were right about him. He had this jar of water on the desk, fiddling with some locks. Marcy flashed her ass at him, sat on the desk. Asked him if he ever sampled the merchandise. He drops a key in the glass of water, and it *disappeared!*"

"I told you not to play with him."

"I *won't*. Does he ever . . ."

"He's not for hire," Michelle snapped. "Now, flash me a smile."

## 161

BAMBI WAS THE LAST one in. "Any special way you want this?" Michelle asked her.

"I've got my own handcuffs. I can twist right out of them if I have to. Can I loop them around the back of this chair?"

"Sure, honey. Go ahead. Bend forward. More. Give your butt a little shake. Beautiful."

Sound of handcuffs clicking. "You don't put me down for it?"

"Why should I?"

"Some of the other girls . . ."

"You got a pimp?"

"No."

"So who's the masochist?"

Bambi laughed.

## 162

THE GIRLS WERE GONE BY one in the morning. "You're next," she told Belle.

I snapped the lead on Pansy, taking her to the basement. The Mole followed me down, shining his flash. "All fixed," he said.

"Okay, Mole. We roll tomorrow for real. Any way I can get Pansy down here without going past the other rooms?"

"Only to the basement, not outside."

"We'll do it that way. Over in that corner," I said, pointing. "Watch where you step from now on."

We went back upstairs. "Try the buzzer," I told him. He hit the switch. I counted in my head. Thirty-five seconds, Morales burst through the door, gun in his hand. "Which way?" he snapped.

"Just testing it," I said.

"Next time make it real. I'm looking forward to it."

# 163

IN THE BACK ROOM. Michelle was working on Belle's face. Cat's-eye makeup, pancaked cheeks, slash of red across her mouth. It didn't look like her. "This is mousse—it'll wash right out," said Michelle, spraying it over Belle's hair, working it through with her fingers. "Let's see . . . You'll turn over your right shoulder"—pancaking that side of her face. "Try it."

Belle peeked over her right shoulder. Her hair was dark, face a stranger's mask.

"Okay, let's do it."

Belle unhooked her bra, knelt before the chair, hands on either side. Michelle wrapped a black scarf around each hand. "Slide further back to me," she said. "Let them swing free. Turn your head. . . . Not so much."

She went over to Belle, pulling the big girl's panties over her rump. Belle lifted a leg to help her get them off.

"Leave them that way—like they've just been pulled down—it'll work better."

Michelle went back to the camera. "Okay, turn your head again. Just a little bit. Can you look a little scared? Oh, forget it—I'll open the lens, blur your face. Nobody'd look past that ass anyway."

Belle giggled. Twin dimples at the top of her butt, strip of black cloth around her thighs. The shutter clicked. Again. She shook her butt at the camera.

"Got it," Michelle said, then snapped off the lights, carried the camera out to the front.

The cigarette burned my mouth. I ground the tip out in the ashtray. Belle was still on her knees, watching me.

"Make you think of something good?" she asked, wiggling again. Then she saw my face. "What's wrong, honey?"

I walked over to her, took the loops off her hands. She put her arms around my neck. I stood up, hauling her to her feet. Reached behind me, pulled the panties back into place.

"Go wash that crap off your face."

"You're mad at me?"

I held her against me. "I'm not mad at you."

"I'm sorry, sweetheart. Truly sorry. I thought it would be a turn-on for you."

"It made me sick to look at it."

Her tears against my face. "I'm sorry. . . . I'm sorry. . . ."

I squeezed her rear with both hands. "Shut up," I said, quietly.

## 164

THE JOINT WAS OPEN and rolling the next afternoon. Michelle was there by eleven in the morning, her arms full of bags. She and Belle worked like maniacs cleaning. The dump even smelled clean when they were done.

I stayed in the back room. The Mole would buzz me if any Hispanic male came in, anyone that could come within a half-mile of Ramón. I checked the periscope a few times on the little TV screen the Mole put on the desk. It worked perfectly.

I spent my time checking my tools. Supermarket shopping cart full of empty plastic one-liter bottles. The kind street bums collect from garbage cans—turn them in for a nickel apiece. I ran a few copies of the *Daily News* through a paper shredder. Packed a half-dozen of the bottles with the paper. I filed the front sight off the long-barreled .38. A couple of tiny slits with a razor blade and the barrel fit deep into the mouth of a bottle of Coke. I felt an ugly smile inside me—the real thing. I wrapped duct tape around the mouth of the bottle, sealing the pistol barrel inside. Pointed it at the wall, holding the bottle in my left hand. Pulled the trigger. It made a sound like snapping fingers. Plaster flew off the wall.

I lined up twelve bullets. Mole specials—super-speed hot loads, mercury tips. Any one of them would total whatever it hit. Six bullets went into the long-barreled .38, another six into the two-inch revolver next to it.

The guns were ice-cold, brand-new. No serial numbers.

A pair of the fragmentation grenades sat on the desk, the blue handles winking at me.

The Mole stashed a new car for me every morning. All along the river, one block apart. We had four cars now. I fingered the ignition key—it would work in all of them.

A tattered khaki raincoat hung on a hook. It would reach well past my knees. A long blond wig was on top of the hook. Straight hair. A blue golf hat, wine-stained. An old pair of white running shoes. Baggy black pants. Black sweatshirt with a hood. Black gloves. A slap-on mustache.

I clipped two nails on my left hand at a sharp angle. A drop of Permabond under each one. I held the razor-filed steel slivers in place against each nail, waiting for the super-glue to dry. It only took a few minutes. I brushed my left hand against a piece of paper. It fell into three pieces.

I slid back the lid on a flat metal box, looked at the colorless paste inside. I'd pass the razors through the paste before I hit the street. Mortay had to get his hands on me to kill me—one scratch, and I wouldn't go alone.

Belle watched me work, cat's-eye makeup on her face.

## 165

BUSINESS BOOMED. MEN got buzzed in, looked through the book. Came and went.

We cleaned up Sunday's business at five in the morning. The Mole was wearing a black silk shirt, red suspenders, cream-colored suit. Dark glasses on his face. Michelle counted a wad of cash and credit-card slips. "You look like death," she told me.

"Good," I said.

## 166

MONDAY, BAMBI TURNED HER first hard trick. The Mole buzzed me—the video screen showed a middle-aged white male, blobby face, light-colored sport coat. Not Ramón. I heard the slash of the belt, cutting through the soundproofed walls.

Later that night, one of the tricks got off the wall. I don't know what he did. I heard Morales' voice in the corridor. "How do *you* like it, motherfucker?" Metal slamming into a face. I heard whining, Morales' voice cutting harsh through it. "Whatever you want here, we got it, see? But we got different girls for different stuff. You want hard stuff, you ask for Bambi, understand? *Bambi.*"

It got quiet after that.

## 167

HE CAME WEDNESDAY evening. Seven o'clock. The buzzer sounded. Ramón's face on the screen. I hit the switch. The light would glow on the Mole's desk.

"It's time," I said to Belle.

She was covered with body makeup head to toe. Fishnet stockings, black spike heels, black panties. She slipped into the red gown, belted it at her waist. A stranger—her face a hard mask.

I watched the screen. Ramón. Wearing a black leather bomber jacket, looking through the book. There was no sound on the screen.

"Monique!" the Mole called.

Belle walked past me into the corridor.

I held the sawed-off shotgun in my left hand, the paint pistol with the phony silencer in my right. Waiting.

I heard them come back. Belle's voice. "I get an extra hundred for hard stuff, honey."

Ramón's voice—couldn't make out the words.

The door to the last room closed.

I sucked air in through my nose, filling my stomach. Let it out, expanding my chest. Stepped into the corridor.

I couldn't hear through the door. The hook-and-eye lock was held in with paste. Every square inch of the room was burning in my mind. I slipped the pistol into a side pocket, cut deep enough to hold the silencer. Counted to five. I hit the door with my shoulder, stepping inside, sweeping the scattergun corner to corner. Belle was on the couch to my right, the red nightgown hiked over her hips. Ramón froze, a thick leather belt dangling from his hand.

The snout of the scattergun froze his balls down to dots. His hands shot into the air, belt still dangling. I stepped to him, the gun leveled at his gut. Five feet away.

"Drop it. Slow."

"Hey, man . . ."

"One more word, I'll blow you all over the walls."

The belt dropped from his hand.

His leather jacket was hanging from a hook in the corner. I could see the shoulder rig inside.

"Got any more guns on you, Ramón?"

He shook his head no.

"Take off your clothes. Real, *real* slow. I want to see for myself."

Belle's voice from the side of the room. "Mister . . ."

"Shut up, bitch!" I snapped at her.

Ramón dropped his pants. Black bikini briefs. Very macho. "Those too," I said. "Watch your hands."

He pulled off his cowboy boots, one at a time, standing on one leg, never taking his eyes from me.

"Sit on the couch," I said quietly. "Next to the cunt."

He sat down. I pulled the handcuffs off my belt, flipped them into Belle's lap. "Put them on. One cuff on your wrist, one on his. Now!"

Belle snapped the cuff on Ramón first, her hands shaking. Her left hand slid to the back of the couch cushion.

I took out the paint pistol. Slowly, letting Ramón get a good look. He didn't want one.

"You know what this is, shooter?"

"I know what it is." His voice shaking like Belle's hands.

"You got two choices. You live. Or you die. Pick one."

"I want to live, man." Thin, weak, soft voice. If he recognized me, he was keeping it to himself. Holding that card.

"Your pal Mortay, he stepped in some shit, understand? Sally Lou's decided to take him off the count."

"But . . ."

"That's the way it plays. I got my money, I got to come back with a head. His head. One more don't mean a thing to me. I'm gonna waste him. Tonight. You tell me what I want to know, you take that fucking diamond out of your ear, and you make tracks. Got it?"

"Man, I don't know where he lives!"

"You're going to meet him. Tonight. Where?"

"He'll *kill* me."

"Ramón, he's a dead man. I don't find him tonight, I find him some other time. But you don't tell me what I want to know, he won't get a chance to kill you."

"Man, I don't know where he is. I'm *serious*!"

"So am I," I said, leveling the pistol at Belle's chest. I pulled the trigger. *Splat*! Belle slammed back against the couch, a red stain running between her breasts. I aimed the gun at Ramón—he never looked at Belle. The sound I made cocking it was the loudest thing he ever heard.

"Where?"

"Under the New York Times clock! Between Seventh and Eighth! On Forty-third! *Don't!*"

"What time?"

"Ten-thirty!" Piss flowed down his legs.

"Who gets there first?"

"He does, man. He *always* does. . . ."

Belle's left hand flashed, plunging the hypo deep into his thigh, her thumb driving the plunger home as I fired a paint ball into his face.

"I . . ." and he was out. Belle rammed the speed key home, unsnapping her cuff. I pulled his free arm behind his back, locked the other cuff. Belle jumped off the couch, rubbing her breasts. I kicked Ramón onto the floor.

"Go get the Mole," I told her.

## 168

MICHELLE AND THE MOLE stood on either side of me. Ramón was in the corner, breathing deeply, out.

"The joint is closed," I told Michelle. "How many of the girls have customers?"

"Just MaryAnne."

"When he's finished, let him out. Tell the girls the show's over—the cops are going to hit in an hour. Get them out the door. You have any trouble, you hit the buzzer, they'll come from next door. Then take off yourself."

She kissed me. "Call as soon as it's over."

"I will."

She went out the door. I knelt down, pulled Ramón over my shoulder by one of his arms, positioned his weight. "The basement," I said to the Mole. Fuck McGowan and his deals—I wasn't going to leave a body around for the cops to hang me with.

He led the way. Pansy met us at the bottom of the steps. "Speak!" I told her, tossed a slab of steak through the air. She caught it on the fly.

"Is the panel truck ours?"

"Yes."

"I'm going to throw this garbage in the back. That shot'll keep him out for hours. You get stopped, it's not a murder beef. He won't testify."

"Where should I dump him?"

"He's the shooter, Mole. One of the Nazis."

He nodded.

"Take Pansy too."

"She won't . . ."

"Yes, she will. That last piece of meat I gave her was laced. She should be asleep by now. Keep her with you—lock her up in one of the sheds. Leave water for her. I'll be back in the junkyard sometime late tonight. Belle will get there before me. Your piece is done."

"The basement?"

"Eleven o'clock. You can do it?"

"Yes. Me and the boy."

"He's a good boy, Mole. You should be proud."

"You too."

"Yeah. Look, Mole. If I don't come back, do something for me. Tell Belle I love her."

He nodded.

"And Pansy, let her loose. Let her run with your pack. Let her and Simba-witz make puppies."

I dumped Ramón's body in the back of the panel truck. The Mole snapped a heavy padlock across the back.

I went back for Pansy. I scooped her up in my arms, carried her to the truck. "Open the front door," I told the Mole. "I don't want her to ride with garbage."

I laid her gently across the front seat. Kissed her snout. "See you soon, girl."

The Mole wrapped his stubby arms around me, squeezed hard. "*Sei Gesund*," he said. Go with God.

## 169

MICHELLE WAS PUSHING THE girls out the door when I slipped back upstairs. It sounded like sorority girls saying goodbye for the summer.

Belle was in the back room, toweling herself off, the cat's-eye mask still on her face.

"You were perfect," I said, holding her close.

"I was scared."

"I still am. It's almost over. Get out of here. Take the Pontiac. Don't leave the office until past midnight. I'll see you at the junkyard."

"Where's Pansy?"

"She's with the Mole. It's okay. Go."

"What'd you do with the freak?"

"He's gone."

"But you're working with the cops, right? They're right next door. He's not dead—why don't you just leave him for them?"

I cupped her chin, making her watch my face. "I'm not working with the cops, Belle. A cop sees me doing my work on the street tonight, I'm going down. McGowan, he can't call off the whole fucking force. He wouldn't do it if he could. I'm not leaving that freak around to tell his story."

I felt a pulse in her throat, just under her chin. Steady beat.

"We're outlaws, little girl. We can step over the line to the other side, but we're not welcome there. We can't stay. The next cop I see, he'll be trying to stop me from coming home."

She nodded, knowing it was the truth. "Burke, it's not even eight o'clock. You have until ten-thirty. Let me wait here with you."

"No."

"I knew you'd say that."

"It's all right, Belle. Smooth as silk. I'll meet this Mortay at ten-thirty, I'll be in one of the cars by eleven. That's when the Ghost Van goes. I'll be with you soon."

"And you'll never leave."

"And I'll never leave."

I lit a smoke, watching her dress.

"Burke?"

"You're going, Belle."

"I know. I will, promise. Remember when you came back to me? After you met that man?"

"Yeah."

"I want you inside me. To keep with me until I see you again. I want my smell on you when you kill him."

## 170

I CARRIED TWO OF THE suitcases out to the back. Tossed in the scattergun. Closed the trunk. I held her next to me.

"Belle . . ."

"Don't you say it! Whatever you're going to say, don't say it. Tell me tonight."

I kissed her. There was blood in my heart.

When she drove away, I was alone.

## 171

IN THE BACK ROOM, I put it all together. Cut two fingertips off the black gloves. Buried the plastic bottle in the cart, pistol handle sticking up, wrapped in black tape. I put on the black pants, the black sweatshirt. Worked the blond wig over my hair, stuck on the mustache. The blue golf cap was a tight fit. The black pants had cargo pockets—I put a grenade in each one. The two-inch pistol in my belt.

Pain plucked at me. Fear. I climbed down into my center. Stayed there, feeling the calm.

Mortay wanted what was mine.

If you can't stand to read the weight, you don't climb on the scales.

Ten o'clock. I pulled on the gloves, ran the two razor-tipped nails through the poison paste.

It was a struggle getting the shopping cart down the stairs.

Then I was in the street. All my people safe behind me. Whatever happened.

I reached down, deep as I could go. Telling myself it would be over soon. I'd be Home Free.

But I knew. Knew why I was pushing a shopping cart filled with homicide through Times Square. No home is free.

# 172

I PUSHED MY SHOPPING cart along, smoking a cigarette, mumbling to myself. The clock in the package store on 43rd said ten-twenty. I slowed my pace.

Three kids came up the street toward me, wearing matching red silk jackets. I watched their eyes, praying they wouldn't think it was funny to tip over my cart. They went on by.

I turned the corner. Moving slow, checking doorways for bottles, picking one up, tossing it into my cart.

The Times clock was a round light in the distance. I pushed the cart ahead of me, one hand on the pistol.

He was standing under the clock. A long white vertical ribbon in the dark doorway. The clock said ten-twenty-eight. I kept rolling.

A hundred feet away. Mortay saw me. A used-up bum, collecting empties.

Fifty feet. I saw his hands hanging loose in front of him. Head turning, scanning the street. Almost home.

I looked him full in the face. Pushed my cart into his life. Felt the chill. His eyes flicked past me, over my shoulder. I pulled the gun loose, snapped off a shot at his chest, the bottle popping off the front of the pistol. A piece of his coat flew as he spun to the side, moving right at me. I kicked the cart toward him, fired again. The gun cracked alive. Missed. Mortay spun in his tracks, shoulder-rolled against the wall. I leveled the gun. He took off, running the other way.

I jumped past the cart and took off after him. Four shots left. Humans jumped off the sidewalk. He wasn't used to running—all his speed was short-range. I was forty feet behind him at the corner of 43rd and Eighth. Mortay glanced west, gave it up, charged across 44th for the Playbill Bar. I was right behind him, the long-barreled pistol looking for his back. He chopped through people, heading for the side door. I fired another shot to clear the way, coming through. The street was clogged. He couldn't lose me.

A cop was on the corner of Eighth and 46th. Mortay took him out with one chop. I jumped over the body, holding the pistol high to clear the street, locked on him.

At 48th I was close enough. He felt it, dodging behind cars, weaving through humans. He was running out of gas. When he turned . . .

Construction site at 49th, high chain-link fence. Mortay ripped his way over the top, white coat flying as I missed another shot.

Couldn't follow him. I raced along Eighth until I found an opening, stepped through, gun up.

I dropped about five feet—they must have started the excavation. No lights. Street noises over my head. Quiet. No sirens.

I was safe there. Scared to be safe. He couldn't come up on me without getting blown away. But if he got out . . .

It was like being back in Biafra. Focus on the sounds, separate the jungle-noises from the man-noises. Breathe shallow. Don't fight the fear.

I heard him, moving west, toward Ninth Avenue. Machine-gun thoughts ripping at me. Did he know how to do this?

Something moved—flash of white in the night. I fired at the sound. The gun barked—the bullet whined close to the ground, disappointed. I heard him move again.

I got to my feet, running right at the sounds he made, cracking off another shot. One left.

Quiet now. I cocked the pistol. Man-sounds to my right.

"I'm still here, pussy." Snake voice hissing out of the night. He wasn't in a hurry.

I dropped to my knees, crawling forward toward the voice. Another flash of white. I fired. Another crack. Then a dry, audible *click!* I pulled the trigger again. Nothing.

I felt my guts lock. "Fuck!" Letting him smell my fear, throwing the empty pistol as hard as I could in the direction of the noise.

"My turn!" he screamed, coming for me.

I ran for my life, pulling the little backup pistol from my belt. I dived for the ground, rolled onto my back, pushed myself backward by driving my legs into the dirt. Making panic sounds. Leaving a blood-spoor.

Begging him to come in my mind.

He flew out of the darkness in a twisting, spinning series of kick-thrusts, a ghost target if I had a knife. I came to my knees, holding the pistol in both hands. He saw the gun, threw himself flat, already tucking his shoulder under to kick upward when the hollow-point slug caught him in the chest, pinning him to the ground.

The noise from the tiny gun was deafening; the dirt bowl we were in made it sound like a cannon. The street noises all seemed to stop at. once. I walked slowly toward Mortay. He was choking on his own blood—the slug must have caught a lung.

I stood over him, legs shaking. His eyes were ice-pick dots under the shelf of bone, holding me the way the slug held him.

"You can't kill me," he whispered. Stone-carved ice. "Death can't die."

"You still want Max?" I asked, cocking the gun.

He launched himself off the ground, the knife edge of his hand extended. I fired twice more, blowing him off his feet.

I heard a siren in the distance. Mortay was on his side. I dropped to my knees next to him. Blood bubbled from his mouth, killing his last words. I pumped two more shots into his chest. His body jumped. I turned him over with my foot. His eyes were open. I fired again, right into the ridge of bone that covered his eyebrows. His eyes wouldn't close.

The sirens were closer. More than one now. I pocketed the gun, pulled the pin from one of the grenades, holding it tightly in my hand. I slammed the metal ball hard into his face, cracking past his teeth, holding it there. With my other hand, I folded his hands so they were on either side of his face.

I let go of the lever and ran toward Ninth Avenue. Passed a white coat, swinging gently from a steel girder. The target Mortay had left while he moved in on me. I was almost to the fence on 50th when I heard the explosion. I hit the fence, sirens screaming to my right.

Dropped over the top, feeling the breath burst out of my lungs. I popped the pin on the last grenade, side-armed it back over the fence, crouching in the dark. The sirens shrieked at each other—wolf-pack sounds, telling each other the prey was dangerous. The grenade exploded, buying me a little time.

I ran up 50th, the pistol in my hand, driving my knees up to my chest, trying for a burst of speed that wouldn't come. I crossed Ninth, heading for the river, still blocks away from any of the cars we had stashed. Tires shrieked behind me. Cops? I dropped to one knee, leveling the gun. Back over the line—me or them. Belle's Camaro smoked to a stop.

"Come on, brother!" The Prof.

I ran for the car, diving headfirst into the window. Belle stomped the gas, charging for the river. She shot through red lights, standing on the brakes to make the car squat at Twelfth, nailed it again, power-sliding around the corner. She pulled off at 45th, right behind the black Cadillac the Mole had left for me. I jumped out, scooping up the Prof. His legs were still bolted together in casts, the scatter-gun steady in his hands. I unlocked the door, threw him in the back.

Blue lights flashed on 45th, couple of blocks away and moving in.

I started the engine. Looked over my shoulder. Where was she? "Belle! Let's go!" I yelled at her.

The Camaro's engine roared an answer as she peeled out. Right up 45th.

The blue lights came closer. A phalanx of squad cars screaming down the block, at least three deep, spread out to block the way. I wheeled the Cadillac across the highway after her. The Camaro's taillights blazed—she was flying at the cop cars. Head on. I heard her little-girl voice, singing hard-edged in my head. Calling to the cops. "Come on!"

The Camaro was a red rocket.

"Hit the brakes! She ain't gonna stop," the Prof yelled.

The Camaro shot right down the middle of the street, going the wrong way. The police car in the lead charged to meet her.

Time stopped. The squad car swerved at the last second. Too late.

It fireballed against a row of cars on the left as the Camaro shot past. Gunfire cut through the siren's song, a roadblock of wreckage in its wake.

"They'll never catch that girl," the Prof whispered. A prayer.

I threw a U-turn and headed for the junkyard.

## 173

ON THE WEST SIDE HIGHWAY I tried to light a cigarette. My hands wouldn't work.

"I can light one for you, bro', but I can't drive the car."

I straightened the wheel. Reached for the smoke he handed me.

"What happened?"

"Girl walks in my hospital room, shotgun in her hand. Comes right in my room. 'What's this?' the doc asks her. 'Jailbreak,' she says. Throws me over one shoulder like a sack of cement, carries me down in the elevator, walks right out the front door. Puts me in that red car. 'Burke needs us,' that's all she said."

Nothing in the rearview mirror.

"She knew I needed it too," the Prof said, hands on the scattergun. "He took something from me. She was giving me a chance to get it back. Said you were going to take out that motherfucker—our job was the cops."

I dragged on the cigarette, seeing the fireball.

The Prof read my thoughts. "Ain't nothing God or the devil put on this earth gonna catch Belle, brother. She's coming home."

## 174

I WHEELED THE CADDY into the junkyard. The gate swung open.

Terry jumped in, steered us through.

"Belle?" I asked him.

"Not yet," the kid said, his mouth hard.

The Mole was waiting. "Where's Ramón?" I asked him.

He pointed at the wolf pack. Fighting over what was left.

I lit a smoke. Carried the Prof out of the Caddy, put him on top of an oil drum. I stood with my people.

"Mortay's dead."

"You make sure?" the Prof asked.

"They'll need a microscope for the autopsy. It's over. You blow the basement?" I asked the Mole.

"You didn't hear it?" Terry said.

"No."

"It'll be on the news," the Mole said.

I looked at the Prof. "She was well away. They weren't looking for her. Why didn't she just run?"

His eyes shone in the fire. "Why didn't you?"

I couldn't answer him. Fists clenched so tight my arms ached.

The little man dragged on his smoke. "Her dice, brother. Hers to hold, hers to roll."

## 175

TORTURED RUBBER screamed on concrete.

"Belle. The back way!" the kid shouted, taking off. We ran to the fence. The Camaro shot through, skidding past us. It stopped where the Prof was sitting. Belle didn't get out.

I ran back to her. Bullet holes stitched the driver's door. I wrenched it open. Belle fell into my arms. The Mole reached past me, unsnapped the seat belt. I carried her to the bunker. "Don't talk," I said, lowering her to the ground.

Her gray sweatshirt was one big dark stain. The Mole cut it away. She was torn to pieces, the blue necklace around her neck. "Get the medical kit," he said to Terry.

I bent close to her. "Hold on, Belle. You'll be okay in just a minute."

Her eyes were closed. They flicked open. "Burke?"

"You're home now, Belle. It's all right."

Her voice was soft. "My race is run, honey. I'm done."

"Shut up! Save your strength."

"Tell me."

"I love you, Belle."

"I'll be waiting for you," she said. Her eyes closed. The Mole shouldered me out of the way, plunged a needle into her chest, his fingers at her neck. I was on my knees, watching him work, begging in my mind.

He turned to me. "She's gone."

## 176

THE LEFT ME ALONE with her then.

I couldn't hold it in me—screaming curses at the night. The dogs went quiet.

I lay down next to her, wrapping her in my arms. Tears on blood.

## 177

THE SKY WAS GETTING light when they came back. The Mole. Terry. The Prof, riding a wheelchair.

I stood next to the little man, my hand on his shoulder. Felt his hand on mine.

"Pull it together, brother. The way she'd want it. She's with the Lord now. And He's one lucky son of a bitch."

The Mole covered her with a prayer rug.

I gripped my brother's hand, and said goodbye to my Blue Belle.

# Hard Candy

They don't give medals on this planet
for courage in urban combat.
But there are silver stars shining in the sky
that the astronomers can't explain.

ALMA HENRY

BESSIE MYRICK

MARY SPENCER

# 1

CITY VULTURES NEVER have to leave the ground.

I was standing on the upper level of the Port Authority Bus Terminal, waiting in the November night. Back to the wall, hands in the empty pockets of a gray raincoat. Under the brim of my hat, my eyes swept the deck. A tall, slim black youth wearing a blue silk T-shirt under a pale yellow sport coat. Baggy pants with small cuffs. Soft Italian shoes. Today's pimp—waiting for the bus to spit out its cargo of runaways. He'd have a Maxima with blacked-out windows waiting in the parking lot. Talk about how hard it was to get adjusted to the city—how he was the same way himself when he hit town. He'd be a talent scout for an independent film producer. If the girl wanted, he'd let her stay at his place for a few days until she got herself together. Projection TV, VCR, sweet stereo. A little liquor, a little cocaine. High-style. The way it's done, you know. Another black guy in his thirties. Gold medallion on his chest under a red polyester shirt that would pass for silk in the underground lights. Knee-length black leather coat, player's hat with a tasteful red band. Alligator-grain leather on his feet. Yesterday's pimp—waiting his turn. He'd have an old Caddy, talk his talk, make you a star. A furnished room in a no-see hotel down the street. Metal coat hangers in his closet that would never hold clothes.

You could go easy or you could go hard.

Two youngish white guys, talking low, getting their play together. Hoping the fresh new boys getting off the bus wouldn't be *too* old.

A blank-faced Spanish kid, black sweatshirt, hood pulled up tight around his head. Felony-flyers on his feet. Carry your bags, ma'am?

A few citizens, waiting on relatives coming back from vacation. Or a kid coming home from school. A bearded wino picking through the trash.

The Greyhound's air brakes hissed as it pulled into the loading port. Night bus from Starke, Florida. A twenty-four-hour ride—change buses in Jacksonville. The round-trip ticket cost $244.

I know—I paid for it.

The man I was waiting for would have a letter in his pocket. A letter in a young girl's rounded handwriting. Blue ink on pink stationery.

> Daddy, I know it's been a long time, but I didn't know where you was. I been working with some boys and I got myself arrested a couple years ago. One of the cops took my name and put it in one of their computers. He told me where you was, but I didn't write for a while because I wanted to have something good to tell you. I'm sorry Sissy made me run away that time without even telling you goodbye like I wanted. I wrote to her but the letter came back. Do you know where she's at? I guess she got married or something. Anyway, Daddy, you'll never believe it, but I got a lot of money now. I'm real good at this business I'm in. I got a boyfriend too. I thought you could use a stake to get you started after you got out, but I didn't want to mail no cash to a prison. Wasn't that right?
>
> Anyway, Daddy, when you get ready to come out, you write to me at this Post Office box I got now and I'll send you the money for the ticket up here. It would be like a vacation

> or something. And I could give you the money I have saved up. I hope you're doing okay, Daddy. Love, Belle.

The slow stream of humans climbed down. Hands full of plastic shopping bags, cartons tied together with string, duffel bags. Samsonite doesn't ride the 'Hound too often.

He was one of the last off the bus. Tall, rawboned man, small eyes under a shock of taffy-honey hair. Belle's eyes, Belle's hair. A battered leather satchel in one hand. The Spanish kid never gave him a second glance. A cop would, but there weren't any around.

I felt a winter's knot where my heart should have been.

His eyes played around the depot like it was a prison yard. I moved to him, taking my hands out of my pockets, showing them empty. He'd never seen me before, but he knew the look.

"You're from Belle?" he asked. A hard voice not softened by the cracker twang.

"I'll take you to her," I promised, turning my back on him so he could follow, keeping my hands in sight.

I passed up the escalator, taking the stairs to the ground floor. Felt the man moving behind me. And Max, shadow-quiet, keeping the path clear behind us both.

## 2

THE PLYMOUTH WAS PARKED on a side street off Ninth Avenue. I opened the driver's door, climbed in, unlocked his door. Giving him all the time in the world to bolt if he wanted to try it.

He climbed in next to me, looked behind him. Saw a pile of dirty blankets.

"No back seat in this wagon?"

"Sometimes I carry things."

He smiled his smile. Long yellow teeth catching the neon from a topless bar. "You work with Belle?"

"Sometimes."

"She's a good girl."

I didn't answer him, pointing the Plymouth to the West Side Highway. I lit a smoke, tossing the pack on the dash. He helped himself, firing a match off his thumbnail, leaning back in his seat.

I turned east across 125th Street, Harlem's Fifth Avenue, heading for the Triboro Bridge.

"You all got nothin' *but* niggers 'round here," he said, watching the street.

"Yeah, they're everyplace."

"You ever do time with niggers?"

"All my life."

I tossed a token in the Exact Change basket on the bridge and headed for the Bronx. The Plymouth purred off the highway onto Bruckner Boulevard, feeling its way to Hunts Point. He watched the streets.

"Man, if it's not niggers, it's spics. This ain't no city for a white man."

"You like the joint better?"

His laugh was short. Ugly.

I motored through the streets. Blacked-out windows in abandoned buildings—dead eyes in a row of corpses. Turned off the main drag heading toward the meat market. Whores working naked under clear plastic raincoats stopped the trucks at the lights. We crossed an empty prairie, tiny dots of light glowing where things that had been born human kept fires burning all night long.

I pulled up to the junkyard gate. Left him in the car while I reached my hand through a gap in the razor-wire to open the lock. We drove inside and stopped. I got back out and relocked the gate. Climbed back inside, rolled down the window. Lit a smoke.

"What do we do now?"

"We wait."

The dogs came. A snarling pack, swarming around the car.

"Damn! Belle's *here?*"

"She's here."

The Mole lumbered through the pack, knocking the dogs out of his way as he walked, like he always does. He came up to my open window, peered inside at the man in the front seat.

"This is him?"

"Yeah."

He clapped his hands together. Simba came out of the blackness. A city wolf, boss of the pack. The beast stood on his hind legs, forepaws draped over the windowsill, looking at the man like he knew him. A low, thick sound came out of the animal, like his throat was clogged.

"We walk from here," I told the man.

His eyes were hard, no fear in them. "I ain't walkin' *anywhere*, boy. I don't like none a this."

"Too bad."

"Too bad for you, boy. You look real close, you'll see my hand ain't empty."

I didn't have to look close. I knew what he'd have in his satchel—they don't use metal detectors on the Greyhound.

The dirty pile of blankets in the back of the Plymouth changed shape. The man grunted as he felt the round steel holes against the back of his neck.

"Your hole card is a low card, motherfucker." The Prophet's voice, low and strong for such a tiny man. "I see your pistol and raise you one double-barreled scattergun."

"Toss it on the seat," I told him. "Don't be stupid."

"Where's Belle? I came to see Belle."

"You'll see her. I promise."

His pistol made a soft plop on the front seat. The Mole opened his door. The man got out, the Prof's shotgun covering him. I walked around to his side of the car. "Let's go," I told him, my voice quiet.

We walked through the junkyard until we came to a clearing. "Have a seat," I said, pointing toward a cut-down oil drum. Taking a seat myself, lighting a smoke.

He sat down, reaching out a large hand to snatch at the pack of smokes I tossed over to him.

"What now?"

"We wait," I said.

Terry stepped into the clearing. A slightly built boy wearing a set of dirty coveralls. "That him?" he asked.

I nodded. The kid lit a smoke for himself, watching the man. The dog pack watched too. With the same eyes.

The Mole stumbled up next to me, the Prof at his side. The little man supported himself on a cane, the scattergun in his other hand.

"Pansy!" I called out. She lumbered out of the darkness, a Neapolitan mastiff, a hundred and forty pounds of power. Her black fur gleamed blue in the faint light, cold gray eyes sweeping the area. She walked toward the tall man, a steamroller looking at fresh-poured tar. "Jump!" I snapped at her. She hit the ground, her eyes pinning the man where he sat.

I looked around one more time. All Belle's family was in that junkyard. All that was left, except for Michelle. And she'd already done her part.

The Prophet handed me a pistol. "Here's the sign—now's the time."

I stood up.

"They got the death penalty in Florida?" I asked the man.

"You know they do."

"They got it for incest?"

His eyes flickered. He knew. "Where's Belle? Let me talk to her!"

"Too late for that. She's gone. In the same ground you're standing on."

"I never did nothin' to you . . ."

"Yeah, you did. I don't have a speech for you. You're dead."

"I got people know where I am."

The Prophet smiled at him. "Motherfucker, *you* don't even know where you are."

"You want the kid to see this?" I asked the Mole.

Light played on the thick lenses of his glasses. "He watched *her* die."

I cocked the pistol.

He kept his voice low. Reasonable. "Look, if I owe, I can pay. I'm a man who pays his debts."

"You couldn't pay the *interest* on this one," I told him.

"Hey! I got money, I can . . ."

"I'm not the Parole Board," I said. The pistol cracked. He jerked backwards off the oil drum. I fired twice more, watching his body jump as each bullet went home.

The Prophet hobbled over to him. The shotgun spoke. Again.

I looked at the body for a dead minute.

We bowed our heads.

Pansy howled at the dark sky, grief and hate in one voice. The pack went silent, hearing her voice.

I didn't feel a thing.

## 3

AFTER THE COPS TOOK Belle off the count, I thought about dying too. Thought about it a lot. The Prophet told me the truth.

"If there's something out there past this junkyard, she'll be waiting for you, brother."

"And if there's not?"

"Then what's your hurry?"

"I feel dead inside me," I told the little man with the hustler's soul and the lion's heart. The man who helped raise me inside the walls. Everyone called him the Prof. I thought it was short for Professor—he knew and he taught. But Prophet was the true root. A man who sees the truth sees the future. He showed me both—showed me how to be a man.

Or whatever it is that I am.

"You know what to do with it," he told me.

I knew. Survive is what I knew. What I know. The only tune I know how to play.

Down here, we have rules. We made them ourselves. Feeling dead inside me—that was a feeling. It wouldn't bring Belle back to me—wouldn't get me closer. But making somebody dead . . . that was a debt.

Belle's father. The maggot who made her older sister into her mother. He loaded her genetic dice. She never had a chance. Her mother died so she could run, and she ran until she died.

I was holding her in my arms when she went, torn to pieces by bullets she took for me. She looked it in the eye when it came for her.

## 4

BELLE DIED IN THE SPRING. I went cold through the summer. Waiting.

Her father was in a prison in Florida, finishing up a manslaughter bit. I did some checking—learned they'd cut him loose in late October.

Michelle wrote the letter, copying Belle's handwriting from a poem the big girl once tried to write.

If her father had any family left to spend Thanksgiving with, there'd be an empty chair at the table.

But the cold was still in me.

## 5

I SLIPPED MY PLYMOUTH through Chinatown, heading for Mama's. The car didn't feel the same since Belle left. I couldn't make it sing the way she could. Her Camaro was cut up into a thousand pieces in the Mole's junkyard. Her body was in the ground. She left her clothes at my office, her life savings stashed in the hiding place in my garage. I burned the clothes. Kept the money. Like she would have wanted.

It was the fourth day I'd made the run past Mama's, checking the dragon tapestries in the window. One red, one white, one blue. Mama's a patriot. But not a citizen. None of us are.

The blue tapestry had been up for days. Cops. The newspapers said the porno theater had been blown up by some extremist group. The searchers found enough evidence to drop Salvatore Lucastro—drop him hard. His snuff-film business was as dead as the little girls he made into movie stars. Sally Lou was looking at a bunch of life sentences, running wild. Some flowers can only grow in the dark. The local badges had a bad attitude. They weren't surprised that the *federales* snatched the evidence. They knew Sally Lou's ass was going to be RICO'd. Continuing Criminal Enterprise. But there was supposed to be something left for them. A couple of bodies. I left pieces of one all over a construction site in Times Square. Took the other one with me to the junkyard. Put it through the recycling program: it turns freaks into dog shit.

That was months ago. By now, the cops knew they'd never find the bodies. But they knew where to find me.

It played the same way it had for the last few dead months. The cops would come around, ask their questions, make their threats, go away.

When they got tired of sending around the hard boys, they sent McGowan.

"I thought we had a deal," he said, his cop's eyes sad and hard at the same time. A good trick. Pimps can do it too. He and his partner, Morales, they had let me run a massage parlor in Times Square with police cover. The perfect bait for a maggot who took his pleasure in women's pain. Blood-orgasms. I was supposed to leave them something when I cleared out, but I took it with me. And left it in a junkyard.

"I don't know what you're talking about."

"Yeah you do. You think you walk away from this, you're wrong. I don't give a good goddamn about another collar. You know that. But you're on the list now. I don't know how you made the shooter disappear, but they found pieces of that karate freak all over the lot."

The karate freak who'd crippled the Prophet to send me a message.

"What karate freak?" I asked him.

"You want to play it that way?"

"I'm not playing."

"Not anymore you're not," he said, getting up to leave.

## 6

THE WHEEL SPUN TOO many times. They'd always be them—I'd always be me. Some cops went bad. I couldn't go good.

I stayed low to the ground for months, waiting for the Greyhound to deliver Belle's father. Didn't get a parking ticket, didn't bet on a horse. Lived like Gary Hart should have.

There was nothing else to wait for.

## 7

IT PLAYED THE SAME way with Max too. He'd sit across from me, make the gesture for "Why?" I'd shrug my shoulders. Who knows? He never pushed it past that.

Mama knew why. Maybe she'd told Immaculata, I didn't know. But she'd never tell Max.

Only the white tapestry was in the window. I pulled into the alley behind the restaurant, just past the Chinese characters neatly marked on the wall. I didn't bother to lock the car.

I went through the back door, barely glancing at the collection of thugs pretending to be the kitchen staff. Took my table at the back.

Mama was saying goodbye to a customer at the front by the cash register. She didn't put her heart and soul into it—the customer had only bought food.

She came back to where I was sitting, waving her hand at the waiter. He knew what to do.

I got up as she approached. Thick glossy hair tied in a rigid bun at the back of her head, plum-colored sheath covering her from neck to ankles, same color nail polish and lipstick. Dignified, not sexy. Mama never got older.

I bowed to her by way of greeting. "Cops all gone?"

"They come back soon."

"I know."

"Something else happen. Soon enough. Police get tired easy."

"Yeah."

The waiter brought a steaming tureen of hot-and-sour soup. Mama filled my bowl first, then hers.

We ate the soup in silence. She filled my bowl again. I finished it. Shook my head no at her unasked question. The waiter took the bowls away.

I lit a smoke. "It's done," I told her.

"All finish now?"

"Yeah."

She bowed slightly. "Soon, be yourself again?"

I tried a smile, watching her face. She knew a three-dollar bill when she saw one.

"Max on his way."

I didn't say anything.

"Time to stop all this, Burke. Max your brother."

"You think I don't know that? It's not my fault. I did the right thing."

It didn't even feel right saying it.

I felt Max behind me. I didn't turn around. Lit a cigarette as Mama bowed to him. She went back to the front desk. He flowed into the booth across from me, watching my face the same way he had ever since he came back from Boston. Where Mama had sent him on a phony mission to clean up some problem she was supposed to be having with a street gang shaking down one of her joints.

Max the Silent doesn't speak. He can't. He was a free-lance warrior until he met Mama. I met him in the jailhouse—he brought me to Mama when we got out. I took a fall that was part his years ago, when the wheels came off a sting we'd put together. I was there when he met his woman, Immaculata. His baby daughter, Flower, was named for another baby—a baby who never lived to grow up. A baby a chubby little blonde fought a death-duel to avenge. Flood was her name. She loved me and she went back to Japan.

I used to dream about her coming back.

I don't have any more dreams.

He didn't ask me today. The waiter brought him a bowl of fried rice and a pitcher of ice water. I watched him eat, smoking another cigarette. I wasn't hungry.

The waiter took the rice bowl away. I got up to split. To go nowhere. Max pushed his hand toward the tabletop, like there was a delicate bubble of air he was holding to the surface. Stay for a minute.

I sat back in the booth. He pointed to the empty place next to me. Floated his hands before me into a kung fu dragon-master opening. I nodded my head. Yeah, a karate-fighter. So?

He pointed a finger to himself—weaved his own hands in an answering gesture.

I nodded again. The man wanted Max. Wanted to challenge him to a duel.

He pointed at me again, made a gesture of dismissal. He flipped a chopstick between his fingers—snapped it like a dry twig. Right again. I'm no *karateka*—no match for a master.

Max took a sip of water, his eyes pinning me. He waved his hands again, another challenge. Shook his head no. Held up his hand like a traffic cop. Shrugged his shoulders. No big deal. Max the Silent didn't fight for fun. He'd just walk away. It wasn't an ego thing.

He spread his hands in the "why?" gesture again.

It didn't matter anymore.

I jerked a thumb to my right, indicating the challenger. I pointed at Max, put my hands on the table in front of him, two fingers down from each fist. Men walking. I had them approach each other. Stop. One finger pawing the air before the other. Turned one hand and had the fingers walk away. Felt his eyes on my hands. I pulled one hand off the table, flattened it into a wall, slammed it down in front of the two fingers walking away. No. You *can't* walk away. His eyes lifted to meet mine. I took the hand that had been a wall and brought it to my chest. Made the sign of rocking a baby. Pointed to him. *Your* baby. I lifted one hand gently to where the baby's head would have been, watching my brother's face. Held his eyes as I slashed a finger across the child's throat. The *karateka*'s ante in the death-game. *Somebody* dies. "I can always make a man fight," the maniac told me.

Max locked my eyes, making it not true in his mind. But he knew. I heard a sharp crack. The water glass popped in his hand. Blood flowed across the knuckles.

My brother bowed slowly to me. And then he was gone.

I lit another cigarette. Mama came back to the booth. A waiter made the blood disappear.

"You tell him, yes?"

I didn't answer her. She left me alone.

## 8

WEEKS WENT BY LIKE that. Slow, gray time. Like being inside. I stayed where I was, not even waiting. McGowan's partner took his shot too. Morales, a thickset Puerto Rican. He got right to it, bracing me in the basement poolroom. I was pushing the balls around the green felt by myself when he walked in. Took a seat and watched me for a while, not saying anything. The stick artists ignored him—the salesmen moved away from our area. There's rooms upstairs you can rent by the hour.

He tilted his hat back, small dark eyes like bullet holes in his head. Watching.

I stroked the bright orange five ball into the corner pocket. The cue ball reversed itself on the short rail and slapped into a cluster of balls, scattering them.

"Nice shot," Morales said.

I chalked my cue. Nudged the four ball into the same pocket.

"You're a good shooter, I hear."

I tapped the thirteen, sliding it toward the opposite corner. Chalked my cue again.

"Funny game, pool," he said. "You shoot a ball, you do it right, and it just disappears right off the table."

I banked the ten ball into the side pocket.

He got up, poked through the racks of standing cues, found one that suited him.

"Let's you and me play a game," he said, sweeping the loose balls together into the triangular rack. Nine balls.

"Five and ten?" I asked him.

He tilted his head toward a dirty hand-painted sign on the near wall. No Gambling.

"It wouldn't be," I told him.

His lips curled. He didn't pretend it was a smile. "One money ball—a dime on the nine?"

I nodded. He reached in his pocket for a coin, started to toss it on the table.

"Do it," I said, sitting down.

Morales broke the balls the way he'd like to break mine. With a hard, straight-ahead slash. Lots of power, no stroke. The balls scattered, running for cover. The three dropped in. He power-slammed the one ball, not even thinking about running the table. A slugger—no finesse. When the dust settled, there were still eight balls on the green cloth.

He sat down, watching. I tapped the one ball down the long rail, leaving myself a clear shot at the two. Dumped it in. I kissed the cue off the four ball into the nine. The yellow-and-white striped ball went home. Morales got up to rack the balls. I raised my eyebrows at him.

"Put it on my tab."

I flicked my eyes to the No Gambling sign.

His face went dark. He took a deep breath through his nose, remembering why he was there. Tossed a crumpled ten-spot on the table. I picked it up, smoothed it out. Left it lying on the rail.

I made the nine ball on the break.

Morales put another ten down on the rail. Racked the balls.

I broke again. Two balls dropped. I lined up on the one.

His voice was light, hard-cored. Honey-coated aluminum. "Upstate, when you come in on a homicide beef, you know what they say about you?"

"Tough luck?"

"They say you got a body. Nice, huh? Some punk snuffs an old lady for the Welfare check, he struts around the block saying, 'I got a body.' You ever hear that one?"

"No."

I ran the rest of the table. Morales put a twenty down, taking back one of the tens. He racked the balls. I chalked my cue. Lit a smoke.

"We met once before, remember?"

"No."

"You remember my name?"

I locked his eyes. "Something with an 'M,' right? Miranda?"

"Smart guy. You got a body, Burke?"

My eyes never left his face. "You guys have one?" I asked.

"See you soon," he said, walking away.

I put his money in my pocket. Went back to pushing the balls around the table.

## 9

I DIDN'T NEED THE cop's cash. There'd been a fifty-grand bounty on the Ghost Van. A killing machine for baby prostitutes. Pimps put up the coin—it was bad for business. Marques Dupree made the offer in a parking lot. Take the van off the street and collect the money. It was supposed to be a four-way split: me, the Prof, the Mole, and Max.

Then it went to hell. A *karateka* who called himself Mortay was bodyguarding the van. The freak was a homicide-junkie. He fought a death-match in the basement of a porno circus. The players liked it even better than watching pit bulls or cockfights. And after that he walked through Times Square, frightening even the hard-core freaks. But the whispers stayed on the street. Max the Silent. The life-taking, widow-making wind of death, as the Prof named him years ago. Max could beat this Mortay.

The freak wanted Max. I tried to talk to him and he raised the stakes. Max fights him or Max's baby goes down.

I dealt Max out. Called in my chips. One of Mortay's boys was gunned down in a Chelsea playground. By El Cañonero, rifleman for the UGL, the underground Puerto Rican independence group headed by my compadre Pablo. Another was dog food. Belle dealt herself in. The van was scrap metal. And Mortay himself—they'd need a microscope to find the pieces.

I had a lot of bodies. And the cold ground had Belle's.

I didn't have to look for Marques. He called Mama—left frantic messages all over the city. Couldn't wait to put the cash in my hand.

I split it with the Prof and the Mole. The junkyard-genius would take care of Michelle. Belle left a stash behind—that was mine too.

Bail money. For a jail I couldn't walk out of.

## 10

BY THE TIME SUMMER left the city, I thought the heat would leave me alone. But even months later, there was no place to go.

I was in a bar off Times Square. Sitting with the Prof, waiting for Michelle. I got up to get the Prof a brew. The place was packed, music screaming so loud the heavy metal clanged. The whole joint was about as much fun as chemotherapy. I bumped into a stud hustler on my way back to the table. He muttered something. I kept moving.

Michelle slipped her way through the crowd. Wearing a white beret, deep purple silk blouse, white pencil skirt, spike heels to match the blouse. An orchid in a sewer. She kissed me on the cheek, her big dark eyes wary.

"How you doing, honey?"

"The same."

The stud hustler I had bumped came over to our table, thumbs hooked in a bicycle chain he used for a belt. Pretty boy. Short spiky haircut. He leaned forward, eyes on me. His buddies behind him a few feet.

"You made me spill my beer."

His voice sounded tough. The way a worn-out car with a bad muffler sounds fast.

I threw a five-dollar bill on the table. "Buy another."

"How about an apology?"

I felt a tiny pulse in my temple. I crumpled the bill in my fist, tossed it onto the dirty floor.

Muscles flexed along the surface of his bare arms. "Get up!"

Michelle lit one of her long black cigarettes. Blew smoke at the ceiling. "Sweetie, go back to whatever you were doing, okay?"

He turned on her. "I don't need no fucking he-she telling me what to do."

Two dots of color on Michelle's cheeks.

The Prof turned his air conditioner on the heat. "There's no beef, Chief. Take the five and slide."

"You got nice friends," the hustler said. "A cross-dresser and a midget nigger."

The Prof smiled. "I'm a thief, boy. I may pull a little vic, but I don't suck dick."

The hustler's face went orange in the nightclub lights. "Let's go outside," he suggested to me, pounding a fist into an open palm.

"He don't have the time, sonny," the Prof answered for me.

"It won't take long."

One of his friends laughed.

The Prof wouldn't let it go. "Yeah it would. About ten to twenty years, punk. Even if they let it slide with manslaughter."

I pushed back my chair.

"Burke!" Michelle snapped.

The place went quiet.

"That's you?" the hustler asked. His voice was a strangulated hernia.

"You know the name, you know the game," the Prof answered for me.

"Hey, man . . . it was a joke. Okay?"

I sat there, waiting. He backed away. He didn't bump into his friends—they were gone.

It wasn't just the cops who knew I had a body. And whose body I had.

## 11

ON THE STREET OUTSIDE the bar, Michelle grabbed my arm. "What the fuck is *wrong* with you?" She wheeled on the Prof. "And what about you? You turning back the clock twenty years? This idiot's back to being a gunfighter and you're his manager, right?"

"My man's in pain, lady. Give us some play, back away."

Michelle's eyes glittered, hands on hips. I put my hand on her arm—she shrugged it off.

"This isn't *like* you, baby. You're making me nervous."

"It's okay," I said.

"It's *not* okay. You want to go back to prison? Over some stupid argument in a bar?"

"I'm not going back to prison. Just take it easy. We'll drive you home."

She turned and walked away, heels clicking hard on the concrete, not looking back.

## 12

THREE MORE DEAD DAYS later, they took me down. Right off the street. The Prof spotted them first.

"Rollers on the right," the little man said under his breath.

"Probably behind us too. Call Davidson," I said. I tossed my cigarette into the gutter, slipped my right hand into my coat pocket to make them think I might not go along nicely, and slid away to draw them from the Prof. I quick-stepped it along Forty-fifth Street, heading west toward the river. Feeling the heat. Unmarked cop car running parallel to me in the street. Spotted a gay-porn movie house. Heard car doors slam as I slid my money through the slot for a ticket. They wouldn't want to follow me inside. Two slabs of beef shouldered in on each side, pinning my arms, pulling my hands behind me. Cuffs snapped home. They spun me around. A cop I hadn't seen before sang their song.

"You're under arrest. You have the right to remain silent. Anything you say can and will be used against you in . . ."

They patted me down before they shoved me into the blue-and-white that pulled to the curb.

Nobody said a word on the ride downtown.

They left me alone in a holding cell for an hour or so. I didn't ask to make a phone call. I did that once, when I was a kid. Just to be doing it—I had nobody to call. Now I knew better. On both counts.

They brought me into the interrogation room. Two detectives I never saw before shouldered in behind me. Street cops. Wash-and-wear suits, bad haircuts, sidewalk shoes. They looked alike. Same size, same weight. Same eyes.

"You want a smoke?" the first one asked.

"How much are they?"

The second one grunted. "On the house," the first guy said.

I nodded. He tossed a pack on the table, pushed a dull metal Zippo across to me. I rolled my thumb carefully across the surface of the lighter, held it up to the light, slid it back to him. The second guy laughed. Threw a book of paper matches at me. I lit a cigarette.

"You want to make a statement?"

"About what?"

"You're busted. Homicide."

I blew smoke at the ceiling.

A knock at the door. The second guy opened it. The new guy was flashier. Younger. Nice suit, silk tie, dimple under the knot. Spent money on his haircut. Mirror shine on his black loafers. Even had tassels on them. The B Team. He took the seat across from me. The street-sweepers stood in the background.

"I'm Detective Lieutenant Swanson. And you're . . ."

"Under arrest."

One of the street cops snorted. The lieutenant gave me a hard look. "I thought you had more sense than that. What's it gonna get you, pal? You know the score. You don't give up your prints, we can hold you forever. You stand for the prints, your rap sheet falls on you and the judge is gonna remand your ass. You're looking at a few months on Rikers Island even if you beat this."

"I already gave you my prints."

One of the rollers laughed. The lieutenant looked unhappy. "Don't play games, okay? You know how it works. We got some homicides, we got a building blown all to hell in Times Square. We got feds taking fucking bows with their big score. We want ours, okay?"

"What's yours?"

"You tell me, pal. It *could* be you. It don't have to be. Understand? You got something to trade?"

I ground out my cigarette.

The lieutenant looked at his watch. Two gold bracelets on his wrist. "Last chance," he said.

I lit another smoke.

"Don't you even want to know who you killed?"

I blew smoke in his face.

He pushed his chair back. "Book him," he snapped to the two street cops, walking out the door.

This time all three of us laughed.

## 13

IT WAS ONE IN THE morning before they brought me downtown for arraignment. The Lobster Shift: they run arraignments twenty-four hours a day in Manhattan. Seven days a week. I spotted Davidson in the front row, dressed like he was going to face a jury, wide-awake. I waited for my name to be called.

Wolfe was arguing with the judge. If she was standing up at a night arraignment, the defendant must be some major degenerate. She was standing by herself at the counsel table, ten pounds of paper spread out in front of her, a guy who looked like a bouncer in a waterfront bar just behind her. Her voice was soft, but it carried.

"Twenty-nine counts, Your Honor. Twenty-nine *separate* counts. Seven complaining witnesses. That's seven *children.* The People respectfully request that the defendant be remanded until trial."

The defendant was sitting straight up, facing the judge. Well-dressed, dignified. Looked outraged to be in such a place. His lawyer was an older man, beautiful shock of white hair falling almost to his shoulders, church deacon's voice.

"Your Honor, if I may be heard. *Doctor* West is a prominent member of the community. A man without a *scintilla* of a criminal record. A family man, whose wife and children are shocked by these obviously false allegations. The People's request for a remand is simply outrageous. I assure you we intend to fight these scandalous charges on the *merits*, and we are contemplating the appropriate civil remedies against the parents of these obviously misguided children. I'm sure this young lady means well . . ."

"Don't patronize me, you pompous clown!" Wolfe's voice lashed out.

"That will be enough," the judge said, looking at Wolfe.

"From who?" she snapped back.

"From *both* of you. The Court has heard enough. Bail is set at one hundred thousand dollars."

The white-haired lawyer smiled.

"Application to surrender his passport, Your Honor"—from Wolfe.

"Your Honor, I really don't think . . ."

"Granted," said the judge.

One of the fancy lawyer's assistants walked over to the clerk to make the bail arrangements as they brought me forward for my turn. The white-haired lawyer walked up to Wolfe. "My client . . ."

"Tell him to go play with his nitrous oxide," Wolfe snarled at him. She looked up as Davidson stepped in next to me. A lovely woman, tall and shapely, her dark hair drawn back from her face, streaks of white like wings sweeping through it. Our eyes met. She said something out of the side of her mouth to the heavyweight who was with her. Swept her papers into a big briefcase and walked away. We all watched her leave, spike heels clicking on the old marble floor.

The heavyweight stepped in next to me, barrel chest against my shoulder. "You got money on the books?" You go down broke, you stay broke. Wolfe knew what you have to do to get cigarette money inside jail. And she didn't want me doing it. The kind of law enforcement they never taught her in the DA's Office.

I nodded. He left to follow Wolfe, covering her back like he always does.

I shook hands with Davidson. "You didn't make a statement," he said, making one of his own.

The ADA who took Wolfe's place was a young guy. Tired-looking. Mustache too big for his face. The B Team detective was standing next to him, looking more like a lawyer than anyone else there.

The judge stared down from the bench. I stared back—I'd seen him before. One of those "why not the best?" political appointees who climbed the ladder using Preparation H for lip gloss. "Gentlemen . . . any point in discussing this?" He wasn't talking to me.

The ADA started to approach the bench.

Davidson stayed where he was. "No" is all he said.

The ADA went back to his stand. "Judge, the charge is Murder Two. The defendant has an extensive criminal history, including the use of firearms to commit violence. He has no roots in the community, and there is a significant possibility he will flee before trial."

Davidson's face was already red. "What trial? There isn't going to *be* a trial, Judge. This was a pretextual arrest, and the People know it. Or they *should* know it. This case won't survive the Grand Jury. I examined these so-called papers I was handed an hour ago," he barked, waving the yellow-backed sheaf that signaled Felony. "My client is alleged to have killed one Robert Morgan, whoever *that* is, several *months* ago. Period. I don't see a *hint* of what this arrest was based on: no statements, no evidence . . . we aren't even told how this person allegedly died . . . was he shot, stabbed, stomped, poisoned . . . what? My client was arrested on the street. If he was going to flee, he's had enough time to circle the globe, much less leave New York. Where's the connection between this Robert Morgan and my client? Where's the motive? Hell, where's the *body?*" he sneered, looking directly at the detective. Telling him he knew.

The judge was unmoved—he only jumped for state senators on up. "Mr. Gonzales?" he asked the ADA.

"Your Honor, Mr. Davidson knows he can file discovery motions and learn the substance of the People's case. This is an arraignment, not a trial."

"Probable cause!" shouted Davidson.

"We don't need probable cause for an arraignment!"

"You need it for a damn *arrest!*"

"Gentlemen! Approach the bench, please."

I couldn't hear what they were saying. Davidson kept shoving his husky body at the ADA, his face turning as dark as his beard. The ADA kept shrugging his shoulders, tilting his head toward the detective. The judge called the detective up front. Listened, a flat, skeptical look on his face.

Davidson came back to the counsel table. Whispered "Three days" under his breath.

The judge swept the tables with his eyes. "The defendant is remanded for three days. Three days, Mr. Assistant District Attorney. During which time there will *either* be a felony hearing *or* this matter will be presented to the Grand Jury. Is that clear?"

"Yes, Your Honor."

"And if it is not, the defendant is to be released on his own recognizance, by agreement of the People. Yes, Mr. Gonzales?"

"Yes, Your Honor."

"Next case."

I shook hands with Davidson again. They took me away.

# 14

WHEN THEY CAME TO my cell the next day and told me I had a visit from my lawyer I knew it wasn't Davidson. That wasn't the way he worked.

They brought me into a private room. Toby Ringer stepped in. Toby's a Bureau Chief in the Manhattan DA's Office. A stand-up guy, killer trial lawyer, homicide specialist. He plays the game square. I don't know how he's kept his job this long, but he'll never be a judge. Neither will Wolfe.

He offered his hand. I took it. And the three packs of cigarettes he pulled out of his briefcase.

"You know why I'm here?"

"No."

"The arrest won't stand up. We all know that, okay? Nobody thinks you smoked this Robert Morgan. Somebody dropped a dime, but the word is that he won't testify no matter what. But we do know Morgan was tied in with the Ghost Van, and we know the Ghost Van's gone. Couple of more guys gone along with it. You know the story."

"So?"

"That was your work, Burke. It's all over the street. Wall-to-wall. The word is you're a gun for hire now. Contract hitter."

I dragged on my smoke.

"I don't think that's true either, okay? But whoever blew up Sally Lou's operation, he left a big fat hole. And the wiseguys are stacking up to fill it. It was his time, anyway."

I looked a question at him.

"Yeah, there was a contract out on him. Four big guys have been hit in the past few months. And the Italians are getting real nervous. They can't figure out who's moving on who."

I shrugged.

"Yeah, right. Why should you care? Here's why *we* care. They're scared, Burke. So they went to the well. Dead bodies. And more coming. Wesley's back to work."

The little room went dark in the corners.

"That's who we want, Burke. Wesley. That's why I came out here. To give you the message."

"You bring any cheese with you in that briefcase?"

He took a breath. Snorted it out. "Save the speeches, hard guy. We all know you're not a rat. I'm telling you this for your own good."

"Sure."

He leaned across the desk, his voice a clean, sharp whisper. "Sally Lou, he was just a pain in the ass. The wiseguys—they could've just warned him away. But he got himself some muscle. Guy named Mortay. A very, very bad guy, I'm told. So bad he wanted a match with Max the Silent."

Nothing moved in my face. Toby didn't waste his time watching. "This Mortay, he went to see one of the big guys. In the middle of the night. Right past the guards, past the dogs, past the alarms. Woke him up in bed. Broke his forearm with one finger. Told him to stop playing with Sally Lou. They went to Wesley."

I watched Toby, waiting.

"Mortay was on Wesley's list, Burke. And Mortay's not around. Way I hear it, you're Wesley's competition now."

I went back to my cell.

Rikers Island. Even when summer's over, just as hot as Hell is supposed to be. I said Wesley's name in my mind and turned my cell into a refrigerator.

## 15

I DIDN'T GET ANY more visitors. They let me out when they were supposed to. I caught a cab back to the city. Switched to a subway, walked the last few blocks to my office. Pansy was right where she was supposed to be too—on guard. She made a growling noise in her throat, so glad to see me she vibrated. Doing a five-day bit wasn't any big deal to her, but she hadn't liked the food any better than I had. I opened the back door and she lumbered up the iron stairs to the roof. I folded the heavy sheets of vinyl I leave spread over a section of the floor into a giant garbage bag and tied it closed with a loop of wire. Opened the back window to air the place out. I had a system for leaving dry dog food and water for her when I had to be gone for a while, but depositing her loads was always a problem. That's what the roof was for. I took an aerosol can of pure oxygen from the bathroom and emptied it into the room she had used. It wasn't the worst thing I'd smelled in the past few days.

## 16

I TOOK A SHOWER. Shaved. Opened the refrigerator and gave Pansy a quart of vanilla fudge ice cream. She snarfed it down while I made myself some rye toast. I fed it into my stomach slowly, sipping ginger ale. Scratching Pansy behind her ears the way she liked. Talking softly to her—praising her for protecting our home while I was gone. Working on calm.

Changed into a dark suit, a pale blue shirt, and a black tie.

Davidson's office is in midtown, a rifle shot from Times Square. The receptionist was a light-skinned black woman with a severe face. When her smile flashed, her face turned beautiful, then went back to business. She goes to law school nights, waiting for her time to come. I gave her the name Davidson and I agreed on. She buzzed back, got the word, told me to go ahead.

The meeting didn't take long. "What they got is a bad bust," he told me. "An unsolved homicide wouldn't make them that crazy, so it's something else running. You know what it is?"

"Maybe."

"Any chance . . . ?"

I knew what he meant. "No," I told him.

"If they need us back in court, I'll get a call."

"Okay. We're square for now?"

"Yeah."

I shook hands and walked out. Davidson would do his piece, but he was a lawyer. For him, survival was a Not Guilty verdict. The jury of my peers was still out.

# 17

IT STAYED THAT WAY for a while. Hard looks. Role-playing. I felt Wesley's chill but it never got close to the bone. I drifted back to the anchor. Calmed down. Davidson said the murder charge would stay open, but they'd never press it. I worked the perimeter, nibbling. Some good scams were cooking all over town, but I didn't see my way in.

Another college kid killed his parents. Said "Dungeons and Dragons" made him do it. A creature killed a woman because she tried to leave him after twenty years. He told the cops she was his. His daughter. A beast slaughtered his girlfriend, raped and killed her teenage daughter, stabbed his seven-year-old son in the heart, and set fire to the apartment. The little boy lived. Identified him at the trial. The jury acquitted him. He went to court and demanded custody of the boy. The Transit Authority set up bulletproof token booths so they couldn't be robbed. Anyone who's done time knows what to do about that—you fill a plastic bottle with gasoline, squirt it through the slot, toss in a match, and wait for the clerk to open the door for you. One of them couldn't get the door open. A youth worker confessed to sodomizing more than three dozen boys over a ten-year period. The judge wanted to sentence him to a speaking tour. Gunfire crackled like heat lightning on streets where the franchise to distribute rock cocaine was disputed by teenage robot-mutant millionaires.

# 18

IMMACULATA SAT ACROSS from me in the last booth. Max's woman. Mama was at her front desk with the baby, bouncing the plump little girl on her lap, telling her how things worked.

"It's okay now," Immaculata said, voice thick with something I didn't recognize.

"Sure."

"Max understands. He was just . . . hurt. That you left him out."

"I had to."

"I know."

"Yeah, you know."

"Burke, why be like this? You made a judgment . . . it was your call to make. It's over."

"But you think the judgment was wrong."

"It was just an ego thing, yes? It's hard to believe this man would have killed our baby just to make Max fight him."

I looked up. Her eyes were veiled under the long lashes but it didn't help. She couldn't make it stick.

"I have to stand with Max," she said.

I bowed, empty. Her eyes were pleading with me. "You still have your baby," I said.

She put her hand over mine. "You still have your brother."

The pay phone rang in the back. Mama walked past, the baby balanced on one hip.

She came back in a minute. Handed the baby to Immaculata, slid in next to her.

"Call for you. Woman say old friend."

A honeycomb of tiny bubbles in my chest. Flood. How could she have known now was the time?

It must have shown in my face. Mama's voice was soft. "No" is all she said.

I lit a cigarette, biting into the filter. The little bubbles in my chest popped—a tiny string of explosions, like baby firecrackers.

"Woman say old friend. Need to talk to you. Very important."

I looked at Mama. Her lips curled, short of a sneer. "Always important. Woman say to tell you Little Candy from Hudson Street. You know her?" Mama asked, handing me a slip of paper with a telephone number.

I nodded. It didn't matter.

## 19

MAX WENT EVERYWHERE I went. Behind me, not with me. Guarding my back. Protecting me from a ghost. His warrior s soul screaming for combat to make it right. Too late for the battle.

We were on a pier near the Yacht Basin, waiting for a buyer to show up. The buyer had advertised over an electronic bulletin board, using the modem on his personal computer. He wanted a little girl. No older than ten. White. Someone he could love. He'd have ten grand with him. To prove his love.

Max took a restaurant napkin out of his pocket, a felt-tip pen from mine. Drew a rising sun, touched his heart gently. Pointed at me, turned the finger around to include himself. We could go to Japan. Find Flood. Bring her home.

I shook my head. She was home. So was I.

The headlights of the buyer's car flashed. Once, twice. Max merged into the shadow next to my Plymouth. I walked over to the buyer's car, a beige Taurus station wagon. The driver's window whispered down, air-conditioned breeze on my face. It didn't make sense for that time of the year until I saw the fat man inside. Ice-cream suit, straw hat, sweating.

"Mr. Smith?" he asked in a pulpy voice.

"That's me," I assured him.

"She's with you?"

"In the car," I said, tilting my head to show him the direction.

I stepped aside to let him out. The light went on inside the station wagon when the door opened. Empty. He took a black attaché case off the seat next to him.

"She's still a little dopey," I said, walking beside him.

"No problem."

I lit a cigarette, the cheap lighter flaring a signal to Max.

"She's inside," I told the fat man, patting the Plymouth's trunk.

"Let's see."

"Let's see the money."

He popped open the briefcase on the trunk lid. Clean-looking bills, nicely banded. And a small plastic bottle with a spray top, some white handkerchiefs, plastic wristbands—the kind they give you in the hospital.

"Got everything you need, huh?"

"Hey, look, pal. This kid isn't for *me*, okay? I'm a businessman, just like you. In fact, you got any more where this kid came from, you just let me know. I got customers waiting."

His fat body slammed into the back of the Plymouth as Max took him from behind—a paralyzing shot just below the ribs, a lightning chop to the exposed neck as he went down. Vomit sprayed onto the Plymouth.

I ripped open his shirt. No wire. Pulled his wallet from an inside pocket, stripped off his watch, passed up the rings, snatched the briefcase. And left him where he was.

It didn't make the morning papers.

## 20

THE GILT LETTERS ON the pebbled-glass door said "Simon J. Rosnak—Attorney at Law." Max and I stepped inside. The girl at the front desk was a cunty brunette with sparkle-dust for mascara and the kind of mouth that would make you throw out the postage meter so you could watch her lick the stamps.

"Can I help you?"

"I want to see Rosnak."

"You have an appointment?"

"No."

"Well, Mr. Rosnak isn't in yet. If you'll leave your name and number . . ."

"He's in. I don't have time." I glanced down at the console on her desk. None of the lights were lit.

"You can't . . ."

I walked past her. "Call a cop," I advised her, leaving Max behind to keep her company.

I found a carpeted hall, followed it to the end. Rosnak was sitting at an old wooden desk, reading some kind of ledger. He looked up when he saw me, a tired-looking man in his forties.

"What?"

"I need to talk some business with you."

"I don't know you. Speak to Mona. I'm busy."

I sat down across from him. Lit a smoke. There was no ashtray on his desk. "I need to speak with you," I said, calm and relaxed.

"Look, buddy, this isn't a supermarket. I don't know who sent you here, but . . ."

"You represent Johnny Sostre?"

"That's not your business."

"Attorney-client privilege, huh?"

"You got it."

"Only one problem. You're not an attorney."

His eyes tracked me. Camera shutters. Waiting.

"You're not an attorney," I said again. "You went to law school, but you dropped out in your last year. You never took the Bar. You've been running a sweet hustle, representing wiseguys. They know you're not a lawyer. You try the case, do the best you can. You win, they walk. You lose, they wait a couple of years, then they discover the truth, right? You get exposed. They file an appeal. And the court lets them walk. Ineffective assistance of counsel, they call it. Never fails. Josephs did the same thing a few years ago."

He watched me, waiting.

I tapped cigarette ash onto his desk. "Only problem is, you got to have perfect timing. This scam works just one time, no repeats. You got . . . what? Ten, fifteen clients now? Got half a dozen guys already upstate doing time. You get exposed at the right time, all the convictions get reversed. And it's a few years later. Witnesses disappear, memory gets soft, people forget, evidence gets misplaced . . . you know how it works. But you move too soon, it's all for nothing. The DA still has everything he needs, and they just try the cases again. Besides, you're in the middle of a bunch of new cases. They discover the truth now, and you're out of business."

He leaned forward. "The people I represent . . . you know who they are?"

"Yeah."

"You know they wouldn't like this kind of thing."

"Don't tell them."

I ground out my smoke, waiting.

He raised his eyebrows.

"One time," I told him. "One time only. Fifty large, and I'm gone."

"You're crazy."

"But not bluffing."

He fumbled with some papers on his desk. "I need some time."

"This is Tuesday. Friday, you get the cash. I'll call, tell you how to drop it off."

I got up to go. Looked down at him. "I'll save you some phone calls. Burke."

"Who's Burke?"

"Me."

Friday, the juicy brunette took a cab to Chinatown at lunchtime. She got out, and the crowd swallowed her up. When she caught another cab, she didn't have her pocketbook with her.

## 21

I WAS AT MAMA'S WHEN a call came in. Julio. I called the old gangster back at the social club he uses for headquarters. His dry snakeskin voice sounded like a cancer ward.

"You did me a service once, I don't forget. So this is a favor, Burke. You stung Rosnak. He went crying to the boys. I squared it, okay? There's no comeback on this one. But give it a rest—stay out of our business."

I let him feel my silence. The phone line hummed.

"You hear what I'm telling you?"

"Sure."

"You found out some things. Okay, a man's entitled to make some money, he finds out some things. You made enough money. Stick to citizens."

I hung up.

## 22

THERE WAS MONEY OUT there. The city was a boom town. Drugs, not oil. The prospectors drove triple-black Jeeps, wore paper-thin Italian leather, mobile cellular telephones in holsters over their shoulders. Music in their brain-dead heads: Gotta Get Paid. Gold on their bodies, paid for with bodies on the ground. Babies got killed in the crossfire. Children did the shooting. Cocaine was the crop, in countries whose names they couldn't spell. And here, crack was the cash. Named for the sound it made when it hit the streets.

"Gold on their wrist, a pistol in your fist," the Prof rapped, trying to pull me in. Easy pickings. It wasn't for me.

I couldn't let it go. I read a copy of the Penal Law Davidson gave me. Incest. The legislature put it in the same class as adultery. I guess they thought a kid should Just Say No.

## 23

I MET MICHELLE IN Bryant Park, next to the Public Library right off Times Square.

"I'm going away for a while," she said.

"Okay."

"To Denmark, Burke. I'm going to have it done."

"You got enough cash?"

"Yes. I've been saving for a long time. You impressed?"

I nodded.

"It has to be. I'm not having my boy grow up an outlaw, Burke."

"You're going to take him from the Mole?"

"I wouldn't do that. He's ours, not just mine. I know that. But that's no life for him. I want him to be something."

"The Mole's something."

Her hand on my forearm, lacquered nails shining in the late autumn sun. "I know, baby."

I lit a cigarette.

"I won't be any different," she said.

"I know."

"But *you* are."

I didn't say anything.

"You don't want me to go, say the word."

"Go."

"You can get me the papers?"

"A passport?"

"And . . . later . . . I want to adopt Terry. Make it legal."

"Why?"

"Why? You know what I am. Trapped all my life in this body. I can change that. Be myself. The boy . . . I don't want him to grow up like . . ."

"Like me?"

"I love you, Burke. You know that. I'd never walk away from you." She kissed my cheek, walked away.

## 24

ONCE I COULD ALWAYS find something on the sweet side of the edge I lived on. It was gone. Even in prison, there were some things you could laugh at. That was then. The Plymouth drifted back to Mama's. I pushed a cassette into the slot. Janis Joplin. Pure estrogen filtered through sandpaper. Begging some man to take her pain, twist it into love. Throwing her soul at a barbed-wire screen until it diced.

I heard Belle's little-girl voice. "Rescue me."

She'd asked the wrong man.

## 25

"SHE CALL AGAIN," Mama greeted me.

I looked a question at her.

"Woman say her name Candy, remember? Little Candy from Hudson Street. Very important."

"Nothing's so important."

Mama's eyes were black, small hard dots in her smooth round face. "Baby important, okay? Baby safe now."

"I thought . . ."

"Yes. You think, you think what is right. Big girl, you love her, she's gone. High price."

"Too high."

"No. Babies die first, soon no people, okay?"

I put my fingers on each side of my head, holding it like an eggshell with cracks. I wanted to howl like Pansy, grieve for my woman. For myself. Nothing came.

Mama stayed with me. One of the waiters came over, said something in Cantonese. Mama ignored him. He went away. I felt the trembling inside me, but it wasn't my old pal this time. Not fear. I wasn't afraid. Too sad to cry. Nothing left alive to hate.

I looked over at the only woman I had ever called Mama. "Max could have beaten him."

"Maybe."

"I didn't know the answer, Mama."

She tapped my hand to make me watch her face. See the truth. "You don't *know* the answer, you must *be* the answer."

"Who said that? Confucius?"

"I say that," she said.

When she got up, she left a piece of paper in front of me.

## 26

I USED A PAY PHONE off Sutton Place. Not my neighborhood, but the best place to call from. The feds wouldn't tap these phones—they might net somebody they knew. I looked at the slip of paper Mama gave me. Seven numbers, a local call. I pushed the buttons, working backward from the last digit. Mama writes all numbers backwards—she says it's Chinese bookkeeping.

She answered on the third ring. In a throaty low purr sweet enough to kill a diabetic.

"Hello, baby."

"You called me?"

"Burke? Is that really you?"

"It's me."

"You know who this is?"

"Yeah."

"Can I see you?"

"Why?"

"I have something for you."

"Nothing I want."

"You remember me?"

"Yes."

"Then you know I've got something you want."

"Not anymore."

"Yes, yes I do. I got something you want. Love or money. One way or the other."

"No."

"Yes. You wouldn't have called otherwise. I know you. I know you better than anyone."

"You don't know me."

"Come over and listen to me. I won't bite you. Unless you want me to. Friday afternoon."

I didn't say anything.

She gave me an address.

I hung up.

## 27

I DROVE BACK TO MY office. My home. Let Pansy out onto her roof. Lit a cigarette and looked out the window, feeling the airborne sewage the yuppies called a river breeze.

I think her real name was Renée. Or Irene. She always called herself Candy. I couldn't bring her face into my mind but I'd never forget her. She was just a kid then. Maybe thirteen years old. But you could run Con Ed for a year on what she *wanted*.

She didn't have what she wanted then. None of us did. So we fought young animals just like us—fighting over what we'd never own. We *called* things ours. Our turf. Our women. The street forked at the end. Where we found what was really ours. Mine was prison.

Girls like Candy were always around. We didn't have pistols or shotguns then. Just half-ass zip guns that would blow up in your hand when you pulled the trigger. But you could break a glass bottle into a pile of flesh-ripping shards. Squeeze a thick glob of white Elmer's Glue into your palm. Twirl a rope through it until it was coated end to end. Then twirl it again, through the glass. Wait for it to dry and you had a glass rope. When you got real close, you could use half a raw potato, its face studded with double-edged razor blades. Car antennas. Lead pipes. Cut-down baseball bats with nails poking through them. Sit around in some abandoned apartment, drink some cheap wine, pour a few of the red drops on the ground in tribute to your brothers who got to the jailhouse or the graveyard before you did. Toke on throat-searing marijuana. Wait for the buzz. Then you meet the other losers. In a playground if they knew you were coming. In an alley if they didn't. The newspapers called it gang wars. If you made it back to the club, the girls were there. If you got too broken to run, you got busted. And if you stayed on the concrete, maybe you got your name in the papers.

When I went to reform school, she wrote me a letter. A poem, just for me. Signed it that way. "Love, Candy. Just for you." Nobody had ever done anything like that for me. The feeling lasted until I found out it was the words from some song she'd heard on the radio.

Little Candy. A whore in her heart even then.

Just what I needed to cheer me up.

## 28

HER BUILDING WAS A co-op in the Thirties, near the river. We watched it for a couple of days, seeing how it worked. The doorman handled both ends of the building. No problem. On Friday, the Prof rang the service bell at the rear. When the doorman left his post, Max and I stepped inside, past the sign that said "All Visitors Must Be Announced." I took the elevator to the sixteenth floor, Max took the stairs. He was there before I was. We walked up five more flights to the top floor. He stood off to the side as I knocked. I heard the peephole slide back. The door opened. "It *is* you," she said.

I didn't know the woman. Candy had been a slim, dark-haired child. Her body hadn't caught up to her hormones then. But I'd never forget her eyes: yellow, like a cat's, tipped at the corners, glowing under heavy dark lashes. This woman looked about thirty—ten years younger than she should have been. Her black hair was as short as a man's, soft and fine, framing her face. Barefoot, she stood as tall as my jaw. Her eyes were a bright, china-doll blue. The woman had an hourglass figure—the kind where the sand takes forever to get to the bottom but has plenty of room to spread out once it arrives. She was wearing a pair of ragged blue-jean shorts and one of those little T-shirts that stop around the diaphragm. Pale flesh covered her stomach, muscle rippled just below the skin when she spoke.

"It's me, for real."

I shook my head. "Who gave you my name?"

"Burke! It's me. You don't recognize me?"

I let my eyes travel over her. "Not a line."

She fluffed her hair, ran her hands quickly over her face, across her breasts, down past her hips, patted the front of her thighs. "It's all new."

"Some things you can't change," I told her, reaching behind me for the doorknob.

"You don't remember me at all," she said, sadness in her voice.

I closed one eye, watching her with the other. Tapped the closed lid. It was the only chance she'd get.

"Oh! Damn! I forgot. Wait a minute."

I didn't move. She put a hand on my arm. Nails cut short, no polish. "Please."

I watched her walk over to the window, tilt her head back, reach into her eyes. Pull something away from each one. "Come here, Burke. Just for a minute . . . okay?"

I went to the window, the carpet soft under my feet. The late afternoon sunlight came through the window. "Take a better look," she said, her voice soft.

The yellow cat's eyes watched me.

"Contact lenses." A little girl's whisper, giggling at soft conspiracies.

Candy.

## 29

THERE WAS A WHITE PHONE on a glass table near the couch. One of those Swedish designer jobs, big round numbers in four grids of three. I left her standing by the window, picked up the receiver, and dialed the number of the pay phone on the corner. I scanned the joint while the phone rang—it looked like the waiting room in an expensive clinic. The Prof answered. "Call you back in fifteen minutes," I said, and hung up.

I sat down on the couch. Lit a cigarette, watching her. Thinking how I should look through the place first. But it didn't feel like a trap. And a woman who could change herself into something new could hide a microphone anyplace.

"What do you want?" I asked her.

She came to the couch, sat at the opposite end, curling her legs under her like a teenager.

"Maybe I just wanted to see you."

"Write me a letter."

She shook her head slightly, a fighter shaking off a punch. "I was just a kid."

I shrugged.

"You're still angry with me?"

"I'm not angry with anyone. I don't know you."

"But . . ."

"I remember you. It's not the same as knowing you, okay?"

"Okay."

"What do you want, Irene?"

"I haven't been Irene for a long time. That's one of the things I changed."

"What do I call you?"

"Whatever you want. That's me—I can be whatever you want. There's all kinds of candy."

"That's what you do now?"

"That's what I do."

I looked her over again, seeing it. "You got a closet full of wigs too?"

Her smile flashed. She scissored her legs off the couch, held out her hand to me. I grabbed her wrist instead, my thumb hard against the nerve junction. She didn't seem to notice. I left my cigarette burning in the ashtray. She led me down a carpeted hall, stepped into a room nearly as big as the living room. One wall was floor-to-ceiling mirrors. "My closet," she said.

One shelf was wigs, carefully positioned on Styrofoam heads. Blondes, brunettes, redheads from soft rose to flame. Every style from flower child to Dolly Parton. A wall of cosmetics: lipstick with all new, gleaming, fresh tips, standing in rows like large-caliber bullets . . . blusher, body powders, eyeliner, prefitted fingernails, polish, false eyelashes. Makeup table with a round padded stool, tiny row of frosted light bulbs surrounding another mirror, this one three-paneled.

The far wall looked flat. She slid back a panel. Fur coats. Fox, ermine, sable, mink, leopard. Others I didn't recognize.

Another panel. Cocktail dresses, formal gowns, yuppie go-to-business outfits. Leather miniskirts. Dresses from silk to cotton. Jumpers and pinafores.

Another section was shoes. Lizard-skin spike heels, black leather boots from ankle to mid-thigh, shoes trimmed with rhinestones, jogging shoes, little girls' shoes with Mary Jane straps, sandals.

Rows and rows of built-in drawers. She opened them smoothly, stepped aside, gesturing with her hand like a wrongly accused smuggler sneering at a customs agent. G-strings, silk panties, bikini briefs, garter belts, teddies, camisoles, cotton panties in a dozen colors. Panty hose still in the original wrappers. Stockings from fishnet to sheer. Push-up bras, front-opening bras, bras with holes for nipples to poke through, bras with straps that crossed over the back. Red, black, white, and a pastel rainbow.

There was another panel to the wall. She slid it back. Riding crops, handcuffs, lengths of thin steel chains, a leather-handled stock, leather straps at the end, like a shortened cat-o'-nine-tails. Leather belts, from spaghetti straps to thick slabs. Something that looked like a black rubber sweatshirt. Dog collars. A leather face mask, laced up the back, the mouth a zippered slash. Hairbrushes, Ping-Pong paddles, some foam-padded, others covered with sandpaper. Rings, clamps, vibrators. Dildos, from pencils to sausages. A bullwhip of braided silk.

"Seen enough?"

Her eyes were a challenge. My face was flat. I nodded.

She held out her hand again, turning it so I could hold her by the wrist. The next room down the hall was a teenage girl's bedroom: Heavy Metal posters on the wall, fluffy quilt on the big bed, stuffed animals, pink telephone. A leather-bound book next to it. It said "My Diary" on the cover in gold. Bathroom off to the side.

Three more bedrooms. A single working girl. A movie star. The last one had a black leather psychiatrist's couch in one corner. Rings bolted into the floor. The walls were lined in dark cork.

She took me back into the front room. My cigarette had burned itself out. I let go of her wrist—lit another one. She walked out of the room. I picked up the phone, hit the * button, watched the thin slash of liquid crystal fill up with the same number I had dialed before. The Prof answered. "Okay so far," I said. Hung up again.

She came back in again. "You think of a name for me yet?"

"There's lots of names for it."

"Money is the name for it. Nothing's changed."

"I haven't got any money."

"Yes you do, bounty hunter. I know what you do. But it's not your money I want. It's money I have for you—something I want you to do."

"There's nothing I want to do."

She took off her top. Her breasts stood out hard as white marble. "Silicone. The very best—envelopes, not injections." She licked her lips. "Collagen. Here too," she said, patting her seamless face. She stood, dropping the denim shorts to the floor in the same motion. "This is mine," patting her butt. "Hard work. Three times a week on the machines." She took a deep breath through her nose—her waist wasped. "I can do more crunches than a bodybuilder. Six days a week." The soft patch between her legs was dark, gleaming, heart-shaped. "Electrolysis. Once a month," she said, holding out her arms for me to see.

"You don't miss a trick."

"Don't be nasty, Burke. I'm proud of you—you got what you wanted. Can't I do it too?"

"What did I want?"

"You think I don't remember? A name. You got a name now. The whole street knows your name. After Mortay . . ."

She caught me looking at her, felt the chill. "I'm sorry. I know better. Don't say anything. I know the rules. There's something I need you to do—something you know how to do. And there's money. A lot of money. Just think about it, okay? And call me. You have the number. I'll come wherever you want . . . tell you what I need."

I stood up. "One more call," I told her. She shrugged, walked over to the window, naked in the light. The glass had a faint orange tint. One-way. I picked up the phone, dialed 958-2222. A recorded voice spat back a phone number. Ma Bell's black box telling the phone repairman that he was working on the right account. It wasn't the number I had called her on. I said "Okay" into the phone and hung up.

She came over to the door with me. "Whatever you want. *And* the money," she whispered. "Call me." Her lips flexed like she was going to kiss me. Saw me watching her face and pulled the punch. The door closed behind me. I took the elevator to the fourth floor, met Max on the stairwell. I pushed an imaginary button with my finger. We split up at the bottom of the stairs. When the doorman went to the back to answer the buzzer I walked out the front door.

## 30

I DROPPED THE PROF off at the edge of the Village, turned the Plymouth toward Chinatown. Max spread his hands, asking me "What?" I shrugged. I pulled over to the curb when we got near the warehouse where Max had his temple. His face was a mask, staring out the windshield to some other place. His hand dropped on my forearm, a leather-colored bone sculpture, a ridge of horned callous raised along the chopping edge, the first two knuckles enlarged, a white slash across the back from an old razor scar. He wasn't going to move. I turned to see what he wanted.

The mute Mongolian took his hand from my forearm, tapped two fingers against my chest. Where my heart would be. He put his fingertips together, elbows extending in a straight line. Slowly opened his fingers, tilted his face up. Sunlight? I looked a question at him. He went through the whole thing again. He wasn't getting through. A thick finger drew a cross in the dust on the dashboard. I watched. He put an arrow at the top of the cross. A compass? He extended the right-hand line of the cross all the way to the end of the dash. East? He made the gesture again. I nodded. The Rising Sun. Japan. I said her name. Flood. His hands came together in a prayerful gesture. Pointed at me. At himself. Extended his arms in a child's gesture of an airplane banking through the sky. We could go to Japan. Find her. Bring her back.

I shook my head. No. Again.

He bowed slightly. The way you do before the fight starts. Opened the door and he was gone.

## 31

WHEN I GOT TO THE junkyard, Terry let me in. "They're fighting," he said, leading the way back to the bunker.

The Mole was a sodden lump, seated on one of the cut-down oil drums he used for chairs. Elbows on his knees, chin in his hands. His coveralls were so dirty they worked like camouflage—his dead-white face looked suspended in air, light shifting on the thick lenses of his glasses as he followed Michelle's swooping circles around him. She was wearing a white raw silk coat that reached past the tops of her black boots. A black cashmere turtleneck sweater and black slacks that puddled over the tops of the boots. Long strand of pearls around her neck. Her hand flicked them back and forth as she snapped at the Mole. Simba sat next to the

Mole, head cocked, ears flared. Fascinated.

She whirled as we came into the clearing, hands on hips.

"Stay out of this, Burke."

"I came to see Mole," I told her.

"You'll see him when I'm finished with him."

"Mom . . ." Terry started.

All the hardness went out of her face. "This doesn't concern you, sweetheart. You know the Mole and I argue sometimes. Soon as we're finished, I'll let you take me out to dinner in town, okay?"

The Mole's head swiveled toward me. "She wants to have the operation."

"Mole!"

"You think the boy doesn't know?"

It went quiet then. I lit a cigarette, waiting. Terry went over to Michelle, took her hand. "It's okay, Mom."

She kissed him hard on the cheek. Pulled away from him. Walked right up to the Mole, leaned into his face. "It's me. I waited for this. I know I kept talking about it, but now's the time."

"It's dangerous."

"It's *not* dangerous. You think this is like a coat-hanger abortion? They know what they're doing."

His head swiveled to me again. "She wants to be a citizen."

"I know."

"None of you know."

The Mole's eyes were liquid pain behind the glass. "You can't live out there, Michelle. It's not for you."

"You just don't want to lose Terry. How selfish can you be, Mole? You want him to spend his life in this junkyard? Never go to school?"

"I go to school, Mom," the kid said quietly.

"Oh, sure you do, honey. I'm sure you know all about tapping telephones and beating burglar-alarm systems. Maybe someday the Mole will teach you how to blow up buildings."

The Mole's head came up. "Tell her," he said, his voice rusty. He didn't use it much.

Terry tapped Michelle's hand, making her look. "Mom, I study physics. And chemistry. And math. I do. Ask me anything. Burke got me the textbooks for all the first-year courses at college. Mom, I *already* know the stuff. Mole is the best teacher in the world."

"And what are you going to do with all this knowledge, baby? Go to med school?"

"I don't want to go to medical school."

"No, you want to live in a junkyard with this lunatic. Well, you're not."

"Mom . . ."

"Don't 'Mom' me, Terry. You want to end up like Burke? You like the idea of going to prison?"

"The Mole doesn't go to prison."

"Ask him why. Ask your *teacher* why he didn't go to prison."

"I know why, Mom. I know Burke took the weight for him that time in the subway tunnel. Mole told me all about it. That's what family does."

"That's what good *criminals* do, honey."

"That's the rules."

She grabbed the boy by his shoulders. Shook him roughly. "I know all about family. My biological parents taught me very well. They weren't family, so I picked my own. And we picked you. All of us, not just the Mole. You're not growing up in the underground. You're not going to spend your life like this."

Tears ran down the kid's face but his voice was steady. "I lived with them once. The citizens. Remember, Mom? Remember how you found me?"

Michelle dropped to her knees in the junkyard, clutching the boy's legs, crying. He patted her head gently, whispering to her. The Mole moved away. I followed him.

"It's not safe" is all he said.

"The operation?"

"The boy. He can't live out there. Maybe Michelle could. Go back and forth all the time. It's not right to split him like this."

We walked through the twilight, jagged shadows spiking from the cannibalized cars. I moved between two of the cars. Stopped short when I heard a snarl. A white pit bull was lying against an old Cadillac, tiny squealing puppies nursing underneath her. Even Simba stepped around her.

"I never saw a pit bull here before. I thought they were all dog fighters."

"Terry found her. They were fighting dogs on the other side of the meat market . . . you know just past where the trucks pull in?"

"Yeah."

"She lost a fight. They left her there to die. We fixed her up. Now she's part of the pack."

"Like Terry."

He didn't say anything for a while. I lit another smoke. We made a wide circle, giving Terry and Michelle plenty of time.

"The boy knows Hebrew too," the Mole said, defensively.

I dragged on my cigarette, remembering the boy's Bar Mitzvah. The kid already knew how to blow up buildings.

## 32

WHEN WE GOT BACK to the clearing, Michelle was perched on the Mole's oil drum, a fresh blanket beneath her. The boy was sitting on the ground, her hand on his shoulder. They were waiting for us.

The Mole went into his bunker.

"I'm still having the operation," she told me, defiance lancing through the fear in her voice.

I bowed.

A half-smile played across her lovely face. She patted Terry's shoulder. "Sweetheart, just tell me you don't want to be like Burke—that's all I ask."

"I want to be like Mole."

"Honey, the Mole's a genius. I'd never take that away from him. And he's a wonderful man in many ways. I know he's taught you a lot. And I know he loves you, although I'm sure he's never told you."

"He told me. He said he was proud of me."

"I know, baby. But . . . to live like this. You'll be a man soon. The Mole . . . I mean, you want to live out here? Never have a girl of your own?"

"I'll have a woman, when I'm ready. A mate. Like the Mole said. A man has to have a mate."

"But the Mole . . . he doesn't . . ."

"Mom, I thought *you* . . ."

It was the first time I ever saw Michelle blush.

## 33

WE WERE CROSSING THE Triboro Bridge before Michelle spoke.

"You think the Mole feels that way about me?"

"You know he does. Always has."

She lit one of her long black cigarettes. "He never said . . ."

"Neither did you."

I hooked the East Side Drive, high-rise lights flashing past us.

"You miss her?"

"I'll always miss her."

"Belle's dead, baby. You know who I mean."

The Plymouth sharked its own way through the light traffic.

"Sometimes," I said.

## 34

I PULLED UP OUTSIDE Michelle's hotel. "You working tonight?" she asked.

"No."

"Take me to the Cellar."

"Who's playing?"

"Who cares? If we don't like it we can split."

"Okay," I said, turning the wheel to slip back into traffic.

"Hold it! Where're you going?"

"You said . . ."

"Honey, I've been in a *junkyard*. Park this car, wait downstairs in the bar. I'll be changed in a minute."

Right.

# 35

THE BAR HAD ONE OF those giant-screen TV sets suspended in a corner. I ordered a vodka and tonic, telling the barmaid not to mix them. Sipped the tonic.

Some pro football game was about to start. Three guys in pretty matching blazers were talking about it like they were about to cover a border dispute in the Middle East. "This is going to be a war," one of the white announcers said. The black announcer nodded, the way you do when you hear irrefutable wisdom. The guys along the bar murmured agreement. Sure, just like the War on Drugs. If it was really going to be a war, one team would blow up the other's locker room. The Mole was right—we could never be citizens. Where I was raised, there's no such thing as a cheap shot.

"What do you see as the key to this match-up?" one of the announcers asked.

The guy he asked said something about dee-fense. Chumps. The key is the team doctor. The only war in pro football is chemical.

The barmaid leaned over to ask me if I wanted a refill, her breasts spilling out of the top of her blouse. I thought of Candy and her silicone envelopes. What's real?

Michelle tapped me on the shoulder. She'd changed to a red-and-black-striped skirt that pinched her knees close, the hem just peeking out under a black quilted jacket with wide sleeves. Her hair was piled on top of her head, most of the makeup gone. She looked fresh and sweet. I left a ten-dollar bill on the bar and a cigarette burning in the ashtray. Nobody watched us leave—it was kickoff time.

# 36

I WAS GOING THROUGH the motions. Playing out the string. Not waiting for full bloom, like I had been all my life. Full bloom had come to me. Just for a visit.

Jacques called me at Mama's. He's a gun dealer, runs a sweet little operation out of a rib joint in Bed-Stuy. I found a pay phone, called him back.

"I have a client for some of my heating units, mahn"—his West Indian accent singing over the line.

"So why call me?"

"This client, he's one of those Haitians, mahn. Spooky, you know. All that zombie-talk . . ."

"Yeah." There's an army of Haitians between Brooklyn and Queens, waiting for the day when they take back their land from the Tonton Macoutes. They don't fear the living, but Papa Doc's spirit still frightens their children.

"I don't travel, mahn. You know this. And they don't come to my place. I need a traveling man."

"I'm not doing any deliveries."

"Of *course* not, mahn. You know how this works. You go there, they pay you. You call me. I tell them where to pick up the units."

"And I wait with them while they send someone to do the pickup?"

"Sure."

"How much you paying hostages these days?"

"Oh, mahn, do not speak like this. Nobody going to cause trouble. These are not drug dealers, you understand?"

"Sure."

"Let us do business, mahn. Good business for me, good business for you."

"How good?"

"Couple of hours of your time, say . . . five?"

"Okay."

"Yes?"

"I'll see you in a couple of days," I told him, hanging up.

I heard the surprise in Jacques's voice. A deal like this had to net him six figures, and I was going cheap. But I had a secret he didn't know about. I didn't give a fuck.

## 37

I LEFT THE PLYMOUTH just off the West Side Highway near Forty-second and walked over to Eighth Avenue to catch the E train for South Jamaica. A young white dude was sprawled on a bench, chuckling over something he was reading in a magazine. I put one foot on the bench, lit a smoke, took a look over his shoulder. An article about how to make your car burglarproof.

I dropped underground, fishing a token from my pocket. A young black woman dressed like a nun was sitting just past the turnstiles, a flat basket full of coins in her hands. Her face was calm, eyes peaceful.

"Help the homeless?" she asked.

"Say something in Latin first."

"Fuck you," she said, her voice soft.

Everybody's got a pimp.

I caught my train. A huge black guy got on at Queens Plaza. Walked up and down the car announcing that this was *his* train. He was a combat-trained Vietnam vet and nobody was going to pull any stuff on *his* train—all the passengers could feel safe with him. Took off his cap and went up and down the row, collecting contributions for his program. Right across from me was a young Oriental, a folded copy of the *Times* in one hand, a small dictionary in the other. The black man collected some change from the lady a couple of seats down from me, checked my face, passed me by. The guy next to me looked like a lab rat. He threw some coins. When the collector strolled back up the other side, I watched the Oriental. The black guy shoved his cap right in the Oriental's lap. The Oriental was stone-faced. The black guy was covering his newspaper with the cap, not moving. The Oriental reached into the cap, took out a handful of change, jingled it in one fist, watching the black man. The black man pulled his cap back. The Oriental tossed the change into it.

The black guy moved on, into another subway car. Maybe he really was a Vietnam vet.

I rode the train nearly to the end of the line. Walked up Sutphin Boulevard, looking for the house Jacques had described to me.

Three young blacks were watching the traffic from a topless white Suzuki Samurai. The driver stared through the windshield, his passenger watched the street. Another draped a casual hand over the padded roll bar to watch me approach. The passenger got out to sit on the hood, cradling a cellular phone in a white leather shoulder bag. Ten pounds of gold around his neck, brand-new orange leather sneakers on his feet. Wearing a white leather jacket with layered lapels. I kept coming, hands out where they could see them. The driver reached under the dash. The largest one climbed out of the back. Three gold rings on his right hand, welded into a slab across the knuckles. He put his hand to his cheek. I read "Stone" in raised gold letters. The one with the cellular phone took off a pair of dark shades, raised his eyebrows, tapped his nose. I looked through him, went on past. Crack dealers, not hiding it. Nujacks, they called themselves. Flashing. The way a fuse does before it reaches the dynamite.

They were marking out territory in the wrong neighborhood. This turf belonged to a Rasta posse. The last crew from Brooklyn had ended up extremely dead. That's the only War on Drugs going down around here.

I found the house. Knocked four times on the side door. Stepped into a basement. Nobody said a word in English—a couple of the men muttered in something that sounded like French. They pointed to a suitcase. Opened it. I looked inside, counted. They pointed to a phone. I called Jacques.

"It's me. They got one twenty-five."

"New or used?"

"Used, not in sequence. But I got no blue light with me, pal."

"That's okay, mahn. Put them on."

The guy who pointed at the suitcase listened to Jacques, said something to the others. They went out through a different door than the one I'd used. I sat down to wait. I'd told Jacques that the cash *looked* good, but I wasn't vouching for it. If it was funny money, I was taking the same risk he was—my five grand would come out of the suitcase.

I sat down to wait. Put my hand in my pocket for a smoke. The guy waiting with me said, "Easy, easy." I took it out real slow. I had the match to my cigarette before I realized the guy wasn't talking to me.

It was less than two hours later when they came back.

I hit the street with the suitcase. Before I got to the corner, a dark sedan pulled over, flashing its high beams on and off. The window came down. An Island voice said, "Burke?"

I got in the back. It took off smooth and easy. At the next corner, an identical car pulled in front of us. There'd be another one behind. I didn't look. We stopped at a light on Queens Boulevard. A guy in the front got out of the car carrying the suitcase. He handed it over to the car in front, got back in as the lead car took off in a squeal of rubber.

They dropped me off in Times Square. Handed me an envelope. I walked to the Plymouth by myself.

## 38

I WALKED BY MYSELF a lot then. The court case was pending, but not hanging over my head. Davidson was right—if I didn't do something stupid, I was okay.

I didn't feel okay.

After a few more dead days, I called Candy.

# 39

SHE OPENED THE DOOR, wearing an apricot sweatshirt that came down almost to her knees, face sweaty, no makeup. No contact lenses either, yellow cat's eyes patient.

The apartment looked the same. Fresh rosebuds in a steel vase on the coffee table. The air smelled sharp, ionized. Like after a hard rain.

I sat on the couch. She curled her legs under her, wrinkled her nose when I lit a cigarette. I waited.

"I have a daughter," she said.

I dragged on the cigarette, watching the glowing tip.

"You don't seem surprised."

"I don't know you."

"I know you. You're the same. So am I."

"Okay."

"She's almost sixteen years old. Always had the best. The very, very best. Designer clothes, dance lessons, private schools. The last school she went to, they even had a rule about boys in the rooms. You had to have one foot on the floor at all times."

Candy's mouth curled—her laugh didn't come from her belly. "Imagine that, huh? I was older than her before I knew people fucked lying down. Remember?"

I remembered. The dark stairwell at the back of the building where she lived with her mother in a railroad flat on the top floor. Candy standing one step higher than me, her back to me, her skirt bunched around her waist. I remembered taking down a drunk in an alley just past a waterfront bar with two other guys from the gang. Thinking my share of the loot would buy her a sweater she wanted. And me another few minutes on those stairs.

"Her name is Elvira. Pretty name, isn't it? I wanted her to have everything I didn't." She waved her hand, taking in the sterile waiting room to her office. "That's what I started all this for."

I watched her lying eyes, waiting.

"A few months ago, she ran away from school. She's staying with this cult. Over in Brooklyn. I don't know much about it . . . even what it's called. The man who runs it, he's called Train. I don't know how he got to her. I went there once. They wouldn't let me speak to her. I told them she was underage, but they must know something about me. Maybe she told them. Call a cop, they said."

I lit another smoke.

"I want her back. She's mine, not theirs. She's too young for this. She needs help. Maybe even a hospital. She . . ."

I cut her off. "What do you want from me?"

She tilted her chin to look up at me. "Get her out of there. Get her back."

"I don't do that stuff."

"Yes you do. You do it all the time. It's *what* you do. What you used to do before . . ."

I looked a question at her.

She pointed a finger at me, crooked her thumb. "Bang bang," she said softly.

I shook my head.

"All you have to do is *ask*, okay? Just go there. See the man. *Ask* him to let Elvira go with you."

"And if he says no?"

"Then I'll do something else."

"Do something else first."

"No! I want to keep my life. Just the way it is, okay? Just ask him."

"Why should he go along?"

"It doesn't matter. He will. I know he will."

I got off the couch, walked over to the window. It was dark outside, lights spotting the building across the street. Nothing was right about her.

"Say the whole thing," I told her.

"You go there. You ask him for Elvira. He gives her up. You bring her to me."

"He says no?"

"You walk away."

"No more?"

"No more."

"What kind of cult is this? They have the girls hooking, begging, selling flowers, what?"

"I don't know."

"How do you spell this guy's name? Train."

"Like a subway train."

I lit another smoke. "You said you'd pay me."

"I said I'd give you whatever you want."

"Money's what I want."

"Tell me the price. I'll have it here for you when you get back."

I smiled.

She didn't. "Half now, half when you come back."

"Five now."

She padded out of the room on her bare feet. I punched the redial number on the white phone, memorized the number that came up on the screen, hung it up gently before it could ring at the other end.

Candy came back in, handed me a thick wad of bills wrapped in a rubber band. I put it in my coat pocket.

"Here's all I know about him," she started, curling up on the couch again.

## 40

I DID IT RIGHT. HABITS die hard. Like the woman I loved. The building was an old meat-packing plant in the shadow of the triangle formed by Atlantic and Flatbush, on the edge of the gentrification blot spreading east from Boerum Hill. A nonprofit corporation owned it. Four stories. The ground floor was a loading bay for trucks. The front-facing windows were new, vinyl-trimmed. The sides were flat-faced brick. The back windows were covered with iron bars. Front door was steel, set a few inches into the frame. The City

Planning Office had the records. The place had been gut-renovated four years ago. The top floor had a domed skylight.

Traffic was light in and out. Most of the visitors were young. White. Empty-handed.

I went to see a guy I know. An ex-cop who doesn't pretend he's honest. For three hundred bucks, he told me the place had six separate phone numbers and two pay phones.

"You want the numbers, the toll calls?"

"How much?"

"A grand gets you the numbers, and one month's bill for each number."

"I'll let you know."

Four cars registered to the corporation. Two vans, a station wagon, and a Mercedes sedan.

Five hundred bought me an IRS scan. The corporation called itself Mission 999. It declared almost three hundred grand last year in contributions, none larger than a couple of thousand. The guy I paid told me that it had never been audited.

I had a picture of Elvira. Pretty little brunette in a school uniform. Looked about thirteen. Smiling a school-picture smile.

It made me think of something. Something that wouldn't come to the surface.

# 41

I TOLD MAX ABOUT the deal. Sitting in my booth in the back of Mama's restaurant, I drew a picture of the house. Max kept tapping the paper, not satisfied until I drew in every detail I could remember. He curled his fingers into a tube, held it to one eye, flicked a finger across the opening at the end. I shook my head—I didn't need photographs of the place. When I was finished, I handed the drawing to Max. He lit a cigarette, took a deep drag, let the smoke bubble slowly out his nose as he concentrated.

He ground out his cigarette. Reached down, gestured like he was pulling a plant out by the roots. I shook my head again. We weren't going to snatch the kid. I took him through the whole bit again. And again. Finally he nodded.

## 42

THE NEXT MORNING WE parked a couple of blocks from the building. Walked the rest of the way. Calm and quiet. I knocked on the steel door. Waited. Max stood next to me, just off my shoulder, centered inside himself, ready.

A young guy just past his teens opened the door. Wearing a blinding white karate gi, black belt loosely tied at his waist, black headband.

"Can I help you?"

"I want to talk to Train."

"Your name?"

"Burke."

"Wait here, please." He closed the door gently. No sound reached us from inside.

It wasn't a long wait. "Please come with me," he said.

The door opened into a long, narrow room. Kitchen sounds to one side. Young people moving around, serene looks, quiet smiles. "This way," he said, turning toward a staircase.

We followed him to the second floor. Sounds of a postage meter, telephones chiming. More people moving around. Nobody gave us a glance.

Another flight. Quiet. All the doors closed. The guy in the karate outfit never looked back.

He opened a door at the top of the last flight. Stood aside, sweeping a hand to show us in. A room the size of a basketball court. Wide-board pine floor, scrubbed so hard it was almost white. The walls were eggshell, the single row of windows blocked by thin aluminum blinds, slanted to make horizontal bars across the floor. The skylight threw an oblong slash of bright light into the center. A teardrop-shaped blob of concrete was placed at the center of the light. The guide led us to it. The center was hollowed out, red and white pillows arranged in the core to form a chair.

"Please wait," he said. He walked across the room, tapped on a door at the far end, came back, and stood next to us. A rainbow formed an arc over the concrete chair. I flicked my eyes to the sky-light, catching a glimpse of a long arc-shaped prism suspended by a thread from the ceiling.

The far door opened. A man came through at the head of a wedge, three men on each side of him. Medium height, dark hair. Barefoot, loose faded cotton pants. He was bare-chested under a flowing white silk robe.

"I am Train," he said to me, ignoring Max.

"Burke."

"Get chairs for our guests," he said to nobody in particular. He sat down, one man on each side of his chair. The other four came back carrying one of the concrete blobs between them. I saw where hand-holds had been cut into the sides. They put the chair down. Went back and returned with another. Nobody spoke. The four men came back, each carrying two black pillows. They arranged the pillows in the hollow of the chairs. I took the chair closest to the windows. Max swept the room with his eyes, sat down next to me. One of the men put a metal bowl between our chairs. The four chair-carriers walked out. Train spoke to me from between his two remaining guards—their eyes tracked me. Nothing serene in them.

"You wanted to speak with me?" His voice was mellow-calm, almost polite.

I reached into my coat, watching his eyes. They stayed calm. I took out a smoke, fired it up, dropped the match into the metal bowl.

"You have a girl here. Elvira. Her mother wants her back."

"Is that your message?"

"Half of it. I'm here to take her."

"Just like that?"

I shrugged.

"Do you want to know *why* she's here?"

"No."

"Or how she got to us?"

"No."

He closed his eyes. Held his hands to his temples like he was waiting for a message.

"Are you a private detective?"

"No."

"What if she wants to stay?"

"She's underage. It's not her choice."

"Everyone makes choices."

"Everyone tries."

He put his fingers to his temples again. "Can we discuss this?"

"What's to discuss?"

"I'm interested in people. Why they do things. It helps me do my work."

I dragged on my cigarette.

"Are you interested in a proposition?"

"Enough to listen to it."

He leaned slightly forward. "I'm interested in you. Why you would do something like this. An hour or so of conversation. Just you and I. We'll talk. You'll answer my questions. And I'll answer yours, if you want. A dialogue. I will have to prepare the girl. You'll come back tomorrow. She'll leave with you. Fair enough?"

My face stayed flat. "Even if you don't like the answers I give you?"

"Yes."

I made a sign to Max. He flowed to his feet, approached the man sitting across from us. Train didn't move. The guards stepped in front of him. Max kept coming. I couldn't hear what Train said, but the guards parted when Max closed in. He took one of Train's hands in his, turned it over, examining it. Stepped back, nodded to me.

Train's eyes flickered in the artificial rainbow. "What was that about?"

"My brother is leaving now. I'll talk to you. Like you said. I'll come back tomorrow. For the girl. Like you said."

"That doesn't answer my question."

"Yeah it does. You keep your word, there's no problem. You don't, my brother comes back to see you. He'll know you when he does."

Train shrugged. Max stepped away from him. Stood behind his own chair. Thrust his fingers into the handholds and lifted the concrete blob off the ground. The only sound in the room was the whistle of air through the Mongol warrior's flat nose.

That wasn't like Max. Muscle-flexing. Maybe none of us would be ourselves again.

He gently lowered the chair to the floor. Bowed to Train. Walked to the door we used to enter the room. The guy in the white karate outfit stepped in his way, looking to Train for a sign. By the time Train shook his head, the guy was on the floor, face a black shade of red, holding his ribs gently so they wouldn't cut into his lungs. And Max was on the other side of the door.

I lit another cigarette. "Let's have that dialogue," I said to Train.

## 43

THE TWO GUARDS HELPED the guy in the white outfit to his feet. Went out the same door, leaving us alone. Train put his hands to his temples again.

Silence.

"What do you call yourself?" he finally asked.

"Burke."

"Not who, what. You say you're not a private investigator . . . you're not a lawyer, not a doctor . . . all of us are something. You're . . ."

"Waiting."

His eyes stayed calm. "A dialogue. As we agreed."

I nodded my head forward, acknowledging. "I'm just a man. I guess you could call me a contractor."

"Could you explain?"

"I make contracts with people. I promise to do something for them, they promise to do something for me."

"Pay you money?"

"Sometimes."

"And other times?"

"It depends. I need certain things. Just like you or anybody else. I do my work to get those things. It's not always money."

"Are you for hire, then?"

"Only by people who know me. Or know my people."

"This girl you want . . . her mother hired you?"

"Yes."

"And you know her?"

"Yes."

"Do you ever work as a bodyguard?"

"No."

"Why not?"

"It's not what I do. A bodyguard does his job by getting hurt. Or dead."

His lower lip flickered. "And you're afraid of getting hurt?"

"Or dead."

The concrete chair was comfortable. I lit another cigarette. Train shifted his weight, leaning forward, elbows on knees. "Do you feel safe? Here, with me?"

"No."

"Why is that? Your . . . *brother,* you called him . . . seems very powerful. Is that why you brought him?"

"He's gone," I pointed out.

"That confused me. It seems that you told him to go as a gesture of faith. As I told my men to leave. We are the only ones here. Are you afraid of me?"

"Not especially."

"Then . . . ?"

"I'm sitting in this chair. Your chair. It could be stuffed full of low-yield explosive. Wired for electricity. Sitting under a sniper's rifle . . . like that."

"But you don't think so."

"No. I don't think so."

"Would you feel more comfortable if we switched chairs?"

"No. It doesn't matter."

"Are you armed? You have a weapon with you?"

"No."

He leaned back in his chair. "Have you ever been arrested?"

"Yes."

"In prison?"

"Yes."

"Were you innocent?"

"Which time?"

A smile came and went so quickly I couldn't be sure I'd seen it. "Do you mind if one of my people joins us for a minute?" he asked.

"Why?"

"She has a special skill. Something that would help our dialogue."

I shrugged.

"You sure you don't mind?"

"We have a contract."

"Ah . . . yes." He snapped his fingers, a brittle crack in the empty room. The door behind him opened and a woman stepped through. Long, thick dark hair gathered into a heavy braid hanging down the front of a pale violet robe. She stood next to Train, her eyes on me. Big eyes, tropic skin, a slash for a mouth. Dark polish on her nails. "This is Reba," he said.

I lit another smoke. Train rested the fingertips of one hand on the back of the woman's wrist. She was a statue.

"Have you ever taken a lie detector test?"

"Sure."

"Did you pass?"

I felt the ghost of a smile, thinking about it. "The cops never tell you."

"I will."

I raised my eyebrows, waiting.

"Reba has the gift. You know how a polygraph works, yes? Galvanic skin response, heartbeat, pulse rate?"

"Sure."

"Reba does that. With your permission . . . ?"

"Okay."

The woman walked toward me, stepping out of the robe without moving her arms. She was naked, barefoot. I kept my eyes on Train as she crossed the room, the violet puddle of silk at his feet. She came to the right side of my chair, dropped to her knees, her breasts spilling against my forearm, pinning it to the chair. Her right hand slipped inside my jacket, unbuttoned my shirt, hovered over my heart, gently came to rest. I felt two fingers of her left hand against the back of my neck. My eyes flicked to the right. The dark hair disappeared over her shoulder, smooth line of her back down to the swell of her butt, the soles of her feet were calloused, deeply arched.

"You know how it works," he said. "Just answer yes or no."

I dragged on my cigarette, flicking the ashes with my left hand.

"Have you ever been in prison?"

"Yes."

"Have you ever killed anybody?"

I just looked at him, no expression on my face. He went on as if I'd answered.

"Have you ever broken the law?"

"Yes."

"Are you a professional assassin?"

"No."

"Do you pay taxes?"

"Yes."

"Did Elvira's mother hire you?"

"Yes."

"Did you ever hear my name before you spoke to her?"

"No."

"Do you mean me any harm?"

"No."

"Have you ever met Elvira?"

"No."

"Are you working for anyone now besides the woman who says she is Elvira's mother?"

"No."

I tossed my cigarette into the metal bowl. I let my eyes follow the arc of the smoke, swept them back across Train's face, let the sweep carry me to the right. A clear droplet of sweat ran down Reba's spine. Her head came up, lips against my ear. "You told the truth," she whispered. Her hand came away from my heart, brushed smoothly across my crotch as she rose to her feet. She walked over to Train, her back gleaming with sweat. His eyes shifted up to her face as she passed. She went through the door without picking up her robe.

Train's hand went back to his temples. "What do you think of my security here?"

"What security?"

"I don't understand."

"Security against break-ins? Telephone taps? Firebombing? What?"

"Oh, I see. I mean my personal security . . . say, if somebody wanted to injure me."

"Seems easy enough to me."

"How so?"

"I walked in here with my brother. We wanted to do it, you were a dead man once you came in the room."

He dismissed the possibility with a wave of his hand. "Forget that. What if you wanted to kill me without getting into the house."

"You ever *leave* the house?"

"Sometimes."

"That'd be the time."

"How?"

"There's too many ways to even talk about. Shooting, stomping, stabbing . . ."

"What if I had bodyguards. *True* bodyguards."

"Bullet-catchers?"

"If you like."

"So somebody pops you from a rooftop. Or blows up a car with everybody in it."

"If I stayed in this house?"

"Set fire to it, you'd come out quick enough."

Train rotated his head on the column of his neck, working out the kinks from sitting so stiffly. A glaze over his eyes. Maybe it was the rainbow. Finally, he nodded. "Do you know what we do here?" he asked.

"No."

"Do you care?"

"No."

"When we were talking before . . . about assassinations? You seem to be saying that if someone wants to kill you, there's nothing you can do about it . . . no way you can protect yourself. Is that right?"

"No."

"What *can* you do, then?"

"Hit them first."

He bowed his head over clasped hands. Like he was praying. Looked up. "You are a man of your word. I will honor our contract. Come back tomorrow. Anytime after seven o'clock in the evening. The girl you call Elvira will be ready to leave with you then."

He snapped his fingers again. The door behind him opened. One of the guards came out. I got to my feet. Bowed to Train and walked to the door I'd come in, the guard at my heels.

The street was dark as I stepped outside. I didn't look back.

I found the Plymouth, started the engine, waited.

The door opened. Max slipped inside. Shook his head. I hadn't been followed.

## 44

BACK AT THE RESTAURANT, I explained what had gone down to Max. His face didn't change, but I could feel the sadness. Wishing Train had refused me the girl. I made the sign of a rifleman on the roof, watching Train through a sniperscope. Max pointed his finger at me, questioning. I shook my head. I left the symbol of the rifleman in place with my left hand, walked the fingers of my right hand up behind it. Knife-edged the right hand, chopped at the symbol, flattened my left hand. Max pointed at me again. Did Train want us to do the job? No.

I didn't know what he wanted. We'd pick up the girl tomorrow and it would be over.

## 45

I FOUND THE PROF working the Living Room—what the army of homeless humans who live in the tunnels and work the corridors call the arena-sized waiting room at Grand Central. He was propped against the wall by the gourmet bakery, a thick blanket beneath his legs, single wooden crutch standing next to him, a paper plate half full of coins in front of him. I bought him a large cardboard cup of black coffee. Hunkered down next to him, back to the wall. Street people stopped by the Prof's station, talking their talk, dealing their deals. Cops strolled past, eyes working from the ground up. Drugs moved in and out faster than the trains. It felt like being back on the yard in prison.

"You know a guy named Train? Over in Brooklyn."

He sipped his coffee, buried inside a winter overcoat that tented around his shoulders, running it through his memory bank. "It doesn't scan, man."

"He's got some kind of thing going. Like a cult, only . . . I don't know. Woman asked me to bring her kid home from there."

"Runaway?"

"I don't think so. The deal was, I just *ask* him, okay?"

"Ask him hard?"

"No. And just once."

"If it's like you say, what's the play?"

"He asked *me* the questions."

"Show me a piece."

"Mostly about his security system . . . did I think it was good enough."

"For what?"

"To protect him, I guess. I thought he was trying to hire a bodyguard at first, but he never really asked."

"He want a favor? Don't he know you only play for pay?"

I lit a cigarette. Told the little man about the lie detector Train used, the karate-man he had at the door, the layout of the house.

I wasn't watching his face but I could feel him nod. The words came out of the side of his mouth. "I ain't read the book, but I'll take a look."

I left him at his post.

## 46

I CALLED CANDY FROM a pay phone in the station.

"He said okay."

"You have my girl?"

"Tomorrow night. I'll bring her to you."

"See? I told you . . ."

I hung up.

## 47

A DOLL-FACED YOUNG girl was working the exit ramp to the subway at Forty-second Street. Soft brown hair in pigtails down the sides of her face, body buried in a quilted baby-blue jacket.

"Mister? Can you help me? I'm trying to get together enough money to go home."

"Where's home?"

"In Syosset—on Long Island."

"That's where I'm going. Come on, I'll give you a ride."

She bit her lower lip. "Twenty bucks."

"What?"

"Twenty bucks. And you can ride me wherever you want, okay?"

Before I lost Belle, I would have taken her with me. Called McGowan.

I walked out into the street.

# 48

THE NEXT DAY IT WAS dark enough by seven, but we gave the night a couple of hours to settle in. I went to Train's place alone. A different guy let me in. I followed him upstairs. Took my seat. Waited.

The door opened and they all walked in. Train was with them. The woman who said I had told the truth came in last, leading a girl by the hand. A short, slender little girl wearing faded jeans with a rip above one knee. A pale green T-shirt with "Zzzzap!" across the chest, plastic strap of an airline bag across one shoulder, denim jacket in one hand.

"Do you know this man?" Train asked the girl.

She shook her head no.

The lie detector opened her robe. She was naked beneath it. Took the girl inside, hugging her close, looked over her shoulder at Train. Nodded.

"This is who you asked for," Train said to me.

"If you say so."

"You don't know her?"

"No."

"But you've seen a photograph . . . had her described to you?"

"Sure."

"And?"

"I can't tell." The girl's yellow cat's eyes watched me.

"Do you want to ask her any questions?"

"No." I lit a cigarette. "If she's not the right girl, I'll bring her back."

His lower lip twisted. Hands went to his temples. The lie detector opened her robe. The girl walked over. Stood in front of me. "Let's go," she said, slipping one arm into her jacket.

I stood up. Nobody moved. She followed me to the door. The new guard stepped aside. We walked down the stairs by ourselves. Opened the front door and stepped outside. She didn't look back.

## 49

SHE WALKED BESIDE ME to the Plymouth. I unlocked the passenger door for her. As she swung her hips into the front seat I slipped the airline bag off her shoulder. She didn't react. I closed the door behind her, walked around behind the car, unzipping the bag, rooting through it with my hand. Nothing in there that could hurt you unless you swallowed it.

I climbed inside, handed her the bag. She put it on the floor, groped inside, came out with a cigarette.

"Can I have a light?" Her voice was soft, like she was asking me for something else.

I fired a wooden match, held it out to her. She wrapped both hands around mine, lit the smoke, eyes on me. "Your hand feels strong."

I wheeled the car down Flatbush Avenue, heading for the Manhattan Bridge. Turned right on thc Bowery, heading uptown.

"My mother sent you?"

"That's right, Elvira."

"Nobody calls me that."

"What do they call you?"

"Juice," she said, flashing a smile. "You think that's dumb?"

"Kids have funny names."

"I'm not a kid."

"Fifteen, your mother said."

"My mother is a liar. She always lics."

I shrugged.

"What if I don't want to go back?"

"Talk to her about it."

"I'm talking to you."

"You're talking to yourself."

I pulled up at a red light on First Avenue. She snapped her lighted cigarette at me and ripped at the door handle, shoving her shoulder against the passenger door. It didn't budge. I picked her cigarette off the seat, tossed it out my window. She pushed her back against the car door, watching me, breathing hard through her mouth.

"You think you're smart—you're not so smart."

"Just relax."

"Will you *talk* to me?"

"About what?"

"Just talk to me. I'm not a package. Not something you just deliver."

"Yeah you are."

"Look, you can keep me in this car, okay? But you have to bring me in the house too."

"I can do that."

"Oh yes. You're a hard man. Momma only likes hard men."

"It's just a job."

Streets passed. Her breathing got calm again. "Can I have another smoke?"

"Sure." I handed her the little box of wooden matches.

"You don't trust me?"

"Why would I?"

"Because I'm not like my mother. I *never* lie. Never, ever. If I tell you I'll do something, I'll do it."

"And so you're telling me what?"

She drew on the smoke. "I'm telling you I want to talk to you. Just for a couple of minutes. Pull the car over . . . anyplace you want . . . just talk to me. Then when we get to my mother's, I'll walk in with you just like I was supposed to. No trouble, no screaming, nothing. Okay?"

I made a right turn on Twenty-third, found an empty slot facing the river under the East Side Drive. An abandoned car, stripped to its shell, was on my right, empty space on the left. I slid down my window, killed the ignition. Lit a smoke. "Let's talk," I said to the girl.

Her smile flashed again, knocking the pout off her face. "What's your name?"

"Burke."

"Are you my mother's man?"

"No."

She shrugged out of the denim jacket, arching her back so her breasts poked at the T-shirt. "Is this what you do?"

"What?"

"Deliver packages."

"Sometimes."

"You like it?"

"It's work."

"But do you *like* it?"

"If I liked it, people wouldn't have to pay me to do it."

"Sometimes you get paid for what you like to do. Like a whore who loves to fuck."

I shrugged. I had never met one.

She took a drag on her cigarette. Handed it to me. I tossed it out my window.

"It's real dark here."

"You're all done talking, we can leave."

"You want me to shut up?"

"It doesn't matter. We have a deal, right? We talk, then I take you home."

"You mean you take me to my mother's."

"Whatever."

"If you wanted me to shut up, you know the best way to do it?"

"No."

"You put something in my mouth. You want to put something in my mouth?" Her voice was bad-little-girl teasing. She knew how to do it.

"No."

"Yes you do. I can feel it." Her hand snaked toward my lap in the darkness.

I grabbed her wrist.

"All done talking?"

"What's the matter, Mr. Burke? You never went back to your girlfriend with lipstick on your cock before?"

"Lipstick, yeah," I told her. "Not bubble gum."

"I'm old enough."

"Not for me."

The car was quiet for a couple of minutes. "I'm done talking," she said, her voice soft and flat.

She didn't say another word until I pulled up outside Candy's apartment building.

"This is it," I said.

"I know."

## 50

"DOES THE DOORMAN know you?" I asked her.

"Sure."

He waved us in as soon as he saw her face. Never looked at mine. She was quiet in the elevator.

The door swung open before I had the button depressed enough to ring the bell. Candy.

"Come in here," she said to the girl, not looking at me.

Elvira walked past her to the couch, dropping her bag on the floor like the maid would get it in the morning.

Candy walked over to me, reached up and put her hands on my shoulders. "Thanks, baby," she stage-whispered. The girl was sitting on the couch, watching her mother's back. Waiting for the truth.

I gave it to her. "Where's the money?"

Her fingers bit into the top of my shoulders, eyes lashed at me. I waited.

She whirled, heels tapping on the parquet floor. Elvira put her fingers to her chin, like she was considering something important. Her mother came back into the living room, stopped two feet in front of me. Handed me an envelope. I put it into my coat.

I heard the door click closed behind me.

## 51

I GOT BACK INTO THE Plymouth, started the engine. Lit a smoke. The door opened and Max slid inside. I handed him Candy's envelope, pulled out into traffic.

He tapped my shoulder. Holding a slab of cash in each hand. Nodded. All there. He put one hand in his pocket, the other in mine. We'd split the front money too.

I spun my finger in a circle, tapped the back of my neck. Anybody follow us?

The blunt-faced Mongol tapped one eye. Shook his head no. But then he shuddered his shoulders like he got a chill. Something. Something you couldn't see.

I checked the rearview mirror, moving through traffic. Max didn't spook at shadows. I pointed north. He nodded. Anyone following us to the junkyard would stick out like a beer drinker at a Jim Jones picnic.

We crossed the Triboro, turned into the jungle. Nothing behind us. I whipped the Plymouth into a tight U-turn, pointed back the way we came. Max lit a smoke for himself, one for me.

Half an hour later it was still quiet. The cops don't have that much patience. I took another route back downtown, dropped Max off near the warehouse, and headed back to the office.

Pansy was glad to see me.

## 52

I FELT BETTER WHEN I got up the next morning. Not good enough to bet on a horse, but like something bad was over. It was still early enough to risk using the phone in my office. My phone is just an extension run from the collection of deservedly unknown artists who live downstairs. They don't know about it—neither does Ma Bell. They probably wouldn't care if they did know—they don't pay their own bills.

"Any calls, Mama?"

"No calls. You come in today, okay?"

"Anything wrong?"

"Someone leave note for you."

"So?"

"Talk later," she said, hanging up.

I took a quarter-pound slab of cream cheese out of the refrigerator, dropped it in the bottom of Pansy's bowl, covered it with her dry dog food. "I'll bring you something good from Mama's," I promised her.

## 53

MAMA WAS AT THE table almost before I sat down. She handed me a cheap white business envelope, the top neatly slit open. The note was typed:

> Burke: Be by your phone at 11:00 tonight. Don't have anybody take a message. Be there yourself. Wesley

I drew a narrow breath through my nose. Let it out. Again. Feeling the fear-jolts dart around inside my chest, looking for a place to land. I lit a cigarette, holding the note against the match flame, watching it turn to ash. Wishing I'd never seen it.

"You see him?"

"A boy. Street boy. Around five o'clock this morning."

"He say anything?"

"Not see me. Push this under the front door, run away."

"You opened it?"

She bowed. It was okay. I knew why she told me to come in. She never met Wesley, but she knew the name. Every outlaw in the city did.

"Burke? What you do?"

"Answer the phone when it rings," I told her.

## 54

I SAT THERE QUIETLY while Mama went to call Immaculata. To tell Max the devil was loose. Wesley never threatened. He *was* terror. Cold as a heat-seeking missile. He took your money, you got a body. Years ago my compadre Pablo told me about a contract Wesley had on a Puerto Rican dope dealer uptown. The dealer knew the contract was out. He went to a Santeria priestess, begging for voodoo heat against the glacier coming for him. The priestess took the dealer's money, told him Chango, the warrior-god, would protect him. She was an evil old demon, feared throughout the barrio. Her crew was all Marielitos. Zombie-driven murderers. They set fires to watch the flames. Ate the charred flesh. Tattoos on their hands to tell you their specialty. Weapons, drugs, extortion, homicide. The executioner's tattoo was an upside-down heart with an arrow through it. Cupid as a hit man.

The priestess called on her gods. Killed chickens and goats. Sprinkled virgin's blood on a knife. Loosed her death-dogs into the street looking for Wesley.

The dealer hid in her house. Safe.

Blazing summer, but the kids stayed off the streets. Winter always comes.

A UPS driver pulled up outside the apartment house where the priestess kept her temple. Her Marielitos slammed him against his truck, pulling at his clothes. Eyes watched from beneath slitted shades. They took a small box from the driver, laughing when he said someone had to sign for it.

They held the box under an opened fire hydrant, soaking the paper off. One of the Marielitos held the box to his ear, shaking it. Another pulled a butterfly knife from his pocket, flashed it open in the street, grinning. They squatted, watching as the box was slit open. Looked inside. They stopped laughing.

They took the box inside to the priestess. A few minutes later, the dope dealer was thrown into the street, hands cuffed behind his back, duct tape sealing his mouth. He ran from the block.

They whispered about it. In the bodegas, in the after-hours joints, on the streets. They said the priestess found the hand of her executioner inside the box, the tattoo mocking her. Chango was angry. So she found a better sacrifice than a chicken.

The cops found the dealer a few blocks away, a tight group of four slugs in his chest, another neat hole in his forehead. Nobody heard shots.

## 55

MAX CAME INTO THE restaurant. Sat across from me. Made the same gesture of getting a chill through his back he'd made when I'd asked him about being followed. Now we knew. Gold tones shot through his bronze skin—the warrior's blood was up. He showed me a fist, stabbed his heart with his thumb. I wasn't dealing him out of this one. Max tapped my wristwatch. Shrugged. I knew what he meant: why wait? I shook my head, held an imaginary telephone receiver up to my ear. If Wesley wanted to come for me, he wouldn't play games. It had to be something else.

Max folded his arms across his chest. I wanted to wait, he was waiting with me.

I told Mama I'd be back before the call came through, catching Max's eyes. No games—I'd be there.

## 56

PANSY TORE INTO THE gallon of meat and vegetables Mama had put together for her. No MSG. I closed my eyes and lay back on the couch. Watching the smoke drift toward the ceiling. Wondering how long it would be before the office got back to its usual filthy state. The way it had been for years until Belle hit it like dirt was her personal enemy.

Wesley. We'd once worshiped the same god. But only Wesley had been true.

It had been a long time.

## 57

I WAS BACK AT THE restaurant before ten. "Max still here," Mama told me. "In the basement."

There's a bank of three pay phones past the tables, just outside the kitchen area. One of them is mine. People call, Mama answers. Tells them I'm not in, takes a message. It's worked like that for years.

The phone rang at ten-thirty. I looked at my watch. It wasn't like Wesley to be cute. I grabbed the phone.

"Yeah?"

"You answer your own phone now?" Candy.

"What?"

"I have to see you."

"I'm busy."

"I know what you're busy *with* . . . it's about that. You want me to talk on the phone?"

"I'll call you when I can come."

"Call soon. You don't have a lot of time."

## 58

AT ELEVEN THE PHONE rang again I picked it up, saying nothing.

"It's you?"

"It's me," I said to the voice.

"We need to talk."

"Talk."

"Face to face."

"You know where I am."

"Not there."

"Where, then?"

"Take the bridge to the nuthouse on the island. Pull over as soon as you get in sight of the guard booth. Midnight tomorrow. Okay?"

"Want me to wear a bull's-eye on my back?"

"I don't care what you wear, but leave the Chinaman at home."

"What's this about?"

"Business," Wesley said, breaking the connection.

## 59

I FELT LIKE CALLING a cop. It passed.

Max didn't like any of it. When he gets like that, he acts like he can't read my hand signals. Everything takes longer.

None of our crew ever messed in Wesley's business. We didn't work the same side of the street. Max knew the myth; I knew the man. They both played the same. Finally, I got through to Max: if Wesley wanted me, bringing him along would just add another target. I played my trump card. Religion. Our religion. Revenge. If Wesley hit me, Max would have to square it. He bowed in agreement. I could always talk him into anything.

And I wasn't going alone.

## 60

IT WAS ABOUT ELEVEN when I pulled out of the garage the next night, heading for the East Side Drive. If the cops stopped me, they'd get license and registration from Juan Rodriguez. I had a Social Security card too. Juan always pays his taxes and his parking tickets. They wouldn't find dope and they wouldn't find a gun. Pansy made a sleek black shadow in the back where I had pulled out the lower seat cushion, growling to herself. Glad to be along. "Keep your voice down," I told her. "You're supposed to be a surprise."

I took the East Side Drive to the exit for the Triboro, paid the toll, and hooked the turn onto the short bridge for Randalls Island. Followed the signs to Wards Island, then to the Kirby Psychiatric Institute. Home to the criminally insane. The Plymouth trolled under the maze of connecting ramps running above us. I spotted the guard booth about a quarter mile ahead. Behind the booth was a network of state institutional buildings, the size of a small town. Huge sewage disposal plant to my left. Everything Wesley needed.

I pulled over, sliding the Plymouth a few yards off the road. Killed the lights. Flattened my hand in front of Pansy's snout to tell her to stay where she was. Left the door wide open. Lit a smoke.

He came out of the night like he must have come the very first time. Wearing military fatigues in dark gray with black camouflage splotches. Dull black jungle boots on his feet, a soft hat in the same camo-pattern pulled down to his eyes. Black slashes below his eyes. Hands covered in dark gloves, held where I could see them. His voice was like his clothes.

"You came alone?"

"My dog's in the car."

"Call it out."

I snapped my fingers. Pansy bounded off the seat, landing next to me on all fours, head tilted up to watch Wesley's groin. If she fired, she wouldn't go higher than that.

My eyes shifted back to Wesley. To the Uzi in his hands, held tight against the strap around his neck. "Tell it to get down," he said, the barrel pointed between me and Pansy, ready to squirt us both into chunks of dead flesh.

I made the sign and Pansy hit the deck.

"Why's the dog here?"

"What d'you care? She can't talk."

"Put her back in the car. And lock it."

I pointed to the car. Pansy jumped into the back seat. I slammed the back door. Put my key in the lock and twisted it, left and right. Stood aside as Wesley tried both doors, Pansy's huge head looming behind the glass, tracking him. The second twist of the key had popped the trunk. If I called her, she'd come out that way.

"Go ahead," he said, pointing into the underbrush. I followed a narrow dirt path, feeling him behind me. We came to an abandoned pickup truck, rusting to death, its nose buried in one of the I-beams holding up the overpass.

"Sit down," he said.

I hoisted myself up to the pickup's open bed, legs dangling. "Can I . . . ?"

He held his finger to his lips. I counted to fifty before he spoke again.

"Yeah, you can smoke. I know you not carrying."

I took one out, bit hard into the filter to stop my mouth from trembling. Fired it up, cupping the flame. Wesley stood facing me, legs spread, hands behind him. The Uzi was gone.

He didn't look like much. If you didn't know, he could walk up to you—you wouldn't know him till you felt him. The same way cancer works.

"Why am I here?"

"You totaled a freak. Mortay."

I waited. A tiny gleam of white at his mouth. Wesley's smile. "You think I'm trying to get you to confess? Working for the Man?"

"I know you, Wesley. You don't ask questions."

"Yeah I do. I always ask who. Never ask why."

"Okay."

"We go back a long way, Burke."

"This a reunion?"

"You know what I do. Ever since I got out the last time. They give me a name, I do my work. This Mortay, he was off the rails. He had to go. I was tracking him when you went nuts and blew him up."

Toby Ringer had told me the truth. Belle died for nothing. If

Wesley was tracking Mortay, all I had to do was wait. All for nothing. "I didn't know," I said, working to keep my voice from cracking. I never said truer words.

"They don't want to pay me," he said. Like God was dead.

"So?"

"So I don't work for them anymore." His body shifted slightly. I thought about the Uzi. Dismissed it—on the best day of my life, I wasn't fast enough. "You got in the way with that freak. You fucked things up. That's one time. It happens. But now the word's all over the street—you're in business. My business."

"I'm not—that's not me."

"I know. You're a hijacker. A sting artist. You got *friends.*" His dead man's voice made the word sound like a perversion.

"What's your problem?"

"Train. You know him."

"Yeah."

"He's on the spot. He has to go down. You've been sniffing around. Either you're working for him or you're looking to take him out."

"No. I had a contract. I pulled a girl out of his joint."

"I saw that."

"That's it. There's no more."

"You know what he does?"

"No."

"Don't find out."

I lit another smoke, watching my hands near the flame. They didn't shake. Wesley took you past fear.

"Wesley, I got no beef with you. You know that. You want to know something, ask me. And let me go."

"You know why I wanted you out here? You're a fucking nutcase yourself, Burke. You got this Jones for kids. I know about the day-care center too. Out in Queens. Why didn't you use the Chinaman on Mortay?"

"He wasn't around."

"Something about a kid, right?"

I just watched him.

"Yeah, you're bent. Remember when we were coming up? Learning the rules? You don't work with drunks, you don't work with dope fiends, you don't work with skinners, right? You don't work with *nobody* who's off the track. Now it's you—you're off the track."

Tracks. I was a kid again in my mind. In a subway tunnel. Me and Rupert facing each other. Chins on the tracks, bodies spread out behind. The rest of the gang waited off to the side. I heard the rumble of the train, felt the track tremble under my jawbone. Watching Rupert. Last one off the tracks was the winner. Sixteen years old. Don't mind dying. I read my tombstone: Burke Had Heart. Better than flowers. Rupert's face a few feet from mine. He'd offered a knife fight, I bumped the stakes with the train tracks—the tunnel. No matter what happened, I'd have a name. It wouldn't hurt, I told myself. The train roared at us, coming hard, a hundred-ton mindless life-taker. Light washed the black tunnel. Rupert jumped back. Me! My legs wouldn't work. Hands grabbed my ankles, jerked me off the track, cracking my jaw. The train shot past.

That night, on the roof, Candy took my cock in her mouth for the first time.

"I was the last off the track," I reminded him.

"Yeah." A robot's voice. He knew the truth. Even when we were kids, Wesley knew the truth. He'd been there. His hands on my ankles. If he hadn't pulled after Rupert jumped back, I'd still be there. "Train's a dead man. My dead man. You get in the way again, you go with him."

"I'm not in the way."

His face moved closer, watching mine. No psychiatrist could read his eyes—you can't take a census when there's nobody home. I held his gaze, letting him in. See the truth, monster. See it again.

He stepped back. "You're not good enough," he said. Not putting me down, just saying it. "You still do that trick? Where you memorize something without writing it down?"

"Yeah."

He said a number. "You call this number. Anytime. Let it ring three times. Hang up. Do it again. Then you wait by the number I have for you."

"I don't need to call you."

"Yeah you will. I know how things work. You used to know too."

He put his gloved hands together, looking down at the temple they made. "Kids . . . what fucking difference does it make, Burke?"

Once I thought it did. Prayed to that god in the orphanage, in the foster homes, in reform school. Somebody would come. Be my family. I found my family in prison. Prayed to another god. Belle in my mind. *Rescue me*. Sure. The first god ignored me. The second came close enough for me to have a good look. "It doesn't make any," I said to him.

"You're a burnt-out case," the monster told me. "You're done."

"Okay." Nothing to argue about.

"Train's safe for a bit. I'll get to him. But first I got a whole lot of Italians to do."

"Do what you have to do—I'm not in it."

His eyes were tombstones. With no date of birth and no epitaph. "I know how things work. You'll get a call, hit man. Then you call me, got it?" The Uzi came into his hands again. "Stay where you are for a few minutes."

He didn't make a sound moving off past the pickup, away from the Plymouth.

I sat staring into the darkness. Counting the years. Lit another smoke. It was snatched out of my hand. Max the Silent held it to his own lips.

# 61

DRIVING HOME, MAX WAS full of warrior's fire. Full of himself. He grabbed my wrist, tapped the face of my watch, shrugged his shoulders. Sneered. "Anytime," he was saying. Anytime we wanted. Max would cancel the undertaker's ticket.

Too many boxes inside too many boxes. If Max could roll up on Wesley in the dark, I wasn't the only burnt-out case on the set.

I dropped Max off and headed back uptown.

## 62

I FOUND THE PROF IN an after-hours joint by the river. He caught my nod. I waited outside for him. The little man hopped in the front seat, tossing his cane into the back. Pansy's snarl swiveled his head.

"Get down, hound. You ain't bad enough to try me."

Pansy made some noise I hadn't heard before. Maybe she was laughing.

I left the motor running, jumped into an all-night deli and ordered three brisket sandwiches on rye, hold everything. In the car, I threw the bread out the window, squeezed the brisket into a ball the size of a melon. Tossed it back into the pit. Pansy made ugly sounds as she finished it off. She ventured an experimental whine, trying for seconds. Saw it wasn't playing with the home crowd, and flopped down to grab some sleep.

I nosed the Plymouth back down to the waterfront, found a quiet place and pulled over. The Prof fired a cigarette, waiting.

"I saw Wesley."

"*Damn!* Up close?"

"Close as you are right now."

"You ain't dead, so you came out ahead."

"Yeah."

"What'd he want?"

"The freak. The freak who wanted the duel with Max. Wesley was on his case. Way before we started."

"So . . ."

"Yeah. If we'd just gone to ground, holed up, it would have passed."

"You couldn't've known, brother. No man knows Wesley's plan."

"I know."

"He knows the freak is dead. He has to know. Fuck, even the cops know. So what's he want?"

"He wants to get things straight. Says the freak was on his list. A contract, right? And the guys who hired Wesley, they don't want to pay."

"That ride is suicide."

"Yeah. Wesley said he's going to be doing a whole lot of Italians soon."

"Who cares? Let him do a few for me while he's at it. They ain't us."

I lit my own smoke. "He gave me the name of another guy he wants. The same guy I took that little girl from a couple of days ago."

"So?"

"So he doesn't want me in the way. He thinks I'm working his beat now. Hitting for cash."

"Oh."

"I think I squared it."

"You must've, man. With Wesley, you fuck around, you're in the ground."

"You think he's crazy?"

"Not middle-class crazy, bro'. Wesley, he's not . . . he ain't got but one button, and he pushes it himself."

I looked out over the water toward Jersey. "Wesley said I was a burnt-out case. You think that?"

"Wesley's the coldest dude I ever met. But that don't make him the smartest."

"What's that mean?"

"Like Michelle said, man. You not being yourself. Ever since . . ."

"I'll be all right."

"Who says no, bro'?"

"Wesley . . ."

"Wesley. Whatever my man's got, they ain't got no cure for. It's like he's got a couple of parts missing. He *looks* like a man, but he's something else."

"Something . . ."

"Else. That's all I can call."

"You don't come like that stock from the factory."

"Don't get on it, Burke. I didn't know Wesley when he was a kid."

"I did."

"Burke, if you *not* crazy, you putting on a great act." The little man lit a smoke. Drew it in slowly, taking his time. Like you do when you got a lot of it to spare.

"This is the one true clue, brother. Wesley, he's the Mystery Train. Nobody knows where he's going, but everybody knows where he's been."

"I . . ."

"You got no case, Ace. I don't know nobody who ever walked away from a meet with Wesley. He's telling you something. Something just for you. Listen to the lyrics, brother."

I threw my smoke out the window.

Time passed. Wesley said I was off the track. And the Prof was saying that's where I needed to be. Out of the way.

"You got it handled?" he asked.

I nodded, thinking about kids.

## 63

I DIDN'T EXPECT ANYTHING to happen soon. Wesley ran on jailhouse time.

Survive. That's what I do. The biggest piece of that is waiting. Knowing how to wait. Before Belle, I was the best at it. Drifting just outside the strong currents, keeping out of the pattern. Moving in on the breaks, never staying long. In and out.

But if you just stayed in your cell—that was a pattern too.

## 64

MAX WASN'T AT THE warehouse when I pulled in. Immaculata was upstairs, in the living quarters they fixed up above Max's temple. She had a stack of mail waiting for me. One of Mama's drivers handles the pickup from my PO box in Jersey, drops it off every few weeks. Mac bounced her baby on her knee while I smoked and went through the pile.

Anything goes through the U.S. mail. It moves more cocaine than all the Miami Mules going through customs. That's why they invented the "American key." Key as in kilo. A true kilo, European-style, is 2.2 pounds. And the Federal Express cut-off is two pounds.

I work a different kind of dope. Some of the letters were from would-be mercenaries, sending their handwritten money orders to me for "pipeline" information. Child molesters sent cash, seeking the "introductions" I promised in my ads. Freaks ordered hard-core kiddie porn they'd never receive. Let them write the Better Business Bureau. Every so often, someone would answer one of my sting ads: "Vietnam vet, experienced in covert actions. One-man jobs only. U.S.A. only. Satisfaction guaranteed." You hire a hit man through the mails, you find out who first wrote that Silence Is Golden. Blackmailers.

The PO box isn't just for suckers. Anyone out there who knows the game I play can use it for a mail drop. One of the envelopes contained only a single page ripped from a doctor's prescription pad. A blank page except for one word. Shela. She was a high-style scam artist who hated the freaks as much as I did. I never asked why. Whenever she ran across a rich one, she'd pass it along.

I left the money orders in a neat stack for Max to take to Mama's laundry, shrugged into my coat, bowed to Immaculata and the baby.

"Burke . . ."

"What?"

"Max can take care of this thing for you."

"What thing?"

"This man . . . the one you met . . . the one with the machine gun."

"Max told you about that?"

Her lovely dark eyes shone under lashes like butterfly wings. "Do you think that was wrong?"

"I'm glad he has someone to tell."

"You have someone too, Burke. You have us. You know that."

"There's nothing to tell. Wesley's not a problem."

"Not like before?"

"Let it go, Mac."

"That's what *you* must do," she said.

## 65

I'M A GOOD THIEF. Two words—two separate things. When I had that name, I was out of the loop. Safe. The old rules are the best rules—you dance with the one who brought you to the party.

I made some calls, put the team together.

## 66

"THIS'LL REALLY WORK?" I asked the Mole. He was bent over a lab table in his workroom, a pile of gold Krugerrands spread out before him.

He didn't answer. Terry was standing next to him, his little face vibrating with concentration, nose two inches from the Mole's hands.

Michelle was perched on a stool, her sleek nyloned legs crossed, smoking one of her long black cigarettes. Heart-shaped face peaceful. She could have been a suburban housewife watching her husband teach their son how to build a ham radio.

Outside, dogs prowled the night-blanketed minefield of junked cars. Ringed in razor-wire and dotted with pockets of explosives. The safest place I know.

Time went by. The Mole's stubby paws worked tiny probes under a huge magnifying glass he had suspended over the workbench. I heard the clink of coins, saw the red laser-beam shoot from a black box. I picked up one of the Krugerrands, turned it over in my hand. It looked like it was minted yesterday.

"I thought these things weren't allowed in the U.S. anymore. No more trading with South Africa, right?"

The Mole looked up. Hate-dots glinted behind the thick lenses. "No *new* Krugerrands. Illegal since 1984. But it's still legal to trade in older coins if they were made before that date."

I looked at the coin in my hand. Gleaming new. "This says it was minted in 1984," I said.

"It was minted a month ago," the Mole said. "This country always looks the other way for its Nazi friends."

Michelle threw me a warning look. Don't get him started. The Mole was never far from critical mass when it came to his reason for living.

I lit a smoke, patted my brother on the back, willing him to be calm, go back to work.

Soon the Mole pushed back his chair. Pointed at a pile of a half dozen gold coins. "Which one?" he asked.

I took them in my hand. Felt their weight. Held them up to the light. Tried to bend them in half. They were all the same. I tried the magnifying glass. Nothing. Handed them back to the Mole.

He picked out the one he wanted. Handed me a jeweler's loupe. "Look around the edge—where the coin is milled."

It took me a minute, even when I knew what I was looking for. A tiny dark dot standing between the ridges. I gave it back to the Mole.

"Go outside," the Mole said to Terry. He handed me the coin. "Hide it," he said.

"Put it in your purse," I told Michelle.

Terry came back into the bunker holding a transmitter about the size of a pack of cigarettes.

"Find it," the Mole said.

The boy pulled a short antenna from the corner of the transmitter. Hit a switch. Soft electronic beeps, evenly spaced. He moved toward the far wall. The beeps separated, a full second between them. The beeping got more intense as he neared the workbench. The boy was patient, working the room in quadrants. When he got near Michelle, the transmitter went nuts. He worked around her, closing in. When he put it next to her purse, the beeps merged into one long whine. "In there," he said, a smile blasting across his face.

Michelle gave him a kiss. "You're going to take Harvard by storm, handsome."

"Will it work through metal?" I asked the Mole.

"Even through lead," Terry assured me solemnly. I lit a cigarette, satisfied.

"This is the way we're *supposed* to work," Michelle said. "This is us. I'll see the doctor tomorrow."

# 67

THE DOCTOR WOULDN'T blink at a transsexual for a patient. He didn't judge his clients, he just wrote their needs on his Rx pad. He sold what the customer wanted, and he didn't take checks. Quaaludes, steroids, amphetamines, barbiturates. That kind of traffic wouldn't make him rich. But the page from the prescription pad told me what I wanted to know: the doctor was selling Androlan, Malogex . . . all the injectable forms of testosterone. Even threw in a supply of needles. There's a new program for child molesters. The shrinks still haven't figured it out—the freaks, they don't *want* to be cured. This new program, it's only for special degenerates. Ones with money. Counseling, therapy . . . and Depo-Provera. Chemical castration, they call it. Reduces the sex drive down to near-zero. Supposedly makes the freaks safe, even around kids. Methadone for baby-rapers. Some judges love it. The freaks are crazy about the program—it's a Get Out of Jail Free card. The maggots do their research better than the scientists and all their federal grants. They figured out that a regular dose of testosterone cancels the Depo-Provera. Gets them back to what they call normal.

Testosterone's not a narcotic. The feds don't check on how much you dispense. The doctor was doing all right. Medicine changes with the times. When I was a kid, the underground plastic surgeons would give you a new face if you were running from the law. Now some doctors will put a new face on a kid—a kid whose face is on a milk carton. It would do until they outlawed abortions again.

Michelle bought such a big supply that the doctor must have figured she was going into business for herself. The word I got was that he'd wholesale the stuff if the price was right. Michelle paid him in Krugerrands. A dozen gold coins, almost six grand.

The doctor lived up in Westchester County. He had two kids—a boy away at college and a fifteen-year-old girl. We watched the Mercedes pull out of the driveway, his wife next to him in the front seat. The girl was already out for the evening. We figured on a few hours.

The back of the house was protected by an unbroken row of thick hedges. Max unscrewed the top of a cardboard tube, the kind you keep an expensive fishing rod in. Pulled out two aluminum poles. They telescoped like car antennas. He cross-latched the two poles with some X-braces, making a ladder. Max went up first, climbing backwards as easy as if he was using a staircase. The Mole followed him, satchel on a strap over his shoulder. I came next—the Mole was no athlete.

It was a short drop to the ground. The windows were free of burglar-alarm tape. The doctor's wife wouldn't like the look. The Mole fluttered his hand—a flag in a breeze. Motion sensors. "Hardwired," he whispered. "Expensive."

"Can you take it out?" I asked.

The Mole didn't answer, looking through the window with some kind of lens held up to his glasses. "There," he said, pointing.

I saw a wooden box in a corner of the living room. Some kind of dark wood, a slim crystal vase standing on top. A tiny red light glowed near the base.

The Mole fumbled in his satchel. Max braced the pane of glass with his hands as the Mole fitted a tiny drill against the surface. He nodded. Scratched an X on the glass with a probe, fitted the drill point into it. Pressed the trigger. A split-second whine. He reversed the drill bit, pulling it free of the glass. Then he threaded a wire through the hole. Attached the other end of the wire to something inside his satchel. The Mole pushed a toggle switch and the red light on the box inside the house winked out. I could have opened the back door with a credit card.

We left Max on the first floor in case somebody came home. The Mole took the upstairs bedrooms, I hit the basement.

The doctor had a nice little home-office setup downstairs. IRS would approve. I pulled the antenna on the same little box Terry had used to show off for his mother and went to work. It only took a couple of minutes. Second-rate wall safe behind a framed painting of assholes on horses chasing a fox. Amateur Hour. I could have knocked off the dial and pried the thing open in twenty minutes.

It took the Mole less than five. It looked like gray putty he pasted around the edges of the safe. Until you saw the fuse. When he touched it off, we stepped back to watch. A soft pop and the door crumpled.

Our Krugerrands were inside. The doctor liked gold. Canadian Maple Leafs, Chinese Pandas, Australian Koalas. American cash in neat stacks. A small leather loose-leaf book. A Canadian passport. The doctor was prepared—but not for us. We took it all.

## 68

AN AMATEUR STEALS ONLY when he's broke. I'm a professional—I work at my trade.

It didn't stop the pain, just put it on hold.

I've had bad dreams all my life. But now it was sad dreams . . . bone-marrow pain. Belle. I never would have left her. Now she wouldn't leave me.

I told Michelle I'd pick Terry up at Lily's. Got there early, looking around. Waiting. Lily came down the corridor at high speed, shrugging out of her parka, long black hair streaming out behind her. "Tell her I'll call her back!" she shouted over one shoulder. She pulled up when she saw me, a busty, glowing woman with a scar over one of her big dark eyes. Lily's old enough to have a teenage daughter, a little heart-breaker named Noelle, but she looks like she's still in college. Noelle's at the age where she's always griping because her mother isn't stylish enough. She tried to get me on her side once.

"Don't you think Mom would look cool with her hair up?"

"Your mother is beautiful, baby. She looks like the Madonna."

"Oh, Burke!" the kid shrieked. "She's not even blond!"

It's not a generation-gap anymore, it's a time-warp.

I waited until she ran up on me. "Hi, Lily."

Her face was reserved, eyes watchful. "Is there trouble?"

"I'm here to pick up Terry."

"Okay." Dubious.

I lit a cigarette, ignoring her frown, moving aside to let her pass.

She wasn't going for it. "She doesn't bring Scotty herself."

"Scotty?"

Her eyes raked my face, looking for the truth. A trained therapist against a state-raised thief. No contest. I knew who she meant. Scotty was the little boy sodomized by a freak who had a feeder deal with a day-care center. The freak took a picture of his fun—took the little boy's soul for a souvenir. The kid never told anybody until he let it slip to the mother of a little girl he played with. The devil stole his soul, so he asked a witch to get it back. Strega. Flame-haired, steel-hearted Strega. I made a promise to her. To never come back. If she and Wesley mated, their child could walk through Hell in a gasoline overcoat.

Immaculata came down the hall, her arms on the shoulders of the pair of ten-year-olds framing her slender body. One kid was black, the other white. Her long nails made bright slashes of color as she emphasized her words, looking for the right chord to play. Her English was perfect, but the Catholic school in Vietnam where she learned it left a few things out.

"Benny, the very last thing on earth you need is *another* model airplane. It would be . . . coals to Newcastle."

She pulled up short when she saw me standing with Lily. Raised her eyebrows in a question. I shook my head.

"Burke, these are my friends. Benny and Douglas."

I shook hands with each of them. Benny tugged at Immaculata's smock.

"What's coals to Newcastle?"

"Cocaine to Colombia," I told him.

A grin flashed. He raised an open palm and I slapped him a high-five. His buddy grinned.

"Maybe you missed your calling," Immaculata said, pulling the kids down the hall with her, leaving us alone.

Lily wouldn't let it go. "You came here to volunteer . . . teach one of our self-defense classes?"

I dragged on my cigarette. Lily wasn't an ex-con, but she had enough patience for a dozen of them. "Can I talk to you for a minute?"

"Come on," she said, charging down the hall to her office. She walked through the open door, tossed her parka on a couch already overflowing with files, plopped herself in a battered old chair next to the computer she only used for video games. She didn't wait for me to work around to it. "What?" she demanded.

"I lost a friend. Somebody close to me."

"How?"

"She was murdered."

"Oh. You know who did it?"

"Yes."

"Is he . . . the perpetrator . . . arrested?"

"No. And he's not gonna be."

"Why?"

I held her eyes until she understood. "And that didn't end it for you?"

"No."

Lily combed both hands through her thick hair, pulling the mane off her forehead. "You don't know about grief, do you, Burke? You pay your debts, it's supposed to be all done, right?"

I nodded.

"Your friend . . . you loved her?"

"Still do."

She watched my face. "And she knew? You told her?"

"Just before . . ."

"That's not too late."

I lit another cigarette, biting deep into the filter, cupping the match to give my eyes a rest from Lily. "She didn't have to die," I said.

"You think it was your fault?"

"It was my fault."

"She was with you? In your life?"

I nodded.

"Then she knew . . ."

I nodded again.

"Burke, listen to me, okay? Some pain's not *supposed* to go away. That's the price. That's what it costs to remember her."

"Aren't you going to tell me to remember the good times?"

Lily's voice was sweet and quiet, but it made you listen. Honey-in-the-rock. "We all know you're a hard man, Burke. If it works so well for you, why did you come here?"

"Nothing works all the time."

"What does that mean?"

"I played all my cards, Lily."

"Then do what you do best."

My eyes flicked up to her face, watching.

"Steal some more," she said, a Madonna's smile so faint I couldn't be sure it was ever there.

## 69

A PLANE CAN RUN ON automatic pilot, but it hits the ground when it runs out of fuel. Nothing was pushing me. I needed to get back to where I was before. Before Belle. The sands shifted—I couldn't find my own footprints. Throwing antacid tablets into a cauldron of boiling lye. Stealing and scamming didn't bring me any closer. Everything worked. The money kept coming in but there was no payoff.

Even Wesley's fear-jolts wouldn't jump-start my battery.

Dead and gone. Dead and gone.

I called Candy.

# 70

SHE ANSWERED THE DOOR, left me there while she walked away. I knew her this time, even with the blond wig and the violet contact lenses. Much taller in four-inch spikes, ankle straps lancing across the seams that ran down the back of her dark silk stockings. She was wearing a wool minidress in some metallic green color, a heavy black chain around her waist as a belt. Swinging the long end of the chain in one hand, a leopard twitching her tail. Waiting.

I walked as far as the couch, flicking the ashes off my cigarette in the general direction of the ashtray on the end table. She twirled, hands on her hips. "Sit down."

I didn't like the sound. "Don't make a mistake," I told her. "I'm not the trick who just left."

A smile blazed across her face. Perfect teeth, as real as the violet eyes. A sociopath's smile. A woman smiles at you . . . for you . . . it's like a rheostat . . . comes on slow until it hits full boost. Little tiny increments. Different every time. Hers was an on-off switch. She came to me, tilted her seamless face up to mine, tried to bring some feeling into those cash-register eyes, wet her lips. "I'm sorry, baby. I was teasing. Some men like to be teased. I just want to talk your language. *Whatever* that is . . ."

"*Dónde está el dinero?*" I said. Thinking of Wolfe. The beautiful prosecutor sitting in her office, a killer Rottweiler at her feet, my rap sheet spread out in front of her. "John Burke, Maxwell Burke, Robert Burke, Juan Burke . . . *Juan?* Say something in Spanish, Mr. Burke." I sang my theme song for her.

Wolfe got it when I said it. Candy lived it. "I promised you a couple of things. You sure you only want the cash?"

"Yeah."

She curled up on the couch, her legs beneath her. I sat next to her, not too close. Her lacquered fingernails played with the buttons on the front of her dress. Opened one. Then another. The black lace bra stopped just above her nipples. "A lot sweeter than when you last saw them, huh? When we were kids. Remember?"

What's real? Candy wasn't a woman before the surgeons did their work. And Michelle, the most woman I'd ever met, even with the spare parts they threw in as a dirty joke.

"I never saw them when we were kids," I told her.

It was the truth. Foreplay was for people with money. People who had doors you could close. Elephants don't fuck the way rabbits do. Predator pressure sets the rhythm.

"You want to see them now?"

"No."

She shifted her hips, moved against me, face in my chest. "Pretend you just got out of prison," she whispered. "You could do all the things you dreamed about every night."

Her perfume was thick, with a sharp underbase, like it came from inside her body. The last couple of times I got out of prison, I knew where to go. What to do. But the first time out . . . it was like she said.

I TOSSED MY duffel bag on the bed in the cheap hotel and hit the street. I needed a gun. And a cabdriver who wouldn't get a tip. But first things first. The skinny whore in the screaming-red dress was waiting in a doorway a block from the hotel. Dishwater blond, hard-boned face, yellowish teeth, blue-veined hands, two bracelets on her narrow wrist, junkie's eyes. She was probably young and plump and dumb and sassy when she got off the bus from West Virginia.

"You wanna have a party, honey?"

I looked at her face.

"Ten and two, baby. I french, I do it all . . . come on."

I felt the street. Every doorway had one like her.

She knew it too. "It might as well be me, mister."

Another hotel. Two dollars to the clerk. No register to sign. I followed her up the stairs to the second floor. She put the key in her purse, left it open, waiting. I handed her the ten bucks. Peeling wallpaper, swaybacked single bed against one wall, bare mattress. She took a yellowed sheet from the top of a pile on a straight-backed chair, flicked it open, covered the bed. She never turned on the light. Street-neon washed against the streaked window. She pulled the paper shade down. Reached down to the hemline, pulled the cheap dress over her head. Dark elastic garters at the top of her stockings, joyless little breasts in the dim light.

"You want something special, honey? A little half 'n' half?"

No need.

"Let me look at you, baby. Milk it down for you one time, okay? Can't be gettin' burned; I got me a big habit to support." Reaching over to me, her thumb hard against the underside of my cock. "You all ready to go, huh, baby? I like a man all ready to go. You ain't no kid all charged up on beer, huh?"

Yes and No.

She fell back on the bed, still holding me in one hand, tied us together, rocked back to the base of her spine, grabbed her knees. "Come here, baby. It's riding time."

It didn't take long.

This. Fucking. Nothing.

"I DIDN'T JUST get out of prison," I told her.

"Just the money?"

"Just the money."

"I know you, Burke. I know you forever." It sounded like a threat.

"We've been through that."

"You're not here just for the money."

"I'm not here at all, you don't tell me what you want."

She took a breath. Her breasts blossomed. "Train," she said.

"What's that mean?"

"Not what you think."

"I don't have time for this." I started to get off the couch. She threw herself across my lap. I reached under the wig to the back of her neck, squeezed. Hard. Pulled her face up to mine. Her eyes were measuring, calculating. "You like that? You want to hurt me?"

My hand came off her neck by itself.

She locked my eyes. Saw the truth. "No, that's not you," she whispered. "Hard man, soft center. I know you. Remember the kitten? I was with you when you found it. In the basement, remember?"

SIMON. HE WAS in the gang with us. A freak. Liked to hurt things. Especially small things. Liked to set fires too. Nobody said anything. Simon was a good man in a rumble, quick with a razor. We weren't running a therapeutic community. The kitten was hanging from a noose made out of a coat hanger, ripped from chin to balls, its guts trailing out all the way to the floor. Making sounds no living thing should make. Candy was with me. We were hurrying down there for the darkness and the sex when we heard the tiny shrieks.

I remembered. I unhooked the kitten. Laid it on the concrete floor. Found a brick. Pounded its head into flat jelly. I didn't know how to stop its pain, so I made it all stop.

I found Simon out on the flatlands that night. Burning something on a spit over a little fire. I didn't want to know what it was. I left him there. When I threw the tire iron into the street it was so slick with pulp that it skidded for half a block.

"I PAID that off."

"Yeah. You kept your name. But I remember. You cried for an hour over that kitten. Cried like a baby. You were shaking so hard I didn't think you'd ever get up. You were going to do the same thing to Simon. Remember how you swore that? And how you told the others it was *your* kitten Simon tortured? Liar! You never had a kitten—you don't even like them."

She sounded like the judge who told me I was a menace to society.

"That never happened," I said, lighting a cigarette. "Your mind is all fucked up."

"I kept your secret. I could have told . . ."

"Who'd listen to a little cunt like you?"

"Anybody who wanted it—and they all did."

"'Cause they paid?"

"That's the way you tell."

"That's the way you tell. That's all you know."

"I know you," she said, the dress sliding off her shoulders.

I got up to leave. She stood before me, stepping into my chest. I remembered the basement. How she watched while I cried. How she never touched me—waiting to see who'd win. It wasn't hard keeping my hands from her body. Just from her throat.

I turned sharply away from her, my shoulder cracked against her jaw.

"You never knew how to hold a woman," she said.

"I know how to hold what matters."

"A gun?" she sneered.

"A grudge," I told her, stepping out of the whorehouse.

## 71

COLD FIRE INSIDE ME. Ugly acid, all the way to my eyes, burning off the haze. I felt them cut through the darkness as I neared my car. Everything in sharp-edged black & white. I wanted to talk to whoever took Belle from me and offered this sociopathic slut in return. Just for a hair-trigger minute.

A lump of shadow against the building wall a few feet from the passenger side of the Plymouth. I stepped forward fast on my left foot like I was going to charge, locked on the pavement, pivoted, and threw myself behind the car, turtlenecking like a gunshot was coming. Heard a grunt, a body slamming into the passenger side. Silence. Steel-palmed hands clapped once, twice. Max.

He was standing on the sidewalk, a body at his feet. His hands went parallel to the ground, palms down, patted the air twice. The body was alive. I knelt down to take a look, Max watching my back.

A small body, wrapped in a Navy pea coat, hooded sweatshirt inside covering the head. Dark gloves. Jeans and sneakers. I pulled the hood away from the face. Elvira, the wolf-child. Eyes closed, face blue-toned in the streetlight. I pinched her lower jaw—her tongue slid out. I looked up at Max. He tapped his diaphragm with two stiffened fingers. Just the wind knocked out of her. I touched the face of my wristwatch. Max's finger made one full circle, flashed his hand open and closed. She'd been waiting over an hour—since I'd parked the car.

I opened the passenger door and we put her into the front seat. I motioned for Max to climb in behind her. He bowed, brought his hands together, and disappeared. He was doing his work, not mine.

## 72

BY THE TIME I GOT near the river she was sucking in ragged gulps through her mouth. I hit the power-window switch to give her some air.

"Breathe through your nose. Shallow breaths. In and out. You're okay."

"I'm going to be sick . . ."

I pulled over. Went around to her side and helped her out. She walked toward the water under her own power. I smoked a cigarette while she left her supper in the parking lot.

Michelle had left one of her old street-trick kits in the back of the Plymouth. I gave the girl one of the premoistened towelettes to wipe her face. Handed her the airline-size bottle of cognac. "Rinse out with this," I told her.

I moved the car deeper into the darkness, backing it in against an abandoned pier. Dropped my own window, listening for sounds a human would make. Nothing. I lit another smoke. She still had some of the cognac left, sipping at it, watching me, color coming back in her face.

"What was that?"

"What was what?"

"What happened to me?"

"You set off the burglar alarm."

"I thought I was going to die."

"You could have—you're playing with dangerous things."

"I had to talk to you."

I snapped my smoke out the window, watching the little red dot through my black & white eyes. "So?"

"I have to go back."

"To Train?"

"Yes."

"So go."

"It's not that easy. She'd send you after me again."

"How d'you know?"

"She said so. You work for her, right?"

"Wrong."

"Oh."

I waited. She sipped the cognac.

"You got money?" I asked her.

"I can get some. How much . . . ?"

"Not for me. For cab fare. I'll drop you off near a good corner. Go where you want to go. I won't be coming after you."

She went quiet again. I lit another cigarette. "What's the rest, Elvira?" I asked her.

"I don't believe you," she said in a quiet, subdued voice. "She never tells the truth."

"It's not her talking."

"And I know about you, Mr. Burke."

"Say what you have to say, little girl. I got things to do. And you're not my friend."

"Can I have one of your cigarettes?" Stalling, like a kid who doesn't want to tell you she did something bad.

I gave her one. Fired a wooden match before she could try the dashboard lighter.

She took a deep drag. "I know what you do," she said.

"That right?"

"Yes, that's right. Danielle told me."

"I don't know any Danielle."

"I don't know what her street name was. We're not allowed to use street names in the family. She was a hooker. You came and took her away. A long time ago."

"Away from what?"

"Her old man. And you brought her home. To a big house on Long Island. Her father paid you to do it."

I shrugged.

"I know you. I know things you know and I know things you don't know."

Her mother's rap, a few years early. "I haven't heard one yet."

She dragged on the cigarette, a soft glow lighting her face for a second. Calm now. Watching me.

"Her old man's name was Dice. A sweet mac—he never made his girls turn hard tricks or anything. Let them go shopping whenever they wanted. You were waiting for them when they came back to the hotel room. You must've had a passkey or something. You pointed a big gun right in Dice's face. Told him you were taking the girl. There was another guy with you. Big guy—he didn't say anything. Dice tried to talk to you and you started whaling on him with the gun. Danielle said she could hear the bones break in his face. She'll never forget it. You took all her old man's money and jewelry. Then you put her in a car and drove her to Long Island."

I shrugged again.

"Why'd you do that?"

"You think it's right to fuck fourteen-year-old girls?"

"Her father did. The man who paid you the money to bring her back. He *loved* to do it. In the basement. Danielle told me he had a special room for it. She only has one nipple—he burned the other one off. To teach her not to run away again."

I didn't say anything. Shuffling the memory cards. Going right past Dice and the sleazy hotel room. Looking for that address on Long Island. The world was still black & white, but a piece was out of place.

"And Train saved her?" I asked.

"Train saved us all. Men like Danielle's father. Powerful men.

They're always after him. It's not that they don't understand. They know. And they hate him. Our family too. They hate us all. And they use men like you to do their dirty work for them."

"How'd he save *you?*"

"You think you're smart, don't you? You think you know everything. You don't know everything. We're saving for a place. Our place. Not in this miserable country. Where we can be free. We're in a war. You make sacrifices in a war. Not everyone will be able to go, but that's all right."

"And you all live in that house in Brooklyn? Raising money for your new country? You sell flowers on the street? Phony magazine subscriptions? Blowjobs in parked cars? What?"

"Whatever we do, that's okay. It would never be as bad as what people did to us."

"Sure."

"Sure. You don't know. You're a mercenary. That's what Train calls you. You only serve yourself—you have no honor. Your god is cash."

"That house must be pretty crowded, what with Train saving the world and all."

"We *don't* all live in the house. Some of the older ones, the best ones . . . if they show the commitment, prove themselves . . . they work other places. For our family. Outriders. The special people. I'll be one someday."

"Danielle's an outrider?"

"No. She lives with us. Outriders are special. I only met one. She went to prison for seven years for the family. And she never said a word. That was her commitment. That proved her true."

"So how come this family let you go?"

"It was a test. I know it was a test. We have to act for ourselves. Train isn't running a mission or a runaway shelter. It's only for those who are worthy. I had to find my own way back."

"Which is why you're running this game on me?"

"It's not a game. I thought if you knew what we *really* did, you wouldn't bring me back again."

"I don't know any Danielle."

"You know me. Maybe you're a good man inside. You wouldn't fuck me when I asked you. Maybe you really thought Danielle's father was sincere."

"I don't think anybody's sincere."

"Yes you do. My mother thinks she knows you. Maybe I know you better. And you don't know her."

"But you . . . you know a lot."

"Don't mock me. You know why my mother wanted me back?"

"To fuck you in the basement?"

"Bastard! You know what my mother is?"

"Your mother's a whore. She was a whore before you were born."

"No. Danielle was a whore. My mother . . . I was on the street when Train found me. I was turning tricks in cars. Like you said. Cars just like this one. My mother didn't care. I was too old then. Fourteen. Too old. When I was a *little* girl, my mother trained me. I thought ice cream was the stuff that shoots out of men's pricks when they come. My mother would hold my face between her legs while one of her customers fucked me behind. I used to scream right into her cunt. And the pictures. I still shake when flashbulbs go off near me. I had so many daddies. I knew how to make nice for them. My mother taught me. But once these grew"—flicking her hand at her breasts—"I was too old for the games. And my mother . . . she can be fourteen herself. She can be anything a man wants."

"No she can't."

"Oh yes. You don't know her. She can change. Like a demon. You know why she wants me back? To *sell* me. I'm hers, she said. Not Train's. I'd die first."

"So you don't turn tricks for Train?"

"Even if I *did*, it wouldn't be the same. Nothing's just for Train, it's for *us*. All of us. Together. It's my life. She doesn't own me."

"How old are you?"

"Seventeen."

"How old, Elvira?"

"Okay, fifteen. I'll be sixteen soon. I was born on Christmas Day."

I lit another smoke. "I'll take you to that cabstand," I told her.

"And you won't bring me back to her?"

"No, I won't. If you'll do something for me."

A knowing smile on her little face. "Whatever you want." Her mother's voice.

"I'm going to give you a phone number. You call it. In one week. And you meet me where I tell you to. And you don't tell anyone."

"And then?"

"You answer some questions."

"That's it?"

"Yes."

She took a breath. "I'll do it. I keep my word. You'll see. Can't you drive me home yourself?"

"I got things to do," I said to the girl. Danielle never told me about the basement, but she'd said she had a younger sister. I wondered which part was true.

# 73

THERE WAS NOBODY I could ask. Elvira was partly right. Candy wasn't a whore. Not a real stand-up, pussy-for-cash whore. I knew one once. Never knew her real name. Everybody called her Mercy. She said she got into the business when she mercy-fucked some poor shlub and he bought her a pearl necklace. She was maybe forty years old. An old lady to me then. "It's show business," she told me. "Mind games. Mystery. There's no old whores, honey. Flesh sags. But money earns interest."

I was sitting in her kitchen, sunlight washing the room. Watching her drink her coffee, listening to her story. Even then, I knew how to listen.

"I just want somebody to talk to him," she said, her voice husky and soft. Thick hair pulled back from her face, held there with a rubber band. Cigarette in her long fingers. A housewife in the morning.

"What do I say?"

"Whatever works. He's an old trick—I've been dating him for

years. The difference between a *good* whore and just an experienced one is repeat customers. Now he wants an exclusive, you understand? He wants me to move into an apartment in this building he owns. Be there when he shows up. Hold dinner for him."

I shrugged. "It doesn't sound so bad to me. One trick instead of a lot of tricks. And he'd pay the same?"

"Sure. But when he changes his mind, I'm out. I don't have a pimp—I don't want an owner." She walked over to the sink, her hips churning under the faded bathrobe. Washed out her coffee cup, talking at me over her shoulder. Patted herself on the butt. "This is mine. I rent it out—it's not for sale. Money lubricates me—it doesn't own me."

"You told him?"

"I'm his toy. I do what he wants. It's not inside his head that a toy makes up its own mind. He thought he was my dream coming true."

"I'll fix it," I told her.

When I went back to see her, she had the money ready for me. "He called me," she said. "He won't be coming back."

"That's what you wanted, right?"

"One of my tricks is a champion bridge player. You know how to play?"

I nodded. I knew how to play chess too. And dominoes. Prison.

"This trick, he told me any game you play with a partner, there's a difference between the best result possible and the best possible result. You understand?"

"What I did . . . it was the best result possible, right?"

"Yeah." She kissed me on the cheek. "You're a good man. Solid, keep your word. I thought they didn't make them like you anymore. In a few years, you ever get to Phoenix, you look me up, okay?"

"Phoenix?"

"I'm buying a little motel out near there. My retirement. Been saving for years. You get too old, the mystery wears thin . . . it gets too hard to do the act."

"You'll never be too old, Mercy."

Her smile mocked my lie. She kissed me again. Goodbye.

Candy was a different breed. That didn't mean her little daughter wasn't a liar too.

## 74

I FELL ASLEEP IN MY office later. On the couch, the little TV set flickering at the edge of my consciousness, Pansy snoring on the floor next to me. When I woke up it was dark again. A piece of light sat like a candle flame in the corner of the room, reflected from someplace past the window. I didn't move, watching it, letting it take me. Splitting off from this mess, disassociating. It works sometimes—you let go, it comes to you. But only if it's out there.

No use asking questions if you don't care what the answer is.

The cops wouldn't just walk away, but they'd find something else to do.

I blew smoke at the ceiling, wondering if I would.

## 75

THE NEXT MORNING, I grabbed a tip sheet from the newsstand and went back to the office. None of the horses spoke to me. I didn't dream about having one of my own one day—the way I used to all the time.

I spent a lot of time thinking about who I could steal from next.

## 76

I DRIFTED BACK TO Mama's. White dragons in the window. She told the waiter something. He brought me a plate of fried rice, beef in oyster sauce. No soup.

"Everything okay now?" she asked, leaning forward, watching.

"Sure."

"You wait for something?"

"You mean . . . here?"

"No. For *something*, okay?"

"I don't think so."

"I think so."

I didn't answer her. After a while, she went back to the cash register at the front.

I was walking out when the pay phone rang. Mama walked past me. I waited.

"Man say tell you watch the papers tomorrow. Sutton Place."

"Anything else?"

"No."

"He say his name?"

"Man who called before. One time. Dead-man sound when he talk."

## 77

I WAS AT THE restaurant before it opened the next day. Mama brought me the four-star edition of the *Daily News*. They put it out on the street by six in Chinatown. I didn't have to search through it. The headline screamed "Bizarre Murder on Sutton Place." A socialite with a WASP name was found murdered by her Wall Street husband when he came home from work around nine o'clock last night. Her name didn't mean anything to me. The newspaper account was short on facts—long on adjectives: grisly, ritualistic, satanic. Hinting at things that only come out on evil nights.

It was too early to call any of the free-lance reporters I know, but I had another solid contact in the press: a West Indian who worked the streets for one of the tabloids. Worked them hard. He'd lost his Island accent somewhere between Newark and journalism school but he was a hard-core risk-taker. He might be on the job.

I found a pay phone on the West Side. I got the reporter's answering machine. "If you know who you're calling, you know what you want to say. Do it when you hear the beep and I'll get back to you."

I heard the beep. "Leave me a message," I said into the recorder.

## 78

I GOT OFF THE STREET before the citizens took over the city. Let Pansy out to her roof. Gave her some of the food I'd brought back from Mama's. Felt her pleasure as she lit into it, her sadness when it was gone. In another couple of minutes, she forgot about both feelings, back to herself. Lucky dog.

Maybe I'd go away for a while. Cruise out to Indiana, visit my old cellmate Virgil. His daughter was almost ten and I'd never seen her.

I could always see Virgil's daughter.

## 79

"ANYTHING?" I ASKED Mama when I called her from the street late that afternoon.

"Come in, okay?"

Max was in the kitchen when I walked in through the back door. He followed me out to my table. Mama sat down next to him, facing me.

"Man call. Black man, sunny voice. Call him at home, seven o'clock tonight."

"That's it?"

Mama's smooth face never changed expression. "Dead man called. Said call him. Hangs up."

I waited.

"Man say his name is Julio. You know him. You call him at his club, okay?"

Julio. Fuck!

"Girl call too. Same girl. Say to call her too. Very important."

"Okay."

"Not okay. Take Max with you."

"To make phone calls?"

"Meetings, yes? All these people?"

"Maybe. Maybe not."

"Take Max."

## 80

THE BASEMENT UNDER Max's warehouse has a tunnel we cut through to the building next door. Some architects own it. I stepped into their basement, flashing the pencil-beam before my feet. Empty, like always. I hooked the field phone into their lines with the alligator clips. Julio first.

The beef-brain who answered took his time understanding I wasn't going to talk to him first. Julio got on the line, the old alligator's voice down to a whisper.

"I want to meet you."

"Take Marcy Avenue all the way until it hits the bridge that crosses the BQE. Seven-fifteen, okay?"

"Why don't you come here?"

"I don't have time."

"You should make time."

"Take it or leave it," I told him, cutting the line.

## 81

I RANG THE NUMBER Wesley gave me, using the code. Three times. Again. Then Candy. She answered on the first ring.

"What do you want?" I asked her.

"To see you."

"Tell me."

"I'll tell you whatever you want to hear. You know that. There's trouble for you. I can help. You believe me?"

"No."

"Come anyway. Listen for a few minutes."

"I'll come tomorrow. Don't be cute. Don't be stupid."

"The only thing I'll be is here."

## 82

WE CROSSED THE Brooklyn Bridge to Tillary Street, left to Flushing Avenue. Ran parallel to the highway through Williamsburg. The sidewalk was thick with dark-eyed girls. Young Jewish beauties from the Hebrew high school in Williamsburg. Walking in tight clumps, chattering like sweet birds. All the brightness was in their faces—their clothes were too old for the way their hair bounced at the base of their necks, the way their eyes snapped at life. Mothers wheeled babies in strollers. Hassidim with their black stove-pipe hats and long coats covered ground with purposeful steps. Laughter was for children. Hebrew writing on the walls, iron bars over the windows. Occupied territory, carved out of other ghettos on all sides. We hadn't walked a block before we picked up cover. Half a dozen men, plain white shirts, dark suspenders, yarmulkes on their heads. Hands in their pockets. One had a coat over his forearm. Israeli soldiers—different uniforms. A clot of young girls passed us, demure but fearless. They were used to strangers.

The group of men watched me as I dialed the pay phone, not making a secret of it. The reporter was waiting for the call.

"Morehouse here."

"You know my voice?"

"Sure."

"You working on anything?"

"Lots of things, man. This a social call?"

"Maybe a trade. You know the shelter by the meat market?"

"Sure."

"Two o'clock coming. On the far corner?"

"Sure."

# 83

THE CADILLAC SEDAN stopped on the east side of the short bridge. The old man stepped out of the back. His driver opened the door, stood outside, watching. The pack watched him. I leaned against the stone wall, Max between me and the west side entrance. Traffic rumbled underneath us—tail end of the rush hour.

I let him come to me.

"Who's this?" he snarled, tilting his head at Max.

"What d'you want, Julio?"

"I want to know who this is."

"Fuck you."

"Burke, don't play with me. You got a pass. One time. You know why. Nobody gets two."

"Save it for the Godfather movies, old man. You don't need to know who this is. You had any brains, you'd already know."

"Why's he here?"

"To memorize your face, okay? So don't threaten me."

Max stood as stony as the wall, eyes slitted on Julio. Camera lenses. The old man's driver put his hand in his pocket, restless.

"Tell him to stay where he is, Julio. My brother wants to hurt somebody bad, and you'll do. That guido driving your car, he comes out with a piece and the Jews make him into chopped liver. Look for yourself."

Julio waved his hand as if he'd just seen an old friend. His driver took out a cigarette, kept his hands in sight. The street was empty like it was four in the morning. Except for the pack. One of them walked over to the same pay phone I'd used. Picked up the receiver.

"We can't stay here long," I told Julio.

He took a breath. "Last night, he hit Torenelli's daughter."

"What?"

"On Sutton Place. That was the don's daughter. She broke away from the family. Years ago. Married a citizen. Gives parties to raise money for the homeless, lives in a two-million-dollar co-op, okay?"

"So?"

He moved in close to me, prison-yard whisper cutting, hands shaking. "The husband, he comes home, finds her on the bed. Staked out like a piece of beef, wrists and ankles wired to the corners. With her head chopped off. *Off!* He shoved the head between her legs, you understand? So her face was looking at the husband when he comes in the door."

"Who?"

"Wesley. Who the fuck else? Who else would do that?"

"A freak."

"Sure. A freak who can get past the security in that joint. A freak that don't leave a lousy fingerprint. Not a trace. It was a pro hit. The fucking detectives threw up just looking at it. The husband—he's in a rubber room."

"What's this got to do with me?"

"It's Wesley's work. A fucking message, right? The don said he wasn't going to pay that maniac. He didn't do the job—he don't get paid. Wesley, he says he don't get paid, he's coming for all of us. Crazy motherfucker. He's a hitter. A contract man. He don't tell *us*, we tell *him*. Now he has to go. We can keep the sicko stuff outta the papers for only so long."

The old man tried to fire up one of his twisted black cigars. He couldn't get it lit—it wasn't the wind. I cracked a wooden match in my palm, held the cup for him. He leaned close to take the flame. A sour smell came off him.

"This ain't the first one. He dropped one of the don's boys. One shot, right in the back of the neck. Calls up, says, 'One down.' Like he's going to pick us off one at a time."

"Do whatever you want."

"No, it don't play like that. *You* started this fucking mess, you clean it up, *capisce?*"

"*I* started it? Where d'you get that? You got things mixed up. Wesley just wants his money, right?"

"He was up front with us, we woulda done that, okay? That

Mortay—we know Wesley didn't hit him. But there was another guy—one of Sally Lou's boys. Our inside man. To watch Mortay. We had it all wired. The way we got it, you had a meet with Mortay in a playground in Chelsea." His deep-set eyes turned up to watch mine. Waited a beat, went on. "Our guy was along for backup. And *he* gets dropped. From the rooftop. Sniper shot. Somebody working with a silencer and a night scope. That's the murder the cops want you for . . . that's what they busted you on, right?"

It wasn't McGowan or Morales who made that bust. They wouldn't have squawked to the other cops anyway. I felt the gears mesh. The city has a compost heap for a heart—why shouldn't gangsters drop a dime on it—maybe grow some dollars?

"I wasn't there," I said quietly. "The judge cut me loose."

"Yeah, you wasn't there. Okay, I'm easy. But it was Wesley on that roof. Nobody else works like that . . . like a fucking hillbilly in the mountains. That puts you and that maniac together."

I watched him, waiting.

"It's good enough for the don," Julio said.

"Why don't you just pay Wesley the money?"

"Now you got it. That's exactly what we're gonna do, pal. And you're gonna deliver it."

"No thanks. I don't do crossfires."

"You gonna do this one. You don't, the don says to tell you you're on his list too."

"Why? What difference does it make?"

"You think . . . after what that fuck did . . . you think the don's gonna be happy just seeing him dead? He gets his hands on Wesley, it's gonna take that *animale* a week to die."

"I'm not meeting Wesley to hand over money—he'd waste the errand boy—you know that."

An alligator's smile. "I told them . . . Burke's too slick to play the chump. We don't care how it's done. We gotta have Wesley. Do whatever you gotta do. But quick."

"I'll get back to you."

"Don't even think about hiding. There's no place you can go in this town. One phone call and you're locked up again. You know what it costs to have a man hit in jail today?"

"You mean one *more* phone call, don't you?" I said, so close to his face I could see the pores. "Goodbye, old man."

The pack watched him walk to his car. Watched it drive away. Watched me use the pay phone again. Mama's voice was soft and clear. "He called. Say, same time, same place. Tonight."

Max and I walked back to the Plymouth. One of the young men in the pack caught my eye. I got the message. Don't. Come. Back.

I'd heard it before.

## 84

WE ROLLED BACK ONTO the BQE, heading toward Queens. Random loops, in case Julio was going to be stupid. Time to kill. Exited at La Guardia and looped around the airport, taking our time. Dark now, headlight patterns in the mirror. Max was watching, face turned to the rear. He made the "okay" sign as we pulled into the parking lot of one of the airport motels. We smoked a couple of cigarettes, watching the shadows dance. Men in shiny, pointy-toed boots with Cuban heels, light bouncing off thick shocks of heavily oiled hair. Bulletproof vests over tropical-colored silk shirts. Cocaine and money switched partners. They work outdoors now. The DEA has the rooms wired. A few years ago, some local Colombian paid a half million cash for the key to one of the lockers in the airport. He opened it up, the spring snapped, and the explosion took out nineteen people. That was back when the Italians still thought they could keep narcotics in the family. Wesley had the contract on the Colombian—the other eighteen bodies were on the house. The *federales* are still looking for the terrorist organization responsible.

Julio was playing it like Wesley was just a shooter, but he knew better. And he knew I knew.

I ran it down for Max. He already had most of it, from watching Julio. The Mongolian made the sign of a man aiming a rifle. Pulled his hand away from the trigger, knife-edged it, and chopped at his own neck. Pointed to my watch. Let's take him out tonight.

I shook my head no.

His hands asked why.

I shook my head again, pointed at my watch. Not now. Wait. I held my palm over my eyes like I was shielding them from the sun, turned my head from side to side. Something else around.

I couldn't say what.

## 85

WE CROSSED THE Triboro from the Queens side. Worked our way to the junkyard. Hours yet until we had to meet Wesley—I wasn't going to wait in a bar.

I shoved a cassette into the tape player, jamming the bass as high as it would go for Max. He put his fingertips on the speaker on his side of the car.

Judy Henske. "High Flying Bird." And "God Bless the Child." I wondered if they let torch singers into heaven—I couldn't see Henske in a choir.

Sonny Boy Williamson. "T.B. Blues."

The sky looks different from the gutter.

Kinky Friedman and the Texas Jewboys. I'd forgotten he was on the tape. Just a bar singer's voice, but his dark-side poetry was diamonds shining through blood. The Texas Tower song—Kinky's ode to America's favorite sniper, Charles Whitman.

*There was a rumor*
*About a tumor*
*Nestled at the base of his brain*

Maybe the Mole knew.

# 86

TERRY LET US IN, leading us through the dog pack. Simba was sitting by himself a few feet from the Mole's bunker. His eyes ignored me, tracking Max. Calm, inside himself. Max stepped to the side, hands flowing to a clasp just below his waist. He bowed to the beast. Not in deference—a warrior on another's ground. Simba flashed a lupine grin and strolled off into the darkness.

We went down into the bunker. The Mole was in his chair, lap covered by an artist's pad. The page was covered with sketches of machinery, formulas and equations scrawled from corner to corner. He grunted a greeting, not looking up.

"Would you like some tea?" Terry asked me, making the sign of a cup to the lips for Max. The warrior nodded his head gravely. "You got any ginger ale?" I asked. The kid gave me a look like the Mole does sometimes. Michelle would be proud of him.

We sipped our drinks. The Mole ignored us. Finally, he dumped his calculations on the floor. Terry was waiting with a cup of tea. The Mole nodded his head absently.

"What're you working on?" I asked.

"A computer retrovirus."

"What?"

"Computer virus . . . you reach a certain point and it eats the data, yes?"

"Okay." I knew what he meant. Pedophiles are really into computers, meticulously recording each victim. They have crash-codes built in. The cops try to access the disc and the whole thing goes down.

"There's a way to use the surge-suppressor . . . part of the line conditioner . . . what they plug in to hold the data if there's a power outage . . . you could use that to eat the virus instead of the data."

"I don't . . ."

"Another module. It goes in the line conditioner. Then you drop the power, just a little bit, and the suppressor kicks in, finds the virus, and eats it. And gets out without a trace."

"How long would it take?"

The Mole snapped his fingers. "A thousandth of that."

"Damn."

"I'm still working on it. It's not ready."

I lit a cigarette, leaving the pack on the table in case Terry wanted one. He took out his own—I guess they weren't expecting Michelle.

"Mole, you know anything about tumors?"

"What kind?"

"Brain tumors?"

"Yes."

"Could a tumor make a man kill?"

"It's not so simple," he said. Annoyed at having to explain. "It could make a man mad. Irrational. It couldn't make a man different from what he is . . . just what he does, you understand?"

He watched my face, got his answer. Went on. "Tumor, it's a growth. Different parts of the brain control different functions. A tumor gets in the way. Changes things. Behavior is one of those things."

"Mole, you know Wesley?"

"Only what people say."

"He kills people. That's what he does. I've known him since we were kids. He doesn't have . . . feelings. You understand? He told me once, you want to kill a man sleeping in a house, you don't go in after him, you set fire to the house. Everybody dies. Makes it hard on the cops. The more bodies, the more motives. You can't be *born* like that, right?"

"Everybody's born like that."

"What?"

"Everybody. Humans are born into the world screaming for what they want. They feel their own feelings. They have no pack instincts, like dogs. A baby is a monster."

"So a baby raised by wolves, it would be a wolf?"

"It would be a man who behaves like a wolf."

I dragged on my smoke. I could never keep the Mole talking for long. Terry was watching, focused. Maybe the Mole wasn't talking to me.

"Wesley was always like that," I told him. "He never cried, never laughed. He has no fear in him. Nothing in him at all."

"That's not what you said at first," the Mole replied, his eyes impossible to read through the thick smudged lenses of his glasses. "Babies have all those things. Babies learn to feel past their *own* feelings—that's what we teach them."

"Psychology . . ."

"This isn't psychology. Not a soft science. Animals adapt or they die. That is a biological law. Sometimes things are left over, vestiges. Like the appendix. We don't need it. Eventually, it will disappear from our bodies. Biology . . . it's like what Max does . . . we have to use power, not resist it. Things get left over . . . we are only here for a short time, so we adapt. Or we die."

"Left over . . ."

"Sex. That's left over." Terry shifted his posture, dragging on his smoke. "You know the orgasmic curve . . . different for men than women?"

"You mean it takes them longer to come?"

The Mole's lips tightened primly. "To reach orgasm, yes. Do you know why?"

"The way they're put together . . . I don't know."

"Herd animals, they mate serially, you understand? There's a fail-safe biological response to every genetic code or the organism dies."

"Come on, Mole. Talk English."

Another annoyed look. "A herd of elk. Mating season. The bucks fight it out. And the winner gets to mate with the entire crop of females, right? That's the genetic code. So the strongest, most powerful stud mates with the females and the babies have the best DNA."

"Yeah . . ."

"What if the strongest male is sterile? What if he has a low sperm count? What happens then?"

I glanced at Max. The Mole hadn't moved his hands once, but the warrior watched as intently as the kid.

The Mole answered his own questions. “The herd dies off. So the fail-safe kicks in. When the females are in season . . . when they are in heat . . . the bucks smell it and they start to fight. The winning buck mates with a female, he discharges his sperm, then he moves off to wait for his power to recharge. But the female, she is still in heat. While the winning buck mates with another, one of the other bucks, one of the losers in the fight, he mounts her too. They all do that. If the first discharge of sperm is potent, the genes from the strongest buck make a baby. But if it isn’t, the next one . . . or the one after that . . . takes. And they have babies. The strongest babies survive, and the pack lives on. Understand?”

“Okay, but . . .”

“If the females reached orgasm faster than the males, they would pull away. Animals don’t commit rape—the females must be willing. The mating wouldn’t be completed. The orgasmic curve is longer. Much longer. Long enough for the first buck, long enough for the bucks to follow.”

“That’s why women take longer to . . .”

“Yes.”

“So one day they’ll get off as quick as we do?”

Something less than a smile ghosted on the Mole’s lips. “Yes. In another half million years or so. You won’t be around to see it.”

I lit another smoke. Thinking about it. How Mercy said money was her lubricant. “Wesley . . . he adapted?”

“To something. I don’t know what.”

“How do you know . . . that he adapted?”

“He has many enemies. And he isn’t dead.”

## 87

THE PLYMOUTH PUSSYFOOTED its way through the maze of twisted little roads. I pulled to the side. Max’s door opened. The interior light didn’t come on. He vanished.

I parked where I had the last time. Got out nice and slow.

"Go ahead and light your smoke." A voice behind me.

I felt him next to me. Turned to look. His hands weren't empty this time.

"Tell the Chinaman to come out. Listen to my voice. I'm telling you the truth, Burke. You don't call him out, I'll waste you right here. Whatever happens, you're dead."

If this was the movies, I'd have heard the sound of the Uzi being cocked. This was Wesley—I knew it already was. They say Wesley files the safety off his guns. I pulled the white handkerchief out of my coat sleeve. Waved it high above my head in a circle, stopped the circle right in front of me. Max was coming whether Wesley killed me or not—this way there'd be two of us. Maybe . . . ?

Wesley was on my right, the Uzi in my rib cage. Max came forward, making enough noise so we'd hear him. He kept walking. A lumbering, thug's walk, giving no hint of the speed and grace in the thick body. A locomotive that makes its own tracks. He stopped ten feet away, right in front of us.

"Close enough," Wesley said.

I held a palm out to Max to keep him where he was. The Mongolian dropped his left shoulder a fraction. If he went, he'd go to Wesley's left. I pushed my weight against the stubby barrel of the machine gun, ready to lock my elbow over it, hug my death close to me if it came. Wesley was right. Close enough. For Max. I'd go first, but Wesley would be right behind me.

"You wanted to talk?" I asked the monster.

"You think I didn't know the Chinaman was here last time?"

"I didn't know myself."

"I know. That's why you got to walk away. But you knew this time."

"Okay."

"Max the Silent, right? That's him?"

"That's him."

"Looks like a real bone-breaker."

"He's here for me, not you."

"I know. Tell him I got a gun on you."

"He knows."

"So why'd he come out?"

"He's my brother."

"Yeah. That's nice. I had a brother too."

"I never knew that. Where is he?"

"Dead."

Like you, I thought, taking the last puff of my cigarette, tossing it away. "What d'you want, Wesley?"

"You like the job on Sutton Place?"

"Why'd you do it?"

"They owe me money."

"I know. I met with one of them earlier tonight. They want you bad. They're going to get word out that they'll pay. They want me to deliver the cash."

"And blow me up?"

"No. They want you alive."

"That's the way I figured it. It takes the heat off."

"*Off?!*"

"Sure, off. They could have paid me. Like they should've. When I hit the first guy, they got scared. So they put out the word. Hit Wesley, right? Any asshole with a gun could do it, he got close enough. Now it's different. They're spooked. I made shit of the *don*—fucked him where he breathes right in front of everybody. They had an open contract out on me before. Now it's canceled, right? Now it's personal."

"There's more."

"What?"

"They think it was you who did the job in the Chelsea playground. They had the whole thing wired—one of the guys working with Mortay, he was theirs. He's the guy who went down in the playground. Sniper fire from the roof. They dropped a dime on me to put on the pressure."

"The cops think it was me on the roof too?"

"Probably do, by now."

"We both know it wasn't. So you got a sniper in your stable too."

"He was a loaner. From a friend. I can't use him again."

"Okay. They won't dime you for the Sutton Place thing. It won't fly."

"How d'you know?"

"I dress in a nice suit, nice trench coat. Eight-hundred-dollar briefcase, Rolex, diamond ring. I'm a lawyer, right? I tell the doorman I got a package for Mrs. Swanson in 21A. From Mr. Torenelli. He makes the call, I go up. No problem. Maid's day off. I know. Ring the bell, she answers it herself. Starts right in on me. 'I told my father I didn't want to have anything to do with his . . .' I cut her off, tell her I just got a couple of papers in my briefcase for her to sign and I'm out of there. She treats me like a servant, turns her back on me. I close the door behind her, follow her to the living room. Open the briefcase. She's still yakking at me when I hook her in the stomach with a set of brass knuckles. She's out—can't get a breath. Anesthetic nose plugs and she goes right to sleep. I take off my clothes, lay them in the briefcase. Talcum powder on my hands, surgeon's gloves. Carry her to the bedroom. Piano wire until she's spread out. I find a chopping block and a set of those Ginsu knives in the kitchen. All those rich assholes have fancy kitchens. I put the block under her neck, pull her hair back, and take the head off. Half a dozen shots is all it took. Blood spurts out all over the back wall. I stick the head into her cunt, facing out. Say hello to her husband when he comes home. I write the number two on the wall in her blood. That's the polygraph key the cops'll use when freaks start confessing. I take a shower. Pop open the drain. Pour three bottles of that Liquid Plumber stuff down, leave the hot-water tap on. I get dressed, put everything back in the briefcase. I go downstairs, tell the doorman the package is too big to lug through the lobby. Mrs. Swanson wants it through she service entrance. Wants him to handle it *personally*, right? Slip him a pair of twenties. I'll drive around into the back alley with the box, he'll meet me there, take it up to her. I drive out back. He opens the door. I put three rounds into him. Pop, pop, pop. Drive away. The papers don't have that body either. But the cops, they know they ain't looking for a maniac. They ain't looking for an amateur like you either. They know."

His voice wasn't chilly, just flat. Not quite bored.

"Why?" I asked.

"I was going to spook them. Kill a few the same way. Make 'em think a freak was after their women. Get them all together in one place to figure out what to do. And blow the place up. But this is quicker."

"They got your message."

He wasn't listening. "I was going to beat off onto the body but with that DNA fingerprinting they use now . . ."

"Cut it out, Wesley. You don't give a fuck about blood types, or fingerprints either. They drop you for this, you're not going to jail. . . . You just couldn't do it."

"Couldn't do what?"

"Beat off on a dead body. I came up with you, remember? I know what you do for a living, but you're still a man."

"I'm a bomb," the monster said. "I'm tired of this place. When I check out, you'll *hear* the sound."

My body was rigid with the strain. He wasn't going to pull the trigger. I stepped away from him, carefully.

"Yeah, go ahead," he said. "I was going to waste you, I'd take the Chinaman first. Always take the hard man first. That's the rules."

"Look . . ."

"You're not a hard man, Burke. Maybe you was once, but you let things get in the way. There's a way out of this. For you, not for me. I don't care. I'm tired. I got to do Train first. I took the money. And the don. Then I'm gone."

"What's my way out? What d'you want from me?"

"You're the link. Like I knew you'd be, remember I told you? I need a cop."

"What?"

"A big cop. High-ranker. The don's gone to ground. I'll never find him. The cops and the mob, they're all in the same bed. You find out where he's at, I'll do the rest."

"I don't know any top cops."

"You know how to do things. Talk to people, work around. I can't do that. Nobody knows my face, but they can feel me coming."

Survivors can, I thought.

"They'll want to set up a meet, tell me I'm getting my money," he said. "I want my money, right? It's going to take a little bit of time. Use it. When I finish my work, everybody's happy . . . the cops'll have their bodies and you'll be off the hook."

"You can't hit them all. They'll always come for you."

"No. I'm going to kill their seeds. And then I'm going where they can't come after me."

"The Program? You can't . . ."

His voice didn't change. You can't insult a monster. "The Witness Protection Program? I already hit two guys that was *in* the Program. I told you, I'm tired. Don't worry about it."

"Same deal—I call you?"

"Yeah." He looked over at Max. "You think he's close enough to take me out, don't you?"

"He is."

"No he's not," said the monster, as he stepped away from me into the dark.

## 88

THE MEAT MARKET IS a triangular slab hacked out of the West Village with the wide end opening onto the West Side Highway. Before they opened a bigger version in Hunts Point, all the city's butcher shops got their supplies down there. Every morning, way before the traffic stream thickens with citizens bound for City Hall and Wall Street, the streets are clogged with refrigerated trucks. By noon it's pretty quiet. In the evening, some of the city's best steak houses do a booming business. Yuppies can walk there from their million-dollar lofts. When they close, the meat market is home to the army of kids who spend the night selling the one thing they have left.

To buy drugs to make them forget what that is.

The shelter is a clapboard shack the kids built out of abandoned packing crates. Scraps of carpeting on the floor, discarded mattresses, sometimes an old broken chair. The street kids drift out of Times Square like vampires being chased by daylight. They made this place for themselves. The cops leave them alone as long as they're back on the street by the time the truckers are gone. Nobody turns tricks in daylight down here. I found more than one runaway there over the years, especially when the winterhawk drops down.

Waiting for Morehouse. An abandoned window fan sat upright in the street, plugged into nothing, its blades rasping as it turned in the night wind.

The reporter's battered Datsun rolled around the corner. Spotted my Plymouth, pulled in behind. We got out to meet him. A dark-skinned man about my height, wearing a khaki jacket over a bulky sweatshirt, unpolished combat boots under a pair of chinos. Subway outfit. He'd been around for a while, but his face was unlined, hair cut close. Morehouse has an athlete's build, rangy. Next to Max, he looked like a stick. He held out his hand, smile flashing. The Island way. He ignored Max—the meeting was with me. The City way.

"This is all on the record, right?" he said. His idea of a joke.

"The Sutton Place killing . . . you cover it?"

"I write a column, man. I can't cover every breaking story."

"That means no?"

"That means I know the facts, but there's no column in it."

"How about this for a lead? Mafia don's estranged daughter snuffed. The number two written in blood on the wall. Head chopped off the body and stuck between her legs. Building doorman found dead. Cops cover up mob connection."

He blew a sharp breath through his teeth. "This is on the street?"

"Not yet."

"So you spoke to the cops. Or the killer."

"I don't just know *how* it went down, I know *why*. Want to trade?"

"Sure. What do *you* want?"

"Torenelli. He's holed up. And he's working with the cops. One of them knows where he is. Probably brass."

"So?"

"That's what I want to know."

"This is deep water, man. Deep and dark."

"Pretend you're back in Haiti." Morehouse had won a journalism award for his coverage of the insanity on that island after Baby Doc fled.

"I have to *live* here."

"It's your choice." I shrugged.

"What do I get?"

"You get the inside story. The why of it all. It wasn't a random murder and it wasn't a sex-freak mob. There's a job war coming down."

"Drugs?"

"No."

"What, then?"

"We have a deal?"

"Sure."

"You first."

"That isn't the way it works, Burke. I give you what I got, you give me what you got. Same time, no taking turns."

"Except you got nothing. Nothing now. You get what I want, let me know, and we'll trade. Deal?"

"You at the same number?"

I nodded.

"Sure," he said, watching the disconnected fan spinning in the street.

## 89

I DROVE THROUGH THE Village streets, working toward Chinatown. Max held his hand out in front of his eyes, rigid as a steel bar, asking a question. I took one hand off the wheel, did the same. My hand didn't tremble. Too many things to be scared of at the same time—my nerves were in a coma.

When we pulled into the warehouse, he made the sign for me to come up with him. Sleep over. I bent my wrists, holding paws in front of my face. Pansy was home—I had to get back. His face didn't change. He knew the beast could get along for days without me. I pointed at my watch, showed him the time I wanted to roll tomorrow. He gestured like he was picking something off a plate, putting it in his mouth. We'd meet at Mama's.

## 90

I ATE BREAKFAST AT my desk the next morning, listening to the all-news station on the radio. An FBI agent was busted for molesting kids. The DEA seized another twenty million dollars' worth of coke at JFK. A group of inmates at Sing Sing were demanding a non-smoking wing. There was a city-wide hunt for a bank bandit. Thirteen hits—total take under twenty grand. He was probably scared to hit the bodegas—they had more cash on hand, but you couldn't push notes across the counter.

Rye toast, cream cheese, pineapple juice. I made it last. I like to eat alone. By myself. That's the worst thing about prison—even worse than the fear-mist that makes it hard to breathe—no privacy. Nothing to yourself Even in solitary, the smells come in.

I thought about what Morehouse said. I have to live here too. I'd had this office a long time, but I wouldn't miss it if I had to go.

Flood drifted around in my thoughts. I pushed her back. I thought when I settled up with Belle's father, it would quiet my mind. I could go to Japan, like Max said. Find Flood. Here in the city, a monster was charging toward a machine. I didn't figure out how to get out of the way, I'd find Belle quicker.

# 91

I CALLED CANDY from the street.

"Buzz downstairs. Tell the doorman you're expecting a package. Two guys'll be bringing it up."

"Now?"

"Yeah."

Max and I carried the giant carton stamped with the brand name of the TV set in big black letters. His sleeves were rolled up, biceps popping with the strain, veins roped on his forearms. I kept my coat on. The doorman took us up in the service elevator, let us out on her floor. I picked up the empty carton by a corner and carried it in one hand as Max faded into the stairwell.

She opened the door while my finger was still on the buzzer. Stepped aside to let me in.

"Where's the other guy?"

"He went back down to the car."

"You brought me a present?"

"It's empty."

"It's the thought that counts."

"Tell me what you want."

She was wearing a red silk slip. Barefoot. Thick brunette wig, yellow cat's eyes patient. "Can we talk in the back?"

I followed her down the hall. The backs of her legs were muscular, hips rolling in a tight round arc. "Any particular room you want?" she asked.

"I don't care," I said to her shoulder. "Where's the kid?"

"Back in school."

She turned into the last room. The only window was masked behind a midnight-blue screen—twilight inside. She tilted her head at a reclining black leather chair in the corner, chrome dish ashtray atop a black tripod next to it. I sat down. Lit a smoke. She propped one leg on the psychiatrist's couch, stood sideways facing me, flexing the muscles in her leg.

"That's the part that goes soft first," she said, patting the inside of her thigh. "Mine're like rocks."

"Great."

"It doesn't do anything for you?"

"Why should it?"

"You're a man."

I thought about Wesley, watching the shadow on the inside of her thigh.

"I've seen it before."

She left the room. I dragged on the smoke, knowing I was there for a reason. Not her reason.

When she came back in, she was naked. This time she had on a fluffy blond wig piled up on top of her head, soft tendrils framing her face. Lavender eyes. Black spike heels, no stockings. A black garter banded her left thigh. Her right hand was full of leather and steel.

"You don't trust me?"

"No."

"I need you to trust me. I can be whatever you want. Any woman you want. Just close your eyes and think of it. Tell me. And it happens."

My eyes slitted until she was out of focus, smoke drifting past my face. Her purring voice was background music.

Belle. The big girl twirling before me in her new outfit, pretty-proud, prom-bound. "Come *on*."

Strega. On her knees but not begging, witch-fire eyes promising threats. "You'll be back."

Flood. The chubby little blonde, scars on her body never reaching her heart. Merry, bouncing flesh. All her debts squared now. "I'm for you, Burke" was how she'd said goodbye.

The music stopped. "You can't be anything I want," I told her.

"Your voice is different. The last time you were here, you said cold things. But they were weak. I know when someone's playing a role. That's what I do. You're not playing now."

"You're a lousy psychologist."

"I know when someone's lying."

"You should."

She tossed whatever she was carrying onto the couch. Bent at the waist, rooted around. She held a circle of chain in her hand for me to see, then she pulled it over her head like a necklace. "You know what this is?"

"No."

She walked over to my chair, hands behind her back. Dropped to her knees on the rug. "It's a choke collar. For dogs. See?" She pulled the ring and the steel noose tightened around her neck.

I waited.

Her other hand came from behind her back. Handcuffs. She tossed the key in my lap. Snapped one of the cuffs on her wrist. Reached her free hand behind her. A leather leash. She snapped the hook onto the collar ring. Put her hands together behind her back. I heard the other cuff click home. She turned on her knees, back to me. Held out her cuffed hands. "See?"

"See what?"

She turned again to face me. "Take the leash. Hold it in your hands. There's nothing I can do. Tug on the leash, I come along. Like a dog. Pull too tight and I can't breathe. Try it."

The leash curled like a snake on my leg. I didn't touch it. "What's this supposed to mean?"

"There's more straps on the couch. You can do whatever you want. There's no way I can hurt you."

"You couldn't hurt me over the phone either."

"You're afraid."

"Not of you."

"Of *you*. Of yourself. Take the leash. Hold it in your hand. Feel the power."

I took the leash in my hand, watching her eyes watch me. Something stirred. "I don't feel anything."

"Yes you do. Don't be afraid of it."

"Tell me what you want."

"I lied. My daughter went back to him. Train. I want her back. I want you to get her back."

"How?"

"Talk to him."

"It won't work twice."

"Yes it will. Just go visit him again. A couple of times. Watch his office. Let him see you. Elvira will know. She'll know you'll always be around. He doesn't want people poking into his business. Another girl won't be worth it to him. Just be around. You don't have to do anything. Just be yourself. Tell Train you're investigating him or something."

"What if it doesn't work?"

"A couple of weeks, that's all. Just a couple of weeks. If it doesn't work by then, give it up. Okay?"

"You're paying for this?"

"Whatever you want."

"Money's what I want."

"What about me?"

"What *about* you?"

"I lied to you. And now I confessed. Don't you think I should be punished?"

"Not by me."

"Don't be afraid. You feel it, I know you do." She pushed her face closer, dropping it into my lap. My mind saw the message Wesley left on the rich woman's bed. I felt her lips against me. I was as limp as the leash in my hand.

She pulled her head back. "I thought . . ."

I climbed out of the chair. "I'll call you," I said.

She struggled to her feet, following me down the hall, hands cuffed behind her, the leash dangling from the choke collar.

"Burke!"

I stopped in the living room, waiting. "Get me out of these handcuffs. Or leave me the key. I don't have another one. I can't stay tied up like this."

Lousy little liar. "Call a friend," I told her.

## 92

WESLEY WOULD BE holed up somewhere in the city. Someplace with no neighbors. He had no baggage, no friends, not even a dog. He could go on the move every night. Carry whatever he needed in a duffel bag. No pressure points on his body—he'd been ready for this all his life. Torenelli's boys didn't have a chance. Trying to catch mist in a butterfly net.

I thought about my office. Pansy. Mama in her restaurant. Michelle in her hotel. The junkyard would be safe, but I'd have to stay once I moved in. Compared with Wesley, I was a citizen.

I called Wesley from Mama's. Worked my way through some hot-and-sour soup waiting for the call-back. He must have been keeping a close watch—the phone rang in twenty minutes. I answered it myself, saving time.

"Yeah?"

"You called."

"I have to go back in. See the man you told me to stay away from. Wanted you to know in front."

"Why?"

I knew what he meant. "It's part of this whole thing—I don't know what yet."

"You're checking on that address for me?"

"Already started."

He hung up.

## 93

I WENT LOOKING FOR the Prof. Slipped a roll of quarters in my pocket. Tolls for the turnpike. I found him on Vanderbilt, just before it dead-ends on Forty-second Street. A big shoeshine box in front of him. No customers.

"Let's take a ride," I said.

"I wish I could, but I'm holding some goods."

I glanced at the shoeshine box. He nodded.

"How long?"

"Quarter to a half."

I propped a boot on the metal last, lit a cigarette while the Prof went to work. He knew how to do it. Taking his time, running a toothbrush around the welt, taking the polish directly on his fingertips, working it in, popping the rag. Misted the leather with a little spray can, flicked it off with a buffing cloth. He was finishing up the second boot when two heavyset black guys rolled up. They leaned against the building wall, watching. Chilly young men. Pups from the same litter.

The Prof finished up with a flourish. Tugged at my pants cuff to let me know.

"There's your shine, and it's damn fine."

"How much?"

"Put down a pound."

"Five bucks?"

"The ride is five. You want the honey, you come to the hive."

The two pups pushed themselves off the wall in case I was going to argue. I handed the Prof his cash, moved off. Didn't look back.

The Prof caught up to me around the corner. His hands were empty. He got into the Plymouth and we headed over to the West Side Highway. Pulled over at the Ninety-sixth Street exit, hooked the underpass, and found a parking spot on the river. I popped the hood, hauled a toolbox out of the trunk. We kept our heads under the hood, playing with the tools as we talked.

"I saw him again."

"Keep it up, you'll be draped in crepe."

"I'm in it. He did that job—the one on Sutton Place. Spit in Torenelli's face. Julio met with me too. They want Wesley. Alive."

"And the heat still wants you?"

"That was Julio. The fucking weasel dimed me to turn up the flame. So I got no room to move."

"When the man's got a gun, it's time to run."

"That's what I should've done. If I'd known Wesley was tracking Mortay . . ."

"You know tomorrow's number, we're all rich."

"I know. This is different. I'm in the middle."

"That ain't the place, ace."

"Tell me something I don't know."

"There's no time for that, brother. They're both on the set, so place your bet."

"Wesley."

The little man turned, leaned back against the Plymouth's grille, looking out at the Hudson River. Lit a smoke, taking his time. "It always was him, wasn't it?"

"What're you talking about?"

"In the joint. When you was just a young fool with gunfighter dreams. That's who you wanted to be like, right? Wesley? The ice man."

"He's got nobody, Prof."

"Nobody dragging him down, you mean. Nobody to cry over when they're gone. Traveling light don't make it right."

"He's not a rat."

"This is true. He wanted your head, you'd be dead."

"Wesley wants his money. You know how he is. The Italians made a mistake. Torenelli's hiding. Wesley wants to know where. Settle up."

"It's over, then?"

"That's what he says."

"What do they say?"

"Who? Who should I ask? What they got, it's a big pile of cheese. They don't care which rat gets to eat. Torenelli don't make the count one morning, somebody else'll step in."

He nodded, dragging deep on his smoke. "Somebody knows where he is."

"Yeah, but who?"

"Torenelli. I remember him. A pussy in his heart. He ain't got the stones to go it alone. He was gonna kill *himself,* he'd use pills."

"That's the way I figure it too."

"Wesley ain't no private eye. Who's looking?"

"Morehouse."

"The reporter? That West Indian is my man! You dig his piece on that dude in Louisiana doing life in the box for a lousy stickup? Where the head of the Parole Board ended up doing time?"

"Yeah. I dealt with him before. I gave him some of the inside stuff from the Sutton Place thing. Hard stuff, right from the scene. From the horse's mouth. Got his nose wide open. He knows brass at NYPD."

"He know why you want the info?"

"He don't want to know."

The Prof dropped his cigarette, ground it out under his heel. "What's my end, friend?"

"They think I got no slack, but there's a knot in the rope. I can unravel it, I got room to breathe. There's a little girl. I need to take her to Lily, take her back when it's all done."

"That's it?"

"There's questions only Lily can get the answers to."

"You got the plan, I'm your man."

I lit my own smoke. "I thought I'd feel better after that motherfucker was gone." Belle's father.

"I know."

# 94

I CALLED THE EX-COP who does the phone work. Met him in a midtown restaurant. Gave him an envelope full of cash and some new phone numbers to check. A new address too.

Called Lily. Waited an extra quarter's worth for them to get her to the phone.

"It's me. Could I ask you a question?"

"Sure."

"If a teenage girl had a story, could you tell if it was the truth?"

She knew the kind of story I wanted her to validate. "It depends. I could probably tell if something happened, but not necessarily when. And I might have trouble identifying the source. You have a history?"

"All out of her mouth."

"I'll take a shot. Or maybe Immaculata could do it if you don't want to bring her here."

"It's not a job for Mac."

"Okay."

"Lily . . . I probably won't be able to make an appointment. She might be . . . annoyed. Not want to talk."

I could feel her shrug over the phone. "It happens."

"Thanks."

Called Davidson.

"Anything?"

"Nothing. My prediction? There'll never be a Grand Jury on this one. It's going to be marked 'closed, one arrest' and fade away. They know you had nothing to do with it."

"I owe you any money?"

"I'm good."

That was the truth.

# 95

I KNOW HOW TO WAIT. When I was in prison, I never thought of going over the wall. I wasn't doing a life sentence, and I wasn't ready to go straight once I was out. I let a couple of days slide by slow. No sense pressuring Morehouse—he'd get it done or he wouldn't.

But if he didn't . . .

The trust-fund hippies who live underneath my office don't stir until midafternoon. I think they call getting high "performance art" now.

Mama answered herself. In rapid-fire Mandarin.

"It's me."

"Letter come for you."

"At the restaurant?" Wesley? Julio's morons telling me they knew where I lived?

"Yes. Last night."

"See you soon."

## 96

AS SOON AS MAMA put it in front of me, I knew it wasn't from Wesley. Or Julio. Thick, cream-colored envelope, felt more like cloth than paper. Nothing on the outside. I flexed it in my fingers. Not a letter-bomb. One sheet inside, matching the envelope.

The words flowed so smoothly onto the paper they could have been squeezed from a tube. Icing on the devil's cake.

"Ask me. I know."

No signature. I didn't need one.

Strega.

## 97

I SMOKED A CIGARETTE, thinking it through. Smoked a couple more. It had to be connected—not one of her witchy games.

I'm not sure how I remembered the number. She answered halfway through the first ring.

"I know who this is."

"Okay. What else do you know?"

"I know what you want to know. Come and see me and I'll tell you."

"Say it now. It'll only take a second."

"Longer than that. Come and see me. You want to do it anyway."

"No I don't. We settled that."

"Nothing's settled. If I wanted to talk on the phone, I would have called you."

I bit into the filter of my cigarette. "I'll meet you. Remember where we first talked?"

"You're afraid to come here."

"Yes."

"Afraid of me."

"That too."

"You can't meet me outdoors. You know better than that. You know what I have to tell you. Make a choice. I'll be here tonight. From when it gets dark to when it gets light."

# 98

THE CAR RADIO SAID it was unseasonably warm. Mid-fifties. I felt the chill coming from her house before I got it in sight. Pulled around behind. Backed the Plymouth into the empty space outside the garage. The connecting door was open. I stepped inside. I knew the way.

She was in her black-and-white living room, perched on the edge of the easy chair, flashy legs crossed, elbow on her knee, one hand cupping her chin. Fire-streaked hair combed back from her little fox face.

"I kept it warm for you," she said, getting to her feet, heels clicking on the marble floor as she closed the distance between us.

I stood rooted. Nothing was going to get me back in that chair again.

She took both my hands, holding them gently, watching my face. She was wearing a white silk T-shirt that came to mid-thigh. The kind women tie a belt around and make into a dress.

"Sit in the chair. Your chair, remember?"

"No."

"No what?"

"No, I won't sit in the chair."

"But you do remember?"

"Yeah."

"I won't ask you again."

"Good."

She led me to the couch, still holding both my hands. Sat down, pulling me down with her. Pulled one of my hands to her mouth, a dark slash in the room, tiny perfect white teeth gleamed. She kissed my hand. Licked it. Turned her face up to watch mine again. Put my hand in her mouth, sucked on my thumb. Bit it, hard.

"You still taste good."

"What is it that you know? That you wanted me to ask you?"

"Julio told me. He tells me anything. He can never pay off his debt. This crazy man—this killer, they want you to deliver money to him so they can grab him. They're going to leave you there."

"You think that's news?"

"They're going to force you. Very soon. They know how to do it."

"What's the hurry?"

"Their little *don,* he's so afraid. Hiding in his little house. In the basement, like a cockroach. He's afraid, so they're all afraid. He can't wait. He wants to go to his nightclubs, ride in his big car, visit his *gumare* . . . big man. Now he can't do that."

"Okay. Thanks."

Her fingers were twisted in my coat. "Julio hates you. Because you know. What he did to me. He knows you know. I never told him, but he knows. He's put it out that you work with this maniac. The one who did the killing on Sutton Place."

"I already knew that. I got arrested for a homicide I had nothing to do with. That was his work too."

"I could have had Julio taken out years ago. I waited. To make him pay. But he could never pay. It's time for him to go."

"Why now?"

"You're *mine*. Remember what I told you? I ate your blood, I swallowed your seed. You're in me."

"I'm nobody's," I told her.

Witches hear only their own chants. "I told that evil old man. I told him I'd never let him hurt you. The last time he talked to me, he whined . . . like the coward he is. Said the don wanted it done. But I know. It's him."

"It doesn't matter who."

"It *does*. If the boss goes down, Julio's still here. And he'll still want you."

"So you want . . ."

"A trade. I'll tell you where the don's holed up. And you do Julio. Yes?"

"I thought . . ."

"Don't you sneer at me! Don't be better than me. You *want* to do it. You think I don't read the papers? I paid you to get Scotty's picture back. You did that. But the man who did it to him . . . that pervert in the clown suit . . . they said they found him with a broken neck. You did that. You're a cold man. A cold man, afraid of my fire."

"You're wrong, Jina. Wrong all over the lot."

Her eyes fired, flickered, glazed over. Singsong witch's chant. "Strega. Strega when you call my name. It's Strega who'll do this for you. Not Jina. Jina's a nice girl. You don't want a nice girl."

"I don't want you."

She licked her lips. "Prove it. Sit in your chair."

"For what?"

"For what you want."

"I want the address."

"Me first."

Bitch. I sat in the chair. Watched her curl herself around my legs, the T-shirt riding up to her waist, strip of blood-red silk between her thighs. She bent forward, the red silk a thong between her buttocks. Her hand on my zipper. Raspy, hard sound. "Mine," she said, thrusting her hand inside. Nobody home. She made a noise in her throat, took my softness between her lips, licking, making sounds to herself, speaking in tongues. A stirring in the softness but . . . nothing. Teeth nipped at the head of my cock, lips sliding over the shaft, sucking. Dead. As dead as Belle. I thought if it ever happened to me, I'd die a bit. It felt like winning.

She gave it up after a couple of minutes. Eyes focused hard now, watching my face. "Why?"

"I don't know—it's just gone."

"Is this the first time?"

I don't know what made me tell the truth. "No."

"Did something happen to you?"

"Yeah."

"You got hurt?"

"Yeah."

"Is it going to get better?"

"I don't know. I don't . . ."

"Care?"

"I don't even know that."

She pulled the zipper up, roughly. "It won't last. I know. I don't care what any doctor says. Don't be . . ."

"Don't be what? Depressed? Depressed is finding out you're a diabetic. I found out I can't get insulin, you understand?"

"You're not scared." It wasn't a question.

"No."

"You were the last time."

"I know."

"You think that's what did it . . . if you were scared again?"

"I. Just. Don't. Know. Okay?"

"Okay." Her eyes looked wet—it must have been the light in that white room.

I got up to go. "Give me the address."

"I don't have it."

"You . . ."

"I *think* I know where he is. But I have to be sure, okay? You can't go twice. Once it happens, they'll know it came from me."

"It could come from anybody. Their own outfit is lousy with rats."

"What about our deal?"

"I sat in the chair."

"I know. I know there's things you can't fake. Especially you. That's not what I mean. Julio."

"Spell it out."

"You have to do them both."

"When will you have the address?"

"Tomorrow, next day. Soon. Couple of days at most. I swear."

"Okay."

She walked downstairs with me, kicking off the spike heels, padding along on the carpet. She stood a step above me. Bent down and kissed me on the lips. Sweet. No biting into me. No witch-fire. She turned to go back upstairs, watching me over her shoulder. I flashed on Candy and years ago. Something stirred. It died when I remembered Candy had never kissed me goodbye when we were kids.

# 99

DRIVING HOME, MY black & white eyes were still working, but the images were reversed. Inside out. Inverted. For me, playing it safe wasn't playing—it was my life. I couldn't find the controls—nothing was where it had been. Terror said it was my partner, but I didn't have my old pal Fear to keep the nerve-endings sharp. Strega the witch was back in my life. Liars gave me their word, sociopaths gave me their trust. Dead people in my zone—some didn't know it yet. Some had my address. Users wanted my blood and vultures waited for my flesh. And I couldn't work up the adrenaline to get off the killing floor. Get off the track before the train came. It wasn't just my cock that wouldn't work. I didn't know if I was lost or gone. In the ground, with Belle.

Freaks use pornography on kids to desensitize them. Break down their natural resistance. Make them think this is the way things are. Drop the thresholds until they can step over them.

Maybe lies and loss work like that too. They don't take your soul, but they made it not worth fighting over.

Like when you're hijacking. You know you're going back to prison, you just don't know when.

It didn't seem so hard to find a way out. Just hard to give a fuck.

# 100

IN PRISON, I USED to make lists. In my head. Draw a bright line down the middle of my mind. Pro and con. The two things I wanted to be.

Some fights you can't get in shape for. I was only in prison with Wesley one time. We kept missing each other on the exchanges. I heard he even went in the Army for a while—when Vietnam was hot and heavy and the judges would give you a pass if you enlisted. There was another guy in the joint with us at the same time. Dayton was his name. A gorilla. Iron-freak. He muscled off the weaker ones, did bodywork for the gangsters. Good time. He didn't seem to give a fuck, but he survived. A life charmed by strength and stupidity. I don't remember how he got into the dispute with Wesley, but I was on the yard with the Prof when it kicked off.

Wesley was standing against the wall. By himself, like always. Dayton rolled up on him. I didn't hear what they said to each other. Dayton grabbed Wesley by the front of his shirt, pulled him close, slapped him hard across the face. Wesley slumped, hands away from his body. Dayton left him there, walking away with his boys.

One of the young Italian guys standing with us laughed. "My man is about to be mondo dee-ceased," nodding his head at Wesley. He said it the same way they say dee-fense at pro football games. The Prof flashed his hustler's smile.

"It won't play the way you say. For one to five, I say my man comes out alive."

Within minutes, we'd booked twenty cartons of cigarettes against a hundred that Dayton wouldn't outlive Wesley.

It was a sucker bet. Dayton was a Dianabol freak. Snarfing the steroids the way other guys in the joint did Talwin, or Valium, or anything else the docs handed out to help you escape for a few hours. They made him massive—bigger than a human should be. When the hacks found him slumped over the pile of weights in the gym, there wasn't a mark on him. But his skin had a nice bluish tone to it. The guys who bet with us thought we got lucky behind an OD. The ones that stayed in prison long enough put it all together. By then, going up against Wesley was an out-bet.

# 101

MORALES BRACED ME as I was coming out of Lily's joint. It had to happen—a pit bull would drop a bite sooner than Morales would walk away on the losing end. It would have been okay, but Max was with me. About four steps behind, in my shadow. Morales is about my height but he goes about two-twenty—none of it fat. He was a born head-cracker, not a gunman. That saved his life.

He snatched a handful of my jacket, shoved me face-first to the wall, running his rap, telling me if I was carrying I was going back to the joint . . . when he went dead-quiet. I looked back over my shoulder. Max had one hand on the cop's arm, the other at the back of his neck, bending him backward at an impossible angle. I spun off the wall, making a "drop it" sign to Max. Morales slumped to the sidewalk. I jammed my thumb back in a hitchhiking gesture, twirling my hand, telling Max to disappear.

I knelt next to Morales. He was trying to catch his breath and draw his gun off his right hip with his left hand at the same time—the right arm hung limp and useless at his side.

"You want me to get it for you?" I asked him.

"Cocksucker!" Almost sobbing with the effort.

"Take it easy. You're okay."

"You're not."

"I already know that. Am I under arrest?"

People passed us on the sidewalk. Nobody stopped. I tried to help him to his feet. His eyes were somewhere between rage and pain. Rage won. He fired the elbow of his good arm at my chest. I stepped back and he chopped air. I left him there. Went back to the wall. Stood facing it. Waiting.

Heard him get to his feet, muscles tightening over my kidneys. Felt the barrel of his pistol jam me just where I expected it. Didn't hurt any less.

"Get in the car."

I walked in front of him. His car was empty. He opened the passenger door. I got in. Watched him walk around to the driver's side. His gun was back in his holster.

"You're under arrest. Assault on a police officer. You have the right to . . ."

"Save it. Do what you have to do. You know I never touched you."

"Not you. Your pals. Whoever they were. I never saw them. But you . . . you're gonna tell me who they are. Where to find them. Right?"

"I didn't see anything. I was facing the wall."

"That's the way you want it?"

"I don't want *any* of this. It's you who want things. Things happened, they happen. Whatever you think, I didn't write the script."

"I heard things about you," he said. Lighting a cigarette with the dashboard lighter, not offering me one. "From my partner. He said you were a man. That you could be trusted. We go in on a thing with you—and you Pearl Harbor us—leave us with our dicks in our hands."

"You ever rap a guy in the head with your nightstick when you were in uniform?"

He didn't say anything—that was my answer.

"What if the guy had an eggshell skull? What if he died?"

"Never happen."

"You mean it never *happened*. There's a difference, right? It *could* happen. And you wouldn't have meant it to come down like that. But the guy would be just as dead."

"You saying that's what happened with you in the massage parlor?"

"I don't know what you're talking about. I'm just saying . . . you plan things . . . sometimes the wheels come off. You do the best you can with it. Survive."

"We found out some things. Since everything blew up in Times Square. The guy we found in pieces in the construction site—there was a contract out on him."

"I don't know . . ."

"Yeah, you don't know what I'm talking about, hit man. I didn't think that was your side of the street."

"It's not."

"There's a mob contract out on a guy. The guy gets dead. We know you did it. We're supposed to think it was personal?"

"Think what you want—that's what you *been* doing."

"Give it another spin."

"Not a chance. You keep playing me for something I'm not. You pulled my jacket—you know I'm not a soldier. I'm not a hired killer, and I'm not stupid."

"We got you tied into that skell. The one that got iced in the playground."

"That was the charge I was arrested on. So how come I'm on the street?"

"I look like a fucking pansy judge to you? You think I give a fuck about probable cause?"

"You say that to say what?"

"We weren't going to be pals, Burke. But you don't want me for an enemy."

"Amen."

"So give me something."

I lit a smoke. Used my own matches. Watching the color drift back into his face. His right arm still hung limp.

"I'll give you something, Morales. I'll give you a couple of things. On the house. One, your source. The one who you say tied me into some homicide in a playground. And the one who told you about a contract on a guy you found in Times Square. They're the same man. The same *family* man. Two, you fucking *know* he's a liar."

"So you say."

"Save it for the first offenders, cop. You believed this guy, you'd take me down. Like you said, we're not pals. But I know you. You thought it was me, you sincerely thought I burned you and McGowan, you'd flake me with a piece instead of just selling me wolf tickets about carrying one."

A smile twisted on his face. "You sure?"

"Yeah."

"Say you're right . . . just to be saying it, okay? What's in it for this guy who dropped a dime on you?"

I crossed my hands in front of my chest, one finger pointing at Morales, the other to my door. "He did it. Not me."

"Yeah. But we weren't looking at this guy. He wasn't a suspect."

"He would be, you kept at it. A cold wind's gonna blow."

"Torenelli's daughter?"

"I look Italian to you?"

"When I thought you were okay, you looked sorta Spanish to me. Now . . . now you look Italian."

"I never meant to offend you. I'm not against you. I just want to do my time. On the street, in the jail, wherever. Just do my time. Be left alone."

"That kind of privacy . . . it costs."

"I can't pay what I don't have. And I don't borrow."

"You already owe something."

"If I do . . . if I get the chance, I'll pay it off. Square it up. Ask around. I pay my debts."

"I think you paid at least a couple. I find out you did it for cash, I'll get you. That's a promise."

I threw my smoke out the window. "So I'm not busted?"

He didn't say anything when I opened the door and climbed out.

# 102

I WASN'T UNDER surveillance. The cops don't have the manpower for that, and Morales was still with the Runaway Squad anyway. He'd probably been prowling Lily's joint, watching to see if any of the kiddie pimps he hated so much were working the corners. When he saw me, he couldn't pass it up.

The phone man was where he said he'd be. We passed each other on the steps of the Federal Courthouse in Foley Square. A quick handshake and we each had what we came for.

## 103

I WAS IN MAMA'S arguing with Max over his stunt with Morales when the phone rang in the back.

"Young girl," Mama sad, sitting down.

I picked up the receiver. "What?"

"It's me. Elvira. You said to call today. I told you I would."

"I need to talk to you. About your mother. About Train."

"Go ahead."

"Not on the phone."

"Maybe you can come here. I'll ask . . ."

"Never mind. I can come there, but I want to talk in private. Tell me where you'll be, I'll pick you up."

"I'm not sure . . ."

"Not sure where you'll be or . . ."

"I'm not leaving here."

"Elvira, I wanted you out of there, you'd be out of there. I'm going to talk with you, one way or the other."

"I'm not afraid of you."

"I don't want you to be afraid of me. I want to talk to you."

"And then . . ."

"And then you go back to wherever you want to go. And you never see me again. Okay?"

A long pause. I wondered who else was listening, signaling to her.

"Okay," she finally said into the phone. "Where and when?"

"Tomorrow morning. On the corner of Flatbush and Tillary. The Brooklyn side of the Manhattan Bridge. Ten o'clock."

"How long will I be?"

"Couple of hours."

"Goodbye," she said. Hung up.

## 104

NEXT MORNING, THE Plymouth an anonymous hulk lurking just outside the remnants of the commuter traffic stream. Max in the back seat, black wool Navy watch cap on his head, heavy gloves on his hands. He was only wearing a gray sweatshirt—it wasn't that cold out.

She must have walked from Train's building. I spotted her a couple of blocks away, stone-washed jeans, a dungaree jacket, hair in a ponytail. A kid cutting school. I stepped out of the car, waved to her. She broke into a clumsy little trot.

I opened the passenger door and she climbed inside, Max moving in behind her like water flowing over a rock. "Huh!" she said, surprised. I was sitting in the driver's seat by then.

"Elvira, this is my brother, Max."

She snuck a sideways look, mumbled "Hi," eyes downcast. I fired up the Plymouth, heading over the bridge.

"Where're we going?"

"To see a friend of mine."

"How come *he's* here."

"Just along for the ride."

"I thought we were going to talk private."

"Max can't hear. He's deaf."

"For real?" An off-key note in her voice.

"Yeah. For real."

We came off the bridge into Chinatown, tunneling through the narrow back streets to Lily's. Elvira fumbled in her purse, brought out a cigarette. Max snapped a wooden match, held it for her. She said "Thank you" in a finishing-school voice. Max bowed slightly.

"Does that mean 'You're welcome'?" she asked.

"Yep."

"Can you . . . talk to him?"

"His name is Max. I can talk to him. So can you, you want to bad enough."

"Oh! How?"

"Think of what you want to say, then act it out. Like charades."

"Can I try?"

"Go ahead."

She curled her feet under her, tapped Max on his forearm. Pointed at him, then at me. Pinched her shoulders against her slender neck, spread her hands, palms up. Max pulled off his gloves, tossed them on the dashboard. Watching her face closely, he pointed at himself, then at me. Waited for her to nod. He tapped his chest over his heart. Reached past the girl, tapped me in the same place. Hard. The finger curled into a fist. The fist slammed into his open hand. That hand wrapped around the fist. The two hands twisted together until the fingers were intertwined.

"He *is* your brother!"

"Sure."

Elvira put her two hands on an imaginary steering wheel, pointed to me, pointed out the windshield, made a questioning look at Max. He shrugged his shoulders, pointed at me, nodded.

"He doesn't know where we're going?"

"He doesn't care. He's with me—that's where he's going."

## 105

WE PULLED UP BEHIND Lily's. Max got out. He'd go inside, tell them to open the back door for us.

I lit another smoke, offering her one. "There's a woman inside. Her name's Lily. She's a good friend. Of me and Max both. She's the one I want you to talk to, okay?"

"About what?"

"She'll do that part. All you have to do is what you say you always do . . . tell the truth."

"Is she gonna ask me about Train?"

"Not the way Reba asks questions."

I got a blank look back. Train didn't tell all his people how his fleshy polygraph worked.

"Never mind," I told her. "Lily's a certified social worker. You know what that is?"

"Like a shrink?"

"Yeah, sort of. Anyway, the point is that she's not allowed to repeat anything she's told. Anything you say to her is confidential. That's the law."

"But . . ."

"Elvira, listen to me, little girl. You think any of those kids running around in karate outfits could stop Max? This talk with Lily—it's for you. I know you don't understand that. I know you don't trust me. You don't have to. We made a deal. I took you out of Train's joint and I let you go back. He can't stop me and my friends. I have to find out some things and I want Lily to talk with you. You do that and we're done."

"What if I don't?" Not pouting, curious.

"Then I'm going to ask Train."

"He said you'd be back. He's never wrong."

"You think about that. You decide *how* I'm coming back." I'd been searching for the right button. Tried one more. "You want to protect Train, talking to Lily's the way to do it, understand?"

"My mother . . ."

"Is *out* of this."

"She says you're hers. Her old boyfriend."

"What does Train say?"

"How did you . . . ? He said you were nobody's child. That's what he said: 'That man is nobody's child.' "

"You know what he meant?"

"Maybe."

I threw my smoke out the window.

"I'll talk to her," the girl said finally.

The back door opened and I led her inside.

## 106

I INTRODUCED LILY and Elvira. Watched for the hundredth time as waves came off Lily, enveloping the kid, excluding me. "She has a calm center," Immaculata explained it to me once. "Like Max." They walked down the hall together.

Max was probably in the gym, wrestling with the kids. That wasn't for me. I had some time to kill, so I found an empty office, put my feet on the desk, closed my eyes. I had things to think about.

When I opened my eyes, Immaculata was sitting on the desk, her hand on my ankle.

"You're awake?"

"Sure."

"Burke, I don't have much time to talk. You must let Max help you. It is very important."

"Help me what?"

"Whatever it is you're doing. It doesn't matter."

"Yeah, big fucking help *he* is. You know what he did yesterday?"

"He told me."

"He tell you he almost turned a lousy roust into a Class A felony?"

"Max is your brother. He is in great pain. Men don't know how to take some things. Some gifts. He cannot forget what you did. To save our baby. What it cost you. He must believe he is helping you or he cannot feel whole."

"Mac, you know what Max does?"

"I am his wife. He is the father of our child. You remember when we met?"

I remembered. A night subway run. Me carrying the goods, dressed like a bum. The Mole at the other end of the train, a satchel full of explosives. And Max the Silent sitting across from me, looking like a tired, drained old man. Three punks got on the train. Looked me over. Wouldn't bother with a wino. Started on Max. Asking him for ten bucks for a cup of coffee, shoving him around. No big deal—we only had a couple of more express stops to go. It was going okay until Immaculata saw the action. Dressed like a Vietnamese bar girl, as out of place on that subway as a clock in a casino. She charged the punks, telling them to leave the old man alone. One pulled out a pair of brass knuckles, giggling at the new prey. Max took them all out quicksilver-fast—just flashes and sounds. He shed his filthy raincoat and the tired old man became the Mongol warrior. Bowed deeply to the woman who had come to save him. He signed, I interpreted. She saw past his strength, he past her beauty. They've been together since.

"I don't care what it takes." Her voice soft and relentless. "Is that clear enough for you? I want my husband back. His daughter needs him back. You know what he is. If you tell a true warrior he cannot make things right, his duty is to die trying."

I lit a smoke, playing for time. Her eyes stabbed. "Don't try and trick me. I know you could do it. For *now.* Max even said so—how you can lie so smoothly."

"How can I . . . ?"

"There is a man you went to see. Your enemy. Max has no fear of him, this little killer with his guns."

"Mac, I'm telling you the truth. Believe it or don't, it's still the truth. The man you're talking about . . . he's not my enemy. I don't know how I know . . . I'm not even sure I knew until I just said it. But I'm not gaming to protect Max."

"You must let him help you." Intractable. No slack in the rope.

"What am I supposed to do?"

"Let him help you find what you're looking for."

"What I lost."

"No. What you seek. Please."

She bent forward, kissed me lightly on the cheek. Her perfume stayed after her.

# 107

MAX WALKED IN, KIDS hanging on him like amateur mountain climbers. Before I could say a word, Lily pushed past Max, holding Elvira's hand. She gave me a "stay where you are" look. Told Elvira, "Go with Max. I have to talk to Burke for a minute before he takes you back."

Elvira obediently held out her hand. It disappeared in Max's. He went back toward the gym, leaving a wake of rowdy kids running to catch up.

I lit a smoke. Lily sat down. Her voice had that distanced, professional tone she uses when the anger laps at the boundaries of her self-control.

"Post-Traumatic Stress Disorder. Long-standing. Original stressor undoubtedly the mother. Compounded by numerous instances of sexual exploitation so frequent that they merged into a real-world distortion pattern. Amoral, almost sociopathic aura to her productions. She imitates affect, but has very little sense of feeling things. Nerve-endings blunted. Some indication of Borderline Syndrome too. She actually . . . physically feels a void inside of her. Relates to mother almost as a rival. Tested clean on the MMPI Lie Scale. Telling the truth. Guiltless. Heavily bonded to this Train individual. And she's pregnant, maybe two, three months gone."

I let her see my eyes, willing her to relax. "All that means . . . ?"

"I don't have time for games, Burke. You know damn well what every single word I said means. You've spent years studying. Just because it wasn't in college doesn't make you a stupid thug."

I held up my hands. "Okay, okay. I wasn't being cute. I meant . . . what's the bottom line? Where she is: it's better than being with her mother?"

"There's no *better* to any of this. Where she is now is just one of the places kids like her end up. Nobody wants you, so you hit the streets. And there, somebody always wants you. For something.

They prove they want you by paying you money. A child like that, she couldn't tell a rescue mission from a cult."

"Is she being abused now?"

"Not in her mind. She's working for this wonderful goal. This island they're going to buy someplace. Where they can all live in peace . . . a big, loving family."

"Yeah, like every pimp is going to let his woman retire someday. Open up her own boutique, right? They have her turning tricks?"

Lily's eyes were dark, soulful. Little dots glowing like plutonium around the iris. Holding something in check.

"No. She was in Germany. Making porno movies. But she's too old now."

"Fifteen."

"Yes, fifteen. All she could bring in as a prostitute would be a couple of hundred a day. And she'd have to work outdoors, take a lot of risks. Train doesn't let his people take risks. No, she's not turning tricks . . . they're breeding her."

"What?"

"Breeding her. Like a brood mare. She told me she was 'mated' to one of the young men in the cult. When she has her baby, Train's going to sell it. You know the going rate for a healthy white baby with a solid medical history, educated parents, the whole works?"

"Fifty K and up."

"Yes."

"Doesn't she want the baby?"

"She doesn't want *any* baby. She expects to have a baby a year for a few years. So Train will love her. He takes the best of care of her. A special diet, exercise, regular visits to a doctor."

"The boys . . . he can't use them all for breeding."

"She's so cold about it, it's frightening. She says boys are worth more than girls. They can earn money even when they're old . . . she means like eighteen, nineteen. They go on the circuit too. The boy she mated with, he was in Amsterdam for a few years, then he came back here to work."

"She told you a lot."

"Don't you get it? She doesn't see anything wrong with it! You know what the words mean. She's not a child in her soul. Hasn't been for a long time. It's *all* okay. Train saved her. He saved all of them."

"She tell you about Danielle?"

"Yes. And she told me you brought Danielle back to her father. Don't blame yourself."

"You think it's true, then?"

"Oh yes. All true."

Wesley's voice in my mind: "They didn't pay me." Somebody owed me too. "Isn't she afraid Train will do something to her when he finds out she talked?"

"She's not afraid. She thinks you're a criminal. She says Train knows you. He's in control. Two of the young men, they're his bodyguards. She says they took one of the girls out of there when the girl went crazy. She wouldn't answer my questions about it—she just assumes the girl is dead. And she says her mother knows you too."

"So she thinks . . ."

"I don't know what's going on in that damaged brain of hers. She thinks you and her mother want to blackmail Train, or that you're going to work for Train, or you have your own organization like Train's . . . or God knows what. It's a simple world to her: the big fish eat the smaller fish. They eat enough little fish, they grow into big fish themselves. Here's what she said: 'Everybody gets used. The way to keep from getting used *up* is to learn to be use*ful*.'"

"That's not her line."

"No. But she recites it like a fundamentalist quoting the Bible."

"You said she was bonded to Train . . . sounds more like bondage than bonding."

"It isn't. The bonding is real. Train is real to her. He saved her. Remember that. She's a bright girl. She knows her life was short on the streets. Drugs, a trick with a razor, a sadistic pimp . . . it doesn't take much to snuff out a candle in a hurricane."

Homicide danced in my mind. "Rescue me." My blue Belle. That was all she'd asked. I took her off the runway and into the ground. Like I took Danielle from her pimp. I ground out my smoke with the tip of my boot. Lily was too focused to even frown at me.

"What happens to her if Train goes down?"

She shrugged. "Elvira would find another."

"There's no place for her?"

"A psychiatric hospital. A prison, maybe. No place good."

"What should I do?"

Lily's hands went to her hips, titanium threads in her soft voice. "You brought her to me for a reason. To find out some things. Are your questions answered?"

"Yeah. Are you making any calls?" Lily was best pals with Wolfe, the head of the City-Wide Special Victims Unit. Wolfe was part of the tribe of warrior-women in the city. I'd met a few of them over the years. Catherine, the beautiful social worker in City-Wide's office who specialized in elderly victims. Storm, the brand-new head of the hospital's Rape Crisis Unit. Queenie, an investment banker who left her lizard briefcase and upscale outfits at home when she volunteered at Lily's joint on weekends. All of them not taking prisoners, slugging it out aboveground. Where it's legal. Where the light doesn't shine for men like me. Wolfe had crossed the line with me once. Just for a minute in time. Then she dropped my hand and went back to her life. I wouldn't ask her again.

"Should I?" she asked.

"Can you stay quiet for a bit?"

"I'm a mandated reporter. The law requires that I report every case of suspected child abuse that comes before me in my professional capacity."

"You just did."

"I'm calling it into the Hot Line. But I don't know her full name or her address."

"Okay."

"I *will* know, Burke. And then I have to call Wolfe."

"Okay."

"*When* will I know."

"Ten days, two weeks."

I lit another smoke, waiting for her answer. So much for me to carry. Dead weight. Unreasonable anger flared in me. Lily, she could do the right thing, sleep easy. She walked the line. Part of me wanted to pull her over it.

"Lily, can I consult you in your professional capacity? As a client?"

"Sure." Absentminded, still thinking about waiting to call the Hot Line.

"I have a problem that's affecting my mental state."

"What?" Impatiently.

"I'm going to kill someone."

She got it. Never flinched. "Ten days, Burke. It's too late for Elvira, but not for the others . . . not for all of them."

But for my love.

## 108

ELVIRA WAS QUIET, sitting between Max and me on the way back.

"Your friend Lily . . . she was nice."

"But you know it was all game, right?"

She flashed the no-soul smile of a little girl who learned to do tricks too soon. I pulled up outside Train's place. Max stepped out, holding the door for Elvira like a chauffeur.

"Tell Train I'll be around to see him soon," I told the girl. "I won't be taking you back. Just one last talk. I want to part friends. Tell him, he'll know what I mean."

She turned to face me. "Did my mother kiss you goodbye the last time you saw her?"

"No."

She slid off the seat without a word. I didn't look back.

# 109

MAX DIDN'T REACT WHEN I passed by Mama's. Didn't change expression when I cruised by his warehouse. I knew the look on his face. Whatever. It. Takes.

I backed the Plymouth into the last slot in the loading bay of what had been a factory years ago. When the landlord rented it out for lofts, he left the last piece to use as a private garage. When I explained to the landlord that his son's identity was safe with me, he gave me a hell of a break on the rent. Free. Threw in the garage too.

We took the back stairs to my office. Max stood well aside as I opened the door. I threw Pansy the signal—she waited patiently to see what I'd brought her. The beast watched Max with her homicide eyes, a soft growl just inside her teeth. Talking about him the way he had talked about Wesley.

Anytime. Anytime you want.

They'd known each other for years. Max never patted her. She never bothered him. He bowed to Pansy, no expression on his face. Pansy watched.

I got her some liverwurst out of the refrigerator, gave her the magic word, watched it vanish. She stretched out in a corner by the couch, bored. I crossed over to my desk, cleared a place so I had a flat, blank table. Gestured for Max to sit in the chair I use for clients.

He made a gesture like he was dealing cards. I shook my head. Our life-sentence gin game wasn't going to be continued tonight.

What was the truth? My promise to Immaculata? Or could Max really know? Why didn't it hurt me more . . . like it should have? How come? Bad pun.

How to explain it? I lit a smoke. Put it on the lip of the ashtray, folding my hands behind my head, looking at the cracked cement ceiling. Max reached over, put the cigarette to his lips, took a deep drag. Smoke fired out his flat nose in two broad jets.

I pointed at myself. Put my hands under the desk, tried to lift it off the floor. Strained. Gave it up. Too much weight for me to lift.

Max hooked two fingers under the desk. It came off the Astroturf I use for carpet like it was floating.

I shook my head. It wasn't a weight someone could lift for me.

He spread his hands. "What?"

I drew an hourglass figure in the air. Made my right forefinger rigid, poked it into an opening I made in my left fist. Again and again. Okay?

He nodded, watching.

I pointed at my chest. At my heart. Stiffened the forefinger. Approached the opening in my fist. The forefinger went limp. Wouldn't go in. Pointed at myself again.

Max pointed at me. Smiled. I was joking, right?

Wrong.

He made an hourglass sign of his own. Made a "no good" gesture. Drew another in the air. Opened his hands. Try another woman.

I drew another woman. Another. One more. Pointed at myself again. Stiffened the forefinger—let it sag limp. It was me, not the women. Me.

He pointed at his groin, shook his head. Tapped his skull. That's where the problem was.

I nodded. Yeah, so?

He pointed at an old calendar on my wall. Since when?

I made the sign of a pistol firing. Looked at the ground. Blew a goodbye kiss. Since Belle.

He made an "it's okay" gesture. Tapped my wristwatch. It would get better.

No.

His face closed. He went off somewhere inside himself, looking. I smoked, watched my dog, let my sad eyes play over this miserable little place I lived in. The last time Belle was there, it had sparkled.

Max got up, went by himself into the back room. Pansy tracked him. Once you got in, you could move around. You just couldn't leave until I told her it was okay. Nothing back there but a hot plate and the refrigerator. Toilet, sink, and stall shower. I waited. He came back with two paper packets of sugar, the kind they give you in diners. Put them both on the desk, side by side. Tapped one closed eye. Pay attention.

He pointed at me. Tore open one of the packets. Emptied it into his palm. Tossed the sugar into the air. Wiped his hands. All gone. Looked at me.

I nodded. Yeah, that was it.

He shook his head. No. Took the other packet and put it in my desk drawer. Pointed at the desk top. Nothing there. Still gone?

I opened the drawer. Took out the other packet.

The warrior nodded. Took it from my hand. Slipped it into my coat pocket. Patted me down like a cop doing a search. Pulled out the packet, held it up to the light. Made a gesture, "get it?"

No.

He took the packet, walked over to the couch. Stuffed it under one of the cushions. Looked around the room, confused look on his face. Where is it?

I pulled it free from under the cushion, held it in my hand.

Watched my brother, watched his eyes. He'd said all he could.

Then I got it. Hell of a difference between something lost and something missing. It wasn't gone—I just didn't know where I'd put it.

I bowed to Max.

He took the packet from my hand. Pointed to my chair. I sat down. He made frantic searching gestures, opening drawers, looking under stacks of paper, rapping the walls with his knuckles, looking for a hiding place. Shook his head. No. Not that way. He leaned back, put his feet on the desk, closed his eyes, folded his hands over his stomach. Pointed at me. I imitated him. It was peaceful lying there. Safe and peaceful. I wondered if the fear-jolts would come back someday too. I hated them so when I was young and doing time. Wished them away. It never worked. Back then, when I wanted to be somebody I couldn't be. Something Candy always knew I wasn't.

Something brushed my face. I opened my eyes. The packet of sugar was lying on my chest. Waiting.

Which is what I had to do.

It would come to me.

I held a clenched fist in front of my face. Yes!

Max tapped my fist with his own.

Sparking flame to light the way.

# 110

WHEN I GOT BACK TO the office after dropping Max off, I let Pansy out to her roof. Turned on the radio. A car bombing out in Ozone Park, Queens. A soldier and an underboss splattered. I had some rye toast and ginger ale, thinking I might like to bet on a horse when this was all over.

Pansy came back inside. I worked on her commands for a half hour or so, just to keep her sharp. Like oiling a gun. Then I went to sleep.

The radio was still on when I woke up around ten o'clock that night. Another bombing, this one in Bushwick, Brooklyn. The wise-guys would be paying people to start their cars for a while.

I went into the street. Called Strega. She was right by the phone, like she knew.

"It's me. You find out?"

"I think so. I'll be sure by tomorrow night."

I hung up. Called Mama. Nothing from Morehouse, the lazy bastard.

Dialed the Mole. Heard the phone picked up. The Mole never speaks first. "I need a car," I said. "You got one?"

"Yes." Terry's voice. The connection went dead.

Terry let me into the junkyard. I slid over and he took the wheel, guiding the Plymouth through the maze to a resting place.

"They still fighting?" I asked the kid.

"Mole says Mom has to make her own decision."

"He tell *her* that?"

"No. But she knows."

The Mole was working in one of the Quonset huts he has scattered around the place. No windows, but it was as well-lit as an operating table. A tired-looking Ford four-door sedan was in pieces on the floor.

"What're you doing, Mole?" I greeted him.

"Working." Mr. Personality.

I remembered the counsel the Prof had given me when I was a kid first learning to do time. Watch. Watch and learn. Pay attention or pay the price. I sat down on an old engine block, lit a smoke.

Terry worked with the Mole like gears meshing. Nothing wasted, quick and clean. Each of them took an end of the Ford's back seat. They slid it back into place. I heard a sharp click. The boy shoved harder, using his shoulder. Another click. The rocker panels were off. I saw what looked like a long, thin shock absorber running parallel to the ground. Where the running board would be if they still used them on cars. The Mole fitted a short length of track between the back and front seats. Fiddled around in the trunk. A sound like something being released. I went closer, peered over his shoulder. The back of the front seat was a solid-steel plate, ugly welds slashed across the corners. The front seat was welded to the chassis around the bottom seams. A brick wall.

The Mole signaled to Terry. They each took an end of the back seat, slid it back and forth on the runners. It reached all the way to the welded steel plate. Terry sprayed the runners with silicon.

"We'll test it," the Mole said.

Terry pointed to a pile of green plastic garbage bags stacked against the wall. "Give us a hand, Burke."

I picked one up. Heavy. Maybe sixty pounds. "How many you need?" I asked.

"Six?" the boy said, looking at the Mole. He nodded, absorbed.

I took a sack in each hand, brought them over to the car. Terry wrapped both arms around one sack and followed me. The Mole watched. One more trip each and we had them all.

"What now?" I asked.

The Mole pointed at the back seat. "Four there, two in front."

I loaded them in. Terry struggled until he had one sack on top of another. Two big lumps in the back, one in the front, behind the wheel. Driver and two passengers.

The Mole threaded a wire from the dashboard through the open car window. Backed up until we were against the wall. He stripped the wire, wound it around a terminal on the workbench.

"Stand back," he said.

The back seat shot forward like it was fired from a rocket launcher, slamming into the steel wall. The car rocked on its tires. The back seat bounced off the steel plate, floating listlessly on the siliconed tracks. We went to take a look. The four green plastic bags were plastered to the steel wall like paint on canvas. It smelled of old smeared death. In the front, the top bag had hit the steering wheel and ripped open. White suet mess inside, blood-streaked.

"It works," the Mole said. "We have to tighten the front seat braces."

I stepped outside to get away from the smell. Waited for the Mole and Terry to join me.

The kid was first out. "What was that mess?" I asked him.

"Just fat they slice off the sides of beef in the meat market. They throw it out in big tubs. The Mole says it's pretty much like people, only without the bones."

Michelle would love it. The Mole lumbered out into the night air.

I looked over my shoulder at the car. "How does it work?"

"Two hydraulic pumps. Compressed air. When you hit the trigger, the back seat releases from the catches and slides forward on the tracks. Very fast. Into the wall behind the front seat."

"So if anyone's sitting in the back seat . . . ?"

"Crushed. No escape."

"And the driver."

"Once it's strengthened, no problem. If you wear a seat belt."

I dragged deep on my cigarette, thinking about what my family had been telling me. About not acting like myself. Thinking about insurance. "Mole, could I borrow that car?"

"It has to be cleaned. Then we have to reset the trigger, wire it to a button on the dash, put slipcovers over the front seat. A lot of work. This was just an experiment."

"But you could do it."

"Yes." He hesitated. "The car, it's a killing machine. For Nazis."

"Mole, you know about Wesley. You know he's back and . . ."

"I know."

"Well? Can I . . . ?"

The Mole's lumpy body stiffened as he looked up into my eyes. "Wesley's not a Nazi, Burke."

"Mole . . ."

"What he does, it's not for freakish fun. Not like them."

"You're saying he's like . . . us?"

"More like us than them," he said as he walked away, the kid trailing behind.

I left the Plymouth in the junkyard. Switched it for a dark blue Buick sedan with clean plates.

By the time I stashed the car in my garage it was four in the morning.

I let Pansy out to her roof one more time. Then I went back to sleep.

## 111

I WAS IN THE RESTAURANT early the next morning. Mama brought me a copy of the *Daily News*. The headline said "Sniper Killing on Staten Island." A middleweight mobster had been shot late last night in the living room of his home in Todt Hill. Watching television with his wife. All she heard was glass breaking. A neat hole in his head, right at the hairline. Police said the sniper must have worked his way onto the grounds, lain prone, and fired at a slight upward angle. There were a half dozen pieces about who the guy was, speculation about what it all meant.

Morehouse was on the money with his column. All the Strike Force charts and graphs don't mean a thing when there's a wild card in the deck. He ended it nicely: "Once the feeding frenzy starts, it doesn't matter where you rank in the food chain."

## 112

THE REPORTER FINALLY called. Mama took the message. I rang him back.

"You got it?"

"Sure."

"Meet me . . ."

"Oh, man. Why can't you be civilized once? You know my address, come to my house."

"Not tonight."

"Okay, man. Talk to me. Be quick now, I got work to do."

"Tomorrow morning. Eleven o'clock. You know where the guys work on their cars under the FDR? Like around Thirty-third?"

"Sure."

"I'll be there."

He made a disgusted noise. Hung up.

## 113

NIGHTTIME. STREGA'S TIME. Could there be a good witch? Compared with Candy, Strega was as pure as driven snow. The kind they drive across the border in ten-kilo shrink-wrapped packages. Ice-pure.

I drove into Queens. Dialed her number from a pay phone.

"I'm waiting for you," was how she answered.

The empty spot in her garage was like the impression your body leaves when you get out of bed. The Buick fit.

She stepped into the garage as I closed the car door. Wearing a steel-gray seamless sheath that stopped at mid-thigh. Matching spikes. A single strand of black pearls. Her hair was wild, face scrubbed clean. Not quite ready to go out on the town. She took my hand, pulling me up the stairs. "Let's tell secrets," she whispered.

The living room was dark, pierced by thin beams from the track lighting mounted on the ceiling. The smoke from my cigarette spiraled up into the light.

She took my coat, slipped it off my shoulders, tossed it on the couch. Sat next to me.

"You don't carry a gun anymore?"

"Julio fixed that. I'm out on bail. I can't afford a fall."

"It doesn't matter. You don't need a gun here—it's safe."

"No man's safe around you."

She smiled a witch's smile—rheostated. "You're mine. I never hurt what's mine. Remember Scotty? Remember why I needed you? I never let anyone hurt what's mine. You wouldn't let anyone hurt me either. I know you."

Yeah, everybody knows me. "We had a deal," I said. "I kept my piece, you kept yours. This is another. Another deal."

"I know. I found him. The compound in Sands Point. It's out on the Island. It's a fortress, soldiers all over the place. Dogs. Electronic stuff. He stays in the basement. Julio said even if you dropped a bomb on the place, the don would be okay."

"Great."

"He can't even talk on the phone. He's too scared. He told Julio this man . . . Wesley? . . . is the devil. The real, real devil. He's going mad in his stone basement. He won't watch television—he thinks this man can see him through the screen. Julio, he thinks it's funny—the don would pay a million dollars for Wesley's head, but he doesn't even know what he looks like."

"Julio saw the don?"

"Oh yes. At the compound. Julio's got his own plan. He's going to make Wesley dead. Do what the don couldn't do. Be the *boss*. He'll never be my boss again."

"So he wins no matter what happens?"

"That's what he thinks. Ugly evil old man. He feels strong when he thinks of the don cowering in his basement, afraid of the dark. But when he thinks of me, his strength is gone. That's why he has to go. He thinks it's my time. Time to free himself But it's his time. I waited long enough."

"He's got to leave that basement sometime." Thinking of Train, safe in his house. With his human polygraph and his bodyguards who made little girls' bodies disappear.

She leaned into me, head against my chest. I'd never seen a black orchid, but then I knew what one smelled like. Her hand went to the inside of my thigh. "I'll tell you a secret now. In the chair."

"Jina . . ."

"Please."

Such a strange word from a witch. I sat in the big chair. She squirmed into my lap, lips against my neck. I heard every word, like she was talking into my brain.

"The don can't stay in the basement. He'd lose it all. The others, they'd know. And you know what happens then. When you drop the leash, the dog bites. So every Monday night, he meets with his captain. On the Fifty-ninth Street Bridge."

"How do they work it?"

"The captain's boys park on the Manhattan side. The don's boys park on the Queens side. Then they *walk* across. Soldiers in front, soldiers behind. They do their business and they go back."

"Every Monday night."

"At one in the morning."

She turned sideways so her thigh was across my lap. "I'm a good girl," she whispered in that witchy little girl's voice. Reaching for my crotch. Nobody home.

"Let the beast out," she said. "I know what to do with him."

"Ssssh" I said in the darkness. Patting her just above her hips, stroking her back. "It doesn't matter. There is no beast. You are a good girl, Jina."

Her hand came away from my crotch, pulled gently at a button on my shirt. "Sleepy," she said.

I shifted my weight. Her skirt rode up. A faint trail of light on her stockings. I wrapped my other arm around her, rocked her gently. "It's okay, girl."

She took my thumb into her mouth. Didn't bite it this time, or suck on it. Just left it there, touching it with her tongue. Made a quiet noise in her throat.

I held her for a long time while she slept.

## 114

"WAKE UP," IS THE first thing I heard. She was still there, face softened by sleep, hair tousled.

"I'm awake."

"It'll be light soon. Time for you to go."

"Yeah."

She got off my lap, pulled her skirt down. Shook her hair loose. The sleep fled her eyes. She bent forward, face inches from mine. The witchy hiss was back. "Julio goes too."

I nodded.

## 115

I WAS AN HOUR EARLY to the meet with Morehouse. Pansy prowled a tiny circle in front of the car while I was doing something under the hood. Nobody came close enough to find out what.

Morehouse pulled up in his Datsun, fifteen minutes late.

"I was looking for your other car, man. Been cruising the area for a half hour. I . . . what the fuck is that?"

"Pansy!" I snapped, throwing her a hand signal. She hit the deck, watching Morehouse like a Weight Watcher about to jump ship.

Morehouse's lip curled. "Was that a dog once? Before it swallowed a car?"

"I thought all West Indians loved dogs."

"No, man, you got it wrong. All West Indians *are* dogs. Just ask my girlfriend. Anyway, I got what you wanted."

"I just hope it's not that fairy story about the old man being holed up in a fortress in Sands Point."

Morehouse was too cool to give it all away, but his eyes slid away from me just far enough to let me know I'd hit the target. "Well, that's what's on the street."

"Yeah. And Donny Manes stabbed *himself* to death."

"Hey, man, that was the word. *Is* the word. From on high."

"From on the pad."

"I didn't say that."

"Okay. Thanks anyway."

"That's it?"

"What else is there?"

"Our trade, man. What is wrong with you? I'm not done—I can still come up with the winner. Italians dropping like World War II out there. You were right. Something's coming. And I want to be in the paper with it first."

"I get it, you'll get it, okay? I may have something else for you too. Interested in a cult that traffics in babies?"

"Adoption ring?"

"No. A breeder farm. Using little girls just about old enough to bleed."

"You know I am."

"Want to help out?"

"How?" Suspicion all over his face.

"Switch cars with me."

"What would you want with this old wreck?" he asked, waving his hand at his city-beater.

I pointed at his license plates. NYP. New York Press. Everyone in this city has special plates: doctors, dentists, chiropractors. Everybody but lawyers—it wouldn't be safe for them. "Your plates go anywhere. And even the Italians won't dust a reporter."

"What's this got to do with the baby-seller?"

"Everything."

He reached in his pocket. Tossed me his keys. "Registration's in the glove compartment."

"Mine too."

Morehouse was born to be a reporter. He walked to the Buick, opened the door, one eye on Pansy. He pulled the papers out of the glove box. "Who's Juan Rodriguez?"

"*Quién quiere saber?*"

He laughed.

I snapped my fingers, opened the door to Morehouse's wreck. Pansy launched herself into the back seat. "I'll call you," I told him.

He stood close to me, voice low. "Burke, there's one thing they say about West Indians that *is* true. We *do* love children."

## 116

I PARKED MOREHOUSE'S car behind the restaurant, let myself in through the kitchen. Stashed Pansy in the basement. Grabbed the pay phone. Rang Wesley's number. Three times. Hung up.

I was on my second helping of soup when the phone rang.

"What?"

"Time to meet."

"You got it?"

"Yeah."

"Tonight. Same deal."

"Right."

"Bring the Chinaman."

When Max came in, I was working on a plate of fried rice with Mongolian ginger-beef. I told him we had a meeting that night. He had his own sign for Wesley: an X drawn in salt spilled on the table.

Mama gave me a gallon container of steaming meat and vegetables to take down to Pansy.

Max showed me a copy of the racing form. I shook my head. No. Not yet. But when he dug out a deck of cards, it was okay. We played gin until it got dark. Immaculata came in with Flower. Max took the child from her, parading into the kitchen to show the assorted criminals working back there his prize.

"Hi, Mac."

She leaned over. Kissed me. "Max is back, Burke. I don't know what you . . ."

I held up my hand. "It's not over yet."

"It doesn't matter. Whatever happens." She bowed. As if to fate.

I took Pansy back to the office. Showered. Changed my clothes. Lit a smoke and watched the darkness outside my window.

# 117

MAX RAPPED A KNUCKLE against the windshield as I pulled off the road. I looked where he pointed—a tiny Day-Glo orange dot glowing to the side. It blinked off as I watched. I braked gently, waiting. The light glowed again. Okay. We left the Datsun by the side of the road, walked in the direction of the light, Max first.

Under the network of girders the wind made hunting sounds. The light didn't go on again, but Max walked like he was following a neon strip in the dark. He stopped when we came to a clearing in the jungle. Broken glass on the ground. Tire carcasses. Rotting pieces of car upholstery. Discarded furniture. Shipping crates. A bicycle without wheels. Max slapped his hand lightly against my chest. Stop. Here.

I lit a cigarette, tiny red light of my own. A siren screamed above us. An ambulance—racing the hospital against the morgue.

Wesley was in front of us, just a thin strip of his face showing.

"How's he do that?" he asked me.

"What?"

"He can't hear, right? But he don't make a sound when he moves."

"I don't know," I told him. Not blowing him off—it was the truth. "That's the real reason they call him Max the Silent."

"That isn't your car."

"Julio, he knows my car."

"Okay." Wesley sat down on one of the crates. I sat across from him. Max stayed where he was. Not watching Wesley, eyes sweeping the area.

"Tell him it's safe here," Wesley said. "I got trip wires strung all around except for the way you came in. And you're sitting on enough plastique to knock down the bridge."

"That's your idea of safe?"

"The cover's too thick. And if they charge, we all go together."

"Great."

Sarcasm is wasted on machines. "You got it?" he asked.

"The don is holed up. They have a compound of some kind in Sands Point."

"I know where it is."

"Yeah. But he never leaves the basement. And the place is set up like a bomb shelter."

"You sure?"

"Sure. He's scared to death. Won't even talk on the phone."

Wesley went as silent as Max. Time passed. Finally he spoke, voice just past a whisper but with no breath in it. "Fire fixes it."

"What?"

"The place burns bad enough, he has to come out."

"If he has it right, he won't have to. The place could burn to the ground, he'd still be okay in the basement. He has the cash to fix it that way. Some of those rich geeks, back in the fifties, they fixed up their basements like the Russians were going to drop the bomb any day. All the survival-freaks aren't living in the mountains. It wouldn't work."

"Yeah. Maybe you're right. I saw one of those basements once. Guy even had the place soundproofed."

"I got one more thing. The don, he has to meet his underboss. And he won't talk on the phone, remember? So every Monday night, he meets. On the Fifty-ninth Street Bridge."

"Out in the open?"

"Yeah." I told him what Strega told me. He made me go over it twice more, taking each word in a single bite, chewing it slowly.

"He probably stands behind the pillars . . . so even if we drove by in a car, there'd be nothing to shoot."

"Sure." Thoughts flashing. Who'd *drive* the damn car anyway?

His voice was calm, talking about the weather. "This was another time, it wouldn't matter. I got him in a box. I got nothing to do but wait. But I'm in a box too. I got to finish my work."

"And get paid?"

"They'll pay me. When my work is done, I'm all paid up."

"Julio, he still wants me to bring money to you. It'll be a trap, but . . ."

"No good. They wouldn't send the big guys. They try something, everybody gets blown up. We don't get to take them with us. Like when I was in the Army. The soldiers die, the generals find new soldiers."

"How come you didn't stay in the Army?"

"When I went in, I did it like doing time, right? Keep your mouth shut, stay out of trouble, wait till they open the gates. I didn't talk, so they figured I was stupid. I was a good shot too. So they make me a sniper. We had this platoon leader, some college kid. He talked to us like we were dogs. Nice dogs, dogs he *liked* and all. But stupid, you know? Especially the blacks. He made things simple for us. Every time we go out there, it's the fucking gooks keeping us from going home. To our *families* and all. One day, we're in a firefight. Charlie's winning—got too much juice for us. Time to split, come back another day. But this asshole, he wants us to hold our position. Wait for the choppers to spray the area. Or until they drop napalm on us. Four of our guys got wasted the last time they did that. It came to me. In a flash-second, didn't even think about it. We was supposed to kill gooks 'cause they was keeping us from going home, right? And now it was this lieutenant keeping us from going home. I put a few rounds into his chest. He goes down, I step up and yell, 'Retreat!' I'm the last one out. I got a Bronze Star for it. I had a good war record. So when they court-martialed me later they let me out with a dishonorable. No stockade time. I stuck up a liquor store the night I got back to the city. Everything went smooth, but the night clerk called the cops when I came back to the hotel. That's when I caught up with you again. In prison."

"What'd they court-martial you for?"

"I was in Japan. On R and R. In a bar. Some Marines got into a fight with some Navy guys. I was halfway out the door when one of them jumped me. I went down. Came back up, chopped the guy in the back of the head with this glass ashtray. He turned into a cripple behind it."

"An accident . . ."

"Didn't make no difference. I was glad to go. I'm not a soldier. Like the scams you run."

"You mean the mercenary thing?"

"Yeah. They talked to me once. Guys with British accents, only they ain't British. Fight communism, right? Sure. I don't fly nobody's flag."

"Does Julio know your face?"

"I don't have a face. I met him once. He gave me the go for this Mortay freak. But it was dark and he was scared—he couldn't pick me out of a lineup. It was like it is out here—you can't see much."

"He's part of this now."

"I know."

"No you don't. I made a trade. For the information I got. About the place in Sands Point. And the meeting on the bridge."

"You got to do Julio?"

"Yeah."

He went into himself I could feel the edges go soft, merging with the darkness as the center hardened. I lit another smoke, cupping the tip. Max watched. He could feel the changes in the air like a blind coroner doing an autopsy.

"That's the one thing I know. Really know," the monster said. "Murders. In some countries, the leaders get whacked all the time. You know why? 'Cause the people doing the killings, they're not professionals. They're willing to fucking *die* to get something done. Trade their life for another. Over here, we never get *close,* you know. Only lunatics do it that way. Remember that guy who shot Reagan? I was that close to him, I'd have so much lead in his body they'd need a crane to get him off the ground. You kill people for money, you have to live to spend it."

"So?"

"Julio's no problem for me—he's a problem for you. Even if this informant of yours didn't want Julio dropped, you know he's setting you up. So it don't make a difference—he's gotta go. And the don—he's no problem for you, right? He don't even know you exist. And he don't care. You ever think of just taking me out . . . ? Max, he's close enough now. Maybe. You bring the don my head, you're off the hook."

"No. I never thought about it."

"You're a dancer, not a killer. You don't understand the way things work. Death makes it right. Wipes the slate clean."

"I wouldn't know." Thinking of Belle. Death hadn't made it all right. Not because the wrong man died—because the wrong man did the killing.

"I know a way to hit the don," Wesley said. "But I need three, four people to make it work. You got the people. You help me, I'll do Julio for you."

"It's just me and Max."

"He's in?"

"Yes."

"You got more people. More *brothers*."

"I have to ask. They're my brothers, not my soldiers."

Wesley's voice dropped just a fraction. "Here's the way it goes down," he said. I listened to his toneless voice, thinking how easy he would have taken Mortay. How I should have jumped off the track.

It took a while. "Okay?" he asked.

"I'll be there. Max too. And I'll have the other stuff in place. I'll ask, like I said. Maybe I'll have the other people. If not . . ."

"It'll still go. Just won't be as safe."

I took a deep breath. "I'm going back in. To see Train. Speak with him. Just so you know."

"He's last. Before I finish up."

"Wesley, you remember a girl from the neighborhood? Little Candy? From when we were kids?"

"No."

Max led us back to the car in the darkness.

# 118

ON THE WAY BACK to the city, I called the junkyard. We stopped in, spoke to the Mole. He'd place the cars. I didn't ask him to do anything else.

It took us a couple of hours to find the Prof. He was working Penn Station, deep in talk with a couple of guys stretched out on sleeping mats made from cut-up cartons. A two-wheeled shopping cart stood between them, full of magazines, empty plastic bottles, a Cabbage Patch doll with only one arm on top. As we closed in on him, I recognized the two pups from the shoeshine stand.

They recognized me too. The bigger one snaked his hand into the cart.

"Chill it, fool," the Prof snapped at him. The pup listened to his teacher. The Prof walked over to us. We stood against the corner as I ran it down.

The little man thought it over. "There's always danger from a stranger."

I thought of what the Mole said about Wesley. "He's not us, Prof. But he's not them either."

"I'll drive. From the far side. Couple of hours. You don't show, I go." Dealing himself in. One piece left.

I rang Michelle's room. "Are you decent?" I asked her.

"No, but I'm dressed."

Max and I went up to her hotel room. She was wearing green Chinese pajamas, makeup in place, hair still up. Smoking one of her long black cigarettes.

She kissed Max on the cheek, reached over, squeezed my hand. "What is it?"

"Monday night, late. I need someone to drive me and Max. Wait for us. Couple of hours. We don't show up, take the car and split."

"What's the risk?"

"Not much. The car'lI be clean when you're sitting in it. We come back on the run, you can still fade."

"Somebody's paying?"

"Somebody."

"I'm in for a piece?"

"We're not stealing, Michelle. Flat rate. You call it."

"I'll have to take the whole night off. Say, two large."

"Okay."

"You're different now. Different again."

"What?"

"You don't feel like a gunfighter to me anymore. But you're not back to yourself. Something's still missing."

I knew what it was: I didn't feel afraid.

## 119

IT WAS GETTING LIGHT when I took Max back to the warehouse. I waited while he got my mail from upstairs. Same old stuff.

Always danger from a stranger. Somehow I knew he'd be awake. I dialed the number from the basement. Told the man who answered the phone what I wanted. Waited.

"Mr. Burke."

"Train. I'd like to make an appointment to see you. Continue our dialogue. Tie up the loose ends."

"What loose ends?"

"Questions you asked me. About . . . security. I believe I have some answers for you. And maybe we could do business."

"I see. Around noon?"

"I'll be there."

## 120

I LEFT MOREHOUSE'S CAR on Remsen Street, where it was legal to park with NYP plates. Max and I walked the rest of the way.

The same young man we saw the first time let us in. No karate outfit this time. The chairs were already in place in the top-floor room.

"My brother will wait outside, with your permission. I don't think anyone needs to hear this."

His eyes were a bright blue. "My staff has rather strong feelings about me . . . about my safety."

"You're safe with me. Sometimes it's safer to talk privately."

"The last time we talked. About security. You said something about me having to leave this place sometime. It seems to me that you're already back inside."

"I'm a businessman, not a kamikaze."

"Very well."

Max stepped outside. We were alone. I rotated my head on the column of my neck. To get the kinks out, break the adhesions. And look around. Glass brick ran in a long loop around the top of the room. I had to play it like they were listening—walk the tightrope.

I lit a smoke. "You have enemies. Personal enemies. I think that's part of the cost of doing business for you. That wouldn't frighten you."

"You think I'm frightened?"

"Concerned, okay? Intelligently concerned. About a problem you have. I think one of your personal enemies realized his impotence. And went to a professional. I don't think your security questions were academic."

"Are you guessing about all of this?"

"No."

The blue eyes honed in. That was his wake-up call. "Are you . . . involved?"

"Not yet. I thought I might be. If we can do business."

"I'm not certain I understand."

"You have a sweet business here. Making wine out of rotten fruit, that's a technique. I admire your insight, your skill."

He bowed slightly, waiting.

"The way it works, you cruise the streets. Look for old furniture that people throw out on the sidewalk. Then you refinish the furniture, remodel it, paint it. You sell the furniture to people who want that kind of stuff in their houses. And it's all profit. Garbage into gold. Dirt into diamonds. Why should anybody be mad?"

"Indeed."

"Once in a while . . . not too often . . . somebody wishes they had their furniture back. But you've got this rule—you won't sell it back to anyone who put it out on the curb in the first place."

"They threw it away. It's not theirs."

"Yes. You're a street-cleaner. A scavenger. But you know how people are—they never miss water until the well runs dry."

"You're a perceptive man. I believe we . . . I misjudged you."

"That happens. You have resources, you can ask questions. You know when the truth is around. When it isn't."

"Yes?"

"The truth is around. Here. Now. One of these people who discarded his furniture, he wanted it back. There was a disagreement of some sort. But this individual, he couldn't go to the authorities. The law's on your side. Once you throw garbage out at the curb, it belongs to anyone who picks it up."

He bowed again. Just a slight movement of his head.

"So this individual, he goes outside the law. To a professional. Somebody wants you. And by now you know it isn't me."

"You came for Elvira."

"And I returned her."

"She told you some things . . ."

"And I brought her back to you. I'm not the man who's looking for you."

"No? Then what are you?"

"I'm the man you're looking for."

"How so?"

"Every profession has competition. You have your work, I have mine. I wouldn't know your competitors, you wouldn't know mine. You thought I was here for a particular reason. You were wrong. But someone is out there. For you. Someone I can deal with."

He made a slight "keep talking" move with one hand.

"I have two professions," I told him. "One of them is finding people. I can find this person."

"And then?"

"My other profession."

"And what of *my* profession?"

"That's your business. It seems you could use a man like me."

"I have people."

"You have children."

His eyes locked in. "*My* children."

"Children deserve protection."

"Yes. I must do what is best for my children. Anything else would be immoral."

"Morality can be costly."

"Whatever . . ."

"Very costly."

"Yes?"

"Fifty thousand."

"All right." Unfazed. "I assume you want some sort of . . . preliminary payment."

"It's not necessary."

"I'm not familiar with these things. I just thought . . ."

"I know where to find you. After it's done."

"How would I know?"

"I'll bring the proof. If you're not satisfied, there's no charge."

He stroked his face, pretending to think about it.

"It's for the children," I said.

"Yes. I have no choice. My obligations. You won't mind if I check . . . ?"

I nodded, knowing what he meant. It didn't matter. Wesley had his work and I had mine. And I was back to it. The day I couldn't scam dirtbags, I'd go straight.

I didn't see the signal. Reba came into the room. A white silk robe with a hood, white sash around her waist. Nothing else. She sat next to me on my left, hooking one thigh over my legs, pulling the robe around her shoulder like she was cold. Her hand found my heart.

Train gazed at the ceiling. His voice went thin, dry-washing his hands.

"Is someone looking for me?"

"Yes."

"To hurt me?"

"Yes."

"You know who it is?"

"Yes."

"You could stop him?"

"Yes."

"Could I stop him?"

"No."

"Would he take money?"

"No."

Reba's hand shifted, shielded by the robe. Fingers trailed across my cock. She wiggled her butt like she was trying to get comfortable. I couldn't see her face.

"Are you the man who is looking for me?"

"No."

"Do you believe Elvira is safe here?"

"Yes."

Reba's hand cupped my balls. A gentle squeeze. Her thumb stroked my cock. It stirred. Stiffened.

"Are you working for Elvira's mother?"

"No."

"Did you ever?"

"When I brought the girl back to her."

"The man who's looking for me . . . is he for hire?"

"Yes."

Reba ran two knuckles of her hand up and down the shaft of my cock. Found the tip with her fingers. Squeezed. It was a piece of steel, threatening the zipper.

"But not by me?"

"Not now."

"Because he's already taken someone else's money?"

"Yes."

"Do you know whose money?"

"No."

"How would he come for me?"

"By fire."

He nodded. Reba slid off me, gathering her robe, whispering, "It's all the truth." I crossed my legs as I reached into my coat for a smoke. Lit it, waiting. Reba padded out of the room.

"You'll tell me when it's done?" he asked.

"I'll show you."

Max was outside, standing alone.

## 121

ALONE IN MY OFFICE, I stroked Pansy's soft fur the way the New Age lunatics rub crystals. Getting apart from myself, wrapping what was left in my own fear. Letting the core speak to me.

Being the answer.

"Nobody knows where Wesley's going, but everybody knows where he's been," the Prof said.

I lit a smoke, replaying every square inch of the chameleon's apartment. Everything I'd seen. Waiting for it to kick in. It would come. Reba knew.

## 122

CANDY ANSWERED her phone.

"It's me," I said quietly. "You were right. I want to get it back. Hold the leash in my hands."

"I don't like the way you left me the last time."

"I did. That's how I knew you were telling the truth."

"That's my baby. Anytime after three, okay?"

"I'll be there."

# 123

THE DOORMAN WAS sneaking a smoke just outside the building. The Prof yelled "Yo', Roscoe my man!" at nobody and the doorman turned. Max and I went inside. I took the elevator to the top floor.

The wig was strawberry blond this time but the yellow cat's eyes were her own. Wearing a white terry-cloth bathrobe. "It all starts back there," she said. "Come on."

We went to the last bedroom. She dropped the robe to the floor. The choke collar was around her neck, leather leash dangling to her knee. I sat on the psychiatrist's couch, pulling hard on the leash. She came to the couch obediently, eyes dreamy. I pulled again. She sat on the couch, slipped onto her hands and knees. I stood up. "Stay there," I told her.

I walked behind her. She dropped her shoulders to the couch, her round butt seemed to shimmer in the dim light. "Stay the way you were," I said.

She pushed herself back up on her hands, saying nothing.

"I know where the stuff I want is. Stay there."

I went to her closet. Found what I needed. When I walked back, she hadn't moved.

"Put your hands behind your back."

The handcuffs were leather-lined. I snapped them home. Looped the leash through one of the rings in the floor.

She licked her lips. Cold cat's eyes. Feral and fearless.

I knotted the leash. Her shoulders came forward, bent, touched the couch. I stepped behind her. Her slim ankles were close together, muscles bunched on the backs of her thighs. I cuffed her ankles together. Held a length of chain in my hands. She crooked her feet back over her butt in an arch, holding her cuffed hands back toward her ankles, waiting to be hog-tied the way another woman would wait for a bus. I linked the chain to the cuffs holding her ankles. But then I pulled back, hard. The front of her calves hit the couch. I tightened the chain around one of the couch legs. She was spread out, on her stomach, chin on the couch. The way I'd been on those subway tracks.

Her body was faintly coated with sweat, like she'd been oiled. I put a tube-shaped leather pillow under her hips.

"I can't move an inch," she purred. Like it was magic words.

I put one knee on the couch next to her. Patted her butt lightly. Slid my hands up to her shoulders.

"There's a mirror. Behind the screen. If you want . . ."

She was still talking when I pushed the ball gag into her mouth, slipped the elastic over her head.

Then I went looking for what I'd come for.

There had to be another room someplace. I found it off the dressing room. A butcher-block desk with one of those tiny designer lamps. A high-tech phone with a row of unmarked buttons down one side. I wrapped a handkerchief over my finger. Pushed each button, watching the stored number come up on the liquid crystal screen. I filed the numbers in my head, hanging up before they could ring even once. Ten buttons. Only four had numbers stored.

I stepped into one of the bathrooms. Flushed the toilet. Candy had it backwards. It wasn't her who knew me. Now.

I was back inside the last bedroom in a couple of minutes. Slipped the elastic off her head. The ball gag popped out.

"You okay now, baby?" she asked.

"Not yet."

"I thought . . ."

"I'm not finished," I said, unlocking the cuffs from her ankles. She wiggled her hips. It wasn't to get the feeling back. I unlocked the cuffs from around her wrists. She waited. I unknotted the leash. Pulled her to her feet.

"Get dressed."

Her eyes were downcast, voice soft, feeling her way. She wasn't good at ad-libs. "Tell me what to wear. Tell me everything—I can't get dressed unless you tell me what to put on."

"A sweater and a skirt."

"Should I wear a bra, honey?"

"Yeah."

"Panties?"

"Yeah."

"What color?"

"It doesn't matter."

"I . . ."

"Pink, okay? Do it quick."

"Should I wear stockings? Heels?"

"No."

"How old am I?"

"You'll see," I said, pulling hard on the leash. "Hurry up."

I pulled her down the hall to her dressing room. Watched as she dressed.

"Where's the key to this place?"

She handed it to me. I put it in my pocket. "Come on," I said, bunching the leash in one hand, holding it behind her neck. Even when we were kids, that was the way I held her—never her hand.

I led her to the front door, opened it, pushed her outside. She didn't say a word. The hall was carpeted. I took her to the stairwell door. One short flight to the roof. Twenty flights below us. A naked red bulb was the only light. Emergency Exit. I prodded her forward. Pulled the leash. She stopped. I was one step behind her.

She knew what to do. Grabbed the railing with both hands as I lifted her skirt from behind. "What if somebody comes?" she whispered. Making it come back.

"Too bad for them." Max one flight below us. Only one person was going to come.

My zipper rasped. Her hands went behind her, thumbs hooking the waist of her panties. She had them down just before I slammed into her.

I felt the muscles inside her grab and hold. I never touched the silicone.

It didn't take long. She made a greedy noise as I shot off inside her. Pulled up her own panties. Never turned around. Like old times.

## 124

BACK IN HER APARTMENT. Candy sitting on her couch, the leash a dark line between her breasts inside the bright yellow sweater.

"You'll get her back for me now?"

"Yes." I took her key out of my pocket, running my fingers over it, rubbing hard. I tossed it to her. It bounced off her shoulder. She never took her eyes from me.

"I always loved you," she said.

## 125

I TOOK THE STAIRS down with Max. The Prof was waiting in Morehouse's car. I handed him the soft plastic block from my pocket. The key to Candy's apartment was sharply outlined on its face.

"Tell the Mole I need two, okay? He can leave them in one of the cars for Monday night."

"It's done, son."

## 126

MONDAY, MIDNIGHT. Max and I pulled off the FDR, leaving the car to the darkness. Michelle was in the back seat. Max waited while I walked along the riverbank with Michelle. She leaned into me, her hand on my arm.

"Here's the papers you wanted," I told her.

"This is pretty thick for just a passport," she said, putting the packet into her purse.

"The rest is from the Mole."

She stopped in her tracks. Slit the envelope with a long thumbnail while I lit a smoke. I saw a wad of greenbacks. And a note on the graph paper the Mole uses for stationery. I left her to herself, smoking in silence. When she turned her face to me, tears streaked the perfect makeup.

"After tonight, I'm gone from here."

"I know."

"When I come back, I'll be me."

"Yeah."

"I love you, Burke," she said. Pulled my face down to kiss my cheek. "You watch out for my boy—you take care of him."

I didn't ask her who she meant. "Come back at one, okay?" I told her. "You'll hear some kind of a big bang. Wait five, ten minutes. We're not here, go. If we're coming, we're coming fast. You see us coming toward you, just walk away, leave the keys in the ignition."

"I'm not running around in this mess in my good shoes."

"I mean it, Michelle. Don't wait. We don't need a driver."

She gave me another quick kiss. "Take care of Max," she said.

The ground felt squashy under my boots as we made our way down to the river. Manhattan is a big island; the East River separates it from Queens, dotted by smaller islands. Welfare Island. Roosevelt Island. Once they used them for insane asylums, hospitals, leper colonies. Now they use them for luxury co-ops. Other islands too. Real small ones. Just clumps of dirt and trees sitting in the river. You could get a good view of the Fifty-ninth Street Bridge from them.

Michelle would wait on the Manhattan side. We couldn't just stash a getaway car in that neighborhood—it wouldn't be there when we needed it. The Prof was in place on the Queens side. When the pressure came, we'd move away from it. If we could.

Wesley was waiting. A darker-than-night shape near the water. He handed me the Uzi. A soft hiss as the rubber boat inflated. He pointed to a pair of duffel bags and a large tool chest with a handle on top. Max took the two duffels in one hand, the tool chest in the other. Wesley didn't seem surprised. We boarded the boat. Wesley sat in front, steering. Max and I alternated strokes with the paddles. The river's only about a quarter mile wide where we were working, with the island sitting in the middle. It didn't take long.

We beached the boat. Wesley set up a pair of tripods in the soft ground, pressing down hard to make sure they were firmly seated. He bolted a spotting scope on top of one, a rifle onto the other. No talking—sound carries over water. No smoking. He pointed to the sniperscope, pointed at me. Blew a sharp puff of air. I nodded. Wesley settled in behind his rifle, making himself at home. He swept the bridge with his scope, nodding in satisfaction. He pulled a bullet from his jacket pocket. Long, slender bullet. A soft snick as he chambered the slug. I was inside his mind. Target rifle. One target, one bullet.

Wesley sat behind his rifle, eyes somewhere else. Nothing to do but wait. A foghorn sounded far down the river. The Harbor Patrol had passed almost half an hour ago. They hadn't even swept the island with their searchlights.

I saw the line of humans moving. Walking the bridge. The spotting scope picked them out. Three up front, a man in the middle, three behind. I swung the scope to the Manhattan side. Four men, walking together. I blew a sharp puff of air, imitating Wesley. He settled in behind the scope, moving the barrel in tiny circles. A snake's tongue. Testing. Waiting. Fangs sheathed.

The two groups came together. The man who'd been in the middle from the Queens side stepped forward. One of the men from the Manhattan side detached himself. They walked on the outside of the bridge, safe from traffic. The two men met near the middle of the bridge, slightly to the Queens side. They stood with their backs to the girders. Then they switched places. I blew another puff at Wesley. "I saw it," he whispered. So low it might have been only inside my head.

I saw what Wesley saw.

The target's eyes were shielded by his hat. I zeroed in on the lower cheekbone—the bullet would travel up, climbing all the way till it met his brain. And blow it out his skull.

They were talking. I heard Wesley take a deep breath. Let it all out in a smooth stream. Felt him go coma-calm. So he could squeeze the trigger between heartbeats. The don's lips stopped moving. He cocked his head slightly. Listening to the underboss.

The don fell forward a microsecond before the earsplitting *ccccrack!* ripped my ears. The underboss ducked.

Wesley was on his feet, breaking down the tripod. Max grabbed my scope and tripod in one scoop. Wesley pointed to the Queens side—standing dark and quiet in the distance. No time to argue. We threw everything in the boat. The muscles in my back screamed trying to match Max's strokes. Sirens shrieked somewhere behind us. I knew Wesley would be working the spotlight in front of the boat, watching for the answer. The boat veered left toward my side, where Max's strokes would do most of the work. We ran aground. Wesley popped the release. The air hissed out of the boat as Max made the run to the car.

I took the wheel. Wesley and Max loaded the stuff into the trunk, climbed into the back seat. I pulled away smoothly, heading for the empty factory district of Long Island City.

"Thanks, Prof."

"It's been fun, but my piece is done," the little man said. Meaning he didn't want to stay along for the ride. I stopped within sight of the IRT. Held out my hand. He grasped it, let go. Opened the door and split. Never looked into the back seat.

## 127

I FOLLOWED WESLEY'S directions to an abandoned factory building off Meserole Street in Brooklyn, not far from the Queens border. Wesley got out, unbolted a heavy padlock. I drove the car inside. Pitch-dark. It even smelled empty.

Max reached into the trunk. Held the stuff up for Wesley to see. Wesley made a "put it down right there" gesture. "I won't be here tomorrow," he said to me.

The freight elevator was a bombed-out void. Wesley walked in the darkness like he could see. We followed the sounds he made. Found my hand on an iron railing. Staircase. Wesley walking ahead. Three flights. The top floor was only half there. No glass in the windows. Light from somewhere came through them. Boxes piled up, some covered with a tarp. Cans of food against one wall. Rats made their scratching escape noises.

I lit a smoke. So did Max.

Wesley sat on one of the boxes.

"No doubt in your mind?" I asked him.

"I hit him. With those bullets, I hit him anyplace, his head's in pieces."

"They'll go crazy looking for you."

"Crazy . . . you ever have a suicide dream, Burke?"

"What's a suicide dream?"

"Where you dream of killing yourself. You ever dream of killing yourself?"

"I did once."

"What happened?"

"I dreamed I was real depressed. Sad like there wasn't any reason to keep on. So I made a list. Of all the people I wanted to take with me. Figured I was gonna die anyway, I'd just start blasting everyone on the list. Sooner or later, one of them would get me. Save me the trouble."

"Did it work?"

"No." I felt crazy laughter bubble in me. "I got through the whole list. Then I didn't want to die anymore."

"My list is too long. Yours too?"

"Not anymore."

"You all settled up?"

I thought about Train. Julio. "Just about."

"What'd you use on that Mortay?"

"Use?"

"To off him."

It was like talking into a machine. But not a tape recorder. "A .38 Special. And I dropped a grenade on his face after he went down."

The machine's voice lightened. Wesley's laugh. "A fucking .38? A pistol? Why didn't you just throw rocks at him?"

"I got it done."

"He was supposed to be real good. Like Max here. You got him with a pistol, he must have been close."

"He was."

"Chump."

"I know. Now. Now's too late." For Belle.

"Anything I can do for you?"

"You mean . . . ?"

"What I do. I'm almost done."

"Just Julio. And Train."

"So I was right. From the beginning. You were on his case."

"No I wasn't. Things changed. I learned something."

"Something about a kid?"

"Yeah."

"That soft spot—it's like a bull's-eye on your back."

"Nothing I can do."

"It's not your problem, right? Not your kid."

"I didn't want it like this. I wanted to be . . . something else."

"What?"

I dragged deep on my smoke, looked into the monster's eyes. "I wanted to be you," I told him.

"No you don't. I'm not afraid. Of anything. It's not worth it."

"Wesley, what do you know about Train? What made you think I was on his case?"

"The guy who hired me. I figured it had to be something like that. He knew your name."

And then he said the man's name. Danielle's father. The man with the special basement on Long Island.

I threw my cigarette on the floor. Ground it out.

The monster knew. "There are no good guys, Burke. You're a thief—go back to stealing."

I didn't like the sound of my voice. "Not just yet."

He read my thoughts. "He's on the house. Keep your list short. I'll meet him after Train's done. To get the rest of my money. I'll leave him where I meet him."

I lit another smoke. "I told Train I'd take care of you."

"Good. They're easier when they're sleeping."

"You need a ride anywhere?"

"No. I got a car stashed just down the street. I'll get rid of the stuff first, then I'm gone."

Max bowed to Wesley. The monster moved his head in return. Stiffly, like he wasn't used to it.

I followed Max down the stairs.

## 128

THE ALL-NEWS STATION had nothing about the killing on the way back to Manhattan, but it was all they were talking about by the time I got up in the morning. Ghost stories. The one I liked best had Colombians blasting the don from a speedboat passing under the bridge.

## 129

I DROVE OUT TO THE junkyard. Sat down with the Mole. Told him about a girl named Elvira. About selective breeding, supervised by slime.

I drove back to the city in a black Ford four-door sedan. Max followed in Morehouse's Datsun.

## 130

IN MY OFFICE, I WENT over the Ma Bell printout the ex-cop had gotten for me. One of Train's six numbers had no long-distance calls at all. Never used up its message units either. A dead line. For incoming.

It was one of the numbers stored in Candy's phone.

## 131

JULIO LEFT A MESSAGE for me at Mama's. I called him at his club.

"What d'you want, old man? You think I'm setting up a meeting now, you're crazy. You got nothing to threaten me with."

He sounded strong, alive. In control. "Who said anything about threats? Cut that out. Talk sense. We're on the same side. Your problem disappeared with my problem, okay? I'm gonna make some moves of my own now. There's one little thing . . ."

"What?"

"The bitch, she has something for me. Something I wrote down once. She says she'll give it back, I give her a present."

"Why tell me?"

"She's a crazy woman, you know that. She has something stuck in her head, there's no talking to her. She wants to give it to you. You bring it to me, you take the present back to her. Then it's done."

"Get somebody else."

"I would. It's *her,* okay? You know what she's like."

"I'm not going to see her."

"Hey! Somebody's gotta do it. I'll take care of you, don't worry."

"And then we're quits."

"On my honor."

## 132

I CALLED STREGA. "You called him?"

"Yes."

"You couldn't leave it alone?"

"Don't be mad. You know I told you the truth. And he wants the letter. It's in the way now. The little man has big plans."

## 133

I HEARD THE SLUG muffle the phone with his greasy hand. "The guy wants Don Julio."

"I'm here," he snapped into the phone.

"She says she'll hand it over to me. Out in the open. She wants to see it happen."

"What's that mean?"

"It means you come. Alone. I come. Alone. She drives up. Hands me what you want while you watch. Goes back to her car. I give you the letter for the present you have for her. You wait while I take it over to her. I get in my car and we all go home."

"My boys won't like me going anywhere alone."

"You're the boss, right? Who cares what they like."

"All right. Where?"

"You know her. Queens it's got to be. You're coming from Shea Stadium, okay? On the Grand Central. Just before La Guardia, there's a gas station. You pull over there, where there's a railing. You can park the car, walk down to the water. Where guys fish in the summertime. Got it?"

"Yeah."

"She says tomorrow. Eleven o'clock in the morning. You park all the way to the right. She'll be there, parked to the left. I pull in between you. Get it done."

"I'll be there."

I called Strega. Told her what tomorrow was going to be.

## 134

WESLEY SAID JULIO WAS on the house. A trade for the don. But the don had been Wesley's killing. All his. Danielle's father had turned me into a dog. A hunting dog that fetched his raw meat back. He had to pay. Wesley said he'd do that freak. In his soundproof basement. Train was a trade. Not all mine, but enough.

I couldn't let Wesley within shooting range of Strega—the monster might feel the heat. And strike. Strega. The witch-bitch. She'd set it up this way. "You wouldn't let anything happen to me." Wesley was out.

At eight-thirty, I swung into the gas station. Told the guy to fill it up. Max got out to go to the men's room. The pump jockey filled the tank, took my money. I drove off alone.

A couple of minutes after eleven, I backed into the lot. Strega's BMW on my left, Julio's Caddy on the right. I swung the Plymouth between them. Got out, opened my trunk, left it open. Walked to Julio's car. His window snicked down. I put my head inside, checked the back seat. Empty.

"Get out, Julio."

He showed me a thick envelope. "I thought you were supposed to get the letter first."

"I am. I want you to open the trunk. Make sure you came alone. Mine's already open, you want to look."

He got out, a sneer on his face. Unlocked the trunk. Empty.

"I'll be right back," I told him.

"Burke, wait a minute." His gloved hand on my arm. "I got no more troubles, you understand? Except her. Crazy people, they're always trouble. They *stay* trouble."

"Why tell me?"

"I know you can get to Wesley. I'm going to make some arrangements. I want to pay him for the last job. The old don, he was a fuckin' idiot. No trap, no games. I give you the cash, you deliver it to Wesley. I don't gotta be around. I just want him to know . . . no hard feelings . . . it's a new regime, like they say. You could do this?"

"Maybe."

"Yeah, you always say 'maybe.' I ask you if you get up tomorrow morning, you say 'maybe.' You can do it. When you see Wesley, you tell him he's all right with me. Aces. I even got a nice easy job for him. Cash up front, how's that?"

"I'll see."

I left him standing there. Walked over to Strega's car, feeling his eyes on my back. She stepped out of the little sedan, wearing a black coat, black scarf over her red hair. She handed me a thin envelope.

"I was right," she said.

"Yeah, you were," I said. "Now get out of here."

"I want to see it." Witchy eyes, even in the sunlight. "I was right . . . about everything."

I walked back toward Julio. The old man came forward, one hand reaching into his pocket. Highway traffic hummed to my right, planes thundered to my left. I held out Strega's envelope to Julio. With his confession inside: how he made a little girl-child dance for him. The child he just sentenced to dance again under Wesley's bullets. He took his hand out of his inside pocket, slipped what I handed him into his coat. Reached back inside. A fat envelope. I took it. Closed my hand over his. He pulled back. "What . . . ?" Max launched off the railing in a dark blur. Julio twisted his neck sharply just as I heard the snap. He fell into me. I slipped his dead arm over my neck, walked him to the railing. Propped him on the bench, emptied his pockets. An old man, sleeping in the sun. Until you got close enough to catch the smell.

I walked back to my car. Closed the trunk on the dark bundle of blankets back there. Followed the BMW out of the parking lot.

The Plymouth shot past Strega, heading for the Triboro Bridge. I thought I saw her wave something at me but the windows of her car were very dark. I couldn't be sure.

## 135

I CHECKED MY LIST. I had to spook him, not tip him off. Called one of the six numbers on the printout. Not the dead line. Asked for Train. He came, quickly.

"It's me," I said.

"How did you come by this number?"

"From the man we discussed."

"A shot was fired through my upper window last night. Nobody heard it. There was a little round hole in the glass. A big chunk of plaster torn off the wall."

"I'll have him tomorrow. If I thought you knew what he looked like, I'd prove it to you."

"I know what he looks like."

It would have chilled me, but I knew how he knew.

"If I can pull it off, I'll call tomorrow night. Take you to him."

"You mean . . . ?"

"Yeah. COD."

## 136

CALLED MOREHOUSE. Got him live, no machine.

"Stay by your phone tomorrow night. Keep the line clear. All night."

"Sure."

## 137

CALLED CANDY.

"Hello, baby," she said into the phone. Breathy. Knowing how old she was supposed to be.

"I want to do it again," I told her.

"Anytime, honey. Just tell me."

"There's something I have to do first. Something real important."

"I know you'll be okay."

"Yeah. I'm just a little nervous."

"Anything I can do?"

"No, I'm covered. He doesn't know . . . oh, never mind. It's too complicated. But when it's done, I'll bring Elvira back."

"Are you going to have to . . . ?"

"No. I'm going to do something for him. Something he really wants. He'll *give* me the kid. No problem."

"Oh, I *knew* you could do it. Didn't I tell you?"

"Yeah. I'll call you soon."

"I love you," she said. Like she had before.

## 138

"I'M ON MY WAY," I told Train over the phone.

"I'll be here."

They let me in downstairs. Two of them went with me, close enough to touch. The two Elvira said had made the crazy girl disappear.

He was standing this time. By the window. The one with the little round hole in it. The monster's word was always good. I stepped close to him, keeping my voice down.

"He's dead."

"You're sure? Who is he?"

"Wesley. I'll take you to him—you said you'd know his face."

"How can I be sure?"

"You'll see for yourself."

"Sure of *you*."

"Ask Reba."

His blue eyes blinked rapidly.

"I don't know how you'll know him," I said, my voice soft, slightly awed, "but I know you will. You can go in my car. Take a couple of your men with you. Hold a gun to the back of my neck all the while, if you want. This is the truth—Wesley is a dead man."

"Where?"

"I left him on Wards Island. I'll show you. I've got a flashlight in the car."

He gestured to the two men. Left me alone in the room. Reba came through the door. I stayed against the window, tapping the ashes from my cigarette onto the sill. She walked against me, wrapping her arms around me, grinding her hips. I slid my hands inside the robe, cupping her buttocks. The globes seemed to swell in my hands.

"Can you work your trick standing up?" I asked her.

"The man is dead?"

"The man is dead."

She pressed against me, a fleshy heat-exchanger. "Will you come back? After you show him?"

"What for?"

"For me. I'll tell *you* the truth."

"Then I'll come."

"Yes," she said, promising.

Train came back in with the same two men who'd taken me upstairs. "I'll go with you. We all will. When we come back, you'll have your money."

I nodded.

"And whatever else you want here."

"Let's go," I said.

## 139

THE FORD WAS HALF a block away. I unlocked it. The overhead light went on. The front seat sagged badly on the passenger side, upholstery ripped, a sharp spring showing through.

"It doesn't look like much," I apologized. "Where we're going, a nice car would stand out."

I climbed in behind the wheel. The damaged front seat hadn't been necessary—the bodyguards played it the right way—their bodies pressed against the one they had to keep safe. One of them got into the back. Train next. Then the last man.

I buckled my seat belt. Pulled away from the curb. Drove past the House of Detention. Took the Brooklyn Bridge to the FDR, heading north.

I glanced at the rearview mirror. Train was sitting quietly in the middle, hands on his knees, staring straight ahead at nothing. The two guys on either side of him were in their early twenties. Looked enough alike to be brothers. Close-cropped hair, flat faces, hooded eyes. The first generation of the breeding program? As I hooked onto Wards Island, I heard the sound of a round being chambered. Felt the pistol nestle into the back of my neck.

"You know what that is, Mr. Burke?"

"Yes."

"No matter what happens, Tommy can do his job. The pistol has a hair trigger."

"Tell him to be calm. We're almost there."

I lit a cigarette, leaning back, pressing my head into the gun. Amateurs.

I pulled over under the girders. "Okay," I said, turning sideways to speak to Train, voice low and conversational. "We'll have to walk from here. I'm rolling down my window. Why don't you have Tommy get out and hold the gun while . . ." I pushed the switch in the middle of the last word, ducking my head. The train hit the wall.

The gun never went off. My breath was gone. The windshield was splattered with flesh and fluid. I let air seep in through my nose until my lungs started to work. I didn't look in the back seat.

Unbuckled my seat belt. Stepped outside. My legs wouldn't work. I sat down outside the Ford, waiting. It would come back.

In a few minutes I started walking. By myself. Fingering the little transmitter in my pocket.

The Plymouth growled alongside me, running without lights. The passenger door opened. I climbed inside. Hit the switch. The window went down. Max drove slowly. The Ford was in sight. I held the transmitter out the window, as high as I could. The Mole said it had a quarter-mile range. We were much closer than that. I pushed the button. The Ford exploded. Flames filled the rearview mirror as Max hit the gas.

He dropped me off where I'd left Morehouse's car.

## 140

I CALLED MOREHOUSE from a phone on the West Side. "You know the Yacht Basin?"

"Sure, man. Where you think I keep *my* yacht?"

"Fifteen minutes."

"I'm rolling."

## 141

HE PULLED IN. SEEMED relieved to see his car still in one piece.

"What's on?"

I handed him his keys. "There's gonna be an explosion tonight. Somewhere on Wards Island. Off the approach road to Kirby. The cops'll find bodies inside. They won't make a connect. You know McGowan and Morales?"

"The Runaway Squad? Sure."

"You call them. You got a tip, right? The connect is to a man named Train. He's running the baby-breeding operation." I gave him the address.

"They'll need more than that for a search warrant."

"Save the bullshit for your column, pal. Let them get a warrant the way they always do. You know that Anonymous Informant? The one they use on every search warrant since the Supreme Court told them they needed one? Time for another guest appearance. Tell them to run it through Wolfe at City-Wide. She'll know what to do. Besides, the joint'll be full of victims, not perps."

"Right on, man. When do I know?"

"You got nothing else to do tonight, right? Maybe you're working on that movie script you're always bullshitting about writing someday. So you're monitoring the police band—I know you got a scanner. You get a call a few minutes after they get theirs."

"I'm off."

"Hold up. There's one more thing. A little girl inside the joint. Her name's Elvira. Or Juice—I don't know which name she'll use. Don't let SSC put her in a shelter or a foster home—she'll run. She knows how to do it. She needs a psychiatric hospital. And she's pregnant."

"Okay. Anything else I should know about her?"

"Yeah. She knows my name."

"Crazy people say all kinds of things. 'Specially on the psycho ward."

"Your car sucks," I told the West Indian, not saying the rest— that his word was good.

We shook hands.

## 142

IT DIDN'T HIT ME TILL later. Alone in my office. No lights. Pansy's dark shape on the couch. When Flood had killed the sadist Goldor in his fancy house . . . killed him to save me . . . she almost came unglued. Got off the track. Shaking so bad. Throwing away the clothes she'd worn like they were diseased. I'd held her to me. Rosie and the Originals on the cassette. Angel Baby. "Remember reform school?" I'd asked her, dancing so slow we weren't moving our feet. Until she came back to herself.

She couldn't come back to me that night.

Not Strega's fire, not Wesley's ice.

I found my way.

Survive.

## 143

I WOKE UP THE NEXT morning by myself. The way I always do. Belle was still gone. The pain in my chest was still there. But now I recognized it for what it was—a tourniquet around my heart, not a stranglehold.

The Plymouth found its way over to Mama's. Judy Henske on the cassette. Singing just to me. An old gut-bucket blues number came through next. I didn't remember the man's name but I know he died young. And hard.

*Too sick to go to the doctor*
*Too tired to go to sleep*
*Too broke to borrow money*
*And too hungry to eat*

And then a sweet girl singer, fronting off some doo-wop group that never had a hit record.

*Your tears in my eyes*
*Your heart in my heart*
*Defeat and disguise*
*Can't keep us apart*

The weight wasn't off, but I could carry what was left.

Mama had the *Daily News*. The story about the bombed-out car on Wards Island was buried on page six. The paper had it down to more mob homicides. Couldn't find a word about Julio. It would take a day or so for the Queens cops to run his prints. And they'd throw the body into the same garbage bag with the rest of the mess Wesley made. Morehouse's column would be out tomorrow.

Max came in. I showed him the story about the firebombed car. He drew his X on the table. Wesley's work. He made a questioning sign. I pulled an imaginary cord a couple of times, made the sign of something rushing past. Train. He bowed.

My brother was right. I'd pulled the switch, but it was Wesley's work. Mine was done.

Almost done.

## 144

MAX PULLED THE RACING form from his pocket. I kicked back to read. The horses' names all looked unfamiliar to me. Soon I was lost in a stakes race for three-year-old trotters. There was a shipper from Illinois. Gypsy Flame. An Arsenal filly out of a Noble Hustle mare. Good lines. Her trainer was bringing her along slowly, but she was tearing up the home tracks. A 2:01 at Sportsman's Park in Chicago in the cold weather—that was flying. I went over her last eight races. She always ran off the pace, charged hard going home. She'd be at a disadvantage at Yonkers with the tight turns and the short stretch, but she always ran clean. No breaks on her record. Morning Line had her at 8-1. Yes.

I looked over at Max, to tell him what our selection would be. His seat was empty. I glanced at my watch. Damn. I'd been lost for almost two hours.

Mama was up front, by the cash register. I went back to the pay phones. Dialed my broker. Maurice snatched it on the first ring.

"What?"

"This is Burke. Give me the four horse in the second race at Yonkers. Two to win."

"Horse number four, race number two. Yonkers. A deuce on the nose. That right?"

"Right. You miss me?"

He hung up.

## 145

THE PHONE RANG BEFORE I could go back to my table. I picked it up myself.

"Yeah?"

"Friday, be sure you're watching TV. It don't matter which channel long as it's a network. Try NBC. They got the fastest crew. 'Live at Five.' That's the best show. Don't wait for the late news—watch it go down."

"All right."

"That car. Last night. In my spot?"

"Yeah, the papers made it sound like a train wreck."

"I'm gonna take a trip. Out to the Island. Pick up my money. Then Friday. Watch TV. I'll wave goodbye to you."

"I . . ."

"Don't say my name. I'm leaving you something in my will. Remember what I said. About kids. Don't let the hunters see the soft spot."

"I won't."

"Goodbye . . ."

The machine sputtered—I couldn't make out the last word as the phone went dead.

## 146

"THIS IS REAL NICE, BURKE. Just like the joint, except for the food," the Prof said, sneering.

We were in Mama's basement. At a long table we made out of an old door. I was playing gin with Max, the scorepad to his left. He owed me almost twenty grand. A nineteen-inch color TV stood on top of a couple of barrels we had piled up. Max brought it with him that day, carrying it in one hand like an attaché case.

Max reached for a card. "Nix on the six, chump," the Prof barked, slapping the Mongol on the arm. Max ignored him. I grabbed it. Turned my hand over. Gin.

"Why you waste time playing cards with this fool, Burke? Just take out a gun, tell him to empty his pockets."

"He wins sometimes."

"Yeah. Whenever a cop gives mouth-to-mouth to a guy who faints in a gay bar."

I lit a smoke, sipped at the cup of clear soup standing next to me. Pansy snarled in the corner—she wasn't used to color TV. And she wanted pro wrestling, not soap operas. She's only a dog—she thinks she can tell the difference.

Max took out a racing form, still pumped up with our last success. Gypsy Flame had destroyed the field, powering overland on the back stretch, clearing the others by the paddock turn, driving home with room to spare—$17.20 to win, more than seventeen hundred bucks to the good on our first bet in months. I waved it away—I couldn't concentrate. Max had picked up the cash from Maurice. Like old times. Moving money, not bodies.

"When's this gonna go down?" the Prof asked.

"I don't know, brother. I told you a dozen times. He called, said to watch the tube. So I'm doing it. You don't have to stay."

"He wasn't my friend, but I'll see the end."

"Okay, then. You want to sit in for Max?"

"No way. Fucking Wesley. You always could pick 'em, Burke."

He acted it out for Max—some of the characters I'd hooked up with in the joint. The Prof had a gift for it—he used to be a preacher.

Time passed. Like it does inside the walls. Except it was safe where I was. Working on my alibi. Mac was upstairs. Lily was going to drop over later. Hell, I was hoping the cops rolled by too. Whatever Wesley was up to, I wanted to be on another planet.

## 147

MAX SAW IT FIRST. Rapped the table to get our attention. A trailer running at the bottom of one of the soap operas. HOSTAGE SITUATION IN RIVERDALE SCHOOL . . . ARMED TERRORISTS SEIZE ST. IGNATIUS . . . POLICE AND FBI ON THE SCENE . . . STAY TUNED.

"No way," the Prof said.

But I knew.

The soap opera played on. At two-fifteen, they broke in for a live report. Guy in a trench coat, hand-held microphone, sound truck behind him.

"We have no details yet. Apparently, an armed team of terrorists has captured the school. The doors and exits are blocked. The terrorists arrived in a rental truck and entered the school disguised in some way. The police were alerted by a phone call from inside. There was machine-gun fire. If the camera will just pan over . . . you can see the truck on the edge of the school yard. This is as close as the police will allow us to go. We understand there has been a telephone hookup to the terrorists, and the Hostage Negotiation Team is in place."

The anchorman from "Live at Five" cut in. I guess they told him to report to work early. Wesley would have been pleased. And the anchorman asked the right question. "Tom, you say shots were fired. Were they fired by the terrorists?"

"We just don't know. The police have a tight ring around the school."

"Tell us something about the school."

"St. Ignatius is an exclusive private school here in Riverdale. One of the oldest prep schools in the area. Grades nine through twelve. Some of the most prominent families in the city send their children here."

I clicked on the radio. They had a crew at the scene too. The reporter said something about a media demand, whatever that meant.

Back to the TV. The field reporter was on camera. "It seems that the terrorists have herded the children into the gymnasium. One of them just broke a window. We can see somebody attaching a bullhorn of some kind. I think they're going to make their demands . . ."

A cop's voice. "You! Inside! What do you want? You can't get out!"

The bullhorn fired back. A measured, unexcited voice. A machine talking through a machine. "I want a helicopter to take us to the airport. I want a fucking 747 to take us to Cuba. You got that, pigs?"

"Crazy bastard thinks it's 1969," the Prof said.

"Let the kids go!" the cop shouted back. "Let the kids go and we'll get you the plane."

"Dumb-ass motherfucker forgot the ransom." The Prof shook his head sadly.

The camera held steady on the school. The field reporter read from a list of famous people whose kids were inside. Tomorrow's judges, politicians, mobsters. The seeds Wesley wanted to burn out of the ground.

"You! Inside!" The cop on the bullhorn again. "We've got the plane for you! Waiting at the airport! Let the hostages go and we'll send in some police officers to take their place! Unarmed!"

The monster's voice cracked back. "Bring more cops! You need more cops! Lots of cops!"

"Oh shit!" the Prof muttered, no questions left.

Camera panned to the SWAT team. Riflemen with scopes. Cops in riot gear—helmets with faceplates, flak jackets, pump shotguns. A cauldron coming to a boil.

The announcer's professional voice came through, just the trace of a tremble inside.

"There's a man on the roof! Get the camera on him."

A man standing there in jungle fatigues, field cap hiding his eyes, gloves on his hands.

The rented truck exploded. A greenish cloud filled the screen. Bursts of machine-gun fire ripped. Screams and shouts from everywhere. The announcer held his ground.

"The unknown man on the roof has apparently detonated the explosion in the terrorists' truck here on the ground . . . the crowd is taking cover. A squad of policemen has gone around to the back of the school to try and gain access to the roof. The darkness you see on your screen isn't your picture . . . apparently some type of gas has been released from the truck . . . we're about five hundred yards from the scene . . . the gas is lifting . . . we don't know how many terrorists are left inside."

The camera focused on the lone madman.

"The man on the roof is lighting something. It looks like a torch. He's holding it high above his head . . . he . . . oh my God . . . he looks like some bizarre Statue of Liberty . . . he's . . ."

The dynamite exploded in Wesley's hand and the screen went blank.

## 148

WE STAYED THERE UNTIL late that night. Flipping channels, checking the radio. Every report made a liar out of the previous one. Seventy-five kids dead. A hundred. Two hundred. School security guards machine-gunned. Grenade tossed into the administration office. One of the surviving kids said he heard explosions, gunfire. Then a voice on the PA system telling all the students to get into the gymnasium. A man was standing at the podium, dressed in military fatigues. They all filed inside. The man put some stuff around the door seams. Dropped duffel bags in all the corners. One of the kids screamed. The man raked the row with the machine gun. The kids shut up after that. The ones still alive. The man was shouting at the cops through the bullhorn. Then he ran out. Everything started to blow up. The kid talked in a mechanical voice from his hospital bed. You could hear his doctors arguing with the cops in the background.

The cops were combing through the human wreckage. So far, they hadn't found a single terrorist.

"You think Wesley's going to Hell?" I asked the Prof. He believes in that stuff.

"If he is, the Devil better be ready."

"Amen."

## 149

THE COPS HIT TRAIN'S operation. Found what they were looking for. Morehouse broke the story. Lily led the team of social workers debriefing the kids. The FBI Pedophile Task Force was in on it. Even Interpol.

I called Morehouse.

"Congratulations on your scoop."

"Yeah, man." He sounded sad, the sun gone from his voice.

"What's wrong?"

"The little girl? The one that needed to go to the psycho ward?"

"Yeah?"

"She went out a window. While the cops were breaking down the front door."

"She's on the loose?"

"It was the top floor, man."

"It's not your fault—she was gone anyway."

"Sure."

# 150

THE PACKAGE ARRIVED A couple of weeks later. A nine-by-twelve flat envelope. Thick with paper inside. Routed from my Jersey PO box, the one I use for mercenary stings. Max handed it to me in the warehouse.

I slit it open. A single sheet of paper. Neatly typed letters. "Put on a pair of gloves before you open the next envelope. Burn this part."

I did.

A dozen sheets of single-spaced typing. On a typewriter they'd never find. Each page numbered. Written in blood so icy it ran clear. My hands trembled. I lit a cigarette.

> *My name is Wesley. You never knew me. None of you did. But you know my work. I killed my first human in 1967.*

He gave the lieutenant's name. Where it happened.

> *Four rounds in the chest. M-16. I killed two men in that prison you put me in.*

Dayton and another guy I hadn't known about.

> *When I got out of prison, I started killing people for money.*

Names, places, dates, calibers. The dope dealer even the Marielitos and Santeria couldn't protect. A blowgun with a poisoned dart. An ice pick in the kidney in the middle of a racetrack crowd. The list went on for pages.

*Marco Interdonanto. Car bomb. Carlos Santamaria Ramos. At La Guardia. A spring bomb in a coin locker.*

The one where the whole crowd died along with him.

*Tommy Brown. I cracked his skull with a lead pipe and set fire to the house.*

Near the end, I got to the part he left me in his will.

*I killed somebody named Mortay. It was a contract from a man named Julio. He works for Don Torenelli. I shot him with a .38 Special, then I dropped a grenade on his face. I killed a man named Robert Morgan. In a playground in Chelsea. A rifle shot from the roof. The same contract. Julio wouldn't pay me. He said it was the don's orders. So I hit Torenelli's daughter on Sutton Place. I cut off her head and stuffed it in her cunt. I wrote 2 on the wall. It was a message. They didn't listen.*

Then he listed the other hits. Queens, Brooklyn, Staten Island.

*Torenelli put out a contract on me for revenge. I shot him on the Fifty-ninth Street Bridge. A .220 Remington with a night scope. Then I killed Julio. I killed a man named Train. I blew up a car on Wards Island with him in it. A man named Morrison hired me to do it. On Long Island. He tried to get out of paying me, so I killed him too. With a .357 magnum, wad cutters. Two in the chest, one in the face. He owed and he had to pay.*

*All my life, I worked for the same people. They had different names, but they were all the same. All bosses. Generals. I was a soldier.*

*I have no love in me for any of you. You have no love for me. You don't need my story. Why doesn't matter. What I did, you did it. You did it to me, I did it to you. I'm tired. I'm tired of all this. I'm not a man. I don't know what I am, but I wasn't born to be it. So I'm dying to be it. What I am.*

*I have no friends and I have no fear. I only stopped because*

*I got tired. You could never have stopped me.*

*I worked for my money. That's what I did. They didn't pay me. So I made them pay. They didn't listen to my warnings. So I'm leaving them one last warning. I don't know where I'm going and I don't care. But they better not send anyone after me.*

*If you're reading this, you're a cop. Some kind of cop. I'm not leaving you this as a favor. It's my last chance to tell you how much I hate you.*

*Pray to your fucking gods that I'm the last one. But you know I'm not. There's more coming. You do things to us, we grow up and we do things to you.*

*I'm signing this with the only name you ever cared about.*

His dark thumbprint was at the bottom of the last page.

## 151

I READ IT THROUGH twice. He wasn't just getting me off the hook, he was warning me. For the last time. Never show them your soft spot. Everyone in the street knew mine. Wesley checked out and took a bunch of kids with him. Seeds. Cards in a stacked deck. They dealt them—the monster played them.

I held the pages in my gloved hands. Knowing the last word Wesley never said to me.

Brother.

I waited until my hands stopped shaking. Then I called Morales.

"It's Burke. Let's play some more nine ball."

"I get off at four."

## 152

I WAS AT MY TABLE when he walked in. In the middle of a rack.

"Take off your coat," I said under my breath. "Just do it, you're not the only guy in the room wearing a gun. When we're finished, go someplace private and read what you find in your pocket."

His mind wasn't on the game. I was up a yard and a half before he split.

## 153

WHEN I CALLED MAMA'S the next day, the message was waiting for me. I met Morales on West Seventeenth, just off Twelfth Avenue. Whore corner. We watched the girls jump into cars for a while.

"What do you want . . . for what you gave me?"

"To get square."

"Most of it's the dead truth. *Most* of it. We checked it out. He knows things only the killer would know. Why would he take you off the hook?"

"I don't know what you're talking about."

"We can clear a couple of dozen unsolved homicides behind this. It means a gold shield for me."

"And for McGowan."

"He's my partner," he said, insulted.

"I'm not."

"No, you're not. But we're square. There was no paper on you anyway."

"I know. It's over."

He held out his hand. I took it.

## 154

IT WASN'T over.

Just Wesley's killing was.

Candy let me in. Wearing a man's button-down dress shirt over toreador pants. Like a hundred years ago. "You want to play?" she asked.

"Not today, outrider."

The cat's eyes narrowed. "What?"

"It was always you and Train. From the beginning. Elvira didn't run from you—you dumped her. Into Train's net. You knew Train was on Wesley's list. You thought I killed this Mortay freak. Thought I was a killer too. You knew Wesley was coming, so you put me on the same track. Facing him."

"I had to find out. I just watch—I don't risk. I didn't know how to find Wesley, so I sent you after Elvira. I knew there was a contract on Train—I knew Wesley was holding it. I know how he works. He watches. He waits. And then he does his work. It was all a play, and I wrote the lines. Wesley sees you hanging around, he figures you're with Train. Then he comes. You get in his way, somebody goes down. Not me. Never me."

"And you fuck the winner," I said. Remembering the subway tunnel, the kitten in the basement.

"Sure. That's the way it works. But I never thought you'd win. And you didn't."

"How long have you been with Train?"

"Since I was nineteen. I was one of his first. His very first. But I'm no outrider. That's a game. For the kids. Nobody leaves. I'm a partner, not a soldier. I made him . . . all that mumbo-jumbo bullshit. He tell you the one about truth?"

"No."

Her voice changed the way her face could. Train's voice: "If there is no truth, saying it *is* the truth. So there is always truth."

She watched my face, smiling. "Pretty good, huh? I gave him that one. He works the place in Brooklyn, I work here."

"Your partner's gone. So's Elvira."

"I'm still here. I know how to do it. There's plenty of kids. I'll always have me. I don't need anybody else."

"You're garbage."

"Am I? You think I loved you? Even when we were kids? It was Wesley I loved. He had the power. You . . . you're a weak, soft man. You were never hard. Me, I *made* you hard. I can do it again. I'm the one that's hard. Like Wesley. You should see your eyes . . . you want to beat me to death right here. But you can't do it. You can't hurt me. I know you. We can go in the back room right now. Tie me up so I can't move. And I'll still be in control."

I didn't say anything, watching her. The love Wesley never knew he had. He was better off where he was.

"You won't go to the cops either. That's not your way. The secret is to *know.* Like I know you. You could never hurt me. Wesley won. He's out there someplace. And I'll find him. I know you. If you were really a killer, you'd kill me."

She turned her back on me, walked out of the room, leaving me alone. Giving me a choice.

I closed the door behind me.

## 155

AS I WALKED DOWN the carpeted hall, a puddle of shadow moved. I nodded. Max drifted silently back the way I came, a key in his hand.

## An Excerpt from
# DEAD AND GONE

"DMITRI?"

"Over there," the squat man said, pointing at a table to the left, where a thick-bodied man in a dark suit sat alone, his back to the wall.

I made my way to the table—I was alone with Dmitri. The Russian didn't offer his hand. Just watched, taking a long, deep drag of his cigarette. The red Dunhills package was on the table to his left.

"So?" is all he said.

"You don't recognize me, old friend?" I asked him.

"No. How would I—?"

"Listen to my voice, Dmitri. Listen close. You've heard it before. On the phone. In person. When we were packing that satchel together a few months ago. Remember?"

"You're . . ."

"In my hand, under the tablecloth, there's a .357 magnum. Six heavy hollowpoints in the chamber. Listen . . ."

The sound of the hammer clicking back was a thunderclap in the silence between us, as distinctive to Dmitri as a cancerous cell to an oncologist.

"We are not alone here," he said, calmly.

"Every one of your men's behind me. They couldn't get between you and the bullets."

"Perhaps not. But you would never—"

"I don't care," I said softly. Giving him time to read my face, see that I meant it.

He nodded slowly. "What do you want?"

"Good," I said, acknowledging his understanding. "You thought I was dead, right?"

"Everybody thought you were dead," he said, shrugging.

"Sure. There's only two ways it could have gone down. Either you set me up, or someone set you up."

"There is another way."

"And what's that?"

"Burke, this was business. You understand? Just business. These people come to me. They say their child is kidnapped. And the man who has him will return him for money. They want me to deliver the money. And they will pay for that service. I tell them, of course, we will do that. I would have sent one of my people. But then they say there is a condition. It must be *you* who delivers the money."

"Me by name, right? So they knew . . . ?"

"That we had done business together? Yes, I think. Otherwise, why would they think I could . . . ?"

"All right. So you knew it was me they wanted. And that it was no kidnapping."

"That I did *not* know. It is all over the street, how you feel about kids. And about those who . . . use them. I thought perhaps they wanted someone who might do more than just pick up the child."

Dmitri was good. That last bit was a slick stroke. "But they didn't approach me themselves," I pointed out, nice and calm.

"If they had, would you have done it?"

"Not without references." I took a slow breath. "So you're saying *that's* what they paid you for, huh?"

"It is all how you look at it. I did not think it was a plan to murder you. Otherwise, why put all that money into your hands?"

"Because if we hadn't counted it—together, remember?—I wouldn't have gone out that night."

"I did not know, I tell you."

"Which means the hit squad wasn't yours."

"If it had been mine, you would not be here."

"They were pros, Dmitri. They just got a little unlucky. And a couple of them got dead."

"Ah. This I have not heard."

"Okay, who was it who hired you?"

"That I could not say."

"You mean, *won't* say, right?"

"It would be bad business. They were clients. They paid for a service. I delivered that service. I have a reputation."

"Me, too."

"Yes. You are a professional, as I am. I don't believe you would attempt to kill me in my own place. And, anyway, what would you kill me *for?* I am not going to tell you their names. And you're alive. . . ."

"They killed my dog."

"Your . . . *dog?*"

"My dog," I said, willing the trembling out of my voice. I wouldn't say her name in front of this . . . professional. "So that's enough. For me, anyway. Enough for me to blast you right here. Either you give up the names, or I pull the trigger."

"That is a child's bluff," Dmitri said gently, spreading his hands wide. "I am sorry, Burke. But you—"

The explosion sucked all the sound out of the room in its wake. Dmitri slammed back into the wall, gut-shot. I stepped out of the chair and walked around to where Dmitri lay on the floor. He looked dead. I put three rounds into his face. His head bounced on the floor. When it came to rest, his brains were outside his skull.

ANDREW VACHSS has been a federal investigator in sexually transmitted diseases, a social caseworker, and a labor organizer, and has directed a maximum-security prison for youthful offenders. Now a lawyer in private practice, he represents children and youths exclusively. He is the author of thirteen novels, two collections of short stories, three graphic series, and *Another Chance to Get It Right: A Children's Book for Adults*. His work has appeared in *Parade*, *Antaeus*, *Esquire*, *The New York Times*, and numerous other forums. For more information visit www.vachss.com.

# You wouldn't use an Angel as a tour guide to Hell

## ANDREW VACHSS

Fiction 6-1/4 x 9-1/4
352 pages Hardcover
ISBN 0-375-41121-6

"Bottomlessly knowledgeable about the depth and variety of human twistedness." —The New York Times

*Available in paperback from Vintage:*

Flood
Burke book 1
ISBN: 0679781293

Strega
Burke book 2
ISBN: 0679764097

Blue Belle
Burke book 3
ISBN: 0679761683

Hard Candy
Burke book 4
ISBN: 0679761691

Blossom
Burke book 5
ISBN: 0679772618

Sacrifice
Burke book 6
ISBN: 0679764100

Down in the Zero
Burke book 7
ISBN: 0679760660

Footsteps of the Hawk
Burke book 8
ISBN: 0679766634

False Allegations
Burke book 9
ISBN: 0679772936

Safe House
Burke book 10
ISBN: 0375700749

Choice of Evil
Burke book 11
ISBN: 0375706623

For more information about Andrew Vachss and his work, visit The Zero at www.vachss.com.